Book One of the Rising

Blood
of
Ravens

Jen McIntosh

Cover Artwork & Illustrations © 2021 by Jennifer Ross

First published in Great Britain 2021

ISBN: HB: 978-1-914434-00-6; PB: 978-1-914434-01-3; eBook: 978-1-914434-02-0

Published by Jen McIntosh

www.jen-mcintosh.com

For Andrew,
Without whom my heart would be but ashes in the wind.

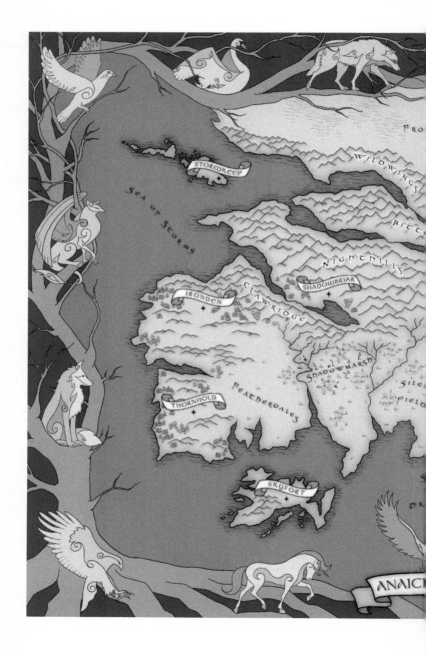

STORMKEEP

SEA OF STORMS

FRO

WILDWINGS

BITTE

NIGHTHILLS

SHADOWBRIAR

IRONDEN

CLAW RIDGE

SHADOWMARSH

SILE

FIELD

THORNHOLD

FEATHERDALES

SKYFORT

OR

ANAICH

PROLOGUE

The raven on the door was scarred, the carving disfigured by long, ragged furrows, cut deep into the aged wood. Running a small, hesitant hand over the destruction, the young boy tried to ignore the trembling in his fingers. His gaze narrowed. These were not deliberate marks just to deface a sigil. Whoever had wreaked this havoc upon his father's crest had done so in a frenzied rage. His hand drifted lower, searching in vain for the handle. He knew the door would be locked, knew he could go no further – wasn't sure what had drawn him here, truth be told. But drawn he had been, beckoned by soft murmurings that never ceased.

His fingers brushed the cold iron of the lock: there was no key, not even a handle. But as his skin touched the metal, it heated beneath his touch, and the lock turned with an audible click. He snatched his hand back, but caution soon gave way to curiosity as the door swung open in silence. Beyond, there was only darkness. The flickering candle in his hand did little to lighten the gloom. Shivering as the chill from within seeped out into the hallway, he drew his coat tighter around his shoulders. Then he took a deep, steadying breath, and the smell hit him – stale air and a hint of damp, along with the faint, musty aroma of old books.

It was this that drew him forward.

The light from the candle was just enough to see by, casting faint shadows on the far wall as he stepped through the door, hardly daring to breathe. There was a torch in a bracket beside the door and, as he raised his candle to light it, heat flared once more in the palm of his hand, and it sparked into life. He jumped back, eyeing the now burning torch with suspicion, sure the flame had not touched it but at a loss to explain how else it had caught. Then he turned around, and the torch was forgotten as uncertainty turned to wonder.

His father's library.

The man had hoarded knowledge, the dusty shelves reaching up to the high ceiling, each one stuffed full of books. There was an armchair by the empty hearth, the once-elegant table beside it buried beneath countless tomes, more stacked on the floor beside it. An enormous desk occupied the alcove opposite the door. He hesitated, but determination steeled his spine. He'd never known his father. Perhaps this was his chance.

A book lay open – a heavy volume, the vellum pages bound in black leather. He didn't dare touch it but could not see through the thick layer of dust. He blew on the pages, noting how his breath misted in the chilled air. But as the dust cleared, curiosity chased the chill from his bones. On one page was a picture. A woman, her arms laden with fruit, and behind her, a vast tree with a snake wrapped around its trunk. The boy studied it, glancing between the artwork and the text across from it – elaborate and written in golden ink. The words were not in a language that he understood, but the picture stirred something in his memory. Whispers of a bedtime story his mother had once told him.

His gaze drifted as he searched the recesses of his mind, his attention snagging on a sheaf of parchment beside the book. Brushing the dust clear, he lifted it to the light. This writing he recognised. And not just for what it said. It was his father's handwriting. He'd seen it before, in the only letter his mother had kept. She'd burned the others after he died but refused to explain why she had spared that one in particular. He didn't understand it either, not even when he'd snuck into her room while she slept and read it by moonlight. It had contained just three words: *'I know',* and then his father's name signed at the bottom.

Ignoring the dust that flurried at his every movement, he climbed up into the too-big chair and, feet dangling, pulled the parchment onto his lap and started reading. The scrawl of his father's handwriting was illegible in places – sharp and savage, as though written in a fit of anger. But as he read on, it was more than the writing that sent a shiver down his spine. These were the ravings of a madman. The words seemed to leap off the page, churning with dark power. The boy glanced up at the raven-feather quill still perched in the now-dry ink pot. Hard to believe something so innocuous could create so much hate.

He threw the parchment away and slipped out of the chair, continuing to search. There was a task unfinished – a reason that murmuring voice had called him here. He glanced at his reflection in the tarnished mirror that hung above the mantle. Through the cobwebs, he could just make out a small, skinny boy with dark hair staring back at him with peculiar, pale eyes. He looked away. They frightened him. Marked him as different. Tainted. *Other.*

A painting of a man adorned the opposite wall. His father. Tall and imposing, with blue-black hair, crowned in iron wrought like ravens' feathers. In his hand was a sword the colour of night, and he looked down at his son with cruel, dark eyes. The boy shuddered. Perhaps it was for the best they'd never met. His mother had said as much. More than once.

Then his gaze fell on the chest. Tucked away in a corner, hidden beneath books and a shield that bore his father's crest of a raven in flight. Something inside him clicked, a key turning in a lock.

Triumph pounded in his veins as he crossed the room and cleared the detritus covering the chest with a sweep of his arm. The chest was wrought iron, inlaid with pieces of darkest ebony – near black, save for the reddish sheen of the grain running through it, and carved like the door to the library. Ravens ... dozens upon dozens of ravens. Certainty settled in his gut. This was why he was here.

The moment his fingers traced over the catch, there was a flash of heat, and it sprang open. He paused, frowning at his hand. Whatever power was helping him, it did not come from him. He was too young. Someone – or something – wanted him here. Magic was a tang on the air, but it could only be a slumbering remnant left behind by his father, now waking at his presence. With a deep, calming breath and lifted the lid.

He was not sure what he'd expected. Not mountains of gold or jewels – his father had been a Prince, not a pirate – but not this assortment of useless items either. A dress of midnight velvet, embroidered with stars of silver thread. A pendant of a crescent moon and a circlet to match. A ring adorned with a black diamond, the setting shaped like feathers. Those he shoved aside without a second thought. A dozen scrolls – maps and sketches of lands and castles he didn't recognise. A pile of letters, folded with seals unbroken. He did not bother opening them. A dagger, sheathed in black leather, the hilt set with obsidian and quillons fashioned like outspread wings. That, he put in his pocket.

Then his eyes fell on it, tucked away at the bottom of the chest: a leather-bound journal, the cover embossed with scattered, silver stars. This was what had been calling him. Its song whispered in his mind, begging to be free. His hands trembled as he reached in and lifted it from the darkness. It was remarkably heavy, as if the gravity of its contents added to its weight. The leather was smooth from years of use and cracked along the spine, the midnight-blue dye long since faded. Lowering himself to sit cross-legged by the chest, he laid the book on his lap and, with shaking fingers, opened it.

This handwriting he did not recognise, yet the graceful lines of ink sweeping across the pages were somehow familiar. He flicked through them, eyes darting across the words which could not have been more different from the ramblings of his father. These were full of quiet grace and steady strength, warm and wise, and the boy felt a peculiar sense of calm settle over him, as though the author of this diary had laid a cloak around his shoulders while he drank in their words. He drifted, floating into the peace of the writing, losing all track of time, all sense of self.

But then he came to the last pages.

I am plagued by dreams. Vivid, tangible visions so palpable they haunt my waking eyes. So it has been every night since I left him. But they are more than dreams. They are prophecy. Glimpses of a past so ancient it has long since moved from the realms of history and into legend, fleeting glances at a dozen different futures, each possibility infinitely more wretched than the last – but futures I may yet help shape.

Others would believe these dreams, these visions, are a gift from my Goddess. That Rionna, Queen of the Night Sky, has smiled upon me. I know better. They are a curse. I wonder if they are my punishment for failing to stop it. To stop him.

Sephiron. I see him whenever I close my eyes. Alone in his tower, bitter and twisted, seeking only the power to destroy those who had wronged him. Power better left bound and buried, banished to the forgotten depths of history for eternity. Instead, he used it to bend others to his will, turning them into something ... other. Not Immortal, not like us. But no longer mortal either. Darklings.

The Council called me in for questioning yesterday. The old fools think he does not understand what he has unleashed, what he risks with this madness. They do not comprehend that he willingly embraces the Chaos – that he revels in it. Even when I warned them, they refused to listen. They still believe he can be reasoned with.

War is coming. There is no stopping it now, though I fear it could rage for generations and, despite our best efforts, innocents will suffer. If we fight, they will die in their millions. But if we do not fight ... their fate will be far worse.

Last night my dreams rang with warnings of that fate. Of the horrors yet to come. I saw Sephiron defeated, his evil contained by children forged by my own two hands. But I saw what followed. And even when I woke, the vision did not leave me. The nightmare haunts my every breath. My children, heir to naught but ashes. Their cities and dreams crumbling. Ravens rising. Darkness spilling across the world. Shadows conquering, bindings breaking. The world drowning in blood, choking on it.

And above it all – Sephiron's heirs upon his throne, smiling at the havoc they wreak. For a moment, hope is kindled. A light, born amongst ashes and shrouded in shadow. And the world trembles as it flickers into life – for it will shine so brightly darkness will flee before it. But even that hope is lost. Crushed and swallowed whole by the night.

Then the voice of my doom speaks.

'Fear not. Sephiron's heirs will rise – and though it may appear that darkness has triumphed, though the Saviour is lost, the sun and the moon will shine on the truth. A tree with deep roots need not fear the storm and not all who fall remain vanquished. An ember may yet raze all to ash. The serpent's seed holds the key and only with faith can the Raven's line be cleansed.'

As it speaks, the nightmare changes. I see what is to come. What I must do. Balance must be restored. The scales must be righted. Fate and destiny are for those too weak to forge their own path, but this task is too important to leave to chance. I will do what is necessary, make whatever sacrifice the Gods demand. Any price is worth paying to end Sephiron's line, to wipe his stain from all memory. If it costs me my life, I will see it done. With Athair as my witness, this I swear.

'Reith!'

His mother's voice echoed from beyond the open door. The boy scowled at the interruption, his gaze lingering on a few words ... *Sephiron's heirs will rise.* His pale eyes skipped down and narrowed further. *An ember may yet raze all to ash ... only with faith can the Raven's line be cleansed ... any price is worth paying to end Sephiron's line ...*

His mother called his name again. He looked up, closing the book with a decisive snap, just as she appeared in the doorway. Her eyes were blazing with fury, her shoulders shaking from the effort of containing herself. He did not think he had ever seen her so angry.

'What are you doing in here?' she hissed. 'How did you get through the door?'

'I wanted to see. I put my hand on the lock, and it opened.'

'Get out.'

He didn't argue. He stood and placed the journal back in the chest. He heard his mother draw in a sharp breath at the sight of it. When he glanced back at her, the anger had gone. Instead, her shoulders slumped in defeat, and there was a look of unfathomable sorrow in her eyes. He crossed the room to stand in front of her and stared up into her face. Tears streaked her cheeks, and she trembled with silent sobs.

'I'm sorry,' she whispered. 'I was just trying to protect you.'

Reith nodded in understanding and put his arms around her. 'I know.'

CHAPTER ONE

B eneath the ancient pines of the Ravenswood, there was only darkness. High above, the moon may well have been full and shining, and the sky littered with stars, but nothing pierced the inky shroud that engulfed the forest.

It was here that Keriath hunted. She drifted through the dense undergrowth, ghosting over the unforgiving terrain. Below the thick blanket of heather, moss and barbed webs of bramble, tangled tree roots coated the uneven ground like a snare awaiting its prey. Beneath her feet, dead branches and scattered pine cones lingered in silent threat – they would betray her presence if disturbed. The grasping thorns of the gorse seemed to reach for her, as if desperate to snarl her in their clutches. She glared, daring them to try.

The cold was not unexpected. It was autumn, and she was a long way north. The sigh of the wind whispered through the trees. Bitter and merciless, seeking every tiny gap in her clothing, it bit into whatever skin it could reach with sharp, icy teeth. The air was thick with damp, the relentless drizzle not heavy enough to qualify as rain, yet too substantial to class as mist. A murky fog soaked everything, sharpening the earthy tang of pine and suffocating what remained of her patience. With a soft curse, she drew her hood lower and pulled her cloak tighter around her shoulders.

It was neither the dark nor the cold that made Keriath so uneasy. It was the silence roaring in her mind.

Forests teemed with life, even during the dead of night. Birds and rodents sleeping, insects scurrying, predators hunting. Her senses should have been ringing with it; the voiceless chatter of their simple minds filling her head with a constant murmur. Instead ... silence.

She rolled her shoulders, trying to dislodge the itch of discomfort crawling down her back. The haunting call of an owl shattered the night. She froze, watching from beneath furrowed brows as the bird drifted overhead on silent wings. Her eyes narrowed, body tensed in readiness.

She'd learned long ago not to trust first appearances. Learned how to differentiate the benign from the malicious. But this time the owl was just an owl. Nothing more than another lonely hunter, searching through the darkness. The only bright spark of life in an otherwise barren wilderness.

Her fingers uncurled from the hilt of the dagger at her belt, and she forced herself to take a slow, deep breath. Willed her body to relax, as every sense screamed in warning, clamouring against the *wrongness* of the place. Had she another choice, she may well have turned and fled. But the choice was not hers to make. For hours, she prowled that forest, ghosting from one shadow to the next, seemingly at random.

It was magic drawing her forward – humming in her veins as she searched for its source. She lifted her nose to the wind, breathing deep, and caught the undercurrent beneath the overwhelming smells of the forest and whatever power drove the living from this place. The tang of magic was unmistakable.

A flicker of life ahead drew her attention. She stilled, senses straining. Too far to see or hear, too far to smell unless the wind changed. But Keriath had other options. She reached out with her mind, further and further, until she found it. One … No. Two. Human. Magically gifted … and trained in concealment, if that was all she could detect. No thoughts, no emotions, not even a sense of their presence beyond the slight ripple of their mental shields. Suspicion trickled down her spine like a drop of snowmelt. Few could hide themselves so thoroughly. Whoever they were, they were not the source of the magic she sought. Nor were they likely responsible for whatever power made her want to flee. That was ancient and terrible. No, they were something else.

She crept closer. At the edge of a clearing, she slid once more into the shadow of a towering pine, pressing herself against the lichen-coated trunk. The seeping damp bled straight through her clothes, chilling her to the bone in an instant. Above her, the clouds shifted, allowing a glimmer of moonlight to break through the canopy of trees and illuminate the clearing. She swallowed a curse and shied back from the light. It would reveal her more surely than any noise.

The clouds moved over, and she peered out to see two familiar figures before her. She sighed with relief. No wonder she hadn't been able to sense them. She'd trained them herself, though not well enough if they were unaware of her presence. She allowed herself a moment to watch. Faolin, tall and proud, and Dorrien, her flowing silvery hair bleached near-white by the moonlight. Her heart ached at the sight of them. It had been so long. Both carried weapons – a sword sheathed at his hip, a pair of lethal-looking poniards belted at her waist – and wore light armour. They stood close together and spoke in whispers. But even the slightest sound carries far in the night.

'I don't understand why we're still wasting our time on this,' Dorrien hissed. Her face was still young and attractive but, in her temper, she had the haughty bearing which only affected those of noble birth.

'You know why. Don't ask questions to which you already know the answer,' breathed Faolin, frowning at a patch of air in front of him.

'This is ridiculous – there's nothing here.'

'There is something,' he corrected. 'Ignore it all you like, but we both sensed it. You know fine well the consequences if we don't find it.'

'There is something *wrong*, Faolin. We're not safe here.'

'That's why it's so important for us to stay.'

Dorrien glared at him. 'We are no use to our people dead.'

'We are no use to our people idle either.'

'It's been days, and we've found no trace. It's time to leave, before someone else comes looking and catches us here.'

Faolin sighed – finally tearing his gaze away – and opened his mouth to reply.

Keriath had heard enough. She stepped out, a mocking grin on her lips as she interrupted, 'Too late.'

Dorrien jumped, hands flying to her waist. But Faolin turned, his face impassive but for a slight warming of that normally fierce gaze.

'Nice of you to join us,' he murmured in greeting.

'Keriath,' welcomed Dorrien, despite the bite of irritation in her voice. Keriath grinned, lowering her hood and opening her arms. Dorrien's frown melted into a gentle smile. The strength of her slender body as they embraced was incongruous but not unexpected, and they clung tight to each other.

'I'm glad to see you in one piece, cousin,' Dorrien murmured. Keriath stepped back, blinking tears from her eyes. Dorrien had aged since their last meeting but was even more lovely for it. She had lost the softness of childhood from her face, leaving high, sweeping cheekbones and a sharp, angled jaw. Faolin too was older, though it was less obvious. Only in his bright yellow eyes, flashing in the darkness, did Keriath see the change. The years were taking their toll.

But none of this held her attention for long. Not when their marks had grown so much since she'd last seen them. Faolin's black tattoos trailed down his neck, across his shoulders, and wrapped their way down his well-muscled arms. A simple design, yet striking and bold. Dorrien's, by comparison, were far more delicate. Shining silver instead of black, they framed her slanted silver-grey eyes and covered her wrists and hands in swirling patterns reminiscent of cresting waves and rushing rivers.

A pang of jealousy swept through Keriath. Her own marks had been damaged beyond repair long ago. Shame prickled at the memory, and she caught the flicker of pity in Dorrien's gaze as her eyes skirted over Keriath's face, over the twisted mess of melted, silvery skin that ravaged the right side of it. Even Faolin's brow creased with sympathy.

Keriath looked away before her humiliation showed, wrapping her cloak tighter. Not that it mattered either way, since they'd both seen the full extent of her ruination years ago. Seen how the scars extended over the entire right side of her body. Shame gave way to panic as the memories rose. The searing heat of the flames, the bitter tang of smoke in her mouth, the stench of burning flesh. And worse, the hooting laughter of her tormentors echoing through the night.

With a deep breath, she forced the memories back. Refused to let them swallow her whole. She focussed instead on the figures in front of her, on the remnants of her shattered family.

Faolin broke the silence. 'What are you doing here, Keriath?'

'Same as you.' Her gaze drifted to the spot Faolin had been studying just moments earlier. The taste of magic was stronger here. The air thrummed with it. Faolin followed her gaze and smirked.

'Told you so,' he murmured to Dorrien, triumph gleaming in those yellow eyes. But it was short-lived, and he sighed in frustration, gesturing at the space. 'There's something here. It keeps tracing back to this one point, but I can't find anything.'

Keriath nodded in agreement, her senses tracking through the air, searching. A frown of confusion creased her brow. Magic did not just happen. There had to be a source. But Faolin was right. There was nothing there. A glance back at Faolin told her he was just as mystified.

Dorrien, meanwhile, was paying no attention to the conundrum. 'You should be in the west, with Taelyr,' she cut in, looking at Keriath. 'Where is he?'

'I don't know,' she admitted. 'We got separated – long story – and when I arrived in Thornhold, there was a Hunt waiting for me at the gates.'

Faolin's fierce gaze snapped to her. 'What?'

'How did they find you?' Dorrien gasped.

'I don't know. But it was well-planned. Too well. I doubt it was a coincidence. I lost them in the Mistwood a few days ago. I was going to search for Taelyr when I sensed this. If it was a child ... I couldn't ...' She broke off with a frustrated sigh, folding her arms across her chest. 'Taelyr can at least defend himself.' She glanced at them both, looking for understanding and assurance that she had done the right thing. The guilt had been gnawing at her for days now. Faolin nodded and gripped her shoulder. Dorrien said nothing, hugging her tight instead.

They stood together in silence for some time until Faolin finally spoke again. 'Have you seen her?'

She didn't need to ask who he meant.

'Yes,' she admitted, 'but it was brief. You know what she's like. There one moment, gone the next.'

His face remained impassive, his voice steady, but emotions warred in his ferocious gaze. 'How was she?'

'As you'd expect – the seasons change, but our blessed Saviour stays the same. Up to her elbows in Darkling blood last time I saw her. A reminder to the King that she was still alive, apparently. Nobody loves a massacre like our dear Kah Resari, but you know that better than anyo—'

She broke off, barely daring to breathe, a sudden ripple of fear and hatred betraying a nearby presence. She reached out with her mind and recoiled. Not human, not alone, and reeking of dark magic. She dropped to a knee, hissing a wordless warning to her companions, and pulled a short knife from her boot.

Behind her, Faolin and Dorrien stilled as they scanned the forest. The sound of a sword being drawn from its scabbard was unmistakable. There was a snarl of recognition from Faolin, as he and Dorrien stepped up to flank her.

Then she saw them ... at least a dozen emerging from between the trees, the element of surprise gone. They looked human – at least at first glance – but she knew otherwise. There was no mistaking that scent. The stench of death and corruption that followed them everywhere. If she were to cut herself with the knife held steady in her hand, their eyes would glow red as the blood from her veins.

Darklings. A whole Hunt of them. There were more shifting in the shadows. Perhaps thirty in total. A manageable number. Just. Anticipation thrummed. The magic building in her veins, driving her to *kill, kill, kill.*

Front and centre was their leader. The Hunter. It was tall and lean, and even at this distance she could tell it was cruel. The stench of a thousand stolen lives soaked its scent, those hands coated in their fear. This was one she'd enjoy ending. Given half a chance, she might even linger over it – though that was not usually her way.

But she didn't have time to dwell on it. Beside her, a low growl was building in Dorrien's throat. To her other side, Faolin's eyes flashed with anticipation as he adjusted his grip on his sword. The same urge, the same impulse drove them all. Spurred all those who shared their power to destroy any Darkling unfortunate enough to cross their path. It was their calling. Their birthright. Death was the song to which their blood danced.

Keriath took another breath, steadying herself to strike. But before she could move, a voice echoed deep within the vaults of her mind.

'They are drawn by the power you seek. Protect it,' it said. It was not a voice she recognised, nor did she have any idea how it had reached through her defences, but it didn't matter. She knew what she had to do.

And she was not alone. Dorrien hurled one of her poniards but didn't even wait to see it embed itself in the skull of one of the Hunt before she turned and fled. Faolin followed, roaring a challenge as he ran. Keriath waited, just a few seconds, until half the Hunt was after them.

Then she sliced her hand open with her dagger and took off in the opposite direction. She'd barely made it to the treeline before the rest of the Hunt caught her scent. They howled in frustration – no doubt torn between their fleeing prey. Darklings were so predictable. Then, like a pack of hounds, they were after her.

She was flying, flowing over heather and fallen tree alike, and resisting the urge to smile. The Hunt could not catch her, not when magic fuelled her flight, though they would continue to try for some time. They crashed through the forest behind her like desperate beasts – weak and starving, driven mad by thirst.

But then she heard it. One that was not stupid or slow, like most of its kind. It was making up ground. It was close behind her, even if she couldn't sense its presence. Well shielded, it was swift, and sure-footed, like the Darklings who had mauled her as a child, who had left her so scarred. It was Graced.

Fear surged. Her legs were burning, although she knew it meant nothing. She'd run all night if necessary; the magic in her veins would see to that. Panic squeezed her chest. It was closer now. So close she could almost feel its breath on the back of her neck. She pushed herself to go faster, but even her gifts had a limit, and she was fast approaching it.

For a heartbeat, everything went silent, then something huge and hard slammed into her back. Dazed, she tumbled down a bracken-clad slope, tangling limbs with whatever had hit her. It was not until the world righted itself and the stench of death reached her that she came to her senses.

She lashed out, kicking at the Darkling on top of her, somehow catching it in the ribs. She felt, rather than heard, bone crunch beneath her foot and smiled as it roared in pain, leaping back and releasing her. Its mind was guarded – too well; she would struggle to overpower it that way. She bared her teeth in anticipation. Brute strength it was then.

Slashing at its throat with her knife, a growl of frustration broke past her lips as it dodged with unnerving agility for one so big. Snarling, it lunged towards her again. It was quick. She grinned. She was quicker. Giving a taunting yell, she danced out of reach, dealing it another savage kick in the gut for good measure. It spun, faster this time, and landed a glancing blow to her shoulder. She fell back, switching the knife to her other hand as she tried to shrug it off. By the Gods, it was strong. Even that slight knock had felt like a kick from a raging stallion. They circled each other cautiously now, each trying to gauge the strength of the other.

It kept its body angled away from her, protecting the side of its chest where she'd landed that kick and no doubt broken a few ribs. She allowed herself a brief glance at its face. It was male and handsome – or at least, it likely had been once. Tall and broad-shouldered, with golden skin and dark hair, but those blood-red, soulless eyes marred its – his – good looks.

She focussed on those, reminded herself that he was a mindless pawn and would stop at nothing to suck the life from her body. She couldn't afford to see him as anything else. In the battle between life and death, there was no room for mercy.

Keriath rushed him again, aiming for his injured side. But this time, she was not so fortunate. Darting to the side, he caught her wrist and, with a feral snarl of triumph, wrenched the knife from her hand. She screamed as the bones shattered, the pain nearly enough to bring her to her knees. Reacting with primal instinct, she lashed out with her other hand and snarled with satisfaction as she felt skin tear beneath her nails. He roared and let go, clutching his face, tainted Darkling blood pouring from where she'd gouged his cheek.

'Now we match,' she spat, gesturing at her own ruined face as she loosed the broad-bladed dagger from her side. He only offered her a withering look and wiped the blood from his face. Then the skin on his cheek knit together, leaving angry weals where she had marked him, and her stomach clenched in fear. Darklings healed fast, but not that fast. Trying to disguise her disquiet, she threw him an equally scornful look and raised her wounded hand for him to see. It took all her concentration, but it was worth it to see its expression as she sent a trickle of magic down her arm to snap her wrist back into place, the bones beneath her skin shifting as they set. But whatever pleasure she took from his discomfort was weighed with a significant dose of pain from the process, followed by a wave of fatigue when the cost of that power took its toll.

'We could be here a while,' he noted with a wry smile.

She couldn't help it. She flinched. In all her years, she'd never heard humour from a Darkling's lips. They were stripped of that the moment they were Claimed. They were nothing but soulless, mindless beasts. Beasts she had been born to destroy. The thought that even a shred of their humanity remained …

She reached for the Casting. Drawing water from the air around her, she shaped it into blades before freezing them in her hand, only vaguely aware of the tell-tale aura surrounding her. Shards of ice shot from her fingertips only to be brushed aside by a blast of icy wind. She snarled in frustration, her gaze snagging on his ears. On his own Casting aura.

Elf. Blessed with the same power she was. Little wonder he'd healed so fast. And then she was on the defensive, dodging a bolt of lightning he Cast at her face. He surged forward. There was no way his power could match her own, and yet she grudgingly gave ground. It was impossible. She had the might of three noble bloodlines in her veins – he should not be able to best her. No Darkling should have that power, mortal or Graced. This was something else. Something *other*.

She scrambled to draw up more magic as she dodged a kick to the chest. The speed and relentless ferocity of his attack caught her off guard, and she tried once more to reach for her power. She delved deep for the strength to finish him, but he only grinned as a black wind gusted towards her, blowing dirt into her eyes. Blinking to clear it, she was too slow to react. His arm swung from nowhere and crashed into the side of her skull. Then all she knew was darkness.

CHAPTER TWO

Deep within the forest, atop the tallest tower of her castle, was a woman. She stood with her head thrown back and her eyes closed, motionless beneath the night sky, wreathed in pure, white light that shimmered through the dark. A younger woman, petite and childlike, with deep burgundy hair, stepped from the shadows, eyes wide.

'Gaelan?' she called, her voice stiff with fright. The woman did not move, but the incandescent light faded, shrinking closer and closer until only the faintest glimmer of distant starlight glittered beneath her skin.

'They're in the forest,' she said, without opening her eyes. 'Darklings. A whole Hunt.'

The young woman paled, the peculiar lights forgotten. 'What do we do if they find us?'

Gaelan opened her eyes, and the magic flickered and died. She turned, her expression calm. 'The castle wards are strong.'

'And if those fail?'

'Then we fight.'

The younger woman nodded in understanding and turned to leave, but Gaelan caught her by the arm.

'What?'

'Look at me,' Gaelan commanded. Their eyes met and the younger woman relaxed into a dazed stupor. When Gaelan spoke, there was an odd tone to her voice – cool and detached, yet controlled and imposing. 'You will forget what you saw. You came up here to watch the aurora, but decided it was too cold. You will return to your bed and remember none of this.'

The younger woman nodded as the commands sank in, retreating into the shadows as Gaelan released her. Candlelight flashed from within as the burgundy-haired woman opened the door and slipped through. Then Gaelan was alone once more.

She sighed in relief and gazed out over the forest.

'Be careful, my children,' she whispered. Then she closed her eyes, and glittering starlight shone once more against the night sky.

Lucan woke screaming. Across the room, Suriya panted in fright. Had she seen it too? He scrambled to sit up and light the candle by his bed. Looking around, his sister was sitting bolt upright, dark blonde hair a tangled mess and nightshirt rumpled. But her huge gold eyes were clear and staring straight at him.

'What did you see?' she asked.

Lucan gulped. 'Darklings. You?'

'The same. And ... a tower. Two women.' She shook her head in frustration. 'I can't remember their faces.'

'And the woman in the forest? With the scars?'

She nodded slowly.

'It's not real,' she whispered, her eyes wide and her hand pressed to her chest as she tried to catch her breath. 'It was just a dream.'

'Yes, just a dream,' he said, rolling his eyes. His throat was sore from yelling, not that he'd share that. He didn't want her fussing over him all night. So he threw his covers back with a sigh. 'Come on.'

She dithered for a moment then scurried across the room and crawled in beside him. He forced himself not to flinch when her icy toes pressed against his leg. She would laugh at him if he did. Besides, he was used to it. She always suffered in the cold.

'Lucan?' she murmured.

'Yes?'

'Why do you think we have the same dreams sometimes?'

Lucan hesitated for a moment. He'd asked himself that question often enough. He had his own theories about it, but she'd never believe them, and he was too tired to argue.

'I don't know,' he sighed. 'Perhaps it's because we're twins.'

Suriya nodded. 'That would make sense, I suppose.'

A change in her breathing, moments later, told him she was asleep. But Lucan couldn't sleep. He lay for hours, staring up at the ceiling, replaying his dream. Who was the beautiful, burned woman? And why were the Darklings chasing her? Where was the tower, and who were those two women? Their faces had seemed familiar, yet he could no longer recall either. Had they said their names? He couldn't remember. And what had they been talking about? Questions continued to race round and round in his head until exhaustion claimed him.

Renila didn't seem surprised to see Suriya snoring away in Lucan's bed when she bustled into their room the next morning. His sister had been restless after their nightmare, so he'd given up on sleep and moved to the armchair by the window to watch the sunrise. He was still there when their nursemaid entered – though nursemaid was perhaps an unfair description of her role in their lives. There had been plenty of times growing up where she'd seemed more like a mother to them than their actual mother. Not that it was hard …

He braced himself for a lecture – she'd nagged for months about how tired he looked every morning before he'd told her about the dreams. Not that it had helped; she just fussed more than ever. It wasn't until he could hear her stripping the sheets off Suriya's unoccupied bed that he dared to glance around.

Shorter than Lucan and skinnier than Suriya, Renila didn't seem much older than the twins at a glance. She had bright amber eyes and hair the colour of red wine, and a smile warmer than hot chocolate by the fireside in winter. As always, she hummed to herself while she moved around the room, pulling clothes from the dresser to lay out for them.

'It happened again,' he mumbled.

She paused and looked up, her face creasing with worry.

'More nightmares?'

He nodded. 'Both of us.'

'What happened?'

'A woman was being chased through the forest,' he began. He broke off, forcing himself not to sound so afraid. 'I think they were Darklings.'

Renila crossed the room and touched a reassuring hand to his cheek. 'It was just a dream. Darklings don't exist, Lucan. They're just a bedtime story.'

Behind her, Suriya stirred, and he looked back out the window. Renila's worry was bad enough. He didn't want to deal with his sister's too.

Suriya was trying very hard to sit still. She ground her teeth in frustration as Renila pulled a comb through the snarls of her dark gold hair. Lucan had shot her a glare when she'd woken, then he'd darted off before Renila could insist on brushing his hair too. Through the open window, Suriya could hear him playing in the courtyard with the other boys. She didn't need to ask what the glare had meant. Sometimes she could almost read her brother's mind.

Say nothing about the dream.

And even though it chafed against her better instincts, she'd do as he wished. It was always her burden to yield to her brother.

'Renila?'

'Mmm?' Renila mumbled, a large hair pin clamped between her lips.

'Would you tell me a story?' she asked. 'Please?'

Renila stuck the pin in her own hair and fixed Suriya with a knowing look. 'Since you asked so nicely. Any one in particular?'

'One you haven't told me before,' requested Suriya, after a beat.

Renila hesitated, her brow furrowing. Then her gaze became distant, as if she was drifting down into the story itself.

'There are many tales of the mighty heroes who have walked this land, many tales of the Graced warriors and their great deeds. But only one speaks of their origins,' she began. 'Destined to be the light in the darkness, they were born during the depths of Sephiron's Rebellion and tempered like steel. Forged in the fires of battle and quenched in the blood of their enemies.

'The Immortals were losing the war. They were powerful, yes. But their numbers were few, and their enemy was many. For every Darkling they destroyed, ten more would take their place. During the darkest days, when hope was all but lost, their leaders sought desperately for the power to end the war. But they knew the price Sephiron had paid for his power, and they refused to sacrifice their souls for that same black magic.

'It was only when, in his madness, Sephiron stole a newborn babe from her crib that the tide began to turn. No one knows why he took the child, but it was like the falling of small stones that begin a landslide. For it was not just any child he stole, but the only grandchild of one of the great Immortal Princes.

'Enraged, the Prince and his son rallied their people and rode out to war and ruin. Left behind, alone with her grief, the child's mother planned her own revenge. She was one of the mightiest daughters of her people – a Princess in her own right, revered by all for her wisdom and power. And now all her rage was turned against the Dark Prince Sephiron and his twisted spawn.

'She alone realised that they could not hope to defeat the enemy by themselves. Not when they were so hopelessly outnumbered. She began to think like her enemy. If magic had created Sephiron's army, it could create one for her.'

A sharp rap at the door broke the spell of Renila's words.

'Lady Suriya!' called a voice from the hall. The Lady's maid. 'Breakfast is ready and waiting.'

Renila shook herself and with deft hands finished the intricate style into which she had woven the girl's hair. Then she pulled Suriya to her feet, checked her dress was clean and not creased, and ushered her outside and down the hall.

'That's not the end of the story,' Suriya objected as Renila guided her towards the stairs.

'I'll tell you the rest later, I promise,' Renila assured her.

Suriya threw her a look heavy with disappointment and trudged downstairs to join her mother in the dining room.

Pausing on the threshold, she studied the Lady of the keep. She sat at the head of the table, her back straight and proud, holding a letter in one hand and pouring her morning tea from the pot with the other. She didn't even glance up from the letter as her daughter entered the room, and Suriya was thankful for that.

Neither Suriya nor Lucan looked anything like their mother – or each other, in truth. She was petite with dark gold hair and eyes, while Lucan had blue eyes and silvery-blonde hair. He was tall and fair-skinned, where Suriya had a distinctly olive cast to her complexion.

Their mother, by comparison, was pale and statuesque – her pure-white hair so at odds with her breathtaking face, unlined and untouched by age. And her eyes ... her eyes were *other-worldly*. As vast and endless as the night sky. Deepest, darkest blue with hints of emerald, magenta, aqua and violet swirling through them – the light of a billion stars glittering in their limitless depths, if Suriya was feeling poetic. Eerie, if she was being more honest about it. She didn't know how anyone who wasn't the Lady's daughter could even bear to meet her gaze.

'Good morning, Mother,' she said, curtseying as she made to sit down.

Those eerie eyes glanced up from the letter. 'Good morning. I trust you slept well.'

Suriya hesitated, instincts raging. Lucan would be furious if she mentioned the nightmares.

But what if their mother could help them?

Her mother raised a delicate eyebrow when she noticed Suriya's hesitation. Cursing her brother and his pride, Suriya smiled and slid into the chair across the table. 'Yes, quite well, thank you.'

Her mother frowned but returned to her letter.

'Where is your brother?' The Lady gestured at his empty place with a jerk of her chin. Suriya shrugged. 'Don't shrug, Suriya, it's not ladylike. Now, where is Lucan?'

'I don't know. He'd already left when I woke up.'

Her mother's scowl deepened, but she said nothing. Instead, she folded the letter, set it aside and began eating her breakfast in silence.

Lucan had, in fact, finished his breakfast hours ago and was hungry enough for a mid-morning snack. Which was how he ended up racing through the kitchens with a large loaf of bread straight from the oven clutched to his chest.

'Master Lucan! You come back here with that!' yelled Mal, the large woman who ran the kitchens. He ignored her, dodging the hands grabbing for him with ease. Then there was an almighty clatter as she slammed her rolling pin on the countertop and knocked over a tower of pans. In amongst a torrent of swearing, she barked after him, 'I'll tell your mother!'

That pulled him up short, but only so he could turn and laugh in disbelief. She wouldn't dare. Everyone in the castle feared his mother. It was an unwritten rule that you didn't speak to her unless she spoke to you first. And that went for her children too.

Mal scowled at him, waving him away.

'You make sure you share that with Erion,' chided the blacksmith, Alec, standing by the door waiting for Mal to hand him whatever she wanted repaired that day.

Lucan just winked at him and darted away.

He raced through the corridors, ducking into rooms and slipping through as many hidden passageways as he could to avoid the few people he might encounter. He knew all the castle's secrets. As soon as he'd been old enough to walk, he'd started exploring, and now he knew every inch. Quite right too, since it would be his one day.

He paused just long enough to make sure no one was watching then slipped into his mother's library, knowing she'd be in the dining room having breakfast with Suriya. He crept over the squeaky floorboards, crossed the room and heaved open the bookshelf beside the fireplace to reveal a long, narrow passage behind it. With a grin, he flitted inside and pulled it closed behind him. He hurried down the dark corridor, despite the darkness, clutching his prize tight to his chest. Still warm from the oven, the smell wafting up into his face making his mouth water.

It didn't take long to reach the end of the passage. He'd learned the hard way to count his steps so he avoided banging his head off the door at the end. He pressed his ear to the door, listening for a moment before knocking. The door creaked open in answer. A pale but serious face appeared in the gap, but once the aroma of warm bread wafted through, the serious expression broke into a broad grin.

Lucan almost laughed. Trust Erion to get excited about bread. He was always hungry. Mal had once said the boy had an appetite like a half-starved bitch with a litter of ten pups. Not that Lucan was much better.

'Took you long enough,' Erion said, throwing the door wide open. He was tall for his age – taller than Lucan – but still built like a skinny little boy. His hair was dark and his face plain. He was almost unremarkable …

At least, if it wasn't for his eyes.

Peculiar didn't even begin to describe them. They never seemed to be one set colour, but instead, changed with his moods. When he was happy, they were a bright amber colour, just like Renila's. When he was angry, they turned a ferocious wolf-yellow. When he was unsettled, they became a deep, stormy grey. Sometimes they were green, sometimes blue, and sometimes they were the colour of amethyst or as pale as the moon.

They'd been friends so long that Lucan barely noticed it. What he did notice, however, were the ever-darkening circles beneath those peculiar eyes. He pushed into the room, turning his back to hide the worry on his face. Erion wouldn't appreciate it.

'I was trying not to get caught,' explained Lucan, throwing himself down on the bed. Erion flopped down next to him and held his hand out. Lucan broke the bread in two and handed the larger piece over without a word, trying not to laugh as Erion bit into it with feverish excitement.

'Mmm, it's still warm,' he mumbled, around a mouthful of fluffy white dough.

Lucan grinned, happy to see him eating again, and began picking at his own piece. 'Mal spotted me,' he said, after a minute. 'Threatened to tell my mother.'

'No chance,' Erion snorted. 'Far more likely to tell mine.'

'Where is Renila anyway?'

Erion shrugged. 'She went upstairs to get you and your sister up, but I haven't seen her since then.'

Lucan grunted and then there was silence, save for the sound of teeth ripping into bread. When they were finished, Erion stood and made to leave, but Lucan didn't move. Instead, he asked, 'What do you know about Darklings?'

Erion looked at him, eyes cold and grey as his fingers played with the ring he wore on his left hand. A family heirloom given to him by his mother, still too big for him, the design of outstretched wings holding a glittering red jewel, fitting only his thumb.

'You mean, other than the things my mother made up to scare us into doing as we're told?' he asked. Then he frowned. 'You and Suriya having the nightmares again?'

Lucan nodded, picking up a piece of string and twisting it round his fingers. 'I'm sure they were Darklings. They looked like people, but their eyes ... they were dark and empty, but when they smelled blood ... they glowed red.'

Erion's eyes changed, and his gaze turned piercing. They were his cat eyes, Renila said, the ones he used when he was trying to stare right into your soul. Lucan fidgeted under the scrutiny. Only a few months separated them, and though it was Lucan who'd always been their leader, Erion was the cannier of the two. Lucan was the intrepid one, though lately he'd become increasingly unsure of himself. Not that he'd ever admit it.

'They're getting worse, aren't they?' Erion asked. Lucan glanced up from the piece of twine in his hands. Erion's dark brows knitted together in concern as he studied his friend, eyes shifting back to dark grey.

Lucan nodded. 'At first they were just flashes. Then they were all strange, like I was watching them through coloured glass. Then they were blurry, like I was seeing them from far away. But last night's was clear. Like I was right there. Except that I can't remember half of it – just that there was a woman being chased by Darklings.'

'Did Suriya have it too?'

'Yeah.'

Erion's eyes narrowed, but he took a deep breath. 'From what I remember of the stories, Darklings are basically people, like you and me, but tainted by corrupt magic. The magic makes them stronger and faster, but it also sort of freezes them in time. I mean, they don't grow old. I don't think they're immortal exactly. They can still be killed, but they need to drink blood – to steal the life-force of others – to survive.'

'But they're just a story?' said Lucan, more a prayer than a statement.

Erion shrugged. 'I've never seen one – have you?'

'No, I guess not,' admitted Lucan.

'There you go. Besides,' he added, 'if Darklings are real, then so are the Graced.'

Lucan looked up and smiled. He hadn't considered that. Even the possibility changed everything. He stood, brushing breadcrumbs from his hands. 'What's the bet that old Mal has got more bread ready for the taking?'

'Or cakes!' laughed Erion, darting across the room.

Lucan tore after him, worries long-forgotten.

Lucan avoided both Renila and his mother for the entire day. He and Erion had returned to the kitchens to steal some sweet cakes, and found Suriya there, covered in flour as she endured a lesson in breadmaking. She'd caught up with them later, having extricated herself from the washing up, and they'd spent the rest of the day racing through the meadow with the other children.

As the sun set, they returned into the castle for their dinner and, attempting to avoid their mothers further, ate with the other children in the kitchens. They gorged themselves on roast chicken with thick onion gravy, carrots, parsnips and mashed potatoes. Mal even gave them the leftover sweet cakes, drizzled with honey, for dessert.

Stuffed and unable to climb the stairs to their room, they retreated to the library where someone had lit a fire. His sister curled up in her favourite chair nearby while Lucan lay stretched out on the rug before it, his eyes closed and his hands behind his head. He was vaguely aware of Erion scanning a bookcase on the other side of the room, and that Suriya was watching their friend closely. No doubt searching for any sign of the sickness returning. She had a tendency to fuss, though for once, Lucan didn't blame her. This last bout had been particularly bad, though Erion seemed to be recovering.

'Did you tell him about the dream?' she whispered.

He opened his eyes with a frustrated sigh, but the spiteful retort died on his lips as he met her gaze. Rolling over to see her properly, the fear in her eyes was clear.

'Yes.'

'What did he say?'

'It's nothing to worry about,' he told her. Then he looked at her suspiciously. 'Did you say anything to Renila? Or mother?'

'No,' she promised. 'I knew you didn't want me to.'

He frowned at her. 'You were upstairs for ages before breakfast.'

'Renila was telling me a story,' she said.

Erion's attention perked at the sound of his mother's name. 'Which one?'

'One she hasn't told us before,' she informed them, voice dripping with smug satisfaction.

Lucan snorted, his disbelief echoed by Erion's laugh. 'Not a chance – she's told them all!'

'Not this one,' she assured them, leaning forward. 'It's about the Graced and where they come from. They were made by an Immortal Princess, whose baby was stolen by the Dark Prince Sephiron.'

Lucan rolled his eyes and looked at Erion who shrugged and flopped down on the floor beside him.

'Right enough, I don't know it,' he agreed. He frowned, trying to remember. 'And I thought we'd heard all the stories about the Graced.'

'Where does she get them from?' asked Lucan, more to himself than anyone else.

'I had an idea,' said Suriya. Lucan looked up at her, his brows arching in surprise. 'What if she gets them in letters?'

Erion frowned. 'I never see her reading any. Besides, who would send her letters from outside the castle?'

'Your father,' Lucan said, without thinking.

The scowl Suriya afforded him was ferocious, and Lucan winced, glancing at his friend. Erion's gaze had become distant, his eyes stormy grey. Still, Lucan wasn't about to apologise. He'd much rather they considered him uncaring than thoughtless. Suriya gave him a look that said she wasn't fooled and warned him to drop it. He stuck his tongue out in response and closed his eyes again.

'Ignore him, Erion,' she murmured.

Fathers were a touchy subject in the castle. Their mother refused to tell the twins anything about their sire – they didn't even know if he was still alive – and Erion's father was never spoken of. Not around the Lady of the castle. That had been a rare, stern warning from Renila when they were younger. Suriya had wondered if their fathers were the same man. Lucan had laughed out loud when she'd suggested it and they both knew better than to ask.

Awkward silence followed, save for the soft crackle of the fire burning in the hearth, but Lucan did his best to ignore it. The sound of his mother calling his name broke the tension.

He jumped to his feet, just as she glided into the room, offering a contrite smile and tentative bow of greeting. Behind him, Suriya and Erion also rose – but while Suriya curtseyed, Erion retreated to the shadows. They all knew the Lady had little tolerance for him.

'Mother,' Lucan said, gesturing to her favourite chair by the fire, opposite Suriya's.

'Shouldn't you both be in bed?' she asked as she sat.

'I was waiting for Renila to come and finish the story she started telling me this morning,' Suriya explained. 'Lucan wanted to hear it too.'

'You're a little old for bedtime stories, aren't you?'

Lucan shrugged and sat in Suriya's chair. 'I suppose so.'

'But it is a wonderful story. You should stay and listen to the rest too, Mother,' said Suriya.

'What would be the point in hearing the end when I don't know how it begins?'

'Lucan didn't hear the start either. But I could tell you – although I don't think I'd tell it as well as Renila. She tells it almost like she was there!'

'Does she indeed?' the Lady laughed, attention fixed on the fireplace. After a moment, she pulled herself away to study them. 'Go on then,

Suriya, tell me how the story begins, and I'll stay and listen to the rest of it from Renila.'

Lucan tried not to laugh as his sister adjusted her posture into something she thought more fitting of a storyteller and began.

'It's the story about the Graced – the story of where they came from. It was during the Rebellion, when the Dark Prince Sephiron rose and created the Darklings. Even though they were stronger, the Immortals were losing the war because they were so outnumbered. But then one night, Sephiron kidnapped a child. Nobody knows why he did it, but it was the baby of an Immortal Princess, so the Princess created her own army to defeat him. That's where Renila left it ...

'Quite a tale,' murmured their mother. But even Lucan could tell her expression didn't match her tone. Her lips were pursed, and her eyes tight. Across from him, Suriya shifted uneasily. He didn't blame her. Perhaps this wasn't a good idea. But before either of them could say anything, their storyteller entered.

'My Lady.' Renila greeted the twins' mother, curtseying.

Their mother inclined her head in response. 'Suriya tells me you have a story for us.'

'I started telling her one this morning but didn't have time to finish it, my Lady,' Renila explained. If she was annoyed, she didn't show it.

Their mother waved a dismissive hand. 'Suriya already told us what we've missed. I'm keen to hear the rest.'

Nodding, Renila seated herself on the low settee by the fireplace while Erion folded himself onto the ground at her feet, trying to avoid drawing the Lady's attention to him.

'Where were we, Suriya?'

'The Princess was making her own army.'

Renila's eyes seemed to glaze over as she stared into the flames before her, toying with the chain around her neck. Nodding again, she began to speak. 'Her lands had been ravaged by the war, her people scattered to the four winds, when Sephiron came for her. Mortal or Immortal, it did not matter to the Dark Prince. He wanted nothing less than the complete destruction of her bloodline and all those loyal to it. Her Immortal kin held the line, stood their ground while she shielded the mortals as they fled. The Darkling horde snapped at their heels all the way to the Glimmering Sea. And there, on the shore, she made her stand, loosed her power upon the descending host and burned them to dust. But by the time she returned to her lands, there was naught left but ash and ruin.

'They say that tears streamed from her eyes, falling like glittering stars, sharing her light with all those who dared reach up and catch them. They say each drop contained a kernel of her power, willingly given to those prepared to fight and die to end the war. Mortals, from the four lands bordering her own, who had sheltered her people from Sephiron, hidden and shielded them at the cost of their own lives, chosen for their bravery, their wisdom and cunning, for their warrior hearts. Each was gifted with a portion of her magic to help them fight the Darkling hordes. Spell-casting, shape-shifting, mind-reading ... immortality. Four powers for the four peoples who had answered her call. And so were born the Graced.

'The Princess stood back from her work, proud of what she had wrought. And so it was that she rode out to join her people, with her army of Graced at her back. Finally, the tide of the war turned in their favour, for the Darklings could not contend with the strength of the Graced.

'The war was won, Sephiron's Rebellion crushed, and when the Immortals faded into the realms of myth and legend, they left behind the Graced to guard against the darkness. And guard they did. For centuries they stood watch, defending humanity from Darklings and worse ... until Sephiron's heirs rose and brought about their Fall.'

Silence roared. Lucan stared at her, so enthralled by the tale that he barely noticed she'd stopped speaking. He glanced around to see his sister and Erion equally entranced. Their mother, meanwhile, looked distinctly less captivated. In fact, he would even say her expression was grim. Renila hardly seemed to notice any of it, staring into the fire. Then without warning, she stirred and looked down at her son.

'Time for bed,' she said with a quick smile.

The twins' mother rose, her lovely face stern. 'I couldn't agree more. Goodnight.'

And then she was gone.

Renila sighed and led them up the stairs to their room. Erion followed. He was quiet, his eyes storm-grey as he watched her get the twins ready for bed. Lucan tried to entice him into conversation, but even though Erion's black moods were few, when one appeared, there was little that could pull him from it. And when Renila moved to tuck them in, Erion slipped from the room without a word. If Renila noticed, she didn't show it, leaning over and pressing a kiss to Suriya's forehead.

Then she crossed the room to Lucan and whispered, 'No more nightmares tonight.'

He smiled and nodded, even though he didn't believe it. Not when his mind was swirling with tales of Immortal Princesses and rebellion ... the birth of the Graced. He'd heard so many stories about the magically gifted warriors. Knew all the names. The legends. Kah Rorrin. Lady Vianka. Queen Benella. Kalielle Half-Elven. But to hear of their creation? Forged like weapons to fight the Darkling scourge.

Maybe Erion was right. If Darklings were real – and he doubted it – then so were the Graced. And that was indeed a comforting thought. Grinning into his pillow, he closed his eyes and let his mind take flight. He lost himself in fantasies, drifting off to sleep, imagining himself as heir to one of those mighty bloodlines.

Renila found the Lady on the drawing-room balcony, her starlight hair snapping in the cool night breeze. Shivering in the cold air, she hugged her shawl tighter around her shoulders and waited.

'What is it Renila?' the Lady said, eventually.

'The children grow curious,' she replied.

'It is not surprising, when you fill their heads with such nonsense,' the Lady admonished, rounding on her.

Renila frowned. 'They're just stories.'

'That may well be the case, but those tales are not fit for the ears of children,' she hissed, pointing an accusing finger in Renila's face. 'They are too close to reality.'

'They deserve to know the truth,' Renila argued. 'The twins are coming into their powers far more rapidly than you said they would. The visions they're having, the nightmares, they're becoming clearer every time. They dreamed of the Ravenswood last night. Captain Farran told me this morning that there were Darklings spotted in the forest, and Lucan said they saw a woman being chased by a Hunt.'

The Lady scowled and turned away. 'It can wait a little longer.'

'I don't think Erion can. I worry about him – he grows weaker with every passing day, and I don't know how to stop it. I don't know what's wrong with him. And he's restless. He wants to know about his heritage, about where we come from, about his father. We all deserve to know the truth.'

'No,' said the Lady, shaking her head. 'Now, I suggest you speak no more of this, or else I might have to reconsider harbouring either of you here at all.'

Renila looked at her incredulously, but as she opened her mouth to argue, the Lady turned to her once more. At the look in her fathomless eyes, Renila closed her mouth. The Lady nodded and breezed past, leaving Renila alone to share her fears with the stars.

CHAPTER THREE

I t was still dark outside the castle. The sun had not yet risen, but Renila was wide awake and staring up at the ceiling, seeking the will to leave her cosy bed. She always woke before the dawn. As usual, she was careful not to wake Erion as she rose, wrapping herself in her dressing gown and slipping from the room in silence. Her slippered feet were soundless on the cool flagstones as she padded through the corridors. She paused in the kitchens, setting a kettle to boil and greeting Mal as the cook arrived to begin her preparations for breakfast. Mal grunted in response and took the mug of steaming tea without a word of thanks. Renila only smiled and slipped through the kitchen like a wraith, dodging bleary-eyed servants arriving to start work.

There was a time when the trek up the hundreds of spiralling stairs to the topmost tower of the castle had made her head spin and her breath catch in her throat. But that was long ago. Now, she glided up.

She reached the top and stepped out onto the turret in silence. Farran, the Captain of the Guard, stood by the parapet, his dark brows creased with concentration as he scanned the lightening horizon. Renila moved to his side and set the other mug of tea on the wall in front of him, before looking out to the forest. The sky had taken on the cold, pale quality which signalled dawn was not far off. It was a relief to note it had stopped raining, though a thick blanket of mist now shrouded the ground between them and the forest. The air itself was still heavy with the damp, but as she took a deep breath, she revelled in the refreshing scent that so often came with persistent rain. Without taking his eyes off the horizon, Farran picked up his mug and sipped his tea, wincing as it burned his mouth. Renila smiled to herself and wrapped both hands around her own mug, savouring its warmth.

This had always been their morning ritual. Every day, for as long as Renila could remember, she had risen before the sun and sought the highest vantage point to watch the dawn. It had not taken her long to discover the turret, nor to befriend the stern-faced Captain. Farran always volunteered for the most dangerous shift, from sunset to sunrise the next morning. Sunlight didn't harm Darklings like it did some other creatures of night, but they had no love for it. If an attack came, it would happen while the sun slept.

Precisely when Farran slept was a mystery. He was on guard all night long and then spent all day training his soldiers. Somehow, he still found time to oversee the fortifications of the castle and then work his way through the mountain of paperwork that seemed to breed on his desk during his absence. Renila did not understand of what the paperwork comprised, only that Farran hated it more than anything and that it was always last on his list of priorities. Second last, since Farran had no time for his wife, vain and selfish as she was.

Perhaps that was why he worked so hard. He made no secret of his distaste for the woman. It had been a match arranged by their parents, long before either of them had come to the castle. The Lady would have never allowed such nonsense on her land. But honour was the code Farran lived by, so he'd tried to be a good husband. His wife had lost whatever beauty she once possessed long ago, but instead of discouraging her affairs, this only increased them. Farran, meanwhile, had never strayed – despite the temptation of many invitations from various women in the castle.

The Captain was an attractive man: tall and lean, with warm brown eyes the colour of tilled earth. His russet skin was weather-beaten and his short, dark hair peppered with grey about the temples. He looked in desperate need of a shave and dark circles shadowed his eyes, but to Renila, these were endearing features.

It was that selflessness which had drawn Renila to him. He was a young man when she'd first met him atop the turret. He had greeted her politely and offered to escort her out of the cold and back to her rooms. She'd smiled and declined, explaining that she wanted – no, needed – to see the dawn with her own eyes. She had stood by his side, wrapped in his cloak, and watched the sun rise over the forest. That was in the days following Erion's birth, a little over twelve years ago now.

She sighed to herself and glanced at Farran. The side of his mouth quirked in acknowledgement, but he was otherwise still as he awaited the dawn. It was not long before the sun deigned to poke its head over the horizon. Over her heart, the pendant she always wore warmed from the touch of those early rays. Beside her, Farran huffed a relieved sigh as he watched its slow, lazy ascent into the morning sky.

'We survive to fight another day then?' Renila asked, a playful smile on her lips. Farran scowled at her as he sniffed at his tea.

'It's no laughing matter,' he admonished her. 'They've never come this far north before. It can't be a good sign.'

'I'm sorry,' she said, dipping her head. 'I shouldn't make light of something so serious. But at least the castle is warded – we're more fortunate than most.'

'The wards can't protect us from everything,' he warned. Renila shivered, but it had little to do with the bitter cold of the morning. Farran gave her a knowing look and glanced out across the forest once more. 'I don't like it,' he said. 'They've never ventured this far into the forest before. And why should they? They're drawn to large, dense populations – not a few dozen souls hidden miles from anywhere. They've no reason to be here, and that's what worries me.' He looked down at her then, his dark gaze mixed with worry. She stepped closer to him, placing a slender hand on his chest.

'They don't know we're here,' she assured him. 'They were just hunting; they followed their quarry into the forest, that's all. There's nothing here that would interest them.' There was a tightness in his eyes that said he did not entirely believe her, that he saw the glimmer of the lie beneath her words. She schooled her face into an impassive mask. It pained her to lie to him, but the children's safety came first.

He covered her hand with his own and held it over his heart, smiling softly. She leaned in a little closer, her smile broadening to a grin as Farran sighed in exasperation and pulled away.

'Come on,' he said, shaking his head in frustration. 'Get inside before you catch a chill. I've never understood why women insist on dressing in such flimsy garments.' Renila laughed and twirled for him, fanning the skirt of the silken dressing gown out around her as she did so.

'For your pleasure, Captain,' she confided with a conspiratorial wink. Farran snorted and looked to the heavens imploringly.

'Go,' he ordered, chasing her back down the stairs. 'Get dressed, see to your boy, and our Lady.'

She blew him an impudent kiss and darted back down the stairs into the kitchen before he could scold her further. The kitchens were in full swing now, with Mal stood in the middle of the room barking orders like a general directing troops on the battlefield. Renila chuckled as she sidled through the throng with practised ease, pausing only to place the mugs on the growing pile of dirty dishes. She threw a sympathetic smile to the young scullery maid sitting nearby eyeing the pile with trepidation, before slipping through the door and back out into the hallway.

She was humming happily to herself as she breezed back into her room and almost danced to the windows to throw open the heavy curtains. But her good humour faltered when she turned to meet the storm-grey eyes of her son. Erion's mood had not lifted then. She squared her shoulders, fixing a dazzling smile on her lips, and pretended not to notice.

'Good morning!' she chimed, straightening the sheets of her bed. 'How are you feeling today? Did you sleep well?'

'Fine,' he grunted, rolling from his own bed and crossing the room to the wash basin. 'And you?' he asked with forced civility.

'I am well, thank you,' she said with a bright smile, adding another log to the fire.

'How is Captain Farran this morning?' he asked as he washed his face. She did not miss the trace of bitterness in his voice; it cracked her heart. He knew that Farran was not his father and no doubt still believed that his father would one day come for them. Renila didn't dare to have such dreams, which was why she allowed herself to have ... well, whatever it was she had with Farran. She forced another smile as she laid out a clean shirt for Erion.

'He's well. Though in desperate need of a hot meal and a good night's sleep,' she said, running a comb through her tangled mane of wine-red hair.

'As ever. You're such a mother hen,' Erion muttered as he pulled his shirt over his head.

'Indeed,' she chuckled, running a fastidious eye over her son, but he darted back out of reach before she could comb his hair. Renila clicked her tongue in exasperation but didn't pursue him. 'Go on, get away with you. Mal should have breakfast ready for you by now.'

Erion's eyes flashed to her own at the mention of breakfast, and he scurried away towards the kitchens. Renila washed and dressed quickly and tried unsuccessfully to tame her hair once more before following him back to the kitchens. She spotted him in the corner nearest the fire with two other children. A boy who worked in the stables with Erion and one of the young housemaids. She was pretty, with soft brown eyes and womanly curves far beyond her years. Renila felt a flash of worry when she noted the girl's hungry gaze on Erion. But he seemed too busy talking horses with the other stable boy to notice those bedroom eyes. The sound of Mal yelling Renila's name interrupted her worries.

'The Lady has requested her morning tea in her room,' Mal instructed, handing Renila a tray laden with the aforementioned tea. There was also enough fresh fruit, toasted bread and honey for at least two people. 'Her instructions were that *you* were to deliver both it and yourself to her as soon as possible. You'll be breaking your fast with her today.'

The tone of Mal's voice told Renila that she did not approve of such special treatment. Renila was a servant, and to dine with the mistress was to rise above her station. Even if she disagreed, arguing with Mal wasn't a good plan. And in any case, it wasn't like Renila had much choice.

She hesitated on the threshold. After their argument the previous night, she'd assumed the Lady would not want to see her again for several days. Her temper tended towards the fury of a midwinter storm, and the aftermath was rarely anything less than total devastation. With a deep breath, Renila knocked on the door and entered.

The Lady was out of bed and stood by the window in the sitting room, brushing her hair and gazing out across the forest. An exquisite robe of embroidered silk shrouded her shoulders and covered an equally beautiful nightgown of chiffon and lace. Her snow-white hair was already smooth and gleaming, but she continued to brush through the length while those starlight eyes considered the view in front of her. The early light of the morning caught on the sharp planes of her face, and for a rare moment, her angled features softened.

She was breathtaking. Hers was a face that stopped people in their tracks. But her demeanour was so cold, so aloof, that it was like gazing up at the distant stars. And on the rare instance that someone dared to meet her eerie gaze, the power that dwelt there was all too often paralysing. She was beautiful, yes, but she was also terrifying.

Knowing her presence had been noted, if not acknowledged, Renila crossed the room to the small dining table in the adjacent room. With practised dexterity, she transferred the contents of the tray to the table and put the tray on the sideboard. Assuming the Lady would speak when she was ready, she crossed back through to the bedroom and began making the bed.

'Leave it,' the Lady commanded. 'Someone else can do it later.'

Renila kept her back to her mistress and finished what she was doing. It didn't seem fair to add to the other servants' workloads when she could do it in moments. 'Will milady require help to dress this morning?'

'I think I can manage.' The Lady was studying her from the dining room. Renila hadn't heard her move from the window, yet there she was – seated at the table, pouring herself a cup of tea, fathomless eyes watching her every move with the predatory glint of a cat surveying a potential meal. Renila tried not to flinch beneath that stare.

'Is there anything else I can do for you, milady?' she asked, desperate to leave. No matter how bitter she was about their exchange the night before, she would die before she let the Lady see it.

The Lady's eyes flashed as she regarded Renila from over the rim of her teacup. 'I'm sorry I lost my temper with you last night,' she murmured. Renila blinked. She'd never heard the Lady apologise. Not in a dozen years. The Lady smiled ruefully and reached for a piece of toast. 'It may well be another dozen before you hear it again, so I would enjoy it while you can.'

Renila forced her face to remain impassive. It wasn't hard. She was well practised in not reacting to the Lady's eerie ability to read her mind.

'Thank you,' she murmured.

'I thought a lot about what you said last night, Renila,' the Lady continued. 'You're right, they deserve to know the truth. But I'm afraid, in my anger, I failed to impress upon you the dangers that come with that truth. Our greatest defence is secrecy. If that fails, everyone in this castle is at risk.'

Renila nodded but could not shake the feeling that she was continuing her earlier conversation with Farran. 'I still don't understand how telling Suriya and Lucan the truth about their power puts that secrecy in jeopardy?'

'Blood calls to blood, magic calls to magic.' The Lady sighed. 'Ignorance keeps those children safe. If they start using their powers, Darklings will sniff them out in days. Magic is rare. Even the weakest remnants of those bloodlines are sought with zealous desperation.'

Renila lowered her eyes as she yielded the point. But after a moment, she continued, her gentle voice desperate. 'What about me? I know nothing about who I am. Where I came from. Why I'm here. And what about my son? I know he's sick, even though he pretends that he's not. How do I make him better when you won't even tell me what's wrong with him?'

'You came to me for protection, and I've given you that,' the Lady replied, her expression darkening at the mention of Erion. 'Your reasons were your own, and you understood the consequences of your decisions. I will not take responsibility for your regrets.'

A gasp of horror escaped Renila's lips, despite her best efforts. 'Why do you hate Erion so much? What could a boy have done to deserve such loathing?'

'Get out,' the Lady snapped, focussing those terrifying eyes on her. 'I don't want to see your face again until you can keep a civil tongue in your head.'

Renila flinched and stood hastily. The Lady could be vindictive when provoked. She wouldn't put it past her to throw both her and Erion out into the cold just for sheer spite. It wasn't a risk Renila was willing to take, even if it stung her pride to back down.

So she swallowed her reply and left with as much dignity as she could muster.

Renila did not trust herself when she was so worked up. It was a rare occurrence, but once roused, her agitation took a long time to settle. She bolted for the stables.

Erion took one look at his mother's face, his eyes flashing to a wild, wolf-yellow, and began saddling her horse – a stubborn but loyal chestnut mare named Copper. She placed a hand on his shoulder and gripped it tightly in silent thanks. He smiled in understanding and handed her the reins.

'Be careful,' he murmured, his eyes flickering like a storm.

She smiled gently, nudging his chin with her fingers. 'Which one of us is the mother hen now?'

He gave her a knowing look as she climbed up into the saddle, and he opened the door of the stall. With a twitch of her heels, she was off, thundering through the courtyard and out into the fields beyond. She heard a familiar male voice shout her name when she passed through the open gates, but she didn't look back. She didn't want to see the exasperation and disappointment on Farran's face.

Copper carried her across the fields with near feral delight and needed no urging from Renila to stretch into a gallop. The mare loved nothing more than a flat sprint across open ground and, for once, Renila let her have her head. The wind surged and whipped around her, and she let her temper rage with it. Copper seemed to sense her mistress's displeasure and whinnied as she charged onward.

The castle and its surrounding land was bordered on three sides by forest – the vast expanse of the Ravenswood. But on the fourth side, the farmlands met rock, a sheer cliff face that rose into the rugged mountains behind it. It was towards that craggy expanse of bare rock that Renila headed now. To the secret path up the cliffs, since nothing calmed her mind quicker than the cold, biting air of the mountains.

Copper needed little guidance to find the path, and she climbed steadily upward without encouragement. As the path narrowed, trapping them between flat rock on one side and a sheer drop on the other, she nickered in discomfort, but a soothing word from her mistress had her moving forward. Renila dared to look down. A familiar rush of primal fear set her heart pounding in her chest as she leaned out across the vast expanse of empty air beneath her. It was a thrill. To face such dangers when your body knew the risks, but neither your heart nor mind cared. One could become addicted.

Copper froze and whinnied in warning as Renila's shifting in the saddle threatened to unbalance her. She leaned in heavily against the wall of stone on her other side, pinning her mistress's leg to the rock with her weight. Renila chuckled at the mare's reproach and straightened herself. Satisfied, Copper moved on with a derisive snort.

Renila dismounted as Copper reached an outcrop. The mare had more sense than to approach the edge, where the ground was liable to crumble, but Renila tied her reins to the withered stump of a gorse bush anyway. Copper gave her a long-suffering look and began to munch on what little tufts of grass she could find growing in the cracks of the rock.

Renila edged closer to the precipice and looked out across the land stretched out below her. It was a rare, fine day, and the bright morning sun had burned away the blanket of fog that had lain so heavy on the land before the dawn. It was cold, as it so often was this far north. The air was clear and crisp, and the smell of the pine forest was on the wind, drawing her gaze from the castle. The Ravenswood was large, but it was just part of the vast expanse of woodland that covered this part of the world. The dark forests to the south were wild by comparison. They blanketed the hills, the valleys and the glens, shrouding the land in mystery. Little wonder legend claimed it as the mythical home of the Fair Folk. How many times had she told the children stories about the hidden court of the Elf-Queen concealed within that forest?

Toying with the chain about her neck, she pulled free the pendant nestled within her bodice. Gold and shaped like a bird in flight, it was set with a tiny ruby for the eye. It was hot to touch, warmed by her body, and it seemed to grow heavy as she studied it in the sunlight. She wasn't sure where it came from, though she'd had it as long as she could remember. It had to have been a gift, beautiful and finely wrought as it was. The Lady didn't pay well enough for Renila to afford such expensive adornments.

Casting the resentment aside, she inhaled deeply, savouring the cool, clean mountain air as it filled her chest. The bitter wind whipped her hair about her and stung at her nose and cheeks, but she revelled in the untamed beauty of it. She threw her arms wide, welcoming its embrace, and let her head fall back to feel the warm rays of the sun kiss her upturned face.

It took some time, but eventually her rage evaporated. The air steamed around her, and like mist dispersing in the morning sun, it caught in the breeze and floated away into the aether. She sighed. There were days, like today, that she wished it were more than just her temper – or even her worries and fears – the wind could carry away. But she was a mother now. Everything she wanted, all her dreams and desires, were secondary. Erion had to be kept safe. So, she would endure.

It was almost midday by the time Renila returned to the castle. Farran was waiting for her at the gate, no doubt having spied her approach from his office window. His dark brows knit in a stern scowl, but he said nothing as he helped her dismount and escorted both her and Copper back to the stables.

It did not surprise her to find Erion sitting in the mare's stall. His stormy grey eyes warmed as she entered, swirling to match her own amber gaze. And though she noted the weary circles under his eyes, she said nothing. He didn't like to be reminded of how easily he tired these days. He hugged her fiercely and took Copper's reins from the Captain, affording Farran a long, flat stare as he did so.

'I can take care of her, Mother,' he assured her, stopping her hands as she reached for the saddle. Then he offered her a cheeky grin. 'You should go wash. You stink of horse.' She resisted the urge to cuff him across the back of the head, instead ruffling a hand through his dark hair. She kissed his brow and smiled as he feigned embarrassment.

'Thank you,' she whispered. The soft smile he gave in return told her he understood all that she was thanking him for. Her son was remarkably perceptive.

Farran took her elbow and guided her from the stables, his grip on her arm firm enough to communicate his displeasure. But despite his temper, she couldn't ignore how the feel of his fingers against her skin made her heart flutter and her breath catch in her throat. He released her as they entered the castle but stayed close to her side while he shepherded her through the hallways to his office. Farran's squire, Olly, stood guard. The Captain's tone was brusque, and his voice clipped as he instructed the boy to ensure they were not interrupted.

He gestured Renila ahead, following her in and closing the door firmly behind him. He crossed the room and removed the cloak from his shoulders, throwing it across the back of his chair without a word. It was a mark of his irritation – the carelessness with which he tossed it. Farran was the sort of man who folded even his socks neatly and had them arranged in the drawer by colour and thickness. Renila repressed a smile when she glanced at his bookshelf – alphabetised by the author's surname, then in order of publication date, if she knew him at all.

He stood at the window with his back to her and sighed as he ran a frustrated hand through his dark hair. She was forced to take a deep, steadying breath as thoughts of those fingers knotting in her own burgundy mane flashed through her mind. He was a married man, she reminded herself firmly. He was not for her.

'Are you going to explain yourself?' he snapped eventually.

'I needed some fresh air,' she answered, betraying no hint of the emotions that had sent her running.

Farran swore as he rounded on her, twitching as if he was fighting the urge to cross the room and shake her. She kept her expression neutral, despite the fist of fear around her heart, and met the blazing fury in his gaze.

'Damn it, Renila!' he raged. 'We had Darklings in the woods not two nights ago – are you trying to get yourself killed?'

'I'm sorry,' she murmured, looking at the floor. 'It was broad daylight, I thought it would be safe.'

'Don't be ridiculous. You know fine well they might prefer to hunt at night, but they're just as dangerous during the day. And what if they'd followed you, hmm? You could have led them straight to us.'

'I would know if I was being followed, and if I had been, I wouldn't have come back here until I'd lost them.'

Farran placed his hands on the edge of his desk and leaned across it, his voice cold. 'You expect me to believe that? That a servant girl, a nursemaid, not only knows when she's being followed by some of the deadliest hunters in the world but is skilled enough to evade them?'

Renila was silent, and though she tried to keep her face blank, she saw the triumphant gleam in his eyes and knew that she had somehow betrayed her shock.

'I don't know,' she whispered. It was the truth. She didn't even know how she'd known that she knew. She winced inwardly. It sounded mad, even to her. She wasn't even sure it made sense. Farran wouldn't believe her. But she wasn't lying. Not even by omission this time.

All she had of her past before the castle were vague flashes of a frantic flight through the forest. Precisely who had led her here, she could no longer remember. But she could remember a steady presence at her side as she fought her way free of the forest. In the dark of the night, she'd staggered, exhausted and heavily pregnant, to the doors of the castle. The Lady had opened the door just as her waters broke. Somehow, through the screams of her labour pains, she'd begged sanctuary for herself and her child before passing out.

She'd woken days later – alone, dazed and confused, any knowledge of her life before gone. Whatever she knew about herself now was a gift from the Lady. She'd told Renila her name and helped her to the nursery, pointing out her sleeping son in a cot beside the Lady's own infant children. She could still remember how her hands had shaken with fear when she first cradled that tiny, fragile baby to her breast. The Lady had helped her name him. Erion. It meant 'hope', she'd said, in an ancient tongue long since forgotten by mortals.

Later, the Lady had explained more. That Renila had run away, fleeing some nameless threat. The Lady, too, was hiding. Her children were in danger, for they were blessed with magic. And though it was perhaps little more than a remnant of some ancient spell, all magic was dangerous and sought by those who craved power. It had to be kept secret until they came of age.

Renila fidgeted with her necklace again, the only thing she had of her life *before*, then took a deep breath. She pushed the black thoughts from her mind, forcing herself to look at Farran. How was she to explain that sometimes, inexplicably, she just *knew* things? How could she explain the vast wealth of knowledge in her head? More knowledge than anyone her age could have learned? Stranger, that she had no memory of learning these things? How could she explain the stories? She didn't know where she'd ever heard them, but she knew them – hundreds of them, as if the words were inked on her heart.

The simple answer was that she couldn't explain any of it, and if she tried, Farran would either think her mad or a liar. She wasn't sure which was worse. So, she bowed her head in submission.

'I'm sorry, Captain,' she said. 'I behaved recklessly ... I will not do so again. I hope you can find it in your heart to forgive me. Now, if you'll excuse me, I must see to the children.'

She curtseyed and left without meeting his gaze. She didn't think she could bear for him to see the tears that threatened to stain her cheeks. It was only the feeling of Olly's eyes on her retreating back that made her walk calmly down the hallway.

Only once she rounded the corner, beyond sight and hearing, did she let that rising wave of emotion wash over her. Crushed beneath it, she crumpled to the ground and wept. She'd never felt so alone ... or so lost.

CHAPTER FOUR

S uriya was glad for a day free of her mother. Neither she nor Lucan had been plagued by the nightmares again, but she was exhausted and in no mood to pretend otherwise. Particularly not for her mother. Why she was so incapable of simple kindness, never mind warmth or tenderness, was beyond Suriya.

With a frustrated sigh, she sat at her dressing table and glowered at her reflection in the mirror. Renila had not been to see them that morning, leaving Suriya to choose her own outfit for the day. She far preferred the velvet tunic, brown leggings and soft, fleece-lined leather boots to the fancy dresses her mother liked her to wear anyway. Particularly if she had any hope of keeping up with the boys.

Her hair, on the other hand, was an unruly mess. It was a wild mass of dark gold curls that fell just shy of her waist. The colour was nice enough, shining almost red gold in the sunlight. But it had a mind of its own, catching in non-existent winds. Mostly whenever her emotions got the best of her. That, combined with her quiet demeanour, seemed to have given her the reputation in the castle of being ... peculiar. Strange. *Other.* People, other children in particular, mostly avoided her. Something about her made them nervous. Uncomfortable.

Even her eyes were strange. Almond-shaped and slanted, they were the colour of molten gold – an odd enough colour to be sure, but sometimes they almost seemed to ... glow. She was, however, safe in the knowledge she was nowhere near as peculiar as Erion. Her eyes at least stayed the same colour. But neither her hair nor her eyes were anything compared to the peculiarity of her ears. Scowling, she pulled her hair over the tapered tips to hide their deformity. She didn't like the way people stared at them.

Cursing at her misfortune to be burdened with such an abnormal appearance, she braided her hair as best she could. Satisfied her ears were hidden, she set out in search of Lucan. Her brother had dressed and gone ahead to the kitchens for their breakfast, since their mother *'did not require their presence'* that morning.

She scowled as the words echoed in her head. What kind of mother *required* their children's presence? Renila had never treated Erion with such cold aloofness. No mother in the castle had. The blacksmith's wife smothered their son with attention, not to mention gifts and food. Suriya shuddered at the thought. There had to be a happy medium between that pampering mare and her own heartless mother.

Lucan was waiting for her outside the kitchens, leaning against the wall with his arms folded across his chest. Unlike Suriya, Lucan was well-admired within the castle. While she repelled people, he drew them in with his effortless charm. Other girls in the castle said the sight of him took their breath away. Suriya could see why. He was still a boy, with the softness of childhood rounding his features, but her brother was stunningly handsome. In years to come, she had no doubt that he would break plenty of hearts.

A shaggy mop of silvery hair covered his brow and fell into his eyes with seemingly careless indifference. Suriya knew better. Lucan had a strange birthmark on his forehead he preferred to keep hidden, for much the same reason as she covered her ears. Most folk in the castle were superstitious, and such defects were considered a sure sign of witchcraft.

Suriya snorted inwardly. A single glance at Lucan's eyes was enough to realise there was magic in him. She wasn't sure how she knew that, and she'd never shared the belief with anyone, but she was certain that Lucan was no mere mortal. By extension, neither was she, since the same blood flowed in their veins. Exactly what they were, she didn't know either … but no mortal boy should have eyes so captivating. He was her brother, and she knew him better than her own heart. But when she met Lucan's gaze, her mind emptied. All she saw were his stunning, pearlescent blue eyes, gleaming like moonstone in candlelight.

Over the years she had learned to avoid looking directly into that particular trap. Instead, she focussed on his eyelashes or his brows or the smattering of freckles across the bridge of his nose that matched her own. Lucan wasn't stupid. He realised she never met his eyes. He just didn't understand why. At some point, he'd decided it was because she was shy – unsure and deferring to her brother to lead the way. It was easier to let him believe that than explain the truth of it.

'Mal is in a black humour today,' warned Lucan as she approached. 'Saw me coming a mile off and chased me out with a rolling pin.'

'I'll do it,' she said, running a smoothing hand over her hair. 'What do you want?'

Lucan snorted and shook his head in disbelief. With a sarcastic bow, he gestured towards the kitchen in challenge. 'Whatever you can get.'

She threw him a withering glance as she opened the door and slipped inside. Mal spotted her as soon as she entered. The woman scowled in annoyance.

'Lady Suriya,' she snapped. 'What are you doing in here?'

Suriya looked at her feet, shifting anxiously in a way she'd learned made others more comfortable in her presence. Though she was already small, she slumped to make herself smaller, appear less of a threat. Anything to fool whatever instincts made people afraid of her.

'I'm terribly sorry to bother you,' she mumbled, curtsying with deliberate awkwardness. 'I was wondering if you had any scraps or leftovers to spare? It's such a beautiful day outside, I thought we could have a picnic? I was hoping to surprise the other children ...' She trailed off artfully, eyes downcast, biting her lip nervously while she fidgeted with the front of her tunic.

Mal crumbled. She fetched the basket herself and filled it full of bread rolls, thin slices of cured meats, cheese, apples, pears, sweet honey cakes and strawberry tarts. There were even two glass bottles of apple juice – pressed that morning with fresh fruit from the castle orchard. Then she covered the basket with a blanket and ushered Suriya out the door, with much advice about the best spot for a picnic.

Lucan was waiting for her on the front steps, his eyebrows disappearing into his hair as he took in the feast she carried. He let out a low whistle and shook his head. 'How did you manage that?'

'I asked nicely.'

Lucan winced but nodded in agreement. 'Fair enough.'

'There's enough for everyone,' she said. 'Mal said it was alright for everyone else to join us, just so long as chores are done by sunset.'

Lucan crowed with delight and tore off towards the stables. 'I'll tell Erion and get the others to spread the word.'

'Alright,' she called back. 'I'll be down by the burn.'

He threw a hand up to show he'd heard before he disappeared into the courtyard. Suriya smiled. For all his quirks, she loved her brother. They were two halves of the same whole – equal and opposing forces that balanced each other out perfectly.

Lucan was racing through the fields with Erion and the other children. Alone on the picnic blanket, Suriya smiled indulgently at their antics. She wasn't sure what they were playing, but it seemed to involve a lot of ferocious yelling and even some screaming. She heaved a sigh and counted her blessings at being left out.

They were on the edge of the orchard, shaded from the sun by a large apple tree. The stream that was the source of fresh water for the castle ran alongside. The pleasant sound of the water gurgling over the rocks was a soothing backdrop to such a beautiful day. Across the stream, the farmers' fields stretched until they met the forest. The paddock closest held a small herd of cows, along with a larger flock of sheep, and a few goats. The one beside that was empty except for the farmer's two placid plough horses. Beyond that, the fields were devoted to crops.

She watched as Erion bowed out of the game, blowing hard from the effort. Lucan mocked him, but even at this distance, she sensed his worry. If she were being honest, she shared it. Erion seemed to grow weaker with every passing day, though nothing seemed obviously wrong with him. They'd asked their mother about it once, asked her to help their friend. She'd told them to mind their own business. To distract herself from her fears, Suriya continued to study the surrounding land.

The castle was self-sufficient – it even had a mill further downstream to grind flour for bread. Once a month, Captain Farran sent a small party out to the nearest market to trade and to hunt for game. But they could survive without such ventures if necessary.

The picnic was a mark of the bounty the land provided. Food and drink for such an unnecessary treat might have been considered wasteful in the dead of winter. But Suriya had known there was plenty to spare, especially when the farmers had been boasting of their harvests for the last fortnight. She wouldn't have asked otherwise.

It hadn't taken the children long to demolish most of the picnic. Unsurprisingly, all the cakes and tarts were long gone. There was still some bread and cheese left, and she handed some to Erion as he approached and collapsed on the blanket, panting with exertion. He mumbled his thanks through a mouthful of fluffy dough and watched Lucan and the others continue the game without him.

'Are you alright?'

'Why wouldn't I be?' he asked with his most endearing smile.

She wasn't fooled. Erion was the only person she'd ever encountered who she and Lucan could not charm, but that immunity seemed to go both ways. He never had been, nor likely ever would be, able to pull the wool over their eyes. She gave him a withering look that said as much. He chuckled but said nothing.

'It's getting worse,' she pressed.

Erion waved her away with a dismissive hand. 'I'm fine. I'm just worried about my mother.'

Suriya recognised a distraction when she saw one, but she couldn't stop herself from asking, 'What's wrong with Renila?'

'She went out riding in an awful rage,' he explained. 'Captain Farran was waiting for her when she came back. He was furious. He took her back into the castle. But I haven't seen her since.'

Suriya frowned. 'She didn't come to wake me and Lucan this morning either. When I asked for her, nobody could find her. What was she so angry about?'

'Not a clue,' he huffed, running a tired hand across his brow.

Suriya took his hand in her own and gave it a reassuring squeeze. Then she stood. 'Would you please ask Lucan to take the basket and blanket back to Mal, once everyone's finished?'

'Of course,' he responded, brows furrowing. 'Where are you going?'

'To find Renila.'

Erion struggled to his feet. 'I'll come with you.'

'It's alright,' she assured him. 'I can manage. You should enjoy the sunshine while you can – winter isn't that far off. Besides, the fresh air will do you some good.'

Suriya checked Renila's rooms first then popped her head into the kitchen to ask Mal if anyone had seen her – they had not. She checked the library, the drawing room and the dining room. Having no success, she dared to approach her mother's chambers. The Lady was out of her rooms, so she was safe to take a brief glance around. No surprise that Renila wasn't there either. The difficult relationship she and the Lady shared was no secret.

Suriya squared her shoulders. Time to face the Captain then.

Olly's baby blue eyes grew wide as she approached. She smiled sweetly at him, using whatever girlish charms she could muster, fluttering her lashes and blushing.

'Can I help you?' he mumbled.

'Oh, could you?' she asked, leaning closer. He swallowed, glancing about nervously. 'I was hoping to speak with the Captain. It's a matter of grave urgency.'

He nodded fervently and scrambled for the door. The poor boy couldn't open it fast enough, and he bowed far lower than necessary as he showed her in. She gave him a shy smile then turned her attention to the man behind the desk.

Captain Farran did not seem impressed by the interruption.

'Olly? What is this?' he snapped, looking up from the mountain of paperwork on his desk and frowning at the intrusion. Evidently his mood had not improved since Erion had seen him with Renila. Olly flushed to the root of his hair.

'Captain Farran,' he stammered, gesturing at her, 'the Lady Suriya.'

Farran's scowl deepened. 'Yes, I can see that. What I want to know is what she's doing in my office?'

Olly's mouth opened and closed several times as he struggled to find an explanation.

'I need to speak to you, Captain,' she insisted, her voice quiet but firm. Farran raised a dubious eyebrow, studying her cautiously. He was one of the few in the castle who didn't flinch from the sight of her. In fact, Suriya could see the glimmer of respect growing in his eyes as she added, 'In private.'

'Out. I'll deal with you later,' he ordered the shamefaced boy. Olly bowed again and left. Farran leaned back in his chair, a finger running over his chin. 'Well, Lady Suriya, how may I be of service?'

She did not miss the hard edge of irony beneath his otherwise mild tone. Clearly, he thought her nothing but a silly girl, wasting his time. But she refused to flinch. 'It's about Renila.'

'What about her?' he asked.

Suriya held his gaze. 'Erion said she ran away from the castle. When she came back, he said you escorted her out of the stables … nobody has seen her since then.'

'I've no idea where she is, if that's what you're asking,' he answered, frowning as he leaned forward. 'She's in the castle – I escorted her back in myself and instructed my men not to let her leave again. I'm afraid I know no more than that.'

Suriya was unconvinced. She cocked her head to the side as she considered him. 'She was upset. Why?'

'I don't know.'

'Erion said you were furious.'

Farran's scowl deepened. It wasn't a question but he answered it anyway. 'She behaved recklessly. Put herself and everyone else at risk.'

'How?'

'It's not my place to say, Lady Suriya. I suggest you ask your mother.'

Suriya resisted the urge to scowl, but her irritation took another outlet.

'Does Renila realise you're in love with her?' she asked innocently.

Farran sat in stunned silence, his jaw hanging open with shock. 'What did you say?'

Suriya repressed a snort.

'I'm sorry, never mind,' she said, trying her best to look abashed. 'Please, forget I said anything. I'll go now.' She turned to leave, then paused. 'Forgive me, Captain, I'm terribly scatter-brained – remind me, what happened with Renila this morning?'

Farran's expression said he knew exactly what she was about, but he gave her what she wanted. 'I don't know what transpired, but this morning I saw Renila storming out of your mother's rooms in a terrible rage. I caught up with her just in time to see her charge out into the fields and beyond, unarmed and unescorted. Anything could have happened. I was angry at her for endangering herself and everyone else. I told her so when she returned – we argued, and she left. That's all I know, my lady.'

Suriya nodded in understanding and curtseyed. 'Thank you, Captain,' she said. 'I'm sure she'll turn up.' She turned on her heel and stalked from the room, ignoring Olly as she hurried down the corridor.

With a deep breath, she forced herself to think it through as she gazed out of a nearby window. Renila had returned to the castle, so at the very least she should be safe when darkness fell. The nights drew in closer with each passing day. The long, dark hours put the entire castle on edge. With the night came the nightmares. Suriya frowned. It was still daylight outside, but sunset was not far off.

Sunset. Of course, she realised, slapping herself on the forehead. She cursed her own stupidity and tore off down the hall, careering through the kitchen with reckless abandon. Mal yelled a torrent of abuse after her, but Suriya paid no heed. She was already charging up the spiral staircase to the top of the tower. By the time she reached the top, she was gasping for breath, and she practically fell through the door as she shoved it open.

Renila was sitting on the ramparts, her feet dangling over the edge as she awaited the oncoming sunset. Her claret hair was caught in the wind, dancing and snapping like a scarlet pennon. In the dying light of the day, her skin glowed with a tawny hue that almost matched her brilliant amber eyes.

She glanced round at the sound of Suriya's inelegant entrance, and red-rimmed eyes said she'd been crying. Without hesitation, Suriya clambered up onto the parapet beside her and they sat in companionable silence for a moment. Then she leaned in close and rested her head on Renila's shoulder. A choked sob escaped her, and she threw her arms around Suriya. She held Renila tight as she cried, and when she was done, she allowed Suriya to dry her tears with a handkerchief. Together, they watched the sun set, bathing the land in a golden glow. It was only when Farran arrived to begin his watch that Renila consented to be led back inside.

The kitchens were in the usual disarray that preceded dinner, so nobody noticed as Suriya guided Renila through the chaos. She led the way, moving quickly and quietly through the hallways, back to the rooms she shared with her brother. Their mother had once insisted they had their own separate chambers. It had lasted precisely a week before she relented, since they'd just slept in the same room anyway.

Suriya allowed Renila to build up the fire in the sitting room as she pulled out two heavy blankets from the chest in the bedroom. Lucan would join them soon, and Erion would be half a step behind him, so she pulled out two more and piled them neatly beside the fire.

Sure enough, the door banged open just as Suriya and Renila settled themselves into the sofa by the fireplace, snuggled together for warmth. Winter was a while away yet, but autumn nights in the north were just as chilly. Lucan breezed into the room with all the subtlety of a tornado, asking a dozen questions in the same breath. Erion followed and went straight to his mother as she opened the blanket and wrapped him inside it with her.

'I'm sick,' Suriya lied, cutting her brother off. He blinked, not understanding. 'I require supper in my room, enough for four because I need company to see to my every whim. Lucan, go and tell Mal.'

He grinned and gave a mocking bow. 'As you command, my lady.'

'You should maybe be a little less liberal with the truth than that,' Renila added as he made to leave, 'or we'll have Old Jayne up here to find out what's wrong with her.'

Suriya winced. She hadn't thought of that. The castle healer was of the belief that her patients would recover faster if she made being unwell unbearably unpleasant. Her examinations were brutal and her remedies even worse. Lucan nodded in understanding and darted from the room. As soon as the door closed behind him, Erion turned to his mother.

'Are you going to tell me what happened earlier?' he asked.

Suriya looked at Renila. She'd said nothing about the cause of her tears, but Suriya would have held her tongue regardless. Those were Renila's secrets to share. Renila's bright, amber eyes stared into the fire dancing in the hearth, and Suriya was struck by the thought that those eyes seemed to glow. Like embers, they flared and smouldered as she considered her words.

'I had an argument with the Lady,' she said, her voice low and cautious. 'I was angry. It was best for me to leave before I said or did something I might later regret. I went for a ride to calm down, and when I returned ... well, let's just say that Captain Farran was rather vexed with me for leaving without a guard. He made his displeasure quite known. Apparently, I put myself and everyone here in danger with my *recklessness*.'

Erion frowned and caught Suriya's eye. She bit her lip and offered a small shrug. It was clearly not the entire story. Suriya was particularly interested in what her mother and Renila had argued about. But neither of them wanted to push her on it. She would tell them when she was ready.

But there was one matter Suriya couldn't let go. 'Why did the Captain think you'd put the castle in danger?'

Renila winced as she realised what she'd said. Suriya watched her face closely. The emotions were easy to read. She was considering telling them the truth, before deciding that it was, in fact, too much for them to bear. But she also didn't have it in her to look them in the eye and lie.

'We live in troubled times, and our greatest defence is to remain hidden,' she told them. 'Captain Farran worries that any excursions may lead strangers to the castle. The secrecy of this place keeps us all safe. But you must say nothing to anyone – your mother would be most upset if she learned that I'd said anything.'

'I promise,' Suriya vowed, snuggling in closer. But all the warmth of Renila's body could not chase the chill of fear from her bones. Two nights before, she and Lucan had dreamed of the Darklings in the Ravenswood. It was unlikely to be a coincidence that their mother and the Captain were now so on edge about security.

Lucan returned moments later, bearing a tray laden with food. His stunning moonstone eyes flickered straight to Suriya, and she saw the worry within them. She smiled softly, to let him know she was alright, but he continued to frown as he set the tray before the fire.

'Venison pies,' he announced, handing a pastry to Suriya. 'Hot out the oven.' Their fingers bumped as she took it, and his touch lingered, as if reassuring himself that she was alright.

'My favourite,' she said, avoiding his eyes.

'I know,' he replied. She glanced at the tray. As well as the pies, there were buttered leeks and carrots, crusty white bread, a wax-sealed round of Suriya's favourite cheese and half a cherry cake dusted with sugar.

'How did you get all that off Mal?' she asked lightly, trying to cheer him up.

It seemed to work. He smirked and collapsed on the sofa beside her, but the worry didn't leave his eyes. 'I asked nicely,' he said, bumping his shoulder against hers.

'You stole it,' she translated.

He grinned and shrugged noncommittally. And though the worry faded from his face, he stayed close to her throughout the meal. Suriya considered his behaviour as she bit into the buttery pastry – delicious, bursting with venison, onion, mushroom, bacon and rich gravy. She and Lucan had always been close. A single look at the other's face was all they needed to know what they were thinking. But of late, they hadn't even needed to look. It was as if they could sense the emotions rolling off the other, like waves crashing against the rocks. She didn't know what to make of it all.

'Tell us a story,' Lucan blurted to Renila.

Suriya suppressed a sigh. He was trying to distract her. It wasn't working.

'What sort of story?' asked Renila, tearing up the piece of bread in her hand.

'Whatever you like.'

She gave him a long look, as if to say she knew what he was about. 'Alright,' she agreed. Her eyes grew distant as she delved into her mental library for options. It took her less time than usual to begin, as though this story had been sitting on the tip of her tongue all day, waiting to be told. 'It is said that worlds are often shaped by wars, but never have those words been so true as during the last days of Sephiron's Rebellion.

'With the might of the Graced at their backs, the Immortals could finally drive back the darkness. They fought tirelessly to end it, to stop Sephiron and those who had joined with him. The death toll was beyond count.

'Eventually, after decades of bloodshed, they found the answer they had sought. Four champions were chosen for the task – one from each of the Graced bloodlines, four chosen warriors who might lead the way to victory.

'They led their armies in the last push against Sephiron's fortress. They slaughtered the Darklings in their thousands. Even the rebel lords could not hold them back. They entered his fortress, leaving only death in their wake. And then the chosen four sought the Dark Prince Sephiron.

'They were Sil Ciaron, jewel of the fierce Dragon clans; Princess Illyol, heart of the Elven forest court; Elucion, whose flame burned the brightest of all the Phoenix; and the Unicorn, Revalla, Lady of the Isles. Fierce were they, and terrible was their rage. And when they found him, they held him – for only when they stood together were these four equal to his might. They held him and bound him where he stood, sacrificing their lives so that Sephiron would never again wreak havoc on the people of their world. The magic it took to bind him was vast and wild. Strong enough to level the surrounding land. It razed his fortress to the ground and left only ruins in its wake. Only that dark mountain Dar Kual, and the keep atop it remained. So poisoned was it by his twisted magic that not even the combined power of the Graced could cleanse it from this world.

'And when all was done, and the Dark Prince vanquished, the rebels lay down their arms and surrendered.

'But Sephiron's heirs still lived, and the scourge of the Darklings could not be erased. They continued to slaughter wherever they went, long after their master was defeated. And so, the Graced delved once more into their magic. They erected cities to the north and south, to the east and west, and they named them for the fallen warriors who had saved them all. And between the cities was the Binding – a barrier of pure magic to contain the plague of the Darklings, to protect the world of mortals.

'As if in answer to the call of that magic, the world itself shuddered and shook. The mountains to the west grew higher. The forests to the north grew thicker. The land to the east crumbled into the sea, and to the south the mountains erupted in fire. Everything within the Binding withered and died and so was born the Barren Lands.' Renila paused and shook herself from her trance. She glanced at the children and, seeing their awe-struck faces, winked. 'And that, children, is how the world as we know it took shape.'

The magic of her tale was broken, and Lucan scoffed. 'That's ridiculous!'

'Aye,' Erion agreed, shaking a disparaging head at his mother. 'How old do you think we are to believe such nonsense?'

Renila laughed, and the three of them fell into comfortable conversation, discussing whatever shenanigans the boys planned for the morrow.

But Suriya stayed quiet, staring into the fire, unable to shake the feeling that there had been ancient truth in those words … and that Renila knew it.

Beneath a starlit sky, standing on a heather-clad hillside, a man waited. He was tall, broad-shouldered and powerful. Tattoos, so black they seemed to gobble up the faint moonlight, swirled over his bare arms and up his neck, curling over the shaved sides of his head. His remaining hair, long and tied in warrior braids, was dark as night and his eyes almost matched. And though he stood motionless, there was something imposing … menacing … about him. Like a sleeping wolf, with the promise of death lurking beneath his bronze skin.

A raven's cry shattered the silence, but the man did not flinch. His black gaze remained impassive, staring steadily out into the night.

Watching.

Waiting.

Minutes passed. Hours perhaps. The rise and fall of his chest the only sign that he was, in fact, living, and not just a statue carved in flesh.

But his patience was rewarded.

Without warning, a woman appeared, as if stepping out of the air itself. Her hair was moon-white and her eyes were as vast and mysterious as the night sky. Yet her face was young and lovely. Breathtaking. Unearthly. Inhuman.

The man seemed unperturbed by either the manner or quality of her appearance. He did not even turn his head to greet her as she joined him.

'You should not have come,' he said, his voice little more than a deep, dark rumble in the night.

'I had no choice. I need your help,' she replied, as cold and distant as the stars.

He snorted. 'Tell me something I don't know.'

'Her power stirs. I cannot keep her hidden much longer.'

'Her power? Or theirs?'

The woman sighed in exasperation. 'Both. They are Awakening. The wards struggle to contain it. Thoran and Adara's children came searching. Kylar's daughter too and, worse still, she was followed. I have healed the crack they found, but others will form and the Darklings will return.'

'You should never have agreed to harbour them. They would be better off with their own kind.'

She sighed once more, this time in defeat. 'Probably. But they are too important to risk. Rionna would not have shown them to me otherwise. Even their people could not guarantee their safety for long. Your brother plays a dangerous game with his Court. Sooner or later, they will uncover his lies, and the war will resume. Better I keep them where I can protect them myself.'

'Only you can't,' he noted, the ghost of a sneer touching his lips. 'Your power is fading, Mother. Why else would you be here begging my aid?'

The woman rounded on her son, teeth bared. 'I ask nothing of you save that you clean up your own mess, boy. You swore to help me end his line, not continue it. Do not make me regret sparing her. I can still change my mind.'

The man turned then, rage and violence churning in his black gaze. 'As can I. Threaten her again. See what happens.'

'She has to go, Layol,' she hissed. 'The boy too.'

'He is not safe in the city,' he objected. 'Not until he is fully into his power. Not while Emalia rules.'

His mother looked heavenward. 'So you said, when you brought her to me all those years ago. But the world out there is no safer for either of them, and right now, his fiercest protector cannot summon enough magic to light a candle. I cannot continue with this task you have set me, Layol. Either take her back to the city or find some other way to protect her.'

Her son was silent for a long time, but eventually, he nodded.

'Alright,' he breathed. 'I will find another way. But as the saying goes, be careful what you wish for, Mother.'

Then he was gone, vanishing through a rip in the world. The woman cursed in frustration, before she too melted into darkness, leaving only the silent stars as witness.

CHAPTER FIVE

To say Lucan was feeling rebellious was an understatement. He wasn't sure where the feelings came from, but bitterness and resentment had his stomach churning. He didn't need to look at Suriya to know she felt the same. Why was that? How was it he always knew what she was thinking? What she was feeling? When he did glance sidelong at his sister, her golden eyes were glowing, her hair near crackling with the tension radiating off her.

Their mother was oblivious to their temper as she tucked into her breakfast. Lucan looked at the plate in front of him, heaped high with bacon, sausage, eggs and toast, and his stomach heaved. He dropped his knife and fork back on the table and pushed the plate away.

'Lucan? Is something the matter?'

'I'm not hungry,' he said.

His mother eyed him coolly while she finished a mouthful of fresh fruit. Then, coming to some decision, she laid her cutlery down with lethal precision and placed her elbows on the table, her hands steepled over the bowl.

She surveyed both Lucan and Suriya over the top of her elegant fingers for a moment before she spoke. 'Tell me, does this sudden lack of appetite have anything to do with some perceived mistreatment of a certain red-headed servant who needs to learn to keep her mouth shut?'

Lucan repressed a shiver at that eerie, mind-reading ability his mother had. After Renila had left, Suriya had told him everything. But their mother couldn't know that. Unease joined the storm heaving in his guts. A glance at Suriya, knuckles white around her spoon, had him straightening in his chair.

'What did you say to upset her?'

The Lady arched a sardonic brow, pinning him with the full force of her terrifying gaze. 'Why do you assume that I am the one in the wrong?'

Lucan glowered at her but said nothing, too scared to push the matter any further. Beside him, Suriya hissed through her teeth, prompting their mother to turn those remarkable eyes on her instead.

'Call it instinct,' his sister murmured.

The Lady scowled, and she leaned back in her chair. 'If you think I'm going to discuss such matters with a pair of children, you will be disappointed,' she told them. 'But if you wish me to treat you like adults, then perhaps it is time I give further thought to your arrangements in this house. If you can stomach these changes like grown-ups then, perhaps, I will consider increasing your involvement in the castle's running – and involving you in such future disputes.'

'What do you want us to do?' Suriya asked, cutting off the terse response that rose to Lucan's lips.

Their mother considered them with indifference, eyes flicking between the two, contemplating. 'In the first instance, I think it's about time that Lucan learned how to handle a sword. I would like you to train with Captain Farran every day.'

'What?' Lucan choked. He'd only been begging his mother to let him learn how to fight since he was old enough to talk. She'd always refused, without ever giving a reason. Beside him, Suriya stilled. He risked a glance sideways and noted the glower on her face. Turning back to his mother, he asked, 'Why?'

The Lady shrugged. 'You're old enough. I think it's appropriate. But it's more than swordsmanship, Lucan. Captain Farran is a good man – organised, capable and a fine leader. I think you can learn a lot from him.'

'And what about me?' Suriya asked.

Her mother's reply was trivial, and even more dangerous for it. 'I would like for you and I to spend more time together.'

'Doing what?'

Annoyance flickered across the Lady's face. 'It's time you learned what is involved in running this estate,' she said, her tone a little sharper than it had been before. She turned back to regard Lucan. 'Two small caveats. Firstly, if you wish to be treated like adults, then you shall each have your own rooms. It is not acceptable for a man and woman to share a bedroom unless they're married, even if you are brother and sister. Secondly, if you no longer wish to be considered children then you have no need of a nanny, so I can assign Renila to other duties within the castle. It is quite a wasted resource having her look after the two of you all the time.'

Lucan stared at his mother, mouth hanging open in shock. Suriya kicked him under the table. He shook himself and looked to her for help. Shy, she might be, but Suriya was far smarter than him. Not that he'd ever admit it. He could almost hear her mind whirring like a spinning top as she thought through their options.

Sure enough. 'Can we think about it?'

Their mother's lips twisted into a small smirk, but she said nothing and nodded. Suriya nudged him again, and at her pointed glare, he wolfed down some breakfast before they excused themselves and bolted for Renila's rooms.

His sister's pacing was making Lucan's head spin, but she was showing no sign of stopping soon, so he closed his eyes and flopped back on Erion's bed. Neither he nor Renila were in their room, but they hadn't expected them to be. Erion would be working in the stables, and Renila was still upstairs in their chambers changing the bedsheets. It was just a safe space to talk. Away from their mother.

'How can you sleep right now?' Suriya snapped.

'I'm not sleeping,' he grumbled. 'Your pacing is just giving me a headache.'

Suriya spun to face him, her hair crackling with static again. Lucan tried not to laugh – he really did – but she looked ridiculous.

'This isn't funny, Lucan!' she exclaimed, throwing her hands up in exasperation.

But Lucan could hardly breathe through the fit of giggles gripping him. 'Sorry,' he choked eventually. 'You just look ridiculous when you're angry!'

The look she gave him was pure death. He stopped laughing and sat up straight.

'I'm sorry,' he said as sincerely as he could manage. 'But I don't understand what you're so stressed about. I know it'll be hard to have separate rooms, but won't it be worth it for her to treat us like grown-ups? She wants me to train with Farran!'

'That's exactly what I'm so stressed about,' Suriya retorted, folding her arms across her chest. 'You're so enamoured with the prospect of learning to fight that you've forgotten everything else she said.'

'What do you mean?' he asked, not really listening as he brandished a broom handle around in mock swordplay. Suriya caught the other end and wrenched it from his grasp.

'I mean that you're so wrapped up in yourself you've forgotten the part where she said we have to get rid of Renila,' she snapped.

'I am not!' he objected, snatching back the broom handle. 'I know what she said. But Renila would still be around. And we're old enough now; we don't need a nanny.'

Suriya dodged as he over-extended and almost thumped her across the head with his mock sword. He knew she was scowling at him, but he didn't care. She was just trying to ruin his fun. She was so boring sometimes.

But she was also extremely stubborn. 'What if she sends Renila away? We'd never see her or Erion ever again,' she persisted. 'If you're training with Farran all the time, you won't be able to spend any time with Erion anymore. He's your best friend, and he's sick, and you're just going to ignore him because you're so selfish!'

Furious, he rounded on her, waving the broom handle in her face.

'You're just jealous that I get to do something exciting while you're stuck inside doing girly things with mother. But you *are* a girl Suriya – maybe it's time you learned how to be one. You act like you're so clever and better than me, but you're wrong. You're just a scared little girl pretending to be something you're not!'

Suriya flinched at his words, and he felt a flash of guilt. But he knew he was right, so he pushed those feelings down deep and looked down his nose at her with smug superiority. He was nearly a man, and she was just a silly girl. She couldn't understand how important it was that he trained with Farran.

'This is what she wants,' she choked. 'She's trying to divide us, because she knows that we're stronger together.'

But the unshed tears shining in her golden eyes only strengthened his resolve. 'No. *You* are stronger with *me*, because alone you are weak and pathetic,' he snarled.

She shoved past him and ran to the door. But she paused on the threshold and looked back at him, tears now staining her rosy cheeks.

'You're nothing but a bully, Lucan, picking on people smaller than you to make you feel better about yourself. You're a coward.'

And then she was gone.

Suriya wiped her cheeks dry as she slipped through the corridors. She wouldn't let anyone else see her cry. Her mind was racing. It wasn't their first argument, but Lucan had said nothing so hateful before. It hurt, even though she knew he hadn't meant it. He was angry and scared. He always preferred to hide from a problem rather than confront it head on. For all his brashness, Lucan hated conflict.

She wanted to scream. Her mother's games were simple enough to see, but there was nothing she could do to fight them. She was just a child, powerless to dictate her own life. It was as though her mother didn't want children at all – just obedient pets.

Suriya scowled, staring out the window at the nearby forest. She wasn't some well-trained dog, kept to perform tricks to entertain her mother. She was her own person, and she was damned if she was going to let anyone else control her life a moment longer.

A vision pierced through her thoughts. It was blurry. As if viewed through the fog of time, or the haze of a dream. An indistinct face hovered just beyond reach and ... were those kind, golden eyes smiling down at her? A woman's voice spoke and, though she didn't recognise it, she felt a warm, safe sense of familiarity when she heard it.

Fate and destiny are for those too weak to forge their own paths, it said.

Suriya blinked, and the vision vanished. Had it been real or imagined? She wasn't sure. But those words tugged at the edge of her memory. Wherever they had come from, they'd struck a chord deep in her soul. Even if unease did coil in her stomach at the whole thing. Dreams were one thing, even daydreams. But visions? Magic? It wasn't possible …

With a deep breath, she set her shoulders and shoved the fear from her mind. No matter what Lucan or anyone else said, she was not weak. And someday, somehow, she would prove it to him.

Suriya's words haunted Lucan for the rest of the day. He didn't like what she'd said, and he liked the fact that he'd had no response even less. There wasn't much he hated more than not getting the last word.

Desperate for vindication, he sought Erion in the stables. The stable master scowled, warning him not to distract the boy from his work. He waffled some promises he had no intention of keeping and dashed off in the direction the old man pointed.

Erion was alone in a stall, brushing down the Lady's coal-black mare. Storm was a vicious-tempered brute, prone to biting and kicking almost anyone who came near her, and as big as some stallions. She'd always behaved for Erion, and Lucan's mother had eventually conceded that his friend had a gift. Allowing Erion to care for her mount was about the only concession she'd ever made for him, so he took his duty seriously, much to Lucan's disappointment. Work was *so* boring.

Storm snorted as he approached, warning him to keep his distance even as the gleam in her eye dared him to get closer. Well-versed in all her tricks, he swiped an apple from Erion's pocket as he entered the stall and held it out as a peace offering. She snatched it from his hand and turned away, grudgingly accepting his presence while she chomped on the treat.

'Bribery,' Erion said, rolling his eyes. 'I was going to give her that as a reward for being good once I'd finished!'

'So give her another one.'

'It's not good for her to have too many.' Lucan just shrugged, perched himself on the small bale of fresh hay in the corner, and didn't apologise. Erion heaved a heavy sigh and shook his head. 'What is it?'

'What do you mean?'

Erion turned and afforded him a long, flat stare. 'You're in a foul mood; you clearly want to talk about it – why don't you just get it over with and tell me about whatever's bothering you?'

'Suriya and I had an argument,' Lucan admitted with a scowl. Erion crossed his arms and leaned against the wall, waiting. Lucan rolled his eyes and elaborated. 'My mother is going to let me train with Farran, but Suriya told me not to do it. She's just jealous, because she's a girl, so she has to do boring girl stuff with Mother. I told her as much, and she called me a bully and a coward – which is ridiculous, because I'm far braver than she is.'

'I'm sure she didn't mean it—' Erion began.

Lucan cut him off. 'Yes, she did. She's mad! She thinks my mother is plotting to split us up and send you and Renila away! All because Mother

51

said that, now we're adults, we should have different rooms and that we don't need a nanny!'

Erion was quiet for a while, toying with his ring. 'What if she's right?'

'Don't be ridiculous,' Lucan snapped.

Erion's eyes flickered from storm-grey to wolf-yellow as his worry gave way to annoyance. 'But what if she is, Lucan?'

Lucan leapt to his feet, anger rising in his throat. 'So now you agree with her? You think I'm being selfish!'

'I didn't say that,' Erion began.

'That's what Suriya said! She said I'm selfish and cowardly, and you think so too!'

'I didn't—'

'Well, I'm not! I'm brave and strong, and I'm going to prove it!'

Turning on his heel, he stormed out, so angry he barely noticed where he was going. But as he passed Copper's stall at the far end of the building, he stopped. An idea formed. His mother had never allowed him a horse of his own, but Renila had taken him out on her placid – if stubborn – mare plenty of times. He glanced around, checking nobody was watching, and slipped inside.

Copper's saddle was slung over the wooden partition separating her from Farran's stallion, and her bridle hung from a peg on the wall. The mare eyed him curiously but accepted his presence.

'Time for an adventure,' he murmured.

Copper was whinnying, as if in warning, as he led her from the stables. He hushed her with a gentle hand, but she continued to push her nose into his shoulder and snort unhappily until they were outside the castle walls. Even when he calmed her enough to mount, he could feel the tension radiating through her body. He briefly recalled Erion talking about how smart some animals were and wondered if the mare could sense the trouble he would be in for breaking the rules. He pushed the thought from his mind. She was just a horse.

She squealed in protest as he dug his heels into her sides, but she did as she was bid. He urged her into a gallop, charging through the farmers' fields towards his shadowy goal.

The Ravenswood. The one place he was forbidden to go, above all others. A place of mystery and nightmares. A place he was tired of fearing. Suriya had called him a coward. Worse, he knew Erion agreed with her. Well, he would prove them both wrong. Only the bravest souls would ever dare to enter that accursed forest.

He slowed Copper to a walk as they approached. His heart was pounding in his chest, his breath catching in his throat while he battled with himself. Beneath him, Copper shivered with apprehension, her footsteps hesitant as he pressed her onward.

Any warmth left in the autumn air evaporated as she stepped into the shadows beneath the tall trees. His senses were overpowered with the tang of pine, and he breathed it deep. It was a soothing smell, and he found himself drawn further into the forest. The light of the afternoon sun filtered through patches in the canopy, bathing the world beneath in a soft, golden glow. The ground was thick with moss and ferns, the last of the heather still in bloom. It was enchanting. Lucan wondered what he'd been so afraid of – and why his mother had banned him from ever setting foot in such a beautiful place.

But Copper's steps were still tentative as she carried him deeper into the wood, and Lucan understood why. The forest was closing in about them, the thickening undergrowth slowing their progress as the world grew darker. He'd proved his point, so he reached for the reins, intending to turn Copper for home. But the mare froze, sniffing anxiously.

She snorted, stepping back, her eyes rolling in fear. Lucan tried to calm her, but she only whinnied in fright, shaking her head as if to clear some disturbing scent from her nose. He gripped the reins tighter, trying to bring her under control as she grew more and more distressed. But it was no use. She screamed in terror, rearing and throwing her rider. Lucan tumbled to the forest floor, letting out a sharp yell of pain as his head cracked off a rock. He tried to stagger to his feet, blinking to clear his blurred vision, but he could only watch as Copper vanished into the shadows.

Nausea churned in his stomach. The world around him seemed altered somehow. The light filtering through the trees seemed too bright, yet everything else seemed darker than it should. And his head hurt quite a lot. He touched it with a tentative hand, probing the newly formed lump on the back of his skull as he tried once more to stand. His legs protested at his weight, and he took a shaky step forward – only to bump into a tree that seemed to have moved into his way. He glared at it as the world swayed and then frowned in confusion as he realised he was once more looking up from the ground. He blinked. He didn't remember lying down. But he was exhausted. Maybe he would just close his eyes. Just for a moment …

'Lucan, where are you?'

Lucan's eyes opened wide at the sound of his sister's voice resounding in his head. He groaned as he sat up, wincing as he touched the sore spot on the back of his head. What had happened? How long had he been lying here?

He staggered to his feet, casting around for some clue as to where he was or how he'd got there, but all he saw was darkness. He must have been out for hours; it had been broad daylight when he'd left the castle.

A rustle of leaves and the flicker of movement to his right made him start, and he turned. But there was nothing there. He whirled as something stirred behind him and froze when he saw a single pair of glowing red eyes peering at him through the gloom.

He ran.

It had been about an hour before sunset when Suriya, fed up with waiting for Lucan to come and apologise, had started searching for her brother.

But he was nowhere to be found. He'd missed dinner with their mother – something she seemed surprisingly smug about – and Mal hadn't seen him near the kitchens at all. When Suriya had finally tracked Renila down, she hadn't seen either Lucan or Erion since before breakfast.

Puzzled, Suriya went down to the stables. The stable master was far from pleased to see her and grumbled under his breath about *entitled noble brats* before pointing her towards the stalls.

She found Erion sitting in the hay in the corner of Storm's stall, worrying at the ring his mother had given him so long ago. The Lady's mare nickered – almost in greeting – before returning to munching her oats. Suriya skirted round the notorious beast as she crossed to Erion's side and flopped down in the hay with him. He looked tired, worn out from his day's work. She felt a flash of worry. He was weakening, no matter how he pretended. His eyes were storm-grey, a sure sign that he was upset, so she waited for him to speak.

'Do you really think your mother might send us away?' he asked.

Suriya bit her lip. She'd said that to provoke a reaction out of her brother, but there had been a ring of truth to her words. 'It worries me she has the power to decide.'

Erion gave her a sideways glance that said he didn't appreciate the very diplomatic answer. But he let it go.

'Lucan can be selfish,' he said instead, 'and impulsive, and reckless. But he's not a coward.'

'I know,' she agreed. 'I was upset.'

Erion snorted. 'Understandable. He always overreacts when he's wrong and can't admit it. What did he say?'

'He called me weak and pathetic.' She sighed. 'He said I was just a silly little girl, and I was jealous of him.'

'You're a lot of things, Suriya,' he told her, taking her hands in his, 'but none of those are on the list.'

Suriya bumped his shoulder, and they fell into companionable silence for a while. 'Where is he anyway?'

'Don't know. Haven't seen him since he ran out of here this afternoon.'

'What trouble is he up to this time?' she muttered, more to herself than Erion. She just wished she could reach out with her mind and ask him, *'Lucan, where are you?'*

His voice rang in her head, screaming in fear, and she flinched with surprise. *'Help!'*

'Suriya?' Erion asked, placing a steadying hand on her shoulder. His voice was thick with concern as he peered at her. 'What is it?'

'I thought—' she broke off, shaking her head as if to clear it. But it was

54

as if Lucan's mind had invaded her own. Like he was inside her head – no, like their minds had become tangled together. His panic, his pure terror, pounding through her veins like it was her own. *'Lucan?'*

Her fear – his fear – made her breath catch in her throat and her chest squeeze tight. She felt light-headed, and her heart was thundering like she'd just finished a race. Erion called her name again, but she held up a hand to silence him as she closed her eyes and tried to concentrate.

Lucan's thoughts were almost incomprehensible – a jumble of emotions and sensations. Images flashed through her mind of shadows and a shapeless menace. Then she saw it. A pair of red eyes glowing in the darkness. Two single words pierced through the chaos of Lucan's terror. *'Darkling. Ravenswood.'*

Suriya gasped aloud, and her eyes flew open. Erion was leaning over her, expression grim as he read the emotions flickering across her face.

'What's wrong?'

She forced herself to meet his eyes, but the words were difficult to force out past the tightness in her chest. And how could she possibly explain something she barely understood herself?

'Lucan. Ravenswood. Danger,' was all she could manage. Erion nodded curtly and helped her to her feet. In different circumstances, she might have noted how composed he was, despite the tension radiating off every line of his body. How the weariness that seemed to hold him in its grip had slipped from his shoulders like a disused garment. But she was barely aware of her surroundings, her mind still entwined with Lucan's as he careered through the forest.

'We're riding,' he told her, reaching for Storm's saddle. Suriya paused, then she squared her shoulders, took a deep breath and helped Erion ready her mother's horse.

Moments later, Erion leapt into the saddle and held out his hand. This time she didn't hesitate. She gripped his forearm, climbed up behind him and wrapped her arms around his waist. Storm pranced impatiently, as if sensing their need for haste, so Erion barely had to nudge his heels into her flanks for her to take off.

The great, black mare thundered out of the stables, across the courtyard and into the fields beyond. With open space in front of her, she stretched her powerful legs into a flat-out run, needing no encouragement from either of her riders. Nor did she appear to need direction, angling towards one section of the woods with unnatural surety. Suriya didn't question it – she couldn't get any sense of location from the turmoil in Lucan's head.

He was hiding now, gasping for breath but trying desperately to be quiet. Something moved in the shadows behind him. He froze. There was a quiet snuffling, like a dog scenting the ground for a trail to follow. He swallowed.

'Faster,' Suriya whispered. Storm heard her pleas. The mare whinnied a challenging call as she launched them into the forest. Darkness engulfed them, but Storm did not miss a step. She tore through the trees with unerring certainty, her long legs making quick work of the uneven ground as she wove through the dense forest. She snorted contemptuously as a tangled net of vines sought to block their path and charged through, the web yielding before her powerful chest.

Through the gloom, they spied a huge, fallen tree blocking their path. Erion didn't have to do anything as Storm checked her stride, gathered herself and leapt. Suriya yelped with surprise and clung to Erion. Somehow, he held them seated while Storm flew through the air and landed smoothly on the other side of the vast trunk. Right in the path of the Darkling.

The mighty mare gave a vicious roar and reared up, striking the creature with her great hooves. Erion clung on, but Suriya was thrown from the saddle. She tumbled to the ground, rolling over and over until she crashed into the narrow bole of a nearby pine. Disorientated and winded, it was only instinct that had her surging to her feet again.

'Suriya!' Lucan's voice cried from the shadows. 'Behind you!'

She whirled to see the Darkling careering towards her. It was small and weak. Little more than a child, and badly wounded. But its blood-red eyes had her paralysed in fear. Storm reared out of the darkness once more, a spectre of shadow and flashing hooves. Erion yelled encouragement and held on as best he could while the mare charged the Darkling down.

But it was fast. It darted out of the way, hissing irritably. Storm was quick to spin and chase after it, but it had heard Lucan's voice and was streaking through the darkness in his direction. Time seemed to stop as Suriya watched in horror.

As the Darkling had turned on Suriya, Lucan had risen from his hiding place in a desperate bid to defend her. Brandishing a branch like he'd wielded the broom handle only hours earlier. But now he was exposed, with nothing between him and the Darkling streaking towards him. He braced himself and held the stick out as if it were a sword. Like a great cat, the Darkling pounced.

Suriya's scream shattered the night. It was fear and wrath and defiance. And like fuel thrown on a fire, it stoked a single, stuttering ember into a raging inferno. Golden flames coalesced around her, twisting and raging through the darkness towards the creature. It screeched as the force of the blaze knocked it to the ground, where it was engulfed in the firestorm. It writhed and shrieked, but Suriya's fury was insatiable – the flames flared, and the Darkling's screams withered to a pitiful wail as it burned. The fire flickered as she hesitated.

'*Hold your ground,*' an unknown, yet familiar, voice snarled in her mind. '*Kill it now.*'

Whatever tenuous control she'd had over the flames disappeared as that presence took over. The inferno raged hotter than ever, and after what felt like eternity, the Darkling fell silent.

Suriya crashed to her knees, utterly spent, as the fire guttered and went out. Nothing remained of the Darkling but a charred, smoking husk. The forest floor was scorched and blackened in a perfect circle surrounding the corpse. Suriya's stomach heaved at the destruction she'd caused. She didn't know how, but whatever magic had conjured those flames had come from inside her. She dropped onto all fours and vomited on the ground.

Steady hands gathered the tangled mane of her hair and held it out of the way while she continued to retch. They were cool and calm as they soothed her through the pain, then held her while she shook and wept. She didn't need to open her eyes to know it was Erion who held her so tight.

'*Suriya?*' Lucan's voice whispered in her mind. Trembling fingers, slick with sweat, laced with her own, and she sensed her brother crouch down beside her. She squeezed his hand but couldn't bring herself to open her eyes, for fear of seeing the devastation again. Her brothers – for they were all family in her heart – held her as she cried herself out. They huddled together for warmth and security. Storm stood over them, herding them between her legs and nuzzling them with her nose now and again, as if reassuring herself that they were unharmed.

It was only when Suriya's tears ran dry that she consented to move. She was numb from shock and unsteady on her feet. The mighty black mare, who had saved all their lives, bowed down low as the boys lifted her onto her back. Then Erion took the reins and climbed up in front of her, while Lucan sat behind her. Together, they promised her, together they would keep her safe. And there, held between the two people she loved most in all the world, exhaustion dragged her down into oblivion.

———

A figure – a sliver of darkness in the shape of a woman – stalked through the gloom. Clad all in black, her feet were silent on the uneven ground, and despite the weapons hanging from her body, she moved like a wraith, slipping from one shadow to the next with a predator's grace. The acrid stench of smoke and burned flesh mingled with damp pine, and she followed it deeper into the woods.

Glancing up, she checked the moon was hidden by the forest canopy before lowering her hood and removing the scarf from about her mouth. Her bronze face was pallid, as though she had not seen the sun for a hundred years, and marked with ink-black tattoos that curled like flames over her skin. And her eyes ... her eyes were wholly black.

She paused, sniffing.

Crouched low.

Those black eyes narrowed. Tugging a glove off with her teeth, she extended a tattooed hand towards the forest floor. To a smoking circle. Scorched and blackened, with a husk of a body at its centre. Bones enough to tell it was human. But not mortal. She would recognise the stench of Darkling anywhere. Even the girl's Casting hadn't been strong enough to erase that stain from the earth.

She bared her teeth in a vicious grin.

It had been easy. So easy, to slip inside her mind. To wield the girl's power as if it were her own and burn the Darkling to ash. She'd lingered long enough to savour its dying screams, before relinquishing control. The girl seemed to have enjoyed the destruction less. Clearly, she knew nothing of her birthright. Still, she would learn.

But where had she come from? Her and the boy. Those bloodlines were rare now. So rare. Strange enough to stumble on one, let alone two. And the other boy – not Graced. At least, not entirely. Not Darkling or Shade either. Something else.

The black-eyed woman pulled her glove back on, covered her face once more.

Time to find out just what was hiding in this forest.

CHAPTER SIX

The castle was in complete uproar as every man, woman and child dashed back and forth, searching frantically. Panic was rising in Renila's chest. Darkness had fallen and neither of the twins, nor Erion, were anywhere to be found within the castle or its grounds. Copper had returned – saddled, riderless and wild with fright – but the Lady's mare was still missing along with the children.

'Renila!' She stopped and turned at the sound of Farran's voice calling her name as she ran through the main entrance hall. His brow wrinkled with worry, and he asked, 'Any sign?'

She shook her head, unable to speak through the lump in her throat. Heedless to the many eyes watching, Farran took her hand in his own and squeezed in reassurance.

The hallway fell silent as an imposing figure appeared at the top of the sweeping staircase. Fury rippled off the Lady in waves as she descended the stairs and stalked straight towards the Captain. Farran released Renila's hand but did not move from her side as he bowed. The Lady inclined her head in response and looked about her with distaste.

'What is everyone doing?' she asked.

Farran glanced either side of him and frowned in confusion. 'They're looking for your children, my Lady.'

'I realise that, Captain,' she snapped, 'but they are evidently not in the castle. Why are you still searching in here?'

'My Lady?'

The Lady's temper flared as she hissed through clenched teeth. 'They are in the Ravenswood. Gather your men, get on your mounts and *find* them.'

Farran blinked for a moment before he recovered. Bowing once more, he turned on his heel and marched out into the courtyard, barking orders.

'How can you know that?' Renila asked, under her breath.

The Lady turned those terrible eyes on her. 'Instinct,' she said. Then, without warning, her attention flashed towards the open doors – but her gaze was distant, as if she were looking beyond the entrance or even the grounds. The surrounding air throbbed and hummed as her brow creased with concentration. 'Come with me,' she ordered, striding after the Captain. The Lady was much taller than Renila, and her long legs carried her swiftly down the steps into the courtyard, sweeping Renila along in her wake.

Outside, the night was bitter and rain fell in icy sheets that soaked through clothes in the space of a breath. Oblivious to the weather, the Lady stopped below the stone archway that marked the entrance to the castle and looked out across the grounds. The watch kept fires going through the night to illuminate the surroundings, but the light only reached so far. Renila hovered behind her, pulling her shawl tighter against the elements as she peered into the gloom beyond, searching for whatever held the Lady's attention.

'My Lady,' came Farran's voice from behind them. 'You need to go inside – it's not safe.' The Lady didn't move. Then her posture relaxed, and she heaved a sigh of relief.

'Stand your men down, Captain. The children are fine.'

And then, as if in answer to her words, the rain parted, and the mighty black mare stepped out of the shadows into the light. Renila cried out as she spied the small, pale form of her son astride Storm. Then the twins came into view behind him. A cheer went up, and even the Lady cracked a small smile. But any delight was short-lived as they took in the expressions on the children's faces. Erion was the calmest of the three, though there was tension in the set of his shoulders. Lucan's gaze darted about beneath his sopping fringe, and he held firmly to Suriya.

But as Renila's eyes fell on the girl, she realised it was not out of fear for himself that Lucan clung so tight. Suriya's pretty face was pale and drawn, her soaking hair plastered to it, and her glorious golden eyes vacant. She swayed, drifting in and out of consciousness, while a desperate Lucan struggled to hold her steady. Her eyes rolled back into her head as she passed out, and Renila leapt forward ready to catch her when she slumped sideways out of the saddle. But then the Lady was between them, and she caught the girl and lifted her into her arms with surprising ease. She looked down at the limp form she held, frowning, then glanced back up at the mare. She patted Storm's nose in thanks and marched back inside without a word.

'Lucan,' she barked over her shoulder, 'come!'

The boy flinched and slid from the saddle, pausing long enough to give Renila a fierce hug before staggering after his mother.

Renila looked up at her own son. His shoulders were slumped with exhaustion, but he gave her a tentative, weary smile and clambered down from Storm's back. She steadied him with a firm hand as he swayed with fatigue and slipped on the wet stones.

'Are you alright?' she asked. He nodded and fell into her arms. Try as she might, she couldn't help the choked sob that escaped her lips as she clutched him tight to her chest. 'I will not ask, and you don't have to tell me.'

'Thank you,' he whispered back. She buried her face in his hair to hide the fear in her eyes. He grew so weak, so tired … She worried about where it was leading and how tonight might accelerate it. At least her tears of fear and joy were hidden by the rain already streaking her cheeks.

Farran wasn't going to let this matter go. There would be a reckoning. And if she'd learned anything in her time at the castle, it was that the Lady would never miss an opportunity to lay blame at Erion's feet. With a deep breath, she stepped back but kept a firm arm around his shoulders and raised her eyes to meet Farran's. He scowled and opened his mouth to speak, but she cut him off.

'My son is exhausted,' she insisted. 'He needs rest. It will wait until tomorrow, if he's well enough. Please?'

But before she could extricate him, the boy turned to the great black mare and rubbed her nose. 'Thank you,' he murmured. Renila wasn't surprised he insisted on finding the stable master, though perhaps somewhat frustrated. Erion was a gentle soul, and he wouldn't consent to be led back inside until he was satisfied that Storm was looked after. All she could do was hover anxiously at his shoulder while he fussed.

By the time they'd made it back to their room, he was so tired he couldn't even change out of his drenched clothes before he passed out on his bed. She smiled. It had been a long time since she had needed to tuck him in, let alone dress him. He'd be a man before she knew it. The thought almost made her want to weep. What need would he have for his little mother then?

In the last two months alone, she'd seen him age more than in the preceding two years. Not just in height either. There was an insight and awareness that hadn't been there before. Nor could it be found in other boys his age. It often caught her off guard, how mature he was for his years. Something terrible had happened to them tonight, yet Erion had maintained more composure than most adults would ever manage. He would outgrow her before she knew it.

She brushed the tear from her eye in frustration and heaved a heavy sigh. She'd just have to savour every moment with him. It was an effort to move him to her dry bed. But when she was done, she tucked the covers around his softly snoring form and added another log to the fire. He would sleep all night long, and she wanted to check on the twins before she made it to bed. Even if that meant facing the Lady. After their disagreement, Renila had stayed out of her way, but some instinct insisted she should make sure the children were well. So, slipping from the room and locking the door behind her, she squared her shoulders, took a deep breath and headed for their rooms.

A soft curse slipped from her lips when she spotted Farran in front of the door to the twins' chambers. He stood, arms folded across his chest and scowling. The scowl deepened as he registered Renila's approach.

'You can't go in,' he said.

Something in her stirred at his tone. Some wild, burning force that had long slept inside her was waking. Her heart pounded in her chest as that rising beast stretched and roared. A glowing ember of defiance catching on the dry tinder of her frustration.

'Farran, please. Stand aside,' she said in a voice that was not her own.

The Captain didn't move. He didn't even flinch.

'Don't be foolish, Renila. Don't let emotions drive you to something you'll later regret.'

Renila glared. 'I have no quarrel with you, Captain, but one way or another I will tend to those children. So I ask again. Please, stand aside.'

Whatever instinct had driven her to confront Farran was screaming now. Something was wrong. There was something in the air that made her stomach churn, her mind freeze with panic. Her fists clenched at her sides as she fought it.

'Renila?' Farran called.

'Let me through,' she demanded, shoving past him. Only barely noticing how the tall, strong Captain staggered from the force of her touch. Only vaguely aware of him shouting her name and following, as she marched into the twins' rooms.

They were both seated on the settee before the fire, the Lady standing over them. Both awake, but far from alert as they stared up at their mother with glazed, vacant expressions. The Lady straightened at the commotion, releasing the children from her gaze, and turned those vast eyes on Renila, just as Farran drew to a halt behind her. The displeasure on the Lady's face was near glacial. He clamped a firm hand around Renila's arm and bowed in apology. 'I'm sorry, my Lady, I tried to stop her.'

The Lady snorted and said scathingly, 'You clearly tried extremely hard, Captain. I find it difficult to believe that a man of your size and training could not bar one small woman from entering a room.'

Farran flushed and made to drag Renila from the room. But she hardly noticed, her attention on the twins. All too easily, she wrenched out of Farran's grip and crossed the room to kneel before the children. And in a move that was both brave and foolhardy, she turned her back on the Lady.

'What's wrong with them?' she asked, as she scanned their pale, drawn faces. The Lady tutted in annoyance and dismissed Farran with a negligent wave of her hand. The Captain bowed and left. Renila didn't even so much as glance in his direction.

'There's nothing wrong with them. They're just tired and need to go to sleep.'

'Lucan. Suriya,' Renila called, taking their hands in her own. They blinked and looked around stupidly, as if waking from a dream.

'Renila?' Lucan murmured, his voice sluggish as he tried to focus on her. Renila frowned, peering into his eyes as she reached up and ran a light, probing hand over his head. The bloody lump on the back of his skull confirmed her suspicions. Suriya groaned and leaned heavily on her brother.

'It's alright, sweetheart,' Renila said, squeezing their hands in reassurance. 'I'm here.'

'What happened?' whispered Suriya.

The girl shivered, despite the heat from the fire. Her teeth chattered, and her lips were tinged with blue. Renila held a worried hand to Suriya's brow and flinched. The girl's skin was ice-cold. Renila was on her feet and moving, shoving past the Lady as she sought dry clothing.

The Lady frowned. 'What is it?'

Renila ignored her as she peeled the wet clothes off the girl, bundled her up in a blanket and carried her to the bed. She didn't care what the Lady did to her. The children needed care. How could the woman not see that? What kind of mother neglected her own children? Without a word, she returned for Lucan and began stripping him out of his wet clothing – taking great care not to jostle his head any further. Once she was satisfied that they were both safely tucked up in their beds, she added a thick fur to each before stoking the fire.

'Renila,' the Lady growled dangerously.

Renila's temper snapped.

'Don't you dare,' she snarled, rounding on their mother. 'Don't you dare presume to question me right now. I don't know what in the name of the Gods you were doing when I came in here, but it wasn't caring for your children.'

The Lady bristled under that furious look. 'I was questioning them about the events of this evening – where they'd been, precisely what had happened. It was important for me to know, Renila.'

'Nothing is more important than their lives!' she yelled. 'Their health and well-being first – above all else, above even your own life! Every mother knows that!'

'You dare—'

'Yes, I dare,' Renila continued. 'Lucan is injured. Suriya is sick. Right now, they need rest, love and care. If you can't provide any of those things, I suggest you leave and send me someone who can.'

It was as if her blazing fury had taken form, but the Lady didn't so much as blink as she turned and stalked from the room. Renila allowed herself one breath – just one – to calm herself, before she turned back to the twins.

Lucan's glowing moonstone eyes were sombre and unfocussed as he watched her. Suriya's eyes were closed – sleeping or unconscious, Renila wasn't sure. There was no colour in the girl's cheeks, but at least her lips appeared less blue.

'Is she going to be alright?'

Renila sighed and began unlacing her own damp garments. At least her shift was still dry. 'I don't know. But she's as strong-willed and stubborn as you are, so I'd bet the answer is yes.'

'She's far more stubborn than me,' he said with a sleepy smile. He looked once more to his sister before closing his eyes as exhaustion claimed him.

But Renila's task was not yet done. Some instinct that she could not explain was screaming at her – just as it had before she'd forced her way into the room. Renila wrapped a blanket around her shoulders for modesty as she reached for the door. Sure enough, Farran was still standing guard outside. His gaze darkened at the sight of her, and he opened his mouth to speak, but Renila held up a hand to silence him.

'Don't,' she pleaded. 'Please, I can't bear the Captain. I just want my friend back – I just want Farran.'

'I never stopped being your friend, Renila – I never stopped being Farran. But I am also the Captain, and I can't disobey direct orders just because you don't agree with them.'

'I know things aren't right between us, and I want to make them right,' she murmured, 'but right now, I need your help. Please.'

Farran studied her for a moment and seemed to find what he was searching for. He nodded. 'What do you need?'

She told him. Her instincts were never wrong. He sighed and hesitated but nodded again, tucking the key she handed him inside his shirt. Certain they were alone, he dared to stroke her cheek with his fingertips, his thumb grazing her lips. Then he turned on his heel and was gone. Another time, Renila might have stood still, delighting in the ghost of his touch. But the children needed her.

So she turned and closed the door behind her.

It was almost dawn when she was woken by Suriya crying out in her sleep. The girl thrashed beneath the blankets, her foot catching Renila in the side as she struggled with her nightmares. Lucan woke at the sound of his sister's distress and struggled out of the bed.

'Suriya!' he called. 'Suriya, it's alright. You're alright, everything's fine. You're safe.'

Golden eyes flew open, and the scream died in her throat. 'Lucan?'

'I'm here,' he assured her with a relieved smile.

Content they were both fine, Renila slid from the bed and padded across the room for the water jug, glancing to the settee by the fire where Erion was stirring.

She was just grateful Farran hadn't argued with her request. Instinct had told her she had to keep her son close. Precisely why still eluded her, but she knew that she could not let him out of her sight. She would guard him with her life if she had to.

It had been not long after midnight when the Captain had appeared at the door with her sleeping son in his arms. Erion had slept on, exhausted, even as Farran helped her tuck him in spare blankets on the settee while the twins snored in their beds. Then the Captain had bowed and departed without a word.

Renila poured a cup of water and handed it to Lucan, trusting the boy to help his sister for a moment as she turned her attention to her son. Storm-grey eyes watched her from over the coverlet. His brow was crinkled with confusion, but he was alert. He glanced around but said nothing. Renila smiled and brushed a lock of dark hair from his forehead.

'I asked Captain Farran to bring you up here,' she told him. 'Lucan hit his head and Suriya is sick. I couldn't leave them, but I needed to keep you close.'

Erion frowned but nodded. 'Are they alright now?'

Renila glanced across the room. Suriya was drinking from the cup and colour had returned to her cheeks. The worst was over, hopefully. Though the girl would need more rest before she fully recovered. Lucan looked better too. Old Jayne had been and gone, doing what she could for Lucan's head and leaving instructions so that Renila could continue to tend to it. Fortunately, the twins healed fast. They always had.

'They'll be fine,' she assured him.

'Good.'

Renila took a deep breath and held his gaze. 'I said I wouldn't ask, and you can hold me to that, Erion, but I need to know what happened to Suriya. Old Jayne wasn't sure what was wrong with her ...'

Erion hesitated as he looked to his friends. 'Suriya used magic,' he breathed. Renila stilled. She forced a cool, impassive expression onto her face and waited for the rest. He continued in a breathless whisper. 'We were in the stables after supper, and she ... I don't know ... knew or sensed that Lucan was in danger. She was in such a panic. We took Storm – she led us right to him – and there was a *Darkling*. It was going to kill him, and Suriya just lashed out. I don't know how to describe it. Fire just erupted out of her and burned the Darkling to ash.'

He fell silent as he glanced across at the twins. There was no fear in his eyes, swirling from storm-grey to feline-green while he studied them. Suddenly struck by how much she loved her son, Renila leaned in and kissed his head. Any other boy would have run if they'd witnessed something like that. But not her son. Erion never judged, never presumed. The prejudices of teenage boys were alien to him. He was simply curious. And he was hers. What had she ever done to deserve such a wondrous child?

She took a deep breath, watching Erion extricate himself from the blankets and join the twins in Suriya's bed. The Lady had warned her that the twins might manifest such powers as they approached adolescence. And although the changes had already begun, the Lady insisted that they did not yet need to know the truth. But Renila knew nothing of magic, save what was mentioned in her stories, so she was of little use.

She glanced around and saw the two boys had sandwiched Suriya between them, pulling the furs up to their chins, and now all three were looking at Renila.

Eyes of gold and amber and pearly blue gazed imploringly at her, and it occurred to her that, despite their differences, the three children were remarkably alike. No other child in this castle would have handled such traumatic events with their courage or composure. Neither Suriya nor Lucan had made any mention of the supernatural happenings in the Ravenswood. Had it not been Erion himself who told her, she might not have even believed the tale – they were so unruffled. Lucan's eyes were bright and merry, his worry gone at the sight of Suriya's rosy cheeks. And though Suriya herself was exhausted, there was no sign of the anguish Renila had seen in her eyes. It was only on Erion's face that even the tiniest trace of their ordeal could be seen. And even then, only to one who knew him as well as she did.

'Tell us a story, Renila,' Lucan begged.

'Please,' Suriya added, her voice stronger already.

Renila laughed and settled herself at the foot of the bed. 'What story would you like to hear?' she asked. Lucan opened his mouth to answer, but Erion cut him off.

'Tell us one about a Phoenix – someone like Laviana or Kalielle.'

Renila threw him an exasperated glance, but Lucan rolled his eyes.

'Why do you want to hear that?' he scoffed. 'We've heard all of those before.'

Erion looked incredulously at his friend, amber eyes swirling back to storm-grey as he held Lucan's gaze. Then he frowned and looked away.

'It doesn't matter,' he said with an indifferent shrug that Renila knew he didn't mean. 'Tell whatever you want.'

Suriya elbowed her brother in the ribs.

'What?' he hissed defensively.

'You always get to choose the story,' she admonished. 'Let someone else pick for once.'

Lucan flushed and glanced surreptitiously at Erion. Renila followed his gaze and realised Erion wasn't paying any attention to the conversation. His dark eyes were churning like the ocean as he stared out of the nearby window, brow furrowed.

'Fine,' sighed Lucan.

Renila nodded in agreement and tore her gaze away from her son. 'Light against the darkness is an ancient battle, a story as old as the earth itself. And there is no greater example of the light than the fire of the Phoenix, the last and greatest of all the Graced.

'The first flicker of the darkness was born in the depths of the Rebellion. Sephiron's heirs, and the heirs of those traitors who joined with him, born to their Darkling lovers. Blessed with their fathers' magic but tainted and corrupted by the blood of their mothers. 'Shade' they were called – for they were little more than a pale shadow of their once glorious lineage.

'Even after the Rebellion was over, and Sephiron was defeated, their numbers continued to grow. For Shade sire Shade, and their stolen magic will always breed true.

'And then there came a time where the Shade rose up to conquer the earth. They were led by Sephiron's five surviving children. The oldest four

– the Princes Revian and Jaxon and the Princesses Elyria and Malia – had all served their father's cause and fought at his side whenever he asked. But it was not until after Sephiron was defeated that his youngest heir came forward. Together, Sephiron's heirs led the Shade to victory. Together, they brought the mighty Graced low. Together, they ushered in the dawn of the Dark Days.

'The Immortal soldiers who had survived the Rebellion turned away, for they were tired of war and ruin. But the Graced were not so easily cowed – the Phoenix least of all. Their magic is powerful, more potent than any other Graced bloodline, but it is not a power to be wielded. They cannot change their form, like Dragons, nor control minds, like Unicorns. They cannot control the elements, as the Elves do. Their gift is simple. Immortality. Not like the Darklings who steal life to defy death, nor like their Immortal creators who cannot be touched by its hand. But when they fall, they rise once more from the ashes of their funeral pyre.

'Blessed as they were, they feared no evil – valuing courage and honour above all else. They shared their lands with the mighty firebirds, but rather than slaying the legendary beasts, they believed the true test of valour was instead to ride them. During the Rebellion, they flew their flaming mounts into battle, dying and rising side by side. And after Sephiron's defeat, when his heirs rose up to claim the world for themselves, still, the mighty Phoenix did not yield. Many of the greatest Graced warriors have hailed from that proud and noble bloodline, but few are more revered than Kalielle Half-Elven.

'Heir to Laviana, the Flame of Elucion, she was born and raised in secret, hidden and protected from all who would seek to harm her. She was not alone in her seclusion, concealed as she was with the Elf-Queen's heir, Diathor, and the future Lady of Revalla, Kylar. For their own protection, they were kept ignorant of their heritage, as the longer they went without touching the magic in their blood, the longer they could remain hidden.

'But that kind of power cannot be contained forever, and the time came when they could hide no longer. Graced children struggle to control their magic at the best of times, but Kalielle was untaught and unaware of her bloodlines. Her magic took on a life of its own, acting purely on instinct and emotion. But like sharks scenting blood in the water, the Shade can sniff out magic from far and wide.

'So Kalielle, Diathor and Kylar sought the legendary Elf-Queen Benella, who had survived the worst of the Dark Days, hidden behind the great walls of her city. They joined with her forces as she readied for war. Of Sephiron's heirs, only Malia and his youngest son remained, their siblings long since slain by Laviana and others. Desperate to stamp out the last smouldering embers of resistance, Princess Malia brought the full force of her might down upon them.

'The battle raged for days, with casualties beyond count, Benella herself amongst the fallen. The problem was not the Darkling hordes – after all, the sole purpose of the Graced is to destroy Darklings – but their Shade masters. Sephiron's heirs were too powerful. That only two remained was down more to chance than any scheme, and the Graced could no longer afford to wait for fate to guide the way.

'So Kalielle determined to forge her own path. She knew she lacked the power to defeat Malia alone. But unable to bear the thought of endangering others, she found another way to remove the threat the Shade Princess posed. Fighting her way across the battlefield, she sought her enemy. By sheer luck, Malia's back was to her. Kalielle raised her sword, but rather than bringing it down upon her foe, she instead turned the blade on herself. She ended her own life ... and loosed the power of her Rising.'

'Malia was consumed by the magic, and when the firestorm was over, there was naught left of the Shade Princess but ashes and dust. Of all Sephiron's heirs, only the youngest Prince remained. Kalielle was whole once more, though her power was spent. But rather than seeking to avenge his sister's death, the Prince laid down his arms and pulled back his forces. He retreated back to the dark fortress, Dar Kual, and took up his father's throne and crown, becoming the Shade King – who still reigns to this day.'

She glanced up at the children. The twins' eyes were wide with wonder, as they always were after a story – no matter how many times they had heard it. But Erion was frowning, staring into space. She could almost see his thought process as he tried to connect her story to what he'd seen in the woods.

Renila smiled sadly. She hadn't the heart to tell him it was a fairy tale. There was some magic in the world, but it was nothing like the vast power in her stories. True, the Lady had said that the twins carried some hint of magic, but it was a remnant of something ancient. They weren't Graced. They couldn't be. The Graced didn't exist.

She paused as a thought struck her ...

Darklings were real. Could that not also mean that the Graced were real?

Her mind became sluggish, and she blinked stupidly. The Graced were dead and gone, she told herself when the fog cleared.

But how could that be, if they were just a story?

The cloud of confusion descended again. None of it was real, she reminded herself.

But it was, a small voice argued. *Darklings are a real threat, and the cities in the stories exist. Even the shape of the world matches ...*

No. They were legends, stories made up to explain naturally occurring phenomena that couldn't be explained by facts.

But—

Her thoughts were interrupted as the door banged open, and an icy wind swirled into the room, making the fire stutter in the hearth. Renila looked round as a familiar figure stormed into the room.

The Lady was in a furious temper. Renila flinched from those frightening eyes that glittered with the light of a billion stars as the Lady took in the scene. Relief seemed to flicker there when she registered the rosy tint to

Suriya's cheeks and the bright gleam in Lucan's eyes. But then her gaze fell on Erion, and she stilled, with all the deadly grace of a wolf eyeing its next meal.

Instinct had Renila on her feet and placing her body between Erion and the Lady before she'd even registered the hatred thrumming around her. She opened her mouth to speak, but the Lady got there first.

'I warned you about filling their heads with nonsense,' she breathed, her hands clenched into fists.

'It's just a sto—' Lucan began.

'Silence,' the Lady snapped, cutting him off. 'You told me you wanted to be treated like adults, and yet you still insist on listening to fairy tales like little children.'

'It was Erion who asked to hear it,' Lucan grumbled under his breath, sulking from the admonishment. Suriya elbowed him in the ribs, but it was too late.

The Lady's livid gaze turned on Erion. 'You again? Why is it you seem so insistent on leading these children astray?'

'Erion did nothing wrong,' Renila growled, pulling her son behind her as if to hide him from those dreadful eyes.

The Lady snorted. 'Other than stealing my horse and leading Suriya and Lucan into the Ravenswood, after spinning them some ridiculous story – one of yours no doubt?'

'That's not how I heard it,' Renila retorted.

'Because that's not what happened,' Erion murmured from behind her.

The Lady's face was inscrutable. 'Well, I'm afraid your son's word does not carry much weight with me. Suriya and Lucan said that is what happened, and I'm inclined to believe them. This is hardly the first time your boy has caused trouble under my roof.'

Renila glanced back at the children. Lucan and Suriya looked uncomfortable, but these were not the shamed faces of two people caught lying by loved ones. Erion's expression was one of total betrayal. His eyes were stormy-black and swimming with unshed tears. Renila frowned. Something did not add up. But before she could speak, Erion exploded.

'That's a lie!' he screamed at the twins. 'Lucan was the one stupid enough to run into the wood when it was nearly dark. And the only reason I took Storm was because Suriya somehow knew he was in trouble. We found him just as he was about to be attacked by a Darkling, and she killed it with magic!'

The look on the twins' faces was utter confusion, and they blinked stupidly in the face of the accusations. They glanced at each other, and Renila could see the alarm in their eyes. She knew her son wasn't lying – she could hear the truth in his voice – but somehow, the twins remembered a different truth. Deep within her mind a glimmer of warning, of understanding, sparked to life. But before she could comprehend it, the Lady distracted her.

'That's the best you can come up with?' she sneered. 'You've got quite some way to go, young man, if you hope to be as good a storyteller as your mother.'

'It's not a story!' Erion shouted, pushing passed Renila. 'It's the truth!'

The Lady drew herself up to her full height and turned her furious eyes on Renila. 'I've had enough of this,' she spat. 'That boy has caused nothing but trouble since the day you arrived. If you cannot keep him away from those children, then you will have to go. I cannot tolerate either of you any longer. I want you ready to leave by sunrise tomorrow.'

She turned and stormed from the room.

CHAPTER SEVEN

Keriath swore as she fought her way free from the cloying darkness of unconsciousness. The reek of magic filled her nose, and she tasted her own blood in her mouth. Her head was pounding, her vision blurred, and she had no sense of anything around her. She blinked, shaking her head to clear the fog as she struggled to stand.

Except she couldn't move. Her back was to a tree and a considerable length of rope bound her to it. They'd tied it tight too. She barely had room to breathe, and it bit into her arms. Her hands were numb; she must have been like this a while. She wiggled her fingers, trying to encourage some feeling back.

Manacles encircled her wrists, a thick chain clinking between them, the cold bite of iron against her skin unmistakable. As was the stench of magic imbuing them. Dark. Corrupted. *Wrong.*

A Shade had made these. Filled them with the power to shackle even the Graced. To contain their might, subdue their magic. A hiss of frustration burst past her lips as she pulled viciously against her restraints, though she knew it was useless. Her captors clearly recognised what she was. Escape would not be easy.

Above her, a calm voice called out in warning. 'She's waking up.'

'Quick, the ruan,' came the response from the shadows, this voice cold and cruel.

She flinched at the word; at what she knew was coming. A hand fisted in her hair, wrenching her head back. She thrashed, ignoring the pain when they ripped a handful of hair from her scalp. Two pairs of firm hands gripped her face, and sharp fingers prised her jaw open. She bit down on them, drawing a satisfying howl from their owner. But they did not relent.

Keriath tried not to swallow as they tipped the bitter liquid down her throat, but they kept pouring it in until she choked. She spat out as much as she could, but when she felt the ruan's icy grip, she knew it was too late. She grasped for her magic, but that ocean of power was now only frozen wasteland. Worse was the panic now coursing through her as it choked off her magical senses. Without them, she couldn't feel those around her – their thoughts, their emotions, their presence. All silent. They might as well have blinded her.

Panting with frustration, she hissed, 'I will kill you for th—'

A hand appeared from the shadows and cracked across her face, leaving her cheek stinging, and she fell silent, glaring up at her captors. Darklings. The Hunt was gathered in close. Their leader, the Hunter, stood over her. It – no, his … Gods, since when did she suffer a Darkling to live long enough to notice or care for its gender – dark eyes were merciless as they considered her. She didn't need her power to know her initial impression had been right. This one was cruel beyond belief.

She glanced past him to the Graced Darkling from the Ravenswood. He was standing back, separate from the Hunt, surveying the scene with feigned disinterest. But where he was huge and broad-shouldered, a warrior born and bred if she were to guess, the Hunter was slender as a rapier. Although judging by her smarting cheek, he was strong enough.

'I know what you are,' the Hunter crooned, drawing her attention back. His voice sent chills down her spine. It was the voice of a creature that delighted in the pain of others. She spat in his face rather than show the fear he stirred. He smacked her again, hard enough to draw blood, before wiping the spittle from his cheek. His head cocked to the side as he considered the mix of blood and saliva on his hand. With a smirk, he licked it clean, his eyes rolling back into his head with exaggerated pleasure. Keriath repressed a shudder. Not just cruel, but mad too. 'I can't help but wonder why three of the Graced are meeting in the dead of night so far into the Ravenswood?'

She stilled, unease churning in her gut. 'Keep wondering, *Darkling*. I'm not about to tell you.'

The Hunter chuckled softly.

'Ah, false bravado,' he hissed. He breathed deeply, as if savouring a sweet fragrance. 'I can smell your fear. You're drowning in it.'

She unleashed a blistering string of curses, refusing to give him the satisfaction of flinching, of letting him know how close to the mark his words had struck. But as the Graced Darkling prowled forward, she trailed off. Dread was an icy fist around her chest, and she thrashed against her restraints. He crouched down beside her, grasping her chin and forcing her to look at him.

'I wouldn't. You'll hurt yourself,' he warned. The Hunter turned and stalked away in disgust. The Graced Darkling ignored him, his eyes flickering up to her brow. To the star-shaped mark she bore there. Or at least what was left of it. Then with a surprisingly gentle hand, he pushed her hair back to reveal the slender, tapered ears that matched his own. Their eyes met, and he let her hair fall, his gaze dark with warning.

'What's your name?' he asked. She tried and failed to suppress a shiver. His kindness was more unnerving than the Hunter's cruelty. Instinct had her pressing her lips into a tight line. He sighed, but let it go. 'Alright, what about the other two?' She stared back at him, face impassive. 'You need to give him something, or he'll kill you.'

'And what? You're worried you won't get to sample the treat?' she sneered. Then she heaved against her restraints, leaning in closer. 'Listen carefully, Darkling, because I won't say this again. I will tell you nothing, and nothing you do to me that will change that. Some things are worth dying for.'

He sighed, his brows knitting together as he scowled at her. 'You're making things very difficult for me.' She gave him a withering look, not unlike the one he'd given her in the clearing before he bested her.

'You'd be worried if I made them easier for you,' she muttered as he stood and walked away. Another shiver of discomfort raced down her spine as she heard him chuckle. Then she was alone.

And unguarded, as far as she could see.

The sound of a branch breaking underfoot nearby drew her attention. She stilled, angling her head towards the source of the noise as a figure emerged from the shadows. But it was dread, not hope, that bloomed in her chest at what she saw.

The Darkling was a young female with lank brown hair and the same bottomless, dark red eyes as the others. But it was small. Weak and starving. Had Keriath been free, she'd have killed it with a single thought. But bound as she was? It would drain her dry and there would be nothing she could do to stop it. She closed her eyes and waited for the inevitable.

Agony ripped through her as the Darkling tore into her throat, her scream of pain strangled at its source. Instead, all she heard was an unpleasant gurgle from the gaping wound where the Darkling was feeding greedily. Darkness gripped her, dragging her into unconsciousness.

From the shadows came the roar of an enraged beast, and the Darkling was ripped from her. Keriath opened her eyes to see the Graced Darkling hurl the weak female across the clearing and into the trunk of a nearby oak. Through the haze of pain, she just made out its head smashing against the wood before it crashed to the ground, stunned but alive. Clambering to its feet, it shrieked, enraged, and staggered towards him like a drunkard. The Graced Darkling crouched over Keriath, hissing furiously, and for once, the stench of stolen life didn't turn her stomach. Then the Hunter was between them. He pulled the female behind him and faced down Keriath's saviour with icy rage in his eyes.

'What do you think you're doing?' he spat.

The Graced Darkling stood to his full height. 'She was going to kill the prisoner,' he said, pointing at the female cowering behind the Hunter.

'This is my Hunt, Alexan. You may not be bound to me, but so long as you are with us, you will respect my authority,' the Hunter breathed.

Alexan smiled coldly, but Keriath stilled as a bolt of recognition hit her, even while she struggled to stay conscious. She knew that name. Knew who he served.

'You mean, like she did?' he asked. The Hunter's lips pursed into a tight line, but he said nothing. 'Your Hunt is weak and starving, Drosta. They're going to get us all killed if you don't do something.'

'I'm not leaving you alone with my prisoner,' snarled Drosta.

Alexan bristled. 'You mean *my* prisoner? I caught her, Drosta. She goes with me.'

'We've been hunting her for weeks – stalked her all the way from Thornhold! She's ours. The Queens' orders are explicit – any prisoners are for Dar Kual.'

Alexan stepped forward, looming over Drosta in silent threat. 'I don't have to listen to your Queens; my orders come from the King.'

Keriath couldn't stop herself – a gasp of horror escaped her lips. Panic laced with pain clouded her vision. Not him. Anyone but him. Alexan glanced round, his expression almost apologetic.

'Your orders don't include her,' Drosta challenged. 'She's mine. If you try to take her, you're poaching, and not even your King can protect you from the consequences.'

Alexan didn't correct him. Keriath didn't let herself consider what that meant. 'Get your Hunt fed, Drosta. She stays with me until then.' He turned and cut Keriath's bindings, lifting her into his arms when she swayed. She was vaguely aware of Drosta's burning gaze on them. There was death in those eyes.

'I'll kill you,' he hissed.

Above her, Alexan cocked his head to one side. 'Go on. I dare you,' he breathed. Drosta glared but didn't move. Alexan snorted dismissively. 'I didn't think so. Half your Hunt is still missing, Drosta. You don't have the numbers to fight me. And you don't have the balls to try it, even if you did.' And then he turned his back on the Hunter and disappeared into the shadows, carrying Keriath in his arms.

'I wish you'd let it kill me,' she whispered, and darkness took her once more.

As she came to, the pain in her head was so sharp Keriath worried someone had buried an axe in her skull while she was unconscious. Running a cautious hand over her scalp assured her that was not the case, so she dared a tentative touch to her throat. The wound was healed, but the chill of magic lingered on her skin.

She groaned, rolling the stiffness from her shoulders as she looked around. She was sitting by a small campfire, unbound and unwatched. Her frown deepened. Standing, she strained her senses for anything that might be a threat.

'I wouldn't bother,' said a quiet voice behind her. She tried, and failed, not to start in fright, doing her best to disguise it as she spun to face the Graced Darkling. Alexan. Gods, was it not enough that she'd failed to kill him, must she really be burdened with his name too? He was leaning nonchalantly against a tree, eating an apple. She forced herself not to shudder as his teeth pierced the rosy flesh. 'You're still under the influence of the ruan and will be for a while. You can't Cast, you can't Enchant, you'll struggle to beat me in a fight and, as you've already found out, you can't outrun me.' He grinned as she snarled in defiance. 'Go ahead and try it though,' he offered, pulling away from the tree and tossing the core away.

She didn't hesitate. Turning on her heel, she bolted for the forest. She'd barely made it two steps before he slammed into her, pinning her to the ground and twisting her arms behind her back. Her shoulders barked in pain, but she thrashed anyway, trying to dislodge him. Not that it did any good. He was strong. Too strong. Even for a Darkling.

But she didn't stop. Even when exhaustion clouded her vision and burned at her already aching muscles, she kept fighting. Surrender was not a word that Graced children were taught. Their creed was victory or death, and this Darkling knew it. He held her there until her body trembled with fatigue and her thoughts had long since lost coherence.

'Give up,' he sighed. 'I don't want to hurt you.'

She snarled again, desperate to keep fighting, but her body defied her. Her screaming muscles refused to move anymore, and she collapsed to the ground, beaten.

Alexan heaved a sigh of relief and he released her, carrying her back to the fire and depositing her in a heap beside it. A blanket, a water skin and some food followed, tossed at her feet. She took them without a word, pulling the blanket about her shoulders and leaning into the warmth of the fire. A tentative sniff of the water told her it was free of poison, but the food she eyed in apprehension. The bread and cheese were probably safe to eat, but there was also a blood-red apple that made her nervous. Too many bedtime stories about poisoned princesses, perhaps.

'You realise saving my life changes nothing?' she asked, distracting herself from the morbid turn her thoughts had taken.

'I would expect nothing less, Keriath,' he replied, grinning as she flinched. 'What? You thought I wouldn't recognise the Shade King's daughter when I saw her?'

'I don't have a father,' she said automatically. But her mind was racing. She'd recognised his name – it was hardly surprising he'd recognised her. The three favoured generals of the Shade King were legendary, though Alexan was the most mysterious of them all. She knew nothing about his life before he'd appeared in the Shade King's Court a hundred years ago. Nothing about why he had joined forces with the monster who had killed his Queen.

The Darkling chuckled at her denial. 'So that part's true,' he mused. His eyes glinted like rubies in the firelight. 'I assume you won't work with me?'

'What do you think?' she asked scathingly.

He shrugged and sighed, running a hand through his hair in frustration. There was a peculiar, circular mark on his palm. Like a strange birthmark. Possibly even a brand. 'It was worth asking. If not, we have a bit of a problem. Drosta has laid claim to you, and if I try to take you by force, I risk starting a war. Relations between my King and the Darkling Queens are …

a little tense at the moment. I can't risk making things worse by getting into it with Drosta. If you're willing to work with me though, I think I can get you out of this mess.'

Keriath arched a sceptical brow. 'Do tell?'

'Claim your birthright,' he said. 'If you were to acknowledge the Shade King as your father and claim your place in the Court, I would be duty-bound to escort you to him in Elucion.'

She gaped at him. She knew what he was talking about. How could she not? Since her first breath, the Shade King had claimed her as his heir. Her and Théon. But where Théon was the result of rape – a child conceived in violence and blood – rumour claimed Keriath's mother had gone willingly to the Shade King's bed. The Lady Kylar had never spoken about the circumstances of the union, but she'd never denied that it had happened. Keriath knew her mother well enough to guess the truth. That Kylar had sought to use her power to ensnare and subdue Sephiron's heir. Had sacrificed herself, body and soul, in the hopes of stopping him. But she had failed.

The Shade King believed that Keriath was the product of that union, but the Lady Kylar had denied it to her dying breath. Keriath knew whose word she trusted more. In a hundred years, she'd never doubted. Never even considered doubting. She'd seen what life as the Shade King's heir had done to Théon. She'd sooner die than suffer that fate.

'You've got to be joking,' she scoffed. But the determination glittering in his eyes said otherwise. She shook her head. 'Not a chance. I would rather die than step within a hundred miles of that city so long as that monster draws breath.'

'Then there is nothing else I can do for you.'

'You could let me go. I'll even promise not to sneak back here and put a knife in your worthless heart.'

He snorted. 'Empty words from a woman so easily bested. Tell me, is your sister as arrogant as you?' Keriath bristled. Even if she didn't believe the Shade King's lies surrounding their parentage, there were few others in the world she cared for as much as Théon.

'Leave her out of this,' she breathed.

Alexan grinned at the threat in her voice.

'Can't,' he admitted with a careless shrug. 'Your father ordered me to find her, turn her or kill her. I can't fight the compulsion – unless you can give me a reason to delay it,' he added. Keriath glared at him. A Darkling's bond to its maker was an evil, twisted thing. The Claiming, they called it. The corrupt magic that blessed them with unearthly strength and unnatural longevity ensured they remained loyal to the one who had created them. They could no more fight the commands than they could stop the sun from rising.

She let out a frustrated hiss. He was trying to barter Théon's life for her own. Well, it wouldn't work. 'You'll never find her. And even if you do, you won't last so much as a heartbeat against her.'

Alexan smirked. 'I wouldn't count on it.' He chuckled, leaning back as his gaze raked over her. But the lust that should have been in his eyes was not there. She kept her face impassive as she tried not to frown. It was rare to meet someone completely immune to her. Even with the burns, most people lost control of themselves when they looked at her. It was the curse of her kind, even if the legends called it a blessing. The beauty of the Unicorns, the gift of her bloodline and the key to the Enchanting power in her veins. A power she'd gladly be rid of.

Her gaze flickered over his ears – the mark of his own powerful lineage. All the Graced were marked, one way or another. Magic could not touch a person and leave them unaltered. Their power was unique to their bloodline. Unicorns had the Enchanting. Elves had the Casting. Keriath knew which power she preferred.

'How did it happen? The Claiming?' she asked.

Alexan's smirk faded, and a wariness crept into his steady gaze. 'It's a long story. One I don't care to relive. But I can assure you, I did not go willingly.'

'I'm sorry,' Keriath said, surprising herself with how much she meant it. She'd never given any thought to a Darkling's life before the Claiming. What must it be like to lose everything you hold dear, only to have it replaced by everything you once feared and hated? Everything you were born to destroy?

'Don't be. I'm stronger and faster. I might even live forever.' They fell quiet for a long time, considering each other in silence. Then Alexan spoke again. 'You should get some sleep. You'll need your strength. I'll keep watch.'

But Keriath could not sleep. Dread, the like of which she had never felt before, gripped her tight. Darklings had always been the greatest source of fear in her life, ever since the attack that had scarred her as a child. Now she was to be bound, drugged and dragged to the stronghold of the Darkling Queens. Keriath did the only thing she could. She curled up under the blanket and wept.

Alexan was surprisingly gentle when he shook her awake. Dawn was near – the sky already pale, but the air still cold and damp with the night. Keriath shivered, though it had nothing to do with the chill of the morning. Alexan handed her food and water, his gaze dark with concern.

'Eat up,' he murmured. 'It'll be the last food you get for a while.'

'Thank you,' Keriath heard herself say, though she could hardly believe it. Here she was, not just showing gratitude to a Darkling, but genuinely meaning it. Because the regret in Alexan's eyes was undeniable. Still, not enough to risk starting a war over her.

'Whatever food or water they give you will be laced with more ruan,' he warned, 'but take it without a fight. If you won't take it of your own volition, they'll just force you.'

'Why do you care?' she asked bitterly.

He flinched. 'Why wouldn't I care?'

'Darklings care for nothing but death and destruction,' she hissed.

He shook his head in disgust. 'You know nothing about me or what I care for. Trust me – I've seen what the Queens do to people. I wouldn't wish that on my worst enemy. You need to keep your strength up if you're going to survive.'

'I'd rather die,' she said, staring blankly at the charred remains of the fire. Alexan grabbed her face and forced her to look at him. Then his gaze drifted once more to her scars, and it filled with sympathy. Scowling, she wrenched her head free and looked away. She wouldn't accept anyone's pity.

'Don't be so melodramatic,' he snapped, forcing her back round. 'I'll send help – or come for you myself if I can.'

Keriath glared back at him. 'And what? I exchange one tormentor for another? Don't waste your time. I won't go to him. Not now. Not ever.'

'You won't be saying that once the Queens have sunk their claws into you,' he promised. 'Just stay alive.'

'I'll do my best,' she promised sarcastically. 'You'd better hurry though. Once Resari gets wind that the Queens have me, she'll descend on that city like a natural disaster.'

'I wouldn't hold your breath,' he said. 'Your blessed Saviour can't save you if she doesn't know where to find you. Drosta hasn't recognised you, and I'm not about to enlighten him.'

Keriath stared at him incredulously. 'Why?'

'If he or the Queens realised who you were, no one would be able to save you,' he warned, his tone dark. He grabbed her roughly by the shoulders. 'Do you understand how desperately the Shade King wants you? What kind of power someone holding you would have over him?'

'I don't care!' she snarled, struggling to get free of his grip.

'You should,' he hissed, shaking her. 'You realise it's only his power keeping the Court in check? If he falters … I can't let that happen, Keriath. Not for you, not for anyone.'

'One day, I will kill you for this and watch with a smile as the crows feast on your heart,' she spat.

He released her and stepped back. 'I'm sorry my orders prevent me from helping you further, but I won't abandon you to this fate. I don't know how long it will take but, one way or another, I'll get you out of there. You have my word, Keriath.' And with that, he leaned down to shackle her wrists once more and led her from their camp. She didn't believe him, but she didn't bother to fight. He was too strong.

Drosta and his Hunt were waiting for them by the treeline. The Hunter's dark eyes flashed as they approached.

'About time,' he hissed, with a hungry smile.

'I see the rest of your little minions haven't returned,' Alexan smirked. 'I guess they bit off more than they could chew.'

'They're dead. We found their bodies this morning. Fucking Dragons.' There was more than desire and hunger in Drosta's gaze – he wanted revenge for what Dorrien and Faolin has done to his Hunt. Keriath allowed herself a smug, if small, smile.

'I assume they're all fed?' asked Alexan, pulling his charge behind him.

Drosta scowled, tearing his gaze away. 'Yes,' he snarled. 'We found a hunting cabin up into the mountains. Slim pickings, but we made do. Now hand her over.'

Alexan didn't move. The Hunt moved restlessly as one. Drosta grinned. He seemed desperate for Alexan to challenge him, desperate for any excuse to kill him. And with his Hunt fed, they might just manage. But Keriath owed Alexan a life-debt. It grated on her pride, but she could not ignore it. And as powerful as he was, she doubted he was strong enough to take on the entire Hunt and win.

With that thought weighing heavily on her heart, Keriath stepped out from behind Alexan and gave herself over to Drosta. She tossed her hair back and stood up straight, inflicting the full force of herself on the Hunter. No amount of ruan could bind this power – nothing could change how she looked. Even burned and scarred, the magic in her veins could stun a man into insensibility if she let it. Drosta drank her in like a man dying of thirst. Then he made his greatest mistake. He met her eyes.

All reason flooded from his face. She was vaguely aware of Alexan reaching for her, of the warning hiss from the Hunt that forced him to hold his ground. She ignored it. Kept her eyes on Drosta, drawing him in. Without the Enchanting, she couldn't take hold of his mind, but she could still unhinge him. Sure enough, once she was within reach, Drosta grabbed her and pulled her close. Pressing himself tight to her, he yanked her head over to expose her throat. His cold lips grazed her skin, and he breathed in deeply. His exhale was ragged, and she could feel the full extent of his excitement against her backside. But she refused to flinch. She held Alexan's gaze, ordering him to stay where he was as Drosta taunted him with her.

But Alexan hardly seemed to notice, warning, 'Drosta.'

'Why are you still here?' the Hunter hissed without looking up. He was caressing Keriath's collarbone with languid fingers. Her skin crawled where he touched her. She didn't need to look to understand what was happening. To know he had been entranced by the luminosity of her skin, by the softness of her hair. Even by the aroma of her unwashed flesh. If it weren't for the ruan, she would have had him dancing like a puppet on a string.

A warning growl from one of his Hunt woke Drosta from her spell, and he looked up to see Alexan looming over him. His hands were balled into fists, as if he itched to pull her free. But that path would only lead to bloodshed.

'Remember what she is,' he warned. Drosta looked down at her as Alexan's words filtered through the fog that Keriath's allure had caused. Then his eyes landed on her star-marked brow, and he pushed her away as if she were a poisonous snake. Alexan chuckled, catching her against his massive chest.

'And how is it you are so immune to her?' snarled Drosta, collecting himself. Alexan looked down at her and brushed her hair back from her scarred face. The heady look in his eyes betrayed him. He was not immune after all.

'It's the burns,' he said, looking to Drosta once more. Even though she realised he was lying, she still flinched from his words. She knew that not even the most gruesome disfigurement could dull the effect of her presence. But the burns – the attack that caused them – had broken her spirit, and that dampened her power. Keriath gave him a baleful look, but she understood what he was doing. Bewitching Drosta without the power to control him would put her in even greater danger.

'Bind her up tight and put her on my horse,' ordered Drosta, pushing her towards his Hunt. They were quick to follow his commands, and soon she was mounted astride Drosta's charger with her shackles looped around the pommel. The Hunter swung himself up behind her, his breath catching as he revelled in their closeness. He reached around her to take the reins and breathed in deeply as he buried his nose in her hair again. 'I'm going to enjoy the feeling of your arse between my thighs girl,' he hissed, 'and if you don't behave, I'll enjoy a lot more than that.' Keriath shuddered and looked away. Alexan was leaning against a tree, his arms folded across his massive chest once more, a muscle pulsing in his jaw.

'Kill her, and you'll answer to worse than me, Drosta,' he warned as the Hunter wheeled his mount around.

Drosta afforded him a cruel smile before he and his Hunt plunged their mounts out into the pale light of the dawn, carrying Keriath with them.

CHAPTER EIGHT

Keriath woke to a trickle of ice-cold water on her face. It was one of the more pleasant awakenings she'd endured since Alexan had handed her over to Drosta. Not that it stopped her lashing out with her foot, trying to catch her tormentor off guard. He chuckled as he dodged, tipping the rest of the bucket over her with a vicious hoot of delight.

'When I get loose, you're a dead man,' she vowed.

He laughed again – a cruel laugh, far more chilling that the water soaking her clothes. She spat in his direction and immediately regretted it when his dark red eyes flashed in anger. She flinched, knowing what was coming next, but with the chains around her limbs, she couldn't move quickly enough to avoid the savage kick in the ribs. A frightened yelp escaped her as she fought for breath through the pain. A broken rib. Maybe two. They'd heal within a few days, thanks to the Graced power in her veins, but until then, riding was going to be painful.

'Time to wake up, my beauty,' Drosta jeered. 'We've got a lot of distance to cover, and we'll never get to Illyol if you keep lying around all night.'

There was more haunting laughter from behind her as the Hunt joined in with his ridicule, but she hardly noticed, her attention snagged on one word.

'Illyol?' she heard herself asking. Why would they be going to Illyol? True, it wouldn't be much of a detour as they travelled south to Dar Kual, but the ancient Elvish city had been abandoned since the Fall. Darklings shouldn't have even been able to penetrate the wards. Unease slipped a little deeper through her gut.

Drosta ignored her.

'When can we next feed?' one of the few females in the group complained – the same one who'd attacked Keriath in the Ravenswood. Not discouraged by the beating she'd got from Alexan, she'd tried twice more before Drosta administered his own brutal brand of punishment. Since then, she'd barely stopped whining.

'When we're closer to the city. Now stop your moaning and load her up,' snapped Drosta's second, Dell – another name Keriath would prefer not to know. Big and brutish and none too bright. She fought back a hiss of pain as firm hands grabbed her about the waist and lifted her up into the saddle, the movement burning her bruised chest. But that was nothing compared to the discomfort of Drosta swinging himself up behind her and sliding his arms past her waist as he reached for the reins. His touch and his scent made her skin crawl and her stomach heave, but she forced herself to remain still and hide the shudder of disgust that would betray her. He took far too much joy from it.

With a barked command to his Hunt, he kicked his heels into the flanks of his black stallion and charged into the night.

After leaving Alexan, they had ridden through the day, hidden from the worst of the sun by the shade of the trees. They'd ridden on through the night, but Drosta had called a halt as the sun rose. He'd been far from happy about it, but he needed the remnant of his Hunt strong if he was to keep his *prize*. Keriath cursed her luck to have been captured by Drosta. He was cruel, but also cunning and efficient. Escape would not come easy.

Escape. The thought chafed at her mind, just as much as those cursed chains chafed at her wrists. She wondered where he'd got them. And more importantly, why. Between that and the ruan, Drosta had clearly come prepared to hunt and capture Graced prey. And from the exchange she'd heard in the Ravenswood, he'd known exactly where to start. But *how*? The lethal edge of some dark, dangerous thought glinted in the periphery of her mind, but she looked away. That wasn't a fear she was prepared to breathe life into. Not yet.

She glanced down at the thick, black mane in front of her and felt a twinge of sadness. He was a magnificent beast – tall and heavily built, and his coat was as black as coal. She was under no illusions where he was from. He was the legacy of a once powerful people. Her people. A descendant of their legendary warhorses. She'd seen her brother take a form like this many times. The thought tore at her heart, worry gnawing at her gut. Taelyr. Her baby brother. Gods, she hoped he was safe.

Keriath closed her eyes and tried to rest. But surrounded by the stench of the creatures that haunted her nightmares, it was a hard ask. Still, the smooth, rolling gait of the horse was soothing, and it was not long until she felt herself floating away into darkness.

Cruel hands pinching at her thigh dragged her from her restless slumber.

'Wake up,' Drosta snarled in her ear.

She shook herself as she focussed in on her surroundings, muttering, 'Have I mentioned I'm going to kill you?'

'Once or twice.'

'It won't be quick either,' she promised.

He leaned in close to her neck and inhaled deeply. 'I wouldn't expect anything else,' he breathed against her skin. Unable to repress her shudder, Keriath leaned away from him. He laughed and squeezed his thighs around her. 'What's the matter?' he crooned in her ear. 'Tried Alexan out for size and discovered you don't like the touch of a Darkling after all?'

'I'd rather be flayed alive.' She tried to elbow him in the gut, but her chains held her tight. Drosta chuckled again and ran his tongue from the top of her shoulder all the way to the bottom of her jaw. Her stomach heaved, and she had to take deep, steadying breaths to stop herself retching all over the poor beast beneath her.

'I can arrange that, you know?' he warned.

Keriath struggled not to flinch, forcing herself to remain calm as she continued to look around her. She had dreamed away most of the night. The sky to the east was pale with the first light of dawn. They had travelled south, drifting up into the eastern foothills of the Wildwings. She frowned at that. It would have been much quicker to skirt around them, even riding through the dense forest. Then her gaze fell on the small, white cottage nestled on the other side of the valley, and she realised what had drawn them so far off course. Realised why Drosta had woken her – why his Hunt was now buzzing with barely restrained excitement. Her heart sank, and she raged against the icy grip of the ruan.

'No,' she breathed, heaving against her chains.

Drosta ignored her. 'Slim pickings,' he said to his second. Dell grunted in agreement. Keriath couldn't bring herself to look at either of them. Her attention was on the little croft across the glen. The farmer was in his field, readying for the hard day of work ahead. A young man – possibly his grown son – helped, while a young woman scattered feed for some scrawny chickens. Then two children came racing out of the house, the boy laughing as he chased the screaming girl towards the barn. A furious snarl ripped out of Keriath's lips, and she wrenched at her chains. Drosta only growled, snapping his teeth near her throat in warning.

A terrified whimper had her tearing her gaze away to the young shepherd girl in the saddle before Dell. Her eyes were wide with fright and tears stained her rosy cheeks. She was staring at the farmhouse, guilt and sorrow weighing on her young shoulders. Keriath followed her gaze back and felt her heart break. A woman, a crying baby in her arms, had appeared at the door of the farmhouse, scolding the children for waking their sibling. But the babe was not the worst. Drosta's Hunt shifted with anticipation at the sight of her swollen womb, at the life that slumbered there. Innocent and undefended. Life for the stealing.

Keriath thrashed against Drosta's grip, trying to get loose. It was an instinct she had little control over, an instinct that ruled all the Graced – to protect, to defend, to destroy. She roared as she fought, desperation blinding her. But those chains held tight, draining her strength from her. She could feel their tainted magic pressing down on her Graced power, containing it, binding it. Drosta shoved her from the saddle in disgust, her chains slipping loose from the pommel, and cuffed her across the face with a swipe of his arm. She was sent sprawling, but she surged up, screaming to the family in warning while she reached for the girl in Dell's grip. Dell offered her a look of withering pity before he planted his boot in her chest and kicked her back into the dirt.

'Stay down,' he advised her. It was counsel she had always ignored, even as a child when she had trained with the legendary Resari. And if she had refused to surrender then, outmatched by power strong enough to challenge the Shade King himself, there was not a chance she would now. She staggered to her feet, spitting blood, rushing the Darkling again. This time Drosta intervened, his hand snaking out and seizing a fistful of her hair. She screamed as he wrenched her head back, thrashing against his grip. He shook her.

'If you don't settle down, I will carve that girl up right here in front of you. She will die screaming in agony, and every tortuous moment will be your fault,' he hissed. Dell squeezed the girl's throat to reinforce the point, smirking at the squeal that escaped her terrified lips. Keriath stilled, her fury thrumming in her veins as she quivered from the effort of restraining it. Drosta snarled with satisfaction and released her. 'That's better. Now, be a good girl and watch quietly.' Then he snapped his fingers and sent his Hunt haring across the glen.

It was a bloodbath. Faolin and Dorrien had thinned Drosta's Hunt, but there were still enough left to make short work of the family. The farmer fought, for all the good it did him. The boy and the girl tried to hide, even as their older brother was torn apart. But there was nowhere the Darklings couldn't find them. The mother tried to run, then she tried to shield her child with her body. Her wails cut the deepest into Keriath's tortured soul – worse than even the shrieking baby in her arms – keening as she was for the defenceless life dying in her womb. The Darklings spared the young woman, at least for a while. Her screams echoed through the hills while the monsters toyed with her.

Keriath could only watch, helpless to intervene. Her breath came in seething pants, her teeth bared as bloodlust boiled in her veins. But as the hills fell silent, she quietened. A deep, unyielding cold had seeped into her bones, freezing her fury into an icy rage. Her mother had once spoken in fear about the wrath of a patient man. Words of warning to her daughter, to always stay on her guard should the patience of the Shade King ever wear thin. Keriath might refute his claims, but she had realised long ago that she could learn more from her enemies than her friends. And the Shade King's patience was legendary, as were the consequences of his careful plotting. How many years had he planned the atrocities leading to the Fall? How many years had he waited and suffered for those schemes to bear fruit? Certainty settled in her gut. Keriath could be patient too. One day she would see the world rid of the Darkling stain. One day she would bathe in Drosta's blood for what had happened here, and she would take a damn long time doing it. One day …

'If you want any, you'd better get a move on.' Dell's voice shook her from her vengeful imaginings, and she glanced round. He was speaking to his Hunter, his expression impassive as he looked back to the farmhouse. Keriath frowned. Dell's expression was too blank, too carefully void of any emotion. She might not be able to sense his thoughts, but it wasn't hard to deduce the emotions roiling beneath the surface. The slaughter didn't sit well with him. She looked back at Drosta, but he was oblivious to his second's discomfort. He was too busy watching her, an unsettling smile on his lips.

His bloody gaze flickered up to his second. 'I'm fine. You take that one. I need you fit in case of any trouble between here and Illyol.' Dell nodded, but Keriath could see the hesitation – the reluctance – in his eyes. Drosta didn't seem to notice, turning his attention back to her. 'Once they're finished, we should ride on. I don't want to risk meeting another Hunt drawn in by the blood.'

Dell nodded in agreement. 'Cloud's thick enough to keep riding for another hour,' he grunted. 'Should be far enough.'

Drosta looked back at the farmhouse, to his Hunt returning. 'Maybe I should have Claimed two or three of them,' he mused. 'Our numbers need replenished if we're to stand any chance of holding her between here and Illyol.'

'You'd have lost at least two if they hadn't fed,' Dell pointed out, 'and at least the same again would be weakened near to useless. You're better off strengthening what you've got and replacing later.' Drosta made a sceptical noise in the back of his throat, contemplating his prisoner once more. Dell huffed another frustrated sigh and gestured at the girl in his lap. During the slaughter, she'd fainted and now lay like a limp doll across his saddle. 'If you're that bothered, turn this one. I'll last. It's only another couple of days.'

'No,' said Drosta, turning on his second. There was something wild, something warped and twisted in his bloody gaze that made Keriath cringe inside. 'No. I won't risk it.' He glanced back to the approaching Hunt. 'Be quick about it, or they'll demand that you share.'

'I don't mind—' Dell began.

But Drosta cut him off. 'I do. Now stop arguing and feed.' His voice was laced with command. Keriath could feel the air vibrating with the force of his order, with the power of the Claiming. Dell crumpled beneath it. She hissed, powerless to stop him as he bowed his head to the girl's throat and drained her of her meagre life. When he was done, he dumped her corpse on the ground with careful indifference. But Keriath saw the glimmer of regret in his blood-soaked eyes. A feral smile touched her lips. A chink. That's what she'd found. A chink in Drosta's armour.

'We keep riding, make camp in an hour,' Drosta called to his Hunt. 'Then you can rest. I want everyone at full strength for the last stretch – I will not have my prize stolen by another Hunt.' His voice was cold and stern. The command of a general, expecting his orders to be followed without question. Sure enough, one by one, they all inclined their heads in acquiescence. Keriath didn't fight as he dragged her back into the saddle.

Patience, she told herself. Patience would reward her sooner than reckless fury.

So they thundered back down into the forest, desperate to escape the dawn. A grim smile twisted her lips, and she took a deep, steadying breath. She just had to bide her time.

They descended into the shadows just before the cloud cleared, and Keriath felt Drosta breathe a small sigh of relief behind her. But it was short-lived, and he called a halt not long after. He barked sharp commands as they made camp, ordering a tent set in the centre.

She was afforded some food and water – not enough to fill her belly or soothe her parched throat, but she knew better than to argue, especially when she noted the dangerous glint in Drosta's blood-red eyes. He was hiding it well from his Hunt, but Keriath could see that he was famished.

Sure enough, he gripped her by the arm and hauled her to her feet, shoving her into the tent. Then, with a snapped order not to disturb him under any circumstances, he followed her inside.

It was comfortable, for makeshift accommodation. The forest floor hidden beneath a blanket of animal pelts, the thickest and softest of them piled beside his bedroll. Sleeping rough had never bothered Keriath. A bed of pine needles was about as good as she ever hoped for, so the soft furs were a comparative luxury.

Then she caught that same dark glint in his eye and realised what had prompted this. She recoiled, swearing viciously, and spat in his face. He blinked once and wiped it away before he lashed out, cracking the back of his hand across her face.

Keriath staggered and tripped on her chains, crashing to the ground with her cheek smarting and jaw aching from the force of his blow. He stood over her, massaging his hand as he considered her, his eyes glowing. She touched her hand to her lip and wasn't surprised when it came away bloody. She forced herself to take a deep breath and stay calm. Then she raised her eyes and met his gaze, unleashing her entire self on him. Not for long though. She couldn't risk bewitching him completely, not without the Enchanting to hold him. But just enough to lower his defences, make him forget the threat she posed, bound or not. And when his eyes glazed and his jaw opened in awe, triumph set her heart racing.

It took more effort than she anticipated to repress a grim smile, but she managed, and lowered her eyes in submission. She knew what was coming next, but she had to endure it or risk raising his suspicion. She wasn't strong enough to make a break for it, would have to rely on stealth. For now, at least.

There was a feral growl as he caught the aroma of blood, and she knew he was in control of himself once more. Sure enough, those cruel hands gripped her once more and slammed her into the ground, pinning her there with the full weight of his body. She closed her eyes and fought against the wave of nausea that roiled in her stomach. His lips brushed her throat.

'What are you?' he hissed against her neck.

'You know what I am,' she gasped, struggling against him.

'You're more than just a Unicorn. What other blood flows in your veins?' he murmured as he bit into the skin. She couldn't help it – she whimpered at the piercing pain. But when she refused to answer, he growled and shook her. Hard. His teeth tore at her throat, and she screamed in agony.

'Elf!' she cried. 'By the Gods, I'm half Elf!'

Drosta laughed and drank from the bleeding wound. A small sob escaped her lips – from fear or from pain. She could hardly tell the difference anymore.

It was long after sunset when Keriath finally moved. Drosta lay sprawled in his bedroll, sated at last. Her skin crawled from the ghost of his touch, and shame pricked behind her eyes. Her birthright was to slaughter Darklings, not to lie still while they fed on her power. But she clamped down on the disgust that threatened to overwhelm her, relegating it to the deepest, darkest depths of herself.

We do what we have to with what we have,' her mother said once. The Lady Kylar had endured worse – some would say her daughter was living proof of that, though Keriath refused to believe it. Rumours and lies, meant to turn her against her family. Her mother had never given so much as an inch to the horrors in her past. Keriath would honour her by doing the same.

So she straightened her clothes as best she could and slipped her hand into the pocket of Drosta's discarded coat. A satisfied smile twisted her lips as her fingers closed around the cold metal of the key. Drosta did not so much as twitch as she eased it free and slid it into the locks of her manacles. Even with the power of her blood now running through him, he was still spent. So predictable, Darklings and their insatiable appetites. Offer them whatever it was they desired, and they would gorge themselves senseless.

He stirred when the manacles clicked open, his eyelids fluttering before he drifted back into oblivion. She eyed the knife on his belt, tempted by bloody vengeance. A risk, and difficult to keep silent – not to mention, a waste to make it quick. He deserved to suffer. But this was neither the time nor the place to indulge herself. Instead, she crept to the back of the tent and pulled out the peg securing it, lifting the canvas up enough that she might roll underneath it. With a final hungry look at her prey and a soft hiss of frustration, she slipped from the tent and into the night beyond.

Shrouded in the shadows, she looked about her. The entrance to Drosta's tent faced the fire in the centre of their camp, around which, most of the Darklings were now sprawled. Drunk on human life, she noted with a silent snarl. She'd seen it before. Were it not for the ruan, Keriath could have swept through their pitiful little camp like a natural disaster, leaving only death and ruin in her wake. But that power was beyond her, her strength drained by hunger and exhaustion. She pushed her frustration aside, turned and crept into the night.

It was so easy to steal away from their camp. To slip between bored sentries and half-hearted patrols too scared of their Hunter to disobey him but too tired to do the job properly. She took those cursed chains with her and dumped them in the first stream she crossed. She retraced their steps north-west, making for the farmhouse. It was a risk. Other Hunts might be drawn in by the lure of blood. But she needed supplies – food, clothing … weapons if she could get them. It grated on her to consider pilfering from the dead, but even she could concede that her need was greater than theirs. Besides, Drosta would be unlikely to consider tracking her back there, and any mortals within a ten-mile radius would stay well away.

So the light of a torch flickering in the night as she approached was somewhat unexpected. Hidden in the shadows, she crept closer, wishing for the bow and quiver full of arrows she'd abandoned on her flight from Thornhold, and spared a moment to curse whoever had sold her out to the Darklings. But she dared not dwell any longer. Not when the truth of that betrayal might just break her.

A fire flared into life, shattering the darkness with its roar and crackle. The farm and fields were bathed in the warm glow and smoke filled the air. Keriath frowned, peering through the sudden brightness to what she thought was a shadowy figure beyond. Then the shape vanished, and she blinked in confusion. Perhaps she'd just imagined it. But the fire hadn't started itself. So she inched forward.

And froze at the cold bite of steel at her throat.

'If you come quietly, we can go back to the camp and say no more about it,' a male voice murmured in the darkness. 'You can fight if you must, but either way, you're going back. If you make me work for it, I'll tell Drosta you escaped and watch with a smile when he beats you bloody.'

Dell. Keriath cursed inwardly. What was he doing here? Not that it mattered. He was one Darkling, alone and mortal. She rose from her crouch, allowing him to keep his blade at her throat. He tracked her movements but didn't lower his guard. 'Don't even think about it,' he warned. 'I am not in the mood.' Something in his voice made her pause.

'What are you in the mood for?' she asked with a suggestive wink.

He glowered. 'Not that. I'm assuming that's how you got loose?'

'I promise he'll say it was worth it.' She smirked, trying to ignore how her skin crawled at the thought of him feeding, leeching the power from her soul.

He gave her a knowing look. 'I don't think you'd say the same.'

'It'll be worth it once the ruan wears off, and I can turn his head inside out,' she said. 'Your Hunter thinks he understands pain and suffering, but he doesn't have my gifts.' The Enchanting gave her so much more than just control. With it she could unravel Drosta's mind, delve deep into his nightmares and drown him in them. It was a warming thought.

Dell's face remained impassive. 'I doubt you'll find his head a pleasant place to linger.'

'And what about your head?' she asked, trying to quell the queasy sensation rising in her stomach. 'What will I find in there? Maybe an answer to why you're out here all alone, cleaning up your Hunter's mess?'

His gaze darkened at that. 'It's none of your business.'

'Does Drosta know you're here?' When he didn't answer, her smile broadened. 'Well then, I think it's more likely you who's for the beating.'

'You should worry less about my hide and more about your own,' he reminded her, the blade at her throat twitching in warning. 'Now are you going to come quietly or are you determined to make my life difficult?'

'What do you think?'

Dell heaved a sigh of frustration and swung. She dodged, her Graced speed allowing her to avoid the blade whistling through the air. But as she swirled away, she had a sudden sinking feeling that she was going to lose this fight. Exhaustion and hunger wore deep into her soul. Even though her Graced might was now loose from those accursed chains, she wondered if it would be enough to save her. The clouds overhead shifted, and a ghostly shaft of moonlight pierced the shadows. A silvery glint of an abandoned knife on the ground had her moving again.

Keriath sprinted for the knife, cursing what the moonlight would reveal. The glamour that dampened the sheer force of her appearance – her power – was ripped away as the light touched her. As a child she'd witnessed her mother unleashed, knew what it looked like. What it revealed. Skin glowing with all the luminosity of the moon itself, the light of a million stars glittering in her captivating eyes. She could feel her raven hair curling and snapping as her aura danced over her skin, crackling like purple fire. She hissed in frustration to have unveiled so much. But she had the knife.

Dell staggered in awe but recovered. He came at her hard, lashing out with fist and blade. She tried to catch his eye, tried to stun him into inertia with her gaze, but he seemed wise to that trick and focussed on her body. Bone crunched beneath her boot as she landed a powerful kick on his leg. But her victory was short-lived; he returned with a heavy punch to her face. She stumbled and only just avoided the singing edge of his blade as it cut through the air towards her throat.

With a yell, she arched back as the blade sliced through the air just above her neck, then straightened, throwing the knife with all her might. The big swordsman roared in pain as it pierced his shoulder, and he staggered back. She didn't hesitate. Darting past, she dug deep for the strength that would allow her to escape. But where there should have been a torrent, there was only a trickle. She cursed and ran. If she could just put some distance between them …

He crashed into her, sending them sprawling in the dirt, and pinned her beneath him with his legs. Then he rose up and drove the point of his sword down through her shoulder, burying it to the hilt, impaling her to the ground. She roared and tried to wrench herself free, but the blade held her fast. Dell staggered to his feet, breathing hard from the exertion, and stumbled towards his horse. At the familiar clink of manacles, Keriath thrashed again, but she only hurt herself further.

'Never seen a Unicorn with Elf-magic before,' he panted, crouching beside her. Keriath gasped an ugly curse and tried to fight him off. But he grabbed her jaw and forced her to face him, squeezing hard enough to make her eyes water. 'Will you just give it up?' he huffed, knocking her hands away as she scrabbled for his face.

'I swear, by the Gods, I will kill you before the end,' she hissed, trying to writhe out of his grip. But he only rolled his eyes and clamped the chains back around her wrists. He grunted in disinterest and chained her ankles too, before standing and pulling the sword from her shoulder in one sharp movement. She screamed and swore, wishing for her magic to soothe the pain. Dell's eyes glowed red at the smell of her blood, and he hauled her up against him.

'Don't die on me,' he instructed her. And then he bent his head to her throat and bit into her skin. The pain was not great, not compared to Drosta's savage feeding. Nor compared to the aching wound in her shoulder. But his tenderness surprised her, and she didn't fight it, even as another wave of self-reproach crashed over her. He took a few quick mouthfuls and then stopped, holding her tight as a wave of lethargy and weakness crashed over her. He kept his face buried in the crook of her neck, his breathing ragged against her skin and his heart thundering against her chest. Her flesh crawled at the contact, her stomach heaving at the stench of his stolen magic. Every fibre of her being recoiled from him.

Then he spoke, and surprise stilled her. 'Sorry,' he murmured. 'Couldn't resist.' He blew out a sharp breath and stepped back. 'Damn, you taste good.' Then he hefted her over his shoulder and threw her up into the saddle. He stormed back to the fire and pulled a burning branch from the pile. From the pyre, she realised as she looked again, for those were the bodies of the farmer and his family in the flames. Then he crossed to the house, opened the door and threw the torch in. It didn't take long for the thatch to catch. Satisfied, he turned his back on the blaze and climbed up behind her, wrapping a muscular arm around her when she swayed.

'Why?' she whispered, clinging to consciousness.

He was quiet for a moment. 'It was all the dignity I could offer them.'

'And the house?'

He hesitated. 'A warning. Mortals should know better than to put down roots this close to the Barren Lands. This should serve as a reminder to those who might forget.' Stunned into silence for the second time that night, Keriath didn't fight as he turned his horse back to the forest. Instead, she gave herself to oblivion.

Dell roused her with a vicious shake, his other hand clamped down hard across her mouth. 'Listen to me carefully, Unicorn,' he whispered, his voice so soft she struggled to hear it. But there was enough tension and fear in his voice that she did as she was bid. 'The camp is just up ahead, and something's got the Hunt all riled up. We might both be in very real danger right now, so I'm going to ask you to do something for me, if you don't mind?' Keriath snorted into his hand, but he continued on, unperturbed. 'On the assumption you'd prefer not to die,' he breathed in her ear, 'I'm asking that you do exactly what I say for the foreseeable future. I don't particularly want to die either, so if it comes down to me or you, I'll carve your heart out myself – but it would be such a waste, so can you just do as you're told. Please?' She didn't respond at first, still dazed from blood loss – not to mention shocked by his good manners. But eventually, she inclined her head, and he released her.

'What is it?' she murmured, following his gaze as he dismounted and peered into the gloom.

He shook his head. 'Don't know. Thought it was just Drosta raging because he'd realised you'd gone, at first, but pretty sure it's something else. Too much tension for it to just be coming from our Hunt. Luckily for you.'

'How is that lucky for me?' she muttered, examining her chains. Spelled, just like the ones she'd dumped in the forest.

'Because if there is something or someone else there, it means Drosta will be distracted. I've been on the receiving end of one of his thrashings. I wouldn't wish that on my worst enemy.'

Keriath snorted. 'If you say so.'

Dell hushed her with an impatient gesture, helping her down off the horse in silence.

'Just stay close to me,' he murmured. Then he was moving, creeping forward through the dense undergrowth. Keriath followed, trying not to set her chains rattling. It was only a few moments later that he paused, head up as if listening. Keriath stilled, ears straining. Then she heard it. Voices ahead.

'This is my territory, Drosta,' a female voice was purring, 'and you're trespassing. I'm well within my rights to kill you and all that's left of your pathetic little Hunt.'

Dell scowled, seemingly in recognition of that voice, but he stayed hidden in the shadows.

Drosta snapped. 'I travel on Queens' orders.'

'Show me.'

'I don't have them – they're with my second. They sent us north to deal with the rising Shade presence in the Silvan Forests.'

'Well, you're doing an outstanding job of it if this is all that's left of your Hunt,' the female sneered. A low growl rumbled through the darkness as Drosta made his irritation known, but he didn't dispute it. 'Where's your second anyway? Dell, isn't it? He's a handsome one.'

Drosta's answering snarl was vicious. 'He's none of your business. If you so much as touch him, I swear—'

'Where is he, Drosta?' she crooned, cutting him off. 'Tell me now, or I start killing.' Dell muttered a low curse and put a hand under Keriath's arm, dragging her forward as he marched into the camp.

'Calm your tits, Maren,' he sighed, his voice heavy with contempt. 'I'm right here.'

The Huntress turned, grinning as he approached. Then her bloody gaze fell on Keriath, and she gaped in wonder that gave way to jealousy faster than Keriath had ever seen. She couldn't help the smug smile that rose to her lips, nor the slight raising of her chin as she looked down at the ugly little woman before her.

Then Dell was between them, fishing a scroll from inside his shirt and handing it to the Huntress. Maren opened it and read, her scowl deepening with every line. Keriath glanced to Drosta and what was left of his Hunt, on their knees, surrounded by the larger force of Maren's Hunt. There was even a hint of fear in Drosta's crimson eyes as his gaze bored into Dell. She repressed the snort that rose in response to that. It wasn't the time.

'Well, this all seems in order.' Maren sniffed, waving a hand to her Hunt. 'Let them up.'

'Can we go now?' snapped Drosta, snatching the scroll from her grubby little hands.

Maren stared at him. 'Who is she?'

'My prisoner. A gift for the Queens. And if you try to take her, I'll press charges of poaching.'

Maren ran an assessing eye over Keriath. 'Quite some gift. How did you catch her?'

'None of your fucking business.'

The Huntress snorted. 'I'm concerned about the state of your Hunt, Drosta. Especially if you're representing our Queens. Since I don't have the authority to kill you, I think I should accompany you back to Dar Kual.'

'That won't be necessary,' Drosta hissed.

Maren gave him a serpent's smile. 'Oh, I'm afraid I must insist,' she said, a hungry glint entering her eye as she looked Dell over. 'Now I suggest you cooperate, before I make someone else suffer for your conduct.'

Drosta snarled at the threat, but his gaze was brittle with fear and anger. Keriath almost laughed to see it. Especially when he bowed his head in submission. 'I am yours to command,' he breathed, not bothering to hide the reluctance in his voice.

Maren beamed. 'Good. Now, pack up camp. We ride out in an hour for Ciaron – as per your orders,' she said. Keriath blinked. Ciaron? That made even less sense than Illyol.

Drosta hesitated. 'And my prisoner?'

Maren's smile turned feral, and she rounded on Keriath.

'How old are you?'

Keriath scowled. 'Old enough.'

'And how many of my brethren have you killed in your long life?'

A smirk touched her lips. 'Not enough.'

'The Graced are wild, unpredictable beasts – not to mention arrogant,' mused Maren, turning back to Drosta. 'We owe it to our fallen kin to see her punished for her crimes.'

Dell's grip on Keriath's arm tightened, and he drew her nearer. 'She's for the Queens,' he reminded the Huntress, unable to keep the concern from his voice.

'Oh, I wasn't suggesting we kill her,' the Huntress purred. 'But we can still have a little fun ...'

CHAPTER NINE

E very step her mount took was agony for Keriath. The wounds from her beating were healing, but those to her pride and damaged soul would take far longer. Since then, Maren had left her alone, mostly. Too preoccupied playing whatever sick games she had with Drosta, as far as Keriath could tell. Gods, the noises coming from their tent at night ... Keriath, meanwhile, had been entrusted into Dell's less than tender care. A small mercy, considering the heavy guard that surrounded them while they travelled south.

But Keriath wasn't stupid. She hadn't missed the long-suffering glances Drosta had exchanged with his second, or the ravenous glint that appeared in his eyes whenever his gaze drifted over Keriath. Drosta feared Maren, and he was doing everything in his power to keep her distracted – away from his prize and from the Darkling who rode behind her.

They had passed through the Silvan Forests without further incident. Maren had seemed keen to spend as little time as possible beneath the boughs of the silver birch and had cut south through the narrowest part of the forest. But instead of continuing south towards Dar Kual, she'd cut east across the northern edge of the Barren Lands towards Ciaron – precisely why was beyond Keriath. It was the wrong direction for Dar Kual, and even under Nightwalker rule, Ciaron was still a dangerous place for a Darkling.

'Where were you to meet your contact?' Maren had asked.

'On the Eastern Wing,' he'd grunted. 'We were told they would find us.'

They were now out on the open expanse of the Barren Lands where the bitter wind was merciless, biting into every cut on Keriath's body like a knife. Her cheeks stung from the force of it, and she shivered with the cold. They continued south-east, hugging the southern edge of the Silvan Forests. Keriath didn't bother to ask why they weren't heading south towards Dar Kual. She didn't want to know.

Relief weighed heavy on her bones when they stopped just before dawn. Maren had finally tired of tormenting her, perhaps believing she'd learned her lesson. She resisted the urge to smirk at the thought. The only thing their mistreatment had taught her was a new level of hatred. She daydreamed of ways to end Drosta, Maren and their Hunts, and repay every injustice committed upon her.

Dell interrupted her fantasies, crouching beside her and handing her the water skin without a word. She took it, ignoring the bitter tang of ruan. Alexan had been right about accepting whatever food and water they offered – she'd found out twice now that they were both willing and able to force it on her. At least if she took it without a fight, it was one less excuse for them to beat her.

'How are your wounds healing?' Dell asked.

Keriath glared at him. 'Why? Bored already?'

Dell said nothing, shrugging to concede her point. His eyes were tracking Maren as she arranged her Hunt around the camp. Drosta was at her side, but sensing their gazes on him, he glanced over her head and rolled his eyes at his second. Dell chuckled then seemed to catch himself and snatched the water skin from Keriath's hands.

Drosta frowned, and he bowed his head to murmur something in Maren's ear. She smiled at whatever he said and nodded, before calling to some of her Hunt and vanishing back into the forest. Drosta sighed, looking relieved, and came to join them.

'That bitch is running me ragged,' he complained, holding his hand out for the water.

Dell snorted, passing the skin. 'Aye, it must be such a hardship.'

Drosta's face split into an evil smile that sent shivers down Keriath's spine. 'She's not my type. Gods, how I'd love to make her scream.'

'She screams plenty,' Dell noted, arching a sardonic eyebrow.

Drosta pulled a face. 'I know. It's enough to make your ears bleed.'

'I thought you liked screamers.' Dell laughed, digging around in his pack.

Drosta grunted, eyeing Keriath with a speculative gleam that made her uneasy.

'Aye, but screams of pain are far sweeter than screams of pleasure,' She looked away, trying to hide the wave of revulsion that swept through her, but judging by his dark laugh, she didn't succeed. With a deep breath to quell her rebellious stomach, she turned to meet his gaze. He smirked at the defiance there but said nothing as he looked back to his second. 'We're already late to meet Mazron's agent. We don't have time to deliver this one to Dar Kual and get back to the Wings – we'll have to take her with us.'

'Not to Illyol then?' Dell asked. Keriath's interest pricked. Why *had* they been heading for Illyol? It didn't make any sense.

Drosta shot him a sharp look. 'No. We can't risk a confrontation. We don't have the numbers to ensure it goes cleanly. And Maren's seen her now, so it would raise too many questions if we didn't deliver her to the Queens.'

'Zorana will be pissed,' noted Dell, more to himself than anyone else.

Keriath forced herself not to react. She knew that name. Zorana was a Shade Princess, a high-ranking member of the Shade Court and strong enough to be a serious threat to the King were she so inclined. She and her brother both. Keriath had recognised that name too. Prince Mazron was well known to those who had survived the Fall. He hunted them with an unholy passion. And Drosta was working for them? Interesting ...

'Well, there's not much we can do about it now. Maren's not the sharpest tool in the box, but even she could put it together if I gifted a prize like that to a Shade. Zorana can make do with another one. If her pet knew where to find this one, he'll know where we can find others.' Keriath stilled. Though she kept her eyes on the ground, the sudden tension in her body drew Drosta's gaze back to her. He gripped her chin between his fingers and forced her face up to look at him. 'Breathe a word of anything you heard, and it'll be you screaming beneath me next,' he said, his voice soft but even more dangerous for it.

The threat of violence in his eyes mixed with barely restrained lust made her want to cower in fear. But she held his gaze, daring him to risk staring too long at her face and losing himself in the process. His hand slipped to her throat, and he squeezed in warning. A movement over his shoulder drew Keriath's attention, and she smirked.

'Your lover wants you,' she breathed. 'Time to go back to playing the whore.'

Drosta's lips pulled back in a silent snarl, and he shoved her away. 'You keep her with you at all times – you don't even leave her alone long enough to take a piss. And keep her away from Maren and the rest of her Hunt,' he snapped at Dell, before turning and stalking back to the freshly fed Huntress.

'You're taking your life in your hands, taunting him like that,' Dell warned, hauling her to her feet and dragging her towards his tent. Keriath snorted and rolled her eyes. With a sigh of exasperation, he pushed her into the tent and threw some food in after her. He followed her in but sat down as far away from her as he could. Then he gestured for her to take his bedroll and settled himself facing the entrance, as if to guard her while she slept. 'I'm serious. Keep pushing, and he might just snap. I don't think you realise what your blood does to us. There's enough power in your veins to drive him mad on a good day, and he's not likely to have one of those with Maren around.'

'Your master was mad long before he tasted me,' she pointed out.

He shrugged but didn't dispute her statement.

'Darkling magic does that.'

'What? Makes men into monsters?'

'He's always been that way,' he said, 'always enjoyed hurting people. The Claiming just gave him the freedom to act on his impulses.'

Keriath was stunned into silence for a while. 'He chose this?'

'He wanted power so he could do whatever he pleased without having to answer for his crimes. And since he wasn't Graced, this was the next best option,' he said with a bitter smile.

'At what cost?' she breathed.

Dell shrugged. 'He'd pay a price a thousand times steeper than the one he paid for this power,' he told her. 'He loves this life. Wouldn't change it for anything. Now go to sleep.'

Keriath rolled over and pulled a hide around herself as she repressed a shiver that had nothing to do with the cold. Drosta was the monster she should have feared as a child – a vicious beast who would do anything for power and control. Alexan had proved that not all Dark-lings were pure evil ... perhaps Drosta proved that not all evil came from Darklings.

She shuddered again and closed her eyes. Sleep would not come easily.

Dell roused Keriath with a gentle shake of her shoulder. Well, all things were relative, she reminded herself, studying the partially healed cuts and bruises on her arms.

'Wake up,' he whispered urgently. Keriath blinked and looked at the sunlight pouring through the crack of the tent flap. It was mid-afternoon, and sunset was still hours away. Something was wrong.

'What?' she snapped, sitting up.

'Get up,' he ordered. Then he rose and slipped from the tent. She crawled over to the entrance and lifted the flap so she could peer out. Dell stood right outside and gestured a warning at her with his dagger.

'You stay right there where I can see you,' he growled. 'If you so much as think about running, I will gut you like a pig.'

She snorted and clanked her chains at him. 'Not going anywhere in a hurry, am I?' she said scathingly. He rolled his eyes and stepped closer to her.

She peered past him to see what all the commotion was about and felt her heart swell with hope. From over the horizon, a dozen riders had appeared. She could tell from here that their palomino mounts were Unicorn warhorses, but that didn't mean much anymore. More interesting was their golden armour, flashing in the evening sun. She'd seen its kind before.

Dragons. And they were headed this way.

Keriath fidgeted with her chains as she watched the Dragons grow closer. Drosta didn't try to retreat – he wasn't stupid; he knew there was no point. She wondered why he'd ever allowed them to get this close to Dragon lands. Even with so few left, they were still dangerous and he had to know they killed Darklings on sight. It was one of their highest laws. For a Dragon to suffer a Darkling to live was a death sentence. It had been ever since the Fall.

Dell let out a warning growl as she itched forward. Maren, standing in the middle of the Hunts with Drosta at her side, glanced round at the sound and scowled at her.

'Don't try anything stupid,' she warned. 'We don't have time to let you heal from another beating.'

Keriath heard the threat beneath the words. They'd kill her before they let her go free.

The Dragons were drawing closer, the long legs of their mounts making quick work of the uneven ground. Keriath eyed them speculatively. Golden mounts. Golden armour. Òr Clan – no other clan would ever be so ostentatious. Loyal to their purse first and kin second, if memory served. But would they help her or hinder her?

The Hunts closed ranks as the Dragons drew nearer. But the riders made no move to draw their weapons. And as the Dragons came closer still, understanding seeped at the edges of her consciousness.

She could not see their skin. Every single inch was covered. They were all hooded and gloved, with scarves drawn across their faces. Then they reined in their mounts as they surrounded the Hunt, and she saw their eyes. Instead of the deep gold that would have matched their armour, they were pure black. Her heart sank.

Nightwalkers. Every single one of them was a blasted Nightwalker. Keriath swore under her breath. She would get no help from these bastards. Murderers. Traitors to their kind, every single one of them. For the Graced, the murder of their own kind was one of their greatest crimes. To have the blood of the Graced on your hands was to become a Nightwalker. Cursed to walk in the dark, never to feel the kiss of the sun's rays on your face again, or else accept the punishment of death.

She should have known. Nightwalkers had ruled Ciaron since the Fall and those still free of the curse were rarely trusted. Not in a group this large and not this far beyond Ciaron's walls. Certainly not armed. She'd been a fool to hope. But curse or no, they were still Dragons. And Dragons hated Darklings above all others.

Sure enough, even despite the coverings across their faces, Keriath could see the distaste in their eyes as they surveyed the Darklings. Their hands rested on the hilts of their weapons, though they made no move to draw. Eventually, their leader spoke.

'Which one of you is the Hunter?' a woman's voice asked from behind her golden scarf. Drosta stepped forward without hesitation.

'What do you want, Nightwalker?' he asked.

Black eyes regarded him impassively from beneath a golden hood.

'Drosta, is it?' she asked.

He gave her a vicious grin. 'I do so love it when my reputation precedes me.'

'Òr Lorian,' she said. 'I was expecting you three days ago.'

Drosta relaxed, motioning to his Hunt to stand down. Maren stared at him incredulously and did not follow suit – a move noted by their visitors.

'My apologies,' he exclaimed, bowing. 'We were delayed.'

Òr Lorian's eyes flickered to Maren, and she nodded in understanding, snapping her fingers at her men. They dismounted and began pulling items from the horses' packs. 'We have business to discuss, Drosta. I would prefer to do so face to face,' she said while her men began erecting a small pavilion with practised ease.

He smirked but inclined his head and followed her into the shade.

Dell hesitated, as if torn between standing at his Hunter's side and standing guard over his charge. Drosta seemed to sense his second's indecision and summoned him with a jerk of his chin. Keriath stumbled as Dell dragged her with him, but Òr Lorian barely spared them a glance.

The Nightwalker lowered her hood and pulled the scarf from around her face, breathing a heavy sigh of relief. She had a sharp, pointed face, but age and weariness had left their mark. As she removed her gloves and rolled up her sleeves, Keriath noted her tattoos, her dragon-marks. Gold, but also small and simple. Keriath smirked. Dragon-marks increased in size or intricacy according to the strength and power of the individual. Òr Lorian was weak. Very weak. A life without light would do that to a person.

'I don't see my goods, Nightwalker,' noted Drosta, looking around. 'You'd better not be reneging on our deal.'

'Your goods are secure, Darkling,' she assured him. 'I've got Dragons guarding them half a day's ride from here – with orders to destroy the lot if I don't return,' she added with a knowing look. 'The price has doubled.'

'Piss off. What?'

'Your delay cost me money. My warriors need to be paid, your livestock need to be fed and housed … you should consider yourself lucky it's not more. They wanted me to charge you triple, the original fee multiplied by the number of days you kept us waiting.'

Maren interrupted before Drosta could say anything. 'Livestock?' she asked. Òr Lorian glanced between them, frowning, but she answered all the same.

'Darkling cattle.' She sniffed in disgust. 'Life for the taking.'

Keriath couldn't help the sharp intake of breath as understanding dawned. Drosta was buying human lives. Slaves to feed the Darkling horde. Drosta and Dell both glared at her, but it was not until those black eyes settled on her that Keriath stilled. The Nightwalker hissed.

'Problem?' Drosta asked, turning back. But Keriath knew him well enough now to hear the warning in his voice.

The Nightwalker glared at him. 'Your prisoner is one of the Graced,' she snarled.

Drosta glanced round at Keriath, feigning surprise. 'Oh? I hadn't noticed?'

Maren snorted at the outrageous sarcasm in his voice, but Keriath didn't find the situation funny at all. Nor did Lorian.

'Hand her over,' the Nightwalker demanded.

Drosta's feigned levity disappeared as fast as it had come. 'No.'

Maren hissed. 'She's going to the Queens, and if you try to stop us, we'll kill you all. I reckon between you, you're enough to keep our Hunts fed for a week, even if Nightwalker blood tastes like mud.'

'Watch yourself, Darkling,' Lorian growled in response. 'Nightwalkers might be welcome here, but our law is clear when it comes to your kind and I've risked my head by not killing you and your Hunt on sight. This is Ciaron – we execute those who fail their duties here. Don't make me regret my decision. Each one of my men is worth a dozen of you.'

Maren shifted her weight from one foot to the other as if readying herself to strike. Keriath fidgeted, despite another warning growl from Dell. She needed them to fight over her – it was her best chance of escape. Drosta seemed to realise this at the same time, and he growled, calling Maren to heel. For once, the Huntress did as she was bid.

Lorian crossed her arms over her chest, considering. 'I've changed my mind,' she announced. 'I'm prepared to negotiate. All of your livestock for her.'

Drosta snorted. 'Negotiate all you like. She's not for sale.'

Lorian exchanged a long look with her second, before turning back to Drosta. Keriath watched them closely, and the Nightwalker studied her in return. Those black eyes lingered on her scars and her star-marked brow. Keriath wasn't sure which was worse – a madman like Drosta, or a woman who would kill her own kind. A woman who traded in human lives. At least Drosta had a vested interest in keeping her alive – Gods only knew what the Nightwalker wanted.

'How much does Drosta owe you?' Keriath asked.

'What does it matter to you?' sneered Drosta.

Keriath shrugged, her chains clanking. 'Just curious to know how much I'm worth.'

Lorian told her. Keriath let out a low whistle. It was an enormous sum. The Nightwalker would only pass up that kind of money if she was confident she could get it back later. And judging by how her black eyes kept skirting over Keriath's star-mark and pointed ears, it wasn't too hard to figure out what she was thinking. Lorian knew how powerful Drosta's prisoner was, even if the Darklings didn't. There was only one place that paid that kind of coin for power. The Nightwalker would sell Keriath to the Shade Court. The King's enemies would pay handsomely for the power to overthrow him. If they ever learned who she was ... perhaps Alexan had been right to stay silent after all.

'The number is irrelevant,' Drosta snarled. 'She's not for sale.'

'It's a low offer, anyway. Even the poorest member of the Court would pay double that,' breathed Keriath. She neglected to mention that the Shade King's enemies, those who believed his lies, would pay ten times that for his supposed heir. The King himself would pay a hundred times that to have her in his grasp. Determined to stir things further, she looked to Drosta. 'How much was Zorana paying you to bring me to her again?'

Drosta whirled, his arm lashing out as his hand cracked across her face. She was sent sprawling on the ground, and he followed up with a hefty kick to her chest. Then he grabbed her by the throat and placed the tip of his knife below her eyeball.

'Drosta!' Lorian barked in alarm.

'I wonder how powerful you'll be once I carve those pretty eyes out of your skull and feed them to you?' he said.

But Keriath would not be cowed. 'Still powerful enough to kill you,' she breathed, gasping as his fist tightened around her neck. He bared his teeth in a silent snarl, and Keriath hissed at the sting of the blade piercing her skin. 'Go on,' she dared him, 'destroy the best evidence you've got of my bloodline.'

'So long as that mark remains on your brow, I've all the proof I need,' he reminded her, the knife cutting a little deeper. His hips dug into her suggestively. 'I can do whatever I like with the rest of you.'

'Drosta, in the name of the Gods, leave her be,' Lorian snapped. 'You've wasted enough of my time as it is. I have better things to do than watch you rutting on some poor girl.'

He relented, stepping back and allowing Dell to haul Keriath back to her feet. He licked the blood from the edge of his blade before sheathing it, his eyes glowing red as he inhaled her scent. Keriath touched a finger to her lip. It came away bloody. She offered it to him, daring him to take it, to provoke them further. But he was too smart for that.

'If your time is so precious, we'd best get moving,' he said to Lorian. 'I want to see the condition of this livestock before I pay for them. Dell, load her up.' And with that he turned and stalked away with Maren following in his wake.

The Nightwalkers exchanged long glances as they covered up once more and dismantled the pavilion. Keriath could feel Lorian's black gaze on her all the way as Dell dragged her back to his horse. Someone else had already dismantled his tent and packed his bedroll. Keriath jerked out of his grip as they approached, tired of being hauled around like a sack of meal, but Dell wasn't having any of it. He shoved her towards the horse, crowding her against its flanks with the size of his body.

There was something dark in his eye as he took her hand in his and lifted it to his lips. He offered her a wicked grin before he sucked her bloody finger into his mouth. Keriath gasped and recoiled, trying to pull away, but he held her fast as his tongue rasped over the pad of her finger. Then he dropped her hand and pressed his mouth against hers. It might have been mistaken for a kiss, but it was her blood that he sought. His mouth closed around her split lip and he sucked hard.

Keriath snarled, her knee jerking up, but there was no room, and Dell only laughed.

'Gods you're sweet,' he breathed against her mouth. 'I can't wait to taste more of you.'

Keriath wrenched her head free. 'Fuck you,' she snarled, wiping her face as if she could wipe away the violation.

He grinned. 'Promises, promises,' he said. Then his hands were on her hips, and he threw her up into the saddle before climbing up behind her.

He wrapped an arm around her waist and leaned in close, whispering in her ear, 'Stop pushing him. It's going to get you killed.'

Keriath snorted. 'Promises, promises.'

Dell's grip on her waist tightened. 'I'm serious,' he warned. 'Drosta is wild and unpredictable at the best of times, and that bitch Maren is doing everything she can to throw him off balance. She wants to present you to the Queens herself. She's ruined enough of his plans already. He'll kill you just to spite her if it comes to it.'

'Why do you even care?' snapped Keriath with a withering look over her shoulder.

His hand drifted a little lower. 'I have my reasons.' She lashed back hard, elbowing him in the ribs. He grunted but removed his hand.

'He'll kill *you* if you keep that up,' she hissed, edging as far away from him as she could. Dell said nothing but manoeuvred his horse closer to Drosta. The Nightwalkers were mounted, their scarves pulled tight across their faces as they wheeled their great palomino horses around. Lorian was still watching Keriath, but she said nothing as she signalled to her men and charged back up the hill they had come from. Hooting with excitement, the Darklings followed.

It was not long until Lorian dropped back to ride alongside Keriath and her ever-present jailor. 'So, what's a member of the Unicorn nobility doing playing prisoner to a mortal Darkling?' Lorian asked, her voice light. Keriath kept her face impassive.

Dell snorted. 'This one? A lady? You've got to be joking.'

But Lorian's eyes were on Keriath's scars.

'It's the eyes. During the Rebellion, before the Unicorns were Unicorns, the people of that region accepted refugees from another land. Legend says their leader had eyes like amethysts, and she married the Lord of the Isles himself. If you believe the legends, which I tend to, eyes like that only turn up in the nobility,' she said. 'Though only the Graced would bother to learn those stories. Darklings can't get much further into the Old Tales than hearing 'Kah Resari' before they wet themselves.'

'I wouldn't have thought Nightwalkers could be much braver after what your kind did to her,' Keriath hissed. An image flashed through her mind – a small, dark-haired child nailed to a cross. She shuddered with disgust and forced the memory from her thoughts.

'We hesitate to cross her path,' Lorian admitted with a shrug. 'She did vow to kill every single one of us after all.'

It was Keriath's turn to smirk. She'd seen first-hand the retribution meted out at Resari's hand. The Nightwalkers were right to fear her. Darklings too. The sickened cast to Lorian's face suggested she knew all too well why Nightwalkers should fear that name.

Keriath chuckled darkly. 'You've seen it. What she does to the likes of you.'

'She killed my mate,' Lorian murmured, staring ahead. 'I've seen nothing like it in all my life. I didn't think anyone was capable of that much savagery.'

Keriath's lips pulled back in a silent snarl. 'It's hardly surprising.'

'We're not all the same, you know,' Lorian snapped. 'The Nightwalkers who did that were the worst of our kind – handpicked by Jenia herself.'

'You'd fit right in,' Keriath spat. 'Trading human lives for coin? To the creatures you were born to destroy?'

Lorian scowled. 'I didn't set up this deal, just facilitated it. I don't like it any more than you do, but I answer to a higher power. He is the one who sourced the mortals, and who arranged the buyer. I'm just the middleman.'

'And yet you were prepared to trade it all for me?' asked Keriath. 'One life for how many? A hundred? More?'

'Graced lives are worth far more than mortal ones,' Lorian said.

Keriath just shook her head in disgust and didn't bother to respond. She wouldn't waste her breath on murderers. Dell seemed to sense her fury and kicked his heels to his horse's flanks, urging the beast onward to put some distance between them and the Nightwalker.

'Thank you,' Keriath said. She meant it too.

Dell chuckled. 'I'm sure you can find some way to repay me.'

Keriath didn't answer. She closed her eyes and tried to sleep.

They rode through the evening and reached the river just before sunset. The Nightwalkers seemed to breathe a sigh of relief at the retreating light, but they didn't dare remove their coverings. Not yet, anyway. Lorian had clearly made this journey many times before – she led them through a maze of narrow gorges and hidden glens without hesitation.

They followed the river for a few more hours to a point where it took flight and plunged over a cliff to the deep pool below. The journey down was treacherous, Keriath's chains catching on rock and root more than once.

There, in the wide pool at the bottom of the waterfall, three boats were moored – one smaller vessel and two large barges. Keriath's lips pulled back in a silent snarl, remembering what the latter were for.

The Nightwalkers guarding the boats were a mixed bunch. In the torch's flickering light, she could see tattoos of crimson and azure, gold and even one with the stark black markings of the Kah clan. She vowed to herself that, if she could get loose, she would kill that one first. There was only one member of her grandfather's clan she could forgive for bringing the curse down upon themselves. All others deserved to die screaming for the shame they'd brought to their clan.

But regardless of their clan allegiance, the Nightwalkers all seemed to answer to Lorian. Their commander barked orders to stand down as she approached. Lorian's warriors obeyed, but there was no avoiding the hatred in their black stares as they eyed the Darklings who followed.

Drosta left Keriath with Dell while he and Maren went with Lorian onto the barges to inspect their *'livestock'.* The word made Keriath's guts heave with disgust, though not as much as the gleeful expression on Maren's squashed face when they emerged once more. Keriath's fury must have shown because Dell laid a restraining hand on her shoulder and shook his head in warning.

There was the clink of gold changing hands, and it was done. Two hundred human lives sold. Just like *that.* Drosta snapped his fingers and ordered the Hunts to load up into the barges – they would sail them down the river to Dar Kual – tossing a set of jailer's keys to Dell as he did so, despite Maren's objections. Keriath was vaguely aware of the big Darkling asking for instructions on what to do with her, but the roaring in her ears was too loud for her to take it in. She fixed her baleful eyes on Lorian, letting all her rage and hatred shine through. The Nightwalker had the sense to look unnerved as Dell hauled his prisoner onto the barge.

Keriath heaved against him as she passed the Nightwalker, stopping long enough to snarl at her. 'When I am free – and don't think for a moment that there is any force in this world that can hold me forever – I will find you. And you will pay for what happened here today.' Lorian flinched from the fury and violence lacing Keriath's voice, a kernel of fear glinting in those black pits she called eyes.

Her hand shot out, gripping Keriath's wrist. 'This isn't my doing,' she insisted in a hushed voice. 'We are not always the masters of our own fate. But if you give me a chance – perhaps I can save you from yours.'

'Fate and destiny are for those too weak to forge their own path,' Keriath spat, wrenching free. Dangerous words. But she was beyond caring.

Lorian's gaze tightened in recognition, but she didn't press. 'We don't all have the luxury of your strength,' she murmured, her gaze flickering over Keriath's scars. 'It's a Shade Prince your Darkling deals with. A Shade Prince who reared those people like lambs for the slaughter. I was just the shepherd he paid to watch over them. Prince Mazron holds my heart in his fist, girl. He'll hold yours too before the end.' Then she turned around and stalked off.

Keriath let her go. It was just as well that ruan held her power in check. Magic was tied to emotions, and right now, her rage was strong enough to level mountains.

Lorian was worse than a murderer. She was a traitor. The Graced were born with a single purpose in life: to wipe out the Darkling scourge. They'd been made – crafted like weapons for their Immortal creators to wield – during the Rebellion, a thousand years ago at least. It didn't matter that there were hardly any of them left. Every fibre of Keriath's being screamed at her to destroy the stain that surrounded her. It was an urge, a compulsion they all shared. That Lorian could not only ignore it but see fit to help the Darklings … a snarl of fury and disgust ripped out of Keriath at the thought.

Dell had the sense to keep her away from the slaves. He stood with her at the prow where the wind could caress her face and whip her hair about her shoulders. He hovered nearby, keeping a watchful eye on her while the fresh air and soft rushing of the river beneath them soothed away her rage. She glanced back as they pushed off, watching Lorian and her men disappear back into the night to which they were eternally cursed.

Then they were moving, the boat rocking beneath her as it drifted with the current. Her fury had cooled, but it had hardened into something else. Determination. There were a hundred mortal souls, chained and bound, in the hold beneath her. They sailed to a fate worse than death. Doomed to spend the rest of their miserable lives locked in darkness, their life-force stolen from them by monsters that had no right to this world. Monsters she'd been born to kill.

She leaned over the edge of the boat, watching the water churning alongside. Her frustration had her clenching her fists so tight her nails cut bloody furrows into her palms. Blood dripped like tiny, glittering rubies from her hands, splashing into the rushing river to be lost forever. She heard Dell's sharp inhalation as the smell of it reached him, but he said nothing. He moved a little closer, but she got the feeling it was more for her protection – or perhaps even a sign of solidarity – than anything else. They stood together in silence for a while, side by side, and she found a strange comfort in his presence. Perhaps he too mourned for the lives below.

Well, she would not let them be taken. Not without a fight. Her chin lifted, and she breathed deep the chill of the river, caught the scent hidden beneath it … and smiled.

Waterhorses. Drawn in by the blood she'd spilled over the side. Blood charmed by their ancient power, blood that carried the same magic that made them so deadly. She could hear the first murmurings of their songs, a music to which she was immune. All Unicorns were. Waterhorses had no true voices – the music they used to ensnare their prey was whispered into unsuspecting minds, drawing them into watery graves. A vicious, elemental, unsubtle form of the Enchanting. A ruthless grin touched Keriath's lips when she saw Maren step from the crook of Drosta's arm and walk towards the edge of the barge, her eyes wide and vacant.

Keriath stepped back, lifting the keys from Dell's pocket as she slipped past him. To leave them within her reach was the first stupid thing Drosta had done. Her chains she dumped in the river with a smirk of relief. Let them try to hold her without them.

She chanced a glance into the river. Dark, liquid eyes stared back at her. An elegant, noble head rose out of the water, the proud curve of a powerful neck following as the beast crested the current. Its hide was silvery white, with a pearlescent sheen to it that was eerie yet enticing. Its mane was white too, like the pale froth that formed where the river crashed over rapids. These were riverhorses then. Not as savage as their sea-dwelling cousins, but more dangerous than those who lingered in the lochans that scattered the eastern coast.

She looked away. Their ethereal song might hold no sway with her, but to stare too long at a waterhorse was to court death. At least they weren't fussy eaters. The Darklings had all moved to the edges of the barge and were staring down into the river below – into the eyes of the riverhorses singing them to their deaths. Only Dell was hesitating, glancing in confusion between Keriath and the creatures calling to him.

She paused, frowning as she considered him. But she didn't have time to linger. It was only a matter of time before the waterhorses convinced the Darklings to leave the safety of the boat. And once they did, the slaughter would begin. She had to get the slaves out, now, before the waterhorses were mad with bloodlust. She turned away. Left the Darklings to their fate.

'Wait,' a hoarse voice called to her. Dell. With a glance back over her shoulder, she saw him step away from the waterhorses, step towards her.

Her eyes widened in shock. That wasn't possible. A muscle was leaping in his jaw as he clenched his teeth against the agony of resisting, but his gaze was clear and steady ... calm. She acted on instinct. 'I have to free them,' she said. She didn't need to explain who she was talking about. 'Help me.'

'Can't,' Dell gasped, tensing against a wave of pain. 'But ... won't stop you.'

Keriath nodded in understanding. It was all she needed to hear. 'Don't bother covering your ears,' she offered as a parting gift. 'The song is in your mind. Focus on something else – drown it out.' His head dipped to let her know he'd heard her, but she was already running.

The slaves were unguarded below deck, their Darkling sentinels drawn away by the ethereal music echoing through their heads. Only the shackles binding them together and chaining them to the boat had kept the mortals from following. Their expressions were vacant as they heaved against their restraints. It was mostly women and children. The former had to be breeding stock to keep up the numbers of the Queens' herd. She shuddered to consider the latter. Children, with their entire lives ahead of them.

Keriath shoved the thought from her mind as she ran an assessing eye over the manacles. Nothing but cold iron, no spells of containment or binding. She smiled.

'If you want to live, you have to listen,' she called, her voice ringing out through the hold. Perhaps a dozen pairs of eyes turned to her, woken from their trance. 'You listen to me and only me, do you understand?' More eyes looked her way. She kept speaking, wishing she had power to force them to listen but having to settle for filling her voice with as much authority and power as she could muster. Slowly – painfully slowly – all eyes turned to her.

'Who are you?' one of the men asked. He was big and strong, and handsome. Chained separately from the others. Keriath's stomach heaved as she contemplated why he might have been chosen.

'I'm one of the Graced,' she murmured, crouching down beside him. 'I'm here to help you.'

A small, pale face appeared at her elbow, peering up at her. It was so caked in dirt and grime that Keriath could hardly tell if it was a boy or a girl. 'Nobody can help us,' the child whispered. Keriath thought her heart might break from the despair in that voice, but she refused to give in.

'I can, and I will,' she promised. Just in time, the screaming started as the boat lurched in the water. The child whimpered, but a bitter smile touched Keriath's lips. She reached out a hand and cupped that small face. 'Don't be afraid. What you hear is the sound of your Darkling masters dying in agony. They just met some of my friends.'

'You're a Unicorn,' a nearby woman breathed, staring at Keriath's brow in wonder.

The child beamed. 'Waterhorses!' Keriath nodded and winked. She stood, scanning the bodies crowded in the hold, making sure that every single one was watching her.

'The waterhorses' magic is broken now that blood has been spilled,' she told them, 'but they'll keep the Darklings distracted. I'll go up first, get the boat grounded on the riverbank.' She pressed the keys into the young man's hands. 'You wait for my signal, and then you run. They'll be right behind us, so you scatter to the winds. Individuals and smaller groups have a better chance at escape. Keep running, and don't look back. Do you understand?'

The slaves were silent, hope and fear shining like slivers of silver in their eyes, but they nodded. The only noise was the gentle clinking of the keys passing from hand to hand, the harsh scrape of them turning in rusty locks as the shackles clanked open. Keriath chucked a finger under the child's chin and winked again. Then she was gone.

Absolute chaos reigned on the deck. It was littered with wounded Darklings. More were screaming as they drowned. Keriath saw Drosta still alive and cursed, but she didn't have time to think about that as she sprinted towards her goal. The boat was listing to the side. The water-horses had put a hole in the side, trying to drown their victims.

She slammed into the Darkling holding the wheel, shoving him into the waiting jaws of the waterhorses below. Her joints screamed in protest as she heaved the wheel around, driving for the riverbank. She held on tight, even as Drosta's eyes fell on her and he began roaring for her death.

The barge shuddered from the force of the rocky riverbed tearing open her underside, crashing into the bank. She screamed for the slaves to run. *Now!* And like a crashing wave, they broke upon the deck. A hundred souls, racing for freedom. She spared a thought for the rest trapped on the other barge. But she knew all too well, it was impossible to save everyone.

Drosta was howling for her blood as he watched his livestock escape, bellowing for someone to bring her down. But Keriath was loose, her chains in the water below. She vaulted over the edge of the barge, knees popping from the impact of her landing. Then she was sprinting through the shallows for the riverbank. The slaves followed. They were so slow, these mortals. She was torn. She had promised to help them, but her own freedom was on the horizon. With a curse, she slowed, losing herself in the seething mass as they fled.

'Split up!' she barked. 'Scatter!' They did as they were bid. Just in time.

The buzz of an arrow had her ducking for cover, and it sailed over her head. But another followed, and then another. She heard a scream of fury. She glanced back in time to see one of the riverhorses rear up out of the water and take the arrow meant for her.

But its sacrifice was in vain. Keriath yelled, one of the barbed heads slamming into her shoulder. Another followed, slicing into her calf and crippling her. She crashed to the ground, swearing as she ripped the arrow from her leg before staggering to her feet once more – only to let out another roar of agony as an arrow punched through her ribs. And *fuck*, she realised. They were coated. She could smell the poison in her blood from where she'd pulled out the one in her leg. Still, she could make it. If she could just get out of range—

'Leaving so soon, sweetheart?' Keriath stopped dead in her tracks. Drosta's crooning voice was far too confident. Dread, ice-cold and certain, gripped at her heart as she turned to face him. He stood on the shore, the pale-faced child in his grasp. The child, a boy – in the moonlight, she could see it was a little boy – was whimpering, Drosta's dagger at his slender throat. Keriath's gaze flicked up to the Darkling's smug face, to the body of the waterhorse spread out on the riverbank behind him. She looked back to the child. 'Stand down, or I kill him.'

She hesitated, hating herself for it with every breath. If she surrendered, Drosta would just kill the boy anyway. But Keriath had enough blood on her hands. She wouldn't add the blood of an innocent to the list. Her shoulders slumped in defeat, and she bowed her head in submission. Tears streamed down her face, but she didn't fight as Darklings closed in around her.

Drosta smiled ... and dragged the blade across the boy's throat. Keriath was vaguely aware that she was screaming as blood loss and exhaustion brought her to her knees. But all she heard were the gurgling, wet gasps of the child's last breaths as he died.

She surged then – a last attempt at escape, at revenge, anything – but it was too late. Something blunt and heavy cracked across the back of her skull, and then there was only darkness.

When Keriath came round, she found she was bound tight – though without spelled chains, nothing would hold her for long. But her body was weak. Whatever they'd coated their arrows with had made her drowsy and lethargic.

Drosta was standing before her, filling her hazy vision. His arms were folded across his chest and his expression was murderous. Maren was nowhere to be seen.

'I would have let you die,' he purred, 'but it would have been too pleasant.'

'Fuck you,' she slurred.

Drosta chuckled. 'Quite possibly,' he breathed. 'We've got about another hour until we arrive, and the Gods know I'm tempted. But I thought you'd like to see your new home from the outside first. Because I promise, you'll never see the sky again once you've gone inside.'

He stepped aside, and Keriath squinted into the night. Rising out of the darkness, illuminated by the silvery light of the moon, she saw the mountain fortress of the Darkling Queens. Dar Kual. The City of Nightmares.

CHAPTER TEN

The poisoned arrowheads had done their job – none of Keriath's wounds had healed. The one in her shoulder had kept bleeding for so long that Drosta had needed to bind it himself so she didn't die of blood loss. And because it was driving the remaining Darklings mad with thirst.

The waterhorses had decimated the two Hunts, and at least half of the survivors were injured. It had pleased Keriath to see Maren amongst the fallen, although her second had survived and seemed just as determined to escort Drosta and his Hunt to the city.

Though they'd recaptured most of the slaves, a precious few had escaped. Keriath might have savoured the minor victory, were it not for the screams echoing up from below deck as Drosta punished the survivors. He'd wanted to make her watch, but Dell had talked him out of it. She wasn't sure what had prompted his mercy, only that it was mercy that drove him and not self-preservation as he claimed.

She was weak and sluggish, yet all too aware of the pain in her body. Drosta was a sick bastard. The poison – whatever it was – appeared to only disrupt the connection between her head and her body in one direction. Her control over her limbs was next to nothing, but she could feel everything with perfect clarity.

Drosta had been nervous ever since they'd been close enough to see the docks. He'd ordered her kept on the barge, under Dell's watchful eye, while his precious cargo was unloaded. Keriath had been glad they hadn't allowed her to witness the sight of almost two hundred innocent souls being marched off the barges and into the endless dark. Another of Dell's mercies. She wondered what she'd done to win over his bitter, twisted heart.

The slaves were long gone by the time Keriath was dragged from the barge and thrown into a saddle. Maren's second had gone with the slaves, along with all that remained of her Hunt. Nobody was sorry to see them go. They'd ridden in close formation through the city, with Keriath mounted in front of Dell while Drosta took the lead. Each step the beast had taken had sent waves of pain crashing through her. But any relief she felt when they dismounted was short-lived.

Unwilling to commit so much as one of his Hunt to carry her, Drosta had made her walk. Her calf was screaming, and every step sent a stinging jolt through her side. Dell was close behind, his hand within striking distance of her arm. Drosta was in front of her, swaggering through the castle with his brutal arrogance.

Keriath had the sense to keep her mouth shut as her eyes darted around, trying to take in her surroundings. Legend claimed this had once been Sephiron's keep. She did not doubt it, not when the walls themselves were evidence of such a dark, corrupted mind. Nothing seemed to make sense. The corridors were a twisting labyrinth – the mythical maze of Dar Kual. It was said that during his reign none but Sephiron's most trusted under-lings could navigate the tangled web of passages.

She could believe it. She'd witnessed first-hand the work of his heirs. The Shade King, the one who claimed her as his own daughter, was the worst of them. She almost smiled to think of the punishment he would inflict upon Drosta if he ever learned the wrongs she had endured.

'What's so funny?' Drosta hissed, grabbing her by the elbow. She gasped in pain as the movement jolted her ruined shoulder and glared at him as best she could. But she held her tongue, would never speak the words that might free her from this purgatory. They would only damn her to an even worse fate. Théon had learned that the hard way.

'We should keep moving,' Dell murmured under his breath, as another Hunt prowled past. Drosta snarled and shoved her forward, sending her staggering and forcing Dell to catch her. The movement was enough to make her scream, but a warning look from Drosta was enough to keep her quiet. Much as she'd like to cause trouble for him, she knew that drawing the attention of other Hunts would only result in her death.

When they were alone in the passage, she mumbled 'Are we there yet?' She saw Drosta's shoulders tense at the taunt in her listless voice, but he said nothing. 'Do you even know where you're going?' she asked, moments later. He whirled on her, snarling, his eyes blazing with rage. She flinched away, but Dell caught her, holding her fast to suffer Drosta's temper.

'I swear, by the Gods, I'll kill you,' he spat, his face inches from hers. Perhaps it was the pain talking, perhaps it was the poison itself loosening her tongue, but something made her brazen.

'Get on with it then,' she slurred. Drosta itched towards her, baring his teeth in silent threat.

But then Dell spoke. 'Just leave it,' he murmured. 'We've got her this far – why waste all that effort to kill her now?' There was no challenge in his voice, but Drosta eyed him in warning, almost looking for an excuse to argue. Finding none, he looked back to Keriath.

'I hope they make you suffer,' he breathed.

'Can't be any worse than you,' she muttered.

Drosta's face split into an evil grin. 'Oh, sweet little Unicorn – you have no idea.'

At the diabolical certainty in his voice, Keriath felt a cold sliver of fear slip down her spine. She stilled, but Drosta's eyes glowed as if he could see the shudder she repressed.

And for the first time since she had woken in that accursed wood, seen the faces of her captors, she considered speaking the words that would set her free. The lies of the Shade King. She'd seen what life as his heir had done to Théon, knew she would sooner die than suffer that ...

But it was not death that she faced. Death would have been easy. Peaceful. Even the slow, painful one that Drosta's bloody gaze offered. Instead, she was to be gifted to the Darkling Queens, a toy for them to play with as they pleased. She knew all too well what that might entail. Théon rarely spoke about those years with her father, but she'd relayed enough about the Queens since then for Keriath to understand what her fate would be. It was not something she was convinced she had the strength to bear.

The Shade King was her way out. All she had to do was claim the birthright the King offered, and this ordeal would be over. Not even the Queens would have the nerve to keep her from him. Only another Shade could risk it and survive, and there were none of those here. Sephiron's heir liked to keep his brethren close. He did not trust them to roam beyond his sight, though some were too powerful for him to bring to heel. No, all she had to do was say it, and all would bow and scrape before her. She could have Drosta's head with a single word, have him beaten and humiliated as he had done to her. She had to admit, it was tempting.

But she couldn't do it. Not when there was so much else at stake.

'Just get on with it,' she said in a dead voice. She felt Dell stiffen behind her but bowed her head in submission.

With a grunt of satisfaction, Drosta turned on his heel and stormed into the gloom. Dell's grip on her arm was gentle as he guided her after his master. She risked a glance up at his face and then wished she hadn't. There was nothing but pity in his eyes.

'Lean on me,' he murmured, so soft she could barely hear him. 'It'll all be over soon.'

Dell's kindness lasted until the moment Drosta's attention drifted back to her, at which point, his grip on her arm tightened to the point of being painful. Keriath allowed herself the slightest whimper, and Drosta's eyes glowed in amusement. As soon as he turned his back, Dell loosened his hold once more. She was not fool enough to believe that he cared for her. Only that he considered the horrors her future held bad enough and did not feel it necessary to add to her discomfort.

They came to the great doors almost by accident when the maze opened out into a large hallway. The doors themselves were perhaps three times the height of a man and made of polished ebony. Carved into the gleaming wood were all manner of monstrous depictions of pain and death. Keriath repressed a shudder as her eyes skirted the most grotesque of these, not allowing her gaze to linger. Her imagination needed no more inspiration than it had already been given.

Four Darkling sentinels guarded the door, armed with long spears and shields, dressed in ostentatious armour. Their eyes were little more than drops of blood glowing from beneath the crests of their helmets, and they remained unmoving as Drosta and his entourage approached. The Hunter drew to a halt just out of reach of those deadly-looking spears.

'I, Drosta of Shadowbriar, request the honour of an audience with their Majesties, the dread Queens of Dar Kual,' he said. In response to his ritual petition, the two central-most guards snapped their heels together and turned to the door. The doors swung open, and the guards marched through. Beyond the doors, Keriath could hear the guards' boots snapping sharply on the hard floor, though she could see little through the Hunt crowded around her. Then a final crack as they drew to a smart halt and slammed the butts of their spears to the ground.

'Dread Queens,' they intoned together, 'the Hunter, Drosta of Shadowbriar, requests the honour of an audience with your Majesties.' There was a pause, and then an exasperated sigh that seemed out of place in such a formal setting.

'What do you want, Drosta?' came a long-suffering female voice from the other end of the room.

Drosta chuckled. 'I bring tidings, dread Queen, from your children in the north – and a gift, a sign of my devotion to you.'

'Send him in,' the resigned voice said. The guards' heels clicked together, and their spears banged once more on the floor, before their footsteps retreated back down the room.

'I don't know why you tolerate him,' another woman muttered, her voice rich and throaty.

'Oh, I don't know,' chimed in a third delicate and girlish voice. 'I find him entertaining. We've had all sorts of fun together down in the Pits.' She giggled, and Keriath shuddered. She already knew which one to fear. The guards reappeared and drew to a sharp halt in their original positions.

'Hail, Drosta of Shadowbriar,' they pronounced together. 'The dread Queens of Dar Kual bid you welcome and grant you the honour of a moment in their divine presence.'

'Divine?' Keriath whispered to Dell.

'Shut up,' he muttered and pushed her forward. The eyes of the sentinels fell on her, and they gleamed as they looked her up and down. But, at a warning growl from Drosta, they parted to allow them entry, and he swaggered forward with deadly surety.

Keriath glanced around, taking in her surroundings rather than look to the three women seated before them. More sentinels, armed and armoured like their counterparts on the door, lined the chamber. The three thrones were elevated upon a great dais at the opposite end of the room from the great doors. There were no windows. The room was lit by torches burning in brackets on the walls. The chamber itself was cavernous, with a high, vaulted ceiling that appeared to have been carved out of the bare rock.

Legend said the whole keep had been carved out of the mountain. It had taken centuries, and a river of blood. With the power at his disposal, Sephiron could have completed the work himself in a fraction of the time. But instead he had used slaves to do his bidding, so he may save his strength for a greater battle. A hundred thousand men, women and children died to make this place. They had stained the rocks with their blood, if the stories were to be believed. Keriath glanced at the strange, reddish cast of the walls and was inclined to believe it.

Some might call it madness, but she knew better. Blood was life, and what was life but power? It was not just the strength of their arms he required, but the power of their lives. Each one had poured their life-force into this place, and now the mountain thrummed with that power. The smell of dark magic was an unnerving scent at the best of times, but here, it was laced with the sharp, metallic tang of blood.

Her stomach heaved. The scent of it alone was enough to make her stagger. But the memory in the stone was crushing. The weight of a hundred thousand souls, screaming to be released from their eternal servitude. Their life-force little more than fuel for the ancient spells Sephiron had placed within the rocks themselves. Not just spells of protection and defence either, but something else … something far darker.

Keriath's attention was dragged back as Drosta drew to a halt before the thrones and dropped to a knee. All around him, his Hunt followed suit, and when Keriath refused, he took far too much pleasure in knocking her legs out from under her. She gasped from the pain that her fall sent shooting through her injured shoulder, her vision fading in and out as she fought to remain conscious. Dell's fingers found her upper arm and pulled her upright so she knelt alongside and could lean against him.

'Rise, Drosta of Shadowbriar,' intoned the long-suffering voice. Keriath tried to focus on the three women in front of her, but the pain and the nausea caused by the corrupt magic around her made it difficult. Drosta stood and stepped forward, though his Hunt remained kneeling.

'Keep your head down,' Dell whispered to her, his voice so soft she was half convinced she had imagined it.

'My Queens,' Drosta purred, bowing. 'To stand in your divine presence makes my heart soar. Had I the soul of a poet, I would sing to the world of your terrible beauty. But I am but a simple warrior, and the only language I speak is that of death and ruin.'

One of them sighed, but another spoke over her. 'Pretty words for one who claims such simplicity,' she mused. Hers was the husky, seductive voice that had spoken second. It was almost as appealing as that of a Unicorn. But unlike those of her people, this Queen's voice was hypnotic in a way that made Keriath's skin crawl – imposing rather than alluring. 'What tidings do you bring from our children in the north?' she asked, her musical voice lulling Keriath. Dell's arm tightened around her waist as if sensing the slight lowering of her defences, but he didn't risk saying anything out loud.

'The Princess Zorana has taken the Oak Throne,' Drosta was saying, 'but she does not have the power to extend her hold beyond the city walls. Your Majesties' forces hold the forests now.' Despite the pain and the overpowering pressure from the dark magic surrounding her, Keriath's attention sharpened at Drosta's words, but she kept her eyes on the floor – anything to avoid drawing their gaze. The Silvan Forests had been overrun since the Fall. Darkling numbers had always been too great for anyone to get close enough to get any useful information.

'Well, it's a start,' the exasperated voice growled.

The high, girlish voice spoke. 'I assume you've ordered them to contain her for now?'

'Indeed,' said that weary voice. 'We will need time to gather our forces, as will they. If we don't strike together, with our full strength, he will crush us. If we allow her to take the north without a fight, the King will know that we are working together against him. He will not risk us joining her in open rebellion – not when his hold is so tenuous. Nor will he wait for us to explain. There will be no mercy, no second chance. Not this time.'

'It is taken care of, Your Majesty,' Drosta assured her, bowing low.

'And what news of the Prince? Will Mazron stand with us?' the beautiful voice asked.

'He sends his regards,' Drosta replied, 'and two hundred souls for your Majesties' pleasure. He could not meet in person, but he sent one of his agents in his stead. She informed me he has wooed most of Ciaron's Nightwalkers to the cause, and that they are nearly ready. All that remains, Majesties, is to consider the expansion of our own forces.'

There was a pregnant pause. 'You want our permission to expand your Hunt?'

'It's big enough as it is, Drosta,' said the irritable, older voice. 'I don't like it when one of my underlings has a bigger army than I do.'

Drosta bowed. 'I can assure you, I am loyal to your Majesties – as all your children are. I only seek to replenish what I have lost. I'm afraid I ran into a little trouble in the Ravenswood. My Hunt is no longer what it was. I thought it may also be beneficial to allow my second to start his own Hunt. While he would remain loyal to me, his children would not be. It would allow me to approach Illyol with the requisite numbers, while still keeping the numbers in my own Hunt at a manageable level.'

'That still leaves you in charge,' the old voice snapped.

'And since you are so loyal to us,' the younger voice added, with just enough sarcasm to convey the lack of belief she had in his allegiance, 'your presence in Illyol, complete with reinforcements, will do very little to convince the King that we are not in open rebellion against him.'

'My reputation precedes me everywhere I go, Your Majesties,' Drosta said with a shrug. 'I'm considered a mad dog ... If he asks, just tell him I got off the leash. I'll deny to my last breath that you ever had any knowledge of what I was up to.'

The Queens were quiet for a long moment while they absorbed his words. Keriath could feel Dell trembling beside her – whether from fear or anticipation, she didn't know. She risked a sidelong glance at him. Jaw clenched tight, he looked annoyed more than anything else, though the reason still eluded her.

'Alright,' the beautiful voice conceded. 'I don't know what game you're playing, and I'm not sure I care.'

'Just play it carefully, Drosta,' the little girl voice added, her threatening tone so at odds with the delicate sound coming out of her mouth. 'I like you, but if you cross us, you'll be begging for death by the time I'm done with you.'

There was a beat and then the older voice spoke. 'You may choose one to become a Hunter. But not your second. I know you well enough Drosta – your second stays here with me, to ensure your good behaviour.'

Keriath looked to Dell once more. He scowled irritably, but there was no hint of surprise on his face. He must have known they would demand this price – known that his Hunter would not argue. She glanced up as Drosta spoke and saw the sardonic smirk on his lips. But it did not reach his eyes; they glinted with malice and bloodlust. The Queens were fools to trust him. He gave a mocking little bow before stepping aside and motioning for Dell to bring her forward. 'I understand, dread Queens, and thank you for this opportunity,' he proclaimed. 'And now, to prove my undying devotion to your magnificence.' Dell's fingers on her arms were trembling as he stood, hauling her up with him. His steps were hesitant, but he did not falter as he pushed her ahead of him. She kept her eyes downcast, not daring to look upon her fate.

'What's this?' the lovely voice asked.

'A gift, Your Majesty,' he said. 'We found her in the Ravenswood, where she met with two Dragons. Sadly, they escaped, but we caught this one. I thought she might please you, so I brought her back for you.'

There was a derisive snort, and then the older one spoke. 'What makes you think we'd be interested in some scrawny mortal? Look at her – she doesn't even have enough strength to keep us sated for an hour, never mind longer.'

'I suggest you look again, Eminence,' Drosta replied. But Keriath heard the hard little edge of smugness creeping into his voice. The irritable Queen did too.

'I don't like your tone, boy,' she snarled. But the one with the beautiful voice hushed her.

'Look at me, child,' she breathed. Keriath shuddered as she tried to ignore the command in those words. But this place trembled with ancient power, and mortal or not, more than Darkling magic had touched that Queen. Keriath was panting with exertion as her chin jerked up against her will. Her lips pulled back, and she bared her teeth in a silent snarl as she looked at the Darkling Queens.

The one in the middle was on her feet. She had an exotic beauty about her – soft, pouty lips and a full, voluptuous figure with dark, sultry eyes that were all too alluring for Keriath's comfort. She'd never seen beauty like that in a mortal before. This had to be the owner of that hypnotic, husky voice. Mortal she might be, but that body thrummed with stolen power.

The two Queens on either side of her could not have been any more different. To her right was an old crone, withered and bent, with eyes like shards of glass and a brittle smile. To her left was a young girl, perhaps only ten years old, with adorable chestnut curls and dimples in her child-like cheeks. But Keriath knew better. These were the Darkling Queens. Sephiron's first and most loyal creations.

Ylain, Talize and Pria. Keriath had heard stories. One spoke of a Unicorn boy and his sister, captured by the Shade. The girl they sent to their harems – a prize mare for breeding. The boy they sent to the cells deep in the mountain, to keep her obedient. They didn't know what he would grow to be. Who he would grow to sire. Taelyr's father and Lord of the Isles before the Fall. Her mother's husband and the only father Keriath had ever known. He had been little more than a child then – too young to interest Talize – and had known nothing of any worth, so Ylain had left him alone. But Pria. Keriath glanced at the youngest Queen and was not surprised by the malevolence roiling in that angelic face. She had heard it in the girl's voice, but it was no less disturbing to see it.

The hellion's eyes were on her now. 'What are you?' she asked, scanning Keriath's ragged form with sadistic curiosity.

'Unicorn,' the crone grunted, her eyes lingering on the faint star-mark upon Keriath's brow then flickering over her pointed ears. 'And more.'

'A royal gift, Drosta,' purred Talize, itching towards his prisoner.

Beside her, Pria giggled and clapped her hands with glee. 'We're going to have so much fun!' she sang.

But Ylain was scowling.

'That bloodline is extinct,' she snarled, silencing the other two with an imperious wave of her hand, 'drowned beneath the water they so revered.'

'Is this some kind of trick then?' asked Talize, turning her sensual gaze on Drosta. He opened his mouth to speak, but the crone cut over him.

'No,' she said. 'She's star-marked alright. I can smell the magic in her from here. I'm assuming you've fed from her?' she added, looking to Drosta.

'A mouthful or two, here and there,' he admitted with an unashamed shrug.

Ylain grunted. 'I might have known. Graced blood is potent stuff – especially to those not born with it in their veins. No, I'd say she's the real thing.'

'It's not impossible,' Talize mused. 'There were plenty of survivors. The Shade rounded them all up and kept them as pets, remember? The harems were full of them. Of all the Graced, they were best for pleasure. And coveted for breeding.'

'The Shade King destroyed those harems,' Pria reminded them. 'He burned their whores alive, along with the bastards in their bellies, and outlawed the practice. None of them survived.'

'Some survived,' said Ylain in a deadly quiet voice. Then she fixed those baleful eyes on Keriath. 'Who is your father?'

Keriath repressed a grim smile. Ylain was not stupid. She knew the Old Stories – knew which bloodlines to watch out for. Keriath's amethyst gaze betrayed her as Unicorn nobility, not peasant stock with their eyes of pearlescent blue or liquid silver. Her brother was fortunate enough to have taken after his father, but Keriath was their mother reborn. Ylain hadn't missed her pointed ears, and it wouldn't take long for them to discover the damaged Dragon-marks on her back. There was only one place those three bloodlines had mixed successfully in the last two hundred years.

'Answer her!' Drosta snarled when Keriath remained silent.

But that was the crux of her dilemma. She knew the words that would end this all now. The Darkling Queens, like the rest of the world, believed the King's claim. But if they were allied with Zorana and Mazron against the King? Well … not even that would save her now. She needed another option.

Drosta's fist collided with her gut when she still did not answer. Dell released her, and she went crashing to the floor, gasping for air as she tried to breathe through the pain. She gritted her teeth and heaved herself to her feet as she fought through the waves of agony crashing through her. Drosta growled in warning as he advanced on her once more, but she halted him with a single, imperious look. She was just glad her brother wasn't here to see what she was about to do. He'd crack a rib laughing.

'I am Olena, daughter of Taelyr,' she proclaimed, throwing her shoulders back as she stared down the Queens. Had she been mortal, the lie would have never worked. But the magic of the long-lived Graced made it all but impossible to discern her real age. She was twelve years older than her brother, but amongst the Graced, she could have passed for either his mother or daughter.

'Well, well,' murmured Ylain with a twisted grin. 'I am so very glad to meet you Olena. You and I have much to discuss.'

'I want to taste her,' Talize breathed, inching forward once more.

'Me too,' giggled Pria. 'I wonder how much punishment that Graced body can take?'

'Later,' Ylain snapped. She signalled to the sentinels lining the walls. 'She may well prove useful, and I don't want either of you to break her before we find out. Take her down to the Pits – the Core should hold her. We can't risk her escaping.'

Cruel hands gripped Keriath and pulled her away. As her gaze was finally torn from the malicious smiles of the Darkling Queens, her eyes fell instead upon Dell and his Hunter. She was not surprised by the sadness in Dell's eyes, nor the unrestrained glee in Drosta's.

She closed her eyes and allowed herself to be taken away. Whatever her future held, it had to be better than giving in to the darkness.

It took four guards to hold her as they dragged her down into the heart of the mountain. Despite the poison coursing through her veins, she was still Graced, and these Darklings were not. It was, she realised, a sign of just how strong Drosta and his Hunt had been. No wonder the Queens feared him.

They led her down through a vast network of caves, a warren just as convoluted as the maze surrounding the throne room. But the reason for it soon become clear as she descended into the Pits. The corridors were lined with recesses, each one sealed off with sturdy iron bars. Whether it was the muffled wails of the doomed begging for mercy or the overpowering stench of human waste that caused the stinging in her eyes, she was not sure. But she was unashamed of the tears streaking her cheeks as they marched her past the unwashed herd of the Queens' prized cattle, doomed to live and die in this awful place.

The hallway opened out into an enormous cavern, two or three times the size of the throne room high above. More cells, recessed into the walls, lined the chamber, and great metal cages dangled from the ceiling on chains. Each one was large enough to hold at least twenty people. The floor was littered with deep sinkholes, each one covered by an iron grate; the agonised screams of the occupants echoed off the rocks above with so much force that Keriath feared her skull would shatter.

She refused to cry then. These were the cells that had held the Graced prisoners of Sephiron's heirs. Just as they had held the slaves who carved out the mountain, now they held the Queens' livestock – human beings, captured and bred in darkness to keep those monsters and their horde of children sated.

But only Darklings, not the Shade nor any form of twisted Graced, guarded this keep now, and none of those cells were strong enough to contain Keriath. So they dragged her to the middle of the cavern where the floor melted away into a spiral staircase descending deeper into the rock.

There was no light down there – the guards carried a torch with them. This far beneath the earth, it was so cold her breath misted in the dank air. At the foot of the rough-hewn stairs was a door of solid oak, carved like the doors to the throne room. But this time, runes of binding and containment infused the wood itself with the dark magic of the mountain.

They paused on the threshold, while one of the guards opened the door. It lowered like a drawbridge into the room beyond – though *room* was perhaps an inaccurate description of the cavity. It was little more than a rough-cut chamber carved into the rock. The floor dropped away into darkness, only a small stone pedestal reaching up to meet the door-bridge. It was to this rocky platform that they led her.

Glancing around, she could just make out what, at first, she thought to be lethal-looking stalactites and stalagmites above and below her. But as she looked closer, she realised that vicious iron spikes had been driven into the walls of the cavern. She shuddered. Whoever this cage had been designed to hold had been far more powerful than she. Once the door-bridge was raised, there would be no way to reach the entrance without impaling herself.

Thick chains descended from the rock above, while more lay strewn on the platform beside her. The guards reached for them, and she flinched away before being overpowered. As soon as the manacles were clamped around her wrists and ankles, she recognised the spell that had infused Drosta's chains – magic to nullify her Graced strength. The chains were long enough that she could reach the door, but as her eyes tracked through the gloom, she noted they could be pulled tighter. She dreaded the day they put *that* feature to use. Satisfied that she was contained, her jailers had hauled the door-bridge up and locked it – taking their burning torch with them.

They stood guard outside the oak door now. She could sense that much, even if she could see nothing. The darkness itself didn't bother her, but the enormous mass of the mountain pressing down from above did. She'd always needed open space around her, ever since the day she'd received her scars. It was possible that just the sheer discomfort of being trapped under-ground would be enough to drive her mad.

But worse than claustrophobia, the disturbing pressure of whatever black magic suffused this blasted mountain was becoming unbearable. The weight of a hundred thousand souls crying out in protest at the corruption of their lifeblood was crushing. Even long after, her kind remained sensi-tive to the imprint of violent death. She could hear screams of the dead echoing up out of the blood-soaked rock. The force of it would have been enough to bring her low, had she not already lacked the strength to stand.

So instead, she lay there and let the skull-shattering pain of it drag her down into oblivion.

CHAPTER ELEVEN

Tracking the Dragons wasn't as hard as Alexan had thought it would be. To be fair, they hadn't been subtle to begin with. They'd left a trail about six-foot wide as they'd smashed through the Ravenswood. Maybe trying to draw Drosta's Hunt away from Keriath, but given what he knew about them, it seemed unlikely. Not when they could've slaughtered that Hunt without working up a sweat.

Any lingering doubts to that vanished when he found their killing field. He laughed out loud. Little wonder Drosta had been so irate. He almost felt a flash of pity for the poor bastards as he looked at the surrounding carnage. They'd never stood a chance. Not against those two. He didn't need to see the evidence to realise Kah Faolin's reputation was well-earned, though it would appear there was more to Sil Dorrien than met the eye. Between the bloodbath before him, and what he'd learned during his own fight with Keriath, he realised there'd been no need for them to run. It had to have been a distraction, an attempt to draw the Hunt away from whatever they'd been searching for in that forest.

It had worked too. He ground his teeth in frustration. The scent of magic lay heavy on the air, and he knew all too well what that meant. But he had his orders, and they did not include investigating Awakenings. He couldn't even linger long enough to explore why there hadn't been a single living thing for over a mile in any direction. Not when the Dragons – the best chance he had at finding the King's daughter – were about to slither back into whatever hole they'd been hiding in for the last century.

Finding the tracks that led out of the battlefield was slightly more challenging. Slightly. The trail of blood wasn't quite six-foot wide, but to his Darkling senses it was about as obvious. One of them was wounded then. Curious that it hadn't healed. He considered his options as he prowled in their wake. They were headed west, up into the mountains. Away from the Barren Lands. And they appeared to be on foot. If he could just catch up before they Changed ...

A pool of blood caught his gaze. He frowned, kneeling to examine the ground. A stream gurgled nearby. A stop to refill supplies then. He ran his tongue over his lips, thinking. Such an obvious trail made him nervous. The Shade King had been trying for the best part of a century to hunt those two down – along with any other remnants of those bloodlines – without success. And not for lack of trying. Even on the rare occasion someone had spotted them, they melted back into the wilderness so fast that, all too often, his scouts wondered if they'd seen them at all. This careless trail? It seemed out of character. He proceeded with caution.

Caution which turned out to be unnecessary when he caught up with them.

Kah Faolin had been wounded in the fight. His bronze face was pale and drawn, his eyes closed – whether unconscious, asleep or resting, Alexan wasn't sure. Only the sound of shallow breathing and a faint heart-beat told him Faolin was still alive.

Sil Dorrien was bent over the fire, cleaning bandages in a pot of boiling water with one hand and digging around in her pack for more food with the other. There was not so much as a hint of panic in that lovely, heart-shaped face. Alexan smirked, watching with interest. There was an awful lot more to the silver-haired woman than either he or the King had realised. He noted it all. The Shade King made it his business to learn as much as possible about all his enemies, and Sil Dorrien had been on the list ever since the Fall.

'Dorrien,' Faolin mumbled, breaking the silence. Alexan noted how her calm facade cracked as she turned to him and reached for the water skin. No doubt, she assumed Kah Faolin would fail to notice through the pain, but to Alexan, the raw fear in those cold, silver eyes was all too clear.

'I'm here,' she said. She helped Faolin lift his head to drink, but even the few sips he managed looked to be an effort for him.

'You lit a fire,' he admonished, his voice little more than a breathless whisper.

She scowled. 'You'll be lucky to make it as things stand. I don't fancy your chances if that gets infected. Besides, I was cold.'

Faolin chuckled at that, but his laughter turned into a hacking cough – the grip of pain showing on his face. Alexan watched as she cleaned and dressed his wound. The strike had missed the Dragon's heart by a fraction of an inch. Between Alexan's shoulder blades, an old scar on his back twinged in sympathy. Faolin was lucky to be alive. He'd be luckier still to stay that way if he didn't get help soon. No matter how skilled Sil Dorrien was, that wound would need Caster-healed if it was to be anything but fatal.

'Where are we going?' Faolin asked.

She did not answer immediately, as though worried how he might react. When she spoke, her voice was quiet but firm.

'I'm taking you to Silvermane,' she said. He opened his mouth to argue, but she spoke over him. 'It's not just because of you – though I won't deny that's the main reason. I'm worried. Something about this doesn't sit right.

He needs to know. We need guidance, and you need healing. The blade was poisoned, Faolin. I've cleaned the wound as best I can, but it will take the Casting to purge it, and more skill than either you or I possess.'

They fell silent for a long time, the air thick with repressed emotions. The tension was palpable. Alexan studied them, searching for any weakness he might be able to use. He couldn't believe he'd got this close. Kah Faolin and Sil Dorrien. The legendary brother and sister who could rule half of Ciaron ... if they were ever brave enough to claim their thrones. Faolin thought his sister was overreacting, judging by the look on his face. Alexan didn't need to get any closer to know she wasn't. It was standard for most Darklings to coat their weapons in poison when they hunted the Graced. Nothing strong enough to risk killing them outright – just enough to slow them down. He'd never bothered, but then he'd been one of them before the Claiming. Gods damn him if he needed a poisoned blade to fight his own kind.

He watched them through the night. Dorrien didn't sleep at all, though she seemed unruffled come the dawn. She woke her brother without a word, cleaned and dressed his wound with fresh bandages, and dismantled their camp with cool indifference. Alexan didn't believe it for a second. It was like watching the surface of a still lake – who knew what those dark depths held? Overnight, he'd watched her sort what little they had into one pack, and she hefted it up onto her shoulders with ease. Then she helped her brother to his feet and slung one of his powerful arms around her shoulders. Alexan smiled at the absurdity of it. Faolin was tall, broad-shouldered and corded in muscle, and though his sister was tall, her body was slight. Had she not been Graced, she would never have managed. Unnatural strength was one of the few gifts that all the Graced shared.

She set a gruelling pace as they passed through the forest and headed up into the mountains – or at least it would be for Faolin. Alexan had no problem keeping up, but he stayed well back.

They made frequent brief stops as the terrain grew more challenging and Faolin's condition worsened. Alexan chafed at their pace, bored by the ease of this hunt and desperate to return to the comforts of Elucion. Though he understood why the King had chosen him for this task – there was no one else who could play this role – it still grated on him. He'd spent a hundred years burying that part of himself. A hundred years drowning those memories in the darkness. He did not relish the prospect of reliving those horrors again.

Two days later, Faolin was struggling to remain conscious. Alexan had kept his distance, following their scent rather than trying to keep sight of them and risk being spotted. From what he'd seen, Dorrien had resorted to carrying her brother. How she was navigating the mountains was beyond him. She must have been exhausted. As far as he could tell, she still hadn't slept, and it showed.

He crept closer while she set up camp, her fire not as well hidden this time. Her grey eyes were ringed with shadow and her golden skin looked just about as pale and drawn as her brother's. The stink of death was closing in. The end was approaching. Unless he reached help soon, Kah Faolin would not survive.

Dorrien seemed to come to the same conclusion later that night. She stood and walked around the fire, leaning down to shake her brother awake.

'Faolin, wake up,' she begged. Alexan forced himself to feel nothing at the sound of her voice breaking. 'I need you to wake up, just for a bit, so I can find somewhere for you to hide while I go for help.'

'Illyandi?' he mumbled.

'No, it's me, Dorrien,' she managed through the tears. 'Faolin you have to wake up now, just stay awake for a few minutes. I'm going to look for somewhere you can hide while I get help.'

'Come … with … you,' he gasped. His voice was so weak Alexan had to strain to hear it.

'You're slowing me down,' she said. 'I'll be quicker alone – we're not far. I can go for help and be back in less time than it would take you to go one way. If we try to go together, you'll never make it. So wake up and stay alert, just for a few moments.'

She was persistent, Alexan gave her that much, dragging her brother up to sitting, leaning him against a rock. She even unsheathed his sword and put it in his hand. As if he had the strength to lift it. Then she shouldered the pack and was gone.

Alexan wasn't stupid enough to follow her. He waited near Faolin, trying to quiet the thrum of anticipation coursing through his body. He was close now. So close.

She returned without the pack and roused Faolin once more. After stamping out the fire, she heaved him up over her shoulder one last time. It looked ridiculous. But she didn't falter. Her expression was one of grim determination as she wove her way through the hills.

Alexan considered what he knew of her as he followed. Heir to the Jewel of Ciaron, she'd been a child during the Fall … when she'd watched her mother butchered by the Darkling Queens. Somehow, she and her brother had escaped the slaughter. He'd always assumed they'd had help. That they'd been saved by some loyalist, like the Elvish Princesses Théon and Illyandi, snatched from danger and hidden until it was all over. But based on what he was witnessing, it wouldn't surprise him to learn she'd fought her way out by herself.

Her reputation was for charm and political manoeuvring – he'd assumed she was nothing more than a figurehead for the Dragons to rally behind. And they would need it. Dragons were a proud, selfish people who cared more for riches and renown than for their own kin. Many – if not most – were Nightwalkers now, and they ruled their mountain territories with an iron fist. Kah Faolin and Sil Dorrien were almost all that remained of a once hopeful lineage.

The King might just have to re-evaluate his assessment of the Dragons. The Change seemed crude compared to the Casting – compared to the finesse required to manipulate the world itself – but it was no less effective on a battlefield. Besides, there was far more happening beneath the surface of the still waters of Sil Dorrien's cool face than he had expected. Perhaps enough even to turn the tide of this war against them.

She was descending out of the hills now, heading for the south-east end of the Nightloch. Alexan paused on the higher ground, watching while she picked her way through the rocks. Then she vanished. He blinked. He'd felt no ripple of magic, and besides, that kind of power was far beyond either of them. He swallowed a dozen oaths and was about to stand when he caught her scent on the wind. Relief crashed over him. She was still there, just hidden somewhere amongst the rocks.

He crept closer, stopping when he was close enough to hear, and prayed the wind didn't change direction and carry his scent right to her.

'Faolin,' she was murmuring. 'I need you to listen. There's water and food beside you, but I can't risk a fire. This place is well hidden, so I hope you'll be safe here, at least for a while.' His response was little more than an incoherent mumble. Then a change in his breathing told Alexan he'd slipped out of consciousness. He could smell the salt water of her tears, but he tried not to hear her whispered farewell. Not when it stirred memories better left alone. 'I love you.'

Moments later, she appeared further down the hillside, rolling her shoulders as if readying for a fight and frowning in concentration. The moon shifted out from behind a cloud, and as the light hit her body, she Changed. Her silver marks glowed in the moonlight, growing brighter and brighter until they almost obscured her entire body. Her form shimmered and shifted, Changing in a way that almost looked to be a trick of the light. But as the moon disappeared back behind the clouds and shadows took her once more, the Change became clear.

Where Sil Dorrien had stood, now was a shimmering bird of prey. An osprey, if Alexan wasn't mistaken. He almost grinned at the sight of it. The power of the Dragons. Rare enough even before the Fall, it was a marvel a hundred years later. Fascinated, he watched as the osprey stretched her wings wide, testing their strength, before she turned her head and checked over her feathers with a careful eye. Then, satisfied, she opened her wings once more and launched herself into the air.

Alexan stayed where he was. He was good, but not that good.

Instead, he settled himself amongst the rocks to keep watch. He didn't dare get any closer, not unless he had to. Dorrien would scent his presence when she returned. The stink of Darkling was unmistakable. It was the stench of death. Of stolen life. Alexan hated it. So he tugged his cloak tighter about his shoulders and waited.

His thoughts drifted. He was impatient to get moving. His orders – the compulsion they were laced with – were a constant drive onward. *Find her.* Théon. The Shade King's daughter. Well, one of them. A shame those orders had been so specific. He would have been well rewarded if he'd delivered Keriath to her father. He snorted with disgust. Served the King right for being so controlling.

Gods, Keriath. It would take days – weeks even – for her to reach Dar Kual. Weeks on the road, with nobody but Drosta and his unruly Hunt for company. Alexan cursed his King, shuddering to consider what she would have to endure. And once she arrived and was at the mercy of the Darkling Queens. How long until he might be able to rescue her? Or send for help, if he could not go himself? He could do nothing for her until her found Théon. He could not risk alerting the Dragons. How long would she have to suffer at their hands? He shoved the thoughts away. Refused to torture himself by remembering all the evil, twisted things he'd not only witnessed being inflicted on the Graced over the last century but had done to them himself.

Instead, he considered what he'd overheard in the Ravenswood before Drosta's Hunt had ruined a perfectly good ambush. They'd spoken of Taelyr – Keriath's brother. Half-brother. Keriath might deny her parentage, and her mother might have dismissed the Shade King's claims, but Alexan just needed to look at her face to know. The King's line had bred true there. He didn't know much about Taelyr, beside his bloodlines and the powers that came with them. Rumour had it he was a waste of good skin, and a serial womaniser. Alexan had seen reports of at least two star-marked children, thought to be his bastards. Neither had survived long. Still, Taelyr seemed to have learned his lesson. There had been no sign of another in the last decade.

It was interesting. Not only had Keriath been with her waste-of-space brother but, on being separated from him, walked right into the waiting arms of Drosta's Hunt. And there was the detail that didn't sit right. Drosta had been prepared to hunt and capture Graced prey, and that didn't happen by accident. Mortal Hunts didn't go after a prize like that without warning, and they didn't carry spelled chains or power-binding potions as standard. Even the weakest remnants of the Graced bloodlines were nigh on impossible to find. Drosta had to have known what she was and where she would be. Not that he'd have anything to show for his efforts if Alexan hadn't captured his prize for him. Someone had betrayed her to Drosta. Alexan had an inclination *who*, but the *why* continued to elude him. Possibilities churned over and over in his mind until sleep claimed him.

The palace echoed with the screams of the dying. Noble and servant alike, butchered in their beds, drenching those sacred halls in the stench of blood. Some begged. Most didn't have a chance. Their murderers laughed. Alexan ignored it all.

The clash of steel rang through the hallways. He ran towards it. Sprinting down corridors he would know blindfolded. Anything unfortunate enough to cross his path died. Blade or Casting, it made no difference. He wanted blood. When he found whoever was behind this ...

The thought was cut off as a woman screamed, 'Alexan!'

He knew that voice. Not even death would have stopped him from answering her call.

His Queen.

Diathor.

He turned the corner. Almost fell to his knees at what he saw.

The Prince was dead. Alexan could see his body, spreadeagled on the bed in the chamber beyond. Throat slit from ear to ear. The sheets stained with blood.

His Queen was still alive.

Barely.

The knife had pierced her heart. Blood poured from the wound, painting her silken nightgown crimson. Bodies piled around her feet. Traitors she'd brought down. Several remained, held at bay by her Casting. It would not last much longer.

Her evergreen eyes met his.

And then he realised. She had not called him here to save her. Not when she had planted herself between danger and her daughters, blocking the main hallway that led to the Princesses' rooms. But there was another. One that only she and he knew about. He nodded in understanding, even as his heart shattered in his chest.

'Save him,' she ordered. 'Save Kah Faolin. And in doing so, save yourself.'

Alexan jerked himself from the dream to find himself drenched in a cold sweat, promptly turning and vomiting into a nearby bush. He heaved and retched until there was nothing to come up but bile, while he tried to force the images from his mind. They did not go quietly. The memory of those evergreen eyes least of all.

He lay back, panting. Tried to ignore his racing heart and violently trembling limbs. How the King would laugh to see him like this …

He swore. Took a deep breath. Forced his body to still. His heart to slow. His stomach to settle. Rubbed a weary hand over his face. Swore again.

It had been years, decades, since that face had haunted his dreams, since he'd endured the guilt and self-loathing that followed. He was under no illusions why it had chosen this moment to resurface.

You broke your vow.

He shoved the thought aside and staggered to his feet. There were some bonds that not even the Claiming could break, and even in death, his Queen held his heart in her fist. He could no more deny her than he could stop breathing. Thank the Gods the Shade King was not there to witness it.

He stumbled down the hill, muttering a dozen oaths beneath his breath. He knew what he was about to do risked getting him killed, but his body seemed determined to try, regardless. Reaching within, he searched beyond the Darkling for the magic below. He'd buried his power deep a long time ago now – hidden it where the King would never find it. Unused and smothered, it was a flicker of its former glory. But even as he roused it back to life, he was reminded why he had worked so hard to conceal it.

It was vast. Dark and mighty, and strong enough to have rivalled the

Elf-Queen herself. Far greater than a motherless wretch should possess. The Casting was a birthright, and the Graced were a proud people. For a power like his to surface outside the Elvish court meant he'd been born on the wrong side of the sheets. He'd learned at a young age to feign limitations he had never known.

But it wasn't until the Claiming that he had realised how different, how *other* he was. The taste of the Casting in his mouth should have made his stomach heave. Elvish Darklings rarely used their power, and with good reason. The magics of the Graced and the Darklings were like fire and ice; neither could exist in the other's presence unchanged. It should have broken him to Cast against Keriath in the Ravenswood. And yet, Alexan's power was not just unaffected by the Darkling curse. He was stronger than he'd ever been. It was unnatural and did not bear thinking about.

He cursed his Queen once more, kneeling beside Kah Faolin. Even in the darkness, Alexan could see the glint of Kah Faolin's jet-black tattoos. The dragon-marks. It was a straightforward code: each clan marking was a different colour, and the more tattoos the individual carried, the stronger they were. Crude and simple. Much like the Dragons themselves.

He leaned closer and pulled back the layers Dorrien had buried her brother beneath. Faolin's eyes flickered open, and Alexan flinched back. But the fierce yellow eyes were unseeing as Alexan examined the wound. It was deep. Dorrien had done a good job of keeping it clean, but the poison lingered in his blood.

Alexan frowned. Bloodrot. It was slow-acting and expensive. How a member of a mortal Hunt had got their hands on it was beyond him. His jaw clenched with frustration while he considered the task before him. There was something about the Graced that repelled his power. It had been bad enough when he'd healed Keriath. This was likely to be far worse.

So he steeled himself against the wave of nausea that was bound to follow and readied himself for the Casting. He reached out with a tendril of magic, seeking out the poison, and purged it from the blood. Faolin hissed as the pain of the process roused him to consciousness. But whatever discomfort Faolin felt was nothing compared to the agony coursing through Alexan in that moment. He growled through clenched teeth as the magic in Faolin's veins raged against the bitter touch of his dark power.

Then the poison was gone. He released the Casting with a sigh of relief, panting from the effort as he stepped back.

'I don't know who you are, or why you helped me,' whispered Faolin, drifting back to unconsciousness, 'but thank you.'

Alexan grimaced and retreated, praying to the Gods that he hadn't just ruined his best chance at finding the King's daughter.

He staggered down the hill until he came to the loch shore, crashing to all fours. Splashing the cool, clear water over his face, he drank deeply then slumped to the ground, still panting. Gods, the mark on his palm was burning too. It always did when he used that power. He shoved it into the icy loch and tried not to notice how the water hissed at the contact, as if it wanted to shy away from that peculiar design. Away from the image of a coiled snake, devouring its own tail.

Turning his hand over so he didn't have to look at it, he groaned and sprawled on the sandy banks of the loch. Soothed by the quiet lapping of the water at the shore, Alexan allowed his exhaustion to drag him into a dreamless sleep.

It was midday by the time he found the strength to move. He staggered back up the hill, cautiously at first, until he realised Dorrien hadn't returned. He risked surveying his work from the night before. Faolin's breathing was easier, and the wound was starting to heal. He was sleeping now. Without the poison slowing him down, Alexan guessed the Dragon would be strong enough to stand soon, though it would take another few days for him to heal fully.

Then he heard it. Hooves crashing like waves over the rocks. A rider murmuring encouragement. Alexan caught a mingled scent, carried on the wind. Horse-that-was-not-a-horse. And something else. Someone else. Dorrien was returning then, and it appeared she had found help. He grinned at his good fortune and ducked down amongst the rocks, waiting.

Sil Dorrien, now in the form of a great dappled-grey mare, charged over the ridge. Rushing down the hillside like a river over rapids, mane and tail churning behind her like a waterfall, with a woman astride her back. Raven hair flying in the wind. Evergreen eyes searching.

His heart stuttered in his chest. He recognised her immediately, of course. How could he not? Those eyes had haunted his nightmares for a hundred years. Her mother's eyes. He wondered if she would even remember him. He almost hoped not. It would be better if she didn't have to see this, see what he'd become. Not after all they'd been through together. But she was the one he had come for.

Théon. The uncrowned Queen of Illyol and the Shade King's daughter.

CHAPTER TWELVE

A lexan couldn't believe his luck. Not as he watched his prey ride right into his hands. Théon. He'd barely dared to think her name for the last century, and here she was. Almost close enough to touch. As Dorrien checked her stride and drew to a halt, Théon dismounted, eyes flashing over the hillside.

'Darkling,' was all she said as she drew her sword. A long, slender Elven blade. Alexan's heart gave another uneasy stutter of recognition. The Sword of the Dawn. Heirloom of the Elvish royal house. Broken in two by the ancient Elf-Queen Benella. He'd watched Théon reforge it in Casting flames after they'd fled Illyol.

There was very little of that broken girl-child left in the calm face before him. As expected, she'd grown into a beautiful woman. She was tall. Though not as tall as her mother, who'd been nearly as tall as he was. And where Diathor had been slender, Théon's body was corded in lean, powerful muscle. A warrior's body. Dark where her mother had been fair. Hard where she had been soft. Fierce where she had been gentle. Her father's daughter, through and through.

Apart from that exquisite face. The straight nose, the elegant jaw, the sharp cheekbones. But it was her eyes that drew Alexan in. Feline. Ever-green. Her mother's eyes.

Eyes that were bright and alert as they darted over the hillside, searching for threats. He wasn't surprised she'd caught his scent – he'd been far too dazed to take any care after healing Faolin, and no doubt, the whole hillside was reeking of him.

Behind her, the mare Changed, shimmering and shifting until the silver-haired woman stood in its place. Dorrien approached, poniard out as she scanned the area for danger. Then she disappeared into the hollow where Faolin was hidden, and Alexan heard her loud sigh of relief when she found her brother still breathing. Théon slowed as she neared the hiding spot, her eyes still roving for the source of that scent. She tucked a stray lock of raven hair behind a pointed ear before she too disappeared. Alexan had to strain to hear, but hidden amongst the rocks above, he could just pick out their hushed conversation.

'A Darkling's been here,' Théon murmured.

'Why would it leave him alive?'

'I don't know,' was the dark reply.

'Dorrien?' whispered Faolin.

'Hush,' Dorrien murmured. 'Théon's here now; you're going to be alright.' There was a hiss of a sword slipping back into a scabbard as Théon sheathed her blade. Then a pause, followed by the quiet rush of a Casting that made the hairs on Alexan's arms stand up on end.

A low groan escaped Faolin, then he sighed with relief. 'Thank you,' he said, his voice low with exhaustion. There was a pause before he asked. 'Théon? What is it?'

'You should be dead, Faolin,' Théon said.

'What? How ...' asked Dorrien, trailing off in confusion.

'I don't know,' said Théon. 'But someone must have intervened. Other-wise, we'd be kneeling over a corpse.'

'The Darkling?' said Dorrien.

There was a rustle of fabric as someone shrugged.

'I thought it was a dream,' murmured Faolin, more to himself than to the others.

'What?' Dorrien's voice was sharp with worry.

'Last night ... I thought it was a dream. It can't have been real.'

'What was it, Faolin?' Théon asked.

'An Elf,' he said, his voice hushed with reverence. 'I mean, he must have been. He used the Casting, but there was something strange about it. It felt different. Powerful but *wrong*. But he burned away the poison. And then he just ... left.'

Alexan scratched absently at the palm of his hand.

'It doesn't make sense,' Dorrien began.

But Théon cut her off. 'It doesn't matter. We need to get out of here,' she said. 'Are you strong enough to move?' she asked Faolin.

'I'll manage.'

'Don't be ridiculous,' Dorrien protested. 'Théon, you can't be serious? He's barely healed!'

'I'm fine,' Faolin insisted. And sure enough, when he appeared a few moments later, he looked fit and healthy once more. Fierce yellow eyes flashed in the sunlight, marks glittering as he stretched and flexed his powerful arms, yawning. A small part of Alexan shuddered. An animalistic instinct that any creature felt in the presence of its predator.

'What's the matter?' asked Théon as she joined Faolin, turning to Dorrien who followed with a sullen frown on her pretty face. 'No faith in me? Don't think I'm strong enough to heal such a grievous wound?'

Faolin snorted, prompting Dorrien to hiss and throw her pack at his face with enough force to make him stagger, before storming away. Yes, Sil Dorrien was more than a figurehead.

'Thanks,' Faolin was muttering to Théon. Her mischievous smile faded as she turned her attention to him.

'Don't thank me yet,' she warned him. She jerked her chin at the Nighthills on the other side of the loch. 'You're walking. I'm not having you ruining my handiwork by Changing too soon.'

Faolin's expression grew rebellious, and he opened his mouth to argue, but when Théon fixed him with a murderous look, he seemed to change his mind.

Alexan didn't blame him. Théon was nothing like the shy girl he remembered. Nothing like her sweet, forgiving mother. Anxiety churned in his gut. He wasn't sure what he'd been expecting, but he didn't have time to dwell on it as Dorrien Changed once more into the gleaming white and grey sea hawk and launched herself skyward. He swallowed a curse as Faolin and Théon set off in pursuit: an aerial scout was going to make following more difficult. Just as well the Shade King had chosen him for this task. No one else in his inner circle would have the patience.

Alexan was exhausted by the time they stopped for the night, and desperate for blood. His head felt like it was being split open with a blunt axe, and every breath was like a knife in his side. The curse of the Claiming. The same magic that made him stronger and faster, sharpened his senses and made him so much harder to kill, was itself killing him. It was a poison in his veins, consuming the life-force of his blood. The only way to survive was to steal more, but he daren't. Mortals made an awful racket when confronted by anyone with red eyes.

Dorrien seemed just as exhausted as he was, so he doubted they'd go anywhere soon. Her Change was sluggish, and she staggered as she adjusted to feet rather than wings. Faolin caught her right before she collapsed, and he carried her the rest of the way.

'You'll reopen the wound,' Dorrien protested.

The long, flat stare Faolin afforded her was resolute. Alexan tried not to grin. They were almost as bad as each other. 'Stay there,' he ordered, lowering her to the ground. Dorrien glared at him but did as she was told. Then he joined Théon and began raking through her pack for food and blankets. 'She's exhausted.'

'And you're not?'

But Faolin scowled at her. 'We shouldn't have pushed so hard today,' he argued. Théon waved a dismissive hand, rolling her eyes in exasperation. Faolin snarled. Alexan didn't blame him. Her flippancy was irritating. She'd been more sincere when he'd last seen her. 'I'm serious, Théon – she hasn't slept in days. She needs rest.'

'She's getting it now,' Théon snapped. 'I'm not an idiot, Faolin. I set the slowest pace I could get away with today. But Dorrien was desperate to get away from there. We'll be back within the wards soon enough, but until then, we need to stay alert. I'll take the first watch.'

Faolin snarled again and stalked over to Dorrien with food and a thick blanket. It was a sign of just how exhausted Dorrien was that she fell asleep within moments. Alexan resisted the urge to snort at the way Faolin's expression softened as he leaned over to tuck the blanket tighter around her slim shoulders. Tenderness from a Dragon was a jarring sight.

'She'll be fine,' Théon assured him.

'I know,' he said. 'I'm sorry about earlier. It just frustrates me when I'm not able to look after her.'

Théon shrugged to show her indifference to his outburst. 'We do what we have to, for the people we love.'

'I'm responsible for her.'

The look Théon fixed him with was piercing, and Alexan was glad that ferocious gaze was not on him. 'She's capable of looking after herself.'

'I know,' he said. 'It's just … hard. After all we've lost, I can't lose her too.'

Théon smiled and nodded. 'I understand. Now get some sleep. I'll wake you in a few hours.'

'You told Dorrien she had second watch,' Faolin reminded, even as his eyelids drooped with exhaustion. Théon smirked again, and Alexan felt his irritation rise once more. Was she incapable of being serious?

'I lied,' she confided in him with a wink. 'Just let her sleep – you were right, she needs the rest.' Faolin rolled his eyes at Théon's scheme, before wrapping himself in his cloak and going to sleep.

It was not the last of her lies. She didn't wake either Faolin or Dorrien. She kept watch herself all night long. And Alexan watched her. Considered the impudent, swaggering woman she'd become. The King would be so proud …

Dawn was long past when Faolin stirred, and the look he gave Théon was filled with pure venom. He opened his mouth to chastise her, but she winked, stood and sauntered off into the forest. His restraint was impressive. Alexan wasn't sure he could have controlled himself in Faolin's shoes. His fingers were already twitching for her throat.

By the time she returned, Faolin had woken Dorrien, and they'd broken their fast with some bread and cheese from Théon's pack. He handed the remaining third of the loaf to her in silence, and even Dorrien did not seem happy to see her. Théon took it with a smile, oblivious to the sour countenances of her travelling companions. The mood had not lightened by the time she was finished, but there was no hint of remorse on her face. Alexan took a deep breath. At what point in the last century had she become so infuriating?

Faolin stayed in his mortal form as they moved out, while Dorrien once more took to the skies to scout ahead. She flew in regular circles above them while they trudged ever onward. They continued on for days, pausing to rest every so often. It was slow going. Despite their breaks, Dorrien was still exhausted, and Faolin hadn't regained his full strength. Alexan followed at a safe distance, glad for their slow pace as weariness sank further into his bones.

If they spoke at all in the days that followed, he didn't hear it. He could rarely get close enough, and when he did, he was too preoccupied with not being spotted. Théon clearly knew she was being followed. She tested him, leading them on and off the paths, through streams and even across a sizeable river at one point. But he had her scent now, and it was beyond her skill to evade him. Not when he'd taught her everything she knew.

It took three days to cross the mountains. It was hard going, but he knew the end was in sight when he crested the hill and looked down on the city of Shadowbriar in the valley below. Mortals had built their homes amongst the ruins of the ancient Immortal city. No doubt believing some lingering remnant of Immortal magic would keep them safe from monsters like him. Fools. Darklings could sniff out life from miles away, and the denser the population, the greater the draw.

Alexan wasn't surprised when Théon avoided the town, skirting round the tops of the hills through the remote edges of the ruins as she led them north. She had more sense than to make her home here – too many eyes to see things they shouldn't, too many voices to raise questions better left unanswered. But it would not be far now.

Then he saw it. Nestled in a secluded glen, surrounded by steep slopes coated in woodland on three sides and a river on the fourth, was a small farmhouse. It was built of roughly cut sandstone, with a thatched roof. Animals browsed in an adjacent paddock and crops grew in the south-facing fields.

He stopped a healthy distance away. The house was warded. A Casting of protection, drawing on natural ley lines of magic. Strong enough to keep out any mortal Hunt, and perhaps more even than that. But they wouldn't keep out the King.

But sitting high in the hills above the glen, he could see and hear all he needed. There was a young woman working in the garden by the house, who started with surprise as Théon passed through the wards and called out in greeting. The woman dropped the basket in her hands and ran, flying over the ground, golden hair streaming out behind her. But it was not to Théon she ran. She collided with Kah Faolin, throwing her arms around his neck as she sobbed with relief.

Even from this distance, Alexan could see the love and wonder clear on Faolin's unyielding face. Could hear the sharp sigh of astonishment that broke from his lips as he dropped his pack, folding the woman into his arms and murmuring reassurance in her ear. She buried her face in his shoulder, trembling while he held her. Tears streamed down his cheeks as they clung to each other, shaking from the force of their emotions.

'What about me?' Dorrien said to the young woman, her voice strained with mock outrage. Giggling, the woman extricated herself from Kah Faolin, dashing away her tears with the back of her hand. Then she threw herself at Sil Dorrien, and the two women crashed to the ground, squealing with happiness at their reunion. Théon shook her head and left them to it, taking the pack from Faolin with a knowing look before continuing down towards the house. Faolin blushed but said nothing as he helped his sister and the girl to their feet, and the three of them descended the rest of the way, arm in arm.

Alexan ignored the twinge of jealousy as he watched. Pushed aside the memories of times gone by when he'd cared for anyone so much that just seeing them alive and unhurt could bring him to tears. Tried not to think how long it had been since laughter – true, unburdened laughter – had left his lips. Refused to consider how much he ached to feel those things again. Buried his grief deep, before it could overwhelm him.

He recognised the girl. of course. Illyandi. Théon's half-sister. Princess of Illyol. She'd been, what, four years old the last time he'd seen her? Five? Those huge, wide eyes staring out at him from a tear-stained face. Her mother's eyes.

Gods, she looked so much like her mother. Far more than Théon. She was taller than her sister. More slender. Softer. Spirited, but with none of the ferocity Théon had inherited from the King. And that braid of wheat-coloured hair tumbling over her shoulder ... identical to the one he'd always yearned to touch. To run his fingers through. To see spread across his chest while she slept.

He pulled himself up short. She'd never been his to consider that way – he wasn't about to think of her daughter like that.

The Shade King was a sick bastard.

His attention was dragged back to the farmhouse below as an old man greeted Théon at the door. His hair and close-cropped beard were silver with age. He was tall and still had the bearing of a warrior, but his shoulders stooped, and he leaned heavily on his staff. Little wonder when almost the entirety of his left leg was missing, his trouser leg folded up over the stump of what remained.

He also bore the star-mark of the Unicorn on his brow. Alexan let out a sharp breath. It explained why, despite his age, he was still stunningly handsome. Why those remarkable violet eyes were so bewitching. Alexan frowned. That bloodline was meant to be extinct. Keriath was the last – her and her idiot brother. The rest had been slaughtered by the Shade King's forces during the Fall. It was a complication. The Enchanting was a far more dangerous and elusive power than he was used to combating. The King relied on another to deal with that magic. He'd have to guard his mind well.

'Silvermane,' Théon said in greeting, inclining her head as she breezed past him into the house.

The old man glowered. 'I hope you brought dinner,' he called after her, his voice caustic. Alexan just caught Théon's reply as it floated through an open window, the sweet, singsong tone at odds with the obscenity she offered him. The old man rolled his eyes and opened his mouth to retort when the Princess Illyandi danced up to him and planted a kiss on his furry cheek.

'They're alright,' she said, her lovely face still stained with tears. Alexan took a deep, steadying breath. This was torture. The Shade King must be punishing him for something to make him endure this.

He tried not to think about it while he watched the old man pull Sil Dorrien into a rough embrace. 'It's good to see you,' he was saying, his voice hoarse. She let out a small sob as she clung to him, and Alexan swore the old man's eyes were damp as he kissed the top of her head. Then he released her, and he held her at arm's length, looking her up and down. 'Go inside and get some rest,' he said, pushing her into the house. Illyandi followed, and Alexan almost sighed in relief. How was he going to endure this pain every day for the foreseeable future?

Then the old man turned to Faolin and extended his hand. The two men gripped each other's forearms in greeting, and Faolin clapped a hand on the man's shoulder.

'It's good to see you too, old man,' he said with a wry smile.

'Less of the old,' Silvermane admonished, cuffing him about the head. 'Now rest and then wash up for supper. You can tell me all about it then.' Faolin nodded in agreement and trudged inside. Silvermane cast a long, sweeping look across the surrounding hills before he too went inside and closed the door behind him.

Alexan loosed a breath as he looked down at the little croft. He'd found her. A hundred years the King had been searching for her, and he'd just found her. Almost by accident. He lay back and looked up at the darkening sky.

Except it hadn't been by accident. The King had sent him north, with specific instructions to search the Ravenswood. Alexan had had more sense than to question it, even if uncertainty had sat like a weight in his gut. The King never sent anyone important to search for Théon: it was dangerous hunting, and they rarely returned. Alexan was too valuable to waste on a whim. But even in his privileged position as one of the King's inner circle, Alexan wasn't told everything. He didn't know why he'd been sent to the Ravenswood, or why the King had chosen that moment to go after Théon.

But instinct told him it was far from coincidence that he'd found one daughter in that forest. Nor was he arrogant enough to believe his skill had allowed him to hunt down the other where so many others had failed. He sensed the Shade King's hand in all of it and trembled to consider the implications. The power required.

He took another breath, centring himself. In the grand scheme of things, the why did not matter. What mattered was that he had a purpose, a reason for hunting her down, and now he was able to accomplish it.

But first. He had a few hours, and he needed blood. He rolled to his feet, stowed his pack amongst some rocks and set off at a jog to find someone to quench his thirst.

Mortal prey, it transpired, was hard to find on the edges of the rugged Nighthills. He didn't fancy raiding Shadowbriar in his current state, and people were few beyond the safety of the ruins. It was just pure chance that he happened upon a pair of lovers coupling in the forest.

Perhaps it was the memory of those evergreen eyes that made him feel something akin to regret when he struck. But he'd spent a hundred years giving in to his darkest impulses, darker now than ever, and it was to those that he surrendered as he tore the boy away. The girl screamed, the shrill noise so piercing to Alexan's sensitive ears that he winced. But he grinned as he bent his head and tore into the boy's throat. He watched her stagger to her feet and run while he drank, anticipation thrumming through his veins. They were weak – he would need to drain them both to slake his thirst.

He felt nothing at all when he dropped the boy's corpse on the forest floor minutes later. The starving Darkling was in control now, and he laughed as he inhaled the scent of his fleeing prey. He didn't always need to kill to survive, but sometimes it was unavoidable. Times like now when he was so thirsty, so desperate, that he lacked the control to stop before killing victims. And sometimes, it was just enjoyable. He'd learned long ago not to stop to think, to just let the monster have its fun. There were days, like today, when it just needed some release for the frustration and suffering it had endured. If he let the beast run wild and hunt down this girl now, there was more chance he could stay in control of it later.

So he didn't hesitate, didn't pause to pity the girl as he bounded after her. She was still screaming as she staggered across the uneven ground of the forest floor, tripping over branches and tree roots alike. It wasn't a fair chase. Even if she'd used the head start to hide, which would have been the more sensible option, he would have sniffed her out. She stank of adolescent angst mixed with female arousal. Not the most appealing scent, but it drove the monster in Alexan wild. He drew the line at surrendering to the urges that rose in response. Not out of honour or principle – he'd yielded to such urges a hundred times before now – but because he just did not have time.

She begged for her life, as his victims often did, but he paid her no heed. Stalking towards her, he savoured her fear. She was pretty, by mortal standards. But she could not compare to the beauty of even the plainest of the Graced. Her light brown hair looked almost golden in the dim light of the forest, and her wide, terrified eyes were moss green. The image of Théon and Illyandi's mother lying dead on the floor flashed through his mind, but the monster paid it no heed. *That Queen is long dead*, it told him, *and this mortal girl is no comparison to her exquisite presence.* Snarling, he obeyed the monster's commands.

But when she was dead, and the monster was sated at last, Alexan fell to the ground and wept. He clutched her corpse to his chest and roared his misery to the skies. He did not weep for the girl in his arms, but for his Queen. Diathor, the granddaughter of the legendary Queen Benella. What would she say to see him now?

He didn't bury their bodies. Didn't even light a funeral pyre. There wasn't time. He left them in the woods for their families to find … perhaps they would serve as a warning to others not to venture too far from their homes. Not that their homes were any safer. Not from monsters like him.

CHAPTER THIRTEEN

The sun was near setting by the time Alexan made his way back to the croft. The Dragons were nowhere to be seen, but Théon was outside with the old man. She was in the paddock, brushing down an iron grey stallion, he propped up against a fence post while they spoke. Alexan once more offered up a brief prayer of thanks for his Darkling heightened senses and settled himself in to listen.

'I don't know what else you expected me to have done, old man,' Théon was saying, her voice tight with anger.

'You could have at least told me you were leaving.'

'And you would have wanted to come with me, but that would have meant leaving Illyandi unprotected so you would have insisted on bringing her along. The whole thing would have turned into some ridiculous expedition that would have taken days,' she snapped, brushing the horse perhaps more roughly than the poor beast deserved.

'We could have worked something out.'

Théon glanced up and gave him a withering look. 'Faolin didn't have time for you to *work something out*. As it is, I've no idea how he survived.'

'Maybe you misidentified the poison—'

She cut him off with a glare. 'Don't patronise me.'

'And don't assume that you are without fault,' Silvermane growled. 'That's something your father taught you. I had hoped by now you might have learned better.'

Théon's eyes seemed to glow with a strange but terrible light – like the eerie pulsing of lightning through thunderclouds. Alexan leaned forward, trying to see. But then the light passed, and her shoulders slumped.

'I'm sorry,' she said. Alexan's lip curled in distaste. Meekness didn't suit her. But the old man didn't seem to notice or care. He just nodded and turned away from her.

'Faolin and Dorrien should be awake soon,' he called over his shoulder, as he hobbled back into the croft. 'You should come back inside – we need to prepare dinner.'

Alexan watched her shoulders slump further. With a sigh, she threw the brush over the fence and emptied a large bag of oats into the trough nearest the horse. She was angry, that much was obvious. It went against the grain for her to take criticism from the old man, but something seemed to be holding her temper in check. He felt his curiosity pique.

Finished seeing to the horses, she hopped the fence with athletic grace and gathered up the brush she'd thrown on the ground along with their various packs. Scowling and muttering to herself, she stomped into the barn where he could hear her clattering around as she put things away. She appeared again, this time carrying a bag of feed which she tipped into a trough for the livestock.

Then, with another heavy sigh, she returned to the house. She kicked her mud-caked boots off at the door, and he heard her calling to Illyandi that dinner would be ready in an hour. Then the door slammed, and her voice was cut off.

Alexan frowned. It was apparent from the calm efficiency with which she went about her tasks that these chores were a daily occurrence for Théon. She did not shy away from manual labour like some of her childhood peers may have done, and she had no problem in running both the farm and the house. But it grated on him. She was the Queen – crowned or uncrowned, it made little difference.

It was hours later before he saw anyone again. Silvermane and Faolin appeared just after sunset, when the sky was a riot of red, and sat on a bench outside the front of the house. The sounds of Illyandi and Dorrien chattering away inside drifted through the open door, but he couldn't make out any words. Not that it mattered. He had little interest in what they had to say. He and Théon appeared to have that much in common at least, as she stood in the doorway, drying her hands with a cloth, listening to the two men talk.

'Tell me about the Ravenswood,' Silvermane was saying.

'I'm not sure what there is to tell.' Faolin sighed in frustration. 'The Silvan Forests are crawling with Darklings, and I think there's a Shade in Illyol – a royal too. None of the other members of the Court would be strong enough to break through Benella's wards. We were about to investigate further when we caught the scent of an Awakening. It was faint though growing stronger every day. We followed it up into the Ravenswood but couldn't find anything. We were about to give up when Keriath appeared. Alone. No sign of Taelyr.'

Silvermane frowned. 'What?'

'She said they were separated on the road,' Faolin explained, shrugging. 'There was a Hunt waiting for her in Thornhold. She got out unscathed and thought she'd lost them, but obviously she was wrong. She'd been about to turn back to look for Taelyr when she scented the Awakening. But she led them right to us. It was a mortal Hunt – there's no way they found us by chance.'

'She won't have led them to you on purpose,' Théon said, jumping in as Faolin paused.

'I never said she did—' he began.

But Théon cut him off. 'No, you didn't,' she agreed. Alexan could see the anger in the set of her shoulders as she glanced at Silvermane. 'But there are others who might look to lay blame at her feet.'

Silvermane sighed. 'Keriath has given no indication that she acknowledges that bond.'

'Neither have I for the best part of a century, but you're still plenty quick to point the finger my way,' she hissed. Alexan sat up a little straighter. This was becoming an interesting exchange.

'Careful, Théon,' the old man growled. 'Keriath has denied that bond her entire life. No matter how many times she's accused of it, she refuses to believe that he is her father. The same can't be said of you.'

Théon leaned forward, her body quivering with repressed rage. But then her eyes pulsed with that eerie light once more, and she backed down. Turning on her heel, she walked away with as much dignity as she could muster. Alexan frowned, considering. There was something about that light that just didn't sit right with him.

'Was that necessary?' Faolin growled, once she was gone.

'Every day is a battle.' The old man sighed. 'She's so much like her father. It's hard to keep the darkness repressed. She is so quick to anger, and each time she battles with her temper, it rears its head once more.'

Alexan didn't disagree. He'd been on the receiving end of the King's temper often enough.

But Faolin didn't know any better. 'She's nothing like him, and it's not fair of you to compare them all the time. She was a child, with no control over what happened. If you want to punish someone over what happened a century ago, maybe you should look in the mirror.'

'Me?' Silvermane exclaimed. 'I did nothing!'

'Exactly,' snarled Faolin. 'We're her family, and we failed her. When we let him take her from us that night, we failed her. Every day we left her with that monster, we failed her. So stop blaming her for the past. She suffers for it enough.'

'You don't know what you're talking about,' Silvermane snapped. 'He took her before you were even born.'

Faolin shook his head in disgust and stood up. 'I know that blood is thicker than water. I know that you don't get to pick your kin, but that you can choose who you call family. She's suffered enough. Let it go.'

And with that, he turned and went inside after Théon. Anger bloomed in Alexan's chest at those words, at the memories they stirred. Memories of a wild, pale-eyed hellion thrashing against her captors. The Shade King's heir, stolen from her bed in the dead of night by Kalielle Half-Elven and returned to her mother, Queen Diathor. Memories of the broken, haunted girl-child left behind when the demon was cut from her. The old man stayed outside as the sky darkened and the moon rose overhead, and all the while, Alexan contemplated ways to kill him.

After what seemed like an age, Silvermane stood and followed Faolin inside, leaving Alexan alone with his thoughts. When his blood had cooled, he leaned back amongst the heather and stared up at the starry sky, toying with the amulet about his neck. He twisted the chain around his hands, running over every detail with his fingers, considering his next steps.

He would require help. There was no way he was getting through those wards without it. No one beyond the King's inner circle could be trusted. That left him thin on options. He would need more information if he was to come up with a plan. He sighed. More watching. More waiting. This hunt was turning out to be very tedious.

And each moment he waited, Keriath drew a step closer to Dar Kual. If she was not there already. How much longer would it be until he was free of this task to rescue her? Or at least send another in his stead? Frustration was a restless urge in his veins, raging uselessly against the King's order. Swearing under his breath, he clenched his fists, crossed his arms tight, and waited.

It was close to midnight when Alexan was roused from a restless doze by soft feet padding through grass and the sound of hushed whispers on the wind. He stirred, frowning at the two figures creeping through the darkness nearby.

Kah Faolin, his jet hair blacker than the night sky, and the Princess Illyandi following, little more than a pale sliver in the moonlight.

Alexan stilled. Hardly dared breathe. If they caught his scent …

'Illyandi, be reasonable,' Faolin hissed, striding away from her. Alexan pressed himself flat to the ground as they neared, buried himself amongst the heather and prayed they stayed too absorbed in each other to notice him. His heart was pounding in his mouth, but they were well past him when her hand shot out. She stopped, grabbing Faolin by the wrist and turning him to face her.

'I *am* being reasonable. Do you have any idea what the last few days have been like? To be left behind, doing nothing, knowing you were out there hurt and alone?'

Faolin extricated himself from her grip. 'I'm fine.'

'But you nearly weren't,' she said, her eyes welling with tears. 'The thought of losing you Faolin … it's more than I can bear.'

He sighed and wiped her cheeks dry. 'I know.'

'So take me with you.'

'No.' His gaze hardened, and he folded his arms across his chest. 'You'd just be a distraction.'

'I can look after myself,' she insisted.

He shook his head at that, leaning over her. 'Shall I show you just how wrong you are, Princess?'

'You can try,' she challenged, but the words did not carry as much swagger as intended – breathless as they were. Alexan was glad for the taste of fear on his tongue drowning out the memories awakened by her face, her voice. Though her mother had never been so emotional.

'If you care that much about my well-being, you'll stay here where you're safe. I'll sleep better for knowing you're out of harm's way. I can't do what needs to be done if I'm worrying about you.'

'And what about my well-being?' she demanded. 'I cannot spend every waking moment sick with fear, not knowing if you're alive or dead. I can't do it, Faolin.'

He sighed again as more tears spilled down her cheeks, but this time, he folded her into his arms and held her while she wept. 'Hush now,' he murmured, pressing his lips to her golden hair. 'I'm here, I've got you.'

'For how much longer though?' she whispered into his chest.

Faolin leaned back to look at her and cupped her fragile face in his warrior hands. 'We leave at first light.' She opened her mouth to protest, but he placed a silencing finger to her lips. 'We can't linger, Illyandi. It's not safe for us all to be in one place.'

'I can't keep living like this,' she whimpered. 'A hundred years of secrecy. A hundred years of running and hiding. How much longer? How long until we take back what is ours?'

'That's not a fight we can win.'

'Better to die on our feet than live on our knees.'

Faolin smiled, but the exasperation was clear in his ferocious eyes. 'Words from another time. Another world. Things are different now. We have to endure. Our people's future depends on our survival.'

'I didn't think I'd ever see the day,' she muttered. 'You counselling caution, while I call for action.'

He snorted and shrugged. 'People change.'

'Clearly.'

The Dragon's eyes gleamed in the darkness. 'Don't kid yourself, Princess. I will never forget what they did to us – what they took. When the time is right, I will bathe the world in the blood of our enemies, and I'll do it with a smile on my face.'

'And what will I be doing, hmm? While you're out fighting, risking your life to reclaim our home, where do you expect me to be? Barefoot and pregnant in the kitchen? Warming your bed, awaiting the return of the conquering hero?'

There was a flash of white teeth as he grinned. 'That last option sounds appealing.'

'You've been spending too much time with Taelyr if you think that's an appropriate response.'

Faolin chuckled and inclined his head in acknowledgement. Then he sobered and held her gaze. 'By my side. When that day comes, and we take back what they stole from us, I want you by my side.'

'Promise me.'

He stepped back and dropped to a knee. He took her hand in his, removing a ring from the little finger of his right hand and sliding it onto her ring finger. Then he held up his left hand to show the matching ring he wore there. 'These belonged to my parents – and my father's parents before them, and my grandmother's parents before that. Spelled by Benella herself, to bind her and Kenor together no matter how far apart they were. The magic is old now, and only a remnant of it lingers. Not strong enough for us to communicate properly, but just enough for each of us to know the other is safe.'

'Promise me,' she repeated.

Faolin stood, cupping her face in his hands once more. 'I promise you, Illyandi, when the time is right, we will take back what is ours. Together.' Then he leaned down and kissed her.

Alexan could only lie there as their embrace grew passionate. And though he refused to watch what followed, there was little he could do to block out the sounds of their coupling. Another time, another pairing, and he may well have enjoyed himself. But the noises coming from Illyandi made him uncomfortable. She'd been a child the last time he'd seen her; now he could hear her moaning as he'd once imagined her mother moaning beneath his touch.

The only consolation he could find was imagining Illyandi's father – pretentious prick that he'd been – turning in his grave at his darling daughter debasing herself with a Dragon. He'd been with enough of them over the years to realise she'd have been hard-pressed to choose a more vigorous lover. At least he was attentive, if the muffled gasps of pleasure echoing in the darkness were anything to go by. And their stamina …

Alexan smothered a groan of frustration and buried his face further into the heather. It was going to be a long night.

They'd lasted until dawn was a pale threat on the horizon. Only then did they get themselves under control long enough to dress and return to the croft. Alexan couldn't do much more than roll over and stare into space. A hundred years he'd been part of the Shade King's Court, a member of his most trusted inner circle with all the horrors that entailed. But spending a whole night listening to a Dragon fuck his Queen's youngest daughter was still the most traumatic thing he'd ever endured.

He wasn't sure how long he'd been lying there, looking up at the lightening sky and trying to make sense of the chaotic tangle of thoughts in his head, when a flicker of movement caught his eye, dragging his attention back to the job at hand. That mess of thoughts and feelings he shoved into a box to sort through later. Preferably never.

His gaze snagged on a dark figure, striding up the hill. Théon. Alexan frowned. It was nearly sunrise. A time when she should have been hidden from view. But there she was, outside the wards, stopping at the top of the hill like she was there to greet the dawn. Her arms were bare, and her face tilted upward, as if in anticipation. Then the sun crested the horizon and the first rays brushed her skin, her glamour slipping from her shoulders like she was casting off a gown.

He swore. She was breathtaking. The morning breeze caught her raven hair, sending it swirling around her shoulders like a waterfall of ebony, revealing her tapered ears, now adorned in glittering jewels. Her cheekbones sharpened, and her eyes angled upward, becoming even more feline than before. Her magical aura – the mark of her bloodline – flickered around her like other-worldly flames of vibrant green.

Little wonder she was out here alone. That she worked so hard to hide this, even from her own family. The glamour had made her appear almost Elven. But now, in the dawn's light, there was nothing there but the feral savagery of her father. Of the Shade. Beautiful, yes. But wild and dangerous. Something inside Alexan stirred, as if in recognition.

There was a smile on her lips while she bathed in the morning sun. She spread her hands wide, as if revelling in the play of the breeze through her fingers. He blinked. How many times had he watched her mother do the same thing? How many times had he stood guard while his Queen welcomed the dawn, stunned into silence, near blinded by the sheer beauty of the woman he loved gilded in the morning light? He took a deep breath, swallowing the lump of grief in his throat. Stood fast against the current as a flood of memories threatened to drown him.

'Théon!' An angry shout fractured the peace and tranquillity of the sunrise, but Théon didn't flinch. He shared her exasperation when he registered the intruder a moment later. Illyandi's expression was furious as she stormed up the hill.

'Illyandi.'

'Don't you *Illyandi* me,' her sister snapped. Joining Théon in the sun, her own glamour slipped away revealing the truth beneath. Unlike Théon, her appearance more Elven without it – any mortal traits vanishing, replaced by the delicate, ethereal beauty of their people. The aura of her magic erupted around her, shimmering like sunlight through oak leaves, gilding her in flecks of green and gold light. Alexan's chest seized in shock. Her mother's aura. He closed his eyes against the onslaught of memories.

'You shouldn't be outside the wards,' Théon was saying.

'Neither should you,' Illyandi scolded.

'I am prepared to deal with anything that comes my way.' Théon smiled and tapped the dagger at her hip.

Illyandi tried to hide it, but Alexan could see her lip curl in distaste. 'Just because I follow Benella's example, doesn't mean I can't defend myself.'

Théon's eyes grew distant and sad beyond measure, and she nodded, turning back towards the house. 'I know,' she said. Then she sighed and looked at her sister. 'What is it?'

'Faolin and Dorrien are getting ready to leave. You should come and say goodbye.'

Théon nodded in agreement and turned to follow her sister. Satisfied that they were returning to the safety of the wards, Illyandi began chattering about a new dress she was making. She said nothing of her night with the Dragon. Alexan wondered what her sister would make of it.

He watched Théon's shoulders slump, and the unbridled, ferocious woman who would risk her life to greet the dawn disappeared beneath the layers of responsibilities weighing on her slender shoulders. She didn't fool him for a moment. A wild animal – captured, broken and tamed to serve – always yearned to run free. He smiled. It was a crack just waiting to be exploited.

An hour later, hidden amongst the rocks high in the glen, he watched on while the Dragons prepared to leave. Kah Faolin and the Princess Illyandi stood close together, their heads bowed as they murmured to each other. Illyandi touched a gentle hand to his face, and Faolin once more folded her into his arms, before handing her over to Dorrien. The two women clung to each other, their faces streaked with tears at their parting. Silvermane kissed Dorrien on the brow and shook Faolin's hand once more. Only Théon stood apart, arms folded across her chest as she watched in silence.

Alexan saw Faolin step away to join her. He pulled her hands away from her chest and clasped them in his own. When she refused to meet his eye, he tilted her chin up with the crook of his finger. His smile was warm and hers shy, making Alexan's stomach churn with jealousy. He refused to consider what that meant.

'Stay strong,' Faolin murmured, squeezing her fingers in his own.

'Be safe,' she replied. He winked at her and gave her a fierce hug before turning back to Silvermane and Dorrien.

'Take care of yourselves,' the old man was saying to Dorrien. 'See what news you can find of Keriath, but your priority has to be finding the source of that magic. There are not enough of us left now to risk losing any to a Darkling Hunt. See if you can get word to Arian and Ornak – they were headed south through Ciaron. They can get word to Resari. We're going to need her.' Alexan arched a brow at the list of names. Arian and Ornak were well known to the Shade Court, but only the King's inner circle knew still to fear Resari. The Dragons nodded in understanding and shouldered their packs.

As they crossed the wards on foot, Faolin glanced over his shoulder. He inclined his head to Théon, but to Silvermane he only frowned. It was a clear warning: treat Théon better or face his wrath. Alexan smirked. In a different life, he and Faolin could have been good friends.

The Dragons Changed together in the morning light: where two fearsome warriors stood, now an osprey preened and, beside her, a fierce-eyed falcon. The falcon screeched once as they launched themselves skyward, and the noise echoed around the valley long after they had gone.

Alexan stood in the dying light, far from the croft, watching the sun set with disinterest while he contemplated the amulet in his hand. What it

145

could unleash. It stung at his pride to even consider using it, but he'd evaluated all the other options, and this was the one most likely to succeed.

It was a simple design. Stark. Brutal. A blood-red gem set within a ring of iron. There were five, worn by the Shade King's inner circle, by those blessed and burdened with his trust. His steward and lover, Jenia – his Queen in all but name. His spymaster and assassin, Seren. And his three most favoured generals. Kieyin. Corrigan. Alexan.

He wondered which one would answer.

Dreaded it.

For whoever answered was likely to be Keriath's salvation. There was an even chance that they would be her doom instead.

With a sigh, he sliced his hand open and pressed his bloody palm to the jewel in the centre, the mark there itching in response to the magic within as it activated, pulsing out across the world. Dark magic. Stolen and corrupt. He'd gone some distance to get far enough away from the croft – from the Graced senses inside – to risk using it.

But now the signal was sent. Help would come. All he had to do was wait. Wait and worry.

He prayed it would be Kieyin. Even Seren would do. Jenia would be a disaster.

He shuddered at the thought. Legend said she'd killed her own sister to prove her devotion to the King. Alexan knew all too well she'd done far worse than that in the long centuries since then. Like trying to kill the King's bastard child, for example. Alexan had seen the damage first-hand, opened the gates and carried that small, broken form into the palace himself. Stood guard for three days while the healers battled to save her. Not that she remembered. If there had been any flicker of recognition in Keriath's gaze, it had only been at his name. The name of the Shade King's Darkling general. Not the Lord Protector who'd given her his strength when her own had failed. She'd been barely ten years old. If Jenia came, if he told her where to find Keriath … She would only rescue the King's daughter so she could kill Keriath herself.

Jenia would be a disaster, but that was at least predictable. The same couldn't be said if Seren answered his call. No one seemed to know anything about the mysterious Darkling with the moon-white hair and ageless eyes. And not for lack of trying. Alexan had spent the best part of the last century trying to discover something – anything – about her. Who was she? Where had she come from? What did she want? He might as well have tried to fathom the stars. All he knew was that her loyalty to the King was absolute. And she was very, *very* good at what she did. But given that consisted of spying and killing, he wasn't sure if she would be a help or a hindrance.

His fellow generals were as bad as each other. On the surface, Corrigan was worst. A cruel Elvish Nightwalker with a mean streak a mile wide. Their hatred of each other ran so deep that they were never left alone unsupervised. But that aside, Alexan could at least appreciate that Corrigan was the more sensible one. He was efficient and far less reckless. And he had nothing to gain where Théon or Keriath were involved. But he had also murdered his Queen, and only the Claiming had stopped Alexan from killing the Nightwalker for the last century. Diathor's ghost haunted him enough without sending her murderer to the rescue of her kin.

Kieyin, meanwhile, had an unbridled love of life and all it offered. The Phoenix-born Shade was a serial seducer with a taste for thieving, wine and violence. A Prince of the Court, living his life on a knife-edge for no other reason than the sheer rush it brought him. But he was also the only reason Alexan hadn't been driven insane by the Claiming. Alexan owed him a life-debt. Several, if he was honest about it. More than that, he trusted Kieyin in a way that he could never trust Corrigan. At least the Shade was honest about what he was.

'Penny for your thoughts?' said a smooth, cultured voice behind him. He didn't jump or turn. He'd sensed the magic of the Transference. Only a Shade had that kind of power. Relief had his legs feeling like water.

'You took your time getting here,' Alexan said, leaning against a nearby tree.

Kieyin snorted as he appeared in Alexan's peripheral vision. 'Still faster than Corrigan,' he noted. Alexan chuckled, conceding the point. Kieyin leaned against another tree. 'I assume you found her? If you've dragged me out here for nothing, I will be seriously fucked off. You would not believe the lovelies I left behind.'

'I'm sure Corrigan will keep them warm for you,' Alexan assured him.

Kieyin scowled. 'That's not funny. I don't think he'd have a clue what to do with one. Frigid bastard.'

Alexan huffed a laugh. 'It's *quite* funny. And he does know what to do with them – they just won't be as pretty once he's finished.'

Kieyin mimed vomiting at the thought. 'Gods, he's a sick fucker.' Then he clapped a hand on Alexan's shoulder. 'I've missed you, brother. I can't believe you left me alone with that cretin.'

'You've got Seren. And Jenia,' Alexan said, laughing at the disgust on Kieyin's handsome face. The Shade was pretty, preening and polished, with a smile that could charm his way into any bed he liked. But behind that urbane facade, Alexan knew all too well that a cunning mind lingered. He hid that sly, scheming intellect the same way he hid his slight but well-muscled physique – beneath the exquisitely tailored clothes, gleaming dark hair that shone red in the light, and glittering crimson jewels that adorned his fingers and pointed ears.

Alexan was proud to call him brother. Of all the horrors he'd lived through since his turning, Kieyin alone had made life bearable. He would almost suffer it all again rather than lose the Shade.

'Don't go all sentimental on me now, brother,' Kieyin warned. 'I didn't travel all this way just so we could hold hands and sing songs around the campfire.'

Alexan chuckled darkly and gripped Kieyin's shoulder hard enough that the Shade winced. 'I found them,' he said, his voice near breathless with excitement. Kieyin's brow arched.

'Well, I should fucking hope so,' he snorted. 'I guess that explains why you've gone all misty-eyed on me.'

Alexan pulled a face, ignoring Kieyin's ribbing. 'No, I found *them*. Théon *and* Keriath.'

Kieyin blinked, stunned into silence for once in his life. Alexan savoured the moment. Then the Shade let out a low whistle.

'You're shitting me.'

'Obviously. I said it just to see that look on your face.' Alexan rolled his eyes. 'I'm being serious, Kieyin. I caught Keriath in the Ravenswood less than a fortnight ago.'

'Well, where is she?' asked Kieyin, glancing around in confusion.

'I lost her to a mortal Hunt.' Alexan spat in frustration. 'They laid claim – said they'd been hunting her for weeks. Threatened to press charges of poaching if I took her. There were too many of them for me to risk it. A bloodbath like that could have launched us back into war.'

Kieyin frowned. 'The King would have understood—' he began.

But Alexan cut him off. 'I know, but there are things the King isn't aware of. Zorana and Mazron are at it again. She's made it into Illyol, and I saw him heading towards Ciaron, of all places. I'm worried the Queens are allying with them and, without knowing for sure, I didn't think it wise to risk starting a war we might not be able to win.'

Kieyin nodded in understanding, his eyes narrowing. 'Mazron has been acting strange, right enough. But that sister of his is something else. Last time she was at Court, she was claiming she'd got some new pet – some remnant of the Graced that she'd corrupted.' He snorted in disbelief then shook his head. 'She's a silly mare. If she's got inside Illyol, she's had help – and that can't be good for us. I'll see what I can find out.'

'Thank you.'

Kieyin waved him away. 'It's fine. How did you catch her anyway?'

Alexan told him. The Shade King's orders. The Awakening. The Dragons. Keriath's arrival. The failed ambush. The chase. The fight that followed. Losing her to Drosta's Hunt.

Kieyin interrupted. 'Drosta? Assuming he's one of the Queens' lot?' Alexan nodded. 'What was he doing hunting someone like Keriath? And how did he find her?'

'I don't know. Seems too convenient though. He was well prepared. I can't be sure who, but I reckon someone gave her up. It reeks of Mazron if you ask me, and that's what worries me. Drosta wouldn't have been bold enough to challenge me if the Queens weren't in bed with someone from the Court.'

Kieyin nodded in agreement. 'Alright. I'll see what I can do. But we don't even know where they've taken her, and if all you say is true, any rescue will require careful planning. And the King will want me to investigate the Awakening—'

'Damn the Awakening, Kieyin. Whether she's gone to Zorana, Mazron or the Queens, I guarantee she's suffering. You have to save her. I'm bound by the King's command to deal with Théon, and it'll take too long for me to do it. Please—'

The Prince cut him off. 'I understand, brother, but you know how this works. If the King wants me to investigate the Awakening first then I must do as he commands. But whatever his orders, I swear, I will not leave Keriath to rot. It may take some time, but I will get her out of there, one way or another. You have my word.' Alexan nearly fell to his knees with relief at the words, but Kieyin continued, oblivious, 'Now what about Théon?'

'I tracked the Dragons. They led me right to her.'

'That was careless,' the Shade observed.

'The Kah heir was wounded in the fight. Nothing permanent – certainly doesn't seem to have affected his … vigour.' Kieyin's eyebrows quirked upward in confusion, and Alexan relayed his night of reluctant voyeurism.

As expected, the Shade howled with laughter. 'You should have asked to join them.'

'I'm not sure they would have said yes.'

A longing grin split Kieyin's charming face. 'Oh, but think how good it would be if they had. Did you know, Dragons can use the Change to make their di—'

'Shut up,' snapped Alexan. Kieyin pouted playfully but let the matter drop. 'They've moved on now anyway. It's just her and Illyandi, and an old man they call Silvermane.'

Kieyin was quiet for a while before he spoke again. 'What's she like?' he asked, his voice soft. Alexan forced a neutral expression on his face. He'd never heard Kieyin speak like that, not about anyone. He resisted the urge to press him on the matter.

'She's nothing like her mother,' he said, hiding his own feelings beneath a cold exterior. The glance Kieyin gave him spoke of understanding but not compassion.

'Did you expect her to be?' he said with a soft laugh.

Alexan shrugged. 'I don't know what I expected,' he answered. Kieyin raised a quizzical eyebrow, inviting him to elaborate. 'Someone more like the King. Composed. Logical. Less reckless.'

'Was she ever any of those things when you knew her as a child?'

'No,' he admitted. 'But it was a long time ago. I assumed she'd grow out of it.'

'Do you think you can convince her to return?' Kieyin asked, his pale gaze frank.

Alexan sighed and rubbed a hand across his eyes. 'I don't know. I need to get closer, get to know her better before I can say for sure.'

'And if you can't?'

'I need to be closer no matter what I do,' he said. 'Tempt her, take her or kill her – it makes no difference. I can't do anything from here.'

'But?'

He smiled. Kieyin knew him well. Too well.

'The house is warded,' he explained. 'Impressively so too. Not like anything I've seen since I left Illyol.'

'Do you have a plan to get through them?' asked Kieyin.

Alexan suppressed the urge to roll his eyes. 'Don't be ridiculous,' he grunted. 'A hundred years and you still think I'm stupid enough to go through something when I can just go around it?'

'I know the effect that beautiful women have on you, Alexan,' Kieyin chuckled. 'Just have to check that you've still got your wits about you.'

Alexan smirked and shook his head. 'No,' he continued. 'We wait for her to come to us.'

'We?'

Alexan nodded. 'I have a plan,' he said, darkness glinting in his blood-red eyes. 'If it works, the wards will cease to be a problem. Théon will take me through them herself.'

'And if it doesn't?' asked Kieyin. There was no fear in his voice, only anticipation.

'We'll die.'

Kieyin grinned, his eyes dancing with dark delight. 'When do we start?'

CHAPTER FOURTEEN

I t was too easy. They hadn't even needed to wait that long – which was just as well. Alexan sent up a silent prayer of thanks for that as he watched his prey inch closer. Patience was not something that Kieyin held in significant supply, and the sooner his part here was done, the sooner the Shade Prince could turn his attentions to retrieving Keriath from the Darkling Queens. If their luck continued to hold, they'd be back in Elucion with both daughters before autumn's end.

Alexan had been counting on someone needing to leave the safety of the wards. Inevitably, they'd need to travel into Shadowbriar at some point, whether to trade at the market or gather information about what was happening in the world beyond their little farm. He had not expected a hunting trip. He certainly hadn't dared to hope to catch Théon alone.

And yet, here they were, shadowing her as she crept through the forest. It was now after sunset, and she'd been out since dusk. There were already two fat pigeons in her game bag, and her lips were stained with the juice from a patch of wild berries she'd raided. Like a child, she'd stuffed half of them in her mouth before she'd deigned to gather some to take back. The small buck she was stalking was a bonus.

She handled the bow well, though that wasn't a surprise. She'd been taught well enough. The Shade King. Her mother. Alexan himself. Her body was taut and loose in all the right places, her soft footfalls near-silent as she crept through the woods. She paused, took a steadying breath, aimed and let the arrow fly.

It buzzed through the air, and the beast's head whipped around. But before it could move, there was a dull thwack as the arrow pierced through hide and flesh, driving straight into the heart. It dropped to the ground, stunned, before adrenaline had it surging once more to its feet and disappearing into the undergrowth. Théon's eyes gleamed in the gloom, but she didn't follow it. Instead, she sighed, slinging her bow back over her shoulder while she waited for the beast to die.

'I see you finally learned how to hunt.' Kieyin's irreverent voice drifted from the darkness.

Alexan stilled. This was it.

Théon started to her feet, drawing the hunting knife from its sheath at her hip. But there was no fear in her eyes when Kieyin stepped from the shadows.

'Better than you,' she responded, in a voice that Alexan barely recognised. The voice of the Shade King's daughter. 'You never had the discipline for it.'

Kieyin chuckled. 'Discipline is for dullards. I prefer life with a little more zest.'

'I can imagine. Seren always said you'd leave a trail of broken hearts across Elucion.' Alexan smiled. Just as he'd hoped. They'd been raised together as children by the Shade King, until Diathor had stolen her daughter back. If she would hesitate for anyone, it would be Kieyin.

The Shade grinned. 'Did I break your heart, little Théon?'

'Hardly,' she snorted. 'I was ten the last time I saw you.'

'Ten-year-old hearts can still be broken,' he assured her. 'Mine was. The day you left.'

Théon rolled her eyes. 'The only person you've ever been in love with is yourself. Tell me, do you still keep a mirror in your pocket?'

'I've found far more interesting places to keep mirrors,' he purred, winking. It was Alexan's turn to roll his eyes. There was an obscenely large mirror mounted on the ceiling above Kieyin's enormous bed. 'I could show you if you like?'

She ignored him. 'How did you find me?'

Kieyin huffed an exasperated sigh, examining his fingernails. 'Sweetheart, we never lost you.'

'What do you want, Kieyin?'

'Daddy dearest sent me to bring you home.'

She stilled. Alexan tensed in readiness. He could feel the magic building inside her. Any moment now. 'Then he sent you to your death.'

She lunged. Kieyin spun, laughing as he danced away from the blade flashing in the darkness. Théon was fast. But Kieyin was faster, swirling towards Théon in a whirlwind of shadow and smoke, knocking the knife from her hand with ease. Théon ducked low, hitting him in the gut with her shoulder, bearing them both to the ground. Kieyin grunted, driving his knee up into Théon's ribs. Théon barked a curse of pain, and Alexan heard her bones crack beneath the force of the blow. But she returned the favour, smashing her elbow into Kieyin's face. Alexan waited.

Then they were up. Kieyin spat out a mouthful of blood as magic flickered to life in his outstretched hands. The Wielding. The power of the Shade. Raw, unadulterated destruction.

Théon was panting, aura flaring to heal her broken bones and summon up a storm, wreathing her fists in light as she readied herself to fight. Kieyin struck first. The Wielding streaked through the darkness, slamming into a shield of solid air. The clash of magic shook the ground beneath their feet, and Alexan could see Théon's jaw clenched tight as Kieyin battered her defences. But she held her ground and hurled a bolt of lightning at his head. There was nothing graceful to it. She was relying on brute strength and aggression. Alexan knew she was skilled, but it was becoming clear to him that emotion had chased all thought of control from her mind. Still, he waited.

Finally, *finally*, Théon began to tire. Her attacks grew more careful, cautious. As if conserving what remained of her strength. Then Kieyin grinned, and shattered the tattered remnants of her shield.

'Get ready,' he whispered in Alexan's mind.

Alexan snorted. As if he needed told.

'You should have come quietly, Théon,' Kieyin goaded. 'Can't say I'm surprised though. You did what your father would have done. Even after all this time, you're still his true heir.'

The Wielding coiling around him, Kieyin readied to strike.

Alexan charged. He surged forward, slamming into the Shade with all he had. Threw him bodily against a tree. Turned to see Théon, stunned and motionless.

'Run!' he roared.

Shaken from her stupor, she did as he bid, turning and racing for the croft, for the safety of the wards. Alexan was aware of Kieyin swearing as he staggered to his feet, rushing to follow. Shaping the Wielding into a bow and arrow. Gods, he was so melodramatic.

'Hurry up,' he hissed at Alexan, drawing and taking aim. But Alexan was already there, running parallel to Théon as she charged through the woods, back towards the farm. *'This is going to hurt.'*

Alexan growled. *'Just make sure you don't hit anything vital.'*

He felt the tremor of magic as Kieyin loosed.

He swerved. Dived at Théon. Shoved her clear of the arrow of Wielding magic arcing through the air towards her.

Took the death blow intended for her. He roared as it struck, at the searing pain that burst through his chest from behind. Stumbled and fell, forcing himself not to swear out loud all the obscenities he wanted to hurl at Kieyin.

'Are you fucking serious!' he roared. It had missed his heart – just – but the magic had still punched a hole the size of a fist through his chest. He'd seen Kieyin train often enough to know it hadn't been an accident.

A ghost of a chuckle echoed through his head. *'Sorry, brother, but this is your best chance. Try not to die.'*

Then that presence was gone, and warm hands were on him. His head was swimming with the agony of his wound, the world around him fading in and out of focus, the strength to heal himself spilling out onto the hillside. He was just glad it was dark. If she saw the colour of his blood, she'd never save him. At least the overpowering scent of Kieyin's Wielding would prevent her smelling it.

'Come on.' Her voice above him was insistent. 'Come on, get up. My home is warded – it's not far, but I need you to get up.'

He coughed weakly, spitting blood onto the ground as he allowed her to haul him up and sling his arm around her slender shoulders. Her fingers closed around his wrist, keeping him there. Even in his semi-conscious state, he couldn't help but notice how callused her hands were. The heat of her Casting wrapped around his chest, holding the wound together and slowing the blood loss.

Then they were moving, stumbling through the darkness towards the house. Alexan could sense Kieyin following, herding them back but not closing so near that he risked another confrontation.

He wasn't sure how long it took to make that frantic flight for the croft, but he caught the scent of the wards on the wind. Felt the magical protection around the house recoil and flare in protest at his presence. But Théon's hand around his squeezed as she pulled him through, the Casting retreating at her presence and command. His stomach heaved as it brushed against the corrupt power in his veins, but then he was through, and the sensation faded.

Théon was panting as she lowered him to the ground, straightening to search the hillside for signs of pursuit. Alexan summoned the strength to lift his head just as Kieyin strolled from the shadows towards them. Hands in pockets, his pale eyes raked over the wards, and he let out a low whistle.

'Impressive,' he admired. 'Won't keep you safe though, sweetheart. Daddy dearest could tear them down with half a thought.'

She bared her teeth at him again. 'Maybe. Beyond you though, isn't it?'

'I can wait.'

Théon snorted in disbelief. 'When you tell him how you failed, make sure none of the Court is there to witness it. He won't be able to spare you if they are.'

Kieyin's face was impassive, but there was a flicker of annoyance in that pale gaze. Then he stepped back and vanished in a ripple of Transference.

Above him, Alexan heard Théon swear in relief before she crashed down beside him. He closed his eyes before she could see them and let out a sigh of relief. The heat of her Casting loosened and grew gentler, softer, as she knitted flesh and bone back together.

'Thank you,' she was murmuring. 'I don't know who you are, or why you did it, but thank you.'

His voice was a breathless gasp, stifled by pain, but he managed to speak the words. The last words he'd spoken to her, a hundred years ago now. 'You need never thank me. I swore my life to the Elf-Queen. It is yours. Forever.'

There was a pause, followed by a gasp of recognition.

'Alexan?' she whispered.

He kept his eyes closed. Held off a moment longer before he revealed the truth. Waited until she'd healed his wound.

'It's been a long time, Princess,' he murmured.

'A hundred years,' she agreed. 'They told me you were dead.'

Alexan steeled himself and opened his eyes. The revulsion on her face, the way she recoiled at the sight of them ... it hurt far more than he'd expected.

'Sometimes I wish I was,' he admitted.

She stared at him in disbelief. 'What happened to you?'

'It's complicated,' he said, sitting up. Kept his hands where she could see them. Wide and open. That universal signal for peace.

'I'm sure I can keep up,' she snapped, doing nothing to hide the distrust and anger in her eyes. Her voice was bitter, filled with a dark, savage rage that he knew too well. Her father's voice. The voice of the Shade King. Her aura flickered to life around her, and he felt the wind stir in warning.

So he tried to find the words. Tried to explain something he barely understood himself. Explain the decisions he'd made since they parted. Weeks after the Fall, when the Darklings had finally hunted them down. Théon. Illyandi. All those other children who had somehow survived. He'd stood his ground, alongside Kalielle Half-Elven and a Unicorn woman whose name he could no longer remember. All to buy those children time to flee. He'd meant to die that day, yet here he was.

'There were too many of them,' he began. 'Someone had to stay behind to hold the line. We knew you'd never agree, so we lied. I lied. We never intended to come with you, Théon. Not when Kalielle had the power to destroy them all and cover your tracks. She couldn't risk being taken, dead or alive. Her plan was always to yield the Rising and take as many Darklings with her as she could. But someone had to keep them off her long enough for you and the others to get clear.'

Those evergreen eyes were lined with silver as they welled with tears. 'How did you survive?'

'I don't know,' he admitted. 'After ... I woke up, and I was alone. The Darklings were dead. Kalielle too. You were long gone, and I didn't want to risk leading anyone to you.' He took a deep, shuddering breath. 'I'd broken my vow, Théon. When I left my Queen behind to get you out of Illyol, I broke my vow. My life was forfeit. I should have died with Kalielle, but I didn't. There was only one reason for me to continue living. I went after the Shade King. I wanted to kill him for what he'd done to my Queen. For what he'd done to you.'

Théon stared at him, shaking her head in disbelief. 'And what made you think you could succeed where so many before you had failed? Where people with ten times your power, skill and experience had failed?'

'I didn't care. I wanted to die, Théon – I deserved to die. All I wanted was to take him with me. But I never got close. You know what your father is. You don't need me to tell you what went through his head when I was presented to him.'

Her expression darkened, but she released the Casting and said in a hollow voice. 'If all you wanted was death, then it would be the last thing he would ever give you. You hated him enough to give your life to try to kill him, so the worst punishment for you would be to let you live. To let you live not only knowing that you had failed but bound in eternal servitude to him. Any actual usefulness you had was just a bonus.'

Alexan nodded. Shoved the memories aside. The Claiming. Everything that followed. A wave of self-loathing threatened to overwhelm any semblance of composure that remained. He shoved that aside too. It wasn't helpful.

'So are you here to kill me, Lord Protector?' she asked, her gaze dead and shoulders slumped. The image of defeat, but he flinched anyway. From that title. The honour it implied. He did not deserve it.

'No.'

'No?' she said. There was no avoiding the disbelief in her voice. 'You saved me from Kieyin. Why?'

'I swore my life to the Elf-Queen,' he reminded her, 'and when your mother died, that title passed to you. When I heard the Shade King was coming for you, I knew I had to act. I broke my vow once. I won't do it again.'

It was a half-truth. He couldn't quite bring himself to lie to her again.

'Why now?' she demanded. 'It's been a hundred years since the Fall – why is he sending people after me now?'

'Who knows why he does anything? He speaks, we obey. I learned not to ask questions a long time ago.'

Another half-truth. She was quiet for a while, considering. 'Alright,' she said, her expression unreadable as she offered her hand. He took it, almost sighing with relief but was careful not to let it show on his face. She pulled him to his feet and offered him a look of warning. 'I'm not sure I believe you, but right now, I need all the help I can get. So I'll spare you, for now. But if your loyalties change, or you have them changed for you, remember – I spent over a decade at my father's side, learning everything he knows about power and pain. You won't win.'

'I understand,' he said, dipping his head in submission even as some part of him itched at the implicit challenge.

She shot him a warning glare. 'Don't mistake this mercy for trust. If you come with me, I can't promise that you'll survive. There aren't many of the Graced who can tolerate a Darkling without bloodshed.'

'I know the risks.'

She looked him over once more, her gaze frank and assessing. She snorted and turned away. 'I hope so.'

As they approached the croft, Alexan spotted the old man blocking the doorway while Illyandi hovered at this shoulder. Théon seemed to note it at the same time he did, huffing out an exasperated sigh.

'This might be interesting,' she muttered. 'Are you armed?'

Alexan nodded. 'Dirk on my thigh and a dagger in each boot.'

Her eyes skimmed his hips and chest.

'And the knife belt under your shirt,' she added with a wry smile. He didn't bother to dispute it. 'I'm going to take them. Better if you just stand still and let me do it. If he sees you drawing a weapon, chances are he'll kill you before I can explain.'

Alexan nodded and kept his hands up as she approached. Her fingers skimmed up under his shirt and divested him of his weapons with practised ease. His heart stuttered in his chest at her feather-light touch, at the heat rising to his cheeks. But when she dropped to her knees before him to free the daggers from his boots, his face turned to flame.

He forced himself to look skyward, gritting his teeth against the images that rose in response to that sight, cursing how much the last century had corrupted his mind. For the love of the Gods, she was Diathor's daughter.

'Anything else I should know about?' she asked, arching an eyebrow as her gaze raked his body once more.

The words were out of his mouth before he could stop them. 'You're welcome to investigate further.'

She was silent for a moment. Then she snorted.

'Oh, Illyandi is going to just *love* you,' she chuckled, before turning on her heel and leading him towards the house. He followed at a safe distance, careful to keep his hands where the old man could see them.

Even silhouetted as Silvermane was against the light, Alexan could see he was furious. He carried his unsheathed sword in one hand, the other leaning on his cane. But even with only one leg, there was no doubt in Alexan's mind that the old man was dangerous. There was something powerful sleeping behind those ancient eyes. He was careful not to meet that gaze. Already, he felt the prying touch of the Unicorn's mind tapping against his mental shields. But Seren and the King had taught him well. He knew how to resist the Enchanting.

Théon drew to a halt just out of reach and motioned for Alexan to stay behind her – an order he was all too happy to follow. Silence seemed to stretch for eternity while she waited for the old man to speak.

'Explain yourself,' he said, grinding the words out from between clenched teeth.

'Grandfather,' she said, her voice just a little too sweet as she gestured between them in introduction, 'Alexan. Alexan, my grandfather.' Alexan tried his best to hide his scepticism. The old man was no relation of Théon's father, and Diathor's father was long dead. Théon seemed to sense his hesitation and glanced over her shoulder at him, smiling. 'I might be a few generations out, but it's close enough. You can call him Silvermane.'

'Théon,' the old man growled in warning. Alexan didn't blame him. Her irreverence in such a tense situation was irritating. His own patience was wearing thin already, given it was his life on the line.

But she continued on, unperturbed. 'Alexan is a Darkling, probably sent by my father to kill me, even if he won't admit it. But I figured he wasn't that dangerous, so I just brought him through the wards, within striking distance of my sister, with no precautions.' Her voice was laden with sarcasm as she dropped Alexan's weapons at her feet.

If the old man had been furious before, he was incandescent with rage now. In his temper, his knuckles turned white around the hilt of his sword, and he bared his teeth in warning. 'Théon!' he bellowed, limping forward. 'If you don't give me a straight answer, I swear, by the Gods, I will kill you both!'

Alexan moved, surging to protect her – even if she didn't deserve it after goading the old man. He lifted her by the waist and tossed her behind him, dropping into a defensive crouch over her. Silvermane brought his blade high and slashed downward, the silver blade flashing like lightning through the dark of the night. The blow should have severed Alexan's head from his shoulders. Instead, it glanced off a Casting of solid air. He glanced back and saw Théon on her feet, wind coiling around her in readiness, her eyes pulsing with that awful light once more.

'Drop it,' she breathed, and Alexan shuddered to hear her father's menace touch her lips again. The old man stepped back but made no move to relinquish his weapon. Her aura flared, and her fingers twitched around it. 'Don't,' she warned him. 'I owe him a life-debt. I can't let you kill him.'

The old man let the sword slip from his grasp. It clattered to the ground with bleak finality, and Silvermane staggered back another step. Illyandi appeared from the doorway in a whirlwind of skirts and golden hair, slipping his arm around her slender shoulders and fixing baleful eyes on Théon. Green, lighter than Diathor's, and flecked through with gold. There was no sign of recognition on that lovely face as she glanced at him. A hundred years was a long time. A Casting flickered between them, glinting like oak leaves in the morning sun. She would shield against her own sister? Interesting.

'You owe Silvermane a life-debt too,' Illyandi was saying. 'Are you going to choose a Darkling over your own grandfather?'

'You can't owe family a life-debt,' Théon snapped, releasing the Casting. 'That's just called family.'

Alexan kept his face impassive. So the old man *was* Théon's kin? If so, she was right. Family were responsible for each other, bound by blood, so the bond of a life-debt was void. That didn't, however, mean that she'd been forced to protect Alexan from Silvermane. Blood was the strongest bond of all. No. For whatever reason, she'd chosen Alexan of her own volition.

'We're your blood,' Illyandi argued. Her voice was lovely, and she did look very much like her mother, but with none of Diathor's warmth and kindness. Théon, by comparison, had her mother's fire. It radiated off her as she stepped up to stand beside him. The gaze with which she pinned the old man was merciless.

'You might be my blood, but it wasn't you who was there for us when we needed you,' she said dispassionately, though Alexan could smell the tension rolling off her.

'And what? This Darkling was?' Silvermane spat.

'Yes!' she snarled.

Stunned silence echoed in response.

'Before the Claiming,' Alexan explained in a dead voice, 'I was a member of the Royal Guard. I swore my life in service to the Elf-Queen and would have gladly given it to defend her. But she bid me save her children instead. Once they were safe, I sought to avenge her death.'

But Silvermane wasn't done. 'And look at what that recklessness has cost you.'

'I knew the risks, old man. I didn't march in there blind, and I regret nothing.'

'You are a fool,' Silvermane hissed, eyeing him with disgust.

Alexan shrugged. He hardly cared what the old bastard thought of him. 'Perhaps. But I'm also still here. There aren't many who've walked into Elucion since the Fall that have walked out again. I haven't survived this long by making rash decisions and acting on impulse.'

'Luck,' the old man spat. 'Nothing but luck and the machinations of a madman. A madman you now serve, General.'

'Skill,' Alexan argued, ignoring the accusation. 'Experience. Cunning. And a tenacity that I learned from a young girl, shamed and shunned by her own family for something beyond her control.'

The old man opened his mouth to argue, but Théon cut him off with an exasperated sigh. 'As touching as all this is, we don't have time for it. Kieyin was here.'

Silvermane gaped, slack-jawed, like she'd slapped him. 'What?'

'You heard. So we don't have time for this. I don't trust a Darkling bound to the King any more than you do, but he saved my life, and right now, we don't have a lot of options. Kieyin will be back eventually with reinforcements, so we need to leave, and I'll sleep a lot better knowing we have another fighter with us on the road.'

The old man hesitated, looking like he wanted to argue but unable to fault her reasoning. 'So be it.'

'A rousing proclamation. Inspiring,' Théon said. She turned to her sister. 'We need to pack. Can you get started while I pull what we need from the byre?' Illyandi nodded and helped the old man back inside, casting a nervous glance over her shoulder at Alexan. Théon blew out a breath. 'That went well.'

'I expected worse,' he admitted. 'The journey will be dangerous.'

She snorted. 'I've been in danger since the moment that monster planted me in my mother's womb. It's my sister I worry about. Even if I trusted you with my life – which I'm not sure I do – I don't know if I can trust you with Illyandi's.'

'I am sworn to defend your family, Théon,' said Alexan. 'I couldn't harm a Princess of Illyol even if I wanted to – no matter who ordered me otherwise.'

Another half-truth. Illyandi was safe enough but, like it or not, Théon was bastard-born Shade-spawn. The oath of the Royal Guard was unlikely to protect her. Still, it seemed to settle some of her nerves at least. He stepped closer and looked down at her with as much reassurance and kindness as he could muster. It wasn't much, but it seemed to help. She smiled sadly up at him.

'Thank you, Alexan. For all of it,' she whispered in a small voice. Perhaps there was some of that shy young girl left in there.

'You need never thank me,' he repeated. 'I swore my life to the Elf-Queen. It is yours. Forever.'

She smiled more broadly now and nodded. 'For my first command – there's a wagon behind the byre. You can hitch one of the horses to it and saddle the other two.'

'Yes, Your Majesty,' he replied with a bow.

She looked him over once more, a wicked grin on her lips. 'I could get used to that. It's always a pleasure to watch handsome men bow to me.'

Alexan blinked. Stared at her in confusion. She only winked and slipped inside, leaving him alone to his tasks.

CHAPTER FIFTEEN

Renila's heart was heavy as she climbed the stairs to the tower one last time. The hours following the Lady's announcement had been most trying. Erion's fury had reached breaking point, and Renila had sent him back to their room before he could say something he would regret. Suriya and Lucan had been distraught but insisted the story they'd told their mother was the truth. There had been no Darkling, no magic, just a childish adventure gone awry.

Renila couldn't believe that her son had done any of the things they said he had, and when she'd spoken to Erion later, he'd stuck by his story. She couldn't bring herself to tell him that the twins had magic, that his story was at least plausible. It would only make their betrayal worse in his eyes.

She'd tried to confront their mother – she was the one who had warned Renila that the twins' magic would surface soon, after all – but the Lady refused to see her. Suriya and Lucan had gone to beg on her behalf, but they hadn't returned. If she knew them at all, they would be too ashamed of their failure to face her.

Not that Renila blamed them. It was unfair to hold children to account for the actions of their parents. The confusion in their stories was frustrating, but the strange thing was that she got the feeling they believed what they were saying. Even more confusing was that Erion wasn't lying. Yet both stories could not be true.

She sighed and stepped out onto the turret. Farran was waiting for her, his shoulders slumped in resignation and his kind, brown eyes weary. He smiled sadly when he saw her and held a hand out. She took it and allowed him to tug her closer. They stood in silence, side by side, watching the sky lighten as the dawn approached.

'I'd offer to speak to her myself, if I thought it would help,' he murmured.

Renila smiled. 'I know you would, but it won't.'

'What happened, Renila?' he asked. She looked up into eyes heavy with frustration, in a kind, handsome face lined with worry, and realised that she loved him. Without any doubt, she loved him. And though he was not hers to love, she decided then to trust him. Besides, what did she have to lose now?

So she told him. Everything. How she had come to the castle. How she knew nothing of her past save what the Lady told her. How the Lady had warned her of the twins' magic and hated Erion with a passion that she could not fathom. Showed him the necklace she wore, the only keepsake from whatever life she had known before. And then she told him what had happened between the twins and Erion, and their conflicting stories of the night's events.

And when she was done, she felt lighter and happier than she had a right to be. Farran was quiet for a long time, his brows lowering as he processed her tale.

'Say something?' she whispered when he remained silent. But he said nothing. Instead, he pulled her to him. With one hand on the small of her back, he pressed her against his chest, while the other cupped her face, tilting it up to look at him. He lowered his head and pressed his lips to hers. The kiss was tender at first, and she froze in shock. But as her surprise subsided, she melted into his arms and sighed in contentment. Her lips parted and Farran groaned as the kiss deepened.

After what seemed like an eternity, he pulled away, resting his forehead against hers and breathing. 'I've wanted to do that since the first moment I laid eyes on you.'

'And now, because I'm leaving, you can,' she murmured without bitterness. He had his reasons, and they were justified. It wasn't fair of her to expect anything else. He was a married man. Cold fear gripped at her heart, and she stepped back rather than tempt either of them again.

'Where will you go?' he asked, keeping hold of her hands.

'I don't know,' she admitted. 'I've never lived anywhere but here. At least not anywhere that I can remember.'

He frowned. 'I have family in Ironden. You could go there. I'll write a letter of recommendation for you – they'll find work for you, I'm sure.'

Renila nodded. 'It's a thought,' she agreed. They fell silent for a while, each memorising the other's face.

'Do you have everything you need?' he asked. 'Food? Water? Warm clothes and blankets?'

She nodded again, fighting against the tears pricking at the back of her eyes, struggling to speak past the lump in her throat. 'Mal sorted us out.'

Frustration was written on his handsome face, and he opened his mouth to speak again. Renila placed her finger against his lips and shook her head. She didn't want to hear the words … not out loud.

She looked past him, her attention turning to the dawn. Sunrise. The time the Lady had set for their departure. But her gaze was drawn away, and she squinted in the early morning sunlight, looking towards the forest.

Out of the rising sun, a rider galloped towards the castle.

His mount was bright, shining white, and he wore light, fine armour that glinted in the dawn. Power pulsed and surged around him, the ground trembling beneath his horse's hooves. Thunder echoed through the keep, a roar of defiance to announce his arrival.

And though she thought she should cower in fear and dread, instead there was only a peculiar swell of hope in her heart.

She didn't need to ask to realise that this wasn't one of Farran's men. His mount was far too fine, and his armour was strange. She was vaguely aware of Farran sounding the alarm behind her. The warning clamour of the bells echoing around the castle grounds, the shouts of the men running to their posts followed by the clatter of the portcullis being lowered. But she paid it little heed, entranced by the approaching stranger.

'Go back to your room and bar the door,' Farran yelled over his shoulder as he bolted down the stairs. 'I'll come for you when it's safe.'

She hesitated. There was a yearning, a desperation, in her chest that she could not explain. But it made her heart pound and her breath catch in her throat as she watched the rider draw closer.

Even from this distance, the barely restrained fury in his face was clear. His storm-black hair snapped behind him like a pennon as he urged his steed faster. But the portcullis clanged shut as he approached, and he pulled up hard with a shout of frustration. Thunder rumbled in the distance, shaking the ground beneath her feet. His horse circled with agitation while he eyed the battlements. A storm raged around him in a peculiar aura that sent chills down her spine. She'd seen something like that before … though where it had been eluded her.

'Gaelan!' he roared. 'I know you're in there! Open this damn gate, or I swear by Athair, I will tear this place down with my bare hands!'

There was a long pause, and his horse continued to pace while he waited. But then, with a reluctant creak, the unmistakable sound of the portcullis being raised echoed up from below. The rider kicked his heels into his mount's flanks, and with a triumphant scream, it thundered into the courtyard.

She ran. Down the stairs and through the kitchen, along the corridors to her room. She threw the door open to find Erion peering out the window at the commotion outside.

'Stay here,' she ordered. Before he could reply, she pulled the door shut and locked it. He wouldn't be happy, but she would deal with his foul mood later. His safety came first. She sprinted down another corridor, to the door that would take her to the side of the courtyard, and slipped out to join the crowd gathered there.

The stranger was in the centre of the courtyard, surrounded by Farran's men, their pikes levelled at him. His horse – a magnificent stallion – pranced and snorted with annoyance but kept out of reach.

But the rider? The rider was perhaps the most beautiful man that Renila had ever seen. He was taller than even Farran, with broad shoulders and the most astonishing face. His hair was as black as night, and his eyes ... his eyes were like a thunderstorm, an ethereal shade that lay somewhere between dark grey and pale purple, churning with power that ached to be unleashed.

Then his gaze fell on Renila, and he stilled. Beneath him, the stallion froze, quivering as the rider's strange aura flickered around them. A sense of familiarity hit Renila like a blow to the gut, and she staggered as though winded from the force of that recognition. But she had no memory of this man.

'Lord Alvar,' came the bitter voice of the Lady. The rider looked away, and his gaze, which had softened at the sight of Renila, turned furious once more. Renila looked towards the source of his ire and saw the proud form of the Lady striding out of the castle, Farran at her side.

'Gaelan,' he snarled.

'Lady Gaelan,' she corrected him, drawing to a halt. 'What are you doing here?'

'You know damn well what I'm doing here,' he growled.

The Lady arched a sardonic brow. 'Stand your men down, Captain,' she ordered Farran. Her gaze found Renila in the crowd, and she scowled.

'Are you sure that's wise, my Lady?' Farran asked. 'We can't be sure that he's trustworthy.'

The Lady snorted, her eyes still on Renila. There was a malicious glint in them that made Renila shiver with fear.

'Of course he's trustworthy,' she said with a smug smile. 'He's my husband.'

The ground had dropped away beneath her feet, stomach lurching as the Lady's words filtered through. But something deep within her chest was screaming with the wrongness of it all. *Liar*, it roared. Heat rose in her cheeks as a rage that she didn't understand coursed through her veins. She couldn't breathe for the fury. Gasping, she staggered backwards, shoving her way back through the crowd. There were eyes on her – Lord Alvar's or the Lady's, she didn't know or care. Unable to see for tears of anger that she could not explain, she grasped blindly for the door.

She stumbled as she slipped back inside. A gust of wind from the court-yard had blown out the torch, but she welcomed the darkness. Hidden from sight and safe once more, she leaned against the wall, savouring the unyielding strength of the stone walls beneath her hands. But as she relaxed and her temper cooled, a fathomless despair came crashing down around her. A broken sob escaped her lips, and she slid to the floor. The icy flagstones were an anchor as wave upon wave of sorrow and guilt surged over her. Threatened to drown her in a sea of emotions that made no sense at all.

When those inexplicable tears had run dry, she wiped her eyes and ran a hand through her hair in frustration. Why had the sight of a complete stranger caused such a swell of hope? And why, then, had hearing the Lady claim him as her husband made her so angry? Why did this Lord Alvar make her feel so much regret that the weight of it threatened to crush her?

With a sigh, she got to her feet. She might not know the answers, but she knew who would. But before she could demand those answers, she had things that needed seeing to. So she squared her shoulders and returned to her rooms.

Erion was sitting in her armchair by the fire, facing the door, wearing a scowl with his arms folded across his chest. Renila regarded him as she closed the door behind her and leaned back against it.

'Someone has just arrived at the castle,' she said. Erion pulled a face that said he'd gathered as much, and he'd rather she just cut to the chase. With a deep breath, she continued. 'The Lady's husband.'

Erion stilled, and his expression faded from one of anger to one of shock, then to one of hurt and jealousy. His eyes swirled between storm-grey and ferocious wolf-yellow as emotions warred within him. Renila could only watch on while he struggled with the revelation. She realised it would hurt him to see the twins reunited with their father when he knew nothing of his, and likely never would. But Renila couldn't shake the hope that Lord Alvar's arrival had brought. Perhaps he might overturn the Lady's decision to cast them out?

'What's he like?' Erion asked.

Renila stared into the fire. 'He seems like a powerful man,' she murmured, thinking back to that flickering aura. Erion's eyes swirled to green as he frowned at her. She smiled and shrugged. 'His stallion's the biggest horse I've ever seen – even bigger than Storm.'

That got her son's attention. 'I don't believe it!'

Renila chuckled at his indignant expression.

'It's true,' she assured him. 'The Lady didn't seem happy to see him. I don't think she'll notice if we delay our departure a little. Besides, he might feel differently about us.'

'So we might not have to leave?'

She heaved a sigh and rose. 'Maybe. I'll try. But I'd prefer it if you'd stay here. You're safer out of sight.'

Erion scowled but nodded in agreement. Renila smiled and squeezed his shoulder in reassurance before turning to leave. She paused on the threshold as Erion spoke, his voice quiet and broken.

'Why does she hate me so much?' he whispered. Renila flinched from the hurt in his voice, even as rage and bitter loathing for the woman who caused him such pain flared. She hesitated. She could lie to him, try to soothe his injured soul. But he had confided in her, and she would not repay that trust with dishonesty.

'I'm not sure,' she admitted. 'But I won't ever let her hurt you, Erion.'

Her son said nothing, but a pale light flickered in his grey eyes, like sunlight shimmering through the thinnest cracks of a thundercloud. Renila drew herself to her full height, pulling her rage around her like armour, before she slipped through the door and locked it behind her once more.

Though the hallways lacked the panic that had filled them the night the twins had disappeared, they maintained the same buzz of nervous chatter that set her teeth on edge. Word had spread, and now everyone was hoping to glimpse the Lady's mysterious husband. Farran was nowhere to be seen, but it was for the best. He wouldn't be happy that she'd defied his orders. Again. She didn't care, any more than she cared for the whispers and open stares that followed her as she stalked through the castle. Let them say what they wanted about her, think what they pleased. All she cared for was Erion's safety.

She flitted into an empty room, leaving the noise of the crowds behind her, and scanned around to get her bearings, then allowed herself a small triumphant smile. The children weren't the only ones aware of the secret passages. She darted across the room and pulled a tapestry aside, sparing a glance at the image. A warrior woman cloaked in raven feathers standing on the field of battle. How appropriate. Then she slipped through the door hidden behind it.

Engulfed in darkness, she moved through the shadows with certainty. As she passed the twins rooms, she paused long enough to open the hidden door a crack and peer inside. A maid was helping Suriya dress while Lucan paced. Despite the tension in their shoulders and worry on their faces, they seemed well enough. No doubt they'd heard of their father's arrival and were anxious about meeting him. She didn't blame them. She couldn't imagine how she'd feel meeting her father for the first time. A pang of regret washed through her. She should be with them. It pained her to think she might not be able to help them through this.

She retreated into the black of the passage and continued onward, navigating the labyrinth by memory. She slowed as she approached the Lady's chambers, the sound of raised voices drifting through the cracks. The Lord and Lady's argument had continued in her absence.

Some instinct told her to quieten her mind and hide it from sight. She didn't stop to doubt it. She'd learned long ago that her instincts were rarely wrong, and the Lady had an eerie ability to recognise what she was thinking. She closed her eyes, turning her attention inward, and stilled her thoughts. Imagined them shrouded in shadow, fading into the darkness like a wraith. She didn't even dare to breathe as she inched closer.

'Will you calm down?' the Lady was hissing. Renila lowered herself to the floor and peered through a crack in the wall. The Lady was sitting in her chair by the fire while Lord Alvar paced in front of her, thunder and lightning flashing around him once more. He growled in response and refused to stop pacing, but the aura faded. With a sharp sigh of exasperation the Lady continued. 'Why have you come?'

'You know damn well why,' he snapped. 'Layol sent me. Once again, you appear to have bitten off far more than you can chew.'

'All I asked of Layol was that he clean up his own damn mess,' she said.

But he ignored her. 'What was that performance about our marital status for?' he snarled, as he rounded on her, those ethereal purple-grey eyes glowing with barely restrained fury. The Lady didn't flinch.

'I realise it was more than a few years ago now, and that you like to pretend it never happened. But there are a few witnesses still with us who remember the exchange of vows at our wedding,' she sneered.

'The woman I made those promises to died a long time ago,' he spat, folding his arms across his chest. 'You're just the cold-hearted bitch who wears her face.'

The Lady smirked, but there was no humour in her eyes. 'I ceased caring for your opinion about the same time you let your father lock me away in that tower. So I suggest you shut your mouth, or I will shut it for you.'

'You didn't frighten me then, and you don't frighten me now, Gaelan,' he breathed.

She stood, drawing herself to her full impressive height as she stared him down.

'Well, I should,' she warned him, her voice quiet and all the more menacing for it, 'because as you so delicately pointed out, I do know why you're here. And it has nothing to do with either me or Layol. She's always been your weakness, Alvar, since the day he dropped her in your lap, and now I hold her life in the palm of my hand.' Lord Alvar was silent as he held her gaze, and Renila could practically smell the emotions warring within him. But then the set of his shoulders changed. It was almost imperceptible, but she recognised defeat when she saw it.

'What do you want?' he said.

The Lady smirked again. 'What I want is for Layol to remove his *mess* from my home, but apparently that is not going to happen any point soon. So I'll settle for you staying here and helping me keep those children hidden, until such time as Layol deigns to do as he's told. Even if that means asking you to play the husband you always failed to be and the father you never were.'

'And if I do that, you'll set her free. You'll give her back to me?' he asked.

The Lady's malicious smile broadened, and she closed the distance between them. She leaned in and hissed in his ear, 'I didn't take her from you. She left of her own accord. Came begging me to hide her. And now you are nothing but a stranger to her. She's free to leave any time she wants – but good luck convincing her to go anywhere with you.'

Renila couldn't see Lord Alvar's face, but the dark glee on the Lady's made her shiver with fear. And as the Lady swept from the room, Renila felt a huge swell of pity for the handsome Lord she left in her wake. Then the door closed behind her and he dropped his face into his hands, fingers fisting in his hair and shoulders shaking with silent sobs.

Something inside her longed to go to him, to hold him in her arms and whisper soft assurances in his ear. But she shook herself. He was the Lady's husband, even if they were estranged. Besides, he was a complete stranger.

Stranger. Renila blinked as the Lady's words filtered through and understanding dawned. *You are nothing but a stranger to her,* she had said. *She left of her own accord ...* Could it be that the Lady was referring to her? Was Lord Alvar the reason she had come to the castle seeking shelter in the dead of night? Did he know who she was? Where she came from?

A cold, sinking feeling crept into her bones. Was he the one she was running from? If she was the one the Lady was referring to, it sounded that way. But as she watched Lord Alvar pull himself together, she doubted it. Some instinct told her he was kind, and as she watched him struggle with his pain, she thought that despite his wrath, he was at heart a gentle soul. But more than that, there was no hiding from the feelings of hope and affection that he stirred in her – inexplicable though they were.

A stranger he might be. But every fibre of Renila's being screamed for her to trust him. The Lady's husband or not ... she had to know the truth.

Captain Farran was pacing outside her door when she returned to her rooms. His handsome face was lined with worry, but that concern faded at the sight of her – only to be replaced by annoyance, no doubt remembering that she'd ignored his orders. Again.

'Are you incapable of doing as you're told?' he growled.

'Sometimes,' she admitted, holding the door open for him. Erion looked up from the book he was reading when they entered and, looking past Farran, raised a quizzical eyebrow at his mother. Renila shook her head, and though his eyes swirled to green, he shrugged and turned his attention back to his book.

'At least you're being honest about it,' Farran grumbled, oblivious to the exchange.

'How can I help you, Captain?' Renila asked. He glanced at Erion, but Renila remained impassive. Whatever he had to say to her, he could say in front of her son. Though she kept a respectable distance between them.

'The Lady has reconsidered your banishment,' he said. 'With Lord Alvar's arrival, she finds she can no longer spare either you or the boy.'

Erion snorted. 'Hard to believe.'

Farran blinked, stunned by the boy's apparent impertinence. But try as she might, Renila couldn't halt the smile that rose to her lips as she swelled with pride. Where grown men might falter, her son continued, refusing to cower to anyone. She could hardly believe he was hers.

'She mentioned you specifically,' Farran said to Erion, when he found his voice at last.

It was Renila's turn to gape in shock. She looked between the grim-faced Captain and Erion whose eyebrows had disappeared up into his hair with surprise.

'What?' she demanded.

Farran shrugged and crossed his arms. 'Lord Alvar requires a squire,' he explained, 'but the only one with any experience is Olly. So she's assigned him to look after her husband and given me leave to select and train a replacement. She suggested Erion.'

'What?' Renila exclaimed again.

Erion closed his book with a snap and held the Captain's gaze, his eyes swirling between green and yellow.

'What's her game?' he asked. 'What's she trying to do?'

Farran frowned and stood up straighter. 'The Lady honours you with such an opportunity. I suggest you show a little more respect.'

Renila held her breath but said nothing as Erion leaned back in his seat and studied the Captain. He had picked this fight. She would not humiliate him by interfering. It was his to win or lose by himself.

'Respect is earned,' he said. 'And you must think highly of yourself, Captain, if you believe I should find training to be your squire an honour.'

There was a muscle leaping in Farran's jaw as he stared the boy down. But there was something in Erion's eyes that made him falter. Pursing his lips, Farran took a deep breath and nodded. 'A fair point well made,' he conceded. 'She wants you kept out of Lord Alvar's way. If you're training with me, you'll be too busy to get underfoot.'

'And Lord Alvar likes to ride, so keeping me busy in the stables won't cut it,' Erion continued for him.

Farran smiled, and Renila could have sworn that respect and a touch of pride glimmered in his eyes when he inclined his head in agreement.

'I think you and I will get along just fine,' he said.

But Erion wasn't finished. 'That depends ... What are you intentions towards my mother?'

'Erion!' Renila scolded, stepping between them. But her son ignored her, his eyes settling to ferocious-yellow as he held the Captain's gaze. She turned to Farran, her cheeks flaming with embarrassment. But the sad set of Farran's mouth stopped her in her tracks.

'I love your mother very much,' he admitted, 'and had we met fifteen years ago, I would have asked her to be my wife.'

'Farran,' Renila breathed.

But he ignored her, speaking to her son as he continued. 'But we didn't, and instead, I was pressured into an arranged marriage. I have no love for my wife, but honour is my code, and I made a vow to her the day I wed her. No matter how much I may wish to take the words back, I don't know that I have it in me to break them.'

'So you have no intentions towards my mother?' Erion asked. Farran glanced at Renila then and smiled, a smile that made her heart flutter, and her breath catch in her throat.

'I didn't say that,' Farran murmured, still looking at Renila. She felt her cheeks warm once more under the intensity of his gaze. He took a deep breath and looked back to Erion. 'But I cannot act on any of my intentions while I am still married.'

Erion nodded in understanding and stood, offering his hand to Farran. 'You're a good man, Captain, and should circumstance ever change, then I would be happy to call you father,' he said.

Farran smiled and shook the proffered hand while Renila blinked in confusion.

'Thank you,' Farran said, clapping a hand on the boy's shoulder. 'Now, off down to the stores with you. I need my new squire properly attired. I'll meet you in the training ground for your first lesson in an hour.'

Erion grinned and darted from the room, pausing to give his mother a fierce hug. As the door closed behind him, Farran chuckled while Renila collapsed onto her bed in shock, throwing her arm over her face to hide her embarrassment.

'I'm not sure I like the thought of you two spending so much time together,' she said darkly.

'He's quite a serious boy, isn't he?' Farran laughed. Renila made an indelicate noise in response. He only laughed harder. The bed shifted as he sat down beside her. She peered out from under her arm to see him looking down at her, mischief glinting in his warm brown eyes.

'If you lied to my son, there will be trouble,' she warned.

Farran grinned and leaned over her.

'I didn't lie,' he promised. Then his lips met hers, and she forgot herself for quite some time.

When she could finally think straight, she said, 'You told him you couldn't act on any of your intentions while you were still married.'

'I didn't intend to kiss you,' he assured her, 'but your lips looked so inviting that I couldn't help myself.'

'Sophistry,' she argued, scowling. 'You're a married man, and you promised Erion that you had no intention of being unfaithful to your wife.'

Farran sighed but rolled over and stood up from the bed, offering a hand to help her sit up. 'I love you, Renila,' he said, 'and my honour demands I remain faithful to Breag. But this morning I thought I would never see you again, and my heart was so hurt by that thought that my honour was pushed aside. And now, I cannot forget the taste of your lips, nor the feel of you in my arms.' He broke off, running a frustrated hand through his hair.

'Farran—' she began, but he cut her off.

'It's not just that,' he continued. 'Erion is the son I always dreamed of having. To be around you both … It feels as though the Gods are giving me a second chance.'

Renila stood and went to him, allowing him to pull her to his chest as she gazed up at him. 'You are our second chance too,' she breathed. 'Be careful with him, will you? He'll try to hide it, and deny it if you ask, but he is sick. He tires easily, and each day is worse than the last.'

'I'll care for him as if he were my own,' Farran promised and then kissed her again.

They were interrupted by a sharp knock on the door. Farran smoothed his hair as he crossed to the door, glancing back to see she had composed herself. The rueful look on his face told her there would be no hiding what had transpired, but he took a deep breath and opened the door.

There, in the hall, stood Lord Alvar.

Farran was the first to react, bowing as he held the door open for his Lord. But Renila was transfixed by those purple-grey eyes that regarded her, noting the disarray of her hair and the just-kissed flush of her lips. Those thundercloud eyes darkened, and Lord Alvar scowled. He turned his attention to Farran, releasing her from the spell of his terrifying gaze. Remembering herself, she dropped into a low curtsey.

'Captain Farran, I presume?' he asked.

Farran straightened and nodded.

'How may I help you, my Lord?'

'You could explain why you're here and not in your office? Or on the training field with your men. Or anywhere else that one might expect to find the Captain of the Guard?' he snapped. Renila didn't dare look up, but she knew Farran's cheeks would be flushed with a mix of anger and embarrassment.

'My apologies, my Lord,' he replied. 'I came to deliver a message from the Lady – Renila's son is to become my new squire.'

Lord Alvar's eyes snapped to Renila. 'Your son?' Renila nodded, keeping her eyes on the floor. The Lord was quiet for a long moment, and when he spoke, his voice was shaking. 'How old is he?' he asked. Renila glanced up then and quailed at the strength and range of emotions churning in those eyes. Rage, grief, guilt, shock, love …

'Twelve, my Lord,' she whispered, unable to find any strength in her voice. He flinched but didn't look away.

'What's his name?' the Lord asked, unshed tears glittering in his eyes.

'Erion,' she answered. Lord Alvar staggered and gripped the door frame for support. Renila and Farran exchanged a worried glance, and Farran reached for the Lord. But Alvar wrenched out of his grasp.

'I'm fine,' he snarled. 'Return to your post, Captain.'

Farran looked between Lord Alvar and Renila, but when the Lord let out a warning growl, he bowed and made to leave.

He paused on the threshold and glanced back at Renila. 'Sorry, I forgot – the Lady also wanted me to tell you to report to Mal in the morning,' he told her with a guilty frown. Then he left. Lord Alvar entered the room and closed the door behind him.

'Get up, Renila,' he ordered. 'I'm not my *wife*. Don't ever grovel in front of me again.'

Renila stood, her legs trembling. She didn't ask how he knew her name. She had once thought the Lady to be terrifying, but this man was something else. If she had run away from him, she was beginning to understand why.

'Yes, my Lord,' she murmured. Lord Alvar crossed the room and gripped her chin between long fingers, forcing her head up to look at him. He was breathtakingly handsome. At a glance, he looked perhaps thirty – perhaps younger – with sun-kissed skin that bordered on bronze. His nose was long and straight, and his lips were pressed into a stern line. His jaw and cheekbones looked sharp enough to cut with, and his eyes were the most terrifyingly beautiful thing she had ever seen. But they were full of unimaginable rage and pain.

She had seen eyes like those before. Years ago, there had been an old man living in the castle. Farran's predecessor – an old soldier who had fought in several wars over his long life. His eyes had always fascinated and horrified Renila. They were eyes that had seen too much and lived too long. Lord Alvar's eyes were the same. Though how such a young man could have eyes that were so old was beyond her.

His fingers were warm against her skin, and she felt something stir in her gut at the contact. Some strange part of her yearned towards it, but the other part – the part that loved Farran – recoiled.

'Don't call me that,' he begged. 'My name is Alvar. Please. Use it.'

'The Lady would have me flogged if I dared to show such familiarity with my Lord,' she warned him, stepping back. Alvar's shoulders slumped, though his eyes flashed again.

'Raiden help me, how did you become so meek?' he whispered, almost to himself. Then he shook himself and held her gaze. 'The *Lady* isn't here, and I won't tell her if you don't.'

Renila hesitated, but she needed to keep him close if she was to find out the truth. 'Alright,' she agreed. 'Please, Lord Alvar, would you like to sit?' He rolled his eyes at her compromise but lowered himself into the proffered chair.

'You never could do as you were told,' he muttered, stretching his long legs out in front of the fire.

Renila blinked and sat across from him. 'How do you know that?'

Alvar glanced up, his eyes filled with unfathomable sorrow. 'It's a long story.'

'I like stories,' she said, with a mischievous grin twitching on her lips. She caught herself and leaned back in her chair. The Lady really would have her flogged if she saw such behaviour. It was not her place.

'I know,' Alvar said, 'but that's not why I'm here. Gaelan and I are dining with the children tonight … I can't imagine it will be easy for them and they shouldn't have to face this alone. The stable boy said you were closest to them of anyone here, so I was hoping you would join us?'

Renila stared. 'The Lady dismissed me from their service,' she explained. 'As you heard, I've been reassigned to the kitchens. It would not be appropriate for me to dine with the family.'

'I don't care about what's appropriate,' Alvar snapped. 'This is my home too – I can override Gaelan's orders and have you assigned to the twins if that's what you want?'

'The Lady won't like it,' she whispered. Alvar leaned forward and held her gaze.

'*Fuck* what the Lady likes,' he breathed. He stood in a fluid, elegant motion and smirked down at her. 'See you at dinner. Wear something nice,' he said with a wink. Then he turned and left.

CHAPTER SIXTEEN

Lucan fidgeted with the cuff of his shirt sleeve while he waited for Suriya to join him. They'd been woken at dawn by the tolling of the warning bell and only learned much later that it had signalled Lord Alvar's arrival ... their mother's husband. Their father.

The Lady had refused to let them meet him so far. Not long after he'd arrived, she had appeared in their room in a foul mood and instructed a legion of servants to remove all the contents of their suite. Their rooms were to be given to the Lord of the castle.

Now they each had a room of their own. In fairness to their mother, they'd at least been allowed to remain close to each other, separated only by a short hallway, in the two rooms nearest each other in the castle that were not part of an adjoining suite. Suriya appeared less pleased about the situation than he was. But then, he was being given lessons with Captain Farran, while she was facing days alone cooped up in the castle with their mother.

As if summoned by the thought, her bedroom door opened, and his sister stepped out into the hallway. His jaw fell open in shock – the maids had been busy. He hardly recognised her.

She was beautiful. Her golden hair was swept up and pinned in a mass of curls and braids on the back of her head. She wore an exquisite gown of rose-gold silk, embroidered with dark bronze thread that covered the fitted bodice in swirling flames. The design caught his attention, some instinct telling him it was important, but he couldn't think why. Around her throat was a necklace he had never seen before. The chain was a delicate rope of rose-gold and, in the pendant, was set a large, dark garnet that seemed to flicker as if a candle burned within.

'Yes?' she snapped.

Realising that he was still staring, Lucan closed his mouth with an audible snap and shrugged. 'Sorry. You just look ... different.'

Part of him wanted to laugh at her for looking so much the part of the

Lady's daughter, but he was stunned – and not a little perturbed – by her transformation. Suriya scowled. She was just as uncomfortable wearing the dress as he was seeing her in it.

'You're not much better,' she retorted, gesturing at his own outfit. He had to agree. He'd been forced into a pair of smoke-grey trousers, which were tucked into a polished pair of boots he hadn't even known he owned. And completing the outfit was a shirt of silver satin and a waistcoat of dark blue velvet embroidered with silver thread. His buttons were all set with moonstones that matched his eyes, and his hair had been brushed until it gleamed. As Suriya's eyes skirted his forehead, he remembered that the maid had smoothed his hair back from his brow. He scowled, ruffling it forward to cover his birthmark.

'Shall we?' he asked, offering her his arm. She took it and allowed him to lead her downstairs.

They'd been summoned to dinner. Given the clothes, they could only assume it was to be with the Lord and Lady. Suriya was nervous. He could feel her hand trembling on his arm, and her breathing was shallow and rapid. If he was being honest, he shared her discomfort. His own heart was hammering in his chest, and he felt like he might throw up at any moment.

'What if he doesn't like us?' Suriya whispered, voicing the fear in both their minds.

Lucan glanced sideways at her but kept walking and tried not to sound too bitter. 'If this is the first time we're meeting the man, I'm not sure he gets to have an opinion. I just hope he lets Renila and Erion stay.'

'Gods,' Suriya swore. 'I'd almost forgotten. Do you think Erion will ever forgive us?'

'I don't know what there is to forgive,' Lucan sighed. 'He's the one making ridiculous accusations. I mean, come on? Magic and Darklings? They're fairy tales, Renila's bedtime stories.'

'But he believed what he was saying,' Suriya said, stopping and tugging him round to face her. 'Erion wouldn't lie, Lucan – not to us.'

He frowned. She wasn't wrong. Something tugged at his memory, but a haze descended, making it hard for him to think. He shook his head to clear it and sighed in frustration. It had become a regular occurrence since their adventure in the Ravenswood. Whenever he tried to remember what had happened, his mind just turned to mush. 'Maybe he's telling the truth. Maybe we're remembering wrong?' he reasoned before the smog thickened once more. He shook his head again. 'Never mind,' he muttered, turning away.

But Suriya held him fast. 'You're getting it too, aren't you?'

He didn't need to ask what she meant. 'It's like the winter fogs … when it gets so thick you can barely see your hand in front of your face.'

'And it clings to every thought, muddles them around when you try to remember what happened?' she continued for him. He didn't need to answer. She knew him well enough to read it on his face.

'What happened to us?' he muttered. Then he ran a hand through his hair in frustration. 'How could anything do that to us?'

Suriya's eyes skirted his birthmark again, and he saw a glimmer of understanding dawn there. But before he could press her on it, she said, 'A better question is, why isn't Erion affected?'

He opened his mouth to answer but was interrupted by the sound of footsteps approaching. Captain Farran rounded the corner, dressed in his uniform with the Lady's crest – a silver owl crowned in starlight against a sky of midnight-blue – emblazoned on his chest. Lucan frowned. The Captain almost never wore his full uniform. But Lucan wasn't given the time to think on it.

'Come on, you two,' Farran said, shooing them down the hall. 'Your mother is waiting.'

The twins sighed with distaste but allowed themselves to be chased into the dining room.

The long table was covered with a cloth of midnight velvet and set with chargers and goblets of solid silver. Tapers flickered in matching candlesticks, and there was a fire roaring in the hearth. The Lady herself was nowhere to be seen, but Lord Alvar stood by the fire staring into its depths. His head was bowed, shoulders slumped, but as the twins entered, he straightened and turned to face them. His expression was grim, but not unkind. Suriya curtseyed while Lucan bowed.

'Please – you need not bow to me,' Lord Alvar murmured. His voice was deep but melodic and enchanting, and though he had spoken gently, Lucan felt his cheeks flush with embarrassment.

'I'm sorry, Father,' he said, looking at his feet. Lord Alvar winced at the address, but he crossed the room and placed a reassuring hand on Lucan's shoulder.

'Don't be,' he said. 'You must be Lucan?'

Lucan smiled and nodded, gazing up into the face of his father. 'Yes, sir,' he managed to whisper. Lord Alvar smiled and ruffled his hair before turning to Suriya.

'Which would make you Suriya?' Unable to find her voice and still trembling, she could only nod once. Lord Alvar frowned as he looked between the two of them. Then he knelt, taking their hands in his own. 'You need never fear me,' he told them. 'I am not the Lady Gaelan, and I will never ask you to be anything other than what you are. I know very little about either of you, but I am already proud of you both.'

'Really?' Lucan whispered despite himself.

Lord Alvar nodded.

'Look at you both,' he breathed, looking up at them in wonder. 'Like the sun and the moon, lighting up the darkness. You have my love and my trust, and I hope that one day you can bless me with the same gifts in return.'

An icy voice spoke from behind them. 'Very sweet. But why is the table set for six?' Lord Alvar's purple-grey eyes darkened, and he stood, turning to face the Lady.

'I asked Renila to join us,' he said, 'after I reinstated her as Suriya and

Lucan's nursemaid. I thought it might be easier for them if they had a kind, familiar face present.'

The Lady's face turned ugly, and there was murder in those terrifying eyes. 'First, Suriya and Lucan have decided that they no longer wish to be treated as children and therefore do not require a nursemaid. And second, that would only account for one of the extra two places. Who is the other one for?'

'My understanding was that Renila had a son – a boy named Erion who is a good friend of both Suriya and Lucan. I assumed he would join us,' said Lord Alvar, but Lucan could hear the hard edge of warning in there.

The Lady, however, ignored it. 'Not a chance. That boy is nothing but trouble. I will not tolerate him at my table.'

'It's my table too, Gaelan,' Lord Alvar warned. Then he paused and took a deep breath. 'Besides, the place is already set.'

The Lady Gaelan opened her mouth to argue, but the door opened once more and through it stepped Captain Farran with Renila on his arm.

Lucan's jaw fell open for the second time that evening. If Suriya was beautiful, Renila was magnificent. Her wild mane of wine-red curls was partially pinned up, barely contained by a few delicate braids while the rest tumbled down her back. She wore a gown of cream velvet, trimmed with gold, that hugged her hips and waist but left her shoulders bare. Around her neck was a chain of fine gold, a pendant shaped like a bird in flight lying over her heart.

Suriya reached over and closed his mouth, elbowing him in the side to get his attention as she looked at Lord Alvar. Lucan glanced over but shrugged in confusion. Their father looked just as surprised by Renila's transformation as the rest of them. Suriya rolled her eyes but let it go.

Renila glanced at Lord Alvar, but the nervousness of that look was nothing compared to the fear in her eyes when she looked to the Lady Gaelan. Lucan followed her gaze and felt his own heart beat just a little faster at the rage in his mother's eyes. He didn't understand it. Was his mother worried that Renila was prettier than her? He'd heard that women worried about such things, but he'd never understood it. His mother and Renila were both beautiful, in their own ways. He wasn't sure one was better than the other. Wasn't it just a matter of opinion?

Suriya nudged him again, though it felt more like she had nudged his mind than his ribs, and he glanced back to Lord Alvar. Then he understood. Lord Alvar thought Renila was more beautiful than the Lady. The thought made Lucan irrationally angry. Was this the reason his father had been absent his entire life? Did Lord Alvar love Renila more than his own wife? Scowling, he crossed the room and sat beside his mother in an impulsive display of loyalty.

The Lady blinked in surprise. She stared at him for a moment before a rare smile twitched on her lips. The transformative power that smile had was astounding. The warmth of it cracked the icy surface that made her so remote, and the light of her shone through. He took her hand under the table and squeezed it. There was a moment of hesitation, but then her cool fingers tightened around his, and she nodded in thanks. They glanced around together, to see if anyone had witnessed the exchange. Lucan knew Suriya had, but Lord Alvar and Captain Farran were still fixated on Renila.

'Will your son be joining us?' Lord Alvar was asking.

'I didn't think that would be a good idea,' she whispered with a nervous glance at the Lady. Lucan felt his mother stiffen beside him, but she remained silent.

'Captain Farran,' Lucan called out. 'Why don't you join us?'

Suriya looked at him incredulously as she slid into the seat opposite him, and the Captain started in shock, looking to the Lady for direction. But she just inclined her head and gestured to the seat next to Lucan.

'Shall we?' asked Lord Alvar, pulling the chair next to Suriya out for Renila. Farran scowled as he watched Lord Alvar seat Renila, but he said nothing as he lowered himself into the place the Lady had indicated. Lord Alvar sat at the end of the table, opposite the Lady. Between Renila and Farran.

Lucan's mother said nothing, but he could sense the tension rolling off her in waves as she raised an imperious hand to signal to the waiting servants. Lucan looked at his sister, who pulled a face in response. This was going to be an interesting meal.

Under different circumstances, Suriya might have sighed in contentment at the pleasantly full feeling in her belly. Dinner had been delicious – a starter of creamy chestnut soup with warm bread, goat's cheese and smoked duck breast; then a course of trout wrapped in bacon with a salad of summer greens; followed by a whole suckling pig stuffed with apples and mushrooms, covered in a rich plum sauce and served with buttered leeks and roasted carrots.

She was fit to burst when the servants entered the room and placed her dessert before her. Pears poached in wine and honey, strawberries and cream, and apple tarts shaped like budding roses. At least Lucan would polish off anything she wasn't able to eat. Her brother had wolfed down everything that had been set in front of him with reckless abandon. The thought of it turned her stomach.

Lucan glanced up and met her eye, blushing. She gave a quiet sigh of exasperation and smiled at him. But inside, she was worried. More and more it appeared he could read her thoughts, even when he wasn't looking at her. And the opposite was also true. Sometimes, it was as if she knew what Lucan was thinking before he did. As if their minds had become entangled somehow, if such a thing was even possible. It had all started—

The fog closed in around her once more, and she shook her head to clear it, but she knew it wouldn't work. Nothing worked. No matter how hard she tried, whenever she thought about that night in the Ravenswood, her thoughts grew muddled and confused. Like she was drowning.

Sensing eyes on her, she glanced up. Her mother was looking at Lucan with a curious expression on her face. At the other end of the table, Farran and Renila were still trying to avoid looking at each other. She almost snorted out loud. Something had changed between them, and they were mad if they thought no one else noticed. She'd known that Renila and Farran had feelings for each other since she was about five years old. While part of her disapproved of Farran's apparent disregard for his vows, a larger part was pleased – they both deserved happiness. But there was a sinking in her stomach that warned that happiness might be short-lived. Lord Alvar seemed less than pleased about the tender glances between the two dinner guests on either side of him. He'd been in a foul temper ever since Renila had entered on Farran's arm. His dark mood had grown more noticeable with each course as Renila paid less attention to him and focussed more on the handsome Captain across from her.

Suriya's gaze drifted to the end of the table, and she saw Lord Alvar watching her. She looked back to her plate as her cheeks warmed with embarrassment, but the prickling sensation on the back of her neck told her he was still studying her. She reached for her goblet – filled only with water – to hide her face while she considered him.

He was not their father, that much was clear to her. He looked nothing like them, with his black hair and strange purple-grey eyes that churned like storm clouds. At least the Lady could, perhaps, have passed for Lucan's mother, but only at a glance. While they shared similar traits in their silvery hair and blue eyes, they were not the same.

Besides, their faces weren't similar. Neither she nor Lucan looked anything like their mother, but they at least looked like each other. Lord Alvar's description of them as the sun and the moon was apt, she realised, as she studied her brother over the rim of her goblet. When they'd been younger, Lucan's face had been like a mirror to her own. Now, the differences were more obvious. But they shared the same cheekbones, the set of their eyes, the full mouth with the top lip almost too plump for the bottom. Apart from their colouring, they were near identical. She had known for years that neither of them looked like their mother, had always assumed that they looked like their father. But whoever their father was, it wasn't Lord Alvar. The man's face was nothing like theirs.

She glanced up at him again and was struck by a sense of familiarity. Though she could not place where, she knew she had seen his face before. She met his eye and his lips twitched, as if he were resisting laughter. She wondered if he could read her thoughts, like her mother sometimes could.

He winked.

Suriya went still.

Instinct had her itching towards her brother. If only there were some way she could speak to him without alerting the Lady.

'Lucan,' she whispered inside her head, praying for her brother to look at her. But out of the corner of her eye, she saw Lord Alvar shake his head imperceptibly, warning her to silence. And when she noticed her mother's attention on her, she realised why.

The Lady was watching her, her brows creased in thought.

'Suriya,' she said, 'are you alright?'

'I think I ate too much,' she admitted, patting her stomach.

Lucan was watching her now, his concern loud enough that it almost seemed he was speaking straight into her mind. *What's wrong?*

She could hear his voice in her head. How was that possible? The fog descended upon her once more, and she shook her head, begging it to clear. It made her sick. It was a sweet, cloying mist that clung to every facet of her mind, making it sluggish. She panicked, thrashing around in her mind as she tried to get free of it.

Quiet, she begged him, fear setting in as the Lady Gaelan tensed beside her. *We must be quiet.*

What's happening? Lucan asked. *Why can I hear your voice in my head?*

Lucan, be quiet! Suriya screamed. *It's not safe!*

'Suriya?' he said out loud, reaching across the table for her.

Beside her, Renila took her hand and squeezed. 'Suriya, what's wrong?'

'I feel sick,' she mumbled, staggering to her feet. There was no way out, no way through the fog as she tried to remember. Her heart was pounding, every instinct in her body screaming at her, but her mind was in chaos. She couldn't think, couldn't breathe. The room was spinning.

Then a pair of strong hands closed around her arms and cool fingers brushed her brow. 'It's alright, I'm here,' Lord Alvar breathed in her ear. Then powerful arms were around her, lifting her and cradling her against a broad, warm chest. Then all she knew was darkness.

Lucan paced in the corridor outside Suriya's room. After she'd fainted, their father had carried her to her room and closed the door behind him. He'd allowed their mother in, but he was clearly furious with her about something. Renila waited outside with Lucan, though Captain Farran had needed to return to his post.

'What's taking so long?' Lucan muttered. He needed to see his sister. Needed to understand what had happened. How he had been able to hear her voice in his head.

'She needs rest,' Renila soothed. 'I'm sure they'll let you in soon.'

'She needs me,' he growled.

'I know,' she murmured. 'But you'd know if there was something wrong.'

Lucan froze, staring at her. 'How can you know that?'

'You're special, Lucan,' she breathed, her gaze distant but her voice certain. 'You're both special.'

Lucan had opened his mouth to ask what she meant when the door to Suriya's room banged open, and the Lady stormed out without a word. Lord Alvar appeared in the doorway with a dark look on his face as he watched her leave. He shook his head and turned to look at Renila and Lucan. His expression softened.

'She's awake and asking for you,' he told Lucan with a smile as he stood back and held the door open for him. Lucan looked back at Renila, but she just shooed him forward. As he passed his father, Lord Alvar asked Renila, 'Are you just going to wait out there all night?'

But Lucan didn't wait for Renila's response. He crept closer to his sister's bed. She was still wearing that ridiculous dress, though someone had at least removed the pins from her hair and loosened the tight lacing around her chest. Her face was pale and drawn, but she smiled when he approached.

'Lucan,' her voice whispered in his mind, as if she were too weak to speak aloud.

'I'm here,' he replied. *'How is this happening?'*

'I don't know,' she said. *'But we have to be careful. I don't think it's safe.'*

'Suriya!' Renila interrupted as she joined Lucan at Suriya's bedside. 'How are you?'

His sister smiled. 'Better,' she assured Renila. Her eyes flickered over Lucan's shoulder to where Lord Alvar hovered. Renila's eyes narrowed, but she let it go.

'Well, we should let you rest,' she said, turning to leave.

'How about a bedtime story first?' said Lord Alvar.

Even Lucan noticed Renila flinch.

'I'm not sure that's a good idea,' she remarked. 'The Lady made it quite clear that she didn't approve of my stories.'

Lord Alvar smirked and settled himself into an armchair by the fire, spreading his hands. 'Don't be such a wuss. The Lady isn't even here,' he taunted with a sly grin. Renila's lips twitched in response, but she folded her arms across her chest.

'Please, Renila,' Suriya whispered. Renila sagged and threw her a disgruntled look. Lucan smiled at the guilty flush on his sister's cheek at the manipulation. At least it meant she'd recovered.

'I thought you two wanted to be treated like adults,' Renila commented. 'Adults don't need bedtime stories.'

'I'm an adult, and I need bedtime stories,' Lord Alvar piped up.

Renila glared at him, but he only grinned.

'Fine,' she hissed, settling herself at the foot of the bed. Lucan whooped, wriggling his way under the sheets with Suriya and made himself comfortable. 'Which one would you like?'

Lucan opened his mouth to answer, but Lord Alvar spoke first. 'Tell us about Kah Resari.'

'That's a long story,' Renila noted.

Lord Alvar shrugged. 'I like stories,' he said, his eyes glowing. Something told Lucan that Lord Alvar was quoting Renila's words back at her, but he didn't know how he knew that. Renila scowled at him – all but confirming Lucan's suspicions – and leaned back against the foot of Suriya's bed, gazing off into the distance.

'It was once against the highest laws of the Graced to mingle the bloodlines. It wasn't bigotry that spawned such an edict, but a desire to protect their descendants from the warning their maker had given their ancestors.

'But then came the time of great darkness, when the Shade rose once more to conquer the world. The old ways were lost. Ignorant of their heritage and unaware of the risks, the divisions between the four bloodlines crumbled. Elf married Phoenix, Dragon mated Unicorn – many children died, consumed by powers they could not control. And then came one, within whose veins flowed the blood of all four.

'There have been many Graced warriors, and even a few who have transcended into the realms of legend, but none are so worthy of note as Kah Resari. For she alone had the strength to battle the Shade.

'Born in deepest midwinter, she was the daughter of Kalielle Half-Elven and Kah Thoran. Kalielle laboured for three nights and three days to bring their daughter into the world. She gave her last breath for her child, and Kah Resari was born shrouded amongst ashes and smoke.

'But Kalielle was a Phoenix, and not even death itself could hold her. When she rose from the ashes, she looked down upon what she had made and was glad. Magic did not consume the child, as it had others, for fate had chosen her. She was destined to become the greatest and most powerful of all the Graced – a light who would shine so brightly all darkness would be driven from the land.

'In the skies above, the stars themselves fell like rain from the heavens to herald the child's arrival, and the mightiest of the Graced fell to their knees at the sign. For her birth had been foretold, and they were thankful that she was come, as only she could end the suffering. Legends rose from their slumber, roused by the birth of such power. They travelled through the night so that they might behold the babe, bringing gifts with which to honour her.

'But there was one who feared her more than all others. He was the master of all shadows and brought death and destruction wherever he went. The Shade King, whose name we do not speak. He knew that one day Kah Resari would rise up, and he and his children would perish.

'The years passed, and she grew in grace and might. The magic in her veins was strong, stronger than any of the Graced who had come before her. Even as a child she was deadly to all creatures of the darkness who happened across her. The earth shook beneath her feet wherever she walked, and all who beheld her trembled.

'Knowing that Resari alone had the strength to defeat him, the Shade King sought to destroy her. He had peered into the future and seen that all he had built would be brought low if he did not act. And though she was only a child and would pose no threat to them for many years to come, he knew he had to strike while she was weak. Before she had mastered her powers.

'He sent his creatures of night to find his enemy and break her. She was barely ten years old. Still strong enough to hold her ground and let her friends escape, but even for one as powerful as she, there were too many.

'It was the Lady Kylar who found her body, broken and bent upon an altar. She wept over the body of the child she had failed to protect, and as her tears mingled with the blood of her fallen saviour, the child stirred. She was no longer the same child who had once blessed the world with her quick smiles and sharp wit. Instead, she drew her rage and despair about her like the strongest armour. But she lived, and the Graced were glad, for without her, hope was lost.

'Deep within his dark fortress, the Shade King smiled, for he had seen the girl's weakness. He looked to the stars, asking how he might one day triumph over fate. A single dark star fell from on high, and he laughed at the solution it presented. And all the world trembled at the sound. He would end the girl, even if it meant bringing the once-mighty Graced to their knees.

'The attacks came simultaneously. Darklings and worse swept across the land, slaughtering any who had the misfortune to cross their paths. Brother and sister fought and died back-to-back. Husbands were cut down as they stood over their wives. Mothers fell defending their children with nought but their bodies as a shield. The world drowned in blood that day.

'The Graced, defenders of mankind, fell, and the child who was destined to save them all was lost.'

'But he was not the only one who had searched the heavens. Kalielle knew that her child's life was in danger, now more than ever, and the stars knew that they could not shine through the shadows. They warned her of the Shade King's plans, and Kalielle nodded in understanding. Her child would fall to endless night – there was nothing she could do to prevent that. But she alone, more than any other, knew that so long as but a single ember continued to smoulder, it was possible to fan the flames of a greater power.

'Legend says that the ember is still out there, biding its time as it glows dimly amongst the ashes. Waiting for the single spark that will ignite the fire once more and allow it to burn bright enough to wipe shadows and darkness from the land.'

Renila fell silent, and Lucan risked a glance at his father. Lord Alvar was studying her, as if waiting for her to say more. But she only sighed and stood. 'That's enough for one night. Time for bed.' Lucan scowled and nestled closer to Suriya, daring her to move him.

'Isn't your room down the corridor?' Lord Alvar asked, getting to his feet.

'I wouldn't bother,' Renila told him, chuckling. 'He'll just sneak back later.'

Lord Alvar gave her a tentative smile. 'Alright,' he said. 'It's late. You should get some sleep.'

'I'll get these two ready for bed first,' she said.

'I'll do it,' he insisted. 'I want to stay and watch over Suriya anyway. Go. Get some sleep. Spend time with your boy.'

Renila gave him a peculiar look but curtseyed in thanks and left without a word.

I hope Erion is alright, Suriya whispered into Lucan's mind.

Lucan nodded, watching the door close behind Renila before he replied in kind. He could sense her unease, her desire to keep their conversation secret. Though how he could sense it was beyond him. *'I'm sure he's fine.'*

'I would be careful with that,' Lord Alvar warned them. 'Suriya was right earlier – it's not safe. Until you learn better control, you risk sharing your thoughts with anyone who has the same abilities.'

They were stunned into silence. Lucan could only gape at his father while Suriya stilled beside him.

'How do we learn better control?' she asked.

Lucan looked at her incredulously. He never could fathom how her mind worked. 'Never mind that! How do you know?'

'Because he can do it too,' she snapped, looking to Lord Alvar for confirmation.

He shrugged and leaned against the wall as he considered them. 'Not as well as I used to. That I can hear you at all tells me there's a problem. Either learn to control it or stop it. You'll attract unwanted attention.'

'How do we learn to control it?' Suriya persisted.

Lucan shook his head again. 'What *is* it?' he asked, cutting her off. 'And what sort of unwanted attention?'

'It takes practice and concentration, not to mention a patient teacher,' Lord Alvar said, ignoring Lucan. 'None of which you're likely to find in the middle of the night. So come along, off to bed with you.'

Lucan scowled but allowed his father to help them change and tuck them into the enormous bed in Suriya's room. He sensed the tension in her shoulders and wanted to ask her about what they had just heard, but Lord Alvar stayed true to his word. He pulled up a chair by the fire and gazed into its depths as he began his vigil.

Despite his best efforts to the contrary, it didn't take long for tiredness to claim Lucan, and he slipped into a deep, dreamless sleep.

Suriya, however, did not sleep. Lucan snored beside her, but her mind would not quieten enough to let her rest. She couldn't stop thinking about what had happened after she'd fainted.

Lord Alvar had carried her to her rooms, whispering reassurances in her ear all the while. Once they'd been alone, the sound of his voice had moved from outside to inside her head while he probed her mind for the source of her sickness. She sensed his disgust as he too became snarled up in the cloying fog. Then he had sighed, and the fog had dissipated as if blown away by a strong north wind. He had not deigned to explain any of it, much to her irritation.

When he'd allowed the Lady to enter the room, he'd flown into a terrible rage. Shouting at her for her incompetence. Accusing her of not caring for the children. For abusing her power. Her mother had lasted less than five minutes under the barrage of abuse before she'd turned and stormed from the room.

Now Lord Alvar was sitting in front of the fire, watching over them as the night closed in around them. She continued to feign sleep, even when someone else entered. From the quiet whisper of fabric, Suriya guessed it was a woman. The woman was silent for a while before she spoke.

'How did you find us, Alvar?' asked the Lady, her voice heavy with regret.

'There was a crack in your wards,' he replied. 'Don't worry – I sealed it behind me once I came through. But seems your power is waning. And not even your wards can hide active magic like theirs. Suriya might have been outside of them when she killed that Darkling, but I don't think they could have contained it even if she'd hadn't been. I found what remained of the Darkling, Gaelan. There wasn't much. She's enormously powerful.'

'They both are,' the Lady whispered.

Lord Alvar sighed. 'No wonder you asked for help. With their bloodlines, at this age – it's a miracle they haven't levelled the castle by now. Why aren't you teaching them to control it?'

'It wasn't your help I asked for. And you know the longer they last without it, the safer they'll be.'

'They don't know.' It wasn't a question.

'Of course not.'

'You realise they're entwined?'

She exhaled sharply in frustration. 'How stupid do you think I am?'

'Stupid enough to meddle with their heads when they're already in such a mess.'

'I did what I had to.'

It was his turn to sigh. 'Fix it. Or I will.'

'Fine.'

There was a pause. 'What about Renila?'

'I told you. She has no memory of you.'

'Your doing?'

'Nature's doing ... but at her request.'

'And the boy? Erion?'

The Lady was quiet for a long moment, and Suriya could sense the anger radiating off her mother at the mention of the boy's name. Then the Lady sighed, and there was the whisper of her dress as she moved again. Suriya opened one eye a crack, peering through her lashes. Her mother was standing by the window, gazing up at the moon.

'She refused to tell me who the father was, but I can guess. He's strong, Alvar. Keeping his power contained is killing him.'

'Damn it, Gaelan—' Lord Alvar started.

But she interrupted him. 'Keep your voice down. It's not my fault.'

'It's entirely your fault,' he snarled.

'You supported it at the time,' she breathed. 'You can't just change your mind a century later because of consequences we couldn't have foreseen.'

Lord Alvar was quiet for a long time, but his breathing was forced as he tried to calm himself. 'Fine,' he conceded. There was a pause before he spoke again. 'What happened, Gaelan? Why is she here?'

'That,' she snapped, 'is between you and her. I'm not getting in the middle of it.'

'You're already in the middle of it,' he growled. 'You're up to your damn eyeballs in it. When Layol told me she'd left, that she never wanted to see me again, he promised she was safe, cared for – but I should have known you were involved from the beginning. This has got your scheming mitts all over it. Why else would she be so meek?'

'I know even less than you do Alvar. He brought her here, asked me to hide her, but wouldn't tell me why. But she would not have stayed hidden had she remained the way she was – mortal women are never so brash.'

Lord Alvar wasn't done. 'Bullshit. You know that boy's mind inside out and backwards, and you've certainly never cared what anyone thinks. Least of all mortals. This is just you trying to get some petty revenge because I chose her over you. Now where's her bloody stone?'

'Safe. She didn't want it.'

'Raiden help me, Gaelan … I will rip this place apart.'

'She didn't want to remember, Alvar. Respect her wishes.'

'Just as you respected her wishes when you banished her from this castle?' he asked.

'She told you.' It was a statement, not a question.

'She didn't have to. The first thing the Captain did after showing me to my rooms was beg me to overturn your decision. He's got quite the soft spot for her.'

'A shame he's married. But I suppose that's her type,' the Lady muttered, so quietly that Suriya almost didn't catch it.

Lord Alvar ignored the jibe. 'She didn't come here for your company, Gaelan, and Layol knows better than to have trusted you with her safety without proper assurances. You gave your word to protect her. Why go back on it now?'

'Will you keep it down?' she hissed. 'Her presence puts Suriya and Lucan in danger. It's too much power in one place and I will not risk them for the sake of her or that wretched boy.'

'Why do you even care?' Lord Alvar shouted. 'These aren't your people, and they're not your children!'

Suriya couldn't help but tense at the words.

Her mother – the Lady – sighed in frustration.

'Now you've done it,' she muttered. She perched on the edge of Suriya's bed and laid a gentle hand on her forehead. Suriya stirred and pretended to wake up.

'Hmm?' she slurred, stretching her arms.

'I just came to check on you,' the Lady murmured. 'How are you?'

Suriya blinked at her, trying with all her might to keep her disgust and mistrust from her face. 'Fine. Can I go back to sleep now?'

'Of course,' the Lady said with a sad smile. And with that, she glided from the room, leaving Lord Alvar to his vigil.

But Suriya did not go back to sleep. She was wide awake and lay glaring at the ceiling.

She smelled the Darklings long before she saw them. The stench of stolen life and twisted magic. It burned her nose, made her teeth itch, set her tattooed hands twitching for her weapons as the bloodlust rose. Even a deep, steadying breath did nothing to quiet the roaring in her ears. Only blood would soothe her now she'd caught their scent. Like a hound after a hare.

Such was the burden of the Graced. Created for the sole purpose of destroying Darklings, the urge to kill was strong in even the weakest of her people. For one as strong as she, it was almost irresistible. It was her birthright. Her sacred duty. Her destiny.

And by the Gods, she enjoyed it.

She crept closer, black eyes searching for her prey. Mouth watering in anticipation. But how to go about it? Normally she would take her time, wring every ounce of exquisite agony from her quarry before finally ending them. Leave their mangled corpses in warning for others. For their bastard King. A bloody, defiant reminder that she still walked the earth – despite his best efforts. But here? Now? Too great a risk that he or his Court might come looking, catch the scent of the Awakening, and whatever else sheltered behind wards not even she could breach.

No. Better to kill them quickly and destroy all trace. Disappointment was a weight in her gut, but she loosed her daggers from their sheaths in readiness.

Then she saw them.

She nearly bit her tongue to stop the vicious oath that rose to her lips. The Hunt was enormous. A hundred strong, at least. All Graced. The Huntress was easy to pick out – they moved around her like ants around their queen. She was Elf-born, like most of her Hunt. The rest were almost all Dragons, with the exception of the male Unicorn hovering at the Huntress's elbow. A glance at the star-mark on his brow had the black-eyed woman checking her mental defences. Even cursed, her power made her presence difficult to hide.

Then a figure stepped from the darkness, appearing as if through a rip in the world. Tall and slender, with wine-red hair and eerie, pale eyes.

Shade.

The woman swallowed another curse as she flinched back. What the fuck was he doing here? A silent snarl of frustration twisted her face. Were the Gods taunting her, to put another target before her like this?

'Sire.' The Huntress greeted her master, bowing low.

He ignored her, studying his surroundings. 'Report.'

'Lord Alexan's information appears accurate. We found the remains of the mortal Hunt not far from here. It would appear the heirs of Ciaron were extremely thorough in their work.'

The Shade grunted. 'Not surprising. Though I doubt either Kah Faolin or Sil Dorrien enjoy their butchery half as much as their bastard sister.'

The black-eyed woman smirked. He was not wrong. Then she frowned. If Faolin and Dorrien had been here, they must have sensed the Awakening. What had happened to them that they'd left it undefended?

'We did find one other body, much closer to the wards. Burned to a husk – a Casting. A strong one.'

187

He shrugged. 'Ciaron's heirs have Elf-blood in their lineage.'

'Not this much. I haven't felt power like this since before the Fall.'

The Prince pulled a face. The black-eyed woman didn't blame him. She'd sensed the power contained within the girl-child. Enormous, untapped potential. Not strong enough to rival her own, but then whose was?

The Huntress continued. 'I suppose it could have been the Princess?'

He shook his head. 'Keriath's Shade, whether she admits it or not. Her Castings would smell different. More like a Wielding. Théon's certainly do.'

The black-eyed woman stilled. There was something in his voice ... no. Surely not?

'Lord Alexan found her then?'

The Shade nodded. 'Ciaron's heirs led him right to her. I got him through the wards. The rest is up to him.'

'And Keriath?'

The Shade grimaced. 'Seren's spies confirmed it this morning. The Queens have her now. I'll deal with getting her back once we're finished here.'

The Huntress swore softly. Then their conversation moved on, discussing the wards before them – what they might contain, how they might be breached.

But the black-eyed woman wasn't listening.

Théon. Keriath. Her sisters in all but blood. At the mercy of Darklings.

She was moving before the thought had even fully formed. The children would have to fend for themselves. She had been no older than they were when the Darklings had descended on her home. Even younger when the Nightwalkers had come for her in the forest. Left her nailed to that altar. She'd survived it all. They could do the same.

Climbing high into the mountains, she Changed. Skin yielded to scales, fingernails gave way to talons, and mighty wings bloomed from her shoulders. Great, yellow eyes looked to the lightening horizon. She would have to be fast. There was perhaps an hour, maybe two, before sunlight would drive her from the skies.

Time to race the dawn.

Without so much as a backwards glance to the children she was abandoning, the ferocious onyx dragon launched herself heavenward.

CHAPTER SEVENTEEN

There was a storm coming. Renila could smell it in the air. It was heavy, crackling with static and tension that set her blood thrumming in her veins. She'd always loved thunderstorms. There was something about their wild, terrifying beauty that made her feel alive in a way that nothing else could. As if the hard edge of fear honed her appreciation for life like a whetstone sharpened a knife.

It was at least a day away – perhaps more – but already, it was like the storm were not building in the heavens, but in her soul. She slept poorly and woke several hours before the dawn. Unable to remain in bed any longer, she rose and slipped from the room.

The kitchens were empty, but she ghosted through them in silence, unable to shake the anticipation thrumming through her. Her heart was thundering in her chest as she hurried up the stairs to the tower. The oncoming storm made her feverish and reckless; she didn't care.

Something had changed within her when Lord Alvar arrived – weeks ago, now. While some things had returned to the way they were, others could not be undone. There was a crack in the dam that held back her emotions, and they were seeping through at an increasing rate.

It was still dark outside when she slipped through the door and crept up behind Farran. She could barely see him, but the moon gave just enough light to make out his silhouette against the night. His hair ruffled in the cold breeze as he stared out across the Ravenswood, unflinching as ever in his vigil.

She inched closer on soundless feet, close enough to smell the lavender soap beneath the stink of his armour. Slipping her arms around his waist, she pressed a kiss to his neck and chuckled when he flinched at her touch.

'Oh dear, Captain,' she laughed. 'Did I catch you sleeping?'

Turning, he pressed her to the parapet with the full weight of his body. 'Hardly. I'm trained to react to threats, not impudent nursemaids with no sense of decorum.'

'Impudent?' She gasped in mock outrage, squirming beneath him even as part of her cringed to be so belittled.

He held still, pinning her in place and looking down at her with a wry smirk on his face. 'Yes, impudent. Bold and brazen too.'

'I don't know what you're talking about,' she said, holding his gaze and placing her hands on his chest, her fingers exploring upwards.

He remained motionless as her fingers dipped below the collar of his shirt, and she raked a fingernail across his skin. But there was a tightness in his voice that told her just what effect she was having on him. 'No,' he said. 'A good girl like you would never dream of seducing a married man.'

'Is that what I'm doing?' she asked, her hands curling around the back of his neck.

'That's exactly what you're doing,' he retorted. 'Temptress.'

'Don't play the innocent,' she whispered, knotting her fingers in his hair as she dragged his head down; 'I am not to blame for your lack of control.'

Their lips touched lightly, tentatively, teasingly, and Farran groaned low in his throat. He threw caution aside, sweeping her into his arms and crushing her to him. Her lips parted as she let out a low moan, and he took his opportunity. His tongue swept in, exploring her mouth, and he ran his hands over her body in slow, indolent caresses.

She pressed herself against him and revelled in his touch as he stroked her spine, her ribs, her hips. He trembled with anticipation as her breasts pillowed against his chest. His fingers slipped between their bodies, and his thumb brushed over the peak as he cupped her in his hand. She gasped at the tiny shivers of pleasure that radiated from his touch and gripped him tighter.

Without warning, the door flew open as a clap of thunder shook the castle.

'Sorry to interrupt,' snapped a familiar voice, laced with sarcasm and throbbing with barely restrained rage. Farran tensed, pulling her to his chest with one arm while his other hand went to his sword. Renila peered over Farran's shoulder to see Lord Alvar standing in the doorway, looking like death.

At Renila's reassuring touch, Farran released her and took half a step back, but he kept her behind him as he turned to face his Lord. She straightened her nightgown and smoothed her hair as best she could. She peered around Farran's shoulders, eyeing Lord Alvar in apprehension. He was furious beyond belief. She hadn't seen him this angry since the day he'd arrived at the castle. Renila had to resist the urge to cower when those purple-grey eyes looked her way. That gaze lingering on every place Farran had touched her, as if the Captain had left fingerprints on her skin that Lord Alvar could see. Those eyes turned to Farran.

'I thought you had a wife,' he snarled.

Farran stiffened at the accusation but didn't flinch. 'I thought you did too,' he replied. Renila glanced up at him. She'd never heard Farran talk back to his superiors like that. It frightened her as much as the barely restrained wrath roiling within Lord Alvar.

'I'm not the one who's just been caught feeling up another woman,' Alvar noted. Renila saw Farran swallow the angry retort that jumped to his lips.

'It was my fault,' she said, stepping around Farran to face Lord Alvar herself. 'I seduced him.' He stilled, surveying Farran with bloodthirsty hunger in his eyes.

'You don't deserve her, Captain,' breathed Lord Alvar.

But Farran wouldn't let it go. 'And you do?' he said, tensing as he levelled the accusation. Lord Alvar snarled, but Farran held his ground. Renila's breath caught in her throat as the two men stared each other down. She had no doubts about who would win if it came to a fight. Farran might be a seasoned warrior with a sword at his side, but instinct said that, even unarmed, Lord Alvar was lethal.

'Get out of my sight,' Lord Alvar spat. 'I will take over your watch, since the task is clearly beyond you. And never let me catch you distracted on duty again.' Farran bowed and made to escort Renila down the stairs, but as they passed, Alvar's hand shot out and gripped her arm. 'Not you,' he growled.

Farran twitched towards his sword, as if he might cut Lord Alvar's hand off to free her. But she shook her head.

'It's fine,' she told him. She didn't want anyone getting hurt over her. Farran's parting glance to Lord Alvar was one of warning, but he bowed again and left. As the door closed behind him, Renila wrenched her arm free, surprising herself with her strength. 'How can I serve you, *my Lord?*'

Lord Alvar flinched from the anger in her voice, but he scowled at her. 'I told you not to call me that.'

'You can't have it both ways.' Renila bristled, anger loosening her tongue. 'You want me to dispense with titles and subservience and yet have no problem throwing your authority around and using it to bully me and the people I care about. So which is it? Are you my Lord, or my friend?'

He was quiet for a moment while her words sank in, but he bowed his head. 'Your friend,' he sighed. 'Always your friend, Renila. I'm sorry. I lost my temper … It's difficult for me … to see you like this. To see you with him.'

Renila blinked, stunned by the implication of his words.

'The Lady … Gaelan—'

Lord Alvar spoke over her. 'Can go fuck herself.' He stepped closer. 'All I want is you.' His fingers trembled as he raised them to her face, stroked her cheek with his feather-light touch. Something buried deep within her cracked at the contact, so profoundly she wondered if it could have been heard a mile away. But there was not so much as a hint of a reaction from Lord Alvar, so perhaps it was only the sound of her soul cleaving in two.

She leaned into his touch and heard his breath hitch. He cupped her cheek in his hand, wiping away a tear with his thumb. Renila hadn't even realised she was crying. There was something so gentle, so tender in his thunderstorm eyes as he gazed down at her, a tentative smile tugging at his lips. It was instinct to return it.

But then Farran's face flashed before her eyes, and she recoiled from Lord Alvar's touch. There was no avoiding the hurt in his gaze at her rejection, but he said nothing, dropping his hand to his side and stepping back. His shoulders curved inward, and his head bowed as he nodded in understanding. Renila couldn't bear to look at him in so much pain, broken by her own actions. That crack in her soul grew a little wider at the sight. Self-preservation kicked in. She turned and fled.

———

She was glad the kitchens were still empty as she sprinted back to her room. She threw the door closed behind her, scrabbling to turn the key in the lock, and slammed the bolt shut. Breathing heavily, she leaned back against the door, just as her legs turned to liquid, and she sank to the floor.

She was thankful Erion wasn't around to witness her meltdown. In the days after Lord Alvar's arrival, she'd returned to her room one evening to find her son packing. As Farran's new squire, he was being allocated his own room next to Farran's. With any luck, he was fast asleep and dreaming in blissful ignorance on the other side of the castle.

That crack in her soul grew a little wider. Emotions and … something else came pouring through. Her shivering turned to trembling, and her trembling became uncontrollable shaking that wracked her entire body while she gasped for air. Like a doll fraying at the seams, she felt herself unravel and wrapped her arms around her chest as if she could hold herself together.

But it was not fear of Alvar that threatened to rip her apart, it was fear of what she felt when she looked into his eyes. The awe, the wonder, the anger, the guilt … the love. She sobbed out loud at the thought. How could she love a man she barely knew?

She loved Farran. That was why she had recoiled from Alvar, because she loved Farran, and she would not betray him. And if Alvar had kissed her, she knew she wouldn't have been able to resist giving herself to him entirely.

It was as if there were two people living within her skin. The tender one that cherished her dear Farran and the reckless, wild one that burned for Alvar. And to make matters worse, both were married men who she had no right to.

Renila pressed her fists against her temples and cried out in anguish. Her thoughts were incoherent, her emotions raging out of control. The fire in the hearth flared in response, but she was too lost in a churning mess of feelings to really notice. She screamed and screamed and screamed as rage and hope, love and despair warred beneath her flesh.

But it was more than just the pain in her soul; her body was on fire. She tasted smoke in her mouth, and her own touch scorched her skin. Her tears of agony hissed and turned to steam as they spilled onto her cheeks, while her lips cracked and blistered from the heat. It was searing, like she was burning from the inside out. And she didn't know how to stop it.

There was someone pounding on the door, calling her name, but it seemed so very far away. They sounded afraid – afraid for her, of what she might do – but she couldn't reach them. Then the hidden door to the secret passage burst open, and the Lady flew into the room like a whirlwind.

'Renila!' she cried, crashing to her knees at Renila's side. A cool hand rested on her forehead as the other shook her. 'Renila, look at me,' she begged. 'Look at me.'

It seemed like an impossible task. Renila could barely bring herself to draw breath, let alone battle her way through the fire. But the Lady – Gaelan – continued to murmur, her cool touch soothing and encouraging, until Renila focussed on the worried face leaning over her, and the flames ebbed.

'Gaelan?' she croaked, her throat parched as though she had inhaled a lungful of smoke.

The Lady sighed with relief. 'It's alright,' she assured her.

'What happened?' Renila whispered, looking around in confusion.

The Lady opened her mouth to speak but seemed to think better of it and closed it again. Her vivid eyes were heavy with regret as she helped Renila up and guided her to the bed, handing her a cup of water to soothe her throat.

'I'm sorry,' she breathed, perching on the edge. 'This is all my fault.'

'What is?'

The Lady took a deep breath. 'It's hard to explain,' she began. 'But it was part of the reason you were brought to me. I can make it go away ... but you won't remember that it happened.'

Renila was quiet for a long time, considering the Lady. 'What else have you made people forget, Gaelan?'

The Lady's eyes flickered with guilt. 'My sins are beyond count,' she admitted, 'but you came to me for help, and I did as you asked. I offer my help again once more.'

'What will happen if you don't?' Renila asked.

The Lady winced at the harshness in Renila's voice, but she held her gaze.

'It's a fate worse than death,' she whispered.

Renila hesitated. She didn't trust the Lady. Not after all that they had said and done to each other. But she thought of Erion. He had no one now, save for her. If something happened to her, he would be all alone. For him, she would sacrifice all of herself.

'Do it.'

The Lady nodded, understanding shining in her glorious eyes. 'You'll forget everything since you woke up,' she explained as she placed a cool hand on Renila's forehead. 'It'll be like falling asleep – and when you wake again, you won't remember any of this. It will just have been a bad dream that fades with the coming dawn.'

'Thank you,' Renila whispered.

'You're welcome,' answered the Lady. 'Now, close your eyes.'

It was not yet dawn when Renila woke. She had slept fitfully, plagued by dark dreams that left her anxious and unsettled. The storm had not yet broken, and the tension of it building set her blood thrumming in her veins. She rose, weak and light-headed, stumbling as she reached for her robe. She frowned, studying her reflection in the mirror. Dark circles shadowed her eyes, and her bronze skin was pale and drawn. She looked ill. Her frown deepened. She was never ill.

She splashed cold water on her face, pulling her gown tight around her, and turned for the door. Her fingers slipped on the cool handle as she hesitated. Something was not right. She tried to shake herself. Nothing had been right for weeks. But this was different somehow ... different, and yet the same.

She walked through the kitchens in a daze, drawn towards the tower by something she could not name. As though the force that called her up that spiralling staircase came from within her own chest, pushing her forward with every heartbeat. Yet it was also outside her body, pulling her in.

It was still dark outside when she stepped out into the cold air. Her eyes snapped to Farran, standing with his back to her. He was nothing more than a shadow in the torchlight, hooded and cloaked against the night. The image caught her attention, like her instincts were trying to warn her. There was something amiss. But as the winds rose, so did her anticipation, and she cast caution aside.

She cleared her throat to get his attention and was surprised that he didn't start at the noise. She hadn't expected him to sense her approach. But as he turned, his face hidden beneath the shadow of his hood, she forgot why she cared.

The storm rumbled over the horizon, though something inside her whispered that it was too soon, and the wind whipped her hair about her shoulders. The savagery of the storm made her impulsive, and she shed her night robe from her shoulders. She could feel his eyes on her, drinking in the sight of the golden skin left bare by her silken nightgown, even if she couldn't see them beneath his hood.

He crossed the distance between them in two steps and swept her into his arms, crushing her to him. Her lips parted as she let out a low moan, and he took his opportunity. His tongue swept in, plundering her mouth while his hands ran over her body.

She writhed beneath his touch, desperate for more. He tore his lips away, and she growled in protest, but then they were on her throat, and she forgot herself entirely. Her hands dipped inside his shirt and caressed the powerful muscles of his chest. She ran her fingers through the fine hair there, and he groaned against her collar bone.

He backed her against the parapet, his hands cupping her backside as he lifted her onto it. It was the most natural thing in the world for her to wrap her legs around his hips and draw him to her.

It was a heady contrast – the cool, open air at her back and the solid warmth of Farran against her front. She gasped out loud as he stroked a broad, callused hand over her legs while the other pulled her nightgown down so that his lips might explore further.

How would they ever stop? She was burning for him. His lips were like fire against her skin, and she moaned when his teeth grazed her heavy, aching breast. Her hands drifted up, curling around the back of his neck, and he groaned again. She knotted her fingers in his silky hair.

'Renila,' he breathed, whispering her name like a prayer.

She froze. He wasn't Farran – his hair was longer, and his voice deeper and more melodic. She tried to push him away, almost falling from the parapet. Strong hands gripped her by the waist and held her fast, but she thrashed for him to let her go. He held on long enough to make sure that she wouldn't fall, then stepped back and released her, raising his hands in surrender.

'You!' she hissed. He pulled his hood down. Black hair glinted in the torchlight, and those thunderstorm eyes regarded her warily. 'What have you done with Farran?' she snarled.

He frowned in confusion. 'I dismissed him over an hour ago.'

'What?' she breathed, shaking her head.

'I lost my temper when I saw you both together,' he said, peering at her. 'We argued, and you left …' He trailed off, concern blooming in those beautiful, terrible eyes.

'I don't remember,' she gasped, clutching her head. She was burning. Smoke was curling in her mouth. She couldn't breathe. Lord Alvar started towards her, his expression filled with worry. 'Don't touch me!' she screamed, flinching away.

He stilled, holding his hands up again. 'Renila,' he breathed, his eyes wide and anxious. 'You need to calm down.'

'Don't tell me to calm down!' she snarled. 'How dare you presume to touch me like that? How dare you pretend to be Farran?'

'I didn't pretend to be anyone, Renila,' he assured her. 'I thought you knew it was me and that you'd changed your mind.'

'Changed my mind about what?' she howled, dropping to the ground as the pain in her head threatened to overwhelm her. The heat was unbearable.

Alvar started towards her again, but the torch flared in its bracket, as if in warning, and he held his ground. 'Renila, please,' he begged, 'you have to calm down.'

'I hate you!' she screamed. Then she collapsed, writhing on the ground in agony. She heard Alvar swear as he dropped beside her and tried to hold her down while she thrashed. But when he touched her bare skin, he flinched away and winced as though she'd burned him.

'*Gaelan!*' she heard his voice roar inside her head. '*Gaelan, I need you!*' She heard him swear again and felt his hands on her. He growled against the pain, like she was burning as much on the outside as she was in her mind. Then the door to the tower flew open, and the Lady was at her side.

'What did you do?' she said, her cool hands touching Renila's brow. She flinched but didn't recoil as Alvar had done.

'What did *I* do? What the fuck is going on?' he snapped.

The Lady ignored him. 'Renila,' she called. 'Look at me. Come on, that's it. Just look at me. Her voice and her hands were so soft, so soothing, Renila calmed at their gentle caress. The flames were receding, their heat dying, and Renila had the strangest sense that she had been through this before.

'That's because you have,' the Lady told her, using that eerie, mind-reading ability of hers, 'but it's alright. I'm going to make it stop.'

'Aren't you at least going to tell her the cost first?' Alvar hissed.

Gaelan snarled and bared her teeth in warning. 'She knows the cost – I've had to do it once this morning already. She agreed then, and she'd agree now.'

'Just make it stop,' Renila begged, her voice barely more than a whisper.

'I will,' the Lady promised. 'This shouldn't even be happening. She should have been out until daybreak at least,' she muttered to Alvar as she soothed the fire down to a barely flickering ember. 'I hope you're pleased with yourself.'

'You think this is my fault?'

'Yes!' the Lady shouted. 'I don't know what set her off the first time, but I'll bet my life it involved you. So much for playing the role of husband.'

'Jealousy was never a good look for you, Gaelan,' he snarled.

'When have you ever known anything as trivial as jealousy to motivate me?' the Lady snapped. 'You need to stay away from her, Alvar. For her own good.'

'You asked for my help and now you're telling me to go?'

If the Lady responded, Renila did not hear the words. She was already falling into the darkness.

It was midday by the time Renila woke. She groaned as the bright light filtering through her window roused her from dark and heavy dreams. She lay still, blinking and staring at the ceiling while she tried to reorientate herself.

Swearing, she scrambled out of bed and found herself weak as a newborn lamb. Her legs went from under her, and she crashed to the floor in a crumpled heap.

The bedroom door opened at the sound of the commotion, and Erion hurried in. He pulled an arm around her shoulders and helped her back up onto the bed with a worried expression on his face.

'Are you alright?' he asked, holding her shoulders while she tried to right herself. Her head was spinning.

'I think so,' she said in a daze. 'What happened?'

The expression on Erion's face said he didn't believe her, but he answered the question. 'You took ill during the night. The Lady said you would be out of sorts for the rest of the day, but that you should be fine by tomorrow morning.'

'I don't … remember.' She winced, holding her head to try and make it stop spinning. 'I think I might be sick.'

'The Lady said that might happen,' he admitted, pointing to a bucket beside her bed. 'But she didn't think it would last very long.'

'Suriya … Lucan,' Renila gasped, trying to rise when she realised that she hadn't checked on them since the previous night. But Erion placed a restraining hand on her shoulder.

'They're fine,' he said. 'They're waiting just outside. I have to go – I have training with Farran this afternoon – but they're going to stay and take care of you.'

Renila slumped back against her pillows in disgust. 'Wonderful.'

'Suriya will keep him in check,' he assured her, chuckling. Renila quirked a quizzical eyebrow at her son.

'You three are speaking again?' she asked.

Erion pulled a face. 'Sort of,' was all he said. Then he kissed her brow and went to the door.

'Renila!' came the sound of Suriya's voice as Erion held it open for the twins to enter. The girl sprinted to Renila's side and threw her arms around her in a fierce hug. Renila let out a faint bark of protest at being jostled, as it sent her head spinning again, but returned the hug as best she could.

'Careful,' Erion admonished.

Suriya flushed with embarrassment and muttered a shamefaced apology, but she didn't move from Renila's side. Lucan eyed Erion cautiously as he passed, joining his sister by Renila's bed. But Erion's expression was cool as he bowed and left.

'He hasn't forgiven us yet then,' Lucan said to Suriya as the door closed behind his friend. Suriya said nothing, but when Renila glanced at the girl, she noted the unease and hesitancy in her eyes. Something was wrong, but Suriya wouldn't share it with Lucan.

'Can we get you anything?' Suriya asked, changing the subject.

Renila smiled and touched her cheek.

'No, I'm alright just now, thank you,' she assured her. 'I'd just like to rest more. Why don't *you* tell *me* a story for a change?'

Suriya's eyes lit up with delight, and she nodded. Lucan sighed and flopped down into an armchair, but he didn't argue. With a smile, Renila closed her eyes and listened to the sound of the girl's voice carry her to a faraway land.

By the middle of the afternoon, Renila was much better, though still very weak. Her head had at least stopped spinning, and she no longer needed to vomit whenever she moved. Unable to lie in bed any longer, she convinced

Suriya to help her wash and dress and Lucan to escort her outside for some fresh air.

The storm still brewed on the horizon, and though it set Renila on edge, she didn't have the energy to lose herself in its savage beauty. It was strange: the stronger the call of the storm, the more lethargic she became. As though the sickness itself fought the wildfire that sought to build in her veins. The rest of the world seemed oblivious to the overwhelming pressure that weighed down on her.

Out in the courtyard, Farran was overseeing Erion's training. Her son was in the sparring ring with a wooden sword in his hand, parrying Farran's gentle strikes. Renila flashed him a smile of gratitude. He knew how her son tired.

Lucan scowled at the sight of it but said nothing as he helped ease Renila onto a low bench in the sunny corner of the yard where she could watch. Suriya sat beside her and wriggled her way into the crook of Renila's arm. Renila looked down at the girl. Whatever the matter was with Suriya, the girl didn't want to talk about it.

With a contented sigh, Renila closed her eyes and breathed deep the clean air. Summer had faded to autumn, though the leaves had not yet turned. The earthy tang of the Ravenswood pines was on the wind, and though it was brisk, it did little to dispel the heavy heat of the oncoming storm. The rich smells from the kitchens wafted towards her as the winds changed. Bread baking in the oven, meat cooking over the fire, and there was something being fried in butter and garlic.

Children's laughter chimed beyond the wall where they played in the fields. Alec the blacksmith was working in his forge, and the sound of his hammer ringing on the anvil echoed through the castle. The shepherd boy was whistling for his dog as he rounded up the sheep in the pasture, and there was the gentle lowing of cattle in the sheds nearby. Farran's steady, reassuring voice drifted over from the training ring, punctuated by the sound of wood striking wood, and made her heart swell with tenderness.

She opened her eyes and saw Erion grin as he blocked an overhand blow from Farran. His eyes were bright, and there was a rosy flush to his cheeks she had not seen in a long time. She could see the pride and happiness on Farran's face too when he praised Erion for his rapid improvements. She looked down at the children curled up beside her. Suriya was dozing, like a cat basking in the sun, while Lucan was watching Erion and Farran.

As she considered what to do about the children's broken relationships, a movement from the other side of the courtyard drew her gaze. Lord Alvar and the Lady stepped out of the castle. Lord Alvar carried a pack over his shoulder and was dressed for riding. Lucan stiffened when he saw it, the tension waking Suriya from her nap. She glowered in suspicion but said nothing as her mother and father approached.

Lord Alvar was watching Erion and Farran sparring in the ring with unashamed envy in his eyes. The Lady noted it, and Renila could have sworn she saw a glimmer of guilt.

'Are you going riding, my Lord?' Renila asked.

He grimaced at the address but left it alone.

'Aye,' he said. The Lady did not look at him, but Renila could see the regret weighing heavy on her shoulders. Renila gave him a look that said he wasn't fooling anyone, and he sighed. But instead of telling the twins the truth, he only looked back over his shoulder at Erion with Farran again. His stunning eyes glittered with unshed tears as he watched them together.

'Why don't you join them?' the Lady blurted. Lord Alvar eyed her with mistrust and incredulity, but she nodded. 'Take Lucan too,' she added, clearly noting the expression of betrayal on Lucan's face. Lord Alvar gave a rare smile that might, under different circumstances and directed at her, have taken Renila's breath away. He dropped his pack beside the bench and held a hand out to Lucan.

'Come on,' he said, grinning. Lucan let out a whoop of excitement and bounded to his feet. But as his father turned towards the training ring, Lucan stopped and looked back at Suriya.

'Can Suriya come too?' he asked. Lord Alvar glanced at Renila, and Suriya tensed under Renila's arm. But Renila nodded, and smiled at Lucan's sacrifice. And it was a sacrifice. He was so desperate to prove himself to his father, yet here he was, offering to share the chance with his sister.

'Of course,' said Lord Alvar.

'But—' the Lady began.

Alvar interrupted her. 'She should be able to defend herself,' he said. 'Unless you'd rather teach her yourself?'

'Mother doesn't know how to fight!' Lucan cried in disbelief.

Alvar snorted. 'The Lady Gaelan is the best swordsman—' He broke off as she huffed in protest. 'Sorry, swords*woman*, in this entire castle.'

'Now you're just being ridiculous,' the Lady scoffed, but she waved Suriya towards the training ring. 'Go on. He's right – they're skills you need, perhaps even more than your brother.'

Suriya frowned, and Renila saw the suspicion and distrust in her golden eyes, but the girl followed Lord Alvar and Lucan towards the training ring without comment. It was just as well she'd worn trousers today, Renila noted.

The Lady sighed and sat beside Renila while they watched Alvar and the twins join Farran and Erion.

'He's leaving then?' Renila asked.

'Yes.'

'He must tell them,' said Renila. 'Leaving without a word will break their hearts.'

'I know,' the Lady murmured. They both fell quiet for a long time as they watched Lord Alvar show both Lucan and Suriya how to grip their mock swords and test the weight of them. Though Farran looked less than happy about Lord Alvar's presence in his training ring, distaste turned to grudging respect when Lord Alvar led them through a series of basic drills. Then respect gave way to wonder, Farran's eyes growing wide with awe as

Lord Alvar drew his own sword – a long, elegant blade, engraved with beautiful, swirling patterns – to demonstrate a particular manoeuvre. After that, the children begged him to show them more and, for once, he obliged.

His movements were as mesmerising as his eyes. Renila had never seen someone move with such grace and elegance, and yet despite the beauty, he was deadly, slipping from one place to another with lethal precision. It was breathtaking to watch.

'Why the sudden change of heart?' Renila whispered.

The Lady didn't take her eyes off the scene in front of her as she said in a weary voice, 'Life is too short.' Lord Alvar glanced up from his exercises as if he'd heard her, though that was impossible. His eyes were shining with tears, and he nodded. In agreement or understanding or even thanks, Renila wasn't sure.

'Not for you,' murmured Renila, though she wasn't sure what made her say it.

The Lady glanced at her. 'No. Not for me,' she admitted. Then she sighed. 'You should take the boy inside. It'll go easier on him if you're both out of sight.'

Renila nodded in understanding, and the Lady called out to Farran. At the Lady's request, he and Erion left the ring and escorted Renila back to her rooms. And though she faced forward, refusing to look back, Renila knew that Lord Alvar's eyes never left her as she disappeared into the shadow of the castle.

CHAPTER EIGHTEEN

The tall, black-eyed man with the warrior braids and tattooed face looked distinctly out of place in a library. He was too big, too wild for the dusty shelves and scholarly splendour of the palatial room. The ceiling was high and vaulted, supported on carved pillars and all of it decorated in exquisite detail. Painted panels, gilt cornicing, marble effigies. Every inch oozed with ancient opulence.

Yet there was no discomfort in his posture as he lounged in a leather-clad armchair by the fireplace, a hefty tome in one hand, a cut-crystal glass in the other. He was alone, save for the snow-white wolf sprawled at his feet like a loyal hound. And despite the vastness of the room, here by the hearth, with the flames crackling and the perfume of woodsmoke and whisky, there was a certain welcoming warmth that not even the iciest voice could chill.

And the voice that shattered the silence was the coldest he had heard in a very long time.

'That was your idea of helping was it?'

The man smirked slightly but did not raise his gaze from the book in his hand when the white-haired woman stepped into the room, appearing as if from thin air. The wolf looked up, glancing between her master and the woman, and huffed a long-suffering sigh. Rising, she stretched and yawned before padding round to sit at her master's side, nudging at his hand until he stroked an absent hand through her fur.

'Hello, Mother. How are you?'

'Don't play games with me, Layol,' she hissed. 'You have no idea how complicated you have made matters with your stupidity.'

'My stupidity?' he asked mildly, sipping from his glass. 'I'm not the one demonstrating powers I shouldn't have. If someone catches you here ...'

She growled, baring her teeth at him. 'I wouldn't need to take such chances had you actually done as I'd asked!'

He sighed, rolling his eyes and putting the book down. 'You asked for help. I sent you some. If you don't like what I sent, maybe next time be more specific?'

'She is burning up,' she said. 'Again. Of all the people you could have sent, you picked the one person she loved enough to dredge her past back to the surface? What were you thinking?'

'I was thinking that you want her and the boy dead, and his presence might be the only thing that would stop you.'

'You really think I'm capable of that?'

'I've seen you do worse.'

She pursed her lips but didn't dispute it. 'He left. Last night. Once he realised the danger to her if he stayed ... but the damage is done, Layol. The boy can stay with me a little longer, but she must leave soon.'

'She'll never agree to that.'

'She doesn't have a choice. She's a danger to herself now. If we don't act, not even the Rising will save her.'

Layol was silent for a long time, staring hard at his mother, his knuckles as white as the wolf fur in his fist. Then, after what seemed like an age, he took a deep breath and loosened his grip.

'Very well. Get her ready. I will be there as soon as I can with her stone to escort her back to Khaladron. Whether she wants it or not.'

The sun was long past set. Suriya stared out of her bedroom window, mind churning. The storm that had loomed for days had finally come. Thunder rumbled overhead, and she could see neither the moon nor the stars for the thick blanket of cloud.

Lord Alvar was gone – vanished into the darkness with the setting sun two nights ago – and with him, all hope of ever learning the truth. But it had been enough. Thanks to him, she'd seen the heart of the Lady. The woman who had lied to them their entire lives with her false claims of motherhood. The woman who had hidden their powers from them, kept them ignorant to keep them obedient. The woman who would have thrown Renila to the wolves rather than ever see her happy.

She knew Lucan had seen something different. He had seen a woman who loved them fiercely, a woman who would do anything to keep them safe. A woman who had been hurt and was forced to act the way she did to protect herself from further pain.

But both women could not coexist within one heart. The lie was too great for Suriya to forgive. Worse, she knew it would be more than Lucan could ever bear. Though she longed to tell him the truth, Suriya could not bring herself to shatter his illusions. She'd sooner turn a knife on her own heart.

With a heavy sigh, she turned her eyes skyward. Once, she would have shared her secrets with Erion, but he'd been so distant since the Ravenswood. Not that she blamed him. He thought they'd betrayed him. That they'd allowed him to take the blame rather than face their *mother's* wrath. She clenched her teeth so hard her jaw hurt. Another of the Lady's schemes, designed to drive a wedge between the twins and the ones they loved.

Lord Alvar had shone a light on the twisted reality the Lady had spun in her mind. Erion was right. Suriya had faced and killed a Darkling to save her brother. And rather than help them, the woman who claimed to be their mother had poisoned their minds so they would never remember. But – either because of Renila's fierce protection or for some other game of the Lady's – Erion's mind was untouched. So he'd taken the blame and, buried beneath the fog of magic, Suriya couldn't help him.

No wonder he'd avoided her since. She hated herself for what had happened; it was hardly surprising he felt the same way. But she couldn't confess to him now, not when it risked turning the Lady's eye on him again. And she couldn't tell Renila – not now she'd found some happiness in whatever it was she shared with Farran. She couldn't risk bringing the Lady's wrath down on any of them.

No. She would have to carry this burden alone.

Thunder cracked, closer this time. Suriya allowed herself a small but feral smile. The fire flickered in the hearth behind her, as if in response to the trill of power that surged through her with the storm.

A bolt of lightning split the sky in front of her, and her heart skipped a beat when light flooded the edge of the forest. Because there was a black-haired rider, mounted on a massive white stallion, thundering towards the castle with reckless abandon.

Lord Alvar had returned.

Lucan's mother was fussing, but he didn't mind. He just watched in bemusement while she moved around his room. She folded his clothes and tidied his things away, drawing the curtains and adding another log to the fire, murmuring a song under her breath. A bittersweet smile tugged at his lips. There'd been a price to pay for this newfound connection with his mother. It was as if the distance between the Lady and Renila were fixed, and he could only move between them. The closer he got to one, the further he drifted from the other.

He sighed. It wasn't just Renila, or even his friendship with Erion, that he missed. Suriya was … different. She'd been distant since their father left. Like she'd retreated inside herself and closed the door behind her. No matter what he'd tried, he couldn't draw her out. He couldn't even read her the same way he used to.

'Why such a heavy sigh?' his mother asked, sitting on the bed beside him.

'It's nothing.' Lucan shrugged. She gave him a sceptical look but didn't press any further. 'What was that song you were humming?'

She looked away. 'It's a lullaby. My mother sang it to me as a child, and I sang it to mine.'

'I didn't know you could sing?' he asked, sure he'd never heard it before.

'You were too young to remember,' she murmured, staring into the fire.

On impulse, Lucan took her hand in his. 'Sing it for me now?'

The Lady glanced at him with a peculiar look in her eyes. She smiled sadly but nodded and did as she was bid. The words were not in a language that Lucan recognised. Though the delicate notes were gentle enough to be a lullaby, something told him it was not for the ears of mortal children. He didn't understand them, but he could hear the longing, the ancient sadness and unending grief in the words. His mother's voice was beautiful – rich and powerful, soaring to the highest notes, and sweeter than a nightingale. He'd never heard anything like it.

She fell silent. He could see the tears clinging to her long, dark lashes, and he squeezed her hand in his. She glanced down at him, her gaze tender, and smiled.

A familiar voice from the door shattered the silence. 'I didn't think I'd ever hear that song grace your lips again,' it said, heavy with emotions that Lucan could not even name. He looked around. Lord Alvar stood in the doorway, his eyes shining with unshed tears. The Lady swirled to her feet as he continued. 'I didn't think you'd sing again, not for all eternity. I'm glad I was wrong.'

She eyed him warily, and though she relaxed, Lucan could see the defensive set to her shoulders.

'He asked. You never did,' was all she said. 'Why did you come back?'

Lord Alvar's gaze was bleak. 'Darklings. They've found a crack in the outer wards. They're headed this way.'

'What?' Lucan barked, scrabbling from his bed. They ignored him.

'How?'

Lord Alvar snarled. 'I don't know, Gaelan. Maybe it's because this keep is bursting at the seams with power, and Darklings can scent magic from a hundred miles away. But that's just a theory.'

'The wards should have hidden it—' she objected.

But Lord Alvar cut her off. 'Well, they didn't. So we need to leave. Now.'

'And go where?' Lucan's mother snapped. 'This is the safest place for us. The wards are strong, and the guards are well trained.'

Lord Alvar stepped closer. 'For fuck's sake, Gaelan, it's a Graced Hunt. A big one. And there's a Shade with them.' His mother's eyes widened in shock, and she sat down sharply. Lucan looked between the two of them in confusion, but his father continued. 'We have to leave, right now. Get him dressed, get Suriya, and make for the stables. I'll get Renila and Erion and meet you there. Then we make for home. I've had the horses readied and loaded up with everything we need for the journey.'

His words seemed to snap the Lady back to herself, and she stood, shaking off her shock.

'That city is not my home. I am not abandoning this place and the people it shelters,' she said. 'They're mortal, Alvar; they don't stand a chance without us.'

'Damn it, Gaelan,' yelled Lord Alvar. The room shook as thunder reverberated through the keep, and lightning sparked over his body, so bright that it obscured him from sight. But then it diminished, like a thunder-storm churning beneath his skin. Lucan swore. Magic. Like the kind in Renila's stories.

'What are you?' he breathed. Lord Alvar's eyes, now burning with the same storm that covered him, flickered between Lucan and his mother. He took a deep breath and then the storm was gone. Once again, Lord Alvar ignored him and turned back to the Lady.

'You don't have a choice. A large Graced Hunt could overpower either of us. They'll drain us dry. Are you willing to risk giving them that power? Are you willing to risk letting Sephiron's heir know that our kind still walk the earth? Because one look at us, and that Shade is going to go running straight back to his master and tell him everything.'

'I can't do it, Alvar. I cannot leave all these people to be fed upon by a scourge I vowed to destroy.'

Lord Alvar shook his head in frustration. 'We've been here before. You can't save everyone, Gaelan. There's always a cost.'

They stared each other down while the silence stretched into eternity. Lucan couldn't look away, even if it felt like he was intruding on a private moment. Lord – if that was even truly his title – Alvar was not human ... and his mother ... she was more than he could have ever imagined. They belonged to a world far away. A world of magic and destruction. And now that this world was intruding on his own, he realised he wanted nothing to do with it.

Alvar crumbled. 'Alright. But we can't hold forever. The best we'll manage is to give them time to escape and then draw the Hunt away.'

'And then?'

He pulled a face. 'I guess we'll cross that bridge when we get to it.'

'Just like old times,' she said with a smirk.

There was no humour in Alvar's answering glare as he opened the door. 'Let's get this over with.'

'Will one of you tell me what is happening?' Lucan shouted, frustration breaking through his self-control. He flinched as Alvar rounded on him. The storm-eyed man winced at the reaction and attempted to restrain his temper.

'Lucan—' he began.

Lucan cut him off. 'No. I don't want to hear it. I don't know what you are, but you're not human, and you're not my father.'

'Lucan,' his mother admonished.

'It's alright,' murmured Alvar, sheathing his sword. 'You're right. I'm not human, and I'm not your father. But you know from Renila's stories that not all monsters are evil. I'm here to help and protect you, Lucan – you and Gaelan and your sister – and I promise that when you're safe, I'll explain everything to you. But I need you to trust me and come with us.'

'You lied to me.'

Alvar cast a dark look in the Lady's direction, a muscle leaping in his jaw. 'I never claimed to be your father, Lucan. That was someone else's inference.'

'But you didn't tell me the truth.'

'I know,' he admitted, 'and I'm sorry for that. My hands were tied and my choices not my own. But I spoke true when I said that I was proud of you, Lucan, and that you had already earned my love and my trust. I may not be your father, but I was there the day you were born. It was my hands that brought you into this world, my hands that helped you take your first breath. I swore to your mother that I would protect you. If you trust nothing else, trust that I will not break my vows.'

Lucan was quiet for a long time, considering his words. Then he nodded and allowed himself to be led from the room.

They flitted down the hallway to Suriya's room and stood guard outside while his mother disappeared inside and helped his sister dress. When they emerged, Suriya's face was pale, and her eyes were damp, but there was a steeliness there that he hadn't seen before. Her jaw was clenched in determination, and she walked straight to him, took his hand in her own and gave a reassuring squeeze. She was wearing the garnet necklace again, but he didn't ask. He was too relieved that the distance that had grown between them had evaporated with her touch. Instinct had him reaching out with his mind, re-establishing their bond once more.

'Do you think we can trust him?' he asked her, relaying the conversation he'd witnessed between Alvar and Lady Gaelan.

She frowned but nodded. *'Everything is going to be alright. I promise.'*

'Take this,' said Alvar, handing a large dagger to Lucan and a smaller one to Suriya. Lucan took it without hesitation, but Suriya paused, eyeing it from beneath lowered brows. It was curved, with an ornate hilt and a large red jewel set in the pommel.

'I've seen that before,' she whispered.

Alvar flinched and looked to the Lady, but their mother only shook her head in confusion.

'You cannot possibly have seen this dagger before, Suriya,' he told her. 'It has been in my keeping for more than a hundred years.'

Lucan blinked. 'How long?'

'Never mind,' Alvar snapped, forcing the dagger into the girl's hands. 'If you recognise this, then it was meant for you, Suriya. Now let's go.'

But Suriya didn't move. She was eyeing their mother with suspicion and disgust while she tested the weight of the dagger in her hand. 'You, I trust,' she told Alvar. Then she turned to her mother. 'But not you.'

Lucan flinched and looked incredulously at her, but their mother got their first.

'There are Darklings approaching as we speak, Suriya. We have to leave,' she said.

'And why should I trust you?' Suriya demanded, her voice deadly quiet. 'You've lied to us our entire lives. *Mother.*'

Lucan grabbed Suriya's hand.

'What are you talking about?' he thought into her mind. At first, he didn't think she'd heard him, but then he felt the wall come down.

'I heard them. The day I collapsed at dinner. She came to our rooms while you

were asleep. They argued. About Renila and the stories ... and us. He said we weren't her children.' Her words in his head were tinged with bitterness, but beneath it, he could sense the hurt. The heartbreak. He turned to his mother in horror, and although she flinched from the look on his face, she didn't deny it.

Then Alvar was between them, cutting the argument off before it could start. 'We don't have time for this. None of us are blameless in this mess, but right now, it's a question of survival. You don't have to trust us, but it changes nothing. I will do everything in my power to keep you alive, even if it means going against your wishes. It'll go a lot easier on everyone if you just do as you're told, but the result will be the same. The four of us – along with Renila and Erion – are leaving this keep and going somewhere safe. Somewhere that not even the Shade King himself can reach. Do you understand me?' Lucan nodded reluctantly, vaguely aware of Suriya echoing his acceptance beside him. 'Good. Now let's go.'

The alarm bells were tolling through the keep. The guards thundered through the castle while the clamour called them to their posts. Captain Farran stood in the middle of the entrance hall barking orders as Suriya descended the staircase behind the Lady.

Farran's words stuck in his throat when his gaze fell on the Lady, and Suriya could only offer him a sympathetic glance. She'd been just as unnerved by the trained efficiency with which the Lady had donned armour as he was at seeing her wear it. The Lady's starlight hair was braided back from her face but the rest was left unbound to tumble over her shoulders. And now, she was fastening a sword belt around her slender hips with practised ease while she took in the commotion.

'My Lady,' the Captain said, choking on his words.

The Lady's face was long-suffering, and she held up a hand to halt his protests. 'Save it. They're through the outer wards already. It won't take them long to reach us. We have to evacuate the castle.'

'And go where, my Lady?' asked Farran, taking the sudden changes in his stride as best he could.

'Up into the mountains,' the Lady replied, her eyes scanning the crowd, searching. 'The Darklings approach from the west, so the path east should be clear. They can skirt north around the Nightloch and head south after that. Make for Shadowbriar.'

'You won't be joining them?'

'They need as much time as we can give them, Captain,' she said. 'We need to hold the Hunt's attention here while we can ... and when the defences fall, we will have to do what we can to draw the Hunt away. Lord Alvar and I will ride north. It's us they're looking for, so they'll follow.'

'And your children?' Farran asked, his voice trembling with tension. The Lady fixed him with the full force of her terrifying gaze, letting the

207

other-worldly power in her veins show through, and Suriya saw the Captain shrink back in fear.

'Suriya and Lucan will stay with my husband and I,' she insisted. She breezed past him and called over her shoulder. 'Give the order, Captain.'

Farran snapped a salute, afforded Suriya a lingering glance, and marched away. Suriya scowled and followed in the Lady's wake. Lucan had gone with Lord Alvar to oversee the defences, so she was left to face the woman they had once called 'Mother', alone. She hurried to close the distance, and as she drew up alongside the Lady, she thumbed the dagger Lord Alvar had given her.

'What about Renila and Erion?' she asked.

The Lady glanced down at her and pursed her lips. 'Where do you think we're going now?'

'Renila's room is that way,' Suriya reminded her, pointing in the opposite direction.

'I'm well aware,' the Lady snapped, before pointing in the direction they were heading. 'Erion, however, is that way.'

Suriya almost stopped in her tracks. She wasn't sure the Lady had ever said his name out loud before, let alone considered him first. The Lady seemed to sense her shock and glanced back over her shoulder.

'You don't have to trust me, Suriya, but at least trust that I wouldn't leave an innocent child to face certain death.'

Suriya had no comeback to that, so she allowed herself to be swept along behind the Lady as they wove their way through the castle.

Erion stood guard outside Farran's chambers, watching a harassed-looking maid pack various gowns for the Captain's wife within. The sight of him in his armour, with a sword strapped to his side, made Suriya want to weep. The harsh planes of his helmet only emphasised the childish roundness to his face, the over-large sword making him appear even smaller. He was a boy. Too young for battle.

His face remained impassive as the Lady approached, with not even a flicker of recognition when he spotted Suriya behind her. Offering a hasty bow, he kept his eyes on the floor. Suriya had to resist the urge to hug him. He wouldn't thank her. Not after what the Lady had made her do to him. A glance at the Lady told her the woman was sorry, but that she didn't have time to fix it.

'You're relieved, soldier,' said the Lady. 'I need you to go down to the stables and see to the horses. Alvar has asked for them to be saddled and packed for a long journey. Please ensure his orders have been followed to the letter.'

Erion's storm-grey eyes swirled to a ferocious-yellow as he held her gaze. To his credit, he didn't blink. 'Who will be travelling, my Lady?'

'Myself, Alvar, Suriya, Lucan,' the Lady said, Erion's brow lowering at every name, 'Renila and yourself.'

He flinched when she finished and opened his mouth to speak.

But Suriya cut him off, clutching at his hand. 'We don't have time, Erion. Please just do as she says.'

The expression on Erion's face made her stomach heave with self-loathing, and when he pulled his hand free of her grip, she thought she felt a piece of her heart wither and die. Then he turned those terrible, wolf-yellow eyes on the Lady.

'One day, my Lady,' he promised, his voice soft and deadly and far beyond his years, 'you will answer for all you've done here.'

Then he bowed again – smoother this time, mocking even – before he turned and left. The Lady stood frozen, staring at the space he had just vacated with a haunted look in her eyes. Tears streaked her cheeks, and she took a deep, shuddering breath that seemed to say she agreed with him.

Suriya kept silent. Even if she'd known the words to comfort the Lady, she would not have offered them. The Lady did not deserve it.

Lucan watched on helplessly while the other inhabitants of the castle made ready to leave. His people, the people who had helped raise him, who had cared for him his entire life. Mal was in the kitchens, booming orders as she oversaw the packing of supplies. Alec was helping the farmers load their wagons in the courtyard. Two of the maids herded the children together in the entrance hall, bundling them up in extra hats and scarves to protect against the cold of the night.

Thunder rumbled in the background, and Lord Alvar strode from the castle into the courtyard. His armour gleamed in the torchlight, and magic was churning beneath his skin. Captain Farran followed behind him, barking orders to his men.

Erion stood in the stable door, his serious gaze watching from beneath the rim of his oversized helmet. Wolf-yellow eyes turned to storm-grey when they settled on Lucan, but he offered a small smile that was oddly reassuring. Slipping through the throng, he crossed the courtyard to Lucan's side.

'The horses are all ready to go,' he murmured.

'Good.' Lucan wasn't sure if it was or not, but he didn't know what else to say.

Erion seemed to sense his uncertainty and scowled. 'We're not leaving with the others?'

'No.'

Erion shook his head in disgust. 'I don't know what game your mother is playing, but it's a dangerous one,' he warned, 'and it's likely to get us all killed.'

'She's not my mother,' whispered Lucan, not daring to glance at his friend.

Erion stilled beside him. 'What?'

Lucan shrugged, at a loss to explain something he barely understood himself. 'Suriya ... she ... she overheard the Lady and Alvar talking. They're not our parents.'

'Then who is?' asked Erion.

'I don't know,' Lucan admitted with a bitter smile. 'Maybe if we live through this, she'll tell me.'

Stunned silence filled the air between them. Then Erion let out a huffed breath and swore, before he burst out laughing. Lucan stared at him for a moment before joining him. They laughed until their sides hurt, clinging on to each other for support while they doubled over. And when Alvar tried to quell them with a murderous glare, they only laughed harder.

They sobered of their own volition, and Erion looked about him. 'So, what's the plan?'

'We hold them here as long as we can while the others escape up into the hills – give them as much of a head start as we can. Then Mother—' He broke off with a soft curse. 'The Lady,' he corrected, 'means for us, Alvar, Renila and Suriya to leave together. She thinks we can outrun them and draw them away from the keep.'

Erion's eyebrows quirked upward. 'That seems unlikely.'

'She's confident.'

His friend smirked. 'Isn't she always?'

Suriya hovered behind the Lady, atop the highest tower, while the Lady peered into the night. The clamour of the chaos down in the courtyard echoed up to them, but the Lady hardly seemed to notice. Suriya glanced to her right, exchanging a worried glance with Renila.

They'd found her in the entrance hall, herding the children together. She'd taken one look at the Lady's murderous expression and gestured for two of the maids to take over, before falling into step behind the Lady without question. She hadn't so much as blinked at the Lady's brutal description of what they faced nor flinched from her blunt explanation of the perilous plan they'd concocted to survive it. Suriya wasn't sure what to make of it. Though Renila was hardly prone to hysterics, her current composure was ... disturbing. Even watching her now, glancing over the parapet to the courtyard below, there was something eerie about it.

Suriya wasn't sure what frightened her more – the looming threat of Darklings, or that people she'd known her entire life now seemed strangers to her. She wished she could be with her brother, but the Lady had insisted on separating them. Gods only knew why. They were fools to trust her.

A muttered curse drew her attention back before her thoughts could spiral any further. Beside her, the Lady frowned while she gazed into the darkness.

'What's wrong?'

The Lady bared her teeth in a silent snarl. 'They're here.'

'I can't see anything.'

'That's because you're looking with your eyes,' she snapped. Then her gaze grew distant, her face glazing with a vacant expression – as though she was no longer present in her own body.

Suriya frowned. What if ... she could speak to Lucan mind-to-mind, could she not? She'd seen through his eyes. Shared his thoughts. Felt his emotions as though they were her own. Perhaps the mind was not so bound by the body as she had once believed. She closed her eyes and tried to reach out with it. It was disturbingly easy, just like stretching out a limb, one she'd never realised she had, but no less a part of herself. Shock almost had her tumbling back into her body. How was this even possible?

Another presence caught her attention, drawing her up into the night sky and out to the edge of the Ravenswood. It was the Lady's mind, watching in silence as the monsters approached.

Darklings.

Dozens of them, swarming like flies around a carcass as they cavorted through the woods. Magic crackling and sparking from fingertips and red eyes glowing like blood in the darkness.

Without warning, one stopped, eyes snapping skyward and honing in on Suriya's mind drifting above them. His brow was marred with that same peculiar star-shaped birthmark that Lucan had, and he was breathtakingly beautiful. He shouted in warning to another. A woman – the leader, judging by how the others moved around her – with the same strange, tapered ears as Suriya. The woman's slanted eyes narrowed, and a barked order had those around her stilling. The ground around her froze, coating her in hoarfrost while daggers of ice formed in her hands. The star-marked Darkling smiled, his lips tinged with blood as he looked back at Suriya. There was only death in that red gaze.

Then the Lady was between them, swallowing Suriya's presence within her own. The Darkling blinked in surprise, frowning in confusion as he scanned around for her. But whatever the Lady had done, he found nothing and broke off with a hiss of frustration. Suriya barely dared to breathe while the Lady's mind held her tight, waiting and waiting for the Darklings to move on. They continued on, and the Lady released an audible sigh of relief.

'What do you think you're doing?'

'I wanted to see.'

'You could have got yourself killed!' the Lady snapped, holding tight when Suriya tried to pull away. 'Be still. They can't sense me, but if you keep drawing attention to yourself, even my shields won't keep you hidden for long.'

Suriya growled but did as she was bid. 'Why can't they see you?'

'Wielding magic is like any skill – it takes time and training to gain proficiency. I've had a lot of both,' the Lady said. Her attention was fixed on the Darklings. With a barked curse, she retreated and called back to Alvar in warning. 'They've reached the wards.'

'How many?' came his terse reply.

'A hundred at least. All Graced. Some are holding back, out of range, in the forest. I can't see the Shade ...' She trailed off. Because there he was. A figure wreathed in flames of shadow, stalking through the Darkling ranks. He came to a halt beside the pointy-eared woman, his head cocked to the side as he considered some unseen force. Then he raised his hands, and the Lady reeled back, shouting out in warning, 'Brace!'

Suriya's mind crashed back into her body, just as the world gave a violent lurch. Shadow-flame slammed into some invisible barrier in the sky above, the noise of the impact drowning out even the booming thunder. The world seemed to shudder at that assault, and somewhere in the recesses of her mind, she heard Lucan swearing as the ground shook beneath his feet. His mind invaded hers once more, his senses overwhelming her while he and Erion grabbed on to the nearest wall to stop themselves from falling. *Alvar was the only one who stayed on his feet, his head thrown up as he snarled in frustration. Lightning split the sky, and thunder roared as if in answer.*

Suriya staggered, shoving Lucan's mind from her own as she stumbled and clutched at the parapet while the world trembled. The Lady didn't even flinch, somehow staying upright while black flames and lightning battled in the sky above. Then the flames retreated, and the reverberations stopped.

'What was that?' Renila asked, hauling herself back to her feet.

The Lady scowled. 'The Shade. He's attacking the wards. It won't take him long to get through them.'

'What do we do?'

The Lady drew herself up to her full height. 'We hold him as long as we can.'

'The wards are under attack,' Alvar was saying while he helped Farran to his feet. Lucan offered a hand to Erion in silence. 'They have to go, now.'

'They need more time,' Farran protested.

'There isn't any. They go now and take their chances in the hills, or they stay here, and they die.'

Farran was silent for a long time, eyeing the handsome Lord with a mixture of admiration and hatred. Then he nodded and gave the order. It was all Lucan and Erion could do not to be swept along in the chaos that followed. Alvar paced, chafing at the slow exodus. The ground shook again, and now it was not just the children who screamed out in fright. Erion was itching to help, but he remained at his friend's side.

Then, without warning, Alvar roared and staggered from some unseen blow.

On the parapet, the winds rose around them, carrying the sound of shouting from below as Farran ordered the evacuation. The ground shook again, and frightened screaming echoed up from the courtyard. Lightning sparked, but this time, the sound of magic battering against the wards overwhelmed the roar of thunder.

'Gaelan!' Lord Alvar roared. 'Help me!'

The Lady looked skyward and squared her shoulders as starlight erupted out of her. Suriya raised a hand, shielding her eyes against its brilliance, but her attention was focussed out beyond the wards. She reached out her mind as far as possible, not daring to leave the safety of her body again. But there was no need – the Shade radiated so much power that it was impossible to miss him. Flames of shadow spewed from his hands, hammering at the invisible wards, but they recoiled as the Lady's starlight reached him.

'Alright,' gasped the Lady, huffing from exertion as she drove him back. 'Tell Farran to go now. I'll hold until they're clear.'

Suriya once more found herself tangled in Lucan's mind as his fear threatened to overwhelm them both.

Alvar straightened, wincing as if movement pained him, and looked to Farran. 'Captain! You need to go now!'

Lucan watched Farran nod before turning to argue with his wife. He could only guess at what was being said, since his ears were filled with the nervous hum of the crowds. A child was howling. The sharp sound pierced through whatever sense of calm he had left, and panic squeezed at his chest. He saw Olly appear at Farran's side and nod while the Captain spoke.

The ground shook with the reverberation of that terrible noise once more, and Lord Alvar swore. 'Captain!' he yelled. 'Go or stay, but you and your men need to decide now!'

Farran embraced his wife one last time and clapped a hand on Olly's shoulder as he gave his last orders. His eyes were damp as he watched them join the throng streaming out the northern gate towards the hills. But when he had taken a deep breath and squared his shoulders, he turned to face the men who had chosen to remain. There was nothing but single-minded determination in his gaze.

'We give them as much time as we can,' he said, his voice carrying despite its softness. From his dark corner in the courtyard, Lucan watched Farran's grim resolve spread, touching every man who remained. It was their families, the people they loved, who were depending on them. Every single one of Farran's men would lay down their lives for their Captain, for their home ... for their family. Even Erion was nodding, his hands clenched tight enough by his sides to turn his knuckles white.

As one, they followed their Captain's example. They each allowed themselves one last look at those they would die to defend. Then they turned away, ready to face their doom.

But neither Suriya nor Lucan could watch as those people disappeared through the gates and into the night. Not when all those they loved were still within the castle walls ...

Suriya pulled herself back into her own body, the clamouring from below growing ever louder as the exodus began. The ground shook from the Shade hammering at the wards once more. Gaelan snarled as she flooded the air with power, strengthening the wards with her own magic. Suriya watched – vaguely aware, through Lucan, of Alvar shouting at Farran to keep them moving. And then, after what seemed like an age, came the sound of the north gate closing with a mighty clang.

Lucan and Erion straightened when Alvar appeared beside them, his purple-grey eyes heavy with worry as the crashing of thunder and magic warred in the sky. The world shook again, hard enough to make his teeth hurt this time. Then again. And again. As if some colossal fiend was pounding its fists against the fabric of existence. Though he cursed himself for it, a small whimper of fear escaped Lucan's lips. Erion's hand found his in the darkness and squeezed.

Shooting stars arced overhead, battling with the darkness that battered the wards. Lightning joined them, but still, that terrible force continued to pound the wards.

The Shade was almost through. Lucan wasn't sure how he knew that, but he did. Alvar swayed where he stood, eyes on the wards.

'Gaelan!' he called in warning.

'I fucking know!' was the only response she offered. Lucan blinked. He'd never heard the Lady swear. Alvar stumbled as the ground shook once more, and it was only Lucan's quick reactions that kept him on his feet. He said nothing as he pulled the Alvar's arm around his shoulders, offering his strength when Alvar's was failing. Erion moved to do the same on the other side.

'Thank you,' Alvar murmured, glancing down at the boys keeping him upright. There was a terrible ripping sound as flames of incandescent light and blackest night battled overhead. But despite all efforts, the light was being forced inexorably backwards. Alvar cursed. 'Come on, Gaelan,' he muttered. 'Just a little longer.'

Suriya wrenched her attention back to her own body, scowling up at the magical battle above. The world shook again, the Shade's attack strong enough to rattle her skull. He struck again. And again. And again. The Lady growled, raising her hand. Shooting stars arced from her palms, battling with the darkness. Lightning joined them, but the Shade continued to pound the wards.

The Lady staggered from a savage blow, and Renila reached out to steady her.

'I'm here,' she murmured as the Lady leaned on her. 'Lean on me.'

The Lady flashed her a grateful grimace and bared her teeth at another vicious barrage. And this time, Renila stood with her. Suriya could only stare in wonder as the two women who had raised her put aside their differences to defend the only thing they shared ... the people they loved.

Suriya stepped up beside them, sliding her hand into the Lady's.

'Together,' she whispered. The Lady glanced down, her expression unreadable. A silver sheen of unshed tears shone in her ethereal eyes, and she nodded. Beside her, Renila squared her shoulders and looked to the wards.

Suriya followed suit …

And loosed a power she barely knew she had.

The Lady guided it, drawing on the magic hidden within. Tongues of fire in shades of gold and amber formed in their outstretched hands, and a single thought from the Lady sent the flames racing across the night. The darkness recoiled, and Suriya thought she caught a frustrated shout as the Shade was driven backwards. He raged against their power, his black magic engulfed in flames of gold, white and amber.

In the courtyard, Lucan could only watch in awe as more power streaked across the sky – flames surging from the topmost tower of the castle, driving the darkness back. Farran and his men cheered at the victory, infinitesimal though it was, while Alvar sighed in relief at the brief respite.

'What was that?' Lucan asked.

Alvar smiled down at him and winked. 'Renila … and your sister.'

A cheer went up from below, and Suriya allowed herself a small, triumphant smile. But their relief was temporary as the Darklings added their magic to the Shade's – ice, wind, fire and more slamming into the wards. A wave of exhaustion crashed through her, flames flickering beneath the barrage, while a murderous growl ripped from Renila's lips as she swayed.

'Alvar,' gasped the Lady. '*The wards are failing!*'

'*Are the mortals clear?*'

'*Almost. But I don't know how much longer we can last.*'

'*Just let it go!*' His reply was terse and filled with worry. '*Save your strength. We can hold their attention here and take out as many as we can until the mortals get away!*'

The Lady nodded to herself, glancing to Suriya. 'When I give the signal, break off and get inside.'

'What about you?'

'Just do as you're told,' she ordered. There was a pause, as if she was waiting for something. Then. 'Now!'

Reliant only on her instincts, Suriya released whatever strange power she had conjured and bolted for the door with Renila right behind her. The Lady roared in agony as the full strength of the attack fell on her. Suriya hesitated. The Lady screamed for her to run, but her limbs locked, refusing to move, refusing to abandon the woman she'd once called Mother. Then Renila's arms were around her waist, and she was thrown inside.

The air above the castle seemed to solidify, glittering like a wall of pure diamond. The earth was shaking constantly now with the force of the attack. Lucan and Erion clutched at each other, trying to stay on their feet. Alvar backed up as he herded the boys behind him, eyes on the diamond dome. A bolt of shadow-fire blasted through the night, arcing towards the castle with lethal precision.

'Farran!' yelled Alvar. 'Take cover!'

But his warning was too late. The black flames struck, the diamond dome cracked, and with that last mighty blow, it smashed into a million tiny shards. But Lucan wasn't watching that. He was watching the shadow-fire streak through the air and slam right into the highest tower – right where Suriya, Renila and the Lady had been standing.

Suriya tumbled, screaming, down the stairs as the building exploded above her. Renila fell with her, their limbs tangling as they crashed towards the ground. A bark of pain escaped Suriya as she was slammed into the wall at the foot of the staircase. The world went black, for a moment, but she didn't have time to dwell on it as Renila surged to her feet and threw her body over Suriya's – just as the rest of the tower collapsed on top of them.

The building exploded and, even through the chaos that followed, he heard his sister's screams. Roaring her name, he took a step towards the castle. Erion was right on his heels, yelling for his mother.

But then Alvar was there, tackling the boys and throwing himself on top of them as the pieces of the wards rained down. Thunder cracked, and the air grew thick and heavy. The shards slowed, as if sinking through water rather than falling through air, and floated to the ground like feathers. Lucan barely noticed. He struggled against Alvar's hold, yelling for his sister, but Alvar would not release him.

Renila roared as a chunk of stonework smashed into her back, but she didn't move an inch, shielding Suriya's body with the sacrifice of her own. Then heat seared Suriya's cheeks as amber flames erupted from thin air, wreathing them in a fire that somehow repelled the falling masonry. She glanced up and saw fire and fury dancing in Renila's amber eyes, the gentle woman gritting her teeth from the effort of whatever magic was keeping them alive.

The reverberations stopped, and Suriya dared to peer out from under Renila. The parapet where they had just been standing was gone, the spiral staircase – at least a dozen steps shorter now – ending in open air. Where the Lady had stood was nothing but the night sky. A choked sob escaped

Suriya's lips. She staggered to her feet, stumbling towards the stairs, but Renila held her back.

'Suriya, no!' she insisted, grabbing her about the waist and hauling her back. 'There's no time! We have to get to the stables!'

Suriya barely heard her. She could only stare at that empty space in disbelief. The Lady was gone. Suriya shook her head. It wasn't possible. Her mind was silent, numb from the shock. There was so much left unsaid … so many questions left unanswered.

'But—'

Renila cut her off. 'Suriya, we have to go. We have to go now. Lucan is waiting for us. He won't leave without you.'

And like that, her tears stopped. Nothing in all the world would ever come before her brother. For him, she would sacrifice herself, body and soul, so she dried her eyes and followed Renila from the ruins.

It was quiet in his head. He'd never noticed it before – that warmth and steady dependability that resonated throughout his mind, that part of him that was Suriya. Hadn't noticed it until it was gone. Panic gripped at his heart … she couldn't be …

'Lucan!' her voice echoed through his head. *'It's alright … I'm alright!'*

Lucan sagged with relief, a choked sob escaping his lips as Alvar let him up, though he kept a tight hold on Erion. *'Renila?'* Lucan gasped. *'Is Renila alright?'*

'Yes, she's fine. She's here.'

'Renila's fine,' he told Erion, gesturing to Alvar to release him. Then he turned his attention back to Suriya. *'What happened?'*

'The Shade got through – followed the magic back to us. Mother … Gaelan … she gave us enough time to get out.' She broke off with a shuddering breath. *'Lucan. She didn't make it out in time. She's gone.'*

Lucan stumbled from the shock. His mother. Gone. The thought left him winded. Alvar's hand was around his arm, steadying him, but the his attention was elsewhere – a dark scowl the only reaction he offered to the news of his wife's demise. Lucan wasn't sure what to make of that, was too absorbed in his own grief to notice.

He couldn't bring himself to speak the words, to explain the anguish on his face to Erion. But his friend seemed to understand, his eyes swirling from storm-grey to gentle gold. He said nothing but gripped Lucan's shoulder in reassurance, before turning to Alvar.

'What happens now?' he asked.

Alvar grimaced. 'Now we see if these bastards bleed.'

CHAPTER NINETEEN

The night echoed with the triumphant hoots and wicked crowing of the Darkling invaders. Lucan stood between Erion and Alvar while, across the courtyard, Farran readied the archers. He was bleeding from his brow but seemed unperturbed as he gave the order, prowling along the parapet above the gate while they fired into the oncoming horde. But it didn't seem to do much to repel their advance.

The Captain swore and gave the order to fire at will before vaulting back down the stairs to the courtyard below and ordering the gates reinforced.

Alvar moved.

'Captain,' he called. 'Get your men back. I'll hold the gate for now.'

The look Farran offered in response to this order was incredulous. Lucan didn't blame him. But Alvar's tone brooked no debate, so Farran did as he was ordered.

There was a mighty boom as something slammed into the gate, the shrieking and cackling of their enemies echoing beyond. The gates were splintering now, giving way beneath a barrage of magic. They exploded inward, and once again, that strange, heavy feeling pressed on the air, protecting them from the worst of the blast.

Alvar stepped into the breach, hands outstretched and expression murderous. Thunder cracked, the storm clouds overhead burst, and the rain came lashing down. The winds were rising, howling through the keep as if answering his call, and lightning sparked from his fingertips.

Five Darklings stepped into the light, blood-red eyes glowing as they breathed deep the scent of their prey. They were huge males – tall and broad-shouldered, with chests like barrels and arms like tree trunks. The darkness behind them shifted with the rest of their forces, teeming like shoals of fish. A hundred, Gaelan had said, yet it looked like more.

Gods help them.

As if in answer to his prayer, lightning split the sky, streaking through

218

the night towards the Darklings. Heat seared the air, and the ground shook from the force as the lightning blasted into the Darkling ranks. Screaming winds followed, pushing them back, and cries of pain filled the air when the rain turned to driving hail. Lucan glanced at Alvar. His face was set in a silent snarl, his eyes churning with power unlike anything Lucan had ever seen. Lightning flashed. Once. Twice. Three times. Twice more. And each time, a Darkling died. More careered through the gate, scenting the blood, and they met only death as Alvar's wrath raged unchecked.

'Lucan, get inside,' he hissed, panting from exertion. 'Get Erion and get out of here. Find your sister and hide!'

'But—'

Alvar cut him off. 'Go!'

Lucan ran, shoving Erion in front of him. From the corner of his eye, he saw Alvar unsheathe his sword, the slim blade glinting in the light of the fires. The sight of him, standing alone to face such an overwhelming force, was enough to make Lucan want to weep. Then Farran stepped up beside him, sword steady in his hand as he faced the nightmare descending on them. Other soldiers joined them, but Lucan only had eyes for the Captain and Alvar.

Thunder roared in challenge as the Darklings surged forward, and Alvar attacked. He was lethal, moving with inhuman grace and speed, striking like the lightning that sparked over his skin. He *became* the storm, dancing through the horde like the winds howling overhead, leaving only death in his wake.

Beside him, Farran was only just managing to stay alive. Lucan had seen the Captain take on five men at once and walk away without a scratch. But these were not ordinary Darklings. *A Graced Hunt*, Alvar had said. A whole Hunt made from the magically gifted warriors from Renila's stories. He spared a moment to pity them – those who had become the one thing they'd been created to destroy. But as he saw the destruction they dealt, the lives they claimed, pity gave way to horror.

He paused on the threshold. Couldn't bear to leave them. Alvar seemed to sense his hesitation and snarled in frustration, dragging Farran from the mêlée and shoving the Captain towards the castle.

'Get them out of here,' he roared. 'Renila and Suriya are inside somewhere. Find them and hide them.' Farran dipped his head once in acknowledgement, pausing just long enough to grip Alvar's shoulder in support before he turned and sprinted for the boys.

His broad hands herded them forward, pushing them inside, despite Lucan's objections.

'Do as you're damn well told,' he barked. Lucan flinched from the rebuke, but Erion gave his friend a warning look that told him to keep his mouth shut. Lucan heeded that advice, and together, the boys helped Farran to close and bar the great oak doors.

And as they slammed shut, Lucan heard Alvar's parting words echo through the Captain's mind. *'Keep them safe, Farran. No matter the cost.'*

Erion didn't hesitate. 'This way,' he said, heading towards the kitchens. Farran raised a sceptical eyebrow but didn't argue, signalling for Lucan to follow while he brought up the rear.

The castle was an eerie place devoid of its usual inhabitants. Footsteps which once would have been lost in the cacophony of bustling life now echoed ominously through the empty spaces. Hushed whispers breathed into ears seemed louder than words shouted across hallways, and every murmur of movement sent a shiver of fear down the spine.

But Erion moved forward without hesitation. Lucan smiled. There was a time when he might have drawn strength from Erion's confidence, but now there was little need. He felt the pull towards his sister just as keenly as Erion was being drawn towards his mother.

Erion froze, gesturing for them to do likewise. Then he sighed with relief.

'It's alright,' he whispered into the darkness. 'It's just us. You can come out now.'

'Erion?' a familiar voice breathed in wonder. And out of the shadows stepped Renila, with Suriya tucked into her side. Renila's amber eyes filled with tears as she drank in the sight of her son, and she pressed her lips to his brow. 'Thank the Gods!'

Then her gaze went to Farran, and there was no mistaking the look of relief on his face. He took two staggering steps and threw his arms around them both.

A warm, firm hand slipped into Lucan's. He looked round to see Suriya appear at his side, her tear-stained face now fixed with a look of grim determination.

'Are you alright?'

She nodded, leaning into him for comfort, their minds twining together once more. *'You?'*

'I'll live.'

Golden eyes fixed him with a look that suggested he was perhaps being a little optimistic, given their current situation, but she let it go. 'What now?'

All eyes turned to Farran, but it was Erion who spoke first. 'I know a place. Somewhere they can't find us ... or at least, somewhere we will be safe. Somewhere they can't get to us.'

Lucan frowned. He knew this castle at least as well as Erion, if not better, and there was nowhere that would protect them forever.

'Where?' he asked, trying not to sound too sceptical. Erion's gaze was distant, eyes swirling so fast Lucan barely had time to register the colours.

'I don't ... know,' he said, taking a faltering step towards the narrow corridor on his left. But there was no hesitation when he continued. 'This way.'

Lucan opened his mouth to argue, but then came the sound he had been dreading – the pounding of magic on wood echoing through the keep. The

Darklings were at the doors. Farran swore, looking around as if for another option. Renila only spared him a glance as she herded the twins behind her.

'Stay with me and stay close,' she murmured. Lucan nodded in understanding and gave Suriya's hand a reassuring squeeze. And then, squaring her shoulders, Renila followed Erion into the shadows. Farran followed, just as the shriek of breaking timber shattered the night.

Erion had sped up, sprinting down corridors so fast that Lucan almost lost all sense of direction. He could only run, pushing Suriya in front of him. Renila reached back and grabbed her hand, dragging her onward. The pounding of Farran's boots behind him, bringing up the rear, was the only reassurance he had. So long as Farran was behind, that meant the Darklings were not.

Lucan could hear them inside the keep now. Their vicious laughter echoed off the stone walls, making it near impossible to judge direction or distance or even numbers. Gaelan had said there were about a hundred of them and, while not all had survived the initial attack, there were clearly a significant number left.

Up ahead, Erion skidded to a halt in front of a large tapestry, one of a black-haired woman, armoured and cloaked in raven's feathers with sword in hand, standing upon a field of fallen warriors. He barely spared it a glance as he threw it aside to reveal the door hidden behind it.

Farran checked himself, frowning in disapproval and opening his mouth to complain. Clearly this was the first he had learned of the hidden passages. Renila cut him off.

'Not the time,' she sighed, herding the twins down the passage. 'I'll make it up to you later.'

He shook his head in frustration even as a choked laugh escaped him. 'If we live through this, you'd better.'

Then he stepped inside and helped Erion pull the door closed behind them.

Engulfed in sudden darkness, Lucan's other senses seemed heightened. Fear was heavy on the air, the hunting Darklings all but drowned out by the harsh breathing of those within the narrow corridor. Heat radiated off Renila standing beside him, like it always did when she was angry. Suriya's palm sweaty in his hand, her fingers trembling between his. But she squeezed in reassurance, leaning closer and lending him her strength. What little she had left.

A flame stuttered into life as Erion took a torch from its bracket. It must have lit itself, for there was no flint in his hand. Lucan stared at him, but his friend seemed unperturbed. No, not unperturbed. Oblivious. As if Erion were not with them, his mind so distant that it seemed to have left his body.

His eyes, now so dark they were almost black, focussed on something in the distance. Not down the corridor, Lucan realised, following his friend's gaze, but somewhere beyond. Somewhere deep within the labyrinth of hidden passageways, something was calling him. He did not even wait to see they were following before he moved off, leading the way once more.

'What's wrong with him?' Suriya murmured.

Lucan shook his head. 'I don't know.'

But he did not hesitate to follow where Erion led.

This deep inside the castle, the hidden passageways were a maze. They'd explored them over the years, but only bothered to memorise the useful ones. Left at the junction ahead would lead them to the passage between the rooms he had shared with Suriya and their mother's – Gaelan's – chambers. But Erion turned right down a passage that he'd never noticed before.

The thunder of heavy footsteps shattered the silence. They froze, ears straining, hardly daring to breathe. Then they heard it. Someone – or something – was sniffing at the hidden door. The sound of it echoed down the narrow corridors, growing louder and louder. Another joined it. Then another. Like a pack of wolves seeking their prey ...

The sniffing stopped.

A low, diabolical laugh rang through the passages. 'Got you,' a male voice chuckled. Then he howled, the others joining him, baying like hounds on a scent.

'Run,' Farran ordered. They didn't need told twice. Erion charged ahead, leading them through the maze. Renila stayed right on his heels, dragging Suriya by the hand. Farran was behind, herding Lucan in front of him.

There was another junction up ahead. The right fork should lead back to the kitchens. Erion turned left. Towards the outer wall.

'That'll be a dead end,' warned Lucan.

Erion glanced back over his shoulder, his black eyes glinting in the torchlight. 'Trust me.'

Lucan nodded and kept going, only to skid to a stop a heartbeat later when they reached the end of the passage. Renila's hand scrabbled at the wall, searching for a hidden entrance. But there was nothing there. She stepped back and shook her head. Farran swore, looking back the way they'd just come. The hooting and howling of Darklings echoed round and round. They were in the passages.

'The kitchens should be that way,' Lucan said, pointing. 'We can get out through there, make for the stables.'

Suriya shook her head. 'Renila and I tried that way earlier. It's buried under all the rubble from where the tower came down. The door's blocked.'

'We're trapped,' hissed Farran, swearing again. Lucan and Suriya looked to Erion. He'd been so sure. But he was only frowning in confusion, studying the dead end in front of him. Then he took a hesitant step forward, hand outstretched.

And as his fingers brushed the wall, stone turned to wood, and a door appeared.

It was heavy, made from solid oak and carved with the crest of a raven in flight. The sigil had been defaced by deep, savage furrows gouged by what Lucan could only assume had been the blade of a knife.

There was also nothing resembling a door handle.

A wrought iron lock, yes, with a keyhole. But no key. Lucan stood in stunned silence for a moment before the jeering of the Darklings roused him once more to action. With a huffed sigh of relief, he pushed past Erion, who was staring at the door with a mixture of awe and horror, and shoved. It didn't open.

'It's locked.'

The taunting shrieks of the Darklings drew closer.

'Try to pick it,' Renila ordered. Another time, Lucan might have tried to protest his ignorance of such a dubious skill, but this wasn't the place. Suriya removed two pins from her hair and handed them to him. They'd done this too many times for her to need instructions. But as he knelt and slid the pins inside, he realised the problem.

'There's no mechanism inside. It's just decorative.'

When his announcement drew nothing but silence, he glanced around … and saw what had drawn their attention.

A Darkling stood at the other end of the passage, blood-red eyes flickering in the torchlight, that maniacal grin broadening as two more stepped up to flank it.

Farran unsheathed his sword. 'Try to force it open.'

Renila caught him by the wrist. 'You can't fight those things. They'll kill you.'

Warm brown eyes flickered down, burning with such intensity that Lucan looked away. He wouldn't intrude on something so private. But he couldn't stop himself from hearing Farran's murmur of goodbye.

'Then at least I'll die with my sword in my hand, defending the people I love.'

And with that he extricated himself from her grip and turned back to face the Darklings. Their eyes lit with feral delight, no doubt at the prospect of toying with their prey, but Farran didn't baulk as he stepped back down the passage to meet them.

Halfway down the passage, he stopped and raised his sword.

It was three against one, the Darklings blessed with Graced speed and strength, and yet within such narrow confines, they couldn't all rush him at once.

He held the passage for as long as he could. Lucan tried to make it count, throwing his weight into the door. Suriya joined him, but it wouldn't budge. She rounded on Erion. His gaze was fixed on Farran, his onyx eyes wide with hopelessness and oblivious to their plight.

'Erion,' she snapped, shaking him from his trance. 'Come on!'

He looked around, his eyes shining with unshed tears. 'What can I do?'

'The door appeared for you,' she breathed. 'Maybe it will open for you too.'

To say that Erion looked sceptical was perhaps an understatement, but he did as he was bid and put his shoulder to the door.

Over the top of his sister's head, Lucan saw the moment Erion's hand brushed the lock. Saw the light flare beneath his palm and heard the click as the lock snapped open. But he was still far from prepared when the door swung open smoothly – yelling in surprise as they went crashing into the room, tumbling through the open door together, torches flaring into life at their presence. Lucan scrabbled to his feet, searching for another exit. But there was nothing. Not even a window. He glanced back to Renila and shook his head.

She nodded, taking a deep breath, and looked back to Farran. His defence faltered. The Darklings had no need of steel, and though the death they offered him was quick, it was not clean. He made his last moments count.

Even when the largest Darkling knocked his sword from his grip, he kept fighting. He drew his dagger with his other hand and sliced across its throat in a single fluid motion. Even when the smallest one slipped through his guard and slashed deep into his side with claw-tipped fingers, he kept fighting. The dagger flickered in the torchlight, finding its heart. But it lodged there, and when it screamed, staggering backwards from the blow, he was left weaponless.

The last Darkling snarled as it closed the distance between them, parrying Farran's fists with unnerving ease. Its hand snaked out and closed around his throat, a grim smile twisting its features as it choked the life from its prey. Erion pushed past his mother, but Renila grabbed his arm and held him fast.

Suriya's voice whispered in Lucan's mind. *'Don't look.'*

But he couldn't tear his eyes away.

The sound of Farran's last breath was haunting, but the scream that ripped out of Renila as she watched the man she loved die right in front of her, helpless to save him, was agony. Heartbreaking enough that Lucan felt she'd physically struck him, and he staggered back from it. That was a pain he couldn't even begin to comprehend.

But as he watched the life ebb from those warm, brown eyes, he knew that he could not let the Captain's sacrifice be in vain. So he turned and ran, dragging Renila and Suriya inside. If they hadn't been able to get the door open, he was willing to bet the Darkling would have the same problem.

'Erion, come on!' he called over his shoulder. Suriya seemed to catch on, scrabbling around the door, ready to close it once they were all inside.

But Erion didn't move. He was standing, staring at Farran's lifeless body.

The Darkling had turned its bloody gaze upon him, but as it looked closer, the smirk faded from its lips, and its gaze grew troubled.

'What are you?' it breathed.

Erion squared his shoulders.

Drew his sword.

Stepped forward.

'Erion,' Renila cried, reaching for her son. Lucan blocked her way, even as Suriya grabbed her about the waist. Unarmed, she would end up bleeding on the floor beside Farran. If only they could reach Erion and pull him back to safety.

The Darkling frowned, but it didn't move. Erion took another step forward. Rage was rolling off him in waves, churning the air around him. Then another step. His grip on the ridiculously oversized sword steadied. Then another. He no longer looked silly, instead he looked dangerous. And another. Until he was within striking distance.

Still the Darkling held its ground. Then Erion raised his sword in invitation. Or was it challenge?

The Darkling pounced.

Renila was screaming for her son, fighting to get past Lucan, but he barely heard her.

Time seemed to slow, and he was sure he was about to watch his best friend die before his eyes. But thunder cracked, and Erion was moving with the same lethal grace as Alvar, slipping through the Darkling's defences and driving his blade up into its heart.

He snarled as the creature died on his sword, savouring its death with dark delight dancing in his black gaze.

And as the life faded from its eyes, he leaned in closer and hissed, 'I guess you bleed after all.'

Relief made Suriya's legs tremble as she watched the Darkling die, and at last, she released Renila. It had taken every ounce of her strength to hold the woman back. Strength she knew should have been beyond her, but she didn't have time to dwell on it. The Darkling might be dead, but there would be more coming. They had to find a way out.

She shivered, breath misting in front of her as she looked around. The air was thick with the smell of dust and decay. Cold and stale, with a hint of damp and the faint, musty aroma of old books.

Little wonder. Dust-coated shelves reached all the way to the vaulted ceiling, each one stuffed full of books. There was an armchair by the empty hearth, the table beside it buried beneath countless tomes. A tarnished mirror hung above the mantle, an equally dirty painting of a man adorning the walls opposite. He was tall and imposing, with blue-black hair beneath his crown, and he carried an evil-looking sword in his hand. He looked down at her with cruel, dark eyes and an imperious expression that made her skin crawl. Yet there was something familiar about his face. Something she could not quite place.

She turned away, glancing back over her shoulder. Renila lingered in the doorway, staring at her son in disbelief. Lucan's expression was similarly stunned. Beyond them, in the hallway, Erion stood over his kill, chest heaving. She looked away. Back into the library.

Her gaze skirted over the loose leaves of parchment scattered on the floor around an enormous desk in the alcove, and at the open chest in the corner, half-buried beneath books and a shield bearing the crest of a raven in flight. It was empty save for a dozen tattered scrolls. Nothing of any use there either.

She frowned. This place was humming with some ancient, terrible power. It burned at her nerves like ice held against wet skin. She shuddered from its touch, shrinking inward as she tried to hide from it. Lucan glanced round, seemingly sensing her distress.

'Suriya? What is it?'

She shook her head, trembling as her gaze darted around, searching for the source of that evil. 'Something's wrong. We shouldn't be here.'

But nobody was listening. Renila moved first, dragging Suriya's attention as she shoved past Lucan. She reached for her son …

And rebounded off an invisible barrier. She tried again, only to stagger back as she slammed into it once more. Tentatively, she stretched out a hand: the air shimmered with resistance when she touched whatever held them there.

'What the—' breathed Lucan, glancing back. Suriya shook her head. She didn't understand it any more than he did. But if they couldn't get out …

Erion stepped back from the Darkling and turned to face them, onyx eyes glittering in the gloom. 'Stop fighting it, Mother.'

Suriya frowned, looking between her friend and the barrier keeping them inside. He was controlling it then, somehow. Renila seemed to reach the same conclusion a moment later.

'Erion, you let me out of here this minute,' she snarled, slamming her fist on the barrier.

He sighed, wiping the blood from his over-large sword with cool detachment. Suriya shuddered to see it. It was like a stranger, wearing Erion's face. 'Please just stay in there where it's safer. There are more Darklings in the keep, but they can't get to you in there. It will hide you, protect you.'

'Listen to me. If you do not get back here, so help me, I will put you over my knee,' she promised, her voice deadly quiet.

Erion sighed again and rolled his eyes, but he began the grudging walk back down the passage towards them. Suriya let out a breath and exchanged a rueful look with her brother. Lucan only shrugged, too busy eyeing Renila with trepidation. She was standing in the doorway, arms folded, fury whipping around her like sparks from Alec's forge as she waited for her son to return to her.

But before he could reach them, a dark chuckle drifted into the silence, and from the shadows behind him, a nightmare stepped.

It was as though he had stepped through a rip in the air itself, and the sight of him chilled her right to the bone. There was something so eerie, so different, so *wrong*, about him. Fear, pounding in her blood screamed at her to run, but something kept her rooted in place. Kept them all rooted in place. Stopped her calling out to Erion, to warn him of the demon at his back.

He was tall but slim, this nightmare. Handsome too, with wine-red hair that shimmered like blood in the torchlight. He stepped smoothly over Farran's body, his hands in his pockets as he surveyed the surrounding devastation with a wry smile on his lips. A red stone pierced his pointed ear, and his shirt was open at the collar, revealing a matching jewel on a chain around his neck.

Then Suriya noticed his eyes. They were pale – so pale that the irises were almost lost in the white, and only his pupils were noticeable. The words from a story Renila had once told them whispered in her mind.

Little more than a pale shadow of a once glorious lineage ...

'Shade,' Renila breathed. From the corner of her eye, Suriya saw Lucan flinch, recoiling from whatever dark power stalked towards them. But the Shade only smirked, his pale eyes raking over the twins with interest. Then his gaze slipped beyond them, to the room behind, and his steps faltered. And in that instant, the spell was broken. Renila screamed, 'Erion! Run!'

He glanced back over his shoulder, his eyes widening in shock at the shadow bearing down on him. He tried to run, moved faster than Suriya had ever seen him move before – faster than should have been possible. But the Shade was faster still.

He swirled through the air like smoke and shadow. One moment he was behind Erion, and then, in less than a heartbeat, he stood before him. Long, delicate fingers curled around Erion's throat, lifting her friend clean off his feet, and that ridiculous sword went clattering to the ground.

Erion thrashed in his grip while Renila screamed for her son, and together with the twins, she pounded against the magical barrier that sealed them inside.

'Now, now,' the Shade chided, his voice as smooth as silk and deadlier than a snake. 'Settle down.'

The Shade studied Erion, his head cocked to the side as he considered his prey. He ran a caressing hand over the boy's face, a strangely gentle gesture. His brows knit with curiosity as he cupped Erion's face in those long, delicate fingers, staring into those whirlpool eyes ... and he flinched from whatever he saw there.

But Renila didn't seem to notice. She only roared at the violation. Suriya reached out, taking Renila's hand in her own, only to be bombarded with all the rage and fury churning beneath Renila's skin.

An ember flaring. Grief and sorrow mingling with wrath and vengeance. An ember sparking. Bloodlust rising. A spark catching. Murder in her heart.

Suriya gasped, flinching back to the safety of her own mind. No, not retreating. Defending. Pushing Renila back out. Because that connection had not come from her. It was Renila who had invaded her mind. The power within her – Gods, she was so strong – raging out of control. Blurring the boundaries of her reality. If she couldn't get it under control … she would kill them all.

'Renila,' Suriya begged, trying to bring Renila back to herself. 'Renila, please. Be careful. You might hurt Erion.'

But Renila barely heard it.

Fury raging in her veins, blazing like wildfire.

Suriya shoved her back, trying desperately to protect her mind as Renila's wrath took form, flames licking along her skin. Her hair shifted and curled in the rising heat, surrounding her face in a flickering halo of scarlet waves while her amber eyes smouldered like hot coals. The heat of the flames burned Suriya's skin, but she didn't let go of her hand.

'Release him,' Renila snarled, her voice crackling with the power of the inferno within.

The Shade smiled, unfazed by the terrifying display. 'Come quietly, and I promise that none of you will come to harm.'

'Release my son, and I promise I will kill you quickly,' Renila countered, flames flaring along her golden skin to emphasise her point.

The Shade snorted in disbelief, smirking as his fingers tightened about the boy's throat. Erion thrashed again, and the Shade huffed a sigh of exasperation. His hand flickered up, brushing over his captive's brow once more, and at that touch Erion went limp, his eyes rolling back into his head as he slumped into unconsciousness.

'That's better,' the Shade said. 'Now, are you going to come quietly, or am I going to need to make this permanent?'

Renila roared again and then, as if in answer, thunder pealed through the castle. The ground shook beneath their feet, and behind the Shade, the passage crumbled. Stone shattered and split, as though huge, unseen hands were tearing the keep apart searching for them.

The Shade whirled, shadow-flame flickering to life in a protective bubble around him as he backed away. Still that power kept coming, and piece-by-piece, the castle was torn away, until Suriya could see the faint twinkling of stars in the night sky overhead.

And as the dust settled, a feral smile rose to Suriya's lips at the familiar figure that stepped out of the shadows. He was battle weary, sweat and blood coating his handsome face, but there was fight left in him yet. She could see it churning in his thunderstorm eyes.

The Shade stilled, his eyes widening at the sight of the approaching Lord and the power he possessed.

'You should have taken her offer,' breathed Lord Alvar, 'because I am going to make you suffer for that.'

The Shade let Erion slump to the floor as he drew the twin swords strapped across his back. 'What are you?'

Thunder shook the ground beneath their feet as Lord Alvar's wrath made itself known. Challenge sparked like lightning in his eyes. 'Why don't you try me and find out?'

Then he struck. The Shade snarled, swirling to meet him. The clash of swords rang through the ruined keep, and the roar of thunder echoed in answer. They were matched, Lord Alvar and the Shade. Both moved with that same impossible speed, handled their blades with an ease that spoke of years of training, struck hard enough to make the other stumble. And yet neither touched the power that set them apart.

At least, not until the howling of Darklings shattered the night. Lord Alvar had not destroyed them all then. They swarmed over the rubble, charging towards their prey with reckless abandon.

'Gaelan!' Lord Alvar roared, battling his way through the horde. *'I need you!'* Lucan looked at Suriya in confusion, but she could only shake her head. She didn't understand either. Gaelan was gone. She'd seen it with her own eyes. Why call out to a dead woman for help?

But then star-fire erupted overhead, and the Darklings looked around to see a statuesque figure striding through the rubble towards them.

Gaelan.

Unharmed, unbroken and very much alive.

Suriya couldn't help but gasp while, beside her, Lucan crumpled with relief. Yesterday, they would have thought it impossible. Today had redefined their understanding of the word.

The winds rose, whipping Gaelan's starlight hair around her face as she drew the long, elegant sword from the sheath at her hip. Celestial lights flared in her eyes and danced along her skin, the same way Suriya had seen thunder churn inside Lord Alvar. They were the same. Whatever they were, Gaelan and Alvar were the same.

She was terrifying. As magnificent and dreadful as the storm that loomed overhead. And as those awful eyes fell on the still, bloody corpse of the Captain, whatever leash she had held on that awesome power snapped. The ground trembled, and the starlight blazed around her. She screamed her fury to the night sky, and the light burned brighter and brighter.

'Close your eyes and get down!' Alvar's command thundered in their heads. They didn't hesitate. Renila shoved them both down and threw herself over them, even as they screwed their eyes shut. But it didn't block out the heat or brilliance of the light that flashed through the castle. There were screams as the Darklings died, burned away to ash by the star-fire that Gaelan's rage had conjured.

And then it was over. Suriya opened her eyes to see Gaelan sag with exhaustion. Alvar was beside her, looping her arm over his broad shoulders. But the Darklings were not finished.

There was no mistaking the Huntress. Flanked by the remaining Darklings, she carried herself like a queen as she stepped over a smoking pile of ash, that had once been a member of her Hunt, with deadly precision. A strange, pale light flickered around her in an aura. Her ears tapered to a delicate point, and her eyes were slanted, sleepy and feline as they considered her prey.

Then the Shade's barked command echoed. 'Get the boy!'

The Huntress glanced at her master and nodded in understanding, signalling to others to deal with Gaelan and Alvar.

Gaelan drew her sword and stepped away from Alvar, her teeth bared in a silent snarl. And together, Alvar and Gaelan raised their blades and charged.

The Huntress slipped around them, deflecting their attacks with magic of her own as she darted through the mêlée to Erion's unconscious form sprawled upon the flagstones.

Other Darklings charged forward, but any who came close to that small, prone body met only merciless death. Consumed in amber flames, they died screaming in pain. Renila's chest was heaving from the effort, but she did not let up.

Not even when those flames collided with a wall of ice and rebounded. Renila snarled, redoubling her attack. Once again it slammed into the magical shield protecting the Huntress. But she did not stop trying. Not even when the Huntress knelt and lifted the boy into her arms.

Renila was screaming his name, shoving against that magical barrier with all her might. Alvar bolted forward, roaring for the boy too, his voice a cacophony of thunder echoing around the castle.

But the Shade was too fast. He vanished through another rip in the world, disappearing out from under Gaelan's falling blade and stepping to the Huntress's side. She handed the boy over to her master, and the Shade nodded in thanks.

Renila screamed, and the flames flared, slamming into shields of wind and shadows. Then Gaelan was there, star-fire searing the air around them. And wherever it went, Darklings died.

The Shade hissed in frustration, torn as he looked between Alvar, Renila and the twins. But Gaelan was little more than a shadow in the centre of that storm of starlight now. There was only the promise of blistering death in her terrible eyes. With a final hungry glance at the twins, he stepped backwards and disappeared into darkness … taking Erion with him.

Alvar was yelling at Renila, but she couldn't hear him. Suriya reached for her hand. The flames were raging out of control now, growing hotter and hotter.

The Huntress glanced up at Renila, fear creasing her face as the inferno spread. Behind her, a Darkling screamed as the flames touched it, and it was reduced to a pile of smouldering ash. All around them, Darklings were being consumed in the blaze, shrieking in agony as they died. But still, the fire could not reach the Huntress, nor the others she sheltered within her shield of ice and magic. Alvar was roaring for Renila to stop, while Gaelan sprinted for the twins.

'Get back!' she barked. But Suriya didn't budge. She clung to Renila's hand, unaffected by the heat.

'Renila,' Suriya begged. 'Renila, please, stop. You're going to hurt yourself.'

But Renila couldn't stop. Her clothes smouldered and turned to ash, and she screamed as the flames turned on her, scorching her skin as they sought more kindling to fuel their rage.

'Get back!' Gaelan shouted again. She was closer, almost there. Sprinting towards them with impossible speed. Lucan's hands gripped Suriya's waist, and he dragged her back into the room. But it was too late.

Renila exploded. Gaelan screamed ... and stepped through a rip in the air, just like the Shade, reappearing right in front of them. She threw her body over them with a roar of pain, shielding them from the blast. Suriya cried out, but the surrounding air glowed as if the light itself sought to protect them. Gaelan was panting from exertion, but the light shield held – nothing more than a small bubble of air in the inferno that had consumed Renila.

'Alvar!' Gaelan roared. 'Stop her!'

Suriya glanced at her brother in confusion. Surely Alvar couldn't have survived that eruption of power? But then Lucan grabbed her wrist and pointed. She squinted against the brightness of the fire, following his outstretched hand, and saw a shadow move within the flames.

Alvar was staggering to his feet, his eyes fixed on the spot where the Shade had vanished, brushing the charred tatters of his cloak from his shoulders. He roared in pain – whether from the blaze scorching him or from losing Erion, Suriya couldn't tell – but where the Darklings had withered and died, he remained untouched. Each step seemed to be agony, and the flames were merciless, as if they tried to stop him. But he continued on, lurching towards Renila with steadfast resolve.

Lucan yelled in alarm as Alvar faltered, and Suriya took his hand.

'It'll be alright,' she promised.

Gaelan gasped as the fire flared again and the shield flickered weakly.

'Help him,' she hissed from between clenched teeth, glancing at Suriya and her brother. Lucan's face was incredulous, but Gaelan was insistent. 'Use your powers – help him.'

Lucan looked between them in confusion, but Suriya only nodded and squared her shoulders, sent her mind out towards Alvar, pulling Lucan's with her.

'We are with you,' she whispered, throwing her thoughts to him like a spear. Alvar growled, the blaze surrounding him, driving him to the ground.

'Get up,' Lucan urged, willing him to stand. 'Please, get up!'

Suriya's brow creased in concentration, throwing her strength, just as she had thrown her thoughts. There was half a heartbeat of hesitation before Lucan joined her. She slumped from the exertion, and Lucan swayed on his feet, but they held fast.

Alvar gave a mighty roar as he surged once more to his feet, drawing on their strength.

They were inside his head, and though most of his thoughts were hidden from them, they could feel his despair.

The sight of the boy in the arms of that monster had been hard enough to bear

... watching him vanish had cleaved his heart in two. Renila was before him, her incandescent eyes vacant and unseeing. He hissed through clenched teeth – it was worse than he'd feared. She hadn't just lost control. She was enthralled by the power coursing through her veins.

He reached out, brushing her cheek with his fingers. His skin burned where they touched, but he did not flinch. 'Renila,' he whispered, begging. 'Come back to me.'

A single tear escaped his eye, turning to steam with a hiss, evaporating in the scorching heat of the flames. But she did not react. She was gone, consumed by some wild, elemental creature that revelled in the destructive power she wielded.

'I'm sorry,' Alvar choked. He gripped her face in his hands, snarling at the pain. A clap of thunder reverberated around the castle, and there was a pulse of near-unbearable pressure, but the shield of starlight held.

Renila cried out once, collapsing into Alvar's waiting arms. And just as she descended into unconsciousness, the fire vanished, leaving only smoke and ash in its wake. Overhead, the thunder clouds broke, and rain began to fall, hiding the tears on his face.

Alvar pushed them from his mind as the grief threatened to overwhelm him, but not before they saw the truth there. The fierce, undying love he felt for the scarlet-haired woman in his arms.

Lucan scowled as they retreated but he turned his attention back to his sister as she sank down beside him. Gaelan sighed with relief as the shield flickered out, and she put a grateful hand on his shoulder.

Then she looked around them, her eyes filling with unfathomable sorrow. Alvar, now pulled off his surcoat and wrapped Renila in it, his gaze growing murderous when he took in the library. He shook his head in disgust, eyes filling with loathing as he turned away. Gaelan opened her mouth, as if to explain, but he cut her off.

'Later,' was all he said, refusing to look at her.

Movement at the corner of his eye caught Lucan's attention, and he turned, raising Gaelan's knife. Beyond the ring of ash, Darklings who had survived Renila's flames were stirring. And they were angry.

His gaze settled on the Huntress, and he saw the bloodlust in her eyes as she took in the devastation before her and counted the dead. The side of her face was angry with blisters. And although it healed with a wave of her hand, it left behind ugly and twisted scars that even magic could not erase. Renila had decimated her Hunt, and she growled as she roused the survivors for battle.

'We have to go,' Gaelan said.

Alvar argued. 'Erion –'

'We'll get him back,' she promised. 'I promise, Alvar. I will do everything in my power to get him back. But we can't do that if we're dead.'

'Fine,' he said. 'Take the twins, make for Khaladron. I'll head south, draw them away from this place, from the children.'

'How do you know they'll follow you?' Suriya interrupted.

Alvar stood, hefting Renila's unconscious form into his powerful arms. *The Huntress will not rest until she bathes in Renila's blood for what happened here.*

'You're going to use her as bait,' said Lucan. It was an accusation, not a question. Suriya laid a gentle hand on his arm.

But Alvar did not reply. He gave a low whistle, never taking his eyes off the Huntress while she tried to regroup. Out of the smoke, his enormous white stallion leapt over the rubble of the keep, head thrown high as he whinnied at the sight of his master. Alvar lifted Renila into the saddle and climbed up behind her, cradling her against his chest as he gripped the reins.

Behind them, Storm appeared from the settling dust with Copper stepping behind her. The huge black mare nudged her mistress with her great nose, as if reassuring herself that Gaelan was unharmed. Gaelan patted her neck, her attention on the Darklings.

The Huntress hissed again, sensing that her prey was about to escape.

'Gaelan, go now,' Alvar said.

Gaelan moved with inhuman speed, shoving the twins up onto Copper's back and slapping a hand to the chestnut mare's rump. The Darklings turned at the noise, but they were too slow. Copper was already galloping into the night as Gaelan swung up into Storm's saddle, kicked her heels to her flanks and thundered after them.

Lucan glanced back just in time to see Alvar roar in challenge before urging his own mount in the opposite direction. The Huntress screamed in frustration, her prey scattering to the winds. But Alvar had been right – there was no hesitation when she ordered what remained of her Hunt after Renila.

Behind Lucan, Suriya was silent as they watched Alvar and Renila disappear into the forest. But Gaelan pressed them onward.

'We ride until sunrise,' she said as Storm cantered to a stop beside them. Lucan glanced across. Her starlight hair was wild and unbound and her eyes heavy with grief. Her clothes were torn, her armour stained with blood and ash, and she still carried her sword in her hand. She was every inch a warrior, power radiating from her like lightning flashing in the night. Whoever Gaelan was, she was not the woman he had known all his life. Her eyes softened as she held his gaze. 'Do not look back,' she whispered.

And with that, she led them into a night as black as their despair.

The mighty, black dragon was soaring high over the mountains when she felt the wards shatter behind her; the magic contained roaring out into the world. Exposed. Defenceless. Guilt flickered in her chest, but she held her course. Blood called to blood. Her blood needed her.

Théon.

Keriath.

Still, she was not entirely without mercy. Groping through her mind, she searched for a single thread. Fragile and well-hidden, but more important to her than anything. Finding it, she swallowed her fear and tugged ...

A familiar presence stirred at the other end.

'I am here. What is wrong?' it seemed to say.

So she told it. Whispered secrets of children, hidden in a forest. Of Darklings and Shade Princes. Of magic she had not sensed in a hundred years. Of her stolen family.

'Never fear, I am near,' it whispered back. 'Do what needs to be done. We will do the rest.'

Then it was gone, and she was alone once more in her quest.

CHAPTER TWENTY

They packed quickly, or at least they seemed to think so. For Alexan, who'd lived his entire life always ready to move at a moment's notice, it was painfully slow. So many decisions. So much discussion. He was clenching his teeth so hard by the end of it he wasn't sure his jaw would ever open again.

Théon, at least, seemed to grasp the urgency. The old man too, though unlike Théon he lacked the deep-seated dread that follows a near-death experience. But neither seemed prepared to impress that need for haste upon Illyandi. If she debated which gowns she *couldn't* leave behind for any longer, she was likely to have her own near-death experience far sooner than she expected. What was it about Diathor's daughters that so tested his patience?

He snorted, packing food and blankets into the wagon. There was too much of their fathers in both of them. The Shade King's arrogance might have manifested as wild recklessness in Théon, but Alexan was under no illusions as to its source. Much like Illyandi's vanity. Prince Sarron had been a proud man. Pretentious. Preening. Alexan had never understood what Diathor had seen in him. It made it easier that they were neither like their mother. Less painful. Even if Illyandi looked enough like his Queen that the sight of her was like a knife in his gut.

'You alright?' Théon's voice dragged his attention back to his surroundings. She was standing nearby, strapping various weapons to her saddle. The steel-grey stallion eyed him warily. Smart beast. Smarter than the coal-black mare he would be riding. Smarter than that prancing lily-white beast of Illyandi's. The Princess had almost wept to see her elegant, fleet-footed mount hitched up to the wagon like some common packhorse. The swine had bitten him twice too.

Alexan sighed. 'I'll be fine once we get moving.'

'She's almost done,' Théon assured him, disappearing into the byre once more.

'You said that half an hour ago,' he muttered.

The old man, lingering by the front of the wagon, glared. Alexan ignored him. Took a deep breath as he watched Illyandi scatter feed for the chickens and open the paddock gate to let the sheep roam free, sobbing all the while. Resisted the urge to swear.

'You understand that she neither wants nor needs your help, Darkling?' Silvermane said, noting his gaze. 'She has no intention of allowing you to serve her.'

Alexan snorted, eyeing him up and down. 'You think I'd waste my time on a child? I serve Diathor's firstborn, the eldest surviving heir of Benella herself.'

'Don't talk down to me about birthright,' the old man growled. 'I was there when Benella birthed Vianka and Velor – I know which one was born first, and I know which took the throne. Sometimes the rightful heir isn't fit to wear the crown. Benella's sister was one, her daughter another. Théon is no different.'

'And why is that?'

'Because she's a damned Shade!' the old man said. 'She's as much Sephiron's heir as she is Benella's.'

'I know a fucking Shade when I see one,' snarled Alexan. 'I've spent the last hundred years serving the bastards – I know the mark of Sephiron's heirs. I also know the eyes of the woman I loved. Eyes I never thought I'd see again. Until I saw *her*.' He jerked his chin to indicate Théon watching from the byre door. Watching with her evergreen eyes. Diathor's eyes, staring at him out of her daughter's face.

'Just because that magic slumbers, doesn't mean it is gone,' Silvermane growled.

Alexan's attention snagged on the comment, but he pushed it aside for later. 'Théon is Diathor's true heir. She's not her father. I know that better than anyone. You can't blame her for what happened. She was just a child. I failed to protect her once before. I won't fail again.'

He walked away before he said – or did – anything he could regret. The old man was going to test his patience, that was for sure. The Princess too. Even Théon was far from what he'd expected. Competent, yes, but ruled by her emotions. She was impulsive. Impetuous. Illogical. It set his teeth on edge.

It was only when his temper had cooled that he dared to return. Théon was helping the old man up into the wagon while Illyandi stared at the cottage, her eyes welling with tears once more. Alexan resisted the urge to scream as he swung up into the saddle. Quite how she had remained so soft after almost a century on the run was beyond him ... Though as he watched Théon place a tender arm around her sister's shoulders, guiding her away, he began to get an inkling.

Finally, they were ready, and Théon took the lead as they headed out of the glen, trusting him to guard the rear. They stopped on the crest of the hill, looking back down on the little croft. In the darkness, it was hard to make out, but Alexan could picture it in his mind's eye. A wisp of smoke curling from the chimney, belying life no longer present. Crops waiting for a harvest that would never come. Sheep still grazing in the paddock, ignoring the freedom offered by the open gate.

It was idyllic. Peaceful. The type of place Alexan had once dreamed of calling home. He'd lived in so many places throughout his life, but none had ever been a home. Not the old shepherdess's cottage where he'd taken his first steps, nor any of the safe havens he'd found throughout his years on the streets. Not the barracks, nor the quarters he'd been assigned as he rose through the ranks. Not the chambers in the palace he'd been afforded as Lord Protector. Certainly not anywhere he'd lived since the Fall. Elucion was little more than a cage. A luxurious cage, right enough, but all splendour lost its shine when viewed through bars.

The farm had that rustic comfort, the security he'd always yearned for. He felt a strange pang of regret that he'd forced them to abandon it. Prayed some mortal would stumble upon it, eventually. But as he passed through the wards, he realised they never would. Théon had built the magic too strong for anyone to ever chance across it.

'It's a shame,' he heard himself saying. 'That's good land – not much of that to go about around here. Seems a pity for it to go to waste.'

From the corner of his eye, he could see Théon studying him sidelong, but she said nothing as she raised her hands. A smile touched her lips, and she summoned the Casting with casual indifference. Unravelling wards was only harder than forging them if yours was not the hand that Cast them. Alexan tensed, waiting for her magic to set his stomach churning, but the nausea he anticipated never quite came.

He frowned. What was it the old man had said? *Just because that magic slumbers, doesn't mean it is gone.* Suspicion crept up the back of his neck. He'd never known how they'd cut the Shade from her. None but Diathor and Kalielle Half-Elven had been allowed to bear witness. Where they'd found the power ...

Doubt was a chill in his veins as he watched the wards crumble into nothing. Sensed the magic Théon wiped away with a wave of her slender hand. Considered the colossal power it would take to have Cast those wards. More power than any of the Graced should possess. Far more than even he could conjure. Not without touching that sleeping behemoth. The mark on his hand prickled at the thought.

There was nothing he could do to stop that cold lump of dread from slipping a little deeper as they turned away from the croft and melted into the wilderness. He'd come hunting the Elf-Queen, not a Shade Princess. If he was wrong ... well, he was about to discover that he was out of his depth.

They rode until dawn. Illyandi had fallen asleep hours ago, her head resting on the old man's drooping shoulders. The reins were loose in Silvermane's gnarled hands, and he wasn't convinced that Illyandi's silly mare could be

237

trusted to follow Théon riding ahead. But she called a halt before he had to intervene. Whether or not she'd actually noticed their weariness, Alexan was just glad he wouldn't need to draw her attention to it. It wouldn't have endeared him to either of them.

It took all his self-restraint to say nothing while she picked out a safe place to set up camp. Keeping his expression impassive was even harder, especially when he looked at the spot she'd chosen. But he drew the line at letting a drowsy Illyandi build the fire.

He shouldered the Princess aside in exasperation, knocking the pathetic pile of twigs apart and starting again. Illyandi yelped in fright and scurried out of the way, earning him a reproachful look from both Théon and the old man.

'She was making a pig's ear of it,' he grumbled.

Théon's frown deepened. 'She was trying her best.'

He bit his tongue to keep from replying. Focussed on coaxing flames from the smouldering tinder in his hands.

'What is that mark on your hand?' the Princess demanded.

Instinct had him turning his hand over to hide it. 'A birthmark.'

Not a lie. He'd had it since birth, and it was a mark …

'Why don't you just use the Casting?' Illyandi asked a moment later. Then she looked away, her face flushing scarlet as if embarrassed to have spoken to him.

He resisted the urge to roll his eyes, answering as calmly as he could. 'I prefer to do it by hand. Any skill requires practice to stay honed, and this is an important skill to have. I never know when I might be caught without the Casting at my disposal.'

'I've never been without the Casting,' she blurted.

He huffed a soft laugh, trying not to notice how prettily she blushed. 'If only we were all so lucky.'

'What's it like?'

Théon shot him a warning look.

He ignored it. 'It's like someone shoving your head underwater and holding it there while you drown.'

Illyandi's lovely face paled, and she looked away with a delicate shudder. Théon glared at him. Satisfaction and frustration warred within him. The Princess was easy to rile. Too easy. How could Théon have sheltered her so thoroughly?

'And what reason would the Shade King have for binding the powers of his own general?' the old man asked.

It was Alexan's turn to glare. Of course the old bastard had known. The question was, had Théon? He didn't need to look to find out the answer. Her silence told him enough. Yet even knowing who he was, what he'd done, she'd still chosen to spare him. He couldn't bring himself to meet those eyes. Didn't want to know what he might see there. Held more than enough disgust for himself in his heart. A deep breath fought that rising wave down.

'It wasn't the Shade King who forced the ruan down my throat,' he said, his voice soft and more deadly for it. 'The Elven Guard was an elite group. Prospective candidates were tested. Thoroughly. How else were they to know if we could fight as well without magic as with it?'

The old man did not flinch from the accusation. 'To guard the Elf-Queen is an honour. It is not a duty that all are suited to.'

Alexan's gaze hardened. Those words had weight for any who had known the burden. All who served knew the cost... The Guard had to ensure that all those around their Queen were up to the task, and so many panicked when stripped of their power. Another trickle of misgiving slid down his spine. *I was there when Benella birthed Vianka and Velor*, Silvermane had said. There were scant few with reason to be present at a royal birth.

'Rare for the Guard to recruit beyond Illyol's borders,' Alexan noted, arching a brow in challenge.

Silvermane's gaze shuttered. 'But not unheard of.'

Alexan said nothing, eyeing the old man over the flames. He was not wrong. There were a handful from the other Graced bloodlines to have served the Elf-Queen. One had even risen to the rank of Lord Protector. Captured the heart of the Queen who owned him, body and soul. Ruled at her side. Fathered her children. It was a story Alexan knew well. A faint hope he'd clung to when he'd learned of Diathor's position. Heir to the Oak Throne. Destined to wear the Hawthorn Crown. Hoping that she – like her great-grandmother, Queen Benella – would fall in love with her Lord Protector. Prince Kenor had been a Unicorn, if a vaguely well-born one. Alexan was at least an Elf, even if he had come from nothing.

'We'll need to get moving in a few hours,' said Théon, breaking the silence as she handed a blanket to her sister. 'Get some sleep. I'll keep watch.'

'She got plenty of sleep in the wagon, and she can sleep again once we get moving,' Alexan interrupted, earning him another glare, but he continued. 'You're the one who needs rest. Going toe to toe with any Shade Prince will take it out of you, and I've been around the Court long enough to know Kieyin doesn't pull his punches. You're doing a good job of hiding it, but you're drained. Don't make it worse by exhausting yourself too.'

Silence followed his accusation. Théon's gaze was blistering, pulsing with that eerie light, while Illyandi's jaw went slack as if in shock that anyone would dare speak to her sister that way.

Silvermane was frowning at Théon. 'Perhaps it is time we heard a little more of what transpired between yourself and Prince Kieyin. And how you came to owe a life-debt to a member of the Shade King's inner circle.'

Alexan said nothing, looking to Théon. He'd find out how the old man was so well informed about the workings of the Shade King's Court later. This was a more important conversation. One that would either save him or damn him.

She relayed the exchange and ensuing battle with dispassionate precision, her voice cool with indifference while she described how close she'd come to losing her life. It was almost chilling, the detachment she exuded while narrating what were almost her last moments. Even when she recounted how he'd saved her, there was no hint of emotion in those ever-green eyes. And nothing even approaching gratitude.

'That explains why you brought him within the wards,' the old man growled when she was finished, 'but not why you didn't kill him when you realised your mistake.'

'Were you not listening? He saved my life. It would be tempting fate to repay that mercy with murder.'

'The mercy would have been to free him from his own fate,' argued Silvermane. 'It's what you were born to do.'

'What *you* were born to do,' she corrected. 'As you so kindly reminded me earlier, my situation is somewhat different.'

The old man bristled. 'That fate is behind you. You have a new destiny now.'

'I'm aware of that, and grateful for it too.' Alexan could scent the lie. Taste the unspoken bitterness lacing her words. The same unsaid resent-ment that had so often coloured his own voice. It chafed at her, to speak of gratitude for a destiny she never chose, a destiny forced upon her. 'But as distasteful as it is, my heritage allows me to look beyond blood prejudice and the inclination towards violence that comes with it. When you look at him, you see only the magic corrupting him. I see it too, but it's not all I see.'

The old man was quiet for a while, considering her – reluctantly, if his expression was anything to go by, but he *was* considering.

'And what is it you see when you look at him?' he asked.

Théon's lovely face was unyielding. 'I see the man who helped me when no one else would, who taught me control when I had none. The man who snatched Illyandi and I from the edge of the abyss. Who pulled us from our beds that night and hid us while they hunted us. Who smuggled us from the city when the dawn broke, shielding us from all the horrors the Fall had left behind. The man who defended our retreat, buying us whatever time he could while we fled. Who then hunted down the monster respon-sible for my mother's death – knowing he was outmatched, that his cause was hopeless, that it would cost him everything; I see the man who tried anyway.'

'You see a fool then.'

'I see strength. I see persistence. I see integrity.'

Alexan flinched from the words. From the praise he had not earned. Fortunately, no one seemed to notice. Silvermane had fallen quiet once more, his brow twisted in reluctance.

'Alright,' he conceded, though the word was clearly a bitter taste in his mouth. Alexan tried not to smirk at his obvious discomfort. 'But I have to question whether it is prudent for him to accompany us any further. Regardless of who he was, he is a Darkling now – slave to the Claiming. To your father. Not to mention his thirst. You must recognise the danger he poses? To you. To your sister.'

The look Théon returned was so withering Alexan counted his bless-ings he wasn't on the receiving end of it. 'Of course I recognise the

240

danger. But I have to weigh it against the other threats we might face. Outside the wards, we're exposed. Vulnerable. I might be able to hold my own, but it wouldn't take much for us to be outnumbered. Illyandi's no fighter, and you were past your prime when Velor sat on the Oak Throne.'

'Watch it,' the old bastard growled.

She ignored him. 'If what Kieyin said is true, the King's known where to find me for years. I don't know why he's chosen now to come after me, but he won't give up that easily. Alexan was Lord Protector of the Elven Guard. You think we can afford to pass on that kind of skill and experience? These hills will be crawling with Darklings before we know it, and I will not risk Illyandi's safety for your pride.'

'It's not about my pr—'

She cut him off. 'Yes, it is. You can call it caution, but I know you better.'

'That's your father talking.'

'That line is wearing thin, old man,' Alexan said. 'Nor are you in any position to make that judgement.'

Silvermane blinked. 'What's that supposed to mean?'

'You know what he's done. I know what he is.' He cocked his head, considering the obstinate bastard. 'Yes, she's as stubborn and proud as he is. Arrogant too. But she's not him. If you believe nothing else, believe that.'

The old man's lip curled in distaste. 'Intimate knowledge of the Shade King's mind is not something I would boast about possessing.'

It was Alexan's turn to sneer. 'Only an idiot would consider understanding an enemy to be a failing.'

'Your enemy? Or your master?'

'The two are not mutually exclusive.'

'And yet you expect us to trust you? When you are bound in servitude to the greatest evil this world has ever known?'

Alexan rolled his eyes and looked sidelong at Théon. 'Does he always speak in superlatives?'

'Fairly often, yes,' she admitted, not quite stifling a grin. She sobered as the old man glared. 'His question is valid though.'

Alexan shook his head in frustration. 'Trust is a luxury that none of you can afford right now. It doesn't matter if you trust me or not – you need me, and that's all that matters.'

They fell quiet while his words sank in. Alexan watched, looking for any sign, but their expressions remained impassive. Illyandi broke the silence first.

'Trust is not something to be given freely. It has to be earned. Perhaps he deserves a chance to earn ours.' Alexan could only stare at her in disbelief. A swift glance at Théon and Silvermane told him they were just as stunned as he was. But judging by their speechlessness, it seemed unlikely they would argue with her pronouncement. He bowed his head in thanks before their astonishment wore off. She smiled in answer and looked to her sister. 'He is right though. You should rest.'

'As should you,' Théon began.

'Why don't you both rest?' The old man intervened before either could disagree. 'The Darkling and I can keep watch.'

Théon looked like she was about to argue anyway but seemed to decide better of it. Neither she nor Illyandi said any more on the subject before tucking themselves up and going straight to sleep.

Silvermane watched them in silence for the best part of an hour, that handsome face unreadable even to Alexan. He left the old man to it, busying himself with tending the horses and checking their immediate surroundings before taking up a position between his charges and the path. His weapons he left within easy reach. Not as comforting as having them to hand, but Silvermane was still uneasy, and he wasn't stupid enough to provoke the old bastard any further.

It wasn't until Théon started snoring that Silvermane stirred. Amethyst eyes watched Alexan from beneath furrowed brows, glittering in the flickering light of the campfire.

'For what it's worth,' Silvermane murmured, 'I am sorry for what you have endured.'

Alexan shrugged. 'Don't be. I didn't choose this, but I knew the risks.'

'I won't insult you further by pretending to understand.' The old man sighed and shook his head. 'You realise how difficult this is? What you are asking of us?'

'You speak like I wasn't once one of you. Of course I know how hard it is. But sometimes we have to endure unpleasant things to survive. I've suffered a lot to get this far, and I'll suffer a lot worse to keep Diathor's daughters alive. What are you willing to sacrifice for that end?'

Silvermane's gaze grew hard. 'I've sacrificed more than you can ever imagine.' Then he sighed in defeat and nodded. 'But I would do it all again to protect them.'

Alexan said nothing but inclined his head in appreciation.

After a while, the old man spoke again. 'Your mind is well guarded.'

'All who serve the King have to learn how to keep his secrets.'

'And what of that which is not secret? You say you know him well ...'

Alexan was quiet for a time, considering what the old man was asking. How well he had phrased the question. He understood the Claiming better than he let on. To offer up the King's secrets would be treason, a betrayal the Claiming would not allow for. But this? To share what he thought of the man? His own observations, judgements? The Claiming would not silence him should he choose to share those.

And the old man knew it.

It was a test. Of his loyalty. To see if he would find any loophole, exploit any chance to prove his loyalty to the Elf-Queen.

He sighed in defeat. 'I'll tell you what I can, but I should warn you – you might not like what you hear.'

The old man quizzed him for hours while Théon and her sister slept. As expected, he didn't seem to like much of what Alexan said. His forehead had more wrinkles than Kieyin's used bedsheets, and his mouth was puckered tighter than a cat's arsehole by the end. But at least he didn't bother to dispute anything Alexan told him. He also had the sense to let the matter drop when Théon stirred and stretched.

'How long did I sleep?' she yawned. At least, that's what he thought she said. It was hard to tell for sure.

'A while. It's just after midday.'

She grunted in acknowledgement and nudged her sister awake with the toe of her boot. 'We should get going.'

'You should eat first,' said Silvermane, pointing at the carcass of a large pheasant Alexan had killed, plucked and roasted over the campfire.

Théon blinked. 'Where did that come from?'

'I borrowed your bow,' Alexan told her, handing it and the quiver back to her. 'Not bad, but it's seen better days. Shame about the state of the arrows too. I replaced the fletching on the worst, but they need new heads and some of the shafts are knackered.'

She blinked again, taking the proffered weapon. 'Thanks.'

'Welcome. Eat up,' he replied, tossing her half of the remaining bird. The other he held out to Illyandi who shuddered at the fat and grease dripping from the meat. He rolled his eyes, warning, 'You won't survive long in the wild living on fruit and leaves, Princess. Your body needs a varied diet to stay strong and healthy.'

'I know that,' she told him, pulling an apple from her pack. 'And if a time comes when I have no other choice but to consume the flesh of living things then I will do so. However, currently, I have other options.'

Alexan didn't bother to point out that plants were living things too. He didn't want to waste the breath.

With a sigh, he got to his feet and cleared up their camp. Théon and her sister stayed out of his way, and he made quick work of it. They would have been on their way in a matter of minutes, but Illyandi insisted on checking over her horse before they left. As if he was not capable of caring for the beast ...

They continued as before, with Théon leading and Alexan bringing up the rear. Illyandi revealed herself not to be entirely self-absorbed and had volunteered to take the reins while Silvermane slept. They did not stop again until well after sunset, when darkness made it all but impossible for Théon to see the path before her.

'I can see it fine,' Alexan told her when she explained the problem.

The look she returned was scathing. 'How nice for you. Tell me again how that helps us?'

'Well, if you tell me where we're going,' he said through clenched teeth, 'I can take the lead and then all you have to do is follow me.'

'We should rest the horses,' she said.

'We can't afford to rest the horses! This isn't some little summer jaunt we're on, out to camp under the stars. Do you have any idea what could be behind us right now?' He didn't mean to snap, but his frustration got the better of him. She flinched and hesitated, glancing to the old man, and Alexan had to resist the urge to shake her. 'You said it yourself – you need me right now, but I can't help you if you don't let me. And if this is because you don't think I can be trusted, can I remind you that my life is on the line here too? I've seen what the King does to traitors. I've dealt out his judgements myself often enough.'

'So you think we should trust you because you want to save your own skin?'

'More or less.'

She bared her teeth in frustration. 'Fine.'

He waited.

'There's a port north-west of here. A ferry to Stormkeep leaves every week, for mortals who can afford the passage. And for any of the Graced seeking safe haven.'

He stilled. 'What?'

'You see why I didn't want to tell you.'

He did. 'How many?'

'Not many. But enough that he can never learn of it.'

He didn't bother to correct her. 'Alright. So you were planning on leaving me behind once you got to the boat?'

'I hadn't decided yet.'

Of course she hadn't. He shook his head in frustration, touching his heels to his mount's flanks, urging her to the front, and took the lead. The path was wide enough for the cart. Just. At least Silvermane had woken up and taken over the reins. He seemed alert enough to ensure Illyandi's silly mare stayed close behind Alexan. If Théon had any sense, she'd be keeping her stallion's nose to the back of the cart. Alexan didn't bother to check.

How in the Gods' name was he going to get on board the boat? More to the point, how was he going to survive more than a handful of heartbeats on an island full of the Graced? Perhaps his plan had backfired. There was little chance Théon trusted him if this is what she'd been considering. What a fucking disaster.

The twang of a crossbow was punishment for allowing himself to be distracted, and he roared in pain as the bolt slammed into his gut. Théon yelled a warning to her sister, but he couldn't make out the words over the pounding of his blood. Fool. Fucking idiotic fool. How had he missed that? They hadn't just appeared from nowhere. Where had his mind been that he hadn't noticed?

He ripped the bolt from his stomach with a vicious curse and threw it aside. Magic roiled in his veins, healing the wound and rousing his temper. Another bolt snapped in the darkness, and he rolled from the saddle to avoid it. Why had neither Théon nor Illyandi Cast a shield? Landing on his feet, he grabbed his sword and spared a glance for his charges. The Princess was hunkered down in the cart, the old man shielding her with his body. Théon stood over them, sword drawn but no Casting to speak of was at hand. Alexan cursed again and scanned the shadows for their enemies.

His gaze fell on a familiar crop of gingery hair. Callan. One of Jenia's lackeys. And there were Finn and Hart flanking him. Fear thundered in Alexan's chest as he sought the blood-red mane of the King's lover. No sign of her that he could see, but that didn't mean she wasn't near. This was her Hunt. All Graced. Phoenix, mostly. Thank the Gods. There were a few Elves and a Dragon too, but he couldn't see any of them here. No Unicorns either. There weren't any in Jenia's Hunt. The King couldn't stand them.

He grit his teeth and summoned a Casting. A mighty storm of dark power that churned in the night. A flicker of guilt twisted in his chest for the friends he was about to kill. But perhaps it was just his wound healing. At least they'd walk it off.

Callan charged, Finn and Hart on his heels as always. Alexan swore and loosed the Casting. They screamed as they died, consumed in the maelstrom, but he had no time to mourn when the clash of steel behind him drew his attention. Théon was being pressed hard by the twins, Aven and Briar, and Silvermane was trying to Enchant Madden. More of the Hunt prowled out of reach, waiting for a chance to strike, while Illyandi cowered between her defenders. Not so much as a hint of a Casting from either sister.

His temper surged again. What were they playing at? The power to end this at their fingertips and neither one willing to touch it? He vaulted over his coal-black mare, reaching for a Casting again, blasting the twins away from Théon before slamming his shoulder into Madden's gut, tackling him to the ground. The Phoenix-born Darkling came up swinging and forced Alexan to give ground.

They traded a flurry of blows before an opening presented itself. Alexan almost laughed. So predictable. Madden made the same mistake every time. The consternation on his face said he knew it too, and Alexan smirked as he drove his blade up into his friend's heart. An enraged scream from behind drew his attention, and he spun just in time to parry a heavy, overhand blow from Nola. Another predictable reaction. She'd always been protective of her lover. He dispatched her with similar ease, ignoring the curse of *traitor* from her lips as she died.

Jenia's Hunt kept coming. The twins had recovered and were now circling Silvermane, trying to avoid the Enchanting, while Théon battled three more of the Darklings. Still no sign of a Casting. Alexan swore in frustration and summoned his own. The shield would not hold forever, but it would buy him enough time to deal with those Darklings already inside it. He allowed himself half a heartbeat to catch his breath and watch Théon cleave Brenna's head from her shoulders, before launching himself at the twins.

It wasn't as strange as he'd thought it would be, to butcher his friends. To drench his hands in their blood. He felt no regret for the slaughter. Just relief that Jenia didn't appear to be with them. He would have been powerless to intervene otherwise. A glance over his shoulder told him Théon had come out on top of her little skirmish, so he turned his attention to those beyond his shield. Still too many for comfort. Jenia's Hunt had always been one of the largest in Elucion.

'Cast!' he barked at the sisters.

'Others will sense it,' Théon objected.

He swore but chose instead to take his frustration out on whoever was unfortunate enough to be nearest. He released his shield, slamming his sword point through Maeve's neck without breaking his stride and kicking Bowen so hard in the chest he heard bone shatter.

'Just do it,' he roared back at Théon. 'And get your sister off her fucking knees and making herself useful!'

Gods, they'd gotten so soft. Théon had been more useful in a fight when she was ten years old. How had she let a hundred years go by without ever teaching Illyandi to protect herself? Finally, *finally*, Théon's Casting roared into life in a storm of lightning streaking through the night. Jenia's Hunt died as it blasted through their ranks, and any who were missed were cut down by Alexan's blade or felled by his own Castings.

And then it was over.

The night echoed with the ragged gasps of their breathing and the ringing silence of death. He wiped the blood from his blade, flinching from the sound of it splattering the earth beneath his feet. His heartbeat was a dull roar in his ears and rage a bitter taste in his mouth. He rounded on Théon, restraining his temper long enough to shove the sword back in its sheath before he started lambasting her.

'What the bloody hell was that?' he snarled, kicking Maeve's corpse out of his path. 'Were you trying to get yourselves killed, or are you just incompetent?'

'Watch your mouth,' growled Théon, helping Illyandi to her feet.

'Answer the fucking question then!'

The old man spluttered in indignation. 'You dare—'

'You're damn right I dare.' Alexan cut him off, gesticulating at Théon and her sister. 'The two of you have the power to level mountains! And instead, one of you relies only on steel and the strength of your arm in a fight while the other cowers like a child and does nothing?'

'Blood calls to blood,' Théon snapped. 'You understand how it works. By using our power we've just announced our presence to anything with magic in its veins for a hundred miles in every direction. Nightwalkers. Darklings. Gods, maybe even a Shade. They'll all be after us now.'

'Better that than dying, don't you think?'

'We had it covered.'

He laughed at that. 'No. *I* had it covered. Now you all owe me a life-debt. Actually, no.' He paused, pointing at Théon. 'You owe me two. Now help me clear the path, and let's get moving.'

She had the good grace not to argue. It took only a few minutes to move the bodies out of their way. They could have done it in less time, but Illyandi refused to help. Didn't want to get blood on her hands. By some miracle he'd controlled his temper at that pronouncement. Just.

The old man caught his eye as he was swinging up into the saddle. 'You knew them.'

It wasn't a question.

'Jenia's Hunt. Or part of it, anyway. I trained most of them myself.'

There was a pause. 'I'm sorry.'

'Don't be,' he snorted. 'They're all Phoenix-born, and we don't have time to hide the bodies.'

Another pause told him the old man understood what he was saying. 'How will she find them?'

'She just will.'

Silvermane let it drop, and they continued on in silence.

CHAPTER TWENTY-ONE

It was almost sunrise when Théon joined him at the front, pulling her steel-grey stallion alongside him. She said nothing, but he could feel the tension rolling off her. Sensed the argument brewing. Didn't bother with tact.

'You need to train,' he said. There was a heavy pause. From the corner of his eye, he saw her lips purse and her fingers tighten on the reins. But when she looked at him, it was with the air of someone waiting for the punchline of a badly told joke.

'You think so?' she asked, unable to hide the amused irony in her voice.

'Yes. Kieyin almost killed you, and you wouldn't have lasted long against that Hunt.' He didn't bother to mention that if Kieyin had been intent on killing her, she would be dead already.

She snorted. 'I would have been fine.'

'Really?' he snapped. 'Then why didn't you use the Casting?'

'I told you why.'

'Bullshit,' he countered. 'You didn't hesitate to rely on the Casting against Kieyin. Why not this time?'

Théon snarled, baring her teeth and a wild, unbroken part of herself. 'I had to use the Casting against Kieyin, but I didn't need it against the Dark-lings. I wanted to feel their lives spill out on the edge of my blade.'

'And that was your first mistake,' he insisted. 'You let your emotions cloud your judgement and almost died as a consequence.'

'I would have used the Casting before—'

'Your second mistake,' he said, continuing as if she hadn't spoken, 'was insisting on doing it all yourself. Illyandi is at least as powerful as you, and you've not trained her to fight. She's reliant on you for survival. Worse than that. You're overconfident, undisciplined and reckless, and one of these days, it's going to get you both killed.'

It was something that had bothered him since he'd first laid eyes on her. Keriath was the same. They were arrogant, the pair of them. That arrogance was likely to be the end of them. Petulant rage crackled in her eyes, that terrible, eerie light pulsing again. But she swallowed it, nodding in understanding.

'Alright.'

It was a minor victory, but he savoured it. 'We'll need to stop and rest soon, but once you've recovered, I want to get an idea of what I'm working with. I don't want to get caught off guard again.'

It was another day before the opportunity to test her presented itself. She was more drained than he'd realised, and it had taken far longer than he'd expected for her to recover. He wasn't full of energy himself, though he did his best to hide it. But when they both had the strength, and felt safe enough to linger a little longer, he pressed the point.

'Let's start with some basic hand-to-hand,' he said. He picked a wide-open space away from the camp, partly to minimise damage but mostly to avoid the old man's steely glare. Her overall fitness and competence were a pleasant surprise, but as suspected, her discipline was lacking. He held off mentioning it until the fifth time he'd knocked her into the dirt.

'Sloppy,' he noted, stretching a slight tightness in his chest muscles. His own lack of condition was concerning, and his body complained at the rough handling. He'd need to feed sooner rather than later. Théon swore at him, spitting blood from her mouth and touching the side of her face where he'd struck her. He stilled as the scent filled his nose. Gods, the power in that blood. She could sustain him for days if—

He shoved the thought away. Some things didn't bear thinking about. He chuckled, trying to hide his discomfort. 'Come on,' he taunted, 'I thought your father taught you everything he knew about power and pain?'

She swore again and launched herself at him, tackling him to the ground. It was all too easy for him to use her own weight and momentum against her.

'You let your emotions control you,' he told her, pinning her down. Tried to ignore the feel of her body against his. 'It makes you predictable. Predictable will get you, and your beloved sister, killed.'

Without warning, she went limp, her eyes sliding from his face to stare at the sky above.

'Let me up,' she said in a dead voice. He blinked, surprised that the fire had gone from her so fast. Part of him wanted to keep pushing, to find out what had prompted the change, to sniff out the potential weakness there. But he'd seen that expression on her face before. Heard that tone in her voice. Knew what it meant. It had shattered his heart then, and it hurt just as much now. She was lost. Despairing. Hopeless. He released her and stepped back, offering a hand to help her to her feet. She didn't take it.

'I'm sorry,' he heard himself say. But she didn't even look at him as she turned and walked away. He didn't follow. Some paths had to be walked alone.

He was more than a little surprised that, when the next opportunity presented itself, she asked to continue training. She'd avoided him after that first session, and he'd kept his distance rather than risk another fight. And although he was pleased she wanted to try again, it was obvious some part of her was still lost in whatever darkness he'd roused.

To be fair, she took his steady stream of instructions without argument or complaint. But her attacks were half-hearted and her defence pathetic. The fight had gone right out of her. Like a candle snuffed out in the snow. And it was his fault. He missed it, that wild savagery. The ferocity. Only the hint of grim determination in those evergreen eyes, glinting every time she picked herself up out of the mud, offered any hope. Downtrodden, yes. Hurting. But not broken. Not yet. He tried to provoke her, to turn that resolve into aggression, but even the most humiliating defeats got only sullen silence in response.

'You're not even trying,' he said, watching her wipe the blood from her face. He held his breath. Folded his arms across his chest to hide his shaking hands. She didn't even bother to deny it. 'Come on,' he goaded her, 'even Illyandi could do better than this.'

Something flickered behind those eyes. 'Leave her out of this.'

He stilled and smiled. There it was.

'Why?' he pressed. 'I was going to wait until we'd made more progress, but she needs this as much as you do. Perhaps more.' The edges of her aura flickered to life as she fought for control.

'Don't. Leave her alone.'

He turned towards the camp. 'She has to learn to fend for herself.'

'She lives by Benella's code,' Théon snarled. He rolled his eyes, not bothering to hide it. He'd already gathered as much, but it made it no less irritating to hear it out loud. The Graced worshipped the ancient Elf-Queen, but her vow of non-violence had left her – and anyone who had followed her example – vulnerable. Illyandi wouldn't kill, even to save her own life. But that didn't mean she shouldn't know how to fight. Besides, the discussion was getting a rise out of Théon. It was too good to let pass.

'She should still know how to defend herself,' he insisted. 'She can't rely on you forever. There are plenty of ways to survive without killing anyone.'

'She knows enough to stay alive,' Théon ground out from between clenched teeth, 'and she can *always* rely on me.'

Alexan shook his head, ignoring the warning tone. 'Knowing and doing are two separate things. She should practise.'

'Alexan. Drop it.' There was no mistaking the pure command in her voice. He repressed a triumphant grin as he turned to look at her, puffing his chest out in a way that he already knew would make her see red.

'If the only instruction she's ever had is from you and the old man, she's likely fucked anyway,' he said. 'She wouldn't last five minutes against a mortal Darkling, let alone someone like Jenia or your father. And if she's taken alive, well ... I've seen first-hand what they do to girls like Illyandi. I wonder if she'd shy away from violence if she knew that was her fate?'

Théon snapped. She flew at him, spitting and snarling like a wildcat. He grinned, whooping in triumph as he met her charge. Once again, he used her own weight and momentum against her, throwing her to the ground with ease and pinning her down with the full weight of his body.

'Once again, Your Majesty,' he jeered, 'emotional and predictable.'

She growled and wrenched a leg free, the hint of a Casting flaring around her as her control frayed with her temper. But yet again, she didn't reach for the magic. She planted her foot, driving up through the hips, and pushed him off her with impossible strength. She twisted quickly, far too quickly, with one of her legs coming down on his neck while the other kicked him beneath his sternum. Winded, he couldn't stop her as she grabbed his wrist and held it tight to her chest. His arm was trapped between her legs, and she jerked her hips skyward with a vicious smile, wrecking his elbow. He yelled out in pain as the joint tore, but she didn't stop, twisting his wrist until the bones in his forearm splintered. Then she was on top of him, her fingers gripping his face as her nails bit into his cheeks.

'This is what happens if I let my emotions control me,' she breathed, squeezing hard enough that he thought she might just rip his jaw clean off. He could smell the blood from where her nails had broken his skin, but the sting of the wounds had been lost amongst the other pain sweeping through his body. 'If I am predictable, it is because I'm too much in control – so tightly bound that I cannot breathe.'

She broke off, releasing him and leaping back like he'd burned her. Alexan took a deep breath, luxuriating in the air filling his lungs. He cradled his ruined arm to his chest, rolling to his feet and trying not to wince.

Though there was regret in her steady gaze, there was no hint of an apology on her face. Something flickered behind her eyes, but it was gone before he could register it. Instead, she held out her hand and sighed with impatience when he hesitated. She took his hand, the gentle rush of a Casting gathering.

A wave of dizziness followed as her power swept through him, healing his wounds. She gripped his good arm and held him upright until it passed. He could have done it himself. Would have, if she hadn't got there first. But he took the gesture as she meant it. A peace offering, if not an apology.

'Thanks,' he grunted, flexing his fingers. She nodded in acknowledgement and turned to walk away without a word. But Alexan wouldn't drop it. He grabbed her elbow and spun her to face him. 'Théon, please,' he begged. 'Don't do this, not again. We've been through this before. I can't help you if you won't talk to me.'

'I'm not a child anymore,' she said, pulling away. 'I don't have the luxury of handing out my trust to whoever I wish.'

'You gave me your trust back then,' he argued. 'Why should it be any different now?'

She rolled her eyes. 'Because back then you weren't a Darkling, bound to my father of all people.'

'I don't want to hurt you, Théon.'

'Whether you want it to or not, it will come down to you or me. Every minute we're together, you're studying me for opportunities, assessing anything you can exploit when you're given your orders. Don't think I haven't noticed.'

He didn't bother to deny it. 'Why do you think I want you to train? I don't want to hurt you, but I might not have a choice. If that happens, you need to be prepared.' She sighed and turned away, running a hand through her hair in frustration. He grabbed her again and forced her to look at him. 'Listen to me, Théon. After everything we went through together ... everything we've suffered since ... I'm not about to turn my back on you now. But I can't help you if you shut me out.'

She held his gaze, emotions warring behind those evergreen eyes. He forced his expression to remain impassive. He'd seen her like this once before. When she'd returned from more than a decade at her father's side. She'd been confused and shy. Timid and broken. Unsure who to trust. Diathor had done her best but trying to entice a daughter she barely knew out of her shell was no simple task. And her husband had been no help – if anything, he'd made matters worse. Sarron had been a hard bastard at the best of times. A Shade child living in his home hadn't improved his manner.

Alexan had witnessed it all. He'd lasted a month before taking the task upon himself. Théon had been taught how to fight by the King, and she'd gravitated towards the training grounds. He'd spotted her there late one evening – long after she was supposed to be in bed – watching him spar. She later confessed that she was plagued by nightmares, and the ring of steel on steel was as close to a lullaby as she'd ever get. So he'd handed her a practice sword and gone from there.

Her voice dragged him back to the present.

'They bound it,' she murmured, 'trapped the power inside, so it couldn't hurt anyone. But it can hurt me. It whispers to me, trying to make me do things I know I shouldn't. Sometimes the spell is the only thing stopping me.'

'What?' he breathed, his fingers tightening around her arms.

Her eyes widened with fright, and she shook her head. 'Nothing.' She gasped. 'It's nothing. I shouldn't have said anything. I'm not supposed to tell anyone. I was never supposed to tell anyone.' She was trembling, tumbling over her words in her panic as she tried to run from him. It was a struggle to contain his rage, but he forced himself to control it while he held her fast.

'Théon,' he said, his voice firm. 'Calm down. You're safe. Nobody's going to hurt you. Now tell me what this is about.'

She was shaking, but she met his gaze and nodded. She took a deep breath, though the fear and anxiety did not fade from her eyes, and when she spoke, her voice was barely more than a terrified whisper. 'When

Kalielle took me from my father ... I fought her. Every step of the way, I fought her. Even once I was back in Illyol, I was always looking for a way to escape – to get back to him. The Shade breed true. Children are always loyal to their lineage. We can't help it. It's blood magic, corrupted to the extreme.

'They couldn't destroy it, not without killing me, so they found a way to suppress the Shade and block the ties binding me to him. It's a spell – an ancient, powerful spell, far beyond my reckoning. It keeps the Shade power, and all that it entails, bound beyond my reach. I don't even know if it can be broken, but I wasn't allowed to tell anyone. Not ever. If word got out, my mother knew that my father would tear the world apart to break the spell. She wouldn't risk that.'

'But it's still there, isn't it? Just biding its time and waiting for an opportunity?'

She nodded. 'At first, I kept it secret because I didn't want to let it go. My mother was a stranger, and I wanted to go home. But as my father's influence over me waned, I saw him – saw myself – as others saw us. Monsters. Monsters that needed to be put down. So I held my tongue out of fear. I was scared that if they ever realised it was still inside me, speaking to me, that they'd kill me rather than risk it breaking free. I realised that the spell couldn't be broken, not from within anyway. But by then I had grown to love my mother ... I didn't want to hurt her by telling her the truth. She was so happy to see me free, even for only those few years.'

Alexan nodded in understanding. He too would have done anything to protect Diathor from harm. But what was it the old man had said? *Just because that magic slumbers, doesn't mean it is gone.* Silvermane understood the inner workings of the spell itself. Théon was still keeping secrets. 'And now?' he asked. 'Why keep lying to them now?'

'Habit,' she admitted. 'Habit and acceptance. There's nothing to be done about it, and I've lived with it this long ... what would be the point in saying something now?'

Alexan failed to repress the growl of frustration that ripped out of his chest at the defeat in her voice. 'The point would be the people you love knowing that you're suffering,' he snarled. 'The point would be the old man understanding your needs and treating you with the respect you deserve. The point would be your sister comprehending that she might need to step up and care for you like you care for her.'

'It's my burden to carry,' Théon said. He threw his hands in the air and turned away. Was there no end to her pigheadedness?

'Not anymore,' he told her. 'I'll keep your secrets, Théon, but don't expect me to just sit by and let you fight this alone. Until the day your father orders me otherwise, I will look after you. Live or die. We'll do it together.'

She hesitated, the remnants of that little girl peering out at him. Desperate to trust, desperate to share the burden. To find a way that she wouldn't have to face this alone. But there was a different woman standing in the way. A woman who stood on her own two feet. Who'd protected and provided for her family for almost a century. A woman reluctant to let go.

'Alright,' she conceded. Then she nodded – more to herself than to him – and dropped into a defensive crouch, raising her hands and crooking her fingers in daring invitation. 'Now, show me what you've got.'

By some miracle, the rest of the journey passed without incident. Alexan offered a prayer of thanks to long-forgotten Gods for that small mercy. Not that it hadn't been eventful.

He'd waited a few days before daring to bring up the subject of Illyandi training again. He wasn't enthusiastic about the prospect. The Princess was a pain, and Théon had almost killed him the last time he'd suggested it. But he had to know the Princess would be able to defend herself.

He'd thought Théon would be the biggest challenge, but when he found the will to grit his teeth and raise the matter again, she'd just nodded. He hadn't been sure the old man would like it, but Silvermane had at least agreed to hear him out.

No, the biggest problem was Illyandi herself. She was naive to the point of stupidity, more stubborn than her sister (if that were possible) and had a flair for dramatics that set his teeth on edge. Worst of all, Théon had realised it would be far easier for her to just sit back and let him deal with the Princess. More entertaining too. He'd wanted to throttle them both. His temper was fraying day by day. Not helped by his thirst, and the pounding headache that grew worse by the hour.

The first time Illyandi had joined them, he and the Princess had traded insults in a blistering argument that'd lasted for half an hour before Théon had intervened. Even then, Illyandi hadn't wanted to bend. It was only when the old man ordered her to do as she was told that they'd been able to get started.

It hadn't been pretty, not by any stretch of the imagination. There'd been tears before the end. From both of them. And a lot of swearing. Also from both of them. But eventually, she was at least able to hold a sword. She'd been so tired afterward that she'd fallen asleep the moment she'd climbed back into the wagon, so he hadn't had to endure any more whining.

He'd been enjoying some of that blissful silence, drinking in the beauty of the setting sun, when they rounded the headland, and he finally laid eyes on the harbour town that was to be his deliverance or his doom. His good mood faded in a heartbeat. Had he done enough to earn her trust? Would it even be her choice? If there were other remnants of the Graced in that town …

His mind raced with the possibilities. Sifting through. Calculating. Problems and solutions. Actions and reactions. A hundred potential scenarios. A thousand different outcomes. Most of them beyond his control. His skin prickled with the discomfort of it all.

They followed the coastal path a little further before Théon called a halt. Too preoccupied with his own anxious thoughts, he was content, for once, to let them set up camp without his supervision. Instead, he rode on a little further, until he could get a good view of their destination.

It was little more than a fishing village, truth be told. A handful of boats bobbing in the harbour; a few rows of houses lining the shore. A little market square, a small tavern nearby. All quiet with night approaching, save for the cry of gulls overhead and the sea lapping at the harbour walls. Pleasant. Peaceful. Probably prosperous once, but now just a remote outpost offering passage to safer lands.

But with all that entailed.

He'd scented the camp first, long before he'd even seen the village, but from his elevated position up the path he could now see the tents on the outskirts.

Refugees. Dozens of them. Possibly hundreds.

Human souls, desperate to escape the Darkling scourge.

His stomach heaved with self-reproach. The King had driven them to this. Alexan, as commander of his Darkling armies, had driven them to this. He knew it was the lesser of two evils. Knew the alternative was far worse. But seeing the consequences of his actions ... seeing their despair with his own eyes ... it didn't make his task any easier.

He turned away. There was nothing he could do for them.

Théon appeared to sense his foul mood when he returned, keeping her mouth shut and eyes averted. And when Silvermane seemed about to quiz him on where he'd been, she cut him off with a pointed cough and less-than-subtle shake of her head. Alexan ignored them both and took up position for first watch. Weapon in hand this time. The old man could shove his distrust up his arse. He didn't even turn around when Illyandi announced that their food was ready. Didn't think he could stomach it after what he'd seen.

The three of them ate their meal in silence, oblivious to his discomfort. Well, mostly. He could feel Théon's steady gaze on him, could sense her concern. It was oddly comforting.

He blinked at the thought. Where had that come from? He had little chance to dwell on it as Théon rose from the fire, wiping her fingers on her trousers and swapping her sword for a pair of lethal-looking daggers. She caught his eye as she pulled on her cloak and paused.

'I'm going to check out the village. See if it's safe.'

He nodded in understanding. This was one task he was ill-suited for. With a sigh, he pulled his own knife from his boot and handed it to her. 'Be careful.'

She smiled, and it perturbed him to see a glimmer of relief in those evergreen eyes. His fingers brushed hers as she took it, and he almost flinched from the shock of it. From the fluttering in his gut that it caused. The heating of his blood.

There was something about her. Something alluring that called to the darkness within. Taunted him. Challenged him. Made him want to behave inappropriately. It had to be the Shade magic humming through her veins. There was no other reason for his body to react the way it did. Was it her power that sang to him so sweetly? Her eyes widened, as if she sensed it too. Perhaps not then ...

But just as soon as it had started, the moment passed, and she busied herself with securing the knife in her own boot. He wondered if he hadn't just imagined the whole thing.

Then she was gone, consigning the safety of the Princess and the old man to his care. The hours she was gone dragged ... Partly worry, but mostly Illyandi's inane conversation. She'd been so unwell of late, she was whining, particularly when she first woke up. She thought it was all the stress of the journey. Maybe it was just Alexan's cooking. It must be the smell of meat roasting over the fire that was turning her stomach ...

He snorted at that, eyeing her in contemplation, but kept his conclusions to himself. Held them in reserve for another time.

Dawn was a pale light on the horizon when Théon returned. Alexan had readied himself at least three times during the night to go and look for her, but each time, the old man had talked him down. Illyandi slept through it all.

Relief had his knees trembling at the sight of that familiar figure slipping back into their camp. A tightness in his lungs he'd barely noticed, now easing at last. Something else pounding in his chest.

Gods, he wanted her. The realisation struck him like a blow to the face as he stared at her. It was nothing to do with her power. Nothing more than male desire that heated his veins. It took all his self-restraint not to drag her against his body and kiss her senseless.

There was no denying it, not with his heartbeat roaring in his ears. Nor could he brush it off as some ghost of his feelings for Diathor. She looked nothing like her mother. It was Illyandi who was Diathor's double, but he could hardly stand the sight of *her*. Nor was it some Darkling corruption, some twisting of his soul by the magic in his veins.

No. He wanted Théon. More than he'd ever wanted any woman in his life. Wanted to taste every inch of her tawny skin, feel her body move in time with his, hear her scream his name.

He pulled himself up short. She was not his to think about like that. Besides, even if she would ever consent to his touch, her father would kill him for the imagined slight.

So he pushed his feelings aside. 'What took you so long?'

'Nice to see you too,' she muttered, warming her hands over the fire. 'I had to check the camp too. Took longer than expected.'

'The camp?' yawned Illyandi.

Théon gave him a warning look. This time he heeded it. 'The village is too small to house all the mortals wanting passage to Stormkeep. There's a large camp on the outskirts.'

The Princess nodded, not taking in the words. Just as well, though she was going to throw a fit when she saw it. An argument for a later time. He turned his attention back to Théon.

'Well?'

'No trace of any magical presence that I could sense.'

'Chances of one you can't?'

'Slim, but possible.'

He grunted. 'Great.'

'I think it's unlikely,' Silvermane intervened, before they started squabbling. 'Only the Unicorns can hide their presence and not even a Shade born of Revalla herself could manage it so thoroughly. And any Unicorn who survived the Fall with that amount of skill or power is unlikely to be seeking sanctuary.'

'What about Darklings?' Théon asked.

Alexan shook his head. 'Graced magic doesn't mix well with Darkling blood. They can't use it for any length of time or with any control.'

'You seem to manage just fine,' she noted.

He winked sidelong at her, trying to hide his unease beneath a sly smile. 'Only for you, Majesty.'

She rolled her eyes and let it drop. He tried not to let his relief show. The last thing he wanted right now was a lengthy, in-depth discussion on the unique nature of his power. Especially not in front of the old man.

'Did you make contact?' asked Silvermane.

She nodded. 'There is a room for us at the inn, and we've to meet the harbour master there.'

Alexan frowned, working hard to hide his disquiet. None of it was a surprise to him. He'd seen plenty of evidence over the years in the King's Court indicating a secret network working to hide and protect those remnants of the Graced that had survived the Fall. He'd assumed mortals were involved, but this appeared to be better organised than either he or the King had anticipated. If the Court got wind of it …

'What about the Darkling?' the old man demanded.

Alexan stilled. This was it. He hardly dared to breathe.

Théon glanced at him, considering. Then she pulled a ring from her pocket and weighed it in her hand. 'I Cast a glamour into this before we left the croft. It should hold, so long as he stays out of direct sunlight.'

'So you propose to take him with us then?'

A pause. Only a few moments, but it felt like aeons. Then she smiled at him, held out the ring in offering, and there was no ignoring the stutter of his heart at the sight of it. Nor at the words that followed.

'Yes. Yes, I do.'

CHAPTER TWENTY-TWO

It was surprising that Darklings hadn't found the village already. Between the sailors coming and going, the locals, and the refugees in the camp, the place was teeming with life. So much life. It made his head spin. He hadn't fed in so long.

His mind was already calculating his options, what opportunities might present themselves, when a startled gasp from Illyandi snapped his attention back to his surroundings. He scanned the street for the threat, a Casting curling like smoke in the back of his throat as it itched to break free. But then his gaze landed on what had drawn Illyandi's attention, and he heaved a sigh that was equal parts relief and exasperation.

The camp. She'd finally noticed it. Her lovely face was slack with devastation as she stared in horror at those poor, desperate souls. Took in their gaunt faces, hollowed out by hunger and hopelessness. Their threadbare clothing and tattered tents. The living conditions scarce fit for livestock, let alone people.

'What is this place?' she asked in a hushed whisper. 'Why are all these people here?'

Théon sighed. 'They're waiting for the boat to Stormkeep.'

'All of them?' Théon nodded in silence. 'But there must be other ships? Bigger ships that could take them all?'

Neither Silvermane nor Théon would look at her. They kept their eyes forward. Averted. Alexan ground his teeth in irritation. Someone had to explain these things to her. Why did it seem that the task always fell to him?

'Passage to the islands isn't cheap, Princess,' he said.

'I don't understand.'

'It's nothing more simple than human greed. No one can get to the islands without a ship. The captains know that. They can charge whatever they like. There's still enough wealth left in mortal hands that they'll be able to find some witless bastard willing to pay it.' He paused, looking over the despair around him. 'Or at least able to pay it. Besides, the lords of Stormkeep will not want dregs like these draining the limited resources of their island sanctuary.'

Her face fell, hand drifting to her stomach. 'How can you say that? There are children here. Babies! What makes them any less deserving of safety?'

'You're naive if you think what people deserve counts for anything in this life. Good people are seldom rewarded. In fact, it's the bastards who take advantage of their kindness who often end up on top. That's just the way of the world. If you haven't figured that out in the last hundred years, then the Gods only know how you'll make it through the next.'

He looked away before he said any more. The desperation to feed was taking its toll on his temper. At least neither Théon nor the old man reprimanded him for his outburst, though he caught Théon's reproachful glare from the corner of his eye.

Fuck her. It was her own fault. It was short-sighted at best to have shielded Illyandi the way she had. At worst, it was sheer stupidity. Either way, inexcusable and in need of rectifying. And if they all hated him by the end of it … well, at least the Princess might be better placed to protect herself. And anyone else who came along.

He kept his mouth shut as they wove their way through the cobbled streets and into the heart of the little harbour town. He smelled the tavern before he saw it: the stink of stale piss and vomit, the stench of unwashed flesh from the brothel upstairs. All of it soaked in the unmistakable scent of cheap ale. A blunt axe to the face would have been more pleasant to his Darkling-heightened senses. Passing the camp had been a bed of roses compared to this cesspit. And Théon was annoyed at him for wanting to dispel Illyandi's sweet illusions? This was going to be entertaining …

Sure enough, from the corner of his eye, he spotted the Princess placing a delicate hand over her mouth and turning an interesting shade of green. 'I think I'm going to be sick.'

The stable boy took their horses, looking nervous at the prospect of wrangling Théon's iron-grey stallion. Smart lad. That silly beast of Illyandi's followed quietly enough. No doubt relieved to be unhitched from the cart. She was woefully out of condition.

The innkeeper met them at the door – a thin, weasely little man whose manner was so obsequious it made Alexan's skin crawl. His daughter was a pretty little thing though. Doe-eyed and busty, with a smile so inviting Alexan wondered if she worked upstairs. She cast an appraising eye over him, that smile widening at what she saw. Easy pickings. Tempting too. And he needed to feed. Even if she flinched when she met his gaze. The glamour could not negate the primal instincts of prey when faced with their natural predator. Not that it had ever stopped him feeding before …

But the wife appeared at her husband's shoulder a moment later, took one look at Alexan and escorted her daughter back inside. Hard to tell whether she sought to protect the girl's virtue or her neck. Not that it mattered; he'd be hard-pressed to get her on her own now. The innkeeper's wife had likely been a bonny girl herself once, but a hard life had eroded any remnant of it. And judging by how her husband scuttled from her path, Alexan guessed her heart was as haggard as her face.

'This it?' she snapped at Théon.

'Yes. Just four of us, like I said.'

The harridan scowled. 'Didn't say nothing 'bout no horses. Nor wagon neither. Ain't no one going to ferry all that over.'

'Well, that's for the ship's captain to decide, isn't it?' Théon replied. The innkeeper's wife glared back but didn't argue. 'Now I believe the harbour master is waiting for us?'

The innkeeper's wife grunted in defeat and turned on her heel. 'Follow me.'

Inside, the smell of the inn was even worse contained in the cramped space and warmed by the fire burning in the hearth. A half-dozen sailors drank in the corner, eyeing up the two insipid-looking whores lounging by the staircase. All bar one were too drunk to note the beauty of either Théon or Illyandi. The one who sat up a little straighter as they'd walked in – a handsome woman with short, dark hair and eyes like cut glass – at least had the sense to turn her attention elsewhere when she noticed Alexan following behind.

'Nice place,' he grunted in Théon's ear. The shrew shot him a nasty look over her shoulder. Why wasn't he surprised her hearing was nearly as good as his? Years of straining for whatever gossip would line her purse, no doubt. Not that he'd been much better as a child. How many secrets had he sold for nothing more than a crust of bread over the years?

The room she led them to was cramped enough to begin with, and it was bordering on claustrophobic once Alexan had squeezed his bulk into the confined space. He kept his hand on the hilt of his dagger. Tight quarters left little room for manoeuvre.

A table divided the room, buried beneath a pile of ledgers, the harbour master sat on the other side poring over them. He didn't look up as they entered. Not even when the old harpy slammed the door shut behind them.

'You'd best have a ship lined up for this lot soon, Harl,' she snapped, taking the only empty seat in the room. 'Don't want their sort under my roof.'

'I'm sure your guests appreciate such gracious hospitality,' the harbour master noted, still not looking up from his ledgers. 'I imagine they're paying enough for it.'

She made a vulgar noise in the back of her throat. 'Not enough if they bring the demons to our doorstep.'

The harbour master looked up, and the confusion on his weary face gave way to dread. His sallow complexion turned ashen as Théon lowered her hood to reveal her tapered ears. Those eyes were near popping from his skull as he took in the mark on the old man's forehead. Sweat beaded on his crumpled brow when he spotted Alexan's hand on his dagger, and his jaw went slack as his gaze fell on the Princess.

He swallowed. Loudly. 'Forgive me. I wasn't expecting ... I was only told to arrange passage for four travellers. They didn't tell me ...'

'How valuable your cargo was?' Alexan finished for him, noting the calculating glint entering his eye. Gods, how easy it would be to snap that scrawny neck and gorge himself on the man's life. He folded his arms to hide how his hands shook from the urge.

The harbour master flinched and plastered an ingratiating smile on his tired face as he tried to backtrack. 'How precious.'

'You mean dangerous,' the innkeeper's wife grunted. 'Their kind's nothing but bad news, mark my words.'

So true. Alexan's teeth itched to sink into her flesh. Savour the life pulsing beneath it, tired and spent as it was. He closed his eyes. Breathed through his nose. Clenched his teeth tight. Anything to keep himself from killing.

'Consider them marked,' Théon was saying, her voice cool. 'Now, to business? We will need at least two cabins made available for us, and we have three horses stabled in the inn, along with a wagonload of supplies to be transported.'

The harbour master nodded. 'Yes, yes, of course. Now let me see ... the *Jackdaw* is due in the day after tomorrow and then should set sail again perhaps three days after that?'

Théon shook her head. 'Too long.'

'*Jackdaw* is the fastest ship sailing out of this port. She'll get you there in no time.'

'We need something leaving sooner,' Théon insisted.

He pursed his lips, rifling through pages. 'You've not got a lot of options, I'm afraid. The *Sentinel* is leaving on the morning tide, but her hold is full. No space for your horses, nor your belongings. The captain might be willing to give up his cabin for you, but I think there's only the one. She's not as fast as the *Jackdaw*, but she'll make good time.'

'No good. We need the horses.'

'You could purchase fresh horses in Stormkeep,' the harbour master offered.

Théon shook her head again. 'Not an option. The horses come too.'

Alexan took another deep breath. He was far too thirsty for this. Dizzy. Off-kilter. The corrupt magic of the Darkling was slowly killing him; the blood of his Shade master little more than poison in his veins, burning the magic of his own life-force from his body. The effect had always seemed slower for him than for others. He had no clue why, whether it was something about the Shade King's magic or his own strange power, but he was grateful for it. Grateful that he didn't need to steal as much life as the rest of his kind.

But even he had his limits. And this room, these people, this entire conversation, were testing them. The harbour master sighed, and Alexan forced his attention back to his surroundings. It felt like trying to catch smoke with his bare hands. The harder he tried, the faster concentration slipped through his fingers.

'The only other thing I can suggest is the *Sea Hawk*,' the man was saying, 'though how those two get away with calling that flotsam *Sea Hawk* I've no idea. She floats, but that's about all I'll say for her.'

'When is she due to leave?'

'Nothing in my books, but there never is. Come and go as they please, those two. Never declare anything either.'

'Pirates?'

'Not in that scow,' he snorted. 'No, I'm afraid they're nothing more than a pair of petty smugglers. You'd be better off waiting for the *Jackdaw*.'

'Where can I find them?'

The harbour master bristled. 'I cannot condone you travelling with their ilk. It is one thing being unable to stop them operating out of my port, but quite another to send business their way.'

Théon ignored him. 'Where can I find them?'

'They will take all you have and leave your bodies for the fish.'

'We can take care of ourselves. Now, do not make me ask again.'

Silence echoed.

A growl rippled through Alexan's chest. Equal parts frustration and hunger. Control was wet hands around a sleek fish. The slightest twitch, and it would be free. Free to feed.

The mortals paled. Shrank from the death in his gaze. The innkeeper's wife spoke first.

'Ana disappeared upstairs with one of the girls about half an hour ago. She'll not be back down for some time yet, and I'm not for disturbing her,' she warned, adding hastily when Alexan growled once more, 'but Mari is in the taproom. She's the one you want anyway. Two capt'ns but only one brain between 'em.'

Théon's gaze was on him, eyes narrowed, as she tossed a handful of coins on the table. 'Thank you.'

His senses sharpened under her scrutiny. Became all too aware of the tension thrumming through the room. The tension in her. In her body, limbs taut and ready to strike. In her magic, dancing beneath her skin, waiting to break free. Perhaps his own prey instincts at work? Maybe something else. His lips parted in anticipation. Of what, he didn't know, but he wanted it with an eagerness that scared him.

Then a gnarled hand took him by the elbow, and her spell was broken. He glanced down to see the old man at his side and felt the light touch of an Enchanting brushing his mind in warning.

'Why don't you go get some fresh air?' Silvermane murmured, guiding him towards the door. He didn't fight it. Not when his self-restraint was so fragile. Nodding, he allowed the old man to usher him out, only vaguely aware of the assurances that they could cope without him for five minutes.

He staggered from the inn, lurching out into the square like a drunkard. Head splitting. Guts heaving. Heart hammering. No, being drunk was more pleasant. Muffled laughter from across the marketplace had him stumbling down the alley beside the inn. Away from whatever mortals were foolish enough to be out after dark. Away from temptation. He braced himself against the wall, breathing deeply as another spasm of searing pain squeezed at his chest.

'My lord?' The girl's voice was a clear bell in the night. But did it chime in welcome or warning? 'My lord, are you alright?'

'I'm no lord, girl. Now go back inside,' he growled, wrestling for control over his instincts, over the impulse to drain every drop of life from her body. She'd deserve it too. Foolish to ignore her instincts. They must be screaming at her to run by now.

But she heeded neither them nor his warning. He could feel the warmth of her as she neared. Scent the blood in her veins. A shudder ran through him at her feather-light touch on his arm. At her soft, enticing voice when she asked, 'Can I help you?'

It was an effort to raise his head. A low groan escaped his lips as he met those soft doe-eyes. Saw the invitation in them.

He ground out another warning from between clenched teeth. 'Go. Back. Inside.'

The girl ignored him, leaning closer. His fingers twitched towards her throat. He needed her. Her warmth. Her passion. Her life.

'Alexan?'

Théon's voice shattered the night. He threw himself away from the girl, pressing his body to the wall and praying to the Gods he could hold himself there long enough for her to escape.

'Leave,' he breathed, panting from the effort of restraint. The girl's face was pale with fear now, and he almost laughed with relief. But he knew the signs. A rabbit about to bolt. A fox unable to resist the chase. 'Don't run. Just turn around and walk away.' She stepped away, not able to take her eyes from him as she retreated backwards down the alley. Too fast. And her face. Her fear. Taunting him. Daring him.

Then Théon was between him and his prey, and all that remained of his control shattered.

The pounding in his head, the shakiness in his legs, faded from his awareness as he lunged for the girl. Théon stepped in, blocking his way, and as he tried to dart around her, the world seemed to tilt beneath his feet. His vision darkened, and he faltered, just as Théon slammed into him. He heard her curse of surprise before his head cracked off the ground.

She was on her knees beside him, calling his name in a clear, crisp voice that brokered no nonsense. Had he had any strength left, he might have laughed. She'd never sounded more like her mother in her life. A Casting flooded over him, pinning him in place. His own magic roiled, itching to break free. She could not hold him for long.

'Put me down,' he gasped, ignoring how his eyes focussed in on her all-too-near throat.

'Don't be ridiculous!'

His knuckles were white as his fingers closed on her wrist, his body itching towards her despite the weakness crippling it. He lunged for her, roaring. 'Théon, do it now!'

A Casting flared, then all he knew was darkness.

He let out a mighty groan as he came to. His skull felt like it was being split open with a blunt axe, and he trembled like a newborn calf trying to stand. He winced as he opened his eyes and looked around. He was inside the inn, judging by the stench, lying on a lumpy bed with a lantern on the table by his head.

Théon – at least, he thought it was Théon – was sitting on the end of the bed. She was little more than a blur, but if he squinted, he could just about make out her face. The dark shape of the old man hovered behind her. He closed his eyes in disgust. This would not be a pleasant conversation.

'How are you feeling?' Théon asked. He could only manage a noncommittal grunt in response. She snorted and laid an affectionate hand on his arm.

But Silvermane was far from amused. 'I don't see how anyone can find this situation funny. You've put us all in terrible danger by letting your thirst get this bad.'

'I had it under control,' Alexan mumbled, his voice weak and hoarse. It was the old man's turn to snort, but there was no humour in it. 'I didn't hurt anyone, did I?' he snapped. He knew he hadn't. Wouldn't still be this weak if he had. And his irritation lent him a little strength at least.

'That's not the point,' Silvermane argued.

'What is the point then?' asked Théon, cutting off the argument before it could start. Silvermane hesitated, and Alexan could hear the reluctance in his voice when he spoke.

'He needs blood if he's to survive.'

There was a pregnant pause, and Alexan prayed to the Gods for the earth to open and swallow him whole. Then Théon stood and nodded. 'Alright,' she said. 'I'll sort it.'

The old man gaped incredulously.

'You can't be serious?' he snarled. But Théon had already breezed past him.

'Perfectly,' she assured him, beaming. And with that she swept from the room. Silvermane lingered, and Alexan could feel the old man's mind brushing against his defences, taking control of his body. Weakened as he was, there was little he could do to stop it, but he was glad. Glad to know Silvermane could stop him if he tried to hurt Théon. Besides, his thoughts and memories were safe. Buried deep. Hidden behind defences that the likes of Silvermane would never breach. One of the few perks of serving the Shade King.

Théon returned some time later, a tankard clutched in her hand. Alexan scented the blood the moment the door opened, and his Darkling impulses had him thrashing against Silvermane's control. The old man held him fast. He was helpless as Théon perched on the bed beside him and cradled his head like a child, raising the tankard to his lips.

'Careful,' hissed Silvermane as those Darkling instincts heaved against his restraints. They were desperate. Frantic. Screaming for him to let it rip Théon's throat open.

'Hold on tight,' Alexan warned. 'They'll only get stronger.' The old man nodded in understanding, a glimmer of pity in his amethyst eyes as he glimpsed the burden of the Claiming.

Relief crashed through him as the blood touched his lips, flooding his body with its life-force as he drank deeply. As a child, he'd once gone swimming in the hidden pools, deep within the Silvan Forests. He'd ventured through waterfalls, exploring underwater caves and secret chambers with his only friend. A she-wolf. But he'd got lost, trapped beneath the water with no way out. His lungs had been burning by the time the wolf had hauled him back to the surface. The air filling his chest as he took his first breath was like being born anew ... just like this weakening of his thirst.

Théon smiled, sensing his relief. Even the old man seemed to relax, although his grip on Alexan's mind tightened. His feeding instincts were roused now, strengthened by Théon's blood and emboldened by her closeness, but Silvermane's control did not waver. As he finished, she placed the empty tankard on the table beside the bed and reached over to wipe a stray drop from the corner of his mouth.

Not even Silvermane could stop him as his tongue flicked over her finger. He felt, more than heard, the sharp intake of breath as she stilled in shock, and his gaze focussed on her with predatory intent. Her eyes were wide, and he could scent the anticipation thrumming in her blood. Gods, he wanted her. And maybe, just maybe, she wanted him as well.

Then the old man was between them, guiding Théon from the room even as his voice was a quiet lullaby in Alexan's mind, pulling him into sleep. The Darkling within railed against his influence, but with only a soft word and a whisper, Silvermane soothed it into submission.

'Rest now,' he murmured, his voice echoing in the vaults of Alexan's mind. 'Passage to Stormkeep has been arranged. We sail on the morning tide, but for now, rest. I will watch over them.'

He stopped fighting it, grateful at last for the ancient one's power and the respite it might bring him. And as he descended back into the darkness, he felt an ember of hope flicker into life.

'You've got to be joking?' Beside him, Théon had hissed but otherwise not deigned to respond. He'd shaken his head in frustration. 'Remind me again, what made you think this was a good idea?'

'She's called the *Sea Hawk*.'

'She could be called *Wavebreaker* for all I care, it won't make her float any better.'

'Don't be so provincial. You know, if you ever choose to open your eyes, you might just find a way out of the mess your life has become.'

He'd stared at her. 'What?'

'There are signs all around us, signals put there to guide our steps towards our destiny. Legend says our futures were written in starlight, and only by fulfilling that fate can we ever hope to achieve true happiness.'

'Superstition and prophecy? That's what you're putting your faith in?'

She'd fixed him with a steely look. 'A jackdaw is a type of crow. As is a raven, which is my father's sigil. His personal guard are called the Sentinels. A sea hawk, on the other hand, is Dorrien's favoured form when she makes the Change. You want to ignore that kind of omen?'

'Fate and destiny are for those too weak to forge their own path,' he'd reminded her, before walking away. She wouldn't be persuaded. More's the pity.

The harbour master's description of the smugglers and their ship had been generous. It was little more than a fishing boat. A leaky one at that. Her co-captains were little more than a pair of lecherous drunks who could hardly tell port from starboard. But they'd accepted Théon's coin and had agreed to leave as soon as possible. Their crew comprised of six hands. A seventh had somehow ended up on the wrong side of the red-headed captain, Ana, and been sold to a bounty hunter. Théon had promised Alexan would take his place on the deck. Delightful.

He'd tried not to watch her as they loaded the ship, but time and time again, he found his gaze drawn to her. Her raven hair caught in the sea breeze. Her cheeks tinged pink by the cold of the morning. Her tawny skin glowing golden in the dawn light.

Worst of all was the memory of her blood. That bittersweet flavour would haunt him for all eternity. The way it had crackled and sparked with power, fizzing like sparkling wine in his mouth. Enough to drive him wild. Even the sight of it pulsing through the thin, blue veins at her wrists tested what control he had over his Darkling instincts.

Instincts he would continue to wrestle with for days. Every time he saw her. Caught her scent. Thought her name. She was a siren in his blood. And in the confines of the ship, he was hard-pressed to ignore her call. He spent what time he could above deck, with the salt and spray to clear his mind. Ironic that he was best able to find peace during the hours spent labouring at whatever menial task the capricious captains had set him. But even they could not occupy him at all hours.

'Are you going to sit out there all night?' her voice drifted from the doorway. He was perched on a low bench outside her cabin, finishing the remnants of his daily rations. He glanced up, chest tightening. She was leaning against the doorframe with a wineskin in hand. Her sleeves were pushed up and her hair was pulling loose from her braid, but she was as beautiful as ever.

He finished his food and rose to leave. 'There. All done.'

'Alexan, wait.' She held out the wineskin. 'Come have a drink with me?'

Gods knew, he was tempted. But he didn't trust himself. 'I'm fine, thanks. There's a keg of something stronger in the hold.'

Where he was sleeping, along with the other sailors. Not trusted to share the cabin with her, Illyandi and the old man. Exiled to a cold and lonely hammock, surrounded by a half-dozen, stinking, snoring sailors. Just as well, given that Illyandi was yet to find her sea legs – or so she claimed. Despite regular cleaning, the cabin still reeked of vomit. He wasn't sure which stench was worse.

Théon's hand flew out and grabbed his arm. 'Something's wrong. What is it?' He suppressed a groan as fire spread across his arm from where their skin met. Too close. That cup of blood might have been enough to keep him alive, but it'd done little to satisfy him. That evergreen gaze was searching, but he held it, trying to hide as much as he could. No such luck. 'You're still thirsty.'

He extricated himself from her grip. 'I'm fine.'

'You're not fine,' she insisted. 'If you needed more blood, why didn't you say something?'

He heaved a sigh of exasperation. 'I don't *need* more.'

'But you want more?' she asked, a soft smile playing on her lips. He made to turn away, but a delicate hand on his arm once more forced him back to look at her, and he felt his resolve crumble.

'If you were dying of starvation, and someone were to give you a piece of bread, you might survive for an extra day,' he explained. All too aware of the tension in his voice. 'But you would still be starving.'

Théon's gaze softened as comprehension dawned. 'How much more do you need?'

'No.' He stepped back. Into the cabin. His first mistake.

She followed him. Herded him further inside. Closed the door behind her. His second mistake. 'Why? You're starving, and I can help you.'

'You don't know what you're talking about,' he warned, his back hitting the wall behind him. His third. 'It's more than just the blood, Théon.'

'I don't care.'

'I could kill you.'

'You won't,' she promised. Then the scent of blood filled the room. She held up her wrist in offering. 'Drink.'

Alexan hardly dared to breathe. 'I can't.'

With a sigh, she took Alexan's hand in her own and placed her bloody wrist in his grip. The mark on his palm burned at the contact. That power stirred in response to her touch. He shoved it back down. Then she pressed her other hand to her blood and raised it to his lips.

'Drink,' she said again. His head swam. The warmth of her skin beneath his fingers. His entire body trembled in response. He closed his eyes, breathing that exquisite scent deep. Delicate fingers touched his lips, his tongue, the blood coating them bittersweet with the magic of life sparking within it.

His mind emptied. He raised her wrist to his mouth, fastening his lips around the open wound and pulled her close. Stars exploded behind his eyelids as he gulped down two quick mouthfuls, her power flooding through him.

She gasped and quivered against him, and desire boiled in his veins. He released her wrist and spun her around, pressing her against the wall and turning her head to expose her neck. He held her arms above her head with one hand, taking her throat in the other with as much tenderness as he could muster.

Without hesitating, he lowered his mouth to her neck and bit into her soft skin. Blood filled his mouth, all his senses sharpening as her life-force poured into him, crackling with power over his tongue. Every inch of her hummed against him. Her heart thundering in her chest. The rapid rise and fall of her breathing. That silky skin beneath his fingers and his lips. Gods, what he wanted to do to her.

'I feel ... strange,' she gasped. He grinned against her throat at the quiver of exhilaration in her voice. He'd tried to warn her. To be fed upon like this created an intimacy that most never expected.

A scream of fury shattered the moment, and Alexan found himself blasted backwards. He slammed into the wall. So hard that the room blurred and went dark. When he could focus again, Illyandi stood between him and Théon, her face that of a stone-hearted killer. The hint of a Casting, bursting to get free, swirled and snapped around her like grass swaying in the wind. Théon tried to surge to her feet, but the Casting pulsed, shoving her back down.

Alexan bared his teeth in a silent snarl, challenging the one thing that stood between him and his prey. Between him and his Queen. Under different circumstances, he might have rejoiced at the terrible, vicious noise that ripped out of the delicate Princess in response. But now was not the time to revel in the discovery that Illyandi could, in fact, be roused to anger and violence. Not surprising though, if his suspicions regarding her current condition were correct. There was true terror in Théon's eyes as she watched her sister struggle with her emotions.

'Illyandi,' she begged. The Casting pulsed again, fainter this time, warning Théon to be silent.

'I will kill you,' she growled at Alexan, her voice shaking as the magic coursed through her. Alexan got to his feet, not daring to break eye contact with her. But he had learned tact and diplomacy at Kieyin's side, and it was the deadly Shade Prince who spoke next.

'I dare you,' he hissed, his eyes dancing. Théon's eyes widened – with anger or fear, he wasn't sure – but Illyandi remained frozen where she was. Alexan let his face split into the slow, wicked smile he reserved for the prey he wanted to send running. Illyandi didn't move. He laughed, a low dark chuckle as he watched her hesitate. 'You don't have it in you, Princess,' he taunted. The Casting surged with her temper, and he found himself thrown back and pinned to the wall. He gasped for breath as she tightened an invisible noose around his throat, hissing her hatred for him. But just as quickly as it had flared, her fury ebbed, and she stepped back, releasing him. He slumped to the floor coughing as he tried to catch his breath. By the Gods, she was strong. Not strong enough to have killed him, not with the power he had at his command, but stronger than he'd realised.

Théon surged to her feet as her sister's enormous power retreated beneath her skin, and placed herself between Illyandi and the Darkling she'd threatened to kill. Silvermane appeared in the doorway, but Théon stopped him dead in his tracks with a look. Her hands were thrown up as she edged closer to Illyandi.

'It's alright,' she was saying. 'I'm alright; he didn't hurt me. Illyandi, look, I'm alright.' She spoke softly, like trying to soothe a startled animal before it bolted. Alexan forced himself to stay still, while inwardly he cursed himself. What had he been thinking trying to provoke her like that?

Silvermane pushed his way between the two sisters. He glanced at the healing wound on Théon's throat before turning his attention on Illyandi.

'I'm fine,' she snapped, before he opened his mouth, her hungry gaze still fixed on Alexan. Silvermane jerked the Princess's head to face him, forcing her to meet his eyes. The tiny changes in expression on her face spoke of the silent conversation going on between the two and, for once, Alexan was glad he couldn't hear what was said. Illyandi nodded, and Silvermane stepped back. The old man took hold of Théon's wrist and held her back as Illyandi approached Alexan.

'Let me go,' Théon protested, struggling. Part of Alexan roared at the violation. At the old man Enchanting her into submission. He wasn't strong enough to hold her by sheer force. Alexan snarled but stood his ground as Illyandi approached. 'Illyandi, leave him alone! It wasn't his fault. I offered my blood freely,' she said, heaving against Silvermane's restraints, both physical and magical.

'More fool you,' said Illyandi, in a voice as unyielding as the stone. She stood toe to toe with Alexan and did not flinch when she met his blood-red eyes. 'I should kill you.'

'Almost certainly,' he agreed. Then he spoke the words he knew would save him. 'But you both owe me a life-debt – your sister owes me two, in fact – so you won't. Besides, you live by Benella's code. So why don't you stop posturing, and just let it go, Princess?'

Illyandi hissed but stepped back. 'Get out,' she spat. 'If I see you in here again, I swear, by the Gods, I'll kill you.'

Alexan smirked and gave her a mocking bow before he turned to leave. He paused just long enough to glance back at Théon and wink, and the sly smile she gave him in return made his heart thunder in his chest.

It was a crack. Now all he had to do was widen it.

CHAPTER TWENTY-THREE

K eriath didn't know how much time had passed before the sound of a key turning in the lock echoed through the chamber, and the bridge creaked down. She sat up as best she could, striving to remain alert through the distractions of her pain and the overwhelming burden of the deaths echoing from the rocks she now carried. Having grown accustomed to the darkness, she squinted against the light spilling in from the hallway beyond. Silhouetted in the doorway was Dell, a water skin in his hand, and a murderous look on his face.

'What do you want?' she snapped, in no mood for any games.

His scowl deepened. 'Nice to see you too,' he grumbled, stalking across the bridge and dropping to a crouch beside her. He threw the water skin into her lap. 'Drink this.' Wincing at the pain, she pulled out the stopper and sniffed at it. Water. Just water. She drank gratefully, choking at the movement.

'What? No ruan?' she asked, gasping from the effort.

'No point,' he grunted. 'This place'll block your power better than any drug. The magic here is something else ... seeps into your soul ... changes you. I reckon it won't be long until your heart is as black as mine.' She didn't respond – didn't know what to say to that. His bloody gaze narrowed, considering her. 'Looks like I'm just as much a prisoner here as you are.'

'Clearly,' she muttered, gesturing to her surroundings with a pointed rattle of her chains.

Dell chuckled. 'Glad to see we haven't broken you. Though I don't like your chances of staying that way.'

'Thanks,' she said, her voice laced with sarcasm. 'What is it you wanted again?'

'Would it surprise you to know that I just wanted to speak to you?' She gave him a look that said it would. 'Sad but true. I can't seem to get you out of my head.'

She grinned. 'Careful. That's how it starts – the madness.' Greater minds than Dell's had been lost to Unicorn beauty.

'Think it's more than just your pretty face,' he admitted, leaning back. 'I've met your kind before – none of them ever had this power over me. You spared me from the waterhorses. And not just with what you told me either. The thought of you was what kept me sane. Kept me alive. But more than that – ever since I first tasted you, I've been different. Felt different. Thinking things about my maker that I shouldn't be able to think. Drosta knew it too, that's why he didn't fight when the Queens demanded I stay behind. It's got me wondering if there isn't more to you than you're letting on. That Nightwalker bitch seemed awfully interested in your heritage, *my lady*. Why is that? Who are you?'

Victory turned to ash in her mouth. 'She thought I was someone else. Someone important. Too bad I'm not even a full-blooded Unicorn, just a bastard half-breed.' He offered her a look that said he didn't believe her, but said nothing. 'What about you? Why are the Queens keeping you prisoner?'

'Trying to keep Drosta under control. They made it clear that if he doesn't toe the line, they'll kill me.'

Keriath arched a sceptical brow. 'And they think that'll work?' Drosta hadn't struck her as the caring type.

'It's about the only thing that might,' he muttered with a scowl. 'Drosta and I were children together – a pair of ragged orphans, fighting for survival in the Nighthills. We had no one but each other. I lost count of how many times one of us would save the other's life. Brothers, in every way but blood. I don't think he's capable of love, but our friendship was the closest he's ever come to it. Then one day he just disappeared, left me to fend for myself ... it was the kindest thing he ever did for me. I got my life together, got a job, found a wife ... She was pregnant with our second child when he came back. He never gave me the choice. He pinned me down and fed me his blood. Once it was done, he ordered me to kill my little boy, then made me watch as he raped and murdered my wife.

'Drosta had always been a sick bastard, but the magic unleashed a monster. I'm the only thing he's ever cared about. He cared enough to come back for me, destroy anyone else who had a claim to me and punish me for daring to consider a life without him in it. I've hated him for decades, but he made me bury those feelings down so deep they were nothing but a distant memory. Until you. Your blood set me free. I might be stuck here for the rest of my miserable life, but at least now my thoughts are my own. I wanted to thank you for that.'

'You're welcome,' she heard herself whisper. She meant it too, was glad to have freed him from such a fate. Nobody deserved that. Still, she didn't let herself linger on how ... for there was more to denying the Shade King than just principle. The cost would be her freedom. Her soul. The bond between a Shade and their sire was not as strong as the Claiming, but it was insidious enough that she would rather die than ever endure its touch.

Shade blood in her veins would explain the change in Dell, where nothing else could – but belief was its own kind of magic, the only power she had left to defy him. If she were to doubt, even for a moment, she would be lost forever. So she shoved the thoughts aside and focussed instead on the consequences of his rather interesting revelation.

Dell seemed to notice the cold cunning that entered her gaze and held up a hand to cut her off. 'No. I'm not helping you escape.'

'Why not? You said it yourself – you're a prisoner here, just like me. Don't you want to get out?'

He shook his head, but she could see the interest sparking in his eyes. 'You couldn't escape Drosta's clutches – and that was before you were wounded. The Queens' guard alone is three times the size of Drosta's Hunt … before you and your friends slaughtered most of it. Not to mention the dozens of Hunts who serve here. You wouldn't even make it out of the Pits.'

'I could if you helped me,' she insisted. 'You said they wouldn't drug me—'

He cut her off. 'Because there's no point. The magic of the mountain is enough to keep you contained all by itself.'

'Down here maybe. But if you get me out of this cell, it'll be a different story.'

'You're also wounded,' he pointed out.

'I'll heal.' He folded his arms over his chest and shook his head in frustration, but didn't argue, didn't seem to want to waste his breath. She had to try something else. 'Come on. You know how potent my blood is. You've felt the effects already. It gave you the strength to break free.'

She saw interest spark in his eyes. 'Go on.'

'The Queens will never let you go, and Drosta knows it. He betrayed you – he's leaving you to rot in this city. Unless you help me. I'm not strong enough to escape by myself. But you know this place, and my blood could make you the most powerful Darkling in this city … Together, we might just make it.'

He pursed his lips. 'I'll think about it.'

Then he was gone, and she was alone.

Submerged in total darkness, it had not taken long for Keriath to lose track of the days. She was weaker than she'd ever been. The poison was still advancing, and she could feel the life ebb from her with each passing breath. She welcomed the thought. Death would be a gentle reprieve – perhaps she'd be reunited with all those who had been stolen from her.

Dell came to her sometimes, bringing enough food and water to keep her alive. He still hadn't agreed to help her escape, but he tended her wounds as best he could, although he was no healer. She told him as much – at length – during a painful changing of her dressings. He'd been right though, there was little need to drug her with ruan. The mountain sapped so much of her strength that her magic was useless.

She could sense most of his thoughts and almost all of his emotions. His mind was simple and uncluttered by imagination, which made things easier. But the Enchanting remained beyond her. Likewise, the Casting required strength and focus that she no longer possessed.

At least he hadn't tried to feed from her again; she was far too weak. The Queens would not be happy if their prisoner died before they'd had their fill. None of them had been to see her since she had arrived in this forsaken place. She thanked the Gods for small mercies.

She wasn't sure she could survive an encounter with one of those monsters in her current state, though it was unlikely they'd bother for the pitiful amount of life in her veins, even if it was Graced.

More concerning was Ylain's realisation that Keriath was more important than just a source of life-magic. That she might be a mine of information about the surviving lines the Shade King and his allies so feared. If Ylain tried to torture the knowledge out of her, in her present state, she wasn't sure she could hold out.

'Will you stop trying to die on me?' Dell hissed, rousing her from oblivion once more. He'd just finished changing the dressings on her wound – again – and was lifting a skin of water to her cracked lips. She coughed and tried to drink. It was so very difficult.

'Will you stop trying to stop me?' she gasped. 'I think death would be better than having to look at your ugly mug.'

He grinned at that, but she could see the worry in his eyes. She didn't need magic to feel it rolling off him in waves. Some people's emotions were just that strong. He'd grown to care for her. Or at least for her survival. And strangely, she felt a similar investment in his well-being growing in reciprocation. That was a disturbing thought. She shuddered. Mistaking it for cold, Dell scowled.

'This is ridiculous,' he muttered, looking around. 'They treat their mortal slaves better than this.'

A bitter smile twisted Keriath's lips. 'Well, see, there's your answer. I'm not a mortal slave.'

'No,' he spat, 'you're far more valuable than that. I don't care how dangerous they think you are. This is just plain stupid. At the very least you need a healer.'

A choked laugh escaped her. 'You know that my people were bred to slaughter yours, right?'

Dell just shook his head in disgust.

'It's just wasteful. You're no use to anyone dead.'

'Careful. Someone might think you care.'

He snorted. 'Careful. You almost sound like you do too.' Then he stood. 'Ylain sent for me yesterday. Had a lot of questions about you – where and how we found you, how we caught you. I don't think she liked my answers. She's ordered your rations cut – no food and no water for three days ... and no visitors.' Keriath said nothing to this for a long while, staring up at the cavern roof.

'Why tell me any of that?' she asked.

His face appeared over her, staring down. 'There's no way you can outlast Ylain. I know what she's like. She's older than Pria or Talize. Far older. The years have made her patient. She'll wear you down slowly. Methodically.'

'What's your point?' she sighed.

He grimaced. 'I don't have one. It was more a case of warning you what to expect.'

'Thanks.' Even dying from a poisoned arrowhead, Keriath could still muster the strength to be sarcastic. Dell only shook his head in frustration and left, slamming the bridge door behind him.

As promised, they left Keriath alone for what she could only assume was the requisite three days without food or water. She was starving and weaker than she'd ever been, but it was her parched throat that bothered her most. Unable to sleep for the discomfort, and the pressure of all that dark magic crushing her mind, she spent most of her time in a restless daze. She slipped in and out of consciousness while the poison continued to work its way closer to her heart. The Graced blood in her veins was fighting it with all she had, but death was inevitable.

Shaken from her stupor by the sound of a rusty key turning in the lock, she was unsurprised to hear Ylain's voice outside the door. The three days were up then. She didn't even bother standing, though she wasn't sure she could have managed it if she'd wanted to. Even the dim, orange light from the smoking torch burned at her eyes, accustomed as she was now to the dark. She squinted towards the doorway and could just make out the old crone stepping into the light. There was no mistaking the intent in those blood-soaked eyes.

But where Dell's mind was an open book, this Queen's mind was guarded. Whether from habit or a deliberate move to shield her secrets from her prisoner, Keriath neither knew nor cared. Dell hovered behind his Queen, brow creased with concern when he saw how much she'd deteriorated since he'd last seen her. She sighed and let her head roll back as she gazed up at the ceiling.

'I would have thought that even a motherless wretch like yourself would know to stand in the presence of a Queen,' Ylain noted.

'I thought you'd prefer it if I grovelled,' replied Keriath, without so much as a hint of sarcasm.

Ylain snorted. 'Is that what this is?'

'Obviously,' Keriath said with a slight shrug. She regretted it immediately, wincing as the movement sent a sharp pain through the wound in her shoulder. Ylain afforded her a cruel smile before snapping her fingers.

Two guards filed in, each one carrying a chair. The gaudy, gold-leafed and velvet-upholstered monstrosity they deposited behind their Queen, while they positioned the rickety wooden stool close to the edge of the pedestal. Keriath slumped against the guards as they hauled her up to sitting. The crone's cold eyes bore into her, lingering on her wounded shoulder – which now oozed through the dressing – and glowing red as she inhaled the scent of Keriath's blood.

'Bloodrot,' she grunted, sniffing. 'Expensive stuff, girlie. You must have put up some fight if you forced Drosta into using that.'

It was Keriath's turn to snort, trying to hide her fatigue behind false bravado as she swayed on the wobbly stool. 'Your boy is an idiot,' she sneered. 'He put me on one of your barges and took me down river.'

'And you called up waterhorses to help you escape,' Ylain finished, nodding. 'I hope you at least killed a few of Drosta's Hunt before they put you down? Death is the only way to deal with such carelessness.'

'Sadly, no,' Keriath replied with a bitter smile. 'I was more interested in escaping.'

Ylain's answering smirk was as cold as it was brutal. 'How disappointing,' she murmured. She glanced back at Dell and tutted, before turning to her prisoner once more. 'Drosta's second has requested a healer for you. What am I to make of that?' Keriath resisted the urge to let her gaze flick to Dell and continued to stare impassively at the Queen.

'He thinks I'd give better sport. I think he's an idiot myself. I'll be far more docile with one foot in the grave.'

'No doubt.' Ylain chuckled, leaning back while she examined her prisoner. 'But I have always found that it requires a certain amount of awareness to extract information from a subject. I imagine it has something to do with needing to understand the gravity of the situation.'

'I understand the gravity of my situation just fine,' Keriath assured her.

'Where did you get those scars, girl?' the Queen asked, changing the subject. Keriath had expected the question at some point, and the memory flashed savagely through her mind. But the Queen could never learn the truth. Ylain had to know that only magic could leave a mark like that. Keriath couldn't hesitate for a second, or she might suspect.

'Beauty is a curse,' she snapped. 'My father knew that better than anyone. He thought this would protect me.'

'And did it?'

Keriath held her gaze. 'What do you think?'

The Queen inclined her head in understanding and let the matter drop. Then she raised her hand and snapped her fingers in summons. Two serving boys trotted forward, each one bearing a silver platter they held out to their Queen. Keriath felt her mouth water as the scent wafting off those trays hit her. She sniffed. Smoked fish served on herb-crusted bread. A selection of cheeses with oatcakes. Mushroom pasties and a tart with cheese and … bacon? She inhaled again. Yes, there was definitely bacon on one of those platters. Her stomach growled while Ylain examined the fare before cutting herself a piece of the savoury tart. The old Queen was smirking as she turned to the source of the noise, slice in hand.

'I'm afraid I have quite a boring palate,' she said, nibbling at the pastry. 'But I suppose if you're starved for long enough, you'd eat anything that was put in front of you? Wouldn't you?'

Irritation gave her some strength, and Keriath folded her arms across her chest, the chains rattling, while she stared dispassionately at the old Queen.

'This is tedious,' she said. 'Why don't you just get to the point?'

'Alright,' the grim-faced Queen conceded. 'You have information I want. You're going to give it to me. We can be civilised about it, or I can carve it out of you one piece at a time. It's entirely up to you.'

A kernel of fear settled deep within Keriath's gut, but she refused to acknowledge it.

'What makes you think I have anything of value?'

Ylain pursed her lips. 'In the last hundred years the once-mighty, all-conquering Graced have become little more than a fairy tale – a bedtime story for children. Your cities lie in ruin, shadows sit upon your thrones, wearing your crowns, and your people are claimed by darkness and night. Only a handful have survived untouched. But I remember all too well how quickly a single spark can incite the fires of war. We must stamp those embers out, or they will rise again and destroy us.'

Keriath stilled at the words. Ylain's knowledge was far greater than she had anticipated, though perhaps the Queen did not grasp the significance. Prophecy without understanding was just a collection of random words.

'I know the history.' Keriath sneered, hiding her unease beneath disdain. 'What I don't know is what you think I can offer.'

'I think you know where we can find those embers.'

Perhaps Ylain did grasp the significance. Not that it mattered. Even if Keriath had the knowledge the Queen was after, she would die before giving it up. Snorting, she shook her head in disgust.

'You think they let us stay together after that day? After you slaughtered our families? They separated us a long time ago – for this very reason. The bloodlines had to be kept safe, and only a fool puts all their eggs in one basket. So, you do what you want to me. I can't tell you a damn thing.'

Ylain sighed. 'I'm sorry you feel that way. I had hoped we could be civilised about this. Pria might delight in such things, but I find torture to be a tiresome task. Unfortunately, she has a tendency to get somewhat carried away, so you're stuck with me. So. Shall we begin?'

Ylain's methods were brutally direct, though somewhat predictable. She tried the ploy with the food twice more before giving up when Keriath commented on her transparency. Then, when Keriath passed out from hunger during Ylain's next visit, she gave up starving her. They weren't feeding her well, even with the extra rations Dell brought whenever he was able, but it was at least regular and enough to keep her strength up.

She needed it. The poison in her blood was creeping ever closer to her heart, making her every breath difficult. Ylain's beatings were savage and left her unable to stand. The old crone was an expert with the lash, and her Darkling strength meant that, more often than not, she cut right through muscle and hit bone. The interlacing mass of scars that ravaged Keriath's side extended across her back: a deliberate attack to mar the marks she bore there. But Keriath didn't need to look to be sure they were untouched.

Only magic could leave a scar on Graced skin. So long as Ylain stopped short of killing her, she could inflict as much damage as she liked.

Dell was standing in the doorway with his back to her. He couldn't watch her being flogged. He flinched at every crack of the whip.

Keriath let out a vicious oath as the lash came down once more. She'd given up trying to stay silent. The chains about her wrists had been pulled tight, so she was forced to stand, arms splayed wide to present an unmoving target for the Queen. Her tattered shirt had long since been destroyed, and she was naked from the waist up, her trousers crusted in blood that had run in rivulets down her back.

'Are you ready to answer my questions yet?' Ylain asked, wiping Keriath's blood from the whip. When Keriath offered only a series of blistering curses in response, Ylain raised the lash once more. Keriath screamed as it fell, the whip licking exposed bone, and she finally passed out.

She wasn't sure how long she had been drifting in oblivion when firm hands shook her awake with equal urgency and tenderness. She groaned as she peeled open her eyes to see Dell standing over her, his brows knit with worry.

'What happened?' she mumbled.

'You passed out. Again.' Keriath nodded. It wasn't the first time, though it was the first time she hadn't been brought back to consciousness with another lash of Ylain's whip. Dell seemed to read her thoughts, and his frown deepened. 'She tried. You didn't respond. She damn near split you in half trying to wake you, but you didn't even flinch. I thought she'd killed you.'

'If only,' she muttered. She tried to sit up, but Dell held her fast. She was glad of it; the movement made her back erupt in agony. She fell back, panting.

'Your back hasn't healed,' Dell explained before she could ask. He shook his head in frustration. 'She fucking knew those arrowheads were poisoned; she just didn't care. Said she needed you weak and pliant, for all the good it's done her. But when you didn't wake ... I got her to agree to send a healer.' He trailed off as Keriath's gaze slid to the figure hovering in the doorway behind him.

A middle-aged Darkling woman stepped forward. 'Her blood's gone bad. I can smell it from here.'

'Shocking,' Keriath muttered, closing her eyes. 'Tell me, was it her pride or stupidity stopping her from intervening earlier? Not much use to her dead, after all, am I?'

The healer woman crouched down and rolled Keriath over. 'You shouldn't bait her so much,' she warned, crouching down to inspect the wound. 'She'll just make you suffer more for it.'

Keriath tried to laugh but lapsed instead into a weak cough as tiredness washed over her. 'I'm going to suffer either way. It makes me feel better to put up a fight.' The cool hands probing into the rough dressing around her shoulder were quick and efficient, but firm enough to make Keriath wince.

'You might suffer less if you told her what she wants to know,' the healer woman insisted. Keriath peered at her incredulously. The blood-soaked eyes of the Darkling were out of place in that kind, round face, but she seemed sincere.

'She's not wrong,' Dell's voice murmured.

Keriath sighed and rolled her eyes. 'Really? So if I just tell them everything, they'll let me go?'

'Sarcasm is a sign of an unrefined mind,' he snapped.

'You should know,' she chuckled. Dell hissed through his teeth and fell silent.

The healer woman had removed the dressing on the shoulder and was cleaning the wound. Keriath gasped at the sting of whatever concoction she was using.

'Sorry,' the woman murmured. 'It needs to be cleaned before I can bind it.'

'You're wasting your time.'

'Time is never wasted. It is death that is wasteful. Death of your kind, particularly so.'

Keriath had nothing to say to that, so she remained silent while the woman tended to her injuries. The cleansing tincture smarted enough to make her eyes water, but the dressing that followed contained a soothing poultice to ease the pain. The Darkling's hands had been deft and methodical, if somewhat forceful, but as she examined Keriath further her touch grew gentle, almost tender. She dared to look up at the woman and was unsurprised to see desire in those blood-red eyes. The healer caught her steady gaze and looked away, flushing with embarrassment.

'Don't,' Keriath whispered, catching her hand. 'It's alright. It's not in your power to control such feelings.'

The Darkling looked back at her. 'I've heard tales of your kind before, but I've experienced nothing like this. What is it?'

Keriath shrugged and sighed, leaning back to look at the ceiling. 'Magic. It's the gift of my bloodline.' The woman was quiet for a while as she packed up her things. She took a small, crystal bottle from her bag and pressed it into Keriath's hand.

'Drink this,' she said. 'It will counteract the poison, but I'm afraid you must heal the rest on your own.' Keriath nodded and closed her eyes. Then, as the woman rose to leave, she spoke again. 'You are right to resist Ylain. Once she has what she wants, she will give you to Talize and Pria. So endure this suffering as long as you can, because when that happens ... well, you will beg for death before the end.'

Keriath nodded in understanding, but the gratitude sat like sour wine in her gut.

'Mortals are more susceptible to my kind than those with power in their veins,' she blurted. 'Don't come back, not if you can help it. Stronger people than you have lost their minds. Don't think about me and don't talk about me to others. Every moment you allow your mind to linger on me, you loosen your grip on your sanity.'

The Darkling fell into stunned silence while she considered Keriath's words. When she spoke, her voice was little more than an urgent whisper. 'Why warn me?' she asked. 'Why not just let me descend into madness?'

'Valid question,' Dell muttered.

She ignored him. 'You saved my life. I refuse to be indebted to a Darkling. Now leave, while you still can.' The woman flinched, her eyes wide with hurt and shock. But she did as she was bid, scurrying from the room.

'I'm surprised you didn't let her suffer,' Dell noted, moving to follow the healer out. 'It would have been her own fault for never learning to guard against the Enchanting. Besides, that way she would have been yours to do with as you pleased. And you need all the allies you can get in this place.'

But Keriath was too tired to care. 'Fuck off back to whatever dark hole you crawled out of,' she told him, rolling over. But he didn't. Instead, he settled down beside her, sharing the warmth of his body with her while she drifted off into an uneasy sleep.

She woke to Dell's fingers tracing over the scars across the side of her face. His touch was gentle, his gaze tender for once, rather than overflowing with lust. Despite the instincts that screamed at her for the *wrongness* of it, she leaned into that touch. She needed every bit of kindness she was offered.

'Was it true? What you told Ylain – that your father gave you these?'

She didn't reply, but for once, she did not flinch as the memories rose unbidden.

A girl, racing through the woods. Her hair snapping behind her like a pennon, her yellow eyes glowing in the darkness. Resari. She and Keriath had been as close as sisters growing up, brought into the world on the same day – along with Théon. Three raven-haired girls, born in darkest night to three noble bloodlines, fated to change the world they stood upon …

The whole idea had been Resari's – a fact that had haunted her cousin for years afterward. The young Dragon had yearned for adventure. Not to mention the attention of her parents, who had been too caught up in their own pain to pay any heed to the child that neither of them had wanted. Resari had wanted to explore the sacred groves of the Ariundle and visit the altars of the old Gods, so she'd persuaded Keriath to join her. Resari thought they could handle anything that came their way. And had they stayed together, that may well have been the case.

But they had lost each other while wandering the sacred woodlands.

Keriath was hunted down and ripped apart by a Hunt of Graced Darklings. A band of Nightwalkers captured Resari, tortured her and left her for dead, nailed to an altar as a warning to her parents.

Resari's mother – Kalielle Half-Elven – had found and rescued Keriath. But it had been Keriath's mother who'd had the misfortune to discover Resari, broken but alive and screaming her rage to the night sky. It was just as well that Kalielle hadn't seen the damage with her own eyes. Even now, a hundred years after her death, Keriath shuddered to imagine her fury.

She shuddered at the memory of her own rage when she first saw the ruin of her face. Only magic left a mark on Graced skin.

Which was why the Shade King's lover had led a Hunt of Elvish Dark-lings to hunt down his supposed bastard spawn. Jenia, daughter and heir to the legendary Flame of Elucion. Keriath knew the Old Tales, had heard Jenia's story from the lips of one who had witnessed it first-hand. A child, born of peace and hope, but corrupted beyond reason by the Shade King. She was a monster, cruel by nature but honed into something far worse by the long centuries at her lover's side.

Jenia had wanted Keriath dead from her first breath. Resari she had feared, had tried to break that night in Ariundle. Théon she had tolerated, had tried to use for her own ends. But Keriath ... Keriath she hated. Hated the rumours, hated even the possibility that Keriath was the product of a consensual union between the King and another. She had led that Hunt after Keriath for one reason and one reason only. Her utter destruction.

The King had sent Jenia north to retrieve Théon, stolen from under his nose in the dead of night. But Jenia, her jealousy at breaking point, had had other plans. She'd sent a Shade to assassinate Théon and paid Nightwalkers to torture and eliminate Resari. The Darklings hunting Keriath she'd led herself. All three girls had proven far more resilient than she'd expected, even years away from fully coming into their powers. Théon had dealt with the Shade herself, and Resari had survived her ordeal, damaged but unbro-ken. Keriath had fought off her attackers long enough for help to come and finish what she'd started.

They had come at Keriath with everything they had. A whole Hunt of Graced Darklings, with the magical auras and pointed ears that marked them as Elves, had hunted her through the ancient forest, baying for her blood, before springing their trap. She had never been more scared in her entire life. Jenia had stepped from the shadows like a nightmare given form and watched with a smile as the others loosed their magic upon her prey. Keriath had Cast a shield, but there were too many of them. Driven to the ground, she lay helpless, eyes closed against the horror, shielding her face with her hands as their Castings burned her flesh. Screaming in agony, she'd waited for the end.

Then it had all been over. There was a flash of searing heat and brilliant light, the dying screams of the Darklings and a frustrated roar from Jenia ... Then silence and warm arms enveloping her. She hadn't been able to bring herself to open her eyes. But she'd recognised the voice that murmured to her, recognised the beat of the proud, steady heart inside the chest she cried into. Kalielle. Resari's mother. But in those moments, she was far more. Keriath had slipped into oblivion and awoken days later in her bed, with Théon and Resari at her side. They'd held her in their arms as she was shown her reflection, had shared in her agony for power lost and innocence taken.

But that was not a story she ever told. Most of those dear to her knew what had happened, but none had ever asked her to recount it herself. Even if she could bring herself to speak the words, it was too dangerous to tell such a tale in this place. So Keriath closed her eyes and whispered a lie.

'I was born long after the Fall. I don't remember my mother. My father took me from her when he found out. She was just some dockside whore who'd caught his eye. When he realised his bloodline had bred true, he gave me the only protection he could offer. He knew I would never be safe, so long as the Shade walk the earth, so he marked me. Did this to diminish my beauty, to diminish my power, hoping no one would ever look at me and recognise what I was. Then he left, and I've been alone ever since.'

Like all good lies, it was laced with enough truth to make it believable. Not her story, not by a long way, but the story of someone who had once been dear to her. Dell said nothing at first, though his arms around her tightened.

'Alright,' he said. She glanced up in confusion. 'I'll help you. Together. We'll get out of here together.'

'Thank you,' she said, fighting back the tears that threatened to overwhelm her. Instead, she laid her hand against his chest in offering. He groaned, his trembling fingers closing around her wrist. There was a flash of pain when his teeth tore through the fragile skin there, but he was gentle as he drank. Any strength she'd found was replaced by a languid relaxation that left her head spinning. She swayed, but Dell's arm snaked round her waist, holding her tight. With nothing between them, she was aware of every inch of his broad, powerful chest against her own, but for once, it did not repel her.

When he was finished, he cradled her in his arms for a moment before releasing her. Then he whispered in her ear, his voice so soft she wondered if she'd imagined it as she drifted into darkness. 'You need a better story. There's far too much power in your veins for you to be nothing more than a half-breed bastard. Once they taste you, they'll know.' His hands were almost tender as he stroked her hair back from her face, and he leaned forward to place a soft kiss upon her brow. 'Sleep well, Olena – or whoever you are.'

And then he was gone. And Keriath was alone in the darkness once more.

CHAPTER TWENTY-FOUR

S he wasn't sure how she'd wandered into Dell's mind, whether she'd been waking or dreaming when it happened, but she lingered anyway. For the comfort of escaping her own reality, if nothing else.

The bridge was down, and he was leaning against the archway with his arms folded across his chest, wearing a dark scowl while he considered his prisoner. She was lying on the ground, completely still. It was only with his heightened Darkling senses that he knew she was still alive. She was weak. Healing those wounds had taken a lot out of her. He took a deep breath, trying to quell the fear rising in his gut. If she died ...

A small smile twitched on her lips. She was strangely touched by his concern.

With a heavy sigh, he glanced back over his shoulder to the two Darklings standing guard beyond the door.

'Go on,' he muttered. 'Away with you both. She'll be down soon enough. No need for you to stay.'

They hesitated. 'You sure?' Dell glanced back at Keriath and grimaced at the sight of her.

'Aye. She's not going anywhere.' The guards chuckled and did as they were bid. Dell stepped inside the chamber. 'Still with us?'

Keriath's eyes fluttered open, and she pulled back from his mind into her own. 'Sadly,' she grumbled, rolling onto her side. But her breathing smoothed, and she heard him wonder if it wasn't partly an act that she appeared so weak. 'It's not.'

'I hate it when you do that,' he said, crouching beside her.

She held out her wrist in silent offering and shuddered as his teeth pierced her skin.

'Then you should have let me die,' she countered, sagging as what little strength she had left her.

His tongue grazed over the wound when he finished, and his eyes glinted as he gazed up at her. 'But then I would be without the delights your beautiful body has to offer.' She snorted and withdrew her arm. 'How are you?'

Keriath shrugged. She was alive. Just. Her body ached from the memory of her wounds, and the absence of her Graced strength was like missing a limb. She felt vulnerable ... mortal. And that was just her body. Her heart was weary and her mind numb. She dared not let her thoughts linger or consider her emotions. It was too overwhelming. Even if she were to survive her imprisonment, even if they were to escape, she wondered if she would ever fully recover.

How long had it been since she'd stood with Faolin and Dorrien beneath the lofty boughs of the Ravenswood? She didn't know. Ylain had not returned. It was a small mercy, but a mercy nonetheless, and she relished it. Somehow, Keriath knew it was the last one she'd ever receive. It was a terrifying thought.

'I'm fine,' she said, catching Dell peering at her. He raised a sceptical eyebrow but didn't challenge her. Time to change the subject. 'So what's happening in the world outside this cell?'

'Death and ruin,' he replied. 'What else? Rumour has it the Shade King's forces are moving again. That's got some people in this mountain a little nervous.'

'I'm not surprised. The Queens are plotting against him, right?'

Dell smirked and nodded. 'They've aligned with Prince Mazron and his sister Zorana against the King. They don't like the limitations he places upon them. Think they're above such rules.' Keriath pursed her lips. She'd gathered as much from conversations she'd overheard since her capture.

'So, what? Mazron's bought the Queens with human slaves to feed their army?'

He shook his head. 'No. The Queens bought him, and the Nightwalkers in his pocket, with their business. Shade Princes don't trust Darklings they can't control. The Queens had to convince him to see the benefits of having our kind as equal allies and not just lackeys.'

'And they sent Drosta north to Illyol to help Zorana see the same thing?'

Dell shrugged. 'Something like that.'

'But he's looking for an opportunity to line his own pockets instead?'

'Drosta isn't interested in anything as mundane as financial gains. He wants power. Zorana can give him that.'

Keriath's lip curled in disgust. 'It's a miracle there's any of you left – you're so quick to stab each other in the back. Almost makes me redundant.' He chuckled at that and didn't deny it. Then his gaze grew sombre, and he wouldn't meet her eye. 'What is it?' He hesitated, looking at the ground. Reaching over, she gripped his chin in her fingers and forced him to look at her. 'Tell me.'

'Ylain's had enough. She's going to let Talize have you,' he whispered.

Keriath flinched, releasing him. She tried to speak, but words wouldn't come. His expression was grim, his bloody eyes filled with regret, but he took her hands in his own and squeezed in reassurance. He opened his mouth to speak, but a voice from the doorway interrupted.

'How sweet,' it crooned. Dell surged to his feet, placing himself between Keriath and the Queen, a low growl ripping out of him. Talize's brows arched in surprise, and she eyed Keriath in admiration. 'You must be very strong to have such power over him this far under the mountain.'

Dell seemed to hesitate, shoulders slumping, but Keriath remained impassive. She'd had nothing to do with Dell's reaction. She'd felt it as clearly as if it had been her own, but she'd had no hand in it. It had been instinctive – driven by a base urge to protect and defend something he considered his own.

He bowed. 'Forgive me, Majesty.'

Talize smiled. It was a smile that sent a shiver of fear racing down Keriath's spine.

'I'll think about it,' the Queen mused. 'Now get out.' This time, at least, Dell had the sense not to hesitate. From the corner of Keriath's eye, she could see him pause on the threshold and glance back, his gaze filled with emotions she could not name. She didn't bother looking inside his head to find out what they were. She didn't want to know. Then he was gone, and her gaze drifted back to the Queen.

The unholy desire and ravenous bloodlust in Talize's dark red eyes told her that things were about to become much worse. The dark-haired Queen was beautiful, even by Graced standards, but there was something almost obscene about that beauty. It was not natural.

Talize sniffed and pulled a face as she scented the room. Two menacing-looking guards flanked her, though Keriath could tell at a glance the Queen had chosen them for looks and not for skill. Their muscle-bound bodies were well oiled but sculpted for aesthetic form, not prowess in combat. The Darkling man who followed behind, however, was something else.

His red eyes were glowing from the scent of Keriath's blood, but there was something cruel about them. More stable than Drosta perhaps, more cunning too, but just as vicious. His exquisite, well-fitted clothes, made of the finest black silk, were immaculate. His skin was pale, and his dark hair had been brushed until it shone. No doubt he considered himself handsome, this preening Darkling, and perhaps by mortal standards, he was. But Keriath, who hailed from a bloodline of legendary beauty and could stop a man dead in his tracks with only a smile, was unimpressed.

'Get her up,' Talize ordered, snapping her fingers at the muscles. They bowed and turned to obey. One went to the pulleys on the left, while the other went to the pulleys on the right. Together they shortened the chains above Keriath, pulling her to standing by her wrists, but they did not stop there. They kept going until she was suspended above the pedestal, dangling – her toes just inches above the ground, but it could have been miles for all the difference it made. Her shoulders screamed in protest, but she didn't have the strength to pull herself up to protect them. She slumped in her chains and gave herself to the pain. Perhaps she deserved it.

'Magnificent,' the pretty Darkling companion murmured, raking his eyes over Keriath's limp form with predatory intent. Something in his voice made Keriath's skin crawl.

'Isn't she just?' Talize crooned. 'A shame about the burns though.'

The pretty Darkling shook his head. 'No,' he breathed, 'they're perfect. An artist works with what they have. Marble, canvas ... flesh. It makes little difference. Art is art, and whoever sculpted those was a master.' Keriath's stomach heaved, and she looked away. She had no wish to see the fevered excitement in his eyes.

Talize murmured in agreement before turning back to the guards.

'Clean her up,' she ordered, 'and the cell too. I can't think for the smell.'

And with that she turned and strode from the room with her pretty pet on her heels.

As soon as the Queen had left, Dell returned to oversee the cleaning of her cell, the need to protect and defend churning beneath his skin. Then he sent for food and water, before banishing the other guards from the room once more.

'She'll kill you if she catches you,' Keriath warned as she allowed him to tip the cool, clear water down her throat.

His scowl deepened. 'She's the one who gave the order. She needs you stronger so that ...' He trailed off.

'So I can endure what she's got planned for me?' she finished for him. He nodded, handing her an apple along with some bread and cheese. Disgust and fear tightened around her throat. 'Delightful.'

Dell only grimaced in agreement. 'When she begins, don't trust your senses,' he warned. 'Ylain's given the order. You're not to be touched ... like that ... but Talize's drugs can make you see and hear whatever she wants, so you won't be able to tell the difference. Trust nothing. Even me.'

Keriath snorted and smirked at him, trying to hide the wave of relief that they would not violate her. 'That shouldn't be too difficult.'

He scowled, but she didn't miss the hurt in his eyes. Wouldn't have missed it even if she'd been unable to sense the pain as her words struck him like a blow. She blinked in surprise and opened her mouth to say something – to take it back, deny it. She wasn't sure what she could say. But she didn't get the chance as he turned on his heel and left her alone with her thoughts.

She frowned. Whatever bond was between them, it was growing stronger. She could sense the work of magic at play. What they had ... it wasn't natural. Whether it was the work of the Darkling corruption or the twisted power thrumming through the mountain, she didn't know. But there was no doubt in her mind that it had nothing to do with her Graced lineage. That magic was the kind that made her hands itch with the need to choke the life out of Dell.

A need that grew stronger when he stood by and watched from the door as Talize's bodyguards entered to do their mistress's bidding. As

Keriath watched them approach with the bucket of water and washcloth, her pride snapped to attention, and she growled in warning at them.

'Don't you fucking dare,' she snarled. Her chains had been loosened, so she could lie on the pedestal once more, and she scrambled to her feet as they neared. She dropped to a defensive crouch, her hands outstretched, warning them away. 'I will gut you like the pigs you are if you even think about it.'

Dell's soft chuckle echoed around the cavern. 'I told you she wouldn't take it lying down.' One had the sense to look nervous, but the other had a mischievous glint in his eye as he looked between the woman and the buckets.

'Have it your way,' he said with an idle shrug of his shoulders. Then he threw the contents of one bucket over her. Keriath shrieked in outrage: the water was ice-cold. He chuckled and turned to leave, but he froze when his gaze fell upon the curvaceous figure silhouetted in the doorway. As one, the two guards dropped to their knees and bowed their heads.

'Majesty,' they murmured together.

Talize tutted as she stepped inside, her bloody gaze raking over Keriath's drenched figure. 'That won't do at all,' she purred. 'Strip her and wash her properly.'

Keriath growled, backing away as much as she could. But there was nowhere for her to go, and the guards captured her without difficulty. They pulled her chains tight once more to hold her fast, her joints burning with the pain. She looked to Dell for help, but he stood fast behind the Queen. His eyes blazed, and she sensed the anger churning in his gut. *Mine, mine, mine*, his thoughts were chanting.

She looked away as the guards reached for her clothes. Her shirt was long gone, but her tough boots and blood-crusted trousers proved hard to remove. Her undergarments followed. Keriath thrashed and swore at the violation, but her humiliation didn't end there. Her cheeks burned as they approached with washcloths and soap in hand. Keriath kept her gaze fixed on Talize, trying to hide her embarrassment behind blistering hatred. But the sly smirk twisting the Queen's lips suggested it wasn't working.

'That will do for now, gentlemen,' the Queen ordered. 'Send in Goran on your way out.' The guards stepped back, reluctance clear on their faces, but they bowed and left. Keriath let her eyes drift to Dell once more, to where he hovered in the doorway. Let her mind blend with his.

He'd folded his arms across his chest to hide his balled fists from the Queen, and his jaw was clenched so tight it was a miracle he hadn't shattered his teeth. The urge to defend was roaring in his blood. But he forced himself to remain still, motionless as a statue. He wouldn't – couldn't – risk the Queen's wrath. Talize followed Olena's gaze and laughed but did not send him away. Another game, no doubt.

A moment later, the Queen's pretty pet entered, a broad smile on his face as he took in Keriath's state. It was hard to tell whether it was her state of undress or the humiliation in her eyes he found so exciting. Keriath shuddered.

'It's a shame she has to stay locked in here,' he said. 'We could have so much more fun in your chambers.'

Talize nodded in agreement. 'I know. But Ylain insists she stays here, and judging by how brazen Drosta was when he delivered her to us, I'd say it's for good reason. He was bursting at the seams with power. Her blood must be potent – I'm dying to taste it.'

'Perhaps a small sample then,' he suggested, 'before we begin.'

Talize hummed, her head cocked to the side while she considered it. 'You first.'

Keriath thrashed as he approached, but her chains held her tight. Dell twitched, struggling to contain his temper, and Keriath threw him a glare, warning him to hold his ground. He was no use to her dead.

Goran grinned as he lowered his head to her breast, his hands skimming her hips. She roared at his touch. Tender, but a far greater violation than Ylain's abuse. He drank slowly, his tongue brushing across her flesh, and her stomach heaved in disgust. Tears ran unchecked down her cheeks while she waited for him to finish. Unable to watch, she kept her eyes on the curved ceiling above her.

Then it was over. Goran stepped back, and she looked once more to Dell.

He was shaking from the effort of his restraint, his eyes tracking Goran and the blood dripping from his mouth as he returned to the Queen's side. Talize crushed her opulent body against his, devouring his mouth, tasting the blood on his tongue.

Keriath's body chose that moment to rebel, and she was sick from the disgust and shame churning in her gut.

The Queen broke away. 'Dell,' she called out. Goran glanced at Keriath and grinned. It was a vicious, chilling thing. 'Come here.' Dell's movements were stiff, forced, but he did as he was bid, and Keriath's heart sank further.

Her stomach heaved again as the Queen turned Dell to face her prisoner and tore his shirt from his chest. His face was like stone, but she could see his unease in the set of his shoulders. He smirked as Keriath's gaze skirted over his muscled chest and winked in reassurance. Talize hissed, drawing Keriath's attention back to her while the Queen ran her hands over his body in a possessive caress. Then she spun him round, and Keriath heard herself gasp. His back was a ragged patchwork of scars that could only have been caused by one thing.

Dell had been flogged. Even if she hadn't seen his shoulders tense, she could sense the stress rolling off him. *Those scars were not something he liked people to see. To have them shown off like this? It made him feel exposed ... vulnerable ... weak.*

The wave of disgust that crashed through Dell echoed in her as though it were her own, and the chamber reverberated with his defiant growl. Every thought, emotion and sensation that Dell had – the hatred towards the Queen for exposing him like that; the disgust at her touch, at Goran's eyes on his body; the jealousy of watching the Queen's pet feed ... Keriath felt it all. And as Goran uncoiled a whip, Dell roared. There was murder in his eyes, but he was powerless to stop it. His rage lent her strength, and she lost herself in the bloody, vengeful thoughts that filled his head.

She closed her eyes. She didn't want to see his pain. Feeling it was hard enough.

The first crack of the lash was the worst, coupled with the shame and fear that crashed through Dell. A wave of memories followed.

The moment of his Claiming. Watching Drosta butcher a pretty young woman. His wife. His hands trembling with defiance as his new master forced him to murder his own child. The flogging Drosta had given him when he realised not even the Claiming could force him to love him the way he wanted. Each strike cleaved open his mind, horrors from his past breaking free with each blow, baring his heart and soul.

Finally, it was over, and Keriath shook with dread. She couldn't bring herself to open her eyes. She could sense Goran stepping back just as someone else came closer, and she shuddered as gentle hands ran lovingly over her ruined flesh.

'Look at me.' Talize's voice whispered in her ear, warm breath tickling her neck. Keriath shuddered, trying to ignore the command in those words. It was just as it had been in the throne room. Against her will her chin jerked up, her lips pulled back, baring her teeth in a silent snarl, and she met Talize's bloody gaze. The Queen beamed at the pain in Keriath's eyes and kissed her prisoner on the lips. 'You are so exquisite,' she murmured against Keriath's mouth. She trailed kisses over her jaw and down her throat, setting Keriath's skin crawling, before sinking her teeth in to feed.

Exhaustion tugged at Keriath's mind, the lethargy of blood loss dragging her down towards the darkness. For the first time, she went willingly, desperate for any reprieve.

'Olena. Wake up.' It was Dell's voice that roused her from oblivion. 'Come on, get up,' he insisted. His voice was harsh and raw, as though he'd been screaming for hours. A pang of sympathy pricked at her conscience.

Swearing, she did as she was bid. She didn't have the strength to stand, so she pulled herself up to sitting. Dell was standing over her, the ragged remains of his shirt in his hand. Talize and Goran were gone, the door-bridge sealed shut behind them. Keriath glanced at Dell, but he seemed unperturbed by his current predicament.

'You look ... different,' she murmured, curling in on herself when she remembered her nakedness. He handed his shirt to her without a word and looked away as she covered herself as best she could. She wasn't sure what it was about him that was different, but there was a certainty, a determination in his posture that hadn't been there before.

He dropped to his haunches in front of her and snorted. 'And you look like shit,' he said. 'But I suppose that's nothing new, is it?'

'Prick.'

He laughed, but the humour didn't quite reach his eyes. 'Come on, don't be like that,' he crooned. 'I'm just trying to help.'

'Then fuck off and leave me alone,' she said.

His grin faded to a bitter smirk, and he sat down beside her. Despite her annoyance, she leaned in to his warmth. 'Not going anywhere,' he murmured, kissing the top of her head. 'Even if I wanted to.'

'And why is that?' she whispered. 'What did I do to warrant such loyalty? Your Queen just tortured you because of me. You're in here because of me. How can you even bear the sight of me?'

'I heard you. In my head,' he admitted. 'As I'm sure you noticed, I've suffered worse.'

Keriath growled. 'You're avoiding the question.'

'Because I don't know the answer,' he admitted. 'Maybe I'm just contrary.'

'Not half,' she snorted, smiling.

Dell chuckled. 'Aye well, decades with Drosta will do strange things to you.'

'You know why he did it?' asked Keriath. He nodded, trembling as the memories surfaced again, the fear drenching him in a cold sweat. 'They don't define you,' she told him. 'What people see of us ... it's just flesh, just skin and muscle and bone. Who we are, what matters, is what we hold inside. My people knew that better than anyone.' She sensed his fear dissipate, his nerves settle as she spoke.

'That what they told you when your father marked you?' he asked.

Keriath nodded. 'They're just scars, Dell. They serve as reminders to us and as warning to others, for they show that we fought a terrible enemy, and that we won.'

He was quiet for a long time while he considered her words. 'It feels like the Claiming,' he said. She blinked in confusion. 'Whatever this is, between us,' he elaborated, 'it feels like the bond a Darkling has with their maker.'

'But the Graced can't make Darklings,' Keriath argued, shaking her head.

He shrugged. 'And Drosta's the one who made me. I know it doesn't make any sense; I'm just telling you what I feel.' She waited. 'I know the Claiming inside out and backwards. I've been trying to find a way around it for decades, without much success. It's not a conscious choice. The urge to protect, to defend – it's a compulsion. Like my own survival instincts, if not even stronger. With Drosta ... if it came down to my life or his, I wouldn't even have a chance to think. I would have sacrificed myself to save him before I even realised what I was doing. That's just how it works. It feels the same with you.'

'Your thoughts are your own,' Keriath pointed out.

It wasn't a question, but he answered it anyway. 'The Claiming doesn't override free thought – at least, not on its own. That requires a conscious decision by the maker. It's possible to make their dominion over their *children* so strong that the Hunt becomes an extension of themselves. Drosta never quite took it that far. It takes too much effort, and there were too many of us to control. But he suppressed any part of me that might seek to defy him, even with my thoughts. He couldn't make me love him, but he did the next best thing.'

She shuddered. She couldn't imagine what it was like to have your mind stolen. Her people had that power, but they rarely used it and never for such selfish reasons.

'I still don't understand how any of that explains this,' she grumbled.

'It doesn't. And even if I understood it, I'm not sure it would make any difference. Talize knows there's something there. She'll try to turn us against each other.'

Keriath frowned. 'Why bother? Why not just kill you?'

'It's not her style,' he replied darkly. She followed his gaze as it tracked over her chains, the door, the iron spikes that surrounded her. 'They're fucking terrified of you, aren't they?'

Keriath collapsed back down on the floor. If only her head would stop spinning for just one moment. 'The Gods only know why.'

'Because you're Graced,' he snorted. Keriath shrugged. He wasn't wrong. They might be the legendary Darkling Queens, but they were still just mortals. They were not blessed with magic – not like she was – and no amount of Shade magic or stolen life would ever change that. Not that it made any difference.

'I'm as good as mortal down here,' Keriath murmured, staring up at the ceiling. 'He built this prison to hold something far stronger than me.'

Dell growled. 'Get a grip,' he snapped. 'Talize doesn't care about what you know. She just wants to see you beg. You're the last descendant of an ancient and noble bloodline. Your ancestors were chosen, above all others, to fight against Sephiron's hordes. You were *made* to kill Darklings, born for it. You're a predator, and she's your prey. Act like it.'

Keriath bristled at the insult, at all it implied. But he was right.

They were interrupted by the sound of approaching footsteps echoing around the cell. Keriath debated whether to remain on the ground. While Ylain had commented on Keriath's rudeness at not standing in her presence, Talize struck her as the kind who preferred to see her subjects on their knees. Keriath staggered to her feet, despite the weakness and exhaustion that had plagued her since she'd set foot on this accursed mountain.

Talize smiled to see Keriath standing, defiance written in every line of her wasted frame. 'I would have thought you'd learned your lesson by now,' she purred, stalking closer. Keriath said nothing. Instead, she stared the Darkling Queen down without fear or apprehension in her eyes. The Queen cocked her head to the side, considering. Then her gaze slid to Dell. 'What about you? Learned your place yet?'

'Inside you?' he taunted with a cocky grin.

Talize's eyes flashed as she looked to Keriath. 'How are you controlling him?' Keriath only gave a lazy smirk she knew would make the Queen see red. 'No matter,' Talize said. Then she snapped her fingers, and her guards came running. 'Take him to my chambers. Tell Goran I will join him there in a moment.' Dell struggled as they hauled him up and dragged him away. But it was four against one, and Keriath knew he wouldn't risk letting Talize see how strong Keriath's blood had made him.

'What are you going to do to him?' asked Keriath.

Talize purred, watching him leave, 'Nothing he won't enjoy ... eventually at least.' Then she turned those dreadful eyes on Keriath. 'I'm going to turn him against you. No matter what it takes, I will break whatever hold you have over him. I will have him for myself.'

'Why not just kill him?' Keriath said. She was already weary of Talize and her games. 'He's just one Darkling. You have hundreds under your command.'

That evil smile widened. 'I think it goes both ways. I think hurting him will hurt you. And there's only one way to find out.'

'And if you're wrong?'

'Then you can watch as I kill him. Slowly and painfully.'

Keriath was silent as she tried to slow her racing heart, the fear rising in her chest. Her voice was steady when she spoke. 'What's the point? I won't tell you anything, and I don't know what else you expect to get out of this.'

'What else?' repeated Talize, her eyes bright with excitement. 'Other than watching you suffer? Or do you not believe that would be reward enough?'

'And what have I done to make you hate me so much? Or do you just delight in pain?'

Talize laughed again. 'I won't deny that I enjoy fear and pain. Nothing makes me feel more alive in this world than seeing people tremble in my presence. But you're Graced – a Unicorn too, even if you are disfigured. You should understand. How many have fallen on their knees and offered to worship you?'

'None, that I am aware of,' Keriath replied, smirking at the bitterness and jealousy in Talize's voice. 'I can't help what I am.'

The Queen snorted. 'No. The mighty Graced would never dare to admit fault.' Her hand snaked out, touching Keriath's cheek in a caress that was both tender and lethal. 'I will break you before the end. I will see you on your knees, bowing before me, begging for my mercy, my favour. By the time I'm finished with you, you will do anything I say, for no other reason than to please me.'

'Don't count on it,' Keriath breathed, jerking her chin up in defiance.

But Talize only smirked again and arched a speculative brow, before turning to leave.

'Sleep well, little Unicorn,' she murmured from the door. 'Tomorrow, we begin.'

Keriath soon longed for Ylain's brand of torture. At least the pain was clean. The drugs that Talize filled her with left her in a cloud of confusion and despair. As Dell had warned, it became difficult to separate dreams from reality. There had been little sign of him since they'd dragged him away, and Talize had not mentioned him again. Keriath assumed that meant he had not yet broken. The Queen would have been crowing about it otherwise. Her growing frustration became increasingly obvious in the torments she dreamed up for her prisoner.

There were the drugs that brought physical agony. Some caused such intense pain that Keriath blacked out. Others built more gradually so she could not escape into oblivion. Some lingered for days. Those were the easiest to deal with – she had become accustomed to giving herself to the pain.

It was the drugs that tortured her mind that she hated. Some brought pain, some pleasure. Talize's favourites were the concoctions that made her see and feel things that weren't there. Some things were terrifying, others were beautiful. Both caused equal suffering when she surfaced from the haze, tormenting her for hours between Talize's visits.

The Queen had a dark mind and a twisted soul. They forced her to watch while they whipped a human who looked like Théon and tortured another that looked like Arian. Warm, kind-hearted Arian. Resari's adopted sister and Kalielle Half-Elven's heir. The four of them had been inseparable as children. She tried not to look. But it was no use. Because even once they were gone, all she could hear were Théon's broken screams as the lash came down, or Arian's terror as her tormentor approached.

Some small part of her whispered that it wasn't real. But it was. Perception was reality, and Talize's drugs altered how Keriath saw the world. Drew on her memories and twisted them into nightmares. And the Darkling Queen knew, somehow, that the pain of those Keriath loved was far harder to bear than her own.

Still, she would not beg. She would be haunted forever, but she would carry those horrors alone rather than submit. Her stubborn pride only incensed Talize further, and her torments became worse by the day. Keriath was sure, if she somehow survived, her memories of this time would leave scars far uglier than those that marred her skin.

Then came the day Talize lost her patience. When she entered the cell, there was murder in her eyes, and she carried a vial of blackest night in her hand. 'I didn't want to do this,' she warned, her voice quiet. 'Know that you have brought it on yourself. Had you only submitted earlier, I would have spared you this.'

'Do what you want. I won't bow,' stated Keriath, though there was ice in her veins.

Talize's answering smile was grim. 'Oh, but you will. Opaele breaks all. A pity. I'm afraid you won't be much use to me after this ... though Pria can still have her fun, no doubt.'

Then she called her guards, and they prised open Keriath's jaws so the Queen could pour the contents of the vial down her throat. Keriath snarled and spat out as much as possible but, much like the ruan, only a little was needed for it to take effect. Her vision grew hazy, and she was vaguely aware of watching Talize's retreating back as the Queen stormed from the cell.

She was floating, cocooned in warmth and happiness. Her peace was absolute. The agonies she had endured were nothing but a distant memory. She had never been more content in her entire life. Relief flooded her tired body, easing sore muscles and soothing half-healed wounds. Her fear and rage dissipated, like mist burning away at dawn, and all the dark things she had seen no longer troubled her. It was paradise.

Ecstasy thrummed through her veins until she thought she might burst from the sheer pleasure of it. She was flying higher than the stars themselves, looking down on their heavenly beauty with dreamy eyes. She didn't know how long she drifted in that world of rapture and delight. It might have been hours. It might have been years. She had no way of knowing, and nor did she care. All that mattered was staying there. She would have spent eternity in that place if she could.

But suddenly it was over, and she was slammed back into reality with an excruciating jolt. She screamed in agony. Somehow her body hurt more for its reprieve, the suffering of her mind greater after respite. She wanted nothing more than to go back to that place. She screamed and screamed and screamed as the real world tore her apart. Nothing had ever hurt as much as this. Nothing.

But she would not give in. Not now. Not after all she had already withstood so much. No matter how much it hurt, she wouldn't bow ... and so Talize returned. She gave Keriath more. The second time was even better than the first. The descent after was even worse. But still, she would not bow. And so the cycle continued, over and over again until it was all she thought about.

She needed more. She'd have torn open her chest with her bare hands and ripped her still-beating heart from it if she'd thought it would take her back to that place. But a pair of red eyes glinted in the doorway, and she knew her torments were far from over.

CHAPTER TWENTY-FIVE

Keriath had not believed she could fall any further. She'd been wrong. Pride and rage were no longer things she could afford if she wanted to survive. So she begged. She pleaded and beseeched and implored. She grovelled and knelt at Talize's feet. She did things she daren't linger upon, her stomach churning with disgust and self-reproach.

But when Ylain returned and demanded answers, still Keriath had not bent. Not when they'd starved her. Not when they'd beaten her until she was barely recognisable for her wounds. Not even when they'd withheld the opaele, and she'd screamed herself hoarse. She would sell her soul to Sephiron himself before she betrayed her kin.

Finally, she was given to Pria – though only after the youngest Queen had promised Ylain and Talize that she would not lose control and kill their prisoner by accident. Not that any of them believed her. So began what seemed like an eternity of suffering. Ylain had been a butcher when it came to inflicting pain. Pria was an artist. She tortured her for no other reason than the joy she took from the suffering of others. It wasn't like with Ylain, who tried to justify her actions with claims of righteousness, or Talize, who only felt strong when she inflicted pain and elicited fear.

No, this was pure madness. Pria was insane. Keriath wondered if she would die from the humiliation and pain that the Queen caused her. Sometimes she hoped Pria would get carried away and end her. But the Queen kept her word. She held Keriath on the brink for hours at a time, until her victim no longer knew the difference between life and death.

Then came the day she'd been dreading. Pria entered the chamber as usual, waltzing in on delicate feet. The angelic smile on her sweet face, so at odds with the malice roiling in those bloody eyes. But this time, she was followed by Talize, and Keriath felt her heart sink. The older Queen was smirking, radiating the satisfied smugness of a cat that'd just swallowed a songbird.

Two male figures flanked Talize. Her pet Goran was to her right. Keriath shuddered as he leered at her, licking his lips in anticipation. But to her left ... that hulking figure was Dell. Or at least, it had been. There was nothing of his cocky arrogance left. None of the decency or practicality that'd prompted him to bring her a healer. Not even a shred of warmth was left in his distant gaze. She reached for his mind and flinched from the hate and desperate need for violence she found there. It might have been Dell's face that stared at her, but there was nothing left of him within.

'What did you do to him?' she gasped.

Talize grinned. 'I have ... expanded his mind,' she purred. 'Do you like it?'

'How?' Keriath growled, swallowing her disgust. Magic should have been beyond her.

The Queen tittered. 'Graced blood carries more than just life-magic. Drink enough of it, and some of it sticks.'

'That would take hundreds of lives,' breathed Keriath, trembling from the horror.

'Thousands.'

Her stomach heaved. 'That's not possible. My people are dead and gone – they have been for a hundred years.'

'Yes, that was a shame.' Talize sighed. 'But Ylain, Pria and I ... we've been feeding from the Graced since they first walked this earth. We even had our own breeding stock for a while. Until the Shade King made us destroy them. So you can appreciate how interested we are in where we might find more of you.'

'The Graced are dead. The Shade King made sure of that,' insisted Keriath, trying to hide her rising panic.

Talize raised a disbelieving eyebrow. 'If you say so.' Then she gestured at Dell. 'I'll leave you to get reacquainted.' She turned and left with Goran on her heels, leaving Keriath alone with Pria and Dell. The youngest Queen giggled and clapped her hands.

'We're going to have so much fun!' she exclaimed, her girlish voice sending shivers down Keriath's spine. But worst of all was the look of diabolical glee spreading across Dell's face as he tested the edge of his knife.

It was getting harder. Whatever Talize had done to Dell, it hadn't broken the bond between them. He still seemed to sense what would hurt her most, what would scare her. With Pria's guidance, he wore away at what little remained of her resolve.

Keriath could only pray to Gods long-forgotten that the others were coming. Resari and Théon. Faolin and Dorrien. Her brother. Even Illyandi. And when they did, the Queens would pay for what they'd done. The last of the Graced would blaze through Dar Kual like a natural disaster, leaving only death in their wake. A faint hope, true enough, but it was all she had.

They'd taken her power and her strength, but that could be fixed. Time would reverse the damage from starvation and torture, and then she could use her powers to purge their poisons from her body. They'd stolen her dignity and her fire. But she had hope. They would come. They would save her from her fate, and she need never look upon another Darkling again. They would make sure of that. They would protect her. As they always had.

She'd clung to that hope while Dell whispered her nightmares into Pria's ear. Even as her chains were tightened, and the Queen approached with knife in hand, and she'd felt the bitter grip of fear around her heart. She'd screamed as Pria carved her face, the blade digging deep and edged with enough magic to ensure the wounds would scar. Talize had taken the magic of the Unicorns, corrupting it for her own ends. But Pria had stolen the power of the Casting from any Elf unfortunate enough to cross her path. It was a dark, twisted thing in her hands. The scent of it, the touch as it cut through Keriath ... her stomach heaved in revulsion.

But when Pria handed the knife to Dell, Keriath's terror surged. She thrashed then, making the ordeal even worse as the knife dragged. But she didn't have it in her to hold still. Not when he trailed that blade down her throat, across her breast and the ravaged hollow of her stomach ... lower. Not when he cut into unmarked flesh, to finish the ruination of her beauty that his brethren had started all those years ago. Not when he licked her skin clean of the blood that flowed from his ministrations.

She was not so far gone that she missed what it sparked in his eyes. But she was too tired to care about the flash of devastation on his face when he looked at the bloody knife in his hand. Pria was too drunk on her pain to either notice or care. Instead, the young Queen shoved him aside and drank her fill, dragging Keriath towards oblivion.

The cold seeped through her body, and Keriath drifted, floating in the darkness. She thought she heard a voice raised in song, but it was little more than a distant memory. A Phoenix. Her clear, pure voice soaring to notes that Keriath could not have imagined, tears rolling down her cheeks as she sang. It was an old song, the lyrics in the ancient tongue. Keriath did not understand the words, but she knew their meaning. It was a song of hope.

It was a legend, whispered around mortal campfires – a story they told their children to send them to sleep. They claimed that the song of a Phoenix gave hope to the strong of heart, while casting fear into the weak. Keriath smiled bitterly to herself, wincing as the movement sent a flash of searing pain through the wounds on her face. Mortals also believed that Phoenix tears had healing powers. But faith was its own kind of magic. So she let the memory of the song fill her until it was almost as though the Phoenix woman stood there. Hope swelled, and somehow, despite the crushing weight of the mountain, her magic flared.

Keriath's hands wrapped their way around the chains above her. Her body, although she did not command it to, heaved itself up to stand tall. It fought off the pain and the weakness, the hunger and exhaustion, and it felt strong. In a last, desperate attempt, she hurled her fury at the weight of dark magic suppressing her power and felt it yield. Magic rushed through her body, healing her, strengthening her. In the same instant, she pulled on the chains and kicked out, planting her feet on the chest of the youngest Queen, sending her flying back towards the door.

Flames of darkest amethyst lashed out at Dell, knocking him to the ground. She screamed in defiance as she ripped the chains from the wall, freeing her arms. But as she reached for the chains about her ankles, the corruption of the mountain pressed against her once more, and her strength crumbled. A shout from the door drew her attention – a dozen guards were rushing towards her.

Defiance never left her lips as she was subdued and ruan poured down her throat again. Still she struggled against them, but they were too many. Then she saw the Queen bearing down on her. Blood oozed from a cut in Pria's head where she'd hit the ground. Dell had blood dripping from his mouth. He wiped it from his chin with the back of his sleeve and snarled.

'I should make you drink this,' hissed Pria, gesturing at her blood.

'It would do nothing to me,' Keriath said. 'Even your blood isn't strong enough to turn me.' The Queen's eyes blazed, and she struck Keriath across the face. Despite the taste of her own blood in her mouth, Keriath smiled. With an insolent smirk, she spat the blood out on the floor. All around her, the Darklings eyes glowed red.

'It may not make you one of us, but I can assure you, it will not be a pleasurable experience,' Pria crooned. She sliced open her wrist with her dagger and approached Keriath, smiling as her guards forced their prisoner's mouth open.

The pain was excruciating. The blood burned the inside of her mouth and scorched all the way down her throat. It hit her stomach like a fireball and exploded outward. Every nerve in her body was on fire. Pain blazed through her entire being, a raging inferno fuelled by her power. She could feel the blood trying to change her, to make her blood more like itself. But she was healing as fast as it could hurt her. And then it went back to hurting what had already healed. She didn't know when – or how – it would end. She heard herself screaming. She could not stop it.

'This pain will endure for as long as you can, *Unicorn*,' sneered the young Queen. The guards released her. She didn't need to be restrained; her agony did that for them. She was writhing on the floor, thrashing against the stones beneath her, desperate to escape.

'I will kill you.' Keriath panted as she fought through the pain.

The Queen only laughed. 'Unlikely. Now, I believe I asked for information on where we might find others like you?' Keriath couldn't even summon the strength to swear at them while her body burned. She screamed again as another wave of agony coursed through her.

'Make it stop!' she gasped.

'Tell her where the others are,' Dell countered over Keriath's shrieks.

'I can't!' she choked as she convulsed.

Then Pria's voice whispered in her ear, soft and cruel like the sound of a snake slithering over stones. 'You have nothing left with which to fight. Tell me what I want to know, and I will end it.' Keriath's body twitched. Her eyes closed. It was more than she could endure. They had broken her, and they all knew it.

'Ciaron,' she whispered in the Queen's mind, unable to find the strength to speak aloud. 'There are still Dragons in Ciaron. The Nightwalkers hide them. Protect them from you.'

'Thank you,' crooned Pria. She gripped Keriath's face, forcing her mouth open as she tipped the contents of a vial down her throat. 'To dull the pain.' Then she stamped down on Keriath's leg, shattering it into pieces. Keriath flinched, but it was nothing compared with the agony of her blood.

Guilt and shame mingled with pain until she was drowning in it. Suffering, on and on, long after her tormentors had turned away. She embraced it without question. She deserved no less for her betrayal.

Keriath was singing when Dell returned. Her voice was not as pure as Arian's, and it was raw and hoarse from screaming. But it was still enchanting. The curse of her bloodline. No matter what they did to her, it was the one thing they could not change. Her lips were dry, and as she sang, they cracked, coating her mouth with blood that made the Darkling's eyes glow. She watched him cross the bridge to her, tried not to flinch as he cradled her face in his hands and stroked the tears from her cheeks. Then, ever so gently, he kissed her. His lips were warm and insistent as they savoured the blood in her mouth.

And when he stepped back, and she saw mischief dancing in his eyes, she sobbed with relief.

He smiled and kissed her again. 'Miss me?' he murmured against her mouth.

'How?' she whispered, pulling away.

'This,' he said, touching a finger to the blood beading on her lip. 'I'm not free of her yet. But soon. I'll get you out of here soon. I swear.' She nodded in understanding and thanks, and turned her head to the side, offering her throat up to him.

'What were you singing?' he asked once he'd drunk his fill.

Though the words were in the ancient tongue, Keriath knew the story well. It was one of the Old Tales; written into song by a small, broken-hearted child. She closed her eyes, remembering the little girl with bright crimson hair sitting by the fire all those years ago. The Phoenix memori-alised everything in song. Even when there was only one left living, she'd insisted on continuing the tradition. It was the Song of the Fall.

Dell inclined his head, not needing her to speak the words to under-stand the fathomless sorrow in her eyes. 'Will you tell me the story?'

Keriath nodded and did as he asked. And as she sang, translating as best she could into the common tongue, the horrors of that day came rushing back. Everything had happened so fast. A hundred years later, and her memories were little more than a jumbled mess.

The attacks had come simultaneously. Keriath and her mother had been outside the city wards when they'd been ambushed by Jenia. They'd been visiting the Lady Kylar's mother in her castle to the north. Both had died so that Keriath could live. The shame of that knowledge was a millstone around her neck. It had been easier for Taelyr. He'd been too young to remember any of the horrors. His father had remained up at the palace in Revalla with his infant son. They'd been ambushed by a single Shade. That had been enough to kill the Lord of the Isles, but his sister had escaped with his son and heir.

While Keriath fled, the Shade King's lover on her heels, Darklings had descended upon Ciaron. The Dragon High Chieftain had fallen. His father too. One of their own had turned on them, stabbing them in front of his children. He'd used his dying breath to warn the other Clans. Faolin had barely escaped with his life. Even then, his suffering paled compared to his sister's. Dorrien had watched the Darkling Queens invade the Temple and tear their mother apart. She'd been six years old with next to no control over her powers. Terrified for her life and already grieving for a mother who still lay screaming in agony, she'd cried out with her mind for help. Every Graced being in the world saw what Dorrien saw that day. The sight of that shredded body still haunted Keriath's nightmares sometimes. She knew that, even now, Dorrien saw it every time she closed her eyes.

Keriath was little better. There wasn't a day went by that she didn't picture her mother's mangled corpse lying on the cobbled streets as a red-eyed, red-haired demon stalked towards her. She'd fled, preferring to take her chances with the waterhorses than Jenia of Elucion.

Théon and Illyandi had fared no better in Illyol. They'd been dragged from their beds by a member of the Royal Guard. Forced to hide while they listened to the dying screams of the Queen and her Prince Consort. Keriath had seen Théon's memories of that night. Seen Théon singing the same lullaby to Illyandi, over and over again, just to drown out their mother's screams. When dawn had broken, and the Nightwalkers had been driven away, a single surviving guard had released them and escorted them from the city. They'd never seen their parents' bodies.

What had happened in Elucion remained a mystery. The Shade King alone had confronted the Phoenix and their mighty firebirds. Only two had escaped, and of those two only one remained. Arian. Kalielle's ward. The last Phoenix in existence. She'd never spoken of what she'd witnessed. Less than a week later, Kalielle had killed herself rather than be taken prisoner by the monster that had caused her so much pain.

The torrent of her nightmares, her memories, stopped as Ylain entered, flanked by Talize and Pria. They ignored Dell as they lunged for their prey, drinking deeply.

Keriath kept singing.

The song Arian had written to commemorate the fallen was full of sorrow, but there was hope there as well. For the Phoenix knew best of all that only by falling might one rise again. They alone knew no fear of death; they believed it was their faith that gave them power over it. As a child, Arian believed that those she'd lost might come back to her. Even now that she knew better, she still lived by the hope she'd written into that song.

For they were the Rising. They were the legacy, the survivors: the children of the fallen. There was no Phoenix blood in Keriath's veins as far as she knew, but she'd been raised amongst them. She shared their beliefs – that faith alone had its own power, so long as it was strong enough.

'For glory does not mean never falling,' breathed Keriath, her strength failing as she finished the song. 'You have seen our descent, now watch us rise.' Ylain flinched at the words. Fear sparked in her eyes, and she snapped her fingers, ordering both Talize and Pria from the room. They complained bitterly, but she would not yield.

Once they were gone, she spoke to the guards. 'Nobody gets back in here without my say so, understand?' They nodded. 'Good. Watch her closely. I fear we might have underestimated our prize.'

Keriath barely noticed the exchange, lost once more in the haze of delirium.

Dell hovered for the days that followed, listening to her sing of ancient battles and star-crossed lovers. Sometimes he lingered by the door, and Keriath would talk in hushed whispers, reminiscing in the darkness, stories of her heritage and the legacy she owed to those who came before. They were more than tales to bolster her faith: they were truth. Stories of real people. Her ancestors, who triumphed no matter how far they fell.

Ylain returned, but she made no move to feed. Instead, she stood in the doorway and eyed her prisoner cautiously. 'I fear I have been a fool,' she admitted.

'You will hear no argument from me,' Keriath whispered.

'There is far more to you than we realised, isn't there?'

Keriath offered a bitter smile. 'I don't know what you're talking about.' Ylain nodded, understanding that there were some secrets her prisoner would never yield. Besides, they had no power over her anymore. They'd done their worst. And she was still here.

'The thing is,' the Queen murmured, stepping into the room and closing the door behind her, 'that even this far inside the Barren Lands, we hear the Old Tales. We know who survived the Fall. I haven't come across many of Elucion's children in my time, but I know a Phoenix proverb when I hear one. And barring one exception, the Phoenix are all dead and gone. So either you keep company with legends, or you heard it before the Fall. Either way, you're no child of Taelyr's. What would Arian of Elucion have to do with the bastard offspring of some Revallan urchin?'

Keriath was quiet for a long time, but she sighed in defeat. 'I cannot fault your logic,' she conceded.

Ylain's eyes widened.

'You must truly despise him, if you would suffer all this rather than admit your birthright,' she whispered in wonder.

'He killed my mother.'

Ylain shook her head in frustration. 'Jenia killed the Lady Kylar.'

'On his orders. And don't think I would forget your part in it all. We all saw what you did to Ciaron.'

Ylain smirked, but there was a glimmer of fear in her blood-red eyes. 'We did what we had to. Anyway, what difference would the fate of Ciaron make to you?'

'You forget – Lady Kylar hailed from more than one noble line.' Keriath sighed, unable to rouse herself to anger. 'I bore the dragon-marks, before Jenia's Hunt tore me apart.'

The Queen fell silent for a while. When she spoke again, her voice was weary with regret. 'I wish you'd told me. I would have spared you Talize and Pria at least.'

'How very generous of you,' Keriath muttered, closing her eyes.

'You will pray for my generosity girl, for now I can spare you nothing,' Ylain snarled, advancing on her.

Keriath opened her eyes and frowned. 'What do you mean?'

'There is a Shade in my throne room demanding your release,' growled the Queen. 'He claims he's here on your father's behalf—'

'He's not my father,' Keriath said.

Ylain gaped at her. 'I think you're missing the point. Prince Mazron's sister is in open conflict with the King – there's no way on this earth that he's here to take you back to Elucion. I don't even know how he found out about you. But there is nothing I can do to stop him from taking you, whatever his reasons.'

'What do you expect me to do about it?' Keriath snapped, stung into irritation by the Queen's tone.

'There is nothing any of us can do about it, child,' the Queen sighed. 'I came to warn you. Come now, he is waiting.'

She snapped her fingers, and the door opened as the guards answered her summons. They unchained Keriath, but it was dread, not hope, that settled in her stomach at the sensation. She was far too weak to walk, let alone stand, so they supported her, one on each side, and half-dragged her from the room. She winced as the light from the torches burned at her eyes, but it was nothing compared to what she'd already endured. As they ascended out of the Core and back into the Pits, the weight of the mountain's dark magic eased, and she breathed a sigh of relief.

They carried her back through the labyrinthine corridors up to the throne room. And though each step they took should have made her feel a little lighter, pure terror closed its fist around her heart.

Ylain paused at the door, as if offering her a moment to compose herself. The look the Queen afforded her was full of pity, but there was also a glimmer of respect sparked, Keriath thought, by the knowledge that all they'd done had not destroyed their prisoner – perhaps Keriath would also survive whatever this Shade had planned.

'Be strong,' she murmured. Then she turned and motioned to the guards to open the doors, and Keriath realised that she could no longer remember the words to the song.

Beyond, pale eyes greeted her, and the earth lurched beneath her feet as fear claimed her. A tall frame, with lean limbs and a handsome face ... and the mark of the star upon his brow. She heaved against the hands holding her as she fought to get away from him. His face split in an evil smile, flashing gleaming white teeth in her direction.

'Hello Keriath,' he purred.

CHAPTER TWENTY-SIX

Renila groaned as her eyes flickered open, the bright sunlight filtering down through the pines stabbing at them like a hot knife. She tried to sit up, but the world tipped and rolled. Her head could have been made of solid lead the way her neck and shoulders protested at taking its weight. Her stomach heaved, and she forced herself to roll onto her side so she wouldn't choke.

Strong but gentle hands gathered her hair back while she vomited on the forest floor, rubbing her back as her body convulsed. Callused fingers scraped her neck and shoulder, massaging the aching muscles there while she trembled. She was too weak to shy away from that touch, and it was so calming she found she didn't want to anyway.

When she was done, those same hands eased her back down and smoothed her hair back from her face in a loving caress. She steeled herself against the inevitable pain and cracked her eyes open to look up at her saviour. Alvar knelt beside her, his purple-grey eyes heavy with worry, but he smiled to see her awake.

'Glad to see you're back with us,' he murmured. 'You had me worried there for a bit.' Renila opened her mouth to speak, but her lips cracked and bled, and her throat was too parched to make a sound. Alvar winced and reached for the water skin, lifting her head so she could drink.

'What happened?' she gasped. Her throat was scorched, and her chest burned as though she'd been breathing smoke. A peculiar sense of familiarity made her shiver – she was sure this had happened before, but she had no memory of it.

An ember flaring. Grief and sorrow driven out by wrath and vengeance. The ember sparking. Bloodlust rising. The spark catching. Fury raging in her veins, blazing through her like wildfire. That wrath taking form, exploding out of her as flames, licking along her skin. Her hair shifting and curling in the rising heat, surrounding her face in a flickering halo of scarlet waves. Her voice crackling with the power of the inferno within.

She shook her head, trying to clear the images flicking through her mind, and glanced down. Someone – presumably Alvar – had dressed her in a tunic and leggings that she was certain she'd never seen before. They were made of fine material, much finer than anything she could afford, yet it was still tough and warm enough for travelling. And they fitted her perfectly. She frowned and looked to him for answers.

Alvar sighed and sat back, leaning against the thick trunk of a pine. 'Darklings found the castle – broke through the wards. We held long enough to give most time to escape, but there were too many.'

'Suriya? Lucan?' she asked.

'They made it out,' Alvar assured her. 'The Hunt is after us, so I think they'll be alright. Gaelan is taking them to my father. They'll be safe with him.'

Renila wanted to ask about this rare glimpse into the mysterious Lord's life, but another memory struck her.

'Farran is dead.'

It wasn't a question.

Alvar bowed his head. 'I'm sorry, Renila. I know you cared for him.'

Grief threatened to crush her, but the tears would not come. Something was nagging at her memory, something more important than Farran, something that made fear pulse through her veins and dread sit like a dead weight in her stomach.

'Erion,' she whispered, her eyes wild. She glanced around, ignoring the nausea that rose in response to the movement, ignoring the pain that threatened to shatter her skull. 'Where is Erion?' Alvar's hands gripped her shoulders and held her still.

'Renila,' he said, his voice heavy with warning, 'I need you to calm down.'

'Tell me where my son is!' she demanded, her cheeks heating. Alvar winced and leaned back from the sudden warmth radiating off her, but he held on.

'Calm down. Now,' he ordered.

'Tell me where my son is!' she shrieked, thrashing in his grip. But his fingers dug into her skin, and he shook her.

'Get it under control, or I swear by Athair, I will make you forget you ever had a son!' he snapped. Renila went limp, panting, fear and wrath searing her heart. His temper steadied, and he loosened his grasp, but he held her gaze. 'Breathe. In through the nose, out through the mouth. That's it,' he said, releasing her as she calmed. But it was a lethal calm that settled about her shoulders as she fixed him with eyes that burned slowly like smouldering embers.

'Where. Is. My. Son?' she said, punctuating each word with a pointed breath. There was a muscle leaping in Alvar's jaw, but his voice was steady when he finally answered.

'I don't know,' he admitted.

'Is he even still alive?'

Alvar huffed a frustrated sigh. 'I don't know that either.'

'What *do* you know?' she snarled, her fingers itching to slap him.

His eyes flared at the threat. 'Calm down.'

'Stop telling me to calm down and tell me what the *fuck* happened,' she said. Alvar closed his eyes and took a deep breath through his nose. She could see his body trembling with the effort of controlling himself.

'I'm sorry,' he said. 'What's the last thing you remember?'

'We were trapped ... in a library?'

His gaze grew dark at the mention of that room. 'Farran fell fighting three Darklings. He took two with him, but there was one left ...'

'Erion – he killed it. I tried to get to him ...' She trailed off as her memory stuttered.

'Erion sealed you in—' he began.

'I couldn't stop them,' she whispered, eyes widening with horror as the memories came crashing back.

Alvar nodded. 'The Shade was very strong. There are few who could face one and live to tell the tale.'

But Renila didn't care.

'You let it escape with my son,' she said.

Alvar scowled. 'There was nothing I could do to stop the Shade. It's called Transference – the way it appeared and disappeared, as if drawn out of thin air. It's a power that's beyond me now, and I would have needed to know where he was going to follow.'

'What *are* you?' she breathed.

Alvar flinched from the fear in her voice, his beautiful eyes dark with sorrow.

'It's a long story,' he said, getting to his feet and busying himself with the supplies. Renila was quiet for a long time, but finally, she found the words.

'I like stories,' she whispered. He glanced over his shoulder at her and smiled at the gentleness of her voice. 'We have to get him back,' she begged. 'Please, I'll do anything. Just help me get him back.'

'We will. I promise.' Her shoulders sagged with relief. Then his eyes snapped to the shadows of the trees, to the endless darkness that surrounded them. 'We've lingered here too long. The Huntress is tracking us with what's left of her Hunt. She'll want you dead for what you did to the rest of it. We need to keep moving.'

Renila tried not to cry out in agony as Alvar helped her to her feet and lifted her into the saddle, but she couldn't stop the pained wince. His tentative smile was apologetic as he climbed up behind her, wrapping a powerful arm around her waist while the other took the reins.

The warmth of his body at her back made her feel safe in a way she could not explain. But the familiarity with which he pressed his thighs against her made her cheeks flame with embarrassment. She tried to edge forward, to create some distance between them, but he held her tight against his broad chest.

'What's his name?' she asked, stroking the stallion's shimmering white mane. It was as soft as silk, like running her hands through a cold mountain stream. He was big, and strong enough to carry them both, pawing at the ground with impatience.

'Starfyre,' he answered, a peculiar note of regret in his voice. Renila felt herself drifting off, a bone-deep tiredness making her eyelids droop. 'Sleep, Renila,' Alvar whispered in her ear as he tapped his heels to the stallion's flanks. 'Sleep while you can. I will watch over you. I will keep you safe.'

She felt his lips brush her hair and then all she knew was darkness.

She woke near midday, the pounding in her head gone. So too was the nausea, chased away by the rolling gait of Starfyre's near-silent canter. As she stirred, Alvar loosened his hold on her but kept her close.

'How are you feeling?' he murmured in her ear.

'Better,' she whispered, somehow knowing she needed to keep her voice down. Then she realised why she had woken – Alvar's body was taut with readiness, as though he expected an attack at any moment.

'Good,' was all he said. He twitched on Starfyre's reins, slowing the stallion to a cautious walk. Renila touched the hand splayed across her stomach.

'What's wrong?' she breathed, her lips barely moving.

'Darkling,' he muttered in response. 'Just the one, but it's close.'

'What do we do?' she asked, looking up at him.

His lips twisted into a sardonic smile, and he winked at her. 'Wait for it to get closer.'

Then his eyes snapped up, looking to his left. He swore, pulling them both out of the saddle as an arrow buzzed over them, breaking her fall with his own body. He huffed as her weight forced the air from his lungs, but he was on his feet in a flash, sword drawn.

Renila moved to follow him, but Starfyre herded her back, keeping his massive body between her and the Darkling. It was like the stallion knew his master's wishes without having to be told. She peered over his broad back and watched Alvar stalk into the shadows after the Darkling. Renila blinked. He moved fast. Too fast. No mortal could move that fast.

There was a screech of terror, the whistle of a blade cutting through air, then the sickening crunch as it sliced through flesh and bone. Alvar appeared a moment later, smiling darkly to himself as he wiped the monster's blood from his sword with a strip of material no doubt torn from its corpse. Starfyre nickered at the sight of his master, and Alvar touched his nose in thanks.

'How did you know it was there?' Renila asked, staring at him in confusion and wonder.

Alvar shrugged. 'I heard it.'

'I didn't hear anything,' she said, frowning. He grinned as he lifted her with ease, and she flinched as she noticed just how strong he was. She was far from heavy, but he lifted her so smoothly she might as well have weighed nothing. He noticed her eyes widen in shock, and his grin faded.

'I'm not mortal, Renila,' he admitted.

'You're one of the Graced?' she breathed, looking down at his beautiful face and trying not to get lost in those thunderstorm eyes.

But Alvar shook his head. 'No,' he said. 'Once, a long time ago, I was something like them. But now I'm just … a shadow.'

Renila tried not to recoil, but when Alvar's eyes glittered with unshed tears, she knew she had failed. At least he had the decency to leave space between them once he joined her in the saddle. He could no doubt sense her discomfort and unease, the same way he'd sensed that Darkling, using whatever unnatural gifts had been given to him.

'Where are you taking me?' she asked.

'South,' he murmured. 'Towards the Barren Lands. It's all we can do. Gaelan was headed north-west with the twins, and the mortals from the castle were headed east. We can't risk the Hunt coming anywhere near either of them.'

She almost didn't want to know the answer, but couldn't stop herself from asking, 'And what about Erion?'

'The Shade didn't kill him, and I doubt very much that he will – not until he's figured out what he is, and that will take him a while. Even then, he'll keep him alive. Erion's too valuable to kill.'

'We have to rescue him.'

'We will. I promise. Wherever they've taken him, whatever dark hole they try to hide him in, I swear, Renila, I will find him and bring him back to you,' he said.

She wanted to believe him. She did. Her instincts begged her to trust him. But she didn't have it in her to trust anyone anymore. Her heart was broken for Farran, for the home she had lost, for all hope of ever getting answers out of the Lady Gaelan.

But most of all, her heart ached for her son – for her beautiful Erion, snatched away by some nightmare to face unimaginable torment.

Alvar had claimed that once they had worked out what her son was, they would consider him too valuable to kill. But she could not fathom what his words meant. Erion was a special boy – special in the way all mothers considered their sons.

Part of her wanted to question Alvar further, to tear the information out of him with her bare hands if she had to. But she could not deny that she was afraid of him. And he had promised to help her find Erion … she was not sure she could risk alienating him with an interrogation.

So she held her tongue and allowed the mysterious Lord to take her deep into the forest.

Alvar kept a steady pace as they wove their way through the forest, keeping only one step ahead of their pursuers, although Starfyre could handle a harder ride. When Renila quizzed him about it, he would only say that he felt safest when his enemies were where he could see them. Renila had no idea how. She couldn't tell where the Hunt was, but he was aware of their location and prepared for every attack that came their way.

Alvar handled them all as he had the first. Slowed enough to let them get close before dispatching them and leaving their bodies as a warning for the rest of the Hunt. Once, Renila thought she heard the frustrated scream of the Huntress behind them – no doubt having found one of her fallen soldiers. Perhaps he had been a favourite.

They rode for the rest of the day and through the night. It was long after dawn the following day before he considered stopping for a rest. Renila winced as he helped her down – for all she was a decent rider, it'd been a while since she'd spent so long in the saddle.

'We can't stop for long,' he murmured, setting her on her feet, 'and we can't light a fire.'

She nodded in understanding and sank down into the soft heather coating the ground beneath the pines. She breathed deep the scent of the forest and felt the tension shift from her shoulders as she lay back, groaning as her aching muscles protested. Alvar handed her water and food, a mysterious smile playing on his lips and a dark glint in his eye.

'What?' she asked, taking the food. He shook his head but kept smirking.

'Nothing. Just some fond memories.'

Renila huffed, chewing on an oatcake. 'Lucky you,' she muttered, more to herself than anything else.

Alvar grimaced. 'Sorry,' he mumbled. 'It can't be easy for you.'

She frowned. She'd never told him about her past, or rather, her lack of one.

'How do you know about that?' she asked.

It was Alvar's turn to frown, but it appeared to be anger that creased his brows rather than confusion or mistrust. 'Gaelan told me.'

Renila fell silent, finishing her oatcakes and cheese while she considered his words.

'She knows,' she said. 'She knows who I am, where I come from … why I was hiding in that castle … but she would never tell me.'

'That wasn't her fault,' said Alvar.

Renila's eyes flashed. 'Whose then? Yours? You seem to know an awful lot about me.'

'Yes,' he admitted. 'The fault is as much mine as it is Gaelan's. And yes, I knew you … before. But your hands are not clean in this mess, Renila. You chose your own fate, for reasons that are now lost to us all.'

'How can you know that for sure? Because Gaelan told you? Can you trust her word?'

Alvar folded his arms across his chest and stared her down impassively. 'Gaelan is my wife. I know damn well what she is. She has her faults – many of them – and lies come as easy to her as breathing. But she wouldn't lie about that. Not to me.'

Something inside Renila crumpled to hear him defend the woman who had caused her so much pain. Perhaps part of her had hoped that their marriage had been a ruse, that Alvar was free to choose for himself. To choose her.

She registered the thoughts a moment too late, and her stomach heaved with self-loathing. She looked at the ground rather than let Alvar see the disgust in her eyes. Farran – sweet, loving Farran – was gone, his body ripped apart by nightmares and monsters. No matter what physical feelings Alvar roused in her, she could not think about him like that. Not when Farran's corpse was barely cold.

'We didn't bury them,' she whispered, realising that they had left the dead to rot.

'There was nothing left to bury, Renila. Their ashes will be carried home on the wind, forever free and forever at peace.'

She dared to glance up at him, her eyes glistening with tears for all she had lost. For all she had done. The kindness and steadiness of Alvar's gaze only caused the tears to flow faster, staining her cheeks as they fell. He tugged her to him, wrapping his arms around her, cradling her against his chest while she wept.

Starfyre whinnied in warning. Alvar spun, pushing Renila behind him and drawing his sword in a single fluid motion.

'How very sweet,' hissed a deadly voice from the shadows of the trees. 'You should envy the dead, for neither of you will know freedom or peace ever again.'

The Huntress stepped out into the dappled sunlight, stretching languidly while she eyed her prey. Her hair was pulled back tight off her face, and she had strange, pointed ears. Pale, eerie light danced around her, bathing them all in its unnatural glow.

All around them, the rest of her Hunt prowled from the darkness, faces cracked in identical grins of diabolical glee.

Alvar faced the Huntress while Starfyre screamed and reared behind him, keeping Renila between them. Renila was shaking with fear, and the Hunt cackled as they scented her terror.

She shivered, an icy wind sweeping over her, and glanced up to see the sun slip behind dark clouds, shrouding the forest in shadow. The Darklings did not seem to notice the changing light – too interested in taunting their prey.

'We're going to have fun with this one!' crowed one of them.

'She's a pretty little thing,' another screeched. 'I'm having her first!'

Renila forced herself not to whimper at the cacophony of jeering and threats ringing round the forest while the Darklings imagined the torments they had in store. The darkness grew deeper as the clouds gathered overhead.

'Enough,' snapped the bitter voice of the Huntress, stalking forward. 'They're both mine. I'll take my time with her – make her suffer for the lives she's claimed. I might even be willing to share. He's a beautiful one though … I think I might keep him to myself. At least for a little while,' she crooned, cocking her head as she looked him over, eyes glazed with lust.

Alvar only snorted, an arrogant smirk on his breathtaking face. 'You couldn't handle it.'

She smiled wickedly at his taunt, licking her lips in anticipation. The wind was rising, stirring Renila's hair about her neck, caressing her cheek like a lover's hand. The Darklings shifted with agitation, sensing the changing weather. Alvar stilled, staring down the Huntress, holding her attention away from her Hunt. She stepped closer, inhaling deeply, her brow creasing.

'You smell ... different. Magical, yes, but not Graced,' she mused. Her eyes flickered over Renila. 'That one will taste of fire and ash. But you, you look like you should taste of cold water and moonlight, but you reek of thunder and lightning and the rising wind howling through the trees. Similar to a Shade, yes, and yet ... not. Something purer. Something more. What are you, beautiful one?'

Renila looked to Alvar's hands. Thunder roiled beneath his skin and lightning sparked from his fingertips. 'I am the gathering storm,' he said with a bleak smile. The Huntress glanced up, just as lightning split the sky and thunder crashed overhead. She snarled, throwing herself clear in the heartbeat before the ground exploded before her. 'Run!' Alvar yelled, pushing Renila up into the saddle. He smacked Starfyre's rump, urging the stallion to flee as more lightning struck the ground, clearing a path for them. Starfyre didn't wait for his master to mount, charging forward without hesitation. Renila looked back over her shoulder, screaming for Alvar as the stallion plunged into the forest without him.

Darkness swallowed them. The thunderclouds high above her were so thick now they blotted out the sun, leaving the forest in deepest night. Lightning sparked, offering Renila momentary flashes of the monstrous faces chasing her, and between the mighty claps of thunder, she could hear their snarling curses close by. Starfyre whinnied in outrage as something snapped near her heel, the Darkling's hot breath on her ankle blown away by the howling wind. Then she felt it – the kiss of rain on her face as the clouds burst.

'*Get down and cover your head!*' Alvar's voice cried somewhere deep within the vaults of her mind. She didn't question it. Ducking her face into Starfyre's neck, she pulled her cloak over her head as the raindrops turned to chips of solid ice. She screamed when one struck her shoulder, drawing blood, then again as the Darklings howled in triumph, catching her scent. Like hounds after a fox, they bayed, desperate for their mistress to unleash them so they might rip their prey apart. Thunder roared in answer.

The ground trembled from the force of the storm, but the Darklings were too many. A muscled chest slammed into Renila, arms of steel banding around her as the monster tackled her out of the saddle. Starfyre screamed, his mighty hooves flashing through the gloom as he reared up to strike the beast. The stallion was fast. The Darkling was faster. He hauled her up, bowing his head and pressing his teeth to her throat. Starfyre understood the threat, dropping to his feet and snorting with frustration.

'I know what you are!' the Huntress crowed from somewhere behind them. 'Stand down, or he'll gut her right now.' Renila whimpered as she felt the Darkling's tongue against her throat, his teeth scraping the delicate skin there.

The thunder fell silent. The sky above cleared. Alvar stepped out of the shadows, fury written in every beautiful line of his mighty body. The storm still churned beneath his skin, the energy of it lifting his hair in a non-existent breeze while his eyes flashed and sparked with raw power. He trembled with the effort of restraining himself, but his sword point was steady as he took in the sight before him.

Renila struggled. She could see defeat in the slump of his shoulders, in the tension of his jaw. He was little more than a stranger, but she knew him better than her own heart – knew that he would drop the sword, would sacrifice himself to save her.

'Don't do it,' she breathed. The Darkling at her neck growled in warning, but she paid him no heed. 'Run,' she begged him.

'Most people think it's the screaming that is unbearable to hear,' the Huntress mused, caressing Renila's cheek, 'but it's the subtler sounds of someone dying in agony that haunt you. The pathetic noises, the ones we don't think about. They're the ones that stick with you; they're the ones you can't escape, that wake you in the night. We put the people we love on pedestals, adore them, worship them above all others, but death makes equals of us all. It's the moment that you realise the one you loved was worthless, and you wasted your devotion. What noises do you think she'll make, Immortal? What sounds will haunt you for eternity?'

Alvar lowered his sword. The Huntress smirked and opened her mouth to speak.

And an arrow slammed straight between her lips, piercing through the back of her throat and straight into her brain. She crumpled to the forest floor. Dead.

The Hunt stood in stunned silence for a moment, staring at the body of their Huntress. From the trees above, a slim, lithe figure dropped. Most of the body was covered and the hood was drawn down low, but Renila glimpsed enough of the face to know it was a woman.

'Run,' the stranger said. Then she nocked another arrow, and the Darkling holding Renila fell.

A mighty roar shattered the silence, and the spell was broken.

The Hunt screamed in outrage, swarming forward, desperate for blood. The sound of something enormous crashing through the forest echoed through the clearing, and they flinched back. Alvar took the opportunity and surged free, grabbing Renila as Starfyre pulled to a halt beside them. He swung up into the saddle, dragging Renila behind him while the stallion charged through the rushing Darklings. Without their leader, they were disorganised and chaotic. The hooded archer killed two more before she melted into the shadows.

Starfyre was thundering through the forest at breakneck speed. Alvar crouched low over the stallion's neck, while Renila tried to stay in the saddle.

'Hold on to me,' Alvar's voice drifted back over his shoulder. She wrapped her arms around his waist and held on for dear life.

'What about her?' she called as they tore away from the Darklings. Renila felt the rumble of his chest when he laughed.

'She'll be fine! I'd worry more about us right now!' he yelled over the pounding of Starfyre's hooves on the forest floor.

Thunder cracked overhead once more, but the Darklings did not heed the warning. Lightning sparked around them, striking anything that came near.

Behind them, ruby flame licked through the forest, leaving only charred remains in its wake.

That beast roared again, followed by the sound of tearing flesh, and Darklings screaming in agony as they died. And then the forest fell quiet once more.

Starfyre slowed to a walk, his sides heaving from exertion, but his foot-falls were quiet as he picked his way through the dense undergrowth. Although the sun was still high in the sky – or perhaps because of it – the darkness beneath the trees was near complete. Though Renila could make out her immediate surroundings, anything further than a few feet was swallowed up by gloom. It was more than a little disconcerting, but Alvar seemed unperturbed. She trembled from the adrenaline coursing through her blood, quivering in both fear and fury. Alvar's steady hand touched her wrist in reassurance, and though she tried to lean back, she found her arms were locked tight about his waist. He glanced over his shoulder, his thundercloud eyes heavy with worry at what he saw there.

Gently, ever so gently, he prised her arms off him and slid from the saddle. His hands went to her waist and lifted her down beside him. The moment her feet touched the forest floor, her knees buckled, and any semblance of emotional control slipped from her grasp. Her breath came in panicked gasps, wracking her lungs as she tried to inhale and found she couldn't. He held her tight while she wept violent, tearless sobs into his chest. He murmured in her ear, the deep rumble of his voice soothing away her fear with its promise of violence. It was not the words he spoke that reassured her, for they were gentle nothings – the kind one might use to calm a startled animal or quieten a frightened child. No, it was the savage hatred and fury heaving against his restraint that gave her strength.

Renila wasn't sure how much time passed before she calmed herself and pulled away. Alvar's eyes were reluctant as he released her, though he smiled when she allowed him to wrap her in a blanket and seat her in the heather once more. The sun was lower in the sky now, though it was likely still a few hours until dusk.

'We shouldn't have much trouble from that Hunt anymore,' he said, busying himself with starting a small fire, 'though they won't be the only danger in the area. We can rest for a few hours and have a hot meal, but come nightfall, we must keep moving.'

Renila nodded in understanding. 'What about the woman? The one who saved us? Who was she? Where did she go?' Alvar smiled at the rush of questions and opened his mouth to answer.

But a grim voice from behind them cut him off.

'I'm right here,' it said, 'and if the pretty Immortal Prince doesn't start talking pretty damn fast, I'm going to shoot his pretty little companion in her pretty little face.'

Renila turned, her eyes widening with shock. There, perched on Starfyre's saddle with her bow nocked, arrow pointed at Renila, was their hooded saviour.

CHAPTER TWENTY-SEVEN

The woman was petite – even shorter than Renila and far more slender. She had a bird-like fragility that seemed quite at odds with the speed and ferocity of her earlier actions. Her face was pretty, though her features perhaps too sharp to consider her beautiful. Under the hood, her hair was wrapped in a headscarf, but the brows above her deep, golden eyes were dark.

Eyes smouldered with anger. Anger directed towards Alvar. But then her gaze landed on Renila, and she staggered backwards, as though the sight of her was a solid blow to the gut. She lowered the bow. Dropped it on the forest floor. Stared, her lips parted in astonishment. Took a hesitant step forward, fingers trembling as she reached for Renila. But then Alvar was between them, sidestepping into her path, his hands held up in warning.

'How?' she breathed, not taking her gaze from Renila. Alvar opened his mouth to respond but closed it again, unable to find the words to answer her. The woman glanced at him and then back at Renila, desperation glinting in her glorious eyes. Desperation that hardened into something else as she stared over Alvar's broad shoulder. 'How did you escape Elucion?' she demanded.

Before Renila could respond, Alvar interrupted, 'She didn't.'

'But—'

He spoke over her. 'She knows nothing.'

The woman blinked and looked again at Renila, scanning her as if searching for something. Whatever it was, she didn't find it, and her expression grew sorrowful – pitying, even. A choked sob escaped her lips, and she covered her mouth with a slender hand as tears streamed down her cheeks.

'I thought I was alone,' she whimpered, her body shaking as she wept.

The tension left Alvar's shoulders, and he crossed the distance between them, taking the woman in his arms. 'I know,' he murmured, as she cried into his chest. 'I know.' Renila watched, unsure what to make of his sudden display of affection. Then the woman stepped back, dashing the tears from her eyes with the back of her hand.

'How?' she asked again.

'She was brought to my people for protection,' he began.

The woman stilled. 'By who?'

'I can't tell you that.' There was regret in his voice, but also resolve. 'I was sworn never to speak of it. My oath would strike me down before I could even utter the words.' The woman's gaze hardened, her eyes narrowing. Renila echoed her glare, fixing Alvar with a look that demanded answers. They both ignored her.

'How long ago?' the woman pressed.

He hesitated, doubt clouding his thunderstorm eyes. And then, even though Renila barely knew him at all, she sensed the moment he decided to trust the strange woman. His breathing steadied. His power quietened. His shoulders squared in readiness. 'Thirteen years before the Fall.'

The words meant nothing to Renila, but the woman staggered back as if he'd struck her, her hand flying to her mouth once more. She stared in horror between the two of them, understanding dawning in her tear-soaked eyes. She shook her head, backing away as the weight of her emotions threatened to crush her. Alvar reached for her, but she flinched out of his grip. Renila looked to him for explanation, but he could not meet her gaze. His attention was fixed on the stranger. His hand had drifted, hovering near the hilt of his sword. The woman noticed it and stilled, her fingers brushing the jewelled hilt of the dagger at her belt.

'Would you strike me down?' she asked.

He frowned, but his gaze was resolute. He would do it. He might hate himself for it, but he would kill this woman before he saw Renila come to harm. Renila hardly dared to breathe as he spoke. 'Yes.'

'You need me,' warned the woman, 'far more than I need you.'

A ghost of a smile twisted his lips. 'Why do you think you're still alive?'

'For all the good it would do you,' she snorted.

Alvar shrugged with indifference. 'There are ways and means.'

She laughed bitterly at that, but some tension eased from her slender shoulders, and she dropped her hand from her dagger. Her gaze flicked back to Renila, considering. Renila itched to demand answers, but instinct told her to keep quiet. Whoever this woman was, she was yet to decide whether she was friend or foe. One wrong word risked making her a dangerous enemy at a time where they needed allies. So Renila held her tongue and kept still while those dark, golden eyes scrutinised her.

'Did she ever know?' asked the woman.

He nodded hesitantly. 'Some of it. Not everything.' The woman pulled a face and blew out a sharp breath.

The woman studied Renila a moment longer, then she seemed to reach some decision. She took a deep breath and looked back to Alvar. 'I will take this secret to my grave, Prince. Not as payment for my debt. Not because you hold my heart in your hand. But because my people knew best of all that hope might be kindled by even the weakest of embers.'

'Thank you,' Alvar murmured, inclining his head.

The woman cut him off with a sharp gesture. 'I understand why, and I do not resent you for your part in it. But know that you cannot conceal it forever, and others have suffered while you stayed silent. So do not think there will not be consequences.'

'I am aware.'

She nodded and reached out a hand in offering. 'Then my sword is yours.' Alvar smiled and shook it, relief clear on his handsome face. From deep within the forest, a mighty roar sounded, and she glanced over her shoulder. She cursed, looking back to Alvar, and whispered, 'Where are they?'

'Safe,' he assured her, his attention fixed on the forest behind her, even as he made sure Renila was safe between himself and Starfyre, the great stallion crowding in close.

'I think you and I have very different opinions about the definition of that word,' the woman muttered, though the knee-wobbling relief in her eyes was clear. Then her attention turned back to Renila, a sudden shyness creeping into her golden gaze. She extended a hand, to Renila this time. 'My name is Arian.'

'Renila,' she supplied, not taking the offered hand.

Arian's gentle smile faltered, and she lowered it. 'It's an honour to meet you, Renila,' she said, voice thick with repressed emotion. Then she took a deep breath and looked around. 'We have to move. There may be more out there, and they'll be drawn to you like moths to a flame.'

The last of Renila's patience evaporated.

'Will one of you please tell me what's going on?' she demanded.

Arian looked expectantly at Alvar, folding her arms across her chest. He just looked at the ground, unable to meet either woman's gaze, shoulders stooped in defeat and shame. Arian shook her head in disgust and looked back at Renila.

'I swear to you, he will explain everything,' she vowed, levelling a baleful glare at Alvar, 'and if he refuses, then I will tell you myself. Trust me, Renila, one way or another, you will know the truth.'

Renila felt her temper flare, and she held Arian's steady gaze. 'Why should I trust you? Why should I trust either of you? I've been torn from my home, hunted like an animal, watched the man I love killed before my very eyes. Stood by as my son was stolen from me, taken Gods only know where …'

She broke off, her throat seizing as fear and hurt and rage threatened to overwhelm her. Arian's expression remained impassive, but there was no hiding her surprise at the mention of Farran and Erion. Nor the swell of pity that followed it.

'A Shade,' Alvar explained, before Arian could ask.

She snarled. 'They poison the world with every breath they take. They should have been stopped long ago.'

316

'Don't,' he cut her off. 'We can't change the past, and there is little to be gained wishing on stars to change our fate.'

'Fate and destiny are for those too weak to forge their own path,' she hissed. Renila blinked. She'd heard those words before, though quite where she could not recall. But before she could ask, Arian spoke again. 'I understand what it is to be hunted, to have all you love ripped away from you,' she said, her voice quiet but firm. 'I understand what it is to live in fear, for nowhere to be safe, to trust no one. It's a lonely road, Renila. Your Prince showed me that, helped me find the strength to take a different path. You don't know me, Renila, and I don't know you, but I can't turn my back on you. Not now. Not ever. You don't trust me? Fine. You don't want my help? That's too bad. I didn't rise from the dead just to let darkness triumph.'

Renila was silent, unsure what to make of the strange pronouncement. She risked a glance at Alvar, seeking reassurance. Worry creased his brow, his lips pursed tight with bitterness and regret. But then, catching Renila's eye, he smiled.

'Arian is a Phoenix,' he explained. 'Death doesn't have quite the same meaning to her.'

There was a mischievous twinkle in Arian's eyes, and she grinned wolfishly at Renila. 'The woman who raised me used to say death smiles at everyone, but only a Phoenix smiles back. I am all that remains, but our people always made for powerful allies.'

Then she held out her hand in offering once more. Renila eyed it, unsure whether to trust either of them just yet. But despite the dangers closing in around them and the strange company she was keeping, she felt safe. And without her memories to guide her, she could only rely on her instincts. They had never failed her yet; she doubted they would start now. So she met that glorious, golden gaze and took the hand extended in friendship.

They continued on foot, resting Starfyre while they could, but it seemed to do little to slow their pace. Arian led the way, making quick work of the rough ground, and Alvar seemed to trust that she was taking them somewhere safe. Renila was too tired to care. She trudged along beside the great stallion, with Alvar guarding her back. Her travelling companions looked like they could have kept up the gruelling pace for several more days. But not long after they'd forded the Blackwater, crossing into the Mistwood – which lived up to its name – Renila stumbled and fell, forcing them to call a halt.

She slept for a few hours, her dreams plagued by visions of shadow and darkness, while Alvar and Arian kept watch. When she woke, it was to the smell of roasting meat. She peered through her lashes, feigning sleep while she took in the scene around the camp. Alvar was crouched over the fire, turning a spit with two fat pigeons on it. Arian reclined nearby with one hand outstretched, her fingers curling and dancing as though she were mimicking the movement of the flames. They were murmuring to each other, voices hushed so as not to wake Renila.

'Is he yours?' Arian was asking.

Alvar shrugged. 'I can only assume so. I can't be sure, but the timing would suggest it.'

'Blood calls to blood – all you have to do is look at him to be sure?' she pushed.

He shook his head. 'The containment spell interferes with the blood bond. If he is mine, I can't sense it.'

'I wasn't talking about blood magic,' she teased. 'If your people are all as dense as you are, it's a miracle they've survived this long. And for a race of people who can't die, that's saying a lot.' Alvar snorted but said nothing. 'So why doesn't she remember?'

'Gaelan said she wanted to forget it all – to forget me, our life together, her heritage. She wouldn't tell me why. All I know is that one morning I woke up and she was gone. I wanted to look for her but ... Layol promised me she was safe, but that she never wanted to see me again. That was – what – twelve years ago? Then out of nowhere, he came and told me her life was in danger and she needed my help. But when I got there ... she didn't even know me.'

He fell quiet, lost in his own thoughts while he waited for her judgement. The silence stretched on, heavy with tension and regret. Arian swore, laughing mirthlessly as she stared into the fire. 'Gods.' She sighed. 'You couldn't make this stuff up.'

'You're one to talk,' he noted. She chuckled darkly, conceding the point, before Alvar continued. 'Besides her, the children were all overflowing with magic. The wards couldn't contain it. Gaelan hadn't taught them any control, and they were bursting at the seams. It's not surprising the Hunt was drawn in, though why they were so deep into the Ravenswood is still a mystery. The girl – Suriya – killed one, not long before I arrived.'

'Suriya fought a Darkling?' Arian cut in, her voice thick.

Alvar nodded. 'And won. She and Lucan are powerful.'

'They would be.' There was a pregnant pause. 'It must have been a strong Hunt to get through those wards.'

'Large too,' he agreed, 'and with a Shade Prince for good measure. We fought as best we could. Renila's lover was killed trying to buy the women and children time to flee.'

Arian interrupted again. 'She had a lover?'

'Lover might be a stretch,' Alvar admitted, unable to keep the irritation from his voice. 'I'm not sure how far things went – he had a wife, so I doubt it went very far at all – but she cared about him a great deal.'

Arian chuckled. 'Jealousy is a good look on you, princeling.' He silenced her with a flat stare.

'Erion was caught up in the attack. The Shade took the boy. Renila lost control. She took out most of the Hunt, but I had to put her down before she killed the twins. Gaelan went east with them, to our people, while I drew the Hunt south with Renila. And the rest you know.'

'Will they be safe there, with your people?' she asked after a moment. Alvar opened his mouth to reply, but at that moment, Renila's stomach gave her away. It gave a loud growl, demanding some of whatever smelled so enticing. He flinched, looking up at her to try and gauge how much she'd heard. Renila stretched, pretending to have only just woken from sleep – though the sly grin playing on Arian's lips said that she, at least, wasn't fooled.

'Hungry?' Alvar offered, gesturing at the pigeons. Renila nodded and took the proffered meat. It was good, given the lack of seasoning and accompaniments. Even Arian hummed in appreciation as she tore into her portion. They ate in relative silence, either too tired or too hesitant to converse, and when they were finished, Alvar rose without a word to pack the saddlebags.

'How far is it to ... wherever it is we're going,' asked Renila.

Arian wiped her greasy fingers on her trousers. 'Not too much further. You'll be able to get some proper sleep soon.'

The petite woman stood and offered Renila a hand up. 'Once you're rested and ready, we move on. It's not safe for us to linger in one place for too long.' Renila opened her mouth to ask another question, but Arian silenced her with a knowing glance. 'Don't worry. I'm not forgetting about your son. And neither is Alvar. I promise.'

Renila nodded in understanding and moved to put out the fire, but Arian waved her away. With a sly wink and the hint of a smug grin, she gestured at the fire. The flames died, smoke curling from the charred remains of the wood. Renila gaped at the other woman in wonder.

'Magic,' she breathed.

Arian just smirked, before turning and sauntering off once more, leading them ever deeper into the forest. And for the first time in a long time, Renila felt the slightest ember of hope kindle in her broken heart.

They were another day in the forest, hugging the northern bank of the Mistwater, following it upstream. The mountains of Ciaron rose like a sleeping behemoth to the south, and Arian led them towards those monstrous peaks.

The climb, even up into the foothills, was brutal, and Renila wondered if she would ever breathe freely again. Her lungs ached from the exertion, and there was no end to the sharp, stabbing pain of a stitch in her side. The icy wind howling off the mountains didn't make things any better, whipping around her in a blast of biting air that left her cheeks raw and stinging. At least it wasn't raining. Yet.

Finally, they arrived, and even Arian sighed with relief.

Tucked tight against a cliff face, the cabin was little more than a hut, a wooden shack that looked like a strong gust would knock it over. A tendril of smoke rose from a crooked chimney, and a brace of lean mountain hares hung from a peg by the open front door.

Renila tensed, seeing a shadowy figure moving within, and Alvar stepped in front of her, placing himself between her and any danger. Arian laid a restraining hand over Alvar's fist as it closed on the hilt of his sword. 'It's alright. He's a friend.'

The man who stepped out of the cabin was wild. He was huge, powerfully muscled, and almost dwarfed Alvar. His arms were as thick as Renila's waist and his legs as big as tree trunks, all banded – as far as she could see – in glittering bronze tattoos. Across his back, he carried two broad axes, with another clenched in his enormous hands. His hair was a tangled mop of reddish-brown hair, and his clothing was tattered and mismatched. Renila would have described him as brutish, had it not been for his plain face and the humour twinkling in his dark bronze eyes. Still, something about him screamed *danger*, so she stayed quiet as he approached.

'You could have fucking helped clean up,' he grumbled, pulling a face at Arian.

She rolled her eyes and gestured at him by way of introduction. 'Hal Ornak.'

'Arian,' he announced, waving back at her with an incredulous expression on his face. He spared a glance at Alvar and snorted. 'So that's what all the fuss was about. You're not long for this world, my son, if you can't hold your own against a wee Hunt like that.'

Alvar bristled at the insult but held his tongue. Arian took a deep breath that seemed to do very little for her patience and turned her back on Ornak.

'I would suggest you just ignore him,' she told them, 'but I've been trying for years without success.' Hal Ornak swore in objection. She didn't so much as blink. 'He curses like a drunk fishwife, and he's barely housetrained, but he's harmless.'

'Just charming, you are,' he snapped, pushing past her. But when his eyes fell on Renila, hiding behind Alvar, he stilled. She flinched from that predatory gaze, hardly daring to breathe. There was nothing but wrath in those dark bronze eyes now.

Then Arian was between them, her hands upraised. 'Would you believe me if I said you don't want to know?'

He bared his teeth, a terrible growl ripping out of him. 'Not a chance.'

'Ornak,' she pleaded, but he cut her off.

'Don't give me that,' he snarled. He hefted the long-handled axe and levelled it at Renila in accusation. 'Is she yours?'

Arian bristled. 'Don't be ridiculous. How could I have hidden something like that?'

'You think I don't notice when you disappear for the best part of a year?'

'And who would the father be, hmm?'

'How in the name of the Gods would I know? And don't change the subject – is she yours or not?'

Arian threw her hands up in exasperation. 'No!'

'Then where did she come from? You said they were all dead!'

'I lied!' she screamed. Ornak flinched from her admission, the forest echoing with his stunned silence. Arian took a deep, steadying breath and shook her head in frustration. 'I lied. That night ... the night Kalielle and I made it out ... it wasn't just us.'

Ornak's face was unyielding as he stared her down. 'Who is she?'

'When Thoran cast Kalielle aside, he took their child away from her ... It left a void. So when the Priestesses found a baby girl on the Temple doorstep one morning, Kalielle volunteered to take her – to raise her as her own.'

Ornak's eyes slid to Renila, doubt shadowing that dark gaze. Renila stared back as calmly as she could, trying to keep the confusion from her face. Alvar's fingers found hers and squeezed reassuringly, but she didn't dare even glance in his direction. She didn't understand any of this.

'So where has she been the last hundred years?' Ornak asked, looking back at Arian.

Alvar stepped forward. 'With me. Kalielle and I ... we shared a mutual friend. She thought the girl would be safe in my care, so she had him bring her to me.'

'And who are you? Why would Kalielle trust you?'

'I am Alvar, Crown Prince of Darkstorm.'

Ornak stepped back as if Alvar had punched him, whistling in surprise, though Arian seemed unperturbed by the announcement.

Renila scowled. She'd had enough. She rounded on Alvar. 'What are you? You said you're not mortal, but you're not Graced either, and you talk about things that happened hundreds of years ago like they were yesterday. Just how old are you?'

Alvar bowed his head, taking a deep and shuddering breath before he spoke. 'I have lived for so long that my age has lost all meaning. I fought during the Rebellion, witnessed the birth of the Graced and watched with a smile on my face as Sephiron was brought low. I am what you would call an Immortal. Mine is the ancient race who unleashed magic on this world, and all the good and evil it brought with it. We were revered as Gods once upon a time – though we were only the playthings of real Gods – but that power is beyond us now. My people are a shadow of what they once were, resigned to hiding in the darkness, lest they lend strength to those who would see the world burn.'

'And while your people cower in the shadows, we're out there bleeding, to finish what you started,' Ornak said, glaring once more at Renila. 'What about the rest of us? She wasn't the only child orphaned and made home-less that day. Why did she deserve your protection and no one else?'

'My people wouldn't have welcomed you,' admitted Alvar. 'You were all too old, too numerous ... too powerful. A single infant I could disguise, smuggle in as one of our own. The rest of you would have been turned away, if you weren't killed on sight. Kalielle realised that – it's why she didn't try.'

Ornak spat out a violent oath and turned his back on them, running a furious hand through his hair as he visibly struggled to contain his temper. Behind him, Arian levelled a pointed look at Alvar. She had warned him there would be consequences to keeping Alvar's secrets. And perhaps, it was time to find out what those secrets were.

'Will someone please explain to me what is going on?' Renila demanded.

Ornak whirled, his eyes blazing. 'She doesn't even know?'

'She used to.'

Ornak looked her over, scanning her as Arian had done. A glimmer of pity entered his gaze. 'What happened?'

'It's a long story,' began Alvar.

Renila cut him off. 'Well, I like stories. So tell me this one. Right now. Why don't I remember anything before Erion was born?'

'Erion?' Ornak asked.

Renila didn't take her eyes off Alvar. 'My son.'

'Your son?' The big man was looking at Arian.

Renila ignored him, staring Alvar down. 'Why don't I remember?'

He hesitated. She hated him for it, hated him for the reluctance in those thunderstorm eyes. Even if she had been his wife and not Gaelan, it did not give him the right to choose for her. It was her life. Her decision. After what seemed like an age, he dipped his head in defeat.

'Because you died,' he admitted. 'You died on the birthing bed, bringing your son into the world.'

The silence that followed was deafening. Renila could only stare at him. 'But—'

'You're a Phoenix,' Ornak snapped. Arian glared at him in reproach, but he just rolled his eyes and muttered, 'Oh, please – as if there was an easier way to break that.'

Renila stared at him. 'What?'

'You're a Phoenix,' he repeated, gently this time. 'One of the four Graced bloodlines. The greatest of the four, if you believe the legends.'

Thoughts were difficult. Words were near impossible. 'How?'

He seemed to understand. 'Do I know? Magic always leaves its mark.'

Then he turned to Arian and nodded. She winced and yanked the scarf off her head, running a frustrated hand through the mass of vivid, scarlet hair that tumbled loose and revealed a pair of delicate, pointed ears. Elf. She was part Elf.

High above, the clouds shifted, and a ray of sunshine filtered down; a shaft of golden radiance bathing the forest floor with its warm glow. With a deep breath, Arian stepped into that pool of gilded light.

Her crimson hair came alive, curling and snapping around her face in a fiery halo, ruby flames licking their way over her tawny skin in a burning aura. But most breathtaking of all were her eyes, the deep golden core turning molten until they glowed with the force of the sun itself. She was glorious – a flame given form.

Renila could only gape in wonder. Then Alvar was at her side and with a gentle hand, he guided her into the patch of sunlight beside Arian. Her necklace grew hot and heavy in the hollow of her throat, as it always did in the sun. With shaking fingers, he brushed her hair aside and made to remove the pendant from around her neck. She flinched and reached up to stop him. She'd never taken it off. Not once. Unease churned in her gut at the prospect. Alvar just held her gaze.

'Trust me.'

Nodding, she lowered her hands. His fingers were warm against her skin as he fiddled with the catch. Then it was off, and he stepped away. She felt the change immediately. Felt the heat sear along her limbs, felt the magic dancing over her skin and pounding through her body. And as their eyes met, she saw herself as he saw her. Her burgundy hair raging about her, flames of brightest amber rippling over her skin and her eyes near incandescent with the power roiling in her veins.

'It's true?' she whispered.

He only nodded.

Arian stepped back out of the light, the magic receding. But even when she wrapped her flaming hair in that ragged scarf, the *otherworldliness* remained. Those golden eyes – dull now by comparison – watched Renila for a moment, before flickering self-consciously to Alvar and Ornak.

'Go on,' she said, jerking her chin towards the cabin. 'I'm sure you have a lot to discuss. We'll give you some privacy.'

Then she gestured for Ornak to follow her and melted back into the forest.

CHAPTER TWENTY-EIGHT

E rion was adrift in the darkness. The pain had not been great – only a brief, sharp pulse. Then ... nothing. He had slipped from waking into oblivion, as easily as falling asleep. He was vaguely aware of arms holding him, cradling him against a strong chest. But something was wrong. The body was too hot, too hard to be Farran. The smell of smoke and ash clung to it and, beneath that, the faint metallic scent of blood. Erion cringed away ...

And was slammed into consciousness as they burst into the light. He wrenched away from the stranger who held him, yelling and thrashing to get free. The stranger let him go, dropping him on the floor with a frustrated sigh. Erion surged to his feet and ran, but within two strides, he fell once more as exhaustion claimed him. He tasted blood in his mouth. A split lip, swelling already. Strong hands turned him over, and he looked up into the handsome face of a man.

But he could not be a man ... not with eyes like those. They were eerily pale, almost lost against the whites of his eyes, and they pulsed with a terrible power. Words from a story his mother had once told him thundered through Erion's mind. Shade, she'd called them. Pale shadows of a once glorious lineage. But they were a bedtime story, a tale told by mothers to their children to scare them into obedience.

'You've heard the stories,' the Shade murmured, 'but didn't think to believe them. Sorry to shatter your illusions.' Crouching down beside him, the Shade cocked his head, considering. His pale eyes flickered to Erion's bloodied lip, and he touched one long, delicate finger to the wound. Erion flinched away, but the Shade held him fast. 'Sometimes, not all monsters are what they appear.' His voice so quiet Erion had to strain to hear it. As though he did not want to risk someone else hearing the words. Erion felt a flash of heat against his lip, and then ... nothing. The Shade removed his hand and leaned back, waiting. Eyeing him nervously, Erion risked touching it. The wound was healed, his lip whole, the skin smooth, and the swelling gone.

'What did you do?' he breathed.

'What do you think I did?' sighed the Shade, rolling his eyes in exasperation. 'I healed you. It'll take a couple more days for you to recover all of your strength.

That was a lot of power you used protecting your friends ... almost too much. But you'll live.'

Erion nodded, showing he understood and allowed the Shade to help him up to sitting. 'Why help me at all? Why not just leave me to suffer?'

'You're brave for one so young,' the Shade noted with a sly smile. 'Smart too. But I'll be the one asking the questions.'

Erion scowled and held the Shade's gaze, trying not to let his fear show. Let his voice ring with challenge as he agreed. 'Alright.'

The Shade chuckled and stood, gesturing to a nearby chair as Erion swayed. It was only then that he looked about him and took in his surroundings. They were in a room. An opulent study with a great wooden desk in the centre and chairs either side of it. Shelves lined the walls and books lined the shelves. Luxurious carpets covered the flagstone floor, and a fire burned in the hearth.

The Shade crossed the room to the door, opening it and snarling orders to whoever stood outside it. Satisfied, he closed the door and removed his sword belt, dumping it on the low bench by the window. Then he dropped into the chair behind the desk and crossed his booted feet at the ankles, resting them atop the papers that littered its surface. His dark burgundy hair gleamed in the firelight and a blood-red stone glinted in his pointed ear, its counterpart on a chain about his neck.

There was a sharp knock on the door, and it banged open, a woman entering without invitation. She was exquisite, Erion thought, with pure-white hair – though she looked no older than his mother – and strange, maroon-coloured eyes. She inhaled, her eyes glowing red, gaze flicking to where Erion's blood had sprayed onto the carpet. A Darkling. He recoiled, but the Shade motioned for him to be still. Her gaze scanned over them with brutal efficiency before she slammed the door closed, locking it behind her. She looked pointedly at Erion, but the Shade made no move to explain. Something seemed to pass between them and then she nodded, as if answering some unasked question. The Shade relaxed, though there was still a wariness in his gaze as he slumped low in his chair.

'What's your name?' the Shade asked, turning to him.

'Erion,' he said.

The Shade smiled. It was not entirely terrifying. 'Nice to meet you, Erion. My name is Kieyin.'

'Pretty name for a nightmare,' Erion noted.

Kieyin gave a bark of laughter and nodded in agreement.

'I didn't pick it,' he said with a shrug, and a quick glance to the Darkling. 'My mother hailed from a much nobler line than my father, and it was she who named me, though his power claimed me.'

Erion cut over him, emboldened by the Shade's openness. 'I want to go home.'

'I'm sure you do,' Kieyin murmured, 'and I do not blame you. Your home seemed like a nice place. But what you ask is not in my power to give, Erion. You are like nothing I have ever seen before. I have a great many questions. It pains me to have separated you from your family. Had they not put up so much of a fight I would have brought them too, so they might shine a light on what you are and how you came to be. Until I have these answers, I cannot let you go. The unknown is dangerous.'

325

'And if I tell you everything that I know? If I answer your questions – can I go home then?'

Something like regret flickered in Kieyin's unnatural eyes, and a muscle leapt in his jaw. He hesitated, glancing at the Darkling woman before looking back to Erion. Then the Shade's brows lifted in surprise, and Erion knew his eyes must have changed as his mood shifted from scared to angry. It was not something he could control, or even sense, though he'd observed it in the mirror. But he'd learned to read it in the reactions of those watching him. Knew the signs of shock, awe and disgust that so often flickered across even the most controlled faces.

'Probably not even then,' the Shade admitted. 'I'm not in control of my destiny, Erion. My actions are not always my own, my decisions not mine to make. My master may demand much of you. I do not believe it will be more than you can bear. I think you are far stronger than you look but know that I will be by your side through all of it. I will do what I can to aid you. You have my word.'

'Fate and destiny are for those too weak to make their own path,' Erion muttered, echoing words he had once heard Suriya speak. Kieyin's gaze snapped to the Darkling hovering behind Erion, as if the words had meaning to them also. The Shade hesitated again, and something once more passed between them.

'Kieyin, please,' the Darkling begged. 'Don't—'

'I don't have a choice, Seren,' he snapped, cutting her off. 'Prepare a room for him – let him rest tonight. We go to Elucion tomorrow.'

For once, it was his sister's screaming that woke Lucan, and not his own. She thrashed beside him, as if it were the dream and not the blanket she was trying to claw her way free from. 'Erion!'

Still half-caught in it himself, he shook her more roughly than he intended, trying to rouse her from the nightmare. Her eyes flew open, and her hands scrabbled for purchase and reassurance, fingers knotting in his shirt as she clung to him.

His own heart was racing in his chest, pounding from the fear and horror of the dream. Erion. He had dreamed of Erion. And some pale-eyed monster … a Shade? They were going to … He shook his head as the memory faded. No, he didn't know where they were going to. He reached for the vision, desperate for any hope. But the tighter he tried to hold on, the faster it dissipated. Like trying to catch smoke with his bare hands. And then it was gone, leaving only raw and inexplicable emotions in its wake.

He took a deep breath, steadying himself while he cradled Suriya in his arms, murmuring soothingly to her. He glanced across their hidden camp-site towards their mother – Gaelan, he corrected himself – only to see the glimmer of her starlight eyes staring back at him. There was a whisper of movement, nothing more than a breath of wind in the night, as she rose and crossed to their side. Suriya recoiled from her touch, but Gaelan was undeterred, turning the girl's face so she could examine her.

'What did you see?' she asked, looking between them. Lucan shook his head in frustration, unable to remember.

'Erion,' Suriya whispered, trembling. 'I saw Erion. He was so afraid.' Her voice broke, tears claiming her, and she said no more as she turned and sobbed into Lucan's shirt. Hushing her, he peered over her head at Gaelan to find her watching them closely.

'It was just a dream,' he protested.

Gaelan frowned and leaned back, lips pursed. Then she stood without a word, dusting herself off and moving to pack up her bedroll and blanket. Storm and Copper were picketed nearby, and Lucan watched in silence while she set about loading the few things they had back onto the horses. They hadn't chanced lighting a fire, so there was little work to be done to hide the evidence of their camp.

It was still dark, but there was enough light on the horizon to warn that dawn was not far away. They had ridden through the night, desperate to put as much distance between themselves and the castle – and the Darkling Hunt – as possible. Gaelan had set a brutal pace, and it was only when Suriya had almost fallen from the saddle with exhaustion that she'd deigned to call a halt. She'd hidden them deep in a thicket, far from any paths and hidden from even the sharpest of eyes. But even then, she'd warned they could only risk a couple hours of sleep and had stood guard over them all night.

If she felt any ill effects for her efforts, she didn't show it. Her movements were as lithe and graceful as ever, her beautiful face unmarred by tiredness. If there was any sign that something was wrong, it was only in the wariness of her starlight gaze and the restlessness with which she scanned their surroundings. Storm was restive, as if she too sensed her mistress's need to keep moving. But Lucan didn't share her enthusiasm.

'Where are Renila and Alvar?' he asked, once the storm of Suriya's weeping had passed. That first question unleashed a torrent. 'Are they alright? Who was that man? Where did he take Erion? Why did he take him? Will he hurt him?'

'So many questions.' Gaelan sighed, not looking up from her packing. 'I don't know where they are, but I'm sure they're fine. That *man* was not a man; he was a Shade. I don't know where he took Erion, but I promise I'm going to find out. The Shade was there for all of us, and he only took Erion because he didn't have time to take anyone else. And no, he won't hurt him. Not yet. He'll try to use him as bait to lure either myself or Alvar into his trap first. Anything else?'

Lucan wasn't sure whether to scowl at her tone or gape at the sudden flurry of answers.

'Will you save him?' Suriya asked for him.

Gaelan frowned. 'If I have to give my life to free Erion, I will do so, Suriya. I promise you that. But I will not endanger myself or either of you by making rash decisions when I don't have all the facts.'

'And what about Renila? Those Darklings will be hunting her now.'

The Lady's lips twisted in a brittle smile. 'Renila will be just fine. Alvar will look after her. Like me, he'll want to get his charge to safety. Unlike me, his charge can look after herself. I suspect they will go after Erion with whatever forces he can muster. Once I'm satisfied you're both safe, I'll join him.'

Suriya opened her mouth to argue, but Lucan cut her off. 'Where are you taking us?'

'I'm not sure you'd believe me if I told you,' she murmured.

'Try me.'

'Far away from here,' she said. 'To the city of my people, of Alvar's people. I cannot tell you any more than that. Not now. Not if there's any chance that a Hunt of Darklings is right behind us. It's a sanctuary. A secret that has cost thousands of lives to keep. I won't jeopardise it to satisfy your curiosity.'

'Alright,' Lucan agreed, before Suriya could object. 'Will you at least give us a general direction and timeframe? If we're going to be in the saddle for the next two months, I'd like to know now.'

Gaelan rolled her eyes at that. 'We head east, out the other side of the Ravenswood and up over the Whitefangs. If we make good time, we should be there in a week, provided nothing goes wrong. We can ride hard until we reach the mountains, and maybe up into the foothills, but further up is almost impassable at this time of year. I know one or two routes through the safer passes, but we must walk most of the way.'

'We're in no fit state to be trudging through snowdrifts in the mountains,' protested Lucan, gesturing at the gaunt, hollow cast of Suriya's face.

'Not to mention we're not dressed for it,' his sister muttered, plucking at her dress.

But Gaelan only sighed and shook her head. 'You'll be fine. I've got you this far. I won't let anything happen to you. You have my word.'

It was a mark of just how angry Suriya was that her temper beat his impulsiveness to the first reply.

'And what is that worth?' she snarled, standing and pushing her way in front of Lucan. 'Why should we trust anything you say ever again? You lied to us. Our entire lives, you've been lying to us. If you would lie about something as important – as *sacred* – as motherhood, then what is safe from your falsehoods?'

Lucan saw the hurt flash in Gaelan's starlight eyes, though it was gone so fast he almost wondered if he'd imagined it. But when she did not reply, he knew he hadn't. She turned away, stooping to tie off the top of her pack, her white hair falling forward to hide her face. But Lucan didn't miss the slight tremor that racked her slender shoulders, nor the quick movement of her hand across her face as she dashed the tears from her cheeks.

He glanced sidelong at Suriya, and though her expression softened, her anger did not fade. Her jaw was clenched tight, muscles working as she ground her teeth in frustration, and her breathing was forced, holding her temper in check. It was only when Gaelan had loaded the last of the packs that she turned to face them once more. Her expression was calm – too calm, given how deep Suriya's words had cut – and resolute.

'Everything I have done, since the day the two of you came into my life, has been to keep you both safe,' Gaelan said. 'Every decision I've made, every action I've taken – it's all been focussed on that one, single goal. You can choose to believe that or not. There's nothing I can do to sway you either way.'

'You could tell us the truth,' Lucan pointed out, herding his snarling sister behind him before she could do anything rash. Gaelan nodded, but her gaze was roving over their surroundings.

'I know,' she agreed, 'and I want to. More than anything, I want to tell you everything. But it's a long, long story, and we are not safe here. Even if the Hunt has followed Alvar and Renila, there are worse monsters than Darklings in this world. Plenty of them roam these forests. If you want to survive, you must make a very simple choice. Trust me and live, or don't and risk whatever fate has in store for you.'

'Fate and destiny are for those too weak to make their own paths,' Suriya whispered, more to herself than anyone else. He glanced down at her, brows knitting with worry. Her anger was gone now, and she seemed distant, so far away that even he could not reach her. The look on Gaelan's face told him he was not alone with his fears.

'She needs rest,' Lucan breathed, 'not to be fleeing for her life over mountains while winter closes in.'

'I know,' Gaelan murmured with a worried grimace, her gaze still fixed on Suriya. 'But I can't help her if she won't let me, and there's very little I can do for her here. We have to keep moving.'

Lucan studied his sister's wan and drawn face one last time, before he took a deep breath and nodded. 'Alright. Let's go.'

As Gaelan had predicted, they made good time on the journey through the Ravenswood. Storm seemed to relish the challenge of charging through the thick undergrowth, trampling heather and bracken alike with her massive hooves. It was only when Gaelan scolded her for leaving such an obvious trail that the mare deigned to take more care with her steps.

They stopped only when they had to. Mostly when Suriya or Lucan were near to dropping from the saddle, or Copper was stumbling from exhaustion, risking throwing them, and once when even Storm frothed at the mouth with weariness. The only one who showed no signs of tiredness was Gaelan, though she never seemed to sleep.

When Lucan grew bold enough to ask, all she replied was, 'I can sleep when I'm dead.'

He didn't have much chance to puzzle over her somewhat cryptic answer as later that day they began the steady climb upward into the Whitefangs. He'd mentioned it to Suriya that evening when they unrolled their bedrolls and set up camp. But she'd retreated so far within herself that she could barely respond. She'd nodded vaguely, but he could tell from the glazed expression on her face she hadn't heard a word he'd said.

In fact, she'd barely spoken since they'd shared that nightmare about Erion. Sleep had not come easily for her since then either. She would toss and turn for hours, often waking from her fitful slumber with a frightened shout. She wasn't eating properly. Not that any of them were, on their limited rations of bread and dried meat. What little food and water she would consent to take was only due to his persistence.

Matters got worse as they climbed through the forest coating the foothills. They were fortunate enough with the weather and rode further into the mountains than Gaelan had expected. But out from beneath the shelter of the trees, they suffered from the bitter winds that swept down from the jagged peaks.

The days were cold, and the nights were worse. They couldn't risk a fire, so Suriya shivered near constantly. At Gaelan's whispered instruction, Lucan had dressed his sister in as many layers as he could, but none of them had been wearing travelling clothes when they'd fled the castle. They were lucky they'd at least been wearing their fleece-lined winter boots, and someone had packed two thick cloaks in the saddlebags so they wouldn't freeze.

But it wasn't enough for Suriya, who'd never coped well with the cold. Every winter, for as long as he could remember, she'd retreated indoors. While other children would be racing outside to play in the snow, she could always be found curled up by the fire with a book.

So every day, Lucan would wrap her in their blanket. Tuck her hands, which were too numb to take the reins anyway, against her chest to keep them warm. Then he would nestle her in the saddle in front of him and wrap his cloak around them both. At night, Gaelan would help him lift her from the saddle. Suriya was now too weak and tired to protest at Gaelan's proximity, and they would settle her between them both to keep her warm. As she huddled close to him, Lucan would try to coax her to eat something while he and Gaelan exchanged worried glances.

But the day came when the weather closed in, and the ground became too treacherous for even the bold Storm and stubborn Copper to manage with riders on their backs. On foot, it was slow going, especially as Suriya stumbled with almost every step. She leaned on Lucan, and he was forced to carry her on his back through the more precarious passes. He sweated from the exertion, despite the biting wind. Even Gaelan was breathing heavily and conceded to calling more regular halts.

But even when the snows came, soaking them to the core and leaving them chilled to their bones, she would not risk a fire. They were forced to huddle between the horses for shelter and warmth, and Suriya grew weaker still. It was only concern for his sister that kept Lucan going, fighting off the sickness he felt clawing at him with every breath.

He lost track of time as they weaved their way across the mountains. They could have been up there for as little as a day or as much as a year for all he could tell. The hours blurred together, ever-present storm clouds merging day into night. Gaelan cursed the weather with growing frequency, her irritation near irrational, as if the storm's existence were a personal affront.

He ceased worrying about Renila and Alvar, or even Erion, as his focus narrowed to keeping his sister alive. But then the storm became a blizzard so vicious she staggered against him, and he no longer had the strength to keep them both on their feet.

Copper's reins were wrenched from his hand as they collapsed on each other, tangling limbs as they crashed down the slope before breaking their fall in a deep snowdrift. Gaelan shouted in alarm, but her voice was ripped away in the wind, and there was only darkness around him.

Suriya gasped nearby, and he scrambled through the snow until his hand found hers, fingers knotting. The wind howled overhead, and Storm roared in challenge as the blizzard worsened. He thought he heard Gaelan screaming their names but was sure he'd imagined it. She would never sound so desperate, so afraid. The cold seemed to seep right into his heart, and he felt the fight in him go out. He closed his eyes and sighed. He was so very tired. It would be nice to rest for a while. Suriya whimpered, her fingers struggling weakly in his, but he could not summon the strength to move.

The ground around them trembled as a terrible voice shattered the night. The words were foreign – a language far beyond Lucan's comprehension, but there was no mistaking their ancient power, nor the fury and censure that laced them. Forces greater than his understanding warred in the sky above him, and he cowered in fear.

Suriya's hand was ripped from his, and he cried out for her, begging her not to leave him. He didn't want to die alone.

'Nobody is dying today,' a familiar voice promised in his ear. Gaelan. It had been her voice cutting through the wind with such despair. Her voice that had thundered through the mountains, challenging the storm to its claim on their lives. Strong hands gripped him, pulling him out of the snow and lifting him up into a saddle. He cracked a single eye open and saw her bend to lift a small, limp form up into her arms before leading Storm back up to where they had fallen from.

'Suriya?' he whispered.

'*She'll live,*' Gaelan's voice assured him, echoing within the vaults of his mind. With a sigh of relief, Lucan slipped back into darkness.

———

There was a fire crackling in the centre of the camp as Lucan clawed his way out of sleep. The blizzard had abated, and though the snow still fell, it drifted down in fat, fluffy flakes that seemed harmless by comparison. He sat up, trying his best to ignore the sudden sharp pain that split his skull, and looked around for Suriya. She was seated across the fire from him, huddled beneath her blanket and sipping from a steaming cup.

Gaelan appeared from the shadows, crouching beside him while she examined his head. 'Careful,' she admonished. Sure enough, he winced as her delicate fingers grazed over the tender spot on his brow. 'You gave yourself quite a bump there. You'll be fine, but you'll have an awful headache for the next few days.'

Lucan nodded to show he'd understood and smiled at her. 'Thank you,' he said. She returned his smile and stood, stepping around him to stoke the fire before handing him a cup like Suriya's, filled to the brim with hot broth. He sniffed at it.

'Sorry,' said Gaelan. 'The packs are thin – it was the best I could manage at short notice.'

But his mouth was watering in anticipation. It smelled delicious. He hadn't even known his mother – Gaelan, he corrected himself again – could cook. He was about to take an enormous gulp when he saw the admonishment in Suriya's gaze.

'It's hot,' she warned with a wry smile. 'You'll burn your tongue.'

He choked with relief to hear the humour, pathetic as it was, in her voice, and the look on Gaelan's face told him she felt the same. Suriya ducked her head as embarrassment flushed her cheeks, and Lucan did not miss the glint of tears in her eyes. She knew then. How distant she had become. How worried they had been for her. And although she might not understand or even recall what had transpired, she remembered enough to feel ashamed. It was unfair of her to judge herself so harshly, but that was Suriya. Whatever had caused her melancholia was gone, and though she was not completely herself again, the worst was now over.

'What happened?' he asked, turning to Gaelan.

She did not answer, looking to the sky as if for guidance. He was not sure if she received any, but she heaved a great sigh and lowered herself with sinuous grace to sit between them by the fire.

'The place that we're going,' she began, 'the city – it's home to an ancient and powerful race of beings. But it's their last sanctuary, the last place in the world that they're safe, so they guard it fiercely. It's protected by powerful magic – wards and spells and enchantments as old as the rocks we're sitting on.'

'How did we get through then?' Suriya asked. Lucan glanced at her, glad to see that her ordeal had not dulled her sharp wits. Had it been the magic that had driven her into such a depression? Would she recover, now they were beyond its reach?

Gaelan sighed again and looked deep into the fire. 'They are my people. I have as much right to claim sanctuary within the city walls as anyone else, so the magic can't keep me away.'

Lucan opened his mouth to speak, but Suriya got there first. 'And what about us? Those spells, they tried to keep us away, didn't they? How are we still here?'

'Because I found a crack,' Gaelan explained, 'and I shielded you long enough for you to pass through it.'

'And now we're through it, we're safe enough that you'll risk a fire and tell us where we're going,' Suriya finished for her.

Gaelan nodded and took a deep breath. 'It's called Khaladron – it means "swan song" in the old language – and it was the crowning jewel of an empire that encompassed the entire world. But that empire is long gone, nothing more than ashes and ruin. Khaladron is all that remains.

'It was chosen to be our final refuge. Of all our great dwellings, it was by far the easiest to defend – and our enemies knew nothing of its existence. The only way in and out is over these mountains or by sea through a narrow inlet. Both are protected by powerful magic.

'It took centuries to build, and longer still to weave the spells that defend it. But most will tell you it was worth it. They say there is nothing in this world now that can compare to Khaladron's beauty – an oasis of peace and tranquillity in a desert of death and destruction. It was our final masterpiece before the waning of our power.' She broke off and snorted. 'Honestly, I always found it a little fanciful for my tastes. Hardly the greatest example of our skill. But it's all gone now. Only Khaladron remains.'

She trailed off, lost in a past that stretched back far further than they could ever imagine. Her eyes glittered with unshed tears as she bowed her head in remembrance, and her knuckles were white where she clenched her fists in her lap. They were all quiet for a time while she composed herself. It was only when she took a deep, shuddering breath and raised her head once more that Lucan dared to speak.

'Your people,' he asked. 'Who are they?'

Gaelan nodded to herself but did not meet his eyes when she answered. 'We have a name for ourselves, in our own language, but you couldn't pronounce it, and it wouldn't mean anything to you anyway. We're mentioned in the stories Renila told you … they call us the Immortals.'

'And Sephiron was one of you,' Suriya added. It wasn't a question. She and Lucan both remembered Renila's stories.

Gaelan snarled, starlight blazing over her skin. 'Never speak that name again,' she hissed. Suriya flinched, and the fire flared between them. Gaelan took a deep, steadying breath and nodded. 'Yes, he was one of us. Our greatest mistake. One that brought us to our knees.'

'You knew him,' Suriya pressed, her eyes glowing with certainty. Gaelan didn't dispute it. 'How old are you, if you were alive during the Rebellion?'

'Old enough that such numbers no longer have meaning for me,' she said, her voice heavy with ancient regret. Then she sighed. 'Do you mind? I don't enjoy talking about that period of my life. Even after all this time, some horrors never fade.'

Lucan nodded before Suriya could object. 'Will you tell us more about your people then? About where you come from?'

Gaelan smiled and leaned back, her eyes lifting to the heavens once more. 'For as long as there has been death, there have been those who sought to defy it,' she began. Lucan knew that he had heard the words before, but now they were given new meaning. One of Renila's stories – the Old Tales, Gaelan had called them once. 'For most, the quest would cost their last breath, but upon a precious few, the Gods smiled. They were blessed with untold power – swiftness and strength beyond measure, unparalleled senses and inhuman beauty, and magic to be wielded as they wished. But greatest of all was the gift of life everlasting.

'And so, the Immortals were born. Thirteen they numbered, revered by all those doomed to die. Centuries passed and our numbers grew. King-doms rose wherever we settled, and mortals flocked to us as sheep who follow their shepherd. Over time, we spawned an empire that would cover the earth, and – if you believe the stories – more just and true rulers it has never known.

'But where there is power, there will always be those who seek it for their own. And whenever evil rose, it was always the mortals who suffered for it. We sought to end the bloodshed. Laws were written, measures were taken, to ensure that none would ever be harmed by Immortal actions again. Vows we all gave, to shelter and to shield, to protect and provide for our *mortal flock* – the words spoken, eternally binding, sealed by the magic in our blood.' She trailed off again, entranced by the falling snow.

Suriya huffed. 'You did an outstanding job. If you're so powerful, how come you couldn't stop those Darklings? Why couldn't you save Erion?'

'Our power is not what it once was,' she admitted. 'Some believe it was judgement handed down by beings more ancient than us, punishment for wreaking so much death and destruction upon this world. Others are convinced it is nothing more than the natural decline of any species past its peak of evolution. Whatever the reason, we don't have the same level of control we once had. The power is still there – I can still feel the magic in my veins. I just can't use it all. Not consciously. Sometimes, when I'm angry or frightened, I can do things. Like protecting the wards or fighting those Darklings. But it's instinct. I don't always control it. Some powers are easier than others – those that we gifted to the Graced, for example.'

'But you can't die,' Suriya protested. 'Alvar too. You're both Immortal. Why did you run?'

Gaelan shook her head in frustration. 'Darklings steal life; they steal power. If even one Darkling had got close enough to feed from either of us, they would have become unstoppable. A mortal life buys them another day on this world. My life, or Alvar's life, buys them eternity. I've seen it happen before, and I swore then I'd never let it happen again.'

Suriya opened her mouth to argue, but Lucan spoke over her.

'You did the right thing,' he murmured. Suriya gaped at him, but he stared her down. 'You saw what one of those things could do on its own. Imagine what it might do with unlimited power at its command.'

She scowled but nodded in understanding.

'Get some sleep,' Gaelan said, rising and pulling her cloak tighter about her shoulders. 'We'll leave at sunrise. If nothing goes wrong, we should make it to the city by midday tomorrow. I don't know what will happen once we get there, so get some rest. You might need your strength.'

And with that she turned and strode into the darkness, leaving the twins to themselves.

Dawn loomed in silent threat. She did not even wait to land before Changing. She didn't have the time. Scales gave way to skin, her knees popping as she hit the ground running. Sprinting for shelter. Throwing her senses ahead of her as she roared for her kin. Dread rising as she realised the wards were down.

'Théon!'

But there was no answer.

The cottage was empty. The croft abandoned. The lingering reek of Darkling still strong enough to make the bloodlust rise. She swore, smashing her fist into the wall. The stone shattered and she swore again, wishing that her bones had yielded instead. Pain would be preferable to this panic. She didn't have time. She never had enough time.

And now she was trapped. Stuck in this human body until the sun set. She would never catch them on foot. Fortunately, the Change was not the only power at her disposal. It was a risk. To her and to others. But she had no choice.

Closing her eyes, she cast her mind from her body. Searching. Not for Théon. There was little point; Silvermane would keep them too well hidden. But there were others who might be able to help. It took far longer than she'd have liked to find her quarry, but she found him at last. Skulking in a Ciaron tavern with the rest of his conspirators. She might have known.

'Faolin.'

He flinched from the sound of her voice in his head. Recovering, he excused himself from the table and stepped outside. His snarl of displeasure echoed through her mind. 'Have you completely lost your mind? Are you trying to get me killed?'

'I'd have good reason,' she hissed. 'You and our idiot sister led the King's Darkling general straight to Théon.'

The silence roaring in his mind was deafening. 'What?'

'You heard. I'm at the croft now – there's no one here and the whole place reeks of Darkling, but there's no sign of a struggle.'

She sensed his gaze rake the early morning sky, and finally, he seemed to grasp her urgency. 'I'll find them.'

'Hurry.' His mind began to pull away, but she snared it once more and held it tight in warning. 'If Théon comes to harm, know you will answer to me, brother.'

Then she released him and returned to her body with a reluctant sigh of relief. Faolin would find them. As much as she despised him, she trusted he would tear the world apart to save his precious Princess. And strong as the Darkling was rumoured to be, dealing with Lord Alexan was within their capabilities.

Rescuing Keriath from the bowels of Dar Kual, however, was not. That was a task she alone could accomplish. Cursing, she pulled her hood lower and stormed back out into the dawn. It was a long walk from here to the Barren Lands, but she could not afford to waste a moment.

'Hold on, Keriath,' she murmured, slinking back into the shadow of the forest. 'I'm coming.'

CHAPTER TWENTY-NINE

G aelan woke them just before dawn, and they led their horses over the summit as the sun rose above the horizon. The storm clouds had dissipated, and the sky was bright and clear. The ground was hard from the frost, crunching beneath their boots while they climbed.

As they crested the hill, they saw it, just as Gaelan had promised. Khaladron. The Immortal City.

It was exactly as Gaelan had described. The ridge they stood upon dropped into a wide lagoon-like basin, the mountains curling around to either side. A narrow gap, through which the sea ebbed and flowed, was guarded on either side by great sentinels carved out of the cliff face itself. And there, perched on an island in the centre, rising out of the water like some ancient leviathan, was the city.

It was breathtaking. Built from white marble that glowed in the light of the morning sun with broad, sweeping avenues and buildings so graceful they looked as though they might break in the wind. The great gates, glittering like diamond, were open, and residents strolled through them unchallenged, wandering in and out of the city down to the shore. A handful of vessels dotted the crystalline water. Small fishing boats, sailing yachts and even a large pleasure barge.

'It's beautiful,' Suriya whispered. Lucan nodded in agreement. Gaelan gave them a knowing smile and sighed as she looked down on the oasis of peace and tranquillity.

'Khaladron might be considered the jewel of the Immortal's empire now, but it was one of many,' she said sadly. 'Each House had a seat of their own. Mountaintop castles carved out of the rock itself, palaces of glass by the sea, mansions in the forest made from solid gemstones. Each one with its own land and holdings. Mortal farmers and tradesmen reliant on the Immortals' grace to keep food on their table and clothes on their back. And our cities ... great centres of learning and art and trade. Places where the

Houses came together for the betterment of us all. But they're gone now. Long gone.'

She bowed her head in sorrow and moved on without a word. The course she chose down from the summit was not as treacherous as the one up had been, but it was still hard going. They continued to lead the horses, not daring to risk either of them stumbling and throwing their rider down the perilous slope. Lucan tripped and fell twice before Suriya reminded him to watch his feet rather than staring at the city like an idiot. After perhaps an hour, they descended into more forest, and the temptation to gaze at the phenomenal view below passed as it disappeared from sight.

It was perhaps midday by the time they came out the other side of the forest. Lucan was not short of breath as he had been on the climb, but his legs trembled, and his knees ached from the repeated impact of trudging down such a steep slope. Suriya looked to be in worse shape, limping and wincing with every step, so it was a relief when he spied a gentler path ahead. He was even more relieved when Gaelan made no move to lead them away from it.

'Are we able to ride now?' he asked, glancing at his sister. Gaelan followed his gaze and nodded, her furrowed brow and pursed lips echoing his worry. At least she had the sense not to help Suriya into the saddle. There was enough hostility rolling off his sister; she still hadn't forgiven Gaelan for her lies. He wasn't sure he had either, but they had more important things to worry about. Whatever she was, Gaelan had raised, sheltered, provided and cared for them all their lives. He had to believe they could trust her.

They continued downhill, though at a far more forgiving gradient, until the surrounding hillside rose around them and the path descended into the bottom of a gorge. At the narrowest part stood two guards, ornate silver armour shining in the sunlight. They each held an elegant-looking spear and upon their gleaming white surcoats were embroidered two swans, bills touching, in silver thread that glinted like light dancing on water. The broad cheek plates of their helmets were fashioned like wings, and the fierce nose guard was a swan's head and neck. They shifted uneasily as the riders approached, but Gaelan gave no sign that she had even noted their presence. In fact, she nudged Storm into a rolling canter, bearing down on them with grim determination.

The guards stepped forward, crossing their spears to bar the pass. 'Halt!'

Gaelan sighed and checked Storm. Then she loosened her grip on the reins, letting her mount wheel and dance around while she glared at the guards from beneath her hood.

'Stand aside,' she commanded.

'Who are you, and what business have you here?' one snapped, hefting his spear.

His companion nudged him, peering up under her hood. 'Don't be daft. Look at her eyes man,' he muttered. 'She's one of us. How else could she have got this far?' The one who had spoken first now looked apprehensive but did not lower his guard. His gaze slid to the twins, and his eyes narrowed beneath the edge of his helm.

'Her travelling companions are not,' he noted. Then he looked back at Gaelan. 'I would still have your name and what you mean by bringing their kind here.' Gaelan snarled at his tone – at the hatred and threat of violence in his voice – and kicked Storm forward. The great mare screamed in annoyance and reared, pawing the air in frustration. The guards braced, but Storm landed just short, snorting angrily. Gaelan pulled her hood down with a savage yank, shaking her hair free and drawing herself up to her full height.

'I am Gaelan, Princess of Brightstar,' she snapped. 'The children are my responsibility and under my protection. Threaten them, and you will answer to me. My business is my own and of no concern to you, nor anyone else beyond the Council. Now I say again – stand aside.'

The guards paled in recognition, though the name and title meant very little to Lucan – or his sister, judging by the look on her face.

'How do I know you are who you say you are?' the guard snapped. 'Gaelan Brightstar hasn't been seen for over a hundred years.' His companion gaped at him, his wide eyes wild. The ground shuddered beneath their feet as Gaelan's temper surged, and starlight danced around her like celestial flame.

'It is custom, is it not,' she said, grinding the words out from between her teeth, 'to kneel before any member of the Council, rather than interrogating them with inane questions?' The anxious one dropped to one knee, bowing his head low in submission. But the other stood fast.

'Their kind are not welcome here,' he insisted, jerking his chin towards the twins. 'Nor are you, if you are the Brightstar. The Council has little love for either you or your husband.'

Gaelan nudged Storm forward, the heavenly flames flaring with her temper. 'Turn either me or those children away, and I will return here with a Hunt of Darklings at my back. The Swansinger is many things but prepared for war doesn't appear to be one of them. With my help, a single Hunt could reduce this city and everyone in it to ashes in a matter of days.'

'You wouldn't!' he said, taking a staggering step back.

'How old are you?' she asked, her voice barely more than a whisper now.

'One hundred and eleven.'

Gaelan's answering smile was vicious. 'Too young to have fought in the war then. Too young to know first-hand just what I'll do for me and mine.' She glanced sidelong at his companion and leaned over. 'I think your friend is a bit older and knows better, don't you?'

The other soldier dipped his head lower. 'I was just a child, not even out of the Academy. But I heard the stories.'

'You can tell him all about it later,' she said, straightening in the saddle. 'I will ensure that the children do not pose a threat to the city or to anyone in it. You have my word on this – does that satisfy the need for security? I wouldn't want the Swansinger to reprimand you for not doing your job.'

'Yes, Highness,' the older one said, standing and pulling his companion to the side. Storm did not need to be told and stepped forward, tossing her proud head in satisfaction. As she passed, the guard murmured, 'Welcome home.'

Gaelan faltered and looked at him in surprise. Opening her mouth to respond, she seemed to think better of it and inclined her head in thanks before gesturing for the twins to follow her.

And so, with Gaelan leading them, the twins passed into the realm of the Immortals.

Lucan looked out across the expanse of water between them and the city. Not long after their encounter with the guards, the gorge had opened out to the beach on which they stood. The sand beneath their feet was pure and white and warmed by the sun, the clear water lapping over it. He breathed deep as the song of those soft waves soothed his anxieties.

'So what now? We swim across?'

Gaelan snorted and rolled her eyes. 'I think I liked you better when you were afraid of me,' she muttered, sounding very unlike herself – or perhaps sounding more like herself then than he'd ever heard. She shook her head in exasperation and gestured towards the city. 'There's a sand bank between here and the island. You can see it at low tide, but it's not difficult to cross even when the tide is in – so long as you don't mind getting your feet wet.'

'That doesn't seem very secure,' he noted with a frown. 'Surely anyone could cross it?'

'Not to mention that it would move over time,' Suriya added.

'It's not going anywhere. It was created using magic, and that same power sustains it. But there's only one safe path across. Step off that and the whole thing will wash away. So stay close, and step only where I step.'

The great mare was unfazed by the water lapping around her knees, but the same could not be said for Copper. Renila's horse snorted, refusing to move any further as the sea brushed her legs. Lucan sighed and kicked his heels to her sides, but she was not for budging. It was only when Suriya leaned forward and whispered reassurances in her ear that the mare took one grudging step forward. Then another. And another. Gaelan had stopped and was watching them from beneath her hood, waiting for them to catch up before she continued. Her expression was inscrutable, but there was something almost akin to regret in them as she watched Suriya coax the reluctant horse onward. Lucan had more sense than to mention it.

The journey across the half-submerged sandbank was slow going, with Gaelan pausing often to make sure they were following close enough. Between that and Copper stopping in a fit of stubborn pique whenever the water lapped higher up her legs, it took them far longer than necessary to make the crossing. Lucan was in poor temper as they approached the city walls.

His irritability faded away as his eyes fell on the great gates before him. They did not just sparkle like diamonds – they were covered in them. Thousands. Each one delicately carved into the shape of a feather and set into the pale wood beneath. They overlapped and swirled upward towards the open sky, like great outstretched wings. Despite his best intentions, his jaw fell open.

Gaelan chuckled darkly and reached over, closing it with one long finger under his chin. 'Ostentatious, isn't it?'

He could only gawk at it, but Suriya's lip curled in distaste. 'I can't believe someone would waste so much of their wealth on something so frivolous. There are people dying out there in the world, and these people are coating their front door in diamonds?'

'Much as I agree with the sentiment, those gates didn't cost anyone anything,' Gaelan assured them. 'They were made with magic, thousands of years ago when the Immortals were at the height of their power. It pains me to admit it, but it does serve a purpose. When those gates are shut, they're nigh on impenetrable. Not all our splendour was so functional.'

'What do you mean?'

'The Immortals were blessed with enormous power, but we hoarded our gifts. Oh, we were gentle masters and ruled with wisdom and compassion. But we were masters still, lording our superiority over those less fortunate, rather than helping them,' she said. She sighed and shook her head in regret. She was quiet for a long time before she spoke again, murmuring more to herself than the twins. 'How many thousands died because we thought ourselves better than the masses? How many might have been spared pain and suffering if we had not been so slow to act?'

She fell silent once more before shaking herself from her trance, as if remembering that she was not alone. Suriya opened her mouth to press her, but Lucan elbowed her in the ribs and shook his head. There were emotions showing in Gaelan's eyes that he could not even name. Those were not mysteries that he wanted to stir up. Let them continue to sleep, buried deep beneath those still waters. At least for now.

Gaelan moved off without a word, trusting them to follow. Copper was only too happy to step out of the water and onto the rocky beach before the gates. More armoured guards stood watch at the gates, reaching for their weapons as Gaelan and the twins approached. But when Gaelan lowered her hood, their captain's eyes widened in recognition, and he barked at his men to stand down.

'Brightstar,' he murmured, bowing low. His men hesitated but followed suit, their movements neither as elegant nor fluid as his.

'Prince Brer Shadowfox,' she said with a broad smile. He straightened and removed his helm, returning her welcome with a wicked smile of his own. Suriya gasped, and Lucan could see why. The man was as handsome as Alvar. His fox-red hair, dark amber eyes and pointed, cunning face seemed appropriate for his name, and he looked out of place amongst so much pale, delicate elegance. Gaelan seemed to agree, because she asked,

'Tell me, what is the Shadowfox heir doing guarding the Swansinger's gates?'

Prince Brer chuckled darkly. 'You don't want to know.' His eyes flickered to his men, and he seemed to consider his next words carefully. 'Things change. Plans. Priorities. People. You know that better than anyone.'

Gaelan arched a quizzical brow, but he shook his head, as if to say he would explain later. She seemed to take the hint. 'It's been a long time.'

'A hundred years at least,' he agreed. His gaze turned to the twins, as if he had only just noticed them – though Lucan suspected that was not the case. It was possible Prince Brer was the most observant person he'd ever met. 'What brings you back?'

'It's a long story,' she said, her lips twitching at some private joke.

Brer rolled his eyes and nodded.

'Of course it is,' he muttered. He jerked his head towards the city and snapped his fingers as he called for his horse. 'Come on then, let's get you up to the citadel.' Gaelan murmured her gratitude, but it seemed they were not gaining entry that easily.

'Prince Brer!' one sentinel objected, pointing at the twins. 'You cannot be considering allowing those *things* entry to our city?'

The Prince didn't even flinch as he swung up into his saddle. 'If you don't like it, take it up with my wife,' he snapped. Then, kicking his heels into his mount, he led Gaelan and the twins through the gates without so much as a backwards glance.

'Thank you,' Gaelan said, once they were out of earshot. 'I know I've taken a risk in bringing them here, but I didn't know where else to go. I hope you won't get in too much trouble?'

Brer snorted. 'Don't thank me yet. The Swansinger will decide whether they get to stay. I'd just prefer to keep them where I can see them until then.' Gaelan nodded and threw a warning look at the twins. It was one Lucan knew well. *Stay close and stay quiet.* If Brer noticed the exchange, he didn't comment. 'So that explains why you've come back, but not why you left wherever it is you've been hiding the last century?'

'Darklings,' was all she offered. He nodded in understanding and didn't press the issue. Changing the subject, she asked, 'Wife?'

Brer pulled a face. 'You won't like it.'

'Try me.'

He sighed. 'After the trial … Andriel wanted to keep an eye on the Swansinger.'

'So?'

'So I decided the best way to do that was to get close to her.'

Gaelan made an indelicate sound of disgust. 'You can't be serious?'

'Perfectly serious. But…'

'But what?'

'I fell in love with her, Gaelan.'

Stunned silence echoed through the streets as Gaelan drew Storm to an abrupt halt. 'Tell me you're joking?'

Brer frowned. 'We were married four summers ago.'

'Brer,' she breathed. 'Be reasonable. You sat right beside me all the way through her trial. The evidence was overwhelming. That she wasn't sealed up in the Graves should tell you all you need to know. The woman is dangerous.'

'No more than you,' he retorted. 'She's proven herself time and time again, and she makes me happy. Which is more than I can say for some of your choices over the centuries.'

And with that, he turned his horse around and led them further into the city. Gaelan glared after him but did not argue, though she continued to mutter to herself as they followed him.

Lucan stayed silent, looking around in wonder.

The city was beautiful. The streets were wide and airy with elegant white marble buildings on either side. A line of trees, heavy with fresh white blossoms, separated the broad avenue, and boxes of white roses and clouds of baby's breath decorated the windows of the houses. Pale ivy climbed up and around delicate pillars, creeping over the walls in swirling patterns. The horses' hooves drummed over cobbled stones, echoing around the otherwise tranquil city. And in the centre of a crossroads was a statue of two great swans carved from white quartz, bills touching with necks arched and wings spread wide.

'It hasn't changed much,' Gaelan murmured, calmer now. Lucan wasn't surprised – the peace of the city permeated right through him, soothing his nerves and cooling his temper almost against his will.

Brer grunted. 'She hates change. Nothing in this city has been altered since she was elected.'

'Marriage seems like a significant change,' Gaelan noted, grimacing. 'I didn't think she even had a heart.'

Brer threw her a dark look, but otherwise ignored her jibe as they approached another set of gates. These were far smaller, though they too had the same wing motif carved into the sun-bleached wood. The pair of sentinels guarding the gates straightened and raised their hands in salute when they noted their captain's approach. Gaelan and the twins remained unchallenged as they passed through the gates and into the large courtyard beyond.

In the middle of the courtyard was a fountain with another quartz swan at its centre. The clear water bubbling from its mouth filled the air with its sweet music. It was beside this fountain that Brer checked his horse and dismounted, handing the reins to a stable boy in white and silver livery who came running up. Two more followed, looking up at Gaelan and the twins.

'The lads can see to your horses,' Brer said, casting a disparaging eye at Storm. 'Even that brute.'

The great mare snorted and pawed the ground in warning, but Brer only chuckled, unfazed by the horse's temper. He turned instead to the twins and reached a hand out to help Suriya down from the saddle. Lucan tensed as his sister flinched away, but Brer only smiled, holding his hand out in offering.

'It's alright,' Gaelan murmured. 'He won't hurt you.'

'The Princess speaks truth,' Brer promised, his dark gaze troubled. 'We don't hurt little girls here. I promise you that, so long as I am near, no harm will come to you within these walls.'

Lucan felt some of the tension ease from his sister's body. But there was still a wild glint in her eye as Brer put his hands to her waist and lifted her from the saddle. Lucan followed her down and, sensing her distress, moved close beside her, wrapping an arm around her slender shoulders when the Prince stepped back. She shivered and leaned in to him.

'I've got you,' he whispered, squeezing her tight. The Prince's eyes, ever sharp, did not miss the exchange nor Suriya's apparent discomfort. He pulled the white cloak from his shoulders and held it out to her.

'For warmth,' he offered, 'and as a token of friendship. It's true, your kind are not well-loved here. But we do not all share those prejudices. I fought alongside your people in the Ironvale and at the Fall of Shadowbriar. Your people saved my life when Sephiron's hordes came for my House. I will never be able to repay that debt, but I can still try.'

Suriya extended a trembling hand and took the proffered cloak. 'Thank you. But I don't know what any of that means.'

The Prince gave Gaelan a startled look. She'd dismounted and was hovering nearby, watching the exchange with interest. But she only shook her head. 'Later. I need to speak with the Council.'

Brer folded his arms across his armoured chest and frowned.

'You'll speak to the Swansinger first, Gaelan. You know how this works. This is her city – if you're going to break the laws, you'll at least have the good manners to look her in the eye when you do it.'

'Emalia will never let them stay,' Gaelan hissed. 'I have a better chance at convincing the Council.'

But the Prince was not for budging. 'My wife is a lot of things, but unjust is not one of them. If you've got good reason, she'll give you due consideration.' Gaelan growled in warning, placing herself between them and Brer. But the Prince stared her down. Then his gaze flickered over Lucan and his sister, and he smirked. 'Besides, she might just surprise you.'

With a wink, he turned on his heel and led them into the citadel. Unlike Gaelan's castle in the forest, the corridors were broad and straight, so there was little chance of them getting lost. There was not so much as a single turn between the courtyard and the set of great doors where Brer paused. These were also wood, and though the wood was pale, it had not been bleached to pure white by the sun. A pair of swans were carved into the doors, each one edged with silver and crowned with gold inlay. Brer reached over and tugged his cloak tighter around Suriya's shoulders. She stilled at his touch but didn't flinch away this time.

'Best you don't speak unless asked to,' Brer advised, 'and even then, only answer the question put to you.' His gaze flickered up to Gaelan. 'And you – try to keep a hold of your temper. You won't help anyone lashing out like your beloved Darkstorm heir,' he warned. 'Stay close.' Then he turned and opened the door.

Suriya gasped. Lucan didn't blame her. Beyond the doors, the throne room was magnificent. Armoured sentinels in gleaming white cloaks lined the room, and the walls were carved with the same wing motif as the citadel gates. But he knew that was not what had taken her breath away. The great, vaulted ceiling was supported on arches shaped like swan necks, the buttresses carved like their elegant heads touching. But the ceiling itself … it was clear glass – huge panes of it that let the sunlight stream in, flooding the room with its brilliance. Water gurgled from swan-shaped fountains on either side of the dais, filling the room with its beautiful song as it flowed down into the two ponds that edged the chamber. The light bounced off those pools, the reflection flickering up on the walls in mesmeric patterns.

But it all paled in comparison to the woman on the throne. She was at least as tall as Gaelan, and almost as beautiful. Her hair was palest gold that shone near-white in the sunlight, and her skin was smooth and white as porcelain. A circlet of white gold and quartz, shaped like feathers, rested atop her head, and though her eyes were so dark they were almost black, they seemed serene. Her gown was exquisite: a bodice covered in real swan feathers and wide, sweeping skirts of layer upon layer of feathered tulle. Clearly she took her namesake seriously.

Brer motioned for them to stay back, drawing to a halt at the foot of the dais and dropping to a knee.

'Hmm,' the woman purred. 'That's a pleasant sight.'

Brer raised his head and grinned. 'I would have thought you'd become used to it by now?'

'I don't think I'll ever get used to it,' she murmured, rising from her seat and holding her hand out to him. Brer stood and went to her, kissing her upon the lips. She hummed in satisfaction and touched a slender hand to his cheek. Then her eyes flickered over Gaelan and the twins. 'Not a social visit then?'

'I'm afraid not, my love,' he said, stepping back down and beckoning them forward.

'Kneel,' Gaelan instructed from the corner of her mouth. Suriya was shaking like a leaf in a storm, and Lucan kept a tight grip of her as they did as they were bid. Gaelan, however, remained standing. She inclined her head, but it was a greeting of equals. The woman on the throne responded in kind, unperturbed by Gaelan's lack of submission. Lucan frowned. What was Gaelan's position here, if she was not required to bow to this enthroned goddess before them?

'Welcome home, Brightstar,' the woman said.

'This has never been, nor will it ever be, my home.'

Brer closed his eyes and sighed.

344

But the woman on the throne only chuckled. 'I see decades in seclusion have done wonders for your manners.'

'My manners went out the window a long time ago,' Gaelan said with an indifferent shrug.

'Your good sense too,' the woman said, arching a delicate brow, 'if you think it's acceptable to disrespect me and my city to my face after you've broken our laws.'

'Those are your laws, not mine, and I have not abided by them in a thousand years. Why would I start now?'

The woman sighed as she looked Suriya and Lucan over with contempt and shook her head in disgust.

'They should have never let you graduate the Academy. Your constant disregard for ancient rules and traditions is disturbing.'

'Your lack of regard for human life is far more concerning, Emalia,' Gaelan snapped. 'We designed those laws to protect our people from harm, not to justify turning innocents out in the cold for the wolves to descend upon.'

Emalia opened her mouth to argue, but Brer spoke over her. 'I would at least like to hear her reasoning. The Brightstar I knew never did anything without good cause, and I think understanding her motivation would go some way towards judging her fairly.'

Emalia pursed her lips but inclined her head to concede his point. Beside Lucan, Suriya shifted as she tried to get a better look at Gaelan's face. He didn't blame her; he was as curious about the Lady's true motivations as everyone else in the room. Gaelan's expression was guarded, and she hesitated, her starlight eyes flickering over the twins. But her voice was clear and firm when she spoke.

'It is true, I have no love for this city or the Council and its laws. But Starfall is long gone. I was content to abide here in peace, even unwelcome as I was. But the Fall changed that. I could not remain here after that, not with what it brought to our doorstep. Alvar's decision was hard enough to take, but when the Council took the coward's route, I knew I could not stay here.

'Where I went and what I did is my business and none of your concern. All you need to know is that almost thirteen years ago these children were entrusted into my keeping by those unable to care for them any longer. I gave my word that I would nurture and protect them both, for so long as I drew breath. But despite my best efforts, I alone no longer have the strength to keep them safe.

'The Darkling scourge is persistent and grows stronger with every day. The Binding is all but gone, and Sephiron's corruption spreads ever further, while we sit and do nothing. I still don't understand how they found us, but they sniffed us out and hunted those children down like hounds after a fox. I don't know how many perished in the attack. We escaped, but our freedom came at a cost, and mortal lives paid the price. The Darklings glutted themselves on the souls of innocents, giving us the chance to flee. Those mortals died so we might live, and their faces will haunt me forever.'

Gaelan stopped then with a slight gasp, for her voice was shaking and her knuckles were white as she clenched her fists at her sides. Celestial flame danced around her as her emotions raged out of her control, and the water in the pools shimmered as the ground trembled with the force of her fury. She closed her eyes, took a deep breath and – with visible effort – brought that ethereal power back under control. When she opened her eyes, they were filled with tears.

'I never got the chance to be a mother to my own child. These children are the closest I will ever come to knowing what it's like. Chances are, I've been more than lacking, and they may well consider their upbringing less than ideal. But they are alive, and they are whole. I want nothing other than for them to remain that way. I ask only for you to help me keep them safe. Their people are gone. I am all they have, and likewise, my life is empty save for them. Emalia, I'm not sorry for breaking those laws, and if I had to do it all again, I would. We have nowhere else to go.' She dropped to her knees beside Lucan. 'I beg you. Send me away if you must but keep them safe. They're just children – innocents in a war not of their making. They should not be made to suffer for others' mistakes.'

Emalia was silent. Then, after what seemed like an age, she tore her eyes away from Gaelan and looked to Brer. The Prince was still, his gaze fixed on his wife, a look of grim determination on his face. There was something in the set of his shoulders that said he was prepared to fight. But for what, Lucan wasn't sure.

Beside him, Suriya was shaking so hard that he reached out and gave her hand a reassuring squeeze. Emalia's dark eyes snapped to them, drawn by the movement, and for the first time since they had entered the throne room, she gave them her full consideration. Her expression was inscrutable as she stood and descended the dais towards them.

She reached down and touched a gentle hand to Suriya's face, cupping her chin and tilting her face up. Lucan stilled, but Suriya did not flinch. Her eyes smouldered with emotions that Lucan could not even name, and her jaw was set tight. He could feel the tension rolling off her like the heat from old Mal's oven, but she said nothing and held fast.

'So much hate and anger for one so young,' Emalia murmured. Her attention flickered to Lucan, and he quailed under the force of that gaze. 'But there is love there also – strong enough to level cities and bring empires crashing down. What have you wrought here, Gaelan? Emotions such as these, left unchecked and armed with this power, will bring death to us all.'

'They are a danger only to themselves,' Gaelan promised, her voice breaking with desperation.

Emalia pursed her lips, looking back to Suriya's glorious golden eyes. 'What is your name child?'

'Suriya,' she said, her voice clear and firm. 'And this is my brother, Lucan.' Emalia frowned and reached for Lucan. He tried to flinch back, but she was too fast, brushing his hair back from his brow. Seeing the mark there, she turned to glare at Gaelan.

'Brother and sister? With those bloodlines?' she said, her serenity evaporating as she swirled away. Brer didn't move from his spot beside them, and he gestured for them to remain still. Eventually, Emalia heaved a great sigh and turned back to face them. 'I'll not have them loose in the city untrained. They enter the Academy. If they graduate, they can stay.'

Gaelan surged to her feet. 'That's ridiculous!' she objected. 'Emalia, be reasonable!'

'I'm being reasonable,' Emalia snapped. 'I have responsibilities, Gaelan, to this city and all who shelter here. The children will be safe in the Academy, and if they don't graduate, then at least they'll be strong enough to fend for themselves.'

'You don't have the authority to allow entry to the Academy from outside the Houses,' Gaelan argued.

'Then convene the Council and beg them. Those are my terms. Take them or leave them.' Gaelan hesitated, her body quivering with tension as she battled with herself. Then she sagged in defeat and nodded. Emalia smiled coolly and gestured for Suriya and Lucan to rise. 'Brer will escort you to your rooms. And Gaelan – they're to be supervised at all times, under guard and within the citadel walls until the Council decides.'

Then she gestured to her husband to remove them from her sight, waving a dismissive hand as she returned to her throne. Gaelan didn't even fight as Brer led them from the hall.

Erion wasn't sure where he was. The Darkling woman – Seren – had woken him sometime late in the evening. She'd brought him a change of clothes and a hot, if hurried, meal while they waited for Kieyin to join them. The Shade had held out a hand to each of them, and sensing that he didn't have a choice, Erion had taken it. Then Kieyin had stepped into thin air, pulling them with him, before appearing again in the outskirts of a sprawling city.

A scream of pure terror shattered the night, and Erion shied away from the wicked hooting laughter that followed. A girl, not much older than he was, ran out of a nearby alley. She was covered in blood, her eyes wide with terror as she scrambled away from the shadows. Her clothes were a tattered ruin that covered very little, and she clutched the rags to her as if the thin fabric could protect her. Two Darkling men, huge and hulking and staggering like drunkards, followed – her blood staining their lips. She screamed again, begging for mercy as they closed in on her.

Erion started towards her, but Seren's hands held him fast. 'Don't be a fool.'
'Help her!'
'She's Darkling prey. Her fate is sealed,' she snapped.
Kieyin glanced over his shoulder, hearing the exchange. His pale eyes lingered on the sobbing girl, and his lips curled with distaste. Faster than Erion believed possible, the Shade moved. One instant he was standing in front of them, the next

he was behind the young girl. His hands clasped either side of her face, and in a single sharp gesture, he snapped her neck.

Erion yelled in frustration, and even though Seren covered his mouth with a hand, she needn't have bothered. The noise was lost in the din as the Darkling men roared, but their protests died in their throats when they saw the Shade standing before them. Kieyin cocked his head to the side, considering them while he wiped the girl's blood from his hand with distaste.

'If you're going to play with your food, do it somewhere more contained … and soundproof,' he said, his voice laced with lethal calm. 'I find the shrieking tedious.'

'Yes, sire,' they murmured, bowing low as he stalked away. Seren scowled at him and opened her mouth to admonish him, but he cut her off with an imperious gesture.

'Death may be certain, but the manner is open to debate,' he said, his pale gaze lingering on Erion. 'Sometimes a quick death is all we can hope for.'

'You could have saved her.'

Kieyin shrugged. 'I could have. But all it would have done was buy her a few more hours in which she could have relived all those horrors. Trust me. Death was kinder.'

'We need to keep moving,' Seren insisted. The Shade nodded in agreement and continued on his way. Seren's hand pressed into Erion's back, urging him to follow. 'Just keep your eyes on Kieyin, ignore everything except the sound of my voice.'

He did as he was bid, studying the twin swords strapped across Kieyin's back while the Shade led the way through the maze of streets. Seren walked close behind Erion, murmuring quiet words of solace as they wound their way through the city.

Elucion, Kieyin had called it. The legendary city of the Phoenix. Other than the girl, he had seen nothing but Darklings – and the occasional black-eyed monsters that Seren called Nightwalkers – since they'd arrived. If the Phoenix had lived here, they were long gone.

'Where are we going?' he asked, his feet growing tired of walking. Exhaustion tugged at the edges of his consciousness, and for once, he was glad of his fear. It kept the encroaching weakness at bay. Seren hushed him, reminding him to keep his voice down. But Kieyin slowed, so he walked beside him and gestured towards the centre of the city. He spared Erion a curious glance, a hint of worry edging his gaze, but he didn't press the matter.

'The King holds Court at the heart of the city itself,' he explained. 'The city is divided into districts. His palace forms the innermost ring, with the servants' quarters around that and then the military barracks around that.'

'Why didn't we just go straight there, rather than start at the edge and walk in?'

'The inner districts are warded against magic. I got us as close as I could. Believe me, I don't want to be walking around this city with a prize like you and only my wits and Seren to guard my back.'

'I didn't realise I was a prize.'

The Shade's pale gaze was serious as he looked down at the boy. 'Most in this city would consider you so.'

'But you don't.'

It wasn't a question, but Kieyin answered it anyway. 'No. I don't.'

'We're almost there,' Seren interrupted. Erion followed her gaze to the set of enormous iron gates looming ahead. Kieyin exchanged a long look with the Darkling woman. 'Make it quick,' she growled, her voice tight as though she were suddenly under great strain. Kieyin halted and crouched so he was level with Erion, resting his hands on the boy's shoulders as he looked him straight in the eye.

'I don't have much time so listen carefully,' he said in hushed tones. 'Once we are inside the palace, I cannot speak freely again. For what it's worth, I am sorry. You are just a child separated from his mother, lost and alone and too far from home. It sickens me that anyone would use someone like you for their own betterment, but there are many such monsters here in Elucion. My King does what he can to contain them, and that is why I serve him. That doesn't mean I always agree with him, but his power is too great for me to go against him.

'I wish I could take you back to your mother. I wish I'd never even gone anywhere near your home in the Ravenswood. But I can't change the past, and I don't have a choice now. If I were to set you free, it would undo everything I have spent decades working to achieve. I'm placing my life in your hands by telling you this Erion, but I trust you, and I need you to do the same for me. I will do all I can to protect you in there, but you have to do what I say, when I say it. Do you understand?'

Erion hesitated. Kieyin seemed honourable, perhaps even kind, but he was a Shade – a nightmare brought to life by magic and dread. Up at the gates, a guard stepped forward, brandishing a torch, trying to make out the shadows lingering in the darkness. And when the light of the flame touched Kieyin he changed. His dark hair shone red, like sunlight on deepest wine, and colour flooded his eyes – no longer pale and eerie, they glowed like molten gold.

Kieyin winked. 'I told you – Shade is not all that I am. My mother hailed from a far nobler line. One I intend to protect.' Then he straightened and turned to face the approaching guard, his demeanour changing. 'Careful where you're waving that thing,' he snarled, menace rolling off him in waves as he extinguished the torch with a blast of dark magic. The guard grovelled when he recognised the approaching figure, but Kieyin just swept past in imperious silence. Seren's fingers closed around Erion's wrist, and she dragged him along in Kieyin's wake.

The Shade led them through the palace with complete confidence, ignoring everyone who dared to even look at them. There were two Darkling guards waiting at the great doors to the throne room, and they bowed as Kieyin approached. Leaning against one of the great pillars on either side was a man with black eyes, pointed ears and a cruel smile.

'Kieyin,' he said, stepping to block the Shade when he moved for the door.

'Corrigan,' Kieyin replied, not bothering to keep the contempt from his voice. 'Again? Recovered from your last beating already?'

'Big words from a man who needs a wee girl to watch his back,' Corrigan said, his eyes dancing as he ran a lecherous eye over Seren. The Darkling woman snarled at the insult.

But Kieyin just smirked, straightening his sword belt. 'Who's in there?'

Corrigan stepped back, sensing the tension in Kieyin's voice. He ran a curious eye over Erion but said nothing. 'Pretty much everyone you'd expect – except Mazron. Don't know where that sick bastard has got to, but the King isn't happy.'

'Still no sign of him?'

Corrigan shook his head. 'No Zorana either. The King grows concerned.' Kieyin grunted in understanding but said nothing. 'Who's the boy?'

'Not sure yet,' the Shade grumbled. 'Watch him a minute while I clear the room, will you?' Without waiting for a response, he gestured for the Darkling guards to open the doors and marched in, leaving Erion alone with Seren and Corrigan. Beyond the doors, Erion heard the murmur of voices go quiet as Kieyin's boots snapped on the hard floors.

There was a brief, quiet exchange before another voice – deep, male and throbbing with power – snarled, 'Get out.'

The buzz of voices grew louder as the crowd inside moved towards the door. Corrigan stepped closer and, together with Seren, hid Erion from view while the Court filed out.

Erion trembled. Every one of them was a Shade. Seren's hand found his in the darkness, and she squeezed. Corrigan glanced at her and snorted.

'Gods, you're pathetic,' he breathed.

A low, warning growl rumbled in her throat, and she herded Erion behind her, keeping her body between him and Corrigan. But there was no need. As soon as the Shade Court had dispersed, that same powerful voice called for Corrigan, and he sauntered off into the throne room with a cruel smirk. Then Kieyin was there, his fingers curling around the back of Erion's neck, pushing him forward into the throne room even as his thumb grazed Erion's cheek in silent apology.

The room was large – longer than it was wide, with high vaulted ceilings – and lined with ornate pillars carved from black marble. At the far end of the room was a raised dais, upon which a man was enthroned.

He was tall with jet-black hair and a sensuous, full mouth. His shoulders were broad and powerful, and a crown shaped like ravens' feathers rested above pointed ears. His brow was marked with the same peculiar star-mark that Erion had once seen on Lucan, and his arms were banded in blood-red tattoos. He was the most beautiful man Erion had ever seen but, like Kieyin, he bore the eerie, colourless eyes of the Shade. Power thrummed around him, unbound and unchecked as he revelled in his might. Erion had never felt anything like it before in his life, and he knew who sat before him.

Sephiron's heir.

The Shade King smiled, and it was a terrifying thing to behold. 'Well, well, well,' he murmured, cocking his head to the side as he studied Erion. 'What do we have here?'

CHAPTER THIRTY

A lexan was a light sleeper at the best of times. He wouldn't have survived this long if he hadn't been. A decade on the streets of Illyol, with only his wits to keep him safe. At least double that in the Guard, with only his training to rely on. A hundred years serving the Shade Court.

If either of the first two had failed to teach him to sleep with one eye open, the latter had done the job. Even after feeding, drinking and whoring his way to his large, comfortable bed in Elucion, he'd still never allowed himself to drift into deep sleep. And there was no chance of it now, lying in his swaying hammock in the hold.

Cold. Resigned. Lonely. The same as he'd been every night since that one. Tossing and turning, haunted by the taste of her blood. The feel of her in his arms. He ground his teeth in frustration, trying to force the thought of her from his mind. She wasn't for him. She was his Queen and, worse than that, she was the Shade King's daughter. Alexan wouldn't live to see another sunrise if the King ever discovered he'd bedded her. He'd be punished enough when the King found out he'd fed from her. No. She was not worth the pain he would endure for such a transgression.

Breathing deeply, he tried to relax and quieten the anticipation that hummed in his veins. But it was no use. An hour later, he gave up on sleep and ghosted from the hold back up on deck.

The moon was fat and round in the inky sky, bathing the sea in her cold light. Mari was at the helm, steering by the stars, and she glowered at him as he passed. He ignored her. At least it wasn't Ana. The red-headed captain had a temper to match her fiery hair and a jealous streak a mile wide. Reminded him too much of Jenia for comfort. Mari was just surly and antisocial.

He crossed the deck to the prow, resting his elbows on the handrail as he leaned into the sea breeze. Drank it deep into his lungs. There was land on the horizon. The largest island rising up from the sea, the scattering of smaller islands clustered around it like ducklings huddling to their mother.

They would make landfall at first light. Mari had moaned bitterly about the difficulty of navigating the Beasts – the rocky formation guarding Storm-keep harbour – and refused to even attempt it during darkness.

Tension was starting to slip from his shoulders when he heard move-ment behind him. Near-silent footfalls of someone crossing the deck, headed in his direction. Théon.

He waited as she crept closer. Feigned ignorance of her presence. Not likely, when he could hear her heart pounding in her chest across the deck; her adrenaline and excitement mixed with night air making his stomach clench in anticipation.

'Dangerous business, sneaking up on a Darkling,' he warned in a low voice.

She checked her stride, and he watched over his shoulder as she dropped into a defensive crouch. With a derisive snort, he lunged. Knocked her feet out from under her. Caught her arms, turning and pinning her against the railing in complete silence. 'Not good enough. I could have killed you at least a dozen times since you left your cabin.'

'I'll scream,' she whispered, her eyes dancing with mirth as she delighted in the apparent game. Her joy was infectious, but he forced himself to resist. Allowed more of his weight to press against her and leaned in.

'I'd kill you before you even opened your mouth,' he assured her. 'The captain too. And then there would be no one to stop me going below decks and killing Silvermane while he slept.'

'Ah, but then you'd have to fight Illyandi,' she pointed out in a breathless gasp as she tensed against him.

'She wouldn't put up much of a fight,' he said with a knowing smirk. 'I could have all kinds of fun with her.'

The laughter faded from Théon's eyes. She bucked her hips and twisted free. He grinned when she tried and failed to break his grip, pulling her close to him again. They struggled in silence for a moment before she went limp in his arms. Her sudden weight threw him off balance, and she wrenched free of his grip. She knocked him down onto the deck and then she was on him. She straddled his chest, pinning his arms with her knees as she drew her dagger from her boot and held it to his throat.

The fight had lasted seconds and taken place in complete silence, but it had her chest heaving with the exertion. His own breath caught in his throat as he stared up at her. Illuminated by the moonlight, she was breath-taking. The fierce pride she felt from besting him wasn't just clear on her face. It showed in every line of her body. He drank in the sight of her, near stunned into insensibility.

'Do you yield?' she breathed. He nodded and grinned as she relaxed and sheathed the knife. As soon as the blade was away, he grabbed her by the waist and rolled, pinning her beneath him again. He sensed her taking a deep breath to shout, so he covered her mouth with one hand and leaned in close.

'Your most important lesson,' he whispered in her ear. 'Never trust a Darkling.' Then he released her, standing and turning away.

'Not even you?' she asked.

Alexan didn't turn. 'Especially not me.'

She stood then and came closer, reaching out a tentative hand. When he didn't flinch from her touch, she gripped his shoulder and forced him to turn and face her, but he kept his eyes rooted on the deck.

'Why not?'

He raised his eyes and met her gaze then. The truth burned at his conscience, but he swallowed his guilt down. It wouldn't help either of them to come clean now. 'You trust me. It makes you forget what I am.'

'You would never hurt me.'

'I would never *want* to hurt you,' he clarified, placing two massive hands on her slender shoulders. She seemed so small in his grip. So fragile. So breakable. 'Remember, my will is not always my own.' He didn't need to elaborate. Understanding dawned in that evergreen gaze. It was more than the King's orders. When he considered what had happened earlier ... he shuddered to think how far he might have gone if Illyandi hadn't interrupted. He blew out a breath and turned away, running a frustrated hand through his hair. 'I could have killed you, Théon. The bloodlust ... it's hard to explain. It's not always a choice. It's very easy for me to lose control in a situation like that.'

'A situation like what?' she asked, arching a brow at him in challenge.

He scowled and released her, stepping back. 'You know what.'

'No, I don't,' she snapped, 'so please enlighten me.'

Alexan sighed in frustration and pushed past her. He couldn't meet her eye for this. He took a moment to settle his nerves before he spoke. 'I was starving. My thirst, hunger, whatever you want to call it ... it's not just physical weakness. It's a survival instinct. You'd be the same without air. You can't think rationally, can't control your instinct. The blood – the life you gave me – was enough to keep me alive. Just. But when you let me drink from you, I needed it so badly I don't think I could've stopped if I'd tried. If Illyandi hadn't intervened, I would have killed you.'

There was a long silence while his words sank in. Still, he couldn't find the strength to look at her. She had to know. Had to understand how it worked. She'd spent long enough in Elucion. She was a Shade, for Gods' sake – might have even made her own Darklings at some point. How then could she ignore the risks?

To be fair, killing wasn't always necessary. But so many Darklings found it difficult to stop. It hadn't been that long ago that they would drain every drop of power and leave nothing but an empty, dried-out husk every time they fed. Short-sighted nonsense, even aside from the morality of it. Human souls were valuable. Their lifeblood was a limited commodity and killing them was wasteful.

It had taken him eighty years to convince the Shade King to deal with the problem. Yes, Darklings needed to consume a certain amount of life-magic, and without it, the tainted power of the Shade would poison them. But that didn't mean they had to kill every victim. When the Graced had been at the height of their power, Darklings rarely lived long enough to realise that they didn't need to gorge themselves with every feeding.

True, mortals varied in strength, and though the Graced carried far more power in their veins, they were long gone. At least in any meaningful numbers. Outside of places like Elucion and Dar Kual it was difficult to find enough prey, especially since feeding would always leave the victim weaker, and it took time for them to recover. It was only after the Fall that prey was plentiful enough for them to consider other options. For the King to realise that instead of draining all the magic from one soul, it was just as effective for his Darklings to take smaller amounts from several.

His announcement that his Court and their Darkling hordes had to take more care of their mortal herd had been met with mutterings of dissent and howls of frustration. He'd stopped short of banning the practice, knowing that to do so would have given his opponents the opening they needed. The Shade King was a force to be reckoned with, but even he couldn't hold back his entire Court should it turn on him. That was why he had sent Alexan after Théon. He needed all the allies he could get.

But she couldn't know that. For now, her loyalty was to another power. If legend was to be believed, the only power that could rival Sephiron's heir. So he buried his thoughts deep and dared to meet her gaze. There was sorrow in her eyes. An ancient, endless grief. But there was not even the faintest glimmer of pity there. Good. He wasn't sure he could have suffered that. Not after what he'd almost done.

'I'm alright,' she whispered, laying a reassuring hand on his arm. 'Alexan, I'm alright.'

He huffed out a breath. 'You almost weren't. Théon ... I don't know what I'd do if I ever hurt you.' He broke off, looking away. Too close, too close to the truth. Those were thoughts he didn't even want to consider himself, let alone share with her. A warm, slender hand slid into his.

'I'll be fine,' she promised. 'I've survived this long, haven't I?' He chuckled weakly in acknowledgement. 'But I don't think we can let things continue as they have been.'

He blinked. 'What do you mean?'

'What we've been doing isn't working. Maybe you need to feed more – take as much as you need. Well, assuming you can do so without killing me anyway,' she added with a sly smile.

Alexan hardly believed what he was hearing. He closed his eyes and took a deep, calming breath. But all that did was exacerbate his awareness of her. She was excited by the prospect of being fed on; the scent of anticipation was on her skin. Her heart fluttered in her chest and her breathing was ragged. By the Gods, he wanted her.

'You don't know what you're saying.'

'We can't afford for you to lose control again,' she insisted, 'and besides, I'd rather you fed from me than Illyandi or Silvermane.'

He groaned. She wasn't wrong. And he wanted so badly to taste her again. Their earlier encounter had sated his thirst enough that he thought he should be able to control himself. Plus, he mused, with any luck, she would find the entire experience so terrifying she would stay away from him. He felt his will crumble as she leaned closer to him and her scent engulfed his senses.

'Alright,' he groaned. He grabbed her and held her still, forcing her to look at him. 'Promise to tell me if I hurt you too much.'

She nodded. 'I promise.'

'Even if you feel weak, strange ... anything,' he continued. She nodded again. 'Promise me, Théon. Tell me to stop if needs be.'

'I promise,' she said again, more forcefully this time. He nodded in acceptance and took another steadying breath. She looked around, shy and awkward as she waited. He suppressed the urge to grin. It had been a long time since he'd had someone so inexperienced. She was in for a surprise. Voluntary feeding was an intimate act. Aside from the physical closeness, she was putting her life in his hands. That level of trust created a bond unlike any other.

'This might hurt,' he warned again, pulling her closer with a pointed look at the captain, watching them from the helm. She nodded, her eyes wide with trepidation.

'I trust you,' she whispered.

She meant it too.

Reverently, Alexan lowered his head to her neck. Pressed his lips to the tender skin and inhaled deeply. Scented the blood rushing through her veins. Parted his lips and pressed his teeth to her flesh. He was vaguely aware of her erratic heartbeat, pulsing against his mouth as he bit through the fine layer of skin into her bloodstream. She gasped at the sensation but did not flinch.

Her breathing was ragged now, coming in sharp gulps. She swayed as she grew more and more light-headed. He caught her about the waist and pulled her closer to him to stop her falling, the image of a lover's embrace to anyone watching. She moaned low in her throat.

He glanced up, staring incredulously. She was enjoying it. She even whimpered when he stopped. He shook his head, forcing her to look at him while he bared his blood-covered teeth. Her eyes were heady with desire, and she moaned, louder this time. He shook his head in exasperation. She would never realise the danger if she enjoyed it. He'd have to go further if he wanted to scare her away.

He gripped her tight enough to hurt and bit down harder. She cried out softly, her eyes rolling back into her head. He growled and continued to drink, taking more than he needed even to sate his lust. Far more than he needed to survive. Better she felt weak in the morning, so she would never offer this to him again. If she did, having tasted how sweet she was now, he would never be able to refuse.

He stopped right before she fainted. Unconscious, she would never learn. Awake, she would remember how helpless she'd been. So he maintained eye contact as he licked the blood from the skin around the bite. She gasped and shivered against him. Once the wound was clean, he summoned a simple Casting to heal it and gathered her in his arms. She was limp against his chest, unable to even raise her head, as he carried her back to the cabin. He did not say a word as he entered, tiptoeing so as not to wake Illyandi or Silvermane. Laid her down and removed her boots. She watched him helplessly as he trailed his fingers higher before breaking off and covering her with the blanket. He loomed over her, his red eyes glowing through the darkness, brushed her throat in warning and left.

He spent the rest of the night above deck. Unable to settle, restless with the desire thrumming in his veins. Body buzzing with pent-up energy, yearning for release. He looked forward to landfall, to Théon's recovery so he could channel this new power into their sparring.

He ran a thoughtful finger over his lips, considering her blood. The power it contained. He hadn't noticed at the time, too caught up in the moment. And before, it had been barely more than a drop, never enough to register its strength. But he realised it now. He'd never felt this strong after feeding. He wasn't even sure he'd ever felt this alive. Not even before the Claiming.

Was Illyandi's blood as strong? Was Keriath's? The Queens had to have fed on her by now. A pang of guilt flickered at the thought, but he shoved it aside. Would they notice? Would they put the pieces together? What if others discovered it? She was hunted enough as it was. She would never find peace if others knew.

He dammed the torrent of thoughts and fears with a curse and turned his gaze to the lightening horizon. Watched in silence as the sailors made ready to dock.

Mari's voice drifted down from the helm. 'What's the matter, poppet? Your sweetheart not satisfied with your performance last night?'

He rolled his eyes and prowled up onto the aft deck to join her.

'I always leave my women satisfied,' he purred. 'If I'd known you were curious, I would have been more than happy to demonstrate for you.'

'Mmm,' she hummed. 'As intriguing as that sounds, poppet, I'm afraid you don't have the right equipment to satisfy me.'

He shrugged. 'Too bad. Reckon you could have taught me a thing or two.'

'Oh, definitely.' She chuckled. 'And even more besides. Ana would have probably indulged you; she's a little less discerning.'

'So I gathered.'

'A shame neither of your lady friends swing my way. I've never been with one of the Graced before – I'm curious to know what the difference would be.'

He almost laughed out loud at the thought of Illyandi's reaction to such a proposition. She'd been so sheltered for the last century. Ironic that she would never consider lowering herself to lying with a mortal but would surrender herself to the Dragon's ministrations. Théon, meanwhile …

'Not that much difference,' he said, pushing the image away. 'More stamina. More robust, if you like it rough. Dragons always seem to like it rough. Elves are a little more refined. A Phoenix can be fun, but if you want a fantastic fuck, you need to find yourself a Unicorn. The things they can do with the Enchanting. Mind blowing. Literally.'

'You speak like you're not one of them,' Mari noted.

He winced at the mistake. 'I've … been alone for a long time. Separated from my people.'

'How long?'

'Not long after the Fall. A hundred years, or near enough.'

'And you've spent all that time hiding what you are? Pretending to be someone else?'

She had no idea.

'I was thinking,' he said, changing the subject, 'if the Beasts are so difficult to navigate, why not make port somewhere else?'

Her face said she wasn't convinced, but she didn't push. 'Your sweetheart paid for passage to Stormkeep, so I'm taking you to Stormkeep. That means navigating the Beasts.'

'And if you were to take us somewhere else? Somewhere more … private? I'm sure you know a place or two along these coasts.'

'I don't know what you're implying,' she replied innocently. 'But yes, there are other places we can drop anchor. It'll cost you though.'

'I'm sure we can come to some arrangement.'

A map was spread out on the deck and a long, narrow sea loch selected as their new destination. Coins clinked as they exchanged hands, orders were barked, and before Alexan could blink twice, they had changed course. They were now heading west along the coastline and away from Stormkeep. Satisfied, he made his way back below deck to inform Théon and Silvermane of the new tack. But it was Illyandi who answered his knock on the cabin door. And she was in a fine mood.

'What did you do to her?' she growled without preamble. He rolled his eyes, folded his arms and waited. Time to widen that crack just a little further. She was painfully melodramatic. He didn't know where she'd inherited it. Diathor had been cool under pressure, serene at peace, and like Théon, unflappable in a crisis. Sarron had possessed a more fiery temper, but even he would never have stooped to such histrionics. It made her predictable. All too easy to manipulate. And it was only going to get worse if his theory was right.

'Nothing she didn't ask for.'

'What did you say?' hissed Illyandi, a Casting flashing around her.

'Get control of yourself, you stupid girl,' he said, gesturing at the offending aura.

The Casting broke free, shoving him back against the wall and knocking him down.

'Don't talk to me like that!' she snarled.

Alexan laughed out loud as he clambered to his feet. She'd used the Casting in unprovoked violence. But his laughter only angered her further, and he hurtled backwards, crashing to the floor again. He hauled himself to his feet, suppressing a groan.

'That's more like it, Princess! I knew you had it in you!' he said, grinning despite the pain. Illyandi froze up then, realising what she had done.

'I hate you!' she spat.

Alexan shrugged. 'I don't care.'

'What have you done to my sister?' she hissed again.

He folded his arms again and studied her. 'I fed from her.'

'I know. I was the one who stopped it, remember? She was fine after that! Now she's all weak and cold! You did something else!'

'Yes,' he said. 'I fed from her again.'

A Casting seeped out from her control again. 'You're a monster.'

'She came to me last night and offered it of her own volition,' he snapped. 'I didn't force her to do anything she didn't want to.'

'That's not the point! She's your Queen, and you're using her like a wine skin! You could have killed her!'

'Get a grip,' he snarled. 'I've been feeding from people for almost as long as you've been alive, Princess. If I'd wanted Théon dead, she'd be dead. I weakened her on purpose, so she learns her lesson. It was a damn foolish thing to do, but she'll not do it again.' Illyandi could only gape at him open-mouthed. He reached over and closed her jaw with one finger.

She shook herself and scowled. 'How long will she take to recover?'

'Not long,' he said. 'Just keep her in bed so she can rest for now and make sure she eats and drinks plenty. By the time we drop anchor, she'll be just fine.'

Illyandi gave him a long, dark look but nodded before turning on her heel and storming back inside. Alexan chuckled to himself. Perhaps Illyandi had inherited Sarron's temper after all.

Silvermane hobbled from the cabin a few moments later, his handsome face reproachful. 'Was any of that necessary?'

'Probably not,' admitted Alexan.

'And the feeding?'

He ignored the flush of warmth spreading up his neck. 'It won't happen again.'

'See that it doesn't.'

And that was the end of it.

'I've asked Mari to find another place to drop anchor besides Storm-keep. We have enough supplies, there's no need to go into the city itself.'

'Why do we need to avoid it?'

'Besides the numerous eyes who might recognise Benella's heirs? This glamour might hide me from mortal eyes, but any of the Graced within the city walls will scent me the minute I step ashore.'

'So you're trying to save your own skin?'

'Don't sound so shocked. Besides, do you think your people will be happy to find out you shared the secret of your little commune with the Shade King's Darkling general? Brought him to its shores?'

'Fine.'

358

Alexan let the pretence drop, smiling sadly. 'The less of this place I see, the better for all those sheltering here. I can't share what I don't know. Hide it from me, for our peoples' sake.'

The old man nodded in understanding. Gripped Alexan's shoulder in sympathy and thanks. Then retired to the cabin without a word.

Alexan made his way back up on deck, watching in silent wonder as the coast drifted by, the dark grey waves breaking into plumes of white froth where they met the jagged teeth of barren rock rising from the sea floor. The patchwork of exposed moorland beyond, just visible beneath the thick blanket of storm clouds gathering. It would be beautiful in the summer. Azure ocean giving way to golden sand, the machair swaying in the salty breeze. All the land, lush and fertile, nourished by the sea's bounty.

He snorted at the thought. This far north, they'd be lucky if the summer lasted more than a week. The mainland to the east wasn't far, but whatever lay to the west was so far away that no one had ever set foot there. There was nothing between these islands and the winter storms that came thundering in off the western ocean. He'd been sent to Thornhold on the King's business often enough to know how violent they could be.

Speaking of violence.

'I need you to do something for me.'

Illyandi's voice was drowning in resentment, and he couldn't help but smirk as he turned to face at her. Sure enough, her face was shrivelled with bitterness. A broad grin rose to his lips at her discomfort.

'And how might I be of service, Princess?'

'I want Mari to do something, but she just laughed at me.'

He was repressing the urge to laugh himself. 'Dare I ask what it is you want from her?'

'I want her and Ana to ferry all those refugees across.'

Gods, she was so predictable. He was just surprised it had taken her this long to work up the nerve to ask. 'That's not a small job, Princess. There were a lot of people in that camp.'

'Not that many,' she argued. 'It wouldn't take more than a month. Two at most. They could even get them all over before the winter storms make the sailing impossible.'

'And who's going to pay? Those people don't have that kind of money. That's why they've been stuck there so long.'

'I thought they would do it for free.'

There was no stopping the bark of laughter that escaped at that. 'No chance those two will do anything for free. Let alone that.'

'But the children—'

He cut her off. Gently, for once. Especially as he spotted her hand lingering on her stomach. Shame churned in his gut. He'd always been cunning – one didn't survive long on the streets without a shrewd and devious mind – and a century serving the Shade King had honed his scheming to new heights. He hated it, but it was a necessary evil. Théon would never leave with him if he did not cleave her from Illyandi, and that wouldn't happen on its own.

'Not everyone has your kind heart, Princess. Mari and Ana will expect payment for their services, and it will not be cheap. As sad as it is, those people are stuck there until they can find the money to pay for passage.'

She hesitated. 'What if I paid for their passage?'

'And where would you find that kind of money?'

She reached inside the pocket of her dress and pulled out a necklace. A chain of gold, finer than gossamer silk, with a huge, leaf-shaped emerald set in golden vines. It was Elvish work. Caster-wrought. Some of the finest he'd ever seen.

It was also a priceless family heirloom.

She seemed to understand his hesitation. 'It's just a necklace. A trinket in exchange for dozens of innocent lives? I remember little about my mother, but I think she'd consider that a fair trade. Don't you?'

He nodded. Of course she would. The first time he'd laid eyes on her, she'd been buying food for some beggar with a pair of her mother's earrings. He'd assumed she'd stolen them. She hadn't looked that dissimilar to him. Just another wide-eyed, hungry child. Another unwanted street urchin. She'd stolen his heart too before he'd found out the truth. Before he realised just how unattainable she was. But even as a girl, she'd valued life over any treasure. Guilt was a noose around his neck.

'Does Théon know?'

'Of course.'

'And she supports this?'

'Yes.'

He held out his hand. Shoved down the rising bile of self-loathing.

'I'll see what I can do.'

As expected, Mari and Ana seemed far more amenable to Illyandi's proposal when he held the necklace up for them to see. Caster-wrought work of any kind, from broadswords to bracelets, had always fetched a good price, and now that it was a finite commodity, its worth had increased exponentially.

The ignorance of mortals had not improved over the last century. It was still easy to convince them that, should they renege on a bargain, he would not only learn of it but punish them, no matter how far they ran. The legends surrounding the Graced had only grown more ridiculous in their absence, so he could be confident Ana and Mari would stay true to their word.

Any expectation of gratitude he might receive from Illyandi was short-lived as she, Silvermane and Théon joined him on deck. The Princess hovered at her sister's shoulder, shooting him looks of pure venom whenever he moved. Needlessly, of course – Théon was fine. Tired and a little pale, but otherwise unharmed. Just exasperated by Illyandi's fussing, as far as he could tell. And though the look she gave him was less than pleasant, it wasn't the pure loathing he'd expected. It did, however, promise that they would discuss all that had transpired later.

At length.

He was glad of their ire. It soothed the brittle edge of self-hatred for the seeds of strife he had sown.

They sailed most of the way up the narrow sea loch and dropped anchor close to land. They could disembark onto a craggy islet, but it would be a cold and wet journey across a half-submerged path of rock and reef to get onto the beach. The horses would not be happy. At least the shore was shingle and not the soft, golden sand he'd seen further up the coast. The cart would have never made it otherwise.

'Do you know where you're going from here?' Ana asked as they readied to leave.

Alexan glanced over the hillside. 'We'll figure it out.'

Mari tutted in exasperation and held out an oiled map roll. 'Here. This should keep you right.'

'Thank you.'

She just nodded absently, watching Théon help the old man up into the wagon. Her gaze flickered to Illyandi, and she winked, grinning. 'I'll miss seeing your pretty face about the deck, sweetheart. If you're ever feeling lonely, come find me.'

And with that she turned on her heel and sauntered back towards the stern, swearing at any sailor unfortunate to get in her way. Illyandi blushed and scarpered up into the wagon alongside Silvermane. Perhaps she was not so ignorant as he'd thought.

Beside him, Ana chuckled. 'She's a skittish one right enough. I hope, whoever he is, he treats her well. Does right by her.' Alexan said nothing, praying his face did not betray him. She was observant, he'd give her that much. Turning, she smiled and extended her hand. 'Forged in war.'

'Tempered in blood.' The customary response to the old Graced saying spilled from his lips before he could even register she'd said it. He took the offered hand and opened his mouth to question where she'd heard it. But she placed a finger on his lips and shook her head. Then, with an enigmatic smile, she turned to join her friend on the aft deck.

He was still mulling the exchange over in his mind, vaguely aware of the transition from the undulating grasses lining the beach to heather-coated moorland and barren rock, when Illyandi called an abrupt halt.

Just as he'd planned.

'We need to talk,' she announced, glaring at Alexan. Then she turned to her sister. 'Théon, this has gone far enough. He can't come with us. This place is a sanctuary, a haven from monsters like him. We were created to defend life from those who would try to steal it, not hand it to them on a silver platter.'

Théon blinked. 'You're the one who said he deserved a chance to earn our trust.'

'And we gave him that chance. He spat on it the moment he decided to feed from you.'

'Illyandi—' Théon began.

But Illyandi cut her off. 'No. I've had enough lies. The Shade King doesn't just lose control of his Darkling general. He's not here by accident.

361

And I don't know if it's us he wants, or something else, but there are people on these islands relying on us to keep them safe. It is our duty to protect them, and the Darkling cannot be trusted. Nor can we allow him to live, not with the secrets he's gleaned.'

Echoing silence followed.

Théon shifted uncomfortably. Unable or unwilling to admit the truth of their discussion.

Time to cleave that crack wide open.

'You're one to talk about lies and secrets, Princess,' he murmured, a pointed look at her belly.

Her lovely face paled, hand flying to her stomach. 'I don't know what you're talking about.'

The old man's gasp of horror was lost amongst the stream of curses that spewed from Théon's mouth. Alexan resisted the urge to smirk. Easy. Too easy. He need do nothing more now. Instead, he just folded his arms and watched.

'Tell me he's wrong,' Théon insisted, forcing her sister round to face her.

Illyandi blushed but, credit to her, raised her chin and looked her sister full in the face. 'He's not wrong. I'm with child.'

'And the father?'

'Faolin.'

An aura sparked to life around Théon. 'I'll kill him.'

'He didn't force me,' Illyandi clarified. 'I love him, Théon. I lay with him willingly.'

Alexan snorted. 'That's an understatement.'

'You knew?' demanded Théon, rounding on him.

He shrugged. Prodded the fracture a little further. 'I was unfortunate enough to stumble across them in the act, so to speak. I didn't know for sure she was pregnant until just now, though I've suspected for a while. I assumed she would tell you.'

Théon swore. Violently. Whirled back to her sister, aura crackling as she said, 'What were you thinking? And don't tell me it was an accident because you know fine well how to use a Casting to prevent it. How could you be so stupid? The Shade Court rules, and we're hunted wherever we go, and you think it's a good idea to bring a child into this world?'

Illyandi was crying now, tears streaming down her lovely face. Alexan had no sympathy for her. Even if he hated himself for what he was doing.

'I love him,' she sobbed, 'and he loves me. We belong together. If he won't stay for me, then at least he will stay for his child.'

Even the old man swore at that. 'Foolish girl. A child will make him even less able to stay. He stays away to protect you. He will sacrifice far more to protect his heir. *You* may need to sacrifice far more.'

'What do you mean?'

'He means your child will be far safer away from you,' Théon snapped. 'Away from all of us. And even then, there's no guarantee. You and Faolin hail from the most powerful Graced bloodlines in the world, and you've

362

been hunted your whole lives because of it. How badly do you think the Shade will want your child when they learn of it? And, believe me, they will learn of it. A power like that does not go unnoticed. Gods, you fucking idiot!'

'That's enough,' the old man murmured, putting an arm around the sobbing Princess, who buried her face in his shoulder. 'We should discuss this later, when tempers have cooled.'

Théon's lip curled in a silent snarl. 'We could be waiting a while.'

'Then so be it. But we should get moving – we should be able to cover a few miles at least before it gets dark.'

Illyandi looked up, eyes puffy and wide. 'What about the Darkling? Just because I was keeping something from you, doesn't mean he can be trusted. He's a monster – I don't want him around my baby!'

A terrible growl rippled up from Théon's chest, and she placed herself between her sister and Alexan. His heart stuttered with triumph at the sudden display of loyalty, followed quickly by the queasy churning of shame in his gut. He didn't deserve her. Not when he had shattered her world.

'I don't give a shit what you want,' she snarled. 'He's not perfect, but at least he's honest about what he is. With me and with himself. Which is more than I can say for you.'

And with that she wheeled her mount around and motioned for him to join her as she led the way across the purple moor.

CHAPTER THIRTY-ONE

The wind was relentless. Not always a forceful battering, but still a never-ending draught that left his face and hands numb. It wasn't surprising either, not when there was nothing between them and the raging ocean but open moor and barren hillside. The tallest tree he'd seen had been shorter than he was. Nothing bigger than a large bush would survive in these conditions, even with the long daylight hours through the summer. And winter ... he shuddered to imagine how savage that would be.

He was trying hard not to notice how pretty Théon looked with her cheeks stained pink by the constant breeze. Or the tendrils of damp, raven hair pulled loose from her braid, coiling against her sea-kissed skin. Or the feral smile that touched her lips whenever she thought no one was looking. Despite what he'd told the old man, she was her father's daughter. The wind and the wild were in her blood. Singing her home.

'Where are we going?' he asked, shoving down the feelings that rose in response.

'There's a Graced commune on one of the outlying islands. It's heavily warded, so Illyandi should be safe there.'

He noted the emphasis of her words. 'And what about you?'

'If she decides to keep the child, I can't be near them. Too much power in one place just draws unwanted attention.'

'And Silvermane?'

She let out a bark of caustic laughter. 'His magic is all but spent. Powerful, yes, but tired and weary. My father wouldn't consider him a threat, even if he knew he was alive, which he doesn't.' He took a mental note of the information but said nothing as she blew out a breath and continued. 'I just hope someone there can get word to Faolin, and that he's not too far away. He's the only one who can talk some sense into her.'

He didn't need to ask – she meant the only one who stood any chance of convincing her to end the life growing in her womb. Most women had to rely on herbs for such a thing, and all the risks that came with them. But not the Elves. Not with the Casting power at their command. A single thought, a flutter of magic, and the problem would be resolved.

'If she won't even kill to defend herself, I doubt she'll be keen for that,' he pointed out.

Théon grimaced. 'I know. Gods, what was she thinking? A child is a burden at the best of times and now is hardly that.'

'Not a view I imagine she shares.'

'No,' she agreed. 'She's been desperate for a child for years. I've never understood it.'

He arched a brow, glancing at her sidelong. 'Really?'

'Do I look like mother material to you?' she asked with a sardonic smile. The image of Théon, belly swollen with his child, flashed through his mind. He couldn't deny it was an appealing thought – though dangerous enough to get him killed. Get them both killed.

He hedged his bets. 'I reckon you'd do a better job than you think.'

She snorted and shook her head in disgust. 'Hard to be a mother when you've never had one. Closest thing I had growing up was Jenia, at least until I was dragged back to Illyol. And my mother was a stranger to me for most of the time I knew her. I hated her for at least half of it. Besides, I swore a long time ago that my father's line would end with me, and I have no intention of ever reconsidering that vow.'

They rode in silence for a while, her words echoing in his head. He didn't blame her. Didn't disagree with her choice either. It wasn't an uncommon one in the Shade Court. Shade childbirth was unpredictable, the magic unstable and often deadly. Most Shade women didn't want to risk it, and he'd known enough Graced women over the years who felt the same. As Théon had said, a child was a burden. One that many were not suited to carry, especially those with magic in their blood. For so many, that power was burden enough. Still, it made him sad to think Diathor's line might end with her. Not that his opinion mattered; it was her body.

'We should make camp soon,' she said, glancing up at the darkening sky. 'Then you and I need to have a chat.'

The slight depression in which they made their camp was the best shelter they could find from the incessant wind. Neither the shrubby heather nor gorse provided enough protection for a fire. And since no one was prepared to use a Casting, their meal was cold. Once the Princess and the old man were settled, huddled together in the relative shelter of the wagon beneath as many blankets as they could find, Alexan rose.

'I'm going to scout ahead. Check there isn't anyone too close who might stumble on us.'

Théon stood too. 'I'll come with you. I want to check the road ahead for tomorrow.'

Her tone brooked no discussion, and Silvermane had the sense to respect it. The Princess, however …

'You're just going to leave us here unprotected?'

Théon didn't even turn. 'You have magic. Protect yourself for once.'

They walked far enough that they wouldn't be disturbed, but not too far that they wouldn't hear any commotion if there was an attack. Not that Théon seemed inclined to save her sister if there was.

He perched on a rock and readied himself. 'Come on then, let's get this over with.'

Her expression was grim as she turned to face him, but it was not as enraged as he might have expected. She seemed more irked than incensed, and he found her irritation … arousing. She was frowning at him as she came nearer, and he waited for her reprimand. But when she spoke, her voice was surprisingly calm.

'You took more from me than you needed,' she said.

'Darkling,' he reminded her. 'I told you never to trust one.'

'You were in complete control. I think you took that much to teach me a lesson.'

'Why would I do something like that?'

She shook her head in exasperation. 'I honestly don't know,' she sighed. 'You do the good-turned-evil act very well, but I don't believe it for a second. You're a good man, Alexan. I don't know why you pretend otherwise.'

'You don't know me, Théon,' he warned. 'You don't know what kind of man I am.'

'I know you're the kind of man who tried to scare me to protect me, even though that meant damaging your standing with me,' she said.

'What makes you think I care about my standing with you?'

'Because you care about me,' she said with a smirk. As he opened his mouth to respond she held up a hand to silence him. 'Don't bother denying it. I can see it written all over your face.'

He grinned then. Gods, the way she sassed him. 'I wasn't going to deny it.'

'What then?' she snapped. But her eyes were twinkling with mischief.

He sighed and leaned back against the rock, folding his hands behind his head. 'What do you want, Théon?'

'I want you to know why you did it,' she said, folding her arms across her chest.

'What makes you think I didn't just like the taste?' he asked with a cheeky smirk.

She grinned, his tone infectious. 'Oh, I know you liked the taste,' she said, 'but you drained me to within an inch of my life, and I want to know why.'

'Leave the dramatics to Illyandi, Théon – they don't suit you,' he said, rolling his eyes. 'I didn't drain you to within an inch of your life.'

She kicked him in the shin, hard. 'Answer the damn question,' she ordered.

He threw his hands up in defeat.

'You were right. I did it to scare you. Offering yourself to me like that last night, when I was half-mad with bloodlust for you already, was a damn foolish thing to do. It's like you're daring me to kill you,' he snapped. 'You were stupid, and you needed to learn a lesson.'

'Alright,' she agreed. She knelt before him, and pulled her hair to one side, baring her throat to him. 'Teach me a lesson.'

Alexan gawked at her. 'What?' he asked in a strangled voice. She was gazing wickedly at him from beneath her long, dark lashes, and it made his head spin.

'You heard,' she said, her voice low and husky. 'You did that to scare me, but I'm not afraid. So you'll have to try something else.'

Alexan couldn't repress the low moan that escaped his lips as her words filtered through. 'You've got to be joking,' he groaned. But she wasn't, and the sight of her on her knees in front of him, offering herself, was enough to make him tremble.

'Come on,' she said. 'Do your worst.'

He couldn't resist. Her power was singing to him, enchanting him. He grabbed her by the shoulders and pulled her against him, bending down to bite into her proffered neck. She gasped out loud and writhed in his grip, but he held her tight. He groaned as he gulped down her blood, revelling in the feel of her body against his, in her power crackling over his tongue. She struggled against him again, and instinct had him subduing her, pinning her down with the full length of his heavy frame. She moaned as she pressed herself against him, her fingers winding their way through his hair while she held him tight. His own hands were roving, with a mind of their own he realised, his fingers running across the flat of her stomach to grip her about the hips.

When he'd taken his fill, he released her, propping himself up on his elbows. Once more, he looked her in the eye as he cleaned the blood from her collarbone and shoulder with his tongue. She held his gaze, squirming beneath him. He grinned and stood up.

'Your sister is going to kill me if we keep doing this,' he said, brushing the wound.

Théon smirked and waved a hand over it. A Casting flared, and the wound was gone.

'Good thing she doesn't have to find out,' she said, standing. 'Still not scared.' And with that, she sauntered towards the camp, leaving Alexan watching her retreating back in confusion.

———

The atmosphere back at the camp was tense. Théon and her sister didn't say a word to each other, and what little conversation they had with either Alexan or Silvermane consisted only of terse replies to direct questions.

It was no better the next day, nor the day after that. If anything, it was worse. As they journeyed west along the islands, Illyandi's sullen silences gave way to an ever-worsening series of spiteful remarks. Still smarting from Théon's assessment of her actions, every time she opened her mouth it was to spew another barrage of passive-aggressive abuse at her sister. Never overt, always subtle, but the inference was clear. Théon, as the daughter of the Shade King, was defective. Deficient. Lesser.

Théon never reacted to the insults, no matter how hurtful, instead withdrawing further and further into herself. It was rage-inducing to watch – even if the wedge the Princess was driving between them played right into Alexan's hands.

'Princess,' he'd growled, unable to take any more, 'if you'd put half as much thought into your actions as you do into your insults, you wouldn't be in this mess, so do us all a favour and just shut the fuck up.'

The Princess's eyes had widened with shock, and he realised that he was likely the first person to ever speak to her so callously. He didn't regret it – even if her scathing comments were now likely to be directed his way.

'Keep talking, Darkling,' she hissed. 'See what happens.'

Alexan snorted. 'That might scare me if I hadn't seen you down on all fours being fucked by a Dragon.'

Illyandi's cheeks flushed with embarrassment, but Théon let out a sharp bark of laughter, which only made Illyandi blush harder.

'You're disgusting,' she snapped. 'Though I guess that would make sense. I can't imagine a monster like the Shade King would waste his time Claiming anyone who wasn't a pervert.'

He couldn't bring himself to dignify such a ridiculous statement with a response, so he shook his head in disgust and looked at Théon who said nothing, her gaze dark and brittle, her temper straining for release. He ignored Illyandi and turned his attention to the other two.

'Sunset is not far off. We should think about making camp.'

But the Princess wasn't done. 'Do you have any preference for the people you murder to save your own worthless hide, or is it just a random choice?'

'Illyandi,' Théon warned.

But Illyandi didn't listen.

'Is anyone off limits to your kind? Lovers you've taken trusting into your bed? Old men too crippled by age to run from you? Children hiding behind their mother's skirts?' He kept his face impassive, tried not to wince at the truth of it. He'd done it all. Nothing was sacred at the King's Court. 'How do you even look in the mirror?' she continued, seeing that she'd rattled him. 'You're a thief of life. Each breath you take is stolen from innocents more deserving of it than you—'

A vicious, feral snarl ripped out of Théon's chest as she rounded on her sister. An aura was raging, and her eyes pulsed, the Shade fighting for freedom. Illyandi quailed in the face of her sister's fury. Even Alexan was uneasy, for there was murder in Théon's eyes. In her rage, she could not even bring herself to speak, growling in warning instead, her body trembling with restraint. He laid a gentle hand on her shoulder and flinched back – her skin was burning. His eyes flickered up to Illyandi.

'Go,' he mouthed at her. She shook her head, but as another snarl ripped from between Théon's bared teeth, Silvermane took the reins – and the decision – from Illyandi's hands. Alexan held Théon's gaze, barely daring to breathe while the old man guided the little white mare past them.

When the wagon had disappeared around the hill, Alexan braced himself for the pain then gripped Théon by the shoulders and turned her to face him. 'Relax,' he ordered. Her eyes pulsed in defiance once, twice … and then it was gone. He caught her as she slumped in exhaustion, holding her tight to his chest while she sobbed. 'Hush,' he murmured, stroking a soothing hand over her hair. 'It's alright. I'm here.'

It took some time for the storm to pass, but she quietened and stepped away, drying her eyes with the hem of her shirt. He took a deep breath as his gaze flickered over a flash of toned stomach muscle, but for once, his instincts stayed silent.

'Gods, I hate her sometimes,' Théon whispered, dropping onto a nearby rock. Sensing she needed to talk, he perched beside her and waited. 'She's just a constant reminder of everything I should be. Perfect Illyandi who can do no wrong. Even when she's been so catastrophically stupid, every time I look at her, I see the daughter I should have been. Someone soft and gentle. Like my mother.'

Alexan snorted with disgust. 'She's nothing like your mother. She might appear innocent at a glance, but your sister is a scheming, manipulative bitch.'

'No,' Théon argued. 'She's just upset. And scared. For herself and for the baby.'

Alexan ran a hand through his hair in frustration. Time to fracture this tie beyond hope of repair. 'She got all the brains, didn't she? She treats you like shit, and you sit there defending her? Open your eyes, Théon. She's jealous of you! Bringing you down is just a way to make her feel better about herself.'

'Illyandi has nothing to be jealous of,' she scoffed.

'You mean, aside from the fact that you're firstborn and will sit on the Oak Throne?' he retorted, trying not to roll his eyes. 'How about the fact that you're more powerful than she is, more intelligent, more skilled and experienced, more charismatic, more beautiful—' He broke off, realising what he was saying. But he couldn't bring himself to regret it. There was a slight flush creeping up her neck and across her sweeping cheekbones, and it was enchanting.

'You think I'm beautiful?' she asked, her voice a breathy whisper.

He looked at his feet, certain that his face wasn't as delightful when he blushed. 'You know you are,' he said, glancing sideways at her.

She grinned wolfishly at him. 'All of the Graced are beautiful. I just didn't think I was your type.'

'And what do you think my type is?' he growled, unable to stop himself leaning towards her. She bit her lip, and Alexan's attention honed in on her mouth with predatory intent. She seemed to sense it, her breath catching in her throat. Her eyes flickered over his face, searching.

'I've seen what pleasures my father's Court has to offer. I would have thought I was plain by comparison.'

And like that, his desire was doused as though she had dumped a bucket of meltwater over him. His hand snaked out and gripped her chin, squeezing tight in his frustration. 'I have no interest in Elucion whores,' he said, 'but if you keep talking like that, I'll make you scream like one.' He released her violently, surprised by the strength of his reaction, and stood.

As he turned his back on her, she asked, 'Is that a promise?'

'Yes,' he growled and swung back up into his saddle. Then he turned his mount away and rode after Illyandi and Silvermane before he could say anything else he might regret.

The old man was waiting for him, leaning heavily on his staff. The Princess was some distance further up the road, seated in the wagon with her nose in the air.

Bitch.

'She will go no further in your company, Darkling,' Silvermane said without preamble. 'Even if she could ignore your questionable conduct, she has the safety of her child to consider. Mercy is no longer a luxury she can afford.'

Alexan tried not to let the surge of triumph show on his face. 'She's never been able to afford that. You were a fool to let her believe otherwise.'

'Careful,' he warned. 'You owe your life to her. I was prepared to kill you that night. It was Illyandi who persuaded me otherwise. She offered you a chance, and you threw it back in her face. It's tempting enough to kill you now for that slight. Don't make my decision to spare you any harder.'

He couldn't help but laugh out loud at that. 'You couldn't kill me if you tried, old man, and you won't even do that for fear of losing Théon. Her trust in you, in her sister, is hanging by a thread, and you know one wrong move will cleave her from you forever. You can't risk that. She's too powerful. You want her bound to you and yours, so you can control her. And more to the point, to make sure her father can't.'

Silvermane opened his mouth to reply but closed it again as the subject of their conversation neared. Alexan dared a glance as she drew alongside him and smirked at the mixture of exasperation and disgust on her face as she surveyed the scene before her.

She rolled her eyes. 'Let me guess – another ultimatum? Something about having the baby to think about? No longer being able to afford mercy? Am I getting warm?'

'Hotter than a Rising,' Alexan murmured.

The old man shot him a dark look but left it alone. 'She is not in any danger now. You must concede that your reasons for bringing him in the first place are no longer valid?'

'Sure,' she admitted. 'Now I just want him here because he's the only one who doesn't treat me like shit all the time.'

Silvermane spluttered in indignation. 'Don't be ridiculous.'

'I've lost count of how often you've put me down or written me off, all because of something I can't control,' she snarled. 'I didn't ask for this power. I didn't ask for these bloodlines. I certainly didn't ask to be conceived by force. Those were my father's choices, not mine, and I'm tired of the two of you making me suffer for them.'

'Théon,' the old man began, 'I know you're upset, and she's said some things in anger that I'm sure she regrets, but she's your sister, and she needs you, now more than ever.' Théon hesitated, face crumpling as her resolve wavered. Silvermane smiled, scenting victory, and held out his hand. 'Come, Théon. Be reasonable. We are your blood ... your family.'

A muscle leapt in her jaw at the imperious tone, and she squared her shoulders, looking him full in the face. 'Blood and family are two very different things. My father taught me that.'

'Théo—'

She cut him off with a hiss. 'No. I've heard enough. You want me to choose? I will not choose someone who would never choose me.'

'And you think a Darkling would?'

She looked to Alexan then, her lovely face impassive, but he could see the fear in her eyes. Scent it rolling off her. The power to break her in the palm of his hand. But the King did not want her broken. She was no use to him like that. Not when it was her strength, her power, he needed. So Alexan held her gaze and nodded.

'Every time,' he promised. 'I swore my life in service to the Elf-Queen. It is hers to do with as she pleases.'

She smiled shyly at his pronouncement, the look she gave him lingering.

Then the moment passed, and she looked back to Silvermane. 'You remember where you're going?'

'Of course,' he growled, not bothering to hide his frustration. 'You forget, this network was my doing. Every sanctuary, every ally, all found and nurtured by me and mine during the Dark Days.'

'I'm well aware of that,' she snapped, 'but it's been a long time, and I wanted to be sure. Just because it's time we went our separate ways doesn't mean I don't care for you both. I'll sleep better at night knowing you're safe.'

His gaze softened at that, and he nodded in understanding. 'I will take care of her, and whoever else comes along. You can be sure of that.'

'You should get word to Faolin sooner rather than later.'

'It's already taken care of.'

Her gaze drifted up the road, to her sister sat proudly in the front of the wagon, and a sad smile touched her lips. 'Keep her safe. Forged in war.'

'Tempered in blood,' the old man replied.

And with those final words, Théon turned away. Left her family behind her. No sign of the certain pain inside showing on her lovely face. No hint of suffering in her steel-straight spine. Just grim determination to forge her own path.

Alexan followed without hesitation, ignoring the mixture of triumph, apprehension and guilt that sent his guts churning.

So close. He was so very close.

———

They made camp on an open beach. The wind had eased, making the sweeping sands habitable for their camp. But even if it hadn't, the location was too beautiful to ignore. Turquoise water lapping over golden sands. The setting sun staining the sky in shades of orange and pink. Marram grass undulating in the breeze. The scent of the wildflower meadow beyond mingling with the tang of salt spray rolling in off the sea.

There was enough driftwood to make a sizeable fire, and Alexan downed a nice fat goose for their supper. Nestled in the dunes, they ate and drank and talked while they watched the sun set beyond their flames. Revelled in the reprieve from the Princess's constant criticism. Soaked in the peace and tranquillity of the world around them.

As the sky darkened, Théon rose. 'Right, I'm going for a swim. I've been desperate for a proper bath for days now. Reckon this is the best chance I'll get for a while.'

'Good plan,' Alexan chuckled. 'My eyes were watering riding downwind from you.'

She kicked him in the shin. 'You can talk. When did you last wash?'

'Fair point,' he conceded. 'You go first. I'll wait with the horses.'

Her look said that hadn't been what she was suggesting, but she didn't push it. Instead, she just shrugged and made her way down the beach to the water. His heart was thundering in his chest by the time she reached the surf and began to undress. She had to know he could see her. The scent of her arousal on the wind just confirmed it.

He leaned back in the grass, propping his hands behind his head, and enjoyed the view. Let her play her games. He was sure he'd be rewarded for his patience. The beauty of the sunset was forgotten while he watched her. Considered those long, sleek limbs. The toned muscles and tawny skin. What it would taste like, coated in salt water. Gods, if only she'd hurry up.

Finally, either clean or tired of taunting, she made her way back up the beach towards him. She wore only her shirt, barely long enough to cover her backside, yet there was a confidence – a boldness – in the way she moved towards him that he hadn't seen before. He opened his mouth to speak, to dissuade her, but before he could say anything, she held up her hand.

'Hush,' she whispered. She stepped closer, pulling her shirt up as she lowered herself onto his lap. He groaned softly at the feel of her heat against his groin and her bare thighs about his waist. She took his hands in her own and placed them on her legs, caressing herself with his hands. He heard his own breath catch in his throat and cursed inwardly. He was far from virginal, and yet she had him feeling like a blushing maiden on her wedding night. Her skin was like silk beneath his hands. He watched her, wide-eyed, as she guided his hands higher and higher. Beyond the curve of her hip. Past the flat of her stomach. Until he felt the swell of her breasts. She released his hands then and removed the shirt.

Alexan growled low in his throat. She was exquisite. Her skin glowed in the moonlight, and her damp hair tumbled over her slender shoulders like a waterfall of midnight sky. She was gazing down at him, her feline eyes glittering while she watched him drink in the sight of her, and he felt his stomach clench in anticipation. He loved a woman who understood the effect she had on a man. They had been few in the last hundred years.

'Bite me,' she whispered, her voice husky with desire. He didn't have to be told twice, grabbing her by the waist and pulling her to him. His mouth went to the swell of her breast and she gasped aloud as he bit into the soft flesh. Sweet and salty, just as he'd imagined. He only allowed himself a single mouthful of blood, before licking the wound clean and moving to her other breast where he repeated the process. He rolled so she was beneath him as he moved lower, biting her hip on one side and then the other. She gasped, with outrage this time, then he turned her over and bit into her pert backside, before working his way down and biting into her thigh. She squirmed beneath him as he ran his fingers up the inside of her leg, as he sucked in a mouthful of her sweet blood. He sat up and rolled her onto her back and spread her legs, biting into the soft flesh on the inside of her thigh.

She was panting now, and he grinned, trailing his tongue higher and higher up her leg. She froze as he came to a stop, hovering over the apex of her thighs. She shivered as his breath brushed over her skin but did nothing to stop him. He could have taken it as an invitation, but he wanted to hear the words.

'Say it,' he breathed.

She knew what he wanted. 'Yes,' she begged. 'Gods, yes.' Alexan pressed his teeth against her hot flesh and bit down. She cried out, and he was forced to stop, to reach up and cover her mouth with his hand.

'Quiet,' he admonished her with a soft growl. 'Graced ears are sharp.'

Théon gasped as he removed his hand, quivering beneath him. She nodded, her eyes wide. Satisfied, he lowered himself back down her body. Gently, he lapped up the blood that had dripped down between her legs and tried not to laugh as she shuddered with the effort of staying silent. He closed his mouth over the wound and sucked hard once, before trailing his tongue across her damp heat. She moaned and writhed beneath him. He pinned her hips still with his hands and continued mercilessly. Vaguely aware that she stifled her cry of pleasure with her own arm as she shook apart beneath his mouth.

Gods, she was exquisite. He let her catch her breath as he trailed his lips back up her body, fingers exploring lower, and grinned when his touch had her panting in moments. What pleasure could he wring from a body so responsive? He was going to take his sweet time finding out—

A male voice shattered the night.

'Théon?'

He made to surge to his feet, but Théon got there first, rolling over and pinning him beneath her. Her hand found his mouth in the darkness and covered it, eyes flashing with warning. It was only then he sensed the Casting – a glamour to shield them from whoever approached. Pride and no small amount of surprise swelled in his chest. She'd reacted so fast. Likely saved his life.

Definitely, he realised, recognising the dark-haired figure striding through the dunes towards their dying fire.

Kah Faolin.

Where the *fuck* had he come from?

She motioned for him to stay where he was, hidden in the dunes, while she dressed quickly. She circled around, so she was across the fire from the fierce-eyed Dragon. Then she let her glamour drop.

'Faolin?' she called out, standing and peering over the flames. 'What are you doing here?'

The Dragon drew to a halt, glancing around in suspicion. 'I could ask you the same thing, though I'm more interested in why you've abandoned your sister in her time of need?'

'You've spoken to Illyandi.'

He nodded, handsome face grim. 'She told me everything. Where's the Darkling?'

'Gone,' Théon lied. 'I sent him away. I knew it wouldn't be safe for him here.'

The Dragon's hand was resting on the hilt of his sword. 'I don't believe you.'

'But you'll believe Illyandi? Who got herself pregnant just to make sure you'd stay with her?'

'Trust me, I'm no more happy about it than you are,' he snapped. 'But that's between Illyandi and I, and it has nothing to do with this conversation. I know her well enough to separate her feelings from the facts, but even then, Théon ... to not only suffer a Darkling to live, but to let it feed on you? To choose a *Darkling* over your own family?'

'News gets around fast,' she murmured. 'How did you find us?'

Faolin held up his hand. Showed her the ring on his finger. The partner to the one Illyandi wore. 'Resari warned me you were in danger. That we had led the Darkling to you. But it wasn't until you let it *feed* from you that Illyandi called me. '

A slender figure appeared at his side. Silver-haired and stormy-eyed. Sil Dorrien. There was disgust on that lovely face, softened only slightly by a mixture of sorrow and concern.

'Just tell us where it is, Théon,' she breathed, 'and we can put this all behind us.'

Théon took a step back. 'He has a name.'

'He *had* a name,' Dorrien snarled, 'and then the King filled his veins with poison, and the man you knew died. That thing just wears his face. It's your father's puppet, Théon. You cannot trust it.'

Such vehement hatred from the otherwise cool and unyielding Dragon was enough to make Alexan flinch. Not that he'd blame her, if the stories were true. If she'd watched, a helpless child, while the Darkling Queens ripped her mother apart.

Théon was still moving. Circling slowly. Inching her way towards him. Placing herself between him and the Dragons in case the glamour failed. Fear was a fist about his throat. For himself. For his lover. For his Queen. Even as her fingers curled round the hilt of her sword, the hint of an aura flickered into life around her.

Faolin seemed to sense the threat of violence brewing in the air. 'Théon, please. At least come back to the safe house with us. Illyandi's waiting. We can be safe behind the wards of the sanctuary in moments, then we can talk.'

'No.' The word was almost unintelligible. A guttural growl ground out from between clenched teeth. 'You think the wards offer safety, but all I see is a cage. One you would lock me in forever, if I gave you the chance.'

'It's for your own good, Théon,' Dorrien warned. 'The Darkling has warped your mind. Made you forget who you are.'

Théon laughed at that. A cold, humourless sound that sent chills down his spine. The Shade King's laugh. 'The old man is the one with the power to warp minds. Even this small freedom has been enough to make me wonder just how much he's been playing with mine over the years.'

The Dragons exchanged a long look, confirming Alexan's suspicions. Silvermane's power wasn't spent, as he had led Théon to believe. It had just been preoccupied with keeping her obedient. It was only as they'd left the safety of the wards that his control over her had begun to waver. Given Alexan the opening he'd needed, even though his blood boiled at the violation.

'We don't want to fight you, Théon,' Faolin began.

She laughed again. 'I don't doubt it – your father taught you how to pick your battles, and you're smart enough to know when you're outmatched. Fortunately for you, I don't want to fight either. I'd rather not dishonour my mother's memory by spilling the blood of her kin. So why don't we all just turn around and walk away?'

'We can't let you do that,' said Faolin gravely. 'Not when you've betrayed our secrets to our enemies. We will find the Darkling, with or without your help, but either way, it is going to die. Even if it wasn't in our blood to kill it, it's too dangerous to be left alive with all the knowledge you've given it.'

Théon smiled, a dark and bitter thing. 'You mean *I* am too dangerous to be left alive.'

The Dragon at least had the good grace not to deny it. 'Only if you give us reason not to trust you, cousin.'

'And choosing my freedom over my idiot sister gives you pause, is that it?' she purred. 'I don't think you're in any position to talk about sibling loyalty, Faolin. I'm not the one trying to usurp my sister's throne.'

'Don't start,' he snarled. 'Resari is bastard-born. The clans wouldn't follow her even if she wasn't a Ni—'

Théon cut him off with a warning growl. 'She did what was necessary. As I am doing now.' She loosed a Casting, a howling wind screaming past her and shoving the Dragons down. Then she spun on her heel – even as they roared and Changed – and looked him straight in the eye. 'Run.'

And though it went against every instinct, he did as he was bid.

CHAPTER THIRTY-TWO

The cabin was tiny. Renila glanced around as she entered. A fire burned in the hearth, a solitary armchair in front of it. There was a table with two chairs, but only one bed – if you could call it that. It would be barely large enough to accommodate someone as tall and broad as Alvar. The ceiling was so low he had to stoop. He heaved a resigned sigh as he pushed his way inside, dumping his pack by the door. Renila followed him, her heart in her throat.

'Close the door,' he ordered. She did as she was bid but hovered anxiously while he pulled the wet cloak from his shoulders and hung it on a peg in the corner. His hands were mesmerising as he divested himself of his sword belt, long fingers sure and strong. She could only watch in awe while he removed the dozen daggers he had hidden about his person with lethal precision. He'd washed his hands of the Darkling blood, but his shirt was still soaked with it. Without realising what she was doing, Renila removed her own cloak and began rummaging in his pack for clean clothes. She found a shirt and handed it to him with trembling hands, all too aware of the vast expanse of his bare chest as he tossed the bloody shirt on the floor.

'Look at me,' he demanded, his voice near guttural. Still shaking, she inhaled and raised her eyes to meet his.

The storm was building. She could see it churning beneath his skin. Outside, the winds were rising, and rain lashed against the tiny window. His bloody shirt lay discarded on the floor, the clean one in his hand forgotten as he watched her with predatory intent. Try as she might, Renila couldn't help herself. She shivered in the force of his gaze. Her blood heated in her veins as she watched the muscles of his chest shift and tense with his breathing. Her body was aching for him, as if it knew beyond any doubt they were meant to be together, even though her heart screamed at the betrayal of Farran.

'How do I know you?' she asked. The words came out sharper than she'd intended, but she was so tired of suffering.

Those thunderstorm eyes shuttered, and he pulled the shirt over his head, the spell broken. 'As I said – you were brought to me for shelter.'

'But that's not all of it, is it?'

'No.'

It was going to be like that then. Right. 'Will you treat with me, Alvar Darkstorm, Prince of Immortals?'

Alvar eyed her with all the caution with which one approaches a live snake. 'What do you want?'

'Answers.'

He scowled. 'I can't tell you everything you want to know.'

'Then I'll settle for honesty. Tell me what you can, but promise you won't ever lie to me,' she demanded.

'I've never lied to you a day in your life. I'm not about to start now,' he told her, his lips twisting with the ghost of a smile. 'What do you offer in return?'

She hesitated. What did she have to offer that he would want? No, that was the wrong question, she realised. The question was, was she prepared to give him what he desired? Only one way to find out. 'Me.'

He blinked, then grinned, crossing the tiny space between them in two steps. He placed his hands on the wall either side of her head and crowded her back against the door, his eyes glinting with menace and mischief. 'Are you a whore now, Renila? Offering your body to get what you want?'

Her breath caught in her throat, and though she felt afraid, it was not the only feeling coursing through her veins. He was close, yes, but he hadn't so much as laid a finger on her – as if he didn't presume to touch her without her permission.

'It's the only thing I have that you want,' she breathed, unable to keep the tremor from her voice. She wished she sounded stronger. He chuckled, leaning in as if to kiss her throat, though once more, he stopped himself short. She gasped at the warm breath that caressed the sensitive skin, part of her desperate to pull away and another part longing to feel it again. But she held firm, even as her body quaked with fear. She wanted answers. Ignorance had only seen her ripped from her home, her son and all that she loved. Alvar pulled back, his face inches from hers while he considered her with those thundercloud eyes.

'If I wanted you, Renila,' he murmured, 'I would want you warm and willing, not shaking like a mortal virgin facing the marriage bed. And certainly not selling yourself to me to extract a promise.' He straightened, giving her space to breathe. 'You want my word? You have it. I ask for nothing in return.'

Then he was gone, retreating to the other side of the room. She closed her eyes and stifled a gasp – whether of relief or disappointment, she wasn't sure. The cold air that rushed in around her only heightened her awareness of his absence, and part of her cried out for the warmth that had radiated from his body. She shuddered and took a deep gulp of air before opening her eyes. Alvar was leaning against the wall across the room, arms folded over his chest, waiting expectantly. She pulled a blanket from her pack and wrapped it around her shoulders for warmth, before sitting at the table. His gaze was impassive, though she could see the muscles rippling along the edge of his jaw as he clenched his teeth. Thunder rumbled in the distance, but Renila did not feel afraid.

She held up the necklace, the bird-shaped pendant. Best to start with something simple. 'What is this?'

'A talisman – a spell, a glamour, to hide your power.'

'My power?'

He nodded. 'You know the stories. Graced magic is revealed by heaven's light.'

'So those stories I told the children … they were all real?'

He nodded again. 'Embellished and overwrought in places, but the Old Tales are grounded in truth.'

She took a deep breath. So much for the straightforward questions.

'Who am I?' she asked, her voice quiet but firm.

'Renila Blackfire,' he said. She waited for him to explain. 'It's another Immortal House – like Darkstorm or Brightstar.'

'But I'm not Immortal?'

He hesitated. 'No. When you were brought to me, I needed a way to hide you. The Blackfire claimed you as her own, so you might be protected as any Immortal child would be. It would have raised too many questions if I had done it myself.'

She didn't stop to let that sink in. Not when she still needed answers. 'So the story Arian told is a lie – I'm not some orphan foundling, claimed by Kalielle and smuggled out of Elucion during the Fall?'

'No.'

'But you know where I come from?'

'I cannot speak of it. I swore that I would take that knowledge to my grave. As I told Arian, my oath would kill me before I could even utter the words – not even my Immortality would save me. All I can tell you is that your parents loved you very much and that giving you up was the hardest thing either of them ever did. You were only a week old when you were brought to my city, when your father begged me to shelter you.'

'And when was that?'

She didn't miss the tightening of his mouth as he battled with himself over his response. 'A little over a hundred years ago.'

Renila exhaled slowly through her nose, trying to calm the racing of her heart.

'Are you going to tell me the truth?'

He didn't even blink. 'No.'

'But you didn't hesitate to tell Arian – didn't hesitate to have her lie for you. Why trust her, but not me?'

He held her gaze. 'There is no lie I could tell Arian regarding your heritage that she would believe. She alone survived the slaughter of Elucion, and she knows that. But it also makes her the only person alive today who could weave a convincing tale about you that others would believe. And the fewer who know the truth, the safer you are. It has nothing to do with trust, Renila, and everything to do with necessity.'

'But it is unnecessary for me to know?' she demanded.

His eyes shadowed with something akin to regret. 'Even if I could tell you all of it, the knowledge would be a cross I do not wish you to ever bear.'

She sighed and shook her head in exasperation. She shouldn't have been surprised that he was making things so difficult. He was the most stubborn man she'd ever had the misfortune to meet.

'Alright,' she said, folding her arms across her chest, 'what about us? What were we to each other?'

He scowled and looked away. After what felt like an age, he spoke. 'We were ... romantically involved.'

She'd gathered as much. 'But you're married.'

'Gaelan and I haven't lived as man and wife for centuries.' He kept his gaze on the door, but she could see how difficult it was for him to speak of such things. 'What happened between she and I was nothing to do with you, and I won't burden you with the weight of it.'

'I would carry it gladly, if it meant that you might walk through life a little lighter,' she heard herself saying. Gods only knew why. Still, he huffed a reluctant laugh and looked at her. There was a tenderness in his eyes that wasn't there before, as though her words stirred some cherished memory inside him.

'You carry enough,' he murmured.

She blinked back the tears that rose unbidden to her eyes and scrambled to turn the conversation away from such inexplicable emotions. 'You don't bother with "till death do us part" then?'

Alvar snorted. 'When you live forever, you learn not to make promises like that. Immortal marriage is a somewhat more fluid union than it is with those doomed to die. It's not uncommon for marriages to be dissolved. People change. It's unreasonable to bind them together forever and expect them to be happy. My people are many things, but we renounced such cruelties a long time ago.'

'So why have you and Gaelan stayed together?'

He rubbed the back of his neck in a nervous gesture that was surprisingly endearing. 'Honestly? It was the only way I could protect her. Gaelan has done some rather ... questionable things in her life. There are plenty who would see her punished for her actions. My father is one, but so long as we're wed, he'll fight for her rather than against her. He's well respected and has considerable influence amongst my people. So long as he stands by her, she's safe.'

'So you still care about her?'

'She's been by my side for more than a thousand years, my wife for more than half that, the mother of my child—' he said, breaking off. He took a deep breath before continuing. 'Of course I care about her. But it's complicated. Sephiron's Rebellion broke us both, and when we were remade, we no longer fitted together the same way. Too much has happened between us for things to go back to the way they were before. There are some things that cannot be forgiven, some things that never should.'

Renila was moved by his confession, but she hadn't missed his slip. Child. As in singular. 'Suriya and Lucan aren't your children then?'

He shook his head ruefully, as if knowing she wouldn't have failed to note his mistake. 'No. We had a daughter, but she was taken from us a long time ago now. Losing her was one of the things that drove Gaelan and I apart. The twins were given into Gaelan's care by one no longer able to care for them.'

'You know who their parents are?'

'Their mother, yes. But she refused to speak of their father – other than to assure us it wasn't a Shade. She was willing to give her life to keep their heritage, their existence, a secret. She wouldn't even allow a midwife to help with the birth. I pulled them both from her womb myself. There was only one other person present in the room that day. The three of us were the only people who ever knew the bloodline from which they hail. We vowed to take that knowledge to the grave.'

'Who was the third?'

'A friend.'

'My friend or yours?'

'Is it so strange to consider they might be both?'

'So you won't tell me who their mother is?'

'No,' he conceded. 'It's better that way. You can't reveal something you don't know.'

Renila felt her chest tighten with apprehension. 'It's that important to keep the knowledge secret?'

Alvar nodded. 'Their lives might depend on it.'

They drifted into silence as the gravity of his words sank in. Renila stared unseeing at her hands folded in her lap. She worried about the twins – how could she not? They were just children, lost and alone in the world, with only Gaelan to guide and protect them.

'And what about Erion?' she asked. 'Where does he fit into all of this?'

Alvar tensed, shifting his weight as if repressing the urge to bolt. His eyes had taken on a wild cast, but when he spoke, his voice was calm. 'I'm afraid I know very little about your son or where he comes from.'

'But you suspect a great deal,' she said, voicing unspoken words. It didn't take a genius to piece together all that she had overheard that night, and she was far from stupid. But she wanted to hear it from him. His expression was pained as he shrugged.

'I can make some educated guesses,' he admitted, 'but I can't prove any of them, and I won't give voice to an unsubstantiated claim. The risks, to myself and others, are too high if I'm wrong. Not even Gaelan knew everything. I'm afraid that, until you get your memories back, Erion's exact origin will remain a mystery, as will the reason you hid him away from the world.'

Renila blinked. 'What do you mean, get them back?'

Alvar pulled a face. 'We live in a world of magic,' he said. 'Almost anything is possible.' Renila didn't bother to push him on such a vague answer, sensing that this was likely one of those things that he wouldn't tell her – whatever his reasons. But she was far from done.

'You said we were romantically involved,' she observed, trying to ignore how her cheeks heated at the thought. 'Is magic why my body seems to remember your touch, even though my mind does not?'

She could see him fighting the wicked smile that rose to his lips, and even though he kept a straight face, his thundercloud eyes twinkled with mischief. 'Not particularly. You could walk and talk without having to relearn the skills, yes?' She nodded. 'Your body remembers things that your mind forgets. You think of them as instincts, but they're just the memories of your flesh. Your body remembers that which brings it pain, brings it pleasure, even if your mind does not.'

'And did you bring me pain or pleasure?' she asked, her spine straightening with the challenge. 'I don't know whether to kill you or kiss you, Alvar Darkstorm, Prince of Immortals – so which is it?'

He stilled, his ancient eyes wary yet hopeful while he considered her. 'No doubt I brought you both over the years,' he conceded. He hesitated. 'I could show you …' He trailed off, looking at his feet. Renila had to fight the impulse to laugh. He looked so much like a shy schoolboy anticipating a scolding. And yet, part of her wanted to go to him, to cradle his head to her chest and murmur soft assurances in his ear.

'Show me what?' she enquired, keeping her tone light. He said nothing for a while, staring at the ground as he wrestled with some internal battle. After what seemed like an age, he raised his glorious eyes to meet hers.

'You have no memories of your life before Gaelan's castle, of our time together,' he murmured, 'but I have plenty. I could share my memories with you – give back some of what you have lost. They will not tell you all, for mine is only one side of our tale, but perhaps they can offer you another piece of the puzzle you wish to solve.'

His eyes were wide, and Renila could see how much it cost him to offer such a fragile piece of himself. If she spoke the wrong words, she might break him. They both knew it. And yet, he did not baulk at the prospect. He was willing to risk whatever pain she might yet inflict in the slim hope that part of her remembered and trusted him. She realised then how much he cared for her. That she alone had the power to break this man, this Immortal god, with something as simple as her regard for him. That he would not only offer her the sword with which to end him but place the blade at his own throat and hold it steady so she couldn't miss. This was a man who would walk through fire, face nightmares, fight darkness itself for her. She could not refuse him.

'Show me,' she murmured.

They knelt facing each other on the floor, foreheads touching as he cupped her face in his hands. His fingers rested on her temples while his thumbs brushed her cheekbones. His breath tickled her chin, and she could almost hear the echo of his heartbeat in her ears. He murmured now and then, his words so soft and disjointed that they were incomprehensible. The memories came in flashes, stuttering and incoherent at first, but slowly, the picture emerged.

A man with hair as black as night and eyes to match cradled a baby in his arms, glaring at the men and women before him. He was furious, spitting with rage as he cursed their people with all manner of obscenities. The Darkstorm – his father – bristled at the insult, but Alvar found himself moving. The words rose unbidden to his lips, an oath of fealty – once spoken, unbreakable. Not even his Immortal soul would save him if he reneged on such a promise. The man handed the infant to him, the hesitation and reluctance clear in those dark eyes. But Alvar barely noticed. His gaze was drawn to the child – to the shock of wine-red hair, and the pair of bright amber eyes smiling impishly up at him.

'Her name is Renila,' the man said. 'Treat her well or you answer to me.'

The image changed.

He watched from the shadows as two figures approached a grand building on the edge of a fairy-tale city. White marble glowing, the lagoon beyond glittering with the silver moonlight. It was not long past midnight, the stars glinting in the sky overhead. It was a good omen, Alvar told himself. He felt safer when the stars shone bright. A petite, ebony-haired woman held the infant Renila in her arms, accompanied by a man with fox-red hair and dark amber eyes. They hesitated on the threshold, glancing over their shoulders just once before they continued, disappearing through the great doors. Alvar murmured a soft prayer before slipping back into the night.

Renila felt as though the ground lurched beneath her as the memory shifted once more.

A toddler with burgundy hair, racing on chubby legs across the room as she chased after a long-suffering cat. The Mother tutting in frustration, cursing the wildness of her charge; Alvar chuckling to himself.

A girl, a little over five, with mischievous amber eyes trying her hardest to look contrite as she received a scolding. He didn't ask about her infraction. He wasn't supposed to care. None of the Guardians at the Academy were.

A hellion, just over ten, refusing to cry despite the beating she must have taken for her face to be so bruised. It must have been inflicted by other students – no Guardian would ever hurt a child like that. He fought the fury rising in his blood as he asked her who had hurt her. But she held her tongue, too afraid to speak out. He found them anyway. Not one would ever graduate.

A young woman, hiding in the library, her amber eyes no longer full of mirth and mischief but weary from the fight. He kept his distance. He could never show preferential treatment.

A woman grown, hair unbound and snapping like flames around her head as it stirred in the evening breeze, eyes glowing in the dying light of the sun. None could mistake what she was. She threw the truth of her existence into their teeth, for

383

none could hurt her now. She was no longer an Aspirant, she was a Graduate –
entitled to Immortality as much as anyone born of the bloodlines.

They walked together on the beach while Alvar explained her history. As much
as he could. She said very little, but as he spoke, she stepped a little lighter – as
though he lightened her burden with each word. She smiled and thanked him for
his kindness. He offered her his home and his protection, such as it was, and she
kissed him upon the cheek in gratitude.

Then the visions grew clearer.

Alvar stood in the centre of the training ring, arms folded across his chest and
smirking, watching a woman with scarlet hair and fiery amber eyes storm towards
him. Renila. And she was furious. But before she could start what was doubtless a
well-rehearsed tirade, he threw a sparring sword at her. She caught it and scowled
at him.

'Training begins at dawn,' he told her. 'If you're late again, I'll make you suffer
for it.'

'I don't need to train,' she snarled. 'We learned plenty in the Academy.'

He struck, driving at her with his inhuman speed and strength – the only part
of his Immortal grace left untouched by that wretched curse. Her eyes widened
with shock, and she leapt back, trying to parry. She was quick, he'd give her that.
She put up a good fight, but it was far too easy for him to send her sprawling on
her arse in the dirt. He looked down at her, fighting not to laugh at the outrage on
her lovely face.

'None of the Guardians at the Academy were alive during the Rebellion,' he
said. 'They know the theory, and they can teach discipline and control, but none of
them know how to harness the rage of battle. None of them have ever looked death
in the eye and fought for their lives.'

'You're Immortal,' she objected, struggling to her feet. 'Death is voluntary.'

'You, however, are not Immortal,' he noted, not bothering to correct her. The
Rebellion had redefined what it meant to be Immortal – but that was a secret few
were aware of. Outside the Council, only those who had survived the Rebellion
would ever know the truth. 'I made the blood-oath to protect you from harm,
Renila. Death will not be voluntary for me if I break it. So you'll train with me
until I'm happy that you're at a level where you can defend yourself against
anything that comes your way. And then we'll train every day after that, so I can
be sure you don't forget. My life depends on it as much as yours.'

She scowled but said nothing, settling herself into a ready crouch and raising
her sparring sword in invitation. He smiled and struck.

Another shift. Another scene.

They faced each other across the pale sands of the Arena, the colour leached
from the ground by moonlight. The cold air was refreshing, and a slight breeze
stirred his hair about his shoulders. He shivered from the simple pleasure of the
wind kissing his face and smiled to himself. Renila's figure was like a splash of
blood on pristine snow, her scarlet hair shifting in the same wind that caressed his
cheek. Even from this distance, he could see her eyes glowing while she watched
him. Raiden damn him, she was beautiful.

He pushed the thought from his mind and gestured for her to begin. The air
around her crackled to life as flames licked along her tawny skin, surrounding her

in a fiery aura. He blinked in surprise. The power radiating off her was enormous. He'd never seen its like outside of the Houses. She saw the shock on his face, and her exquisite face cracked into a wicked grin as she realised that here she would not be so easily outmatched. And at the sight of that ferocious glint in her amber eyes, his breath caught in his throat. After all this time ... had he at last found a kindred spirit? Another wild, untameable soul who would not flinch in the face of the storm? For the first time in a long time, he felt a glimmer of hope.

And again.

They sat in complete silence, staring at each other as they tried to break into each other's mind while defending their own. They'd been at it for hours. Too evenly matched for either to gain the upper hand long enough to break through. He'd never admit it, but he was impressed. It had taken him millennia to learn the composure and control he exerted. She wasn't even eighty years old. Her mind was a fortress. He'd tried everything he could think of, from distracting her with one thought while trying to sneak in with another to bringing all his might to bear, bombarding her defences, hoping somewhere a crack would appear. None had. Sometimes it had taken all his strength to keep her out. She was a tenacious and cunning adversary.

They were both exhausted now, but each too proud to admit defeat. Their attacks were half-hearted, requiring very little effort, and he found his attention wandering as he drank in the sight of her. They sat by the fire, and he could see the flush across her golden cheeks from its warmth. The light danced over her scarlet hair, breathing life into it as it surrounded her beautiful face like living flame. Her lips were parted, and she had her tongue caught between her teeth in concentration. Her eyes were distant, but they glowed like miniature suns. Then they focussed on his face, and she smiled triumphantly. His attention snapped back to his defences, inspecting them. He frowned in confusion. There was nothing wrong, no crack that he could see, no sense of her in his mind. Why then was she grinning with her victory?

She moved faster than anything he'd ever seen. One moment she was sitting across from him, flush with success. The next she was in his lap, her hands dragging his face to hers and her lips crushing against his. Her breasts pillowed against his chest, and his stomach clenched in anticipation as she claimed his mouth. Raiden help him. The woman knew how to kiss. She scattered his thoughts with her lips, her hands holding him tight so he could not escape. Not that he wanted to.

She chuckled against his mouth, stroking an invisible hand over his mind. She'd breached his defences. He cursed in surprise, pushing her off him as he recoiled. She'd won. She'd fucking won. His mental walls slammed down, but the damage was done. She was inside now, able to wreak whatever havoc she wanted.

'You cheated,' he said, wiping his mouth on the back of his sleeve.

She grinned the feral grin of the fox who had just broken into the henhouse. 'There are no rules when it comes to life and death,' she breathed. 'You taught me that.'

'Get out,' he snarled, trying to extricate her from the inner workings of his mind. She didn't budge, but nor did she delve any deeper. Instead, she stood and prowled closer. Alvar backed away, afraid for perhaps the first time in his life. This wasn't right. She was his charge, not his lover. His back hit the wall, and he threw up his hands to ward her away. She stopped, just out of reach, and he breathed a sigh of relief.

She smirked. 'What's wrong? I thought you were enjoying yourself?'

'Only because you manipulated my mind into thinking I was enjoying myself,' he challenged.

She grinned again and edged closer. 'Would you believe me if I told you I had nothing to do with it?' she purred.

He scowled. 'Unlikely.'

'Alright,' she conceded with a chuckle. 'I might have escalated things slightly. But all I did was exploit a weakness.'

He opened his mouth to argue, but there was an edge of bitterness in her voice that stopped him in his tracks. He reached out and cupped her face. There was no point denying it now. She was in his head – could read the truth in his thoughts. 'Loving you is not a weakness,' he assured her. 'You give me strength when I am on my knees, shine a light into my darkness ... I would have been lost long ago without you in my life.'

She smiled, dashing the tears from her eyes. 'And I thought you just wanted my body,' she said, trying to hide how his words had affected her behind that fiery bravado.

It was his turn to smirk. 'Well ... not just your body,' he promised. And with that, he kissed her.

The scene switched, and her cheeks heated at the feelings rising in response.

Bodies tangled together in the sheets, skin against skin, they explored every inch of each other. She dragged a groan from his lips as she ran her hands over him and kissed him until he forgot his own name. It was only much later when, in her pleasure, she screamed it out loud that he remembered.

The scenes blurred together once more, as Alvar lost himself in his memories.

A picnic in the meadow – he fed her strawberries from his hand. She flicked her tongue over his fingers, drawing one deep into her mouth. He groaned and kissed her, covering her body with his while they lay together beneath the sun.

They danced together at a ball, finer than any fairy tale. Her gown, cream velvet and embroidered with gold, swirled around her as they spun across the floor. His father looked on in disapproval. He couldn't have cared less. She led him to the edge of the dance floor, spinning them out into the gardens. They danced together beneath the moonlight, drinking in the sight of each other.

They sat in his library in front of the fire, she in the chair and he on the floor at her feet. His head rested against her legs, and she ran her slender fingers through his hair while she read aloud to him. He'd never been so content.

They sparred together, greeting the dawn. Her chest heaved from the effort, her face flushed from the exertion. They came together, swords locked, and he couldn't stop himself from kissing her. She dropped the sword, throwing her arms around his neck as they collapsed to the ground in a heap.

They walked together, hand in hand, through the market. She looked lovely, her cheeks still rosy from their lovemaking earlier that morning. He'd had her twice since *sunrise, but he wanted her again. She was like fine wine – once he'd tasted her, he only ever wanted more. She sensed the desire heating in his blood and glanced over her shoulder at him with a wicked smile on her lips and a mischievous glint in her eyes. Before he knew it, she'd dragged him down a side street and was kissing him senseless. He lifted her up, wrapping her legs around his waist and bunching her skirts about her hips. She moaned at his touch, burying her head in the crook of his neck to silence herself while he took her against the wall. His own climax almost brought him to his knees, and she covered his mouth with her own, swallowing his roar of pleasure.*

Renila jerked out of the memory, breathing deep to slow her racing heart. But Alvar dragged her back under.

'I love you,' her voice whispered in the darkness. *'Nothing will ever change that.'*

Alvar smiled sleepily. 'I know.'

'No matter what, promise me you'll never question that. Promise you'll always remember this moment, no matter how dark things get, and know that I love you more than anything in the entire world.'

'I promise,' he murmured, pulling her body against his as he kissed her into insensibility. *She melted against him, yielding to him completely.*

Renila pulled back, scrambling away from him as tears flooded her eyes. She had sensed the bitterness with which he recalled the memory, but more than that – she remembered the pain it had caused her. She didn't understand why, but speaking those words had been like driving a knife into her own heart.

'Those were the last words you ever spoke to me,' he said in a dead voice, unable to meet her gaze. 'When I woke in the morning, you were gone.' She pressed a hand against her mouth, unable to find the words to comfort him. He heaved a great sigh and looked up at her. 'Now you know.' She shook her head, unable to speak. What agony had she caused this man, this beautiful, brave man who had given so much for her? But there was no reproach in his eyes, only his own guilt for whatever he had done to push her away. 'You should get some sleep.'

With that he stood and strode from the room.

When Renila found the courage to leave the cabin, she found Arian and Ornak had returned. Arian had built up a campfire, having deemed the paltry hearth within insufficient, and was now raiding Ornak's pack – though for what was a mystery. The tattooed man sighed in exasperation at the liberties she took with his possessions, but he said nothing. Instead, he took her bow and arrow from where she'd dumped them by the door and disappeared off into the mountains. An hour later he returned with the carcass of a young buck slung over his shoulder.

'It's a bit skinny,' Arian observed.

Ornak's grin was feral.

'Perhaps you'd prefer to go hungry?' he suggested.

She smiled sweetly, but her eyes flashed in warning. 'That's the point. I've seen your appetite and that won't feed all of us.'

'Have a little faith,' the big man said, handing her a knife. 'Now make yourself useful while I get started on supper.' Arian scowled and did as she was bid, flashing a grateful smile at Alvar when the Immortal offered to help her skinning the poor beast. It didn't take long for the meal to come together and before she knew it, the smell coming from Ornak's cooking pot had Renila's stomach growling in protest. She was starving. Ornak chuckled and handed her a rough oatcake to tide her over.

'Thank you,' she murmured, nibbling on the edge while she studied him. 'Who are you?'

His eyebrows quirked upward. 'My name is Ornak – I'm a friend of Arian's.'

'That's one way of putting it,' Arian muttered, picking dried blood out from under her nails with the tip of her dagger.

'We were children together,' he clarified. 'I served Kah Thoran – High Chieftain of Ciaron, leader of all Dragons.'

Renila glanced at his tattoos. 'Is that what those are? Dragon-marks?'

Ornak nodded, flexing an arm so they caught the light. 'Youngest son of the Hal Chieftain, but the only one born into the clan. My brothers are all Az Clan, like their mother.' Renila stayed silent, unsure what to make of that pronouncement – understanding neither what it meant nor why it had caused Ornak's gaze to shutter. Arian seemed to notice his disquiet and kicked him in the shin. He shook himself with a snort and continued. 'Arian was raised by Kalielle Half-Elven. She and Thoran were lovers for a time – they had a child together, so even when they broke with each other, we still spent a lot of time together.'

Renila glanced over at the Phoenix, not daring to meet Ornak's eye any longer. 'So you're Kalielle's daughter?'

'Adopted daughter,' she explained without looking up. But there was no hiding the pain in her voice. 'I was a foundling, probably an orphan. Kalielle's daughter was about my age, so she took me in. I stayed with her even when Thoran took Resari to live with him in Ciaron.'

'Ciaron was a better place for her, and Thoran was always kinder than Kalielle anyway,' said Ornak. 'Not that it matters. They're both gone now anyway.' Renila's eyes narrowed, her memory stirring at the mention of that name. But it made no sense. Resari was gone. Just like Kalielle and Kah Thoran and all those other names of myth and legend.

'What happened?' asked Renila.

'The Fall. The day the Graced were brought to their knees, slaughtered in their thousands by the Shade King and his armies. There were survivors, but they were few and far between.'

'We're hunted,' Ornak said. 'We've been hunted every day since the Fall. Darklings want our power, to steal our life-force for themselves. Night-walkers want to sell us to the highest bidder. The Gods only know what the Shade are after, but I can guarantee you it's not good.'

Arian scowled at him and settled on a rock across from Renila. 'Don't frighten her,' she admonished. 'Darklings are strong and fast, but so are we. Nightwalkers are many, but they're weakened by their curse. The Shade are powerful, but they're not Immortal. Not like us.'

Renila nodded in understanding and finished her food in silence. The sun was long since set, and though the night closed in around them, their camp was flooded with moonlight. She wondered if that was perhaps deliberate. The chilly night air had her shivering, so she didn't complain when Alvar offered her his cloak for warmth. She moved no closer than that though, unsure what to make of the memories he'd shared. The revelation of who she used to be mingled with the grief of losing Farran, losing Erion, the guilt within her ... She wasn't sure she'd ever make sense of her emotions.

'Will you tell me about them? The Phoenix?' Renila asked, looking to Arian. 'Our people?'

Arian shrugged. 'What do you want to know?'

'Anything. Everything.'

So Arian told her. Stories of fearless warriors riding birds of pure flame into battle. Of a city of glass, warmed by a mountain of fire. Of a proud and noble people who had smiled in the face of death long before they had the power to defy it.

'How does it work?' Renila asked.

'We call it the Rising,' Arian began. 'It doesn't start until your body is burned. Fire isn't necessary, but it's the easiest way – the body has to be destroyed in order for the magic to be released. Once it has, the resurrection begins.

'The Rising is ... it is the best and worst thing you will ever experience. The power flowing through you is euphoric. You're defying death. You feel like a god. But the rest of it ...' She shuddered. 'I've been through about a half-dozen, and the worst ones are always the ones you're not expecting. The moments right before death stay with us through it all. Everything we feel as we die, we feel when we come back – only stronger. Fear, anger, love, hate. All of it.

'You're aware through the entire process. It hurts more than anything you can imagine, and it's ... confusing. The magic doesn't bring back our memories, so most of us use a memory stone,' she explained, touching the blood-red gem adorning her finger. 'It's an ancient magic – one that can survive a Rising – that acts as a repository for memories, for our thoughts and feelings. The things that make us who we are. Everything I am is stored in this stone. So long as I'm wearing it when I Rise, I'll remember everything ... eventually.'

'I used to have one,' said Renila.

Alvar nodded. 'You gave it up, before your last Rising. Gaelan told me. You had a hard labour with Erion; you knew you wouldn't survive, and you wanted to forget everything – forget whatever drove you to her. You gave her the stone, told her to keep it from you so you'd have a fresh start when you Rose again. Then you died. That's why you remember nothing from before Erion's birth.'

'I remember some things.'

Arian was toying with the fire again, her fingers curling and flickering as they mimicked the dancing flames. 'A Riser can walk and talk without having to relearn the skills. A body remembers things that the mind forgets. We think of them as instincts, but they're just a different memory.'

'You said magic meant it might be possible to get my memories back – this is what you meant?'

He nodded again. 'If Gaelan has the stone you wore before your last Rising, you can get those memories back.'

'Looks to me like she took some precautions though,' added Arian, eyeing the pendant in Renila's hands. Renila held it out for the Phoenix woman to inspect. She tapped the ruby eye and nodded. 'Memory stone.'

'Gaelan must have given it to you after your last Rising, just in case,' Alvar breathed with a wry chuckle. 'I might have known.'

'That's no ordinary talisman,' said Arian, studying the bird – the *firebird*. 'It's spelled with more than memories and glamours. There's a shield-casting in here too, even some basic healing magic … and something else.' She recoiled, frowning. 'I've never seen magic like that before.'

Renila blinked. 'Why go to all that trouble if I can't be killed?'

'We're not Immortal,' admitted Arian, still eyeing the talisman uneasily. 'Our bodies weren't designed to contain that much power. The magic required for a Rising is immense. The resurrection alone is confusing, not to mention that much power coursing through your veins. And even with a stone, memory recall isn't instantaneous. The Rising is dangerous … for everyone.'

'There's nothing more deadly on this earth than a Riser,' Ornak murmured. 'Not even the Shade King would dare to face one.'

Arian grunted in agreement. 'Worst of all, magic runs on emotion, and a violent death leads to a violent Rising. That's how Kalielle defeated the Shade Princess Malia. She killed herself in the middle of the battlefield, used the power of her Rising to take Malia with her.'

'A single Phoenix woman, untrained and barely out of girlhood, turned the tide of that war,' said Alvar. 'Imagine what an entire army of them could do.'

'Don't.' Arian cut over him. 'Just don't.'

'What happened to them?' asked Renila.

'The Fall,' Arian sighed, leaning back and looked at the stars above, unwilling to elaborate.

Ornak nudged her. 'Sing for us?'

She smiled softly and did as she was bid. Her voice was rich and throaty, full of hope and wonder. Renila did not understand the words, but she knew a lullaby when she heard one. It wasn't long before she drifted into an uneasy sleep, wishing only for strong arms to hold her through the night.

CHAPTER THIRTY-THREE

Gaelan had stayed remarkably calm. She'd allowed Brer to lead them from the throne room without a fight and been delighted when he'd led them to a suite in one of the soaring towers. She and Brer had then exchanged hurried whispers before he'd left, promising to return as fast as he could.

The rooms were exquisite. Airy and opulent without being ostentatious. Suriya had noted Gaelan's touch in everything from the decor to the artwork, the layout of the rooms and even the soft furnishings. The walls were the same white marble as the rest of the city, but most of them had been covered in the most incredible tapestries and paintings she'd ever seen. A mountain, capped with snow, beneath a night sky littered with stars, a castle of pure starlight perched atop it. A ballroom filled with dancers, their glittering gowns swirling around them like the northern lights.

The windows were framed by curtains of midnight velvet embroidered with silver thread, while silk cushions and white fur throws adorned the plush armchairs and chaise longue. Rich carpets covered the marble floor, and there was even a thick, white, bearskin rug before the fireplace. There was no fire burning in the hearth, but the room wasn't cold. In fact, Gaelan had crossed straight to the full-length windows and thrown them open, before stepping out onto a balcony beyond.

Suriya and Lucan had lingered in the entrance. Her brother had looked around nervously, unsure of where to go, but she hadn't been able to muster the strength to care. There were rooms beyond – bedrooms, a dining room, what looked like a painter's studio – but she couldn't summon the energy to investigate. She didn't know how long they stood there, waiting for Gaelan to remember them. When she returned from the balcony, there was an air of contentment about her Suriya had never seen. She hated her for it. How could she remain so calm after all they had endured?

Gaelan had seemed to sense her rage. Either that or Lucan's anxiety. 'Are you alright?'

Beside her, Lucan nodded, but Suriya said nothing. Didn't even acknowledge the question. She didn't know what she felt beyond exhaustion. Gaelan's gaze lingered on her, but for once, she didn't press.

'What's going on?' Lucan demanded. 'Why does everyone seem so afraid of us? What does she mean, enter the Academy? And who is the Council?'

Gaelan heaved a great sigh, her eyes filled with regret, but Suriya saw no lie in them when she answered. 'There are thirteen great Houses – each one ruled by a single leader, chosen by the rest of the House. The Council consists of those elected representatives – a committee that governs what's left of our people.'

'And you're on the Council, aren't you? Is that why they called you Brightstar?'

Gaelan nodded. 'The leader of each House is given the title of Prince or Princess, but we rarely use it. It's more common to refer to us by the name of the House we represent – the Swansinger, the Darkstorm, or in my case, the Brightstar.'

'And Brer is the Crown Prince of Shadowfox.' It wasn't a question.

Gaelan answered it anyway. 'It has become something of a custom to nominate an heir after a certain length of time on the throne, though the succession must still be ratified by general election. Brer's father, Prince Eris, is the current Shadowfox. If anything were to happen to him, Brer would take his place until they could hold the vote, either ratifying his position or choosing his replacement.'

'But Prince Eris is Immortal,' Lucan objected. 'What could possibly happen to him?'

'Just because we are Immortal does not mean that we cannot die. You'll learn more about it in the Academy, but there are none of that first generation of Immortals still living today.'

'And what is the Academy?'

'It is where our children learn control and discipline,' she explained. 'No child is born Immortal, and none can have that power bestowed upon them until they have graduated from the Academy.'

'So they want to make us Immortal?' Lucan asked.

Suriya snorted. 'No, they just want to control us.'

Gaelan's face remained impassive as she leaned back and considered them both. Suriya held her gaze. She was done cowering before this woman.

'I don't have a lot of time to explain all of this,' Gaelan said. 'We don't even have time to eat, bathe or change. Brer has gone to call a Council session and could return any minute. When he does, you must come with me. I don't want you out of my sight until we've got a decision from the Council. Once we enter the chamber, you must stay quiet. No questions, no arguing. Don't speak unless spoken to directly. Do you understand?' They nodded. 'Good. Bringing you here was the best chance I had at keeping you safe, but that security will come at a price – to you and me. It's against our highest laws to bring strangers into our lands – especially people like you.'

'People like us?' asked Lucan.

'She means the Graced,' Suriya supplied, her gaze fixed on Gaelan, challenging her to dispute the claim. She had, after all, once claimed the Graced were only a fairy tale. A bedtime story for children. So many lies. It would be a wonder if the woman could tell the difference between them and reality.

But Gaelan only nodded. 'Yes. My people created your kind as foot soldiers to fight in our war. But your power has surpassed ours, and now many, if not most, of my people fear you far more than they fear the real dangers. Emalia doesn't want to turn you away – she's too curious – but she knows that letting you stay has its challenges. The Academy is her best option. You'll be trained to use your powers, so nobody can argue that you pose a danger, and you'll be out of the public eye. After a couple of months, most people will probably forget about you.'

'But only Immortal children can enter the Academy,' Suriya continued for her, 'and only the Council has the power to grant an exception.'

'Pleased as I am that you've been paying attention and taking everything in,' said Gaelan, 'you should probably learn to keep your observations to yourselves. My people don't like being shown up by those they deem inferior.'

'Maybe your people need to redefine what they perceive as inferior,' Suriya murmured, her voice deadly quiet.

But Gaelan only grinned in response. 'On that matter, you and I are of a similar mind.'

Then there came a sharp rap at the door, and Prince Brer entered without waiting for an invitation.

'They're ready,' he said, his sharp face tense. Gaelan nodded and stood, gesturing for them to follow her. But Brer held up a hand in warning. 'They're not happy, Gaelan. None of them. Emalia won't go against them for you, and I don't hold as much sway with my father as I once did.'

'I'm guessing that marrying Emalia has much to do with that,' Gaelan noted. He winced at the rebuke in her voice but didn't argue. So she set her shoulders and led the way from the room without a word.

That had been half an hour ago. Now they were seated on a pair of low benches in the antechamber of the topmost tower. The climb up the stairs had left Suriya with a sharp pain in her ribs and such a heat in her cheeks she was sure her face was bright red, but Gaelan was unperturbed. She was seated across from them, hands resting in her lap as she stared ahead.

Her composure grated on Suriya. How could she be so calm? And how could she say so much and yet so little at the same time? It rankled her pride to stay quiet. To place her trust in Gaelan. Unquestioning loyalty and blind faith had never sat well with her, but this was something else. The nerve of the woman, to ask it of them. To ask it of her …

She wiped a weary hand across her face. Gods, she was so tired. Yet despite it all, something in her roared for blood. After all she'd given, all she'd sacrificed, she deserved answers. They both did. The only reason she hadn't burned this city down around them was the faint hope that these people would shelter them. Shelter Lucan. There was no price she would not pay for his safety, not even her own pride. So she'd swallow her rage, let them see the scared little girl they expected. And if they turned them away … left Lucan to the wolves … well, Gods help them.

But thoughts of violence were pushed from her mind when Brer appeared at the door and called them in – offering her a wink as he did so.

Gaelan took a deep breath and stood, running an assessing eye over them and giving a reassuring smile. *'You'll be fine,'* she promised, whispering in their minds. *'Just stay close.'*

She turned to the door, and Suriya watched as all compassion faded from her stern gaze. Once more, the terrifying Lady stood before them. Suriya blinked. Had she changed so much that it was a shock to see that heartless woman once more? A glance at Lucan said that he'd seen it too.

But before they could question it, Gaelan swept into the room with all the bearing of a queen, leaving them to follow in her commanding wake. The Council chamber was nowhere near as grand as the throne room downstairs, but it was imposing enough in its own way.

The room was round, with full-length windows covering half of the wall. As with Gaelan's tower, glass doors opened out onto a large balcony and two elegantly dressed men stood outside, their heads bowed together, deep in conversation. Gaelan's lip curled in distaste at the sight of them.

'Princes Nuada and Vanir – the Skyrider and the Wavebreaker. They will not welcome you. One has seen too little of war, the other too much. It was a Princess of Wavebreaker who sheltered most of my people when Sephiron came for us. They paid dearly for that loyalty. Those losses have left them bitter and jaded. And the Skyrider … his House cowered like children, safe on their island while the rest of us bled for their freedom.'

In the middle of the room was a huge, ring-like table with thirteen high-backed chairs – each emblazoned with a different crest – placed around it. The Princess Emalia was already seated beneath her crest of the two intertwined swans, while Prince Brer stood by her right shoulder. To her left was another man, seated beneath a sigil of an eagle with a thunderbolt in its talons. He looked enough like Alvar that Suriya didn't need to ask if they were related. But father or brother? She was inclined towards the former. His face was unlined and his storm-black hair untouched by the silver of old age, but there was an ancient power in his thunderstorm eyes.

'The Darkstorm. Prince Andriel is Alvar's father. He never liked me,' Gaelan noted without regret, confirming Suriya's suspicions. Sure enough, the Darkstorm scowled as his eyes fell upon Gaelan, deepening further when he noted the twins' presence. He opened his mouth, perhaps to object, but

a pointed cough from Prince Brer cut him off. Suriya glanced at Brer, just in time to see him give her another subtle wink. She ignored him.

To Emalia's right was another man, with a wolf-pelt about his shoulders and keen yellow eyes that saw far too much. He gave Gaelan a predatory grin which, to their great surprise, she returned – even blowing him a mocking kiss.

'Tiberus Frostfang,' she said with a smirk. 'He's annoyed with me because I got you through the mountains. His seat, Wolfstone, was on the northern edge of the Whitefangs before the Rebellion. Just a ruin now, although the wards are still strong. He's a hard bastard, but he's fair.'

Gaelan led them left, around the table, making her way to her own chair. Suriya had spotted her starry crest the minute they'd stepped into the room. The Darkstorm would be seated on her right. To her left was another man, seated beneath the sigil of a fox, who must be the ageing father of Prince Brer. The ancient weariness was obvious in his eyes, there for all to see.

'The Shadowfox – Prince Eris. Stay on your guard around him – Brer inherited his cunning from his father, but any compassion he has he got from his mother. And don't be deceived. Like any animal that's old and weak, he's even more dangerous for it because he has nothing to lose.'

The three chairs beside him were empty. One bore the crest of a dove, carrying a branch of thorns, another was a white stag and the last an armoured bear. It wasn't hard to figure out which of the three people standing on the periphery of the room belonged in which seat. There was a man dressed all in white with a crown of antlers upon his head and a woman, dressed in an exquisite grey gown with a skirt of feathers. They spoke to a woman wearing a dress of iron chain mail, with an armour-plated bodice.

'Prince Herne and Princesses Colma and Artianna – the Whitehart, the Dovethorn and the Ironclaw. I knew Prince Herne's mother very well. She was a good friend to both Alvar and myself, but she died during the Rebellion.' Gaelan's voice broke off, but she couldn't stop the overwhelming sense of loss from seeping through the linking of their minds. 'He was only a boy – not even graduated from the Academy. I think if she'd lived longer, he might have become a great man. But her loss broke him.'

As they passed behind one of the seats nearest the door, a woman rose and stepped into their path. She was petite – at least a head shorter than Gaelan, with a slight, compact figure that reminded Suriya of the hawks she used to see soaring over the castle. Her skin was a glowing golden colour, her hair coal-black, and her eyes dark and smouldering like embers. Despite her somewhat grave expression, she opened her arms in offering and laughed with relief as Gaelan embraced her.

'Endellion!' Gaelan exclaimed, hugging the smaller woman to her. 'Gods, it's been too long!' Endellion laughed again and returned the fierce embrace.

'And whose fault is that?' snapped another voice behind them. They turned to see another woman standing waiting, arms held out expectantly.

She was taller than Endellion, though not as tall as the statuesque Gaelan, with pale hair, pale eyes and skin the colour of bone. Gaelan laughed and threw herself into the outstretched arms.

'Anwyn!' she cried. The woman rolled her eyes in exasperation and gave Endellion a long-suffering look before they crushed Gaelan between them, laughing all the while. Finally, they stepped back, though they kept their hands linked.

Then Endellion's gaze drifted over Gaelan's shoulder and landed on Suriya. She held the gaze, too tired to care. Endellion frowned and exchanged a long look with Anwyn, before stepping around Gaelan and stretching out a hand to Suriya.

Suriya forced herself not to flinch when the Immortal woman's hand cupped her chin. But unlike Emalia's cool touch, Endellion's fingers were warm and firm as she stared right into Suriya's soul.

'Suriya, Lucan,' Gaelan said, her voice steady despite the uncertainty in her eyes. 'This is Endellion, Princess of Blackfire,' she explained, 'and Anwyn, Princess of Mistfury.'

Endellion stepped back, releasing her grip, and Suriya's eyes slid to Anwyn. Unlike the other women in the room, she wore trousers and a tunic. While finely made, they were simple, practical garments – more appropriate for an afternoon of hard labour than speaking with Princes. Three hounds appeared at Anwyn's heels, all massive and black with gleaming red eyes. Suriya flinched back, though nobody else seemed perturbed by the vicious-looking dogs. Gaelan even scratched one between the ears.

'An honour to meet you, Suriya and Lucan,' Endellion murmured, inclining her head. From across the room, there was a snort of disagreement. The strange tenderness in Endellion's mysterious gaze vanished as she turned on the spot to face the source.

The Princes Vanir and Nuada had returned from the balcony to reclaim their seats and were now watching the reunion with disgust. Anwyn placed herself between the twins and the two Princes, folding her arms over her chest while her dogs growled in warning. Further round the table, Prince Tiberus's wolfish grin broadened, and he leaned back in his chair with the air of a man about to watch something entertaining.

Prince Andriel's voice cut in. 'Save your breath, Mistfury. We've heard it all before.' Suriya glanced round to see him staring at her, but his thunder-cloud eyes slid away as if she were little more than a speck of dust on the floor. Instead, his attention lingered on Prince Vanir. 'Manners cost you nothing, Wavebreaker. If you think it's appropriate to insult a pair of homeless, desperate children then I question how you graduated the Academy, let alone deserve a seat on this Council.'

Prince Vanir flushed with embarrassment and opened his mouth to reply, but Anwyn let out a loud bark of laughter and spoke over him. 'There's that famous Darkstorm temper,' she crooned. Then she glanced back at Gaelan. 'I knew there was a reason I'd missed you. He's such a bore without you here to rile him up.'

'Shut up,' the Darkstorm snapped. Anwyn only snorted again and moved to take her seat between Prince Vanir and Prince Tiberus. As she dropped into her chair, the hounds gathering at her feet, she offered the former a hiss of contempt and the latter a mischievous wink. Likewise, Endellion slid back into her chair beside Prince Nuada without deigning to acknowledge him, instead making a great show of examining her nails. The three seats to the left of Prince Eris were now filled. But as Gaelan moved to take her seat, Suriya realised there was still one empty chair between Endellion and Vanir. Opposite Gaelan.

The sigil was a raven in flight, though it looked as though someone had slashed across it with a knife. There was enough dust gathered on it for Suriya to know that it had not been used in a very long time. And although none seemed perturbed by its presence, nobody would look at it. Endellion and Vanir even seemed to lean away from it.

'The last person to sit in that chair was Sephiron, Prince of Ravenscar,' Gaelan whispered into their minds. *'He was the last of his House. We leave the seat there as a reminder ... and a warning to not repeat our past mistakes.'*

Suriya studied Gaelan's expression surreptitiously, and something about it told her the placement of that chair was not accidental. Not when that same crest had adorned the hidden door in the castle. Whatever her history with the legendary Dark Prince, someone on the Council did not want Gaelan to forget it. But Suriya did not have time to think on it more, as Prince Tiberus cleared his throat.

'Alright, Brightstar,' he growled, leaning back in his chair. 'You called this meeting. What do you want?'

Gaelan opened her mouth to respond, but Prince Vanir spoke over her. 'I think a better question would be where has she been for the last century? And why has she deigned to return after all this time? I find it remarkable that she disappears for so long and then has the nerve to show up on our doorstep demanding our aid.'

'Nobody asked for your opinion,' Anwyn snapped. 'You've made an ass of yourself once already today, and we've only been in here for five minutes. You should pace yourself better.'

'The Wavebreaker's questions are valid,' objected Prince Nuada. 'I, for one, am most curious to know what the Brightstar has been up to all these years.'

'The Brightstar's business is her own,' Endellion spat. 'How would you like it if I were to pry into your private affairs?'

'I'm not the one who brought down a curse upon her own people,' Prince Nuada hissed. 'How do we know she's not here to bring more death and destruction down on us?'

Gaelan did not so much as flinch at the accusation, but Suriya could see the tension in the set of her shoulders. Even Prince Andriel offered her a sympathetic grimace before rounding on the Skyrider.

'The Blackfire is correct,' he interjected, cutting off the argument. 'This Council was founded on mutual trust and respect and, most importantly,

397

equality. If we are to demand knowledge of the Brightstar's movements over the last century, then we too must share our own.'

'I have nothing to hide,' bristled Nuada, getting to his feet – though the ruddy flush to his pale face said otherwise.

'Perhaps not, but I'm not sure any of us want to hear it,' Emalia said in a bored voice. 'This is my city, and I have afforded the Brightstar – and the two children in her care – safe passage to attend this Council meeting. I would not have done so without ascertaining her loyalties and motivations, so unless you are suggesting that I would knowingly and willingly put my own people at risk or that I am so unwitting as to allow someone who would do us harm into my city, perhaps you should shut up and sit down.'

Behind her, Brer grinned, amber eyes twinkling. His father shook his head in despair, but there was a glimmer of satisfaction in his gaze too.

'If you're all finished discussing me like I'm not even here,' Gaelan said, leaning back in her chair. She folded her arms across her chest, cocking her head to the side as she considered them all. 'I've been a member of this Council for longer than some of you have been alive. I spoke at the Dovethorn's graduation; I taught the Ironclaw during her first years at the Academy; I helped the Whitehart take his first breath. I stood side by side with the Blackfire and the Mistfury when Sephiron came for them. I fought on the front lines with the Darkstorm heir when Wolfstone fell. I stood with the Swansinger's predecessor when she gave her life to buy us enough time to hide this city. So don't you dare accuse me of ever trying to bring harm to our people. I have given everything I have, everything I am, for them – for you.'

There was a pregnant pause, before Prince Vanir sneered, 'That is open for debate.'

'No, it is not,' the Darkstorm cut in. 'The Brightstar may not have been my first choice to wed my son, and I have not agreed with all – if any – of her actions. But her motivations are beyond reproach, her dedication to our people beyond question.'

'With all due respect, Darkstorm,' Vanir argued, 'you are hardly an impartial judge of her character. She's the mother of your grandchild. An ineffective one perhaps, but I suppose you had to forgive her inadequacy.'

There was a sudden intake of breath from around the table, and even the Frostfang paled. Beside him, Anwyn's temper flared as she turned her murderous eyes on the Wavebreaker – the air around her shimmering, mist curling from her fingertips. And Endellion was no better. The room shook as black flames erupted from beneath her skin, her smouldering eyes sparking while she clenched her fists against the table. But none were so fearsome as the thunder that rumbled ominously overhead or the warning growl that ripped from the Darkstorm's lips.

'I have killed men for lesser insults, Wavebreaker,' he breathed. 'The Brightstar has as much right to sit at this table as you or me and should be treated with the respect due her as a member of this Council. Listen to me very carefully, Vanir. If I ever hear you speak to someone like that again, let alone me or mine, I will have you sealed up in the Graves. Do you understand me?'

The light in Anwyn's eyes turned feral, and she grinned at Vanir, as if daring him to argue. Across the table, Nuada opened his mouth to argue, but the flames surrounding Endellion flickered in warning, and he had the sense to close it. After what seemed like an age, Prince Vanir inclined his head in acquiescence.

'Wise choice,' Tiberus murmured, unable to hide the smirk on his lips. 'Now back to the original question – what can we do for you Brightstar?'

Gaelan leaned forward, resting her elbows on the table as she steepled her fingers in front of her lips. She paused, gathering her thoughts, gazing at the empty chair across from her. Then she took a deep breath and lowered her hands. 'I was chosen guardian upon their parents' deaths. I claim them as my own, as is my right, and seek to have them enrolled in the Academy.'

Silence followed her pronouncement.

Brer's father recovered first. 'Only children from the Houses may enter the Academy,' he said, the boredom in his voice at odds with the glint of amusement in his eye. As though he too had just pieced together Gaelan's scheming. She smiled sweetly at him.

'But they are,' she simpered. 'Suriya and Lucan Brightstar. I am the only mother they have ever known. They're as much mine as Brer is yours.'

'That's ridiculous,' the Dovethorn snapped. 'Raising them doesn't change the blood in their veins. They're not even the same species as you. Mortals are as different from us as a songbird from an eagle.'

'They're not mortal – they're Graced,' Gaelan corrected. 'Falcons perhaps, rather than eagles, but still closer to us than say'—she paused, an evil grin touching her lips as she gazed sidelong at the Dovethorn—'a pigeon.'

Princess Colma flushed, but the Whitehart laid a restraining hand on her wrist and leaned forward. 'They could be firebirds, for all I care. You can't just give your name to whoever you please.'

'Actually, I can,' said Gaelan. 'There are no restrictions surrounding entry into the Houses – but adoption must be ratified by unanimous vote. Which it was.'

'That's a technicality,' Princess Colma hissed. 'Affiliation to the Houses – entry into the Academy – is a sacred honour. You can't just go about handing it out to whoever you please.'

Gaelan leaned back in her chair and smiled. 'Why not? The Darkstorm heir made it happen.'

All eyes swivelled to Prince Andriel.

'That had nothing to do with my House, and you know it. If you want someone to blame for that fiasco, I suggest you look to the Blackfire,' he said, pointing at Endellion.

Gaelan snorted. 'Don't kid yourself. It was all Alvar's idea. He might have acted against your wishes, but you did nothing to stop it. And I have to say – she was a wonderful addition to your family. You must be terribly proud of him.'

Thunder rumbled outside as the Darkstorm glared at her. Deservedly so. There was no mistaking the sarcasm in her voice.

'You are not helping your case,' he ground out from between clenched teeth, struggling to rein in his temper. Gaelan winked at him and looked back to the table.

'It doesn't matter – this is a formality. There's nothing any of you can do to stop me enrolling my children at the Academy,' she said, stretching and leaning back in her chair. The consternation on the various faces around the table was a satisfying sight to behold.

'They're too old,' the Shadowfox breathed. 'The law is specific. All Aspirants must be enrolled within a year of birth – and we only allowed them that time so children could be weaned before removing them from their mothers.'

'So make an exception. You've done it before. If memory serves, there were so many discrepancies in the records regarding the Swansinger's time at the Academy you even put her on trial,' she retorted, gesturing at Emalia. 'And despite the overwhelming evidence, you have allowed her to reign here unchallenged ever since.'

The Swansinger let out a low hiss. 'How dare you? I vouched for you – granted you safe passage into this city, offered you and your mutant spawn shelter in my own home – and this is how you repay me? You want to steal my throne from me?'

'I have little interest in your throne, Emalia,' Gaelan purred, 'beside how unfit you are to sit in it.'

'Enough,' the Darkstorm rumbled, cutting off Emalia's outraged snarl. 'We have digressed somewhat from the subject at hand. The Brightstar and her *children* must be weary from their journey. Perhaps it would be best if you retired. Go back to your chambers to rest while we deliberate.'

Gaelan's gaze flickered over the room, as if taking stock of her enemies and her allies, then came to rest on Prince Andriel. Something passed between them, and reluctantly, she inclined her head. She rose, motioning for Suriya and Lucan to follow her, and swept from the room. But she paused on the threshold and looked back.

'Say whatever you will about their heritage, but remember they are just children. We created those laws to protect the innocent. Such is the burden of our power. Do not let them suffer for our sins.'

And with those words still echoing through the chamber, they slipped through the door and closed it behind them.

The Council deliberations would take hours – perhaps even days – so there was plenty of time to wash, eat and rest. Gaelan showed them to separate bathrooms and laid out fresh clothes for them. When Suriya emerged, clean and warm for the first time in weeks and dressed in garments far too big for her, she found a hot meal waiting for her in the dining room.

The fare was simple but delicious, and she was far too tired to ask where it had come from. Even Lucan didn't question it. They wolfed down as much as they could stomach while Gaelan sat in silence, brushing her damp hair. She wore a gown of midnight-blue chiffon – far more revealing than anything she'd ever worn before – encrusted with thousands of tiny jewels, glittering like stars at her waist. The circlet upon her head was made of silver filigree and set with diamonds – she looked as if she were crowned in starlight. A Princess of Brightstar indeed.

After they'd eaten their fill, she led them back to the sitting room where she had started a fire. Gesturing for them to take their pick of the chairs positioned around the hearth, she crossed to the sideboard and poured herself a glass of clear, sparkling wine. Suriya picked the chair closest to the flames and nestled herself into the fur blanket laid over the arm.

'Do you think they'll let us stay?' Lucan asked.

Gaelan shrugged. 'It's hard to tell. Endellion and Anwyn will side with me – and likely, the Darkstorm too. He may not care much for me, but he holds no prejudice against the Graced. Alvar has brought in enough strays over the years that he hardly notices any more. I think Andriel will fight for you to avoid alienating his son, if nothing else.'

'And the others?' Lucan pressed. 'How many will have to side with us?'

'At least six,' she said, 'not including myself. Unless someone abstains. There are only twelve of us on the Council, and the petitioner cannot vote.'

'Is anyone likely to abstain?' asked Suriya.

Gaelan shrugged again. 'The Shadowfox. The Swansinger. Emalia's never liked me, and Eris is very conservative, but Brer would never forgive them if they voted against me in this. They'll just keep their heads down and stay out of it.'

'So you only need two of the others to vote in our favour,' Suriya extrapolated.

Lucan frowned. 'How do you figure that?'

'There's eleven on the Council, not including Gaelan,' she explained, 'so you need six votes to win. But if two abstain, then you only need five. She said that Alvar's father, Princess Endellion, and Princess Anwyn would vote for us – so we only need two more to win.'

Gaelan smiled and sipped from her glass. 'The Frostfang will probably vote in our favour. He enjoys causing mischief and upsetting the likes of Colma and Artianna. They'll go against, as will Vanir and Nuada.'

'But you think Prince Herne might be swayed,' Suriya continued. 'You said he was a child during the Rebellion, when his mother died. That's why you said those things about children and innocents before we left. You think that appealing to those memories – that sense of helplessness – will influence his decision.'

Gaelan's eyes twinkled with something akin to pride, and she nodded. Then she heaved a sigh. 'Go on, get some sleep.'

Lucan nodded, stifling a yawn as he stood.

Suriya didn't move.

'What is it?' he asked her.

She didn't look at him. Her eyes were on Gaelan. 'Those things you said in there, about our parents, being chosen as our guardian. Was any of it true?'

Gaelan didn't flinch, though Suriya could see the question had cut her deeply. But her voice was steady when she answered.

'Not all of it,' she admitted. 'I'm afraid I know nothing of your beginnings. Alvar brought you to me, begged me to keep you safe. He swore you weren't his but wouldn't tell me anything else about where you came from. Not that it mattered. Not to me. I gave him my word that I would care for you as if you were my own, and he left.'

'Why couldn't he care for us himself?'

Gaelan didn't so much as blink. 'That's not my story to tell. I will keep that promise though. I didn't have a chance, before we went in there, to ask what you want. But my offer still stands – I know you no longer trust me and that you might never trust me again. I know I'm not your mother, and perhaps you have never loved me as one. But I have loved you as my own since the day I set eyes on you. I offer you my name, with all the protection it brings. I offer you my body, to shield you from all it can – as any mother would. I offer you my heart, though it may mean nothing to either of you. I give you it all freely and ask for nothing in return.'

The words were formal, ritualistic almost – as though they meant far more than she was saying. Suriya glanced up at her brother, but he was still watching Gaelan. There was infinite longing in his moonstone eyes, and Suriya knew that her decision had been made for her. She could not go against her brother. Not now. Not ever.

She'd rather die.

She'd come close enough crossing the mountains. Pouring every ounce of energy she could spare into him, just as they had with Alvar when he'd tried to reach Renila. It had almost killed her to do it, but she'd die a thousand times over rather than see him come to harm. He was all she had, and she would give anything for him, including her pride.

She nodded and took a deep breath. 'Alright. I accept your offer.'

Gaelan's eyes widened in wonder and filled with tears as she looked between them in disbelief. But before she could reach for them, Suriya turned for the door. She wasn't ready for that. Not yet.

'I'm going to bed,' she announced. She didn't even wait to see if Lucan followed her.

The Shade King never raised his voice. That was what unnerved Erion the most. Even more than his inhuman eyes or his imposing size. Even more than the terrible power that rippled and surged around him. Even more than the knowledge of who he was and what he'd done. It was the calm, cool and detached way he asked questions.

'What is your name?'

'Erion.'

'And how old are you Erion?'

'Twelve.'

Always the same. Simple questions with simple answers. Where did he come from? How long had he lived there? Did he have any brothers or sisters? What was his mother's name? But always with the same oppressive weight of the Shade King's mind hovering over him. Never pushing, never prying. But lingering nearby, a silent yet ominous threat. Then came the more difficult ones.

'Who is your father?'

'I don't know.'

'How did you find your way into the library?'

'It told me where to find it.'

'What are you?'

'I don't understand.'

A pause. 'Who taught you to guard your mind so well?'

'I don't know what you mean.'

And on and on. The King never rebutted Erion's answers, even on the rare occasion that his dreadful eyes tightened infinitesimally in displeasure. Occasionally, the black-eyed Elf Corrigan would interject – add another question. Too scared to refuse, Erion answered those too. Seren remained silent, standing behind the King with her arms folded and a disapproving look on her face. Only Kieyin stayed with him, offering what little comfort he could with the warmth of his presence at his back. Hours must have passed, and he swayed with exhaustion and horror as his situation pressed down on him.

'Enough,' Kieyin interrupted. 'He's tired. Let him rest.'

The Shade King cocked his head to the side, considering. Those terrible eyes bored straight into him, staring right down into his soul, and the weight of his presence grew heavier still. Erion's legs buckled from the force of it. Then it was gone. And the King inclined his head in acquiescence.

'Very well,' he purred. 'But Kieyin ... keep him close.'

And with that Erion was led from the room.

CHAPTER THIRTY-FOUR

'Mazron, is it?' Keriath asked, eyeing the Shade uneasily.

'Now, now,' he chided, 'let's not forget our manners. *Prince* Mazron. I would have greeted you properly, Your Highness, but I'm assured you refute your claim to that title.'

Keriath's lip curled in distaste, but she didn't deign to reply as she studied him. He was tall – at least as tall as her brother, though shorter than Kah Faolin – and leaner than either of them, though more muscled than the skeletal Drosta. He was handsome, this Shade. Not enchantingly beautiful, like Taelyr, nor strikingly masculine, like Faolin. But the Unicorn blood in him was obvious. There was something so appealing, so captivating about him. He moved with sinuous grace, like a cat stalking its prey. Slow, deliberate and confident. But it was his eyes that caught her attention. They were a Shade's eyes – eerie and pale – but they burned with an intensity that she had never seen before. They danced with fire and rage. He was terrifying and yet unbearably alluring.

She could feel the brush of his mind against her own, quiet probing touches to test her defences. She did her best to shield herself, but she was so weak, and even from that tentative contact, she could tell he was powerful. He smirked as he read the thought and winked in acknowledgement before turning his attention back to the Queens.

'That's her alright,' he assured them. 'I saw her once, before Revalla fell. She was only a child, but those scars are unmistakable. Although there are several more than I remember ...'

Ylain and Talize fidgeted, but Pria bristled. 'We didn't know. She didn't tell us.' Mazron pinned her with a look that was lethal; even Keriath shuddered at the sight of it.

'I would have thought, *Majesties*, that after all this time you should at least be able to recognise your sovereign's heir. If not, then a wanted criminal and enemy of the state,' he breathed. Had she been any stronger, Keriath would have snorted. Her only crime was existing, and she was an enemy to a state that had butchered its way into existence. Mazron shot her a warning glance over his shoulder, and the talons of his mind scraped against her defences in silent threat. The message was clear. *Hold your tongue, or I'll cut it out.*

'I hope the *King* will find it in his heart to forgive us for our transgressions,' Ylain replied, cutting over whatever tart response was rising to Pria's lips. The pointed irony of her statement was not lost on anyone in the room, for they all knew Mazron had no intention of handing his prize over.

The Shade's handsome face darkened at the implied threat, but he only offered a twisted smile and said, 'I'm sure. Now, I will require rooms and a servant or two to see to our needs until we are ready to depart.' Ylain inclined her head and snapped her fingers.

'Escort Prince Mazron and his prisoner to the guest chambers,' she ordered the Darkling that came running. 'I will select someone suitable and send them up to relieve you, but in the meantime, please ensure that our guests have everything they need.'

The Darkling bowed once to his Queens, and with that Keriath and her new jailer were escorted from the throne room.

The rooms to which they were taken were sumptuous, though that wasn't surprising. The suite was large, but that wasn't surprising either. Complete with separate sitting and dining rooms, a library with a writing desk, a dressing room, an obscenely large bedroom – containing an obscenely large bed – and an adjoining bathing room.

The furniture was lavish, the walls coated with rich tapestries. Luxurious carpets littered the polished wooden floors, and the mirror over the mantle sat within a gilded frame. The armchairs were covered with azure velvet, and the crimson bedsheets were made of pure silk. The table was set with chargers and goblets of solid silver, and tapers flickered in matching candlesticks. There was a fire roaring in the hearth, as though the room was in a state of perpetual readiness while it waited for occupants.

After so long in the Core, the sight of such luxury turned Keriath's stomach. Besides, she knew all too well that every extravagance came at a price. And all of these had been paid for in blood. The blood of her people. She squared her shoulders and turned to face Mazron.

'*Prince* Mazron,' he corrected her, tapping a pointed talon against her shields. Keriath didn't so much as blink. She couldn't even summon the energy to swear at him. The Shade tutted in disapproval. 'I have to say, I'm a little disappointed. I expected more … well, *more* from someone of your reputation, Keriath.'

Keriath held his gaze. '*Princess* Keriath,' she corrected. 'And if you wanted better sport, you should have got here a little sooner.'

His eyes danced as he realised his prey was not entirely broken.

'If you want niceties, then you will have to claim your birthright. And I don't think you're prepared to do that. Not even now. Not even when it might give you the power you need to get through me and escape this place.' He broke off, considering her. 'As to getting here sooner, I'm afraid the message regarding your capture was somewhat delayed. I assure you, I came as fast as I could. I am keen that we get to know each other, Keriath ... very keen indeed.'

Her skinned crawled at the implication, but she was excused from replying by a sharp knock at the door. Mazron growled at the interruption and wrenched the door open with a savage yank.

'What?' he snarled at the offending Darkling waiting on the other side.

The Darkling handed him an envelope. The seal was broken. 'A missive from the Princess Zorana arrived for you. The Queens request your presence back in the throne room to discuss its contents.' Mazron stilled as he studied the broken seal, barely restrained rage creeping through every line of his lithe frame.

'Who opened this?' he said, in a voice that promised only violence and death.

The Darkling stuttered, and Keriath felt a swell of pity for him. Mazron, however, offered neither pity nor mercy.

She felt the wave of pressure building and cried out in warning. But there was no defence the Darkling could muster against such an attack. Keriath's stomach heaved, and she watched in horror, helpless to intervene, as Mazron melted the Darkling's mind within his skull. And in less than the space of a heartbeat, the Darkling crumpled to a heap on the floor, dead.

'Wait here,' Mazron ordered, stepping over the corpse with casual indifference. And with that he left, slamming the door behind him. She heard the key turn in the lock, and then she was alone.

The crushing weight of fear and exhaustion chased the strength from her legs. She sank to the floor, the impact cushioned by the embroidered carpet, and wept.

She didn't know how long she lay there, curled in a ball in front of the fire while terrified sobs racked her ruined frame. At first, they came in ragged gasps, leaving her unable to catch her breath through the engulfing panic. Then came the tears she feared would never end, streaming down her face like a river in flood. At last, they quietened to an exhausted whimper, and she could not find it in herself to care how pathetic she sounded.

Then the sound she'd been dreading: a key turning in the lock. But she no longer had the strength to stand. Instead, she curled up a little tighter and closed her eyes.

The hand that stroked her hair was surprisingly gentle. And callused. Keriath frowned: Mazron didn't strike her as the type to have ever used his hands. She opened her eyes and peered up through her fingers at the familiar figure crouched over her.

Dell. A choked cry of relief escaped her, and she threw her arms around his neck, sobbing into his chest.

'I know,' he murmured, his hand steady on her back in reassurance. 'I know. But it's alright. I'm here now.' After a moment, he leaned back and looked down at her. His thumb grazed the ragged lines of her new scars. 'I'm sorry—'

She cut him off. 'Don't.' She didn't want to remember. Didn't want to hear him ask for the forgiveness that she did not have it in her heart to give. He nodded in understanding and ran his other hand over her old scars.

'Keriath,' he breathed, his voice full of wonder. 'I wish you'd told me … Princess.' She repressed a shudder. There were so many girls in the world who craved such a title. All raised on fairy tales stuffed full of knights on white steeds and palaces made of rainbows and moonbeams. Stories about magic slippers and wicked witches, talking bears and dancing swans, and all the other nonsense. For Keriath, it was nothing more than a curse.

'Just get me out of here,' was all she said.

He dipped his head in submission and stood, pulling her to her feet. She staggered, leaning against him as he looped her arm around his neck and half-carried her from the room.

Free from the crushing weight of the Core, Keriath had enough strength to expand her awareness, allowing her to warn Dell of passing servants or approaching patrols. It was one benefit of being held inside the mountain – only the Queens and their household lived within the castle itself. Most of the Darkling horde was down in the city that sprawled around the foot of the mountain. Between Keriath's ability to scout ahead and Dell's knowledge of the twisted labyrinth of corridors within, they made easy ground.

But it was too good to last, and eventually, they came upon a group of guards they could not avoid. Keriath conjured what little magic she could to hold them in place while Dell swept through them like a whirlwind of blood and death. It was a sign of just how much the power in her veins had strengthened him that he could kill so many so fast. Hope swelled in her heart. They continued on as before, creeping from one shadow to the next.

Until there was a door ahead of them. Wide open, the dying light of the day spilling into the hallway. Sunlight. A source of healing and restoration for the blessed Graced. A gust of cold wind blasted in through the entrance, and Keriath thought that air had never tasted so sweet. An easterly wind, bringing with it the scent of ocean spray. The scent of her childhood home, of freedom. But even with freedom so close, a wave of exhaustion sent her crashing to the floor, a gasped sob of frustration escaping her as her body failed her.

Then Dell was there. 'No, you don't,' he breathed. 'Not when we're this close.' His arms slid around her, and he lifted her up, tucking her against his chest. Her eyes drifted closed, the rolling motion of Dell's gait lulling her towards oblivion.

His steps faltered. She peered up through her lashes, and her gut clenched at the fear on his face. She didn't think she had ever seen him look so afraid. And yet, as she probed around them with her mind, she sensed nothing. She hissed from the effort, lifting her head and following his gaze. To the figure barring their way, silhouetted against the sunset pouring in through the open door.

Mazron. No wonder she hadn't sensed him. He was shielding himself from her – hiding his presence with his mind. Doing it so well, in fact, that Keriath wondered if he had not set her up for this exact moment. The serpent's smile he offered suggested he had.

'Despair is never so sweet as when all hope is ripped away,' he crooned.

And in that moment, all that remained of the woman Keriath had once been withered and died. Her soul had never been vibrant like Théon's, battered and bruised as it was. But she had clung to life, fought for it with a desperation that had made her strong. Now, that desire was gone; all that remained of her shattered heart were ashes and dust.

Dell set her on her feet, though her legs could not hold her. He kept an arm around her, taking most of her weight as she leaned on him.

'You have something of mine,' Mazron said, advancing on the Darkling.

Dell growled in response. 'She belongs to me.' Mazron pulled up short, cocking his head to the side as he studied his prey. Then he laughed.

'I'm afraid it's the other way around,' he chuckled. 'She could order you to jump off a cliff right now, and you would not refuse her.'

'What are you talking about?'

'You don't even realise, do you?' cawed Mazron. 'It's the blood bond. She's Claimed you – her blood overpowered that of your maker. How could it not? He is only mortal, after all ... and she is a Shade.'

Keriath trembled at the accusation but smothered the doubts that crept so insidiously into her head, saying nothing. She hardly had the strength to draw breath. Dell was staring at her, eyes wide with a mixture of awe and incredulity. 'That's why your blood freed me from Talize,' he breathed. 'Why I feel so strong. The power dilutes over generations. The closer to the source you are, the stronger you are.' His eyes skipped to Mazron. 'I'm Shade-made.'

'Yes,' agreed Mazron. 'And had it not been for this somewhat unique situation, you would never have discovered these secrets. For what Darkling would ever dare to feed upon a Shade?' He smiled. 'But I cannot allow you to live with such knowledge. Even if I were to ignore the fact that you tried to help my prize escape, I can't risk that information falling into the hands of the Queens. Nor the other secret you're keeping.'

'I don't know what you mean.'

Mazron's smile was diabolical. 'Yes, you do. You've wanted to tell her. Every moment you've been alone with her it's itched to break free ... but you were too scared to ever speak the words.'

'What is he talking about?' Keriath whispered, edging away from Dell.

He glanced down, his jaw set with determination. 'Nothing.'

'Oh, come now,' crooned Mazron, inching closer. 'Time's up, Dell. You wanted to tell her – now's your chance. She wants to know. It's been bothering her since you ambushed her in Thornhold. Go on, put her out of her misery. Tell her who gave you the information.'

Dell growled. 'Your bitch sister sent us after her.'

'Stick to the facts, Dell,' Mazron taunted. 'Zorana gave the order, but who told you where to look?'

Keriath stepped clear of him, her legs trembling from the effort of staying upright. 'Dell?'

The big Darkling's face was a mask of resolve, but there was pain beneath it. Mazron hissed, and she sensed the talons of his attack driving into Dell's mind. The Darkling – her Darkling – screamed and crashed to his knees.

'Tell her!' roared Mazron. Dell screamed again as the razor-sharp blades of the Shade's attack cut into him. 'Look her in the eye and tell her who betrayed her!'

Dell's neck shuddered from the strain of resisting as his head was forced round to look at Keriath. Veins bulged across his face as he fought the pain, but the Shade was too strong.

'Taelyr!' he gasped. 'Gods forgive me. It was Taelyr. Your brother betrayed you, Keriath. I'm sorry. I'm so sorry.'

Keriath swayed from the shock. There was a roaring in her ears, over which she barely heard Dell's strangled apologies or Mazron's vicious laughter. Taelyr. Her baby brother. Betray her? It couldn't be. Her eyes went to Mazron.

'Why? What did you do to him?'

But the Shade only smiled and looked over her shoulder at the two Darkling guards now approaching. Enchanted by Mazron, they were like blank-faced puppets as they bound Dell's hands behind his back and hauled him up.

'Much as I would like to deal with you myself,' Mazron whispered, 'I'm afraid I can't go killing your Queens' subjects in their own castle. It wouldn't be prudent, what with us being allies and all. I apologise – I would at least make it quick – but I expect the Queens would prefer a traitor's death to *linger*.' Mazron smiled as Dell flinched, then he reached for Keriath. 'And as for you, I've already told you twice. It's *Prince* Mazron. Don't make me tell you again.'

Then his hand fisted in her hair, and he pulled her close, kissing her thoroughly. Her skin crawled at the violation, and she tried to pull away. But then he was in her head, soothing away her complaints and stirring up her blood until she was desperate for more.

He broke away, leaving her gasping for breath, and glanced at Dell with a smug, satisfied smile. Keriath could not bring herself to look at the Darkling ... *her* Darkling. She could sense his rage boiling in his veins, taste his wounded pride and bitter regret. But it was the wrenching despair in his heart that hurt her the most.

So she didn't fight when Mazron gestured to the Darkling puppets he had commandeered. She didn't fight as they dragged Dell away, his feet trailing behind him when his legs refused to hold his weight any longer.

She didn't fight when Mazron's hand went to the small of her back and guided her back under the mountain.

The sentinels guarding the throne room did not challenge their approach. Nor did the Shade Prince make any move to request an audience, as Drosta had done. Whether through his dark powers or out of fear, the sentinels did not hesitate to open the doors and grant him entry.

The Queens bristled at the unannounced intrusion, but as they looked more closely at the figures striding down the chamber towards them, their irritation faded to incredulity.

'Your little pet here was trying to make off with my prize,' Mazron announced, with the air of someone commenting on the weather. Keriath almost admired the audacity of it. 'I stopped them. Also, I hope you don't object – I appropriated two of your guards to aid in his capture. And I trust you don't object, but I altered their minds to ensure they didn't disobey their orders.'

Ylain straightened. The old crone's imperious gaze swept the room once, taking in the commotion with a slight curl of her lip, and she snapped her fingers in dismissal. 'An unnecessary but understandable precaution. But they are no longer required, so I would ask that you release them now.'

'If you insist,' said Mazron, rolling his eyes. The guards shoved Dell down to kneel before the Queens then joined the line of servants and guards filing from the room.

Keriath was permitted to remain standing, though Mazron kept a proprietary grip on her arm. She paid him little heed, her eyes on Dell. Guilt gnawed at her gut. She had done this to him. First with her beauty and then with her blood. Stolen his will, his chance to choose for himself. She was no better than the Queens. No better than Mazron. Even now, Dell was gazing at her with love and loyalty in his eyes. But it was a lie, a perversion of a once pure magic. The worst kind of corruption imaginable. It made her stomach heave just to look at it.

Ylain cleared her throat and stepped forward. 'I assume you want him executed,' she said without preamble.

'He betrayed you, helped your prisoner escape, tried to steal my prize. The punishment for such transgressions can only be death,' noted Mazron with a cruel smile.

'He is *my* subject,' she snarled, 'and it is for *me* to sentence him.'

'And do you judge differently?'

'Of course not,' she hissed. 'But I would have preferred to handle it with more tact.'

The Shade smirked. 'Because he is only here to ensure his maker's good behaviour? A Hunter whose loyalty you doubt?' The Queen flinched from the accusation, for that was why Dell had remained while Drosta returned north. To Zorana. 'We're all on the same side, aren't we?' he purred. 'I would hate to think you were spying on my sister, Ylain.'

'Don't be ridiculous.' The crone bristled. 'Anyway, I'm not the one keeping secrets,' she added with a pointed look at Keriath.

Mazron offered an irreverent shrug. 'What can I tell you, Ylain? Your boy got lucky. Why would he have brought her here instead of taking her back to Zorana if he was planning to betray you?' Ylain paused at that, but she let the matter drop.

'We are, perhaps, drifting off topic,' Talize interjected, sidestepping Ylain. The smile on Talize's full lips was forced and tight as she tried to remain polite, but bitter rage rolled off the Queen in waves. 'Despite our differences of opinion, I think we can all agree that the traitor must die. While it might have suited us better to have been more discreet about it, the damage is not irreparable. Drosta might find the death of his second inconvenient, but there is no need to anger him any further with the humiliation of a public execution. I say we kill him now and get it over with.'

Pria nodded. 'I agree.'

'Agreed,' grunted Ylain.

'As you wish,' the Shade purred. 'Although I'm surprised the infamous Darkling Queens would offer a traitor a quick death.'

Talize descended the steps, her eyes filled with blistering hate. 'Oh, do not fear my Prince. I have no intention of rushing this. His suffering will linger, I promise you that.'

'He will tell them everything before he dies,' Keriath hissed into the Shade's mind as Talize's talon-like fingers yanked Dell's head back by his hair, baring his throat. Mazron only chuckled.

'Given that he is already under the influence of the Enchanting, I find that unlikely.'

Keriath glared at him. *'If you can stop him from speaking, why bother having him killed?'* Mazron prowled closer, running a possessive hand down her cheek. She flinched from that proprietary touch, and the Shade chuckled at her discomfort.

'Because he tried to take what was mine,' he breathed. *'And now you will watch him die.'* Keriath flinched away, but Mazron only smirked, turning and leading her up the dais. He sat in one of the empty thrones, pulling Keriath down into his lap. One arm snaked around her waist, pulling her to him while the other caressed her throat. Bile rose from her stomach, her skin crawling at his touch, but he held her fast. *'You will watch every moment, and you will remember it all in exquisite detail whenever you close your eyes. His death will haunt your nightmares forever,'* he purred, the words weaving commands in her mind that she was powerless to counter. *'This is your punishment for trying to run. Consider it a mercy. The last one you will ever receive from me.'*

Mercy was perhaps not the word Keriath would have used, but even without Mazron's command, she would not have looked away. She owed Dell that much. He looked so small and fragile, kneeling at the bottom of the dais. As vulnerable and shattered as her dying heart. But deep down, she knew that the wrench of despair at seeing him so helpless had nothing to do with anything she felt for him. She felt nothing for him – save her guilt at robbing him of his choice. He was just another Darkling. If the Queens or Mazron didn't kill him, Keriath would have done it herself. No, what she felt was the keen edge of desperation at having all hope ripped away. Hope that Dell had given her.

So she watched. She watched in silence as Ylain and Pria descended the dais, and the Queens began their torment. Watched as they beat him with their bare hands. Watched as Pria and Talize held him fast while Ylain whipped his back into bloody ribbons. Watched as they carved into his flesh, cutting him up piece by piece.

And while she watched, Mazron whispered in her mind. What he told her, what he showed her … It made her blood run cold.

Taelyr, with his silvery hair and his moonstone eyes. Her baby brother, who she loathed and loved with equal measure. Or rather, someone else wearing his face. Because the things she saw him do – that was not her brother.

Her brother would never have helped the Shade take Illyol, would never allow them to taint his ancestral home. Her brother would never suffer a Darkling to live in his presence, let alone sit back and watch as they feasted on the lifeblood of every mortal they could find. He would never have tolerated the hunting and killing of the Graced children, too young to suppress their powers … would have died himself before he saw one come to harm.

And yet, that was Taelyr she saw drawing up plans of Illyol and handing them to the Shade. That was Taelyr smiling while Darklings slaughtered the mortals who sheltered within the wards. That was Taelyr leading the Hunts through the city, searching for any remnants of the Graced bloodlines that might have lingered beyond the Fall. That was her baby brother handing a little girl with pointed ears and an aura like sunlight on water over to the Darklings.

The images were punctuated with the sound of Dell's gasping breaths, and the wet thud of tearing flesh as the lash cut into his back. Keriath's eyes did not leave his tortured face.

'What did you do to my brother?' she hissed. 'Taelyr is a lot of things, but this isn't him. You did something. You changed him.'

'Did I?'

Dell's blood was running in rivulets down his legs, staining the stone beneath his feet. It was black, tainted by the poison of the Shade magic … her Shade magic. She shoved the thought away as Mazron flooded her mind with more pictures of her brother.

She watched as Taelyr bowed before the Oak Throne, bowed to the Shade Princess he'd helped to claim it, with that same beautiful, arrogant smile he'd had since boyhood. She saw that same cruel glint in his eye, the scheming expression on his breathtaking face when a plan was forming in his wicked mind. Rumours might claim Keriath to be the child of shadows, but Taelyr was the one with the soul as black as night.

She watched the Princess take him by the hand, leading him to her bed, and felt nothing. For Taelyr, the choosing of lovers had little to do with attraction or even morality; it was just a question of what he might gain from his liaisons. His actions and their consequences were always meticulously considered, and his motivations were never anything but self-serving. He would readily debase himself with someone like Zorana if he thought he might benefit from it. While it was a flaw she had long ago accepted, Keriath had no desire to witness it. Mazron showed her anyway.

She watched as Zorana tore Taelyr's shirt from his chest, those all-too-familiar tattoos swirling over his shoulders. Simple, yet striking – black dragon-marks to honour their grandfather. To see a Shade run her hands over those shoulders, over those hallowed symbols, in such passionate caresses ... it broke her heart.

She watched him tell the Shade Princess where she could find his sister.

Dell was screaming now as Pria sawed off his little finger with a blunt knife. Then his other fingers. His toes. Other parts. Keriath watched, the image seared into her memory, but her mind was racing. It had not been her brother whispering in the night to their enemies. It looked like him. It sounded like him. But someone else looked out from those pearlescent eyes. Someone she did not recognise ... a monster wearing his skin.

'He did it to himself,' whispered Mazron. 'Your baby brother did it to himself. He opened the door and invited it in. Stood by and watched as it made its home in his heart.'

She shivered. 'You're lying.'

'Am I?' challenged Mazron. 'Your brother is strong. Too strong for me to Enchant. Definitely too strong for me to Enchant from afar. And Zorana is Elf-born, so you can be sure she had nothing to do with it. Besides, your brother came willingly. His mind was already altered beyond recognition when he found us.'

Keriath forced herself to ask, choking on the words, 'How?'

'You know how. The power all star-marked share. We can Enchant the minds of others – why not our own?'

Keriath flinched. Such power was forbidden. All Unicorn children knew that. They were taught to fear it long before their powers ever manifested. It was the worst type of self-harm – the deliberate murder of one's own self. How could he have become so lost that he would even consider such a thing? Her heart broke anew. For whoever Taelyr was now, he was no longer the brother she knew. He was just the monster that had killed him.

'Why?'

Mazron laughed at her pain. 'He knew the innocent boy he was could not hope to survive this world unscathed. He was weak and foolish, driven by emotion and sentiment. So the man killed the boy. Replaced him with someone strong and proud, so nothing could ever hurt him again. Now all he values is power, and my sister can give him that. So he does what she asks and does not care for the consequences.'

Tears streamed unchecked down her cheeks. Taelyr had been the last hope of their people. If he too had fallen, what chance was there? If the Lord of Revalla was gone, replaced by some monster wearing his face, then what had she fought for? Anguish was a knife twisting in her gut.

She looked at Dell, at the ruined body where her only hope of salvation

413

had once been. He was still alive. Just. His body was so covered in blood that she could hardly recognise him. His breath came in wet, pitiful gasps, but his eyes were still on her.

'I'm sorry,' she whispered into his mind. His lips twitched as he tried to smile. His thoughts were incoherent, weak and confused as he slipped in and out of consciousness. But she could read enough.

There was nothing for her to be sorry for. He did not regret any of the choices that had led him to this place. Even knowing that sometimes his choices were not his own, he did not blame her for his suffering.

Guilt and rage and anguish swelled, her power rising in her veins. Magic was fuelled by emotions, and Mazron had just stoked hers to boiling point. She was weak, and it was near impossible to direct her power where she wanted it. Mazron scrabbled for his defences, trying to control her mind. She hissed through gritted teeth, becoming like water – fluid and free, slipping through his fingers as she gathered up all the power she could muster. Panting from the effort, she dug deep, even as Mazron yelled in warning to the Queens. He threw her from his lap, and she crashed to her knees at the top of the dais, but she didn't take her eyes off Dell as her power built. Because it was not for her own benefit that she called it forth.

'Thank you.' And then she poured all that she could muster into Dell's head. It was a painful death she offered him, but at least it was quick. He cried out once, his body spasming from the agony, and then he was still.

Silence filled the room. The Queens stared down at the corpse in shock. They were not alone. Behind her, Mazron was breathing hard with the effort of restraining himself. Keriath hardly noticed. She stared down at Dell's corpse. It had been a meaningless act of defiance, with no benefit to herself save soothing her guilty conscience. No doubt Mazron would make her suffer for it later. A choked sob escaped her lips. *What had she done?*

Three pairs of blood-red eyes turned on her and, as one, the Queens hissed in outrage. Then Mazron was between them, placing his prize behind him, his hands just a little too firm as he fought to maintain a hold of his temper. He squeezed her wrist once in warning, hard enough to make the bones groan. She took the hint and stayed silent.

'You were going to kill him anyway,' he said, cutting over whatever the Queens were about to say.

Ylain bristled. 'That's not the point.'

'She interrupted our fun.' Pria growled, staring at her intended prey.

A vicious growl ripped out of Mazron. 'I don't give a shit. She's mine, and if you try to take her, you'll meet the same end as your little friend here,' he warned, gesturing at Dell's corpse.

'You're not strong enough to take all three of us,' hissed Talize, itching forward.

'And you're not strong enough to kill me,' he snapped. 'You kill her, and I'll tell the King she was here. And I won't stop him when he tears this place down and buries you beneath it.'

Talize and Pria growled at the threat, but Ylain saw it for what it was: a promise. She silenced the others with a sharp wave of her hand, inclining her head towards the Shade. 'Fine. But I want her gone from here as soon as possible.'

'We will leave at dawn,' Mazron offered.

'You will leave now,' snarled Talize.

The Shade turned his pale gaze upon her, and Keriath almost smiled as the Queen flinched in terror. 'We will leave at dawn,' he repeated, 'for you and I have unfinished business to discuss.' It was Talize who had opened Zorana's missive then. The Queen blanched, glancing to the others in supplication. But Ylain only sniffed and turned away. Pria shook her head in frustration and followed suit.

'So be it,' Talize spat, barely repressing the violent trembling that had overtaken her luscious frame.

Bowing, Mazron dragged his prize from the room without a word.

The sentinels beyond the chamber were still in place, but they did not even glance in their direction as Mazron hauled Keriath away. As soon as they were alone, he stopped, slamming her against the nearest wall by the throat.

'That,' he hissed, 'was incredibly stupid.' She stared back into his eerie eyes and said nothing. His grip about her throat tightened, like he was fighting the urge to choke the life from her. Then he deflated, shaking his head in frustration. 'Was he worth it? Your Darkling? Was he worth wasting the last of your power? And for what? The mercy of a quick death?'

Keriath kept her face impassive. 'I wouldn't expect a Shade to understand.'

'Shade is just the magic in my blood,' he said, smirking; 'it has nothing to do with my heart.'

'I wasn't aware you had one.'

Mazron chuckled, ghosting the breath of a kiss against her cheek. 'I understand mercy and guilt, love and loyalty,' he whispered against her skin. 'I just don't waste time on them.' Then his hand slipped higher, squeezing her jaw in his crushing grip as he pressed the full weight of his body against her in warning. 'And for the last time, it's *Prince* Mazron. I suggest you remember, or things will become increasingly unpleasant for you. Now come. Time to get you cleaned up.'

CHAPTER THIRTY-FIVE

They lingered another three days at the cabin. Three days for Renila to regain her strength. The nights were cold and long, and growing longer. She and Arian had shared the tiny bed, huddled together for warmth. Ornak had tried sleeping on the floor by the fire for all of an hour before storming out, grumbling that bare earth wasn't just softer but also had fewer splinters. As far as Renila could see, Alvar hadn't slept at all. Not that it seemed to affect him.

Renila dreamed of Erion every night. Dreamed of thunder and starlight. Flame and shadow warring in the sky. The hum of some ancient, terrible power – burning like ice held against wet skin. Air shimmering. A barrier between them. And eyes. Brown eyes. Pale eyes. Black eyes. All watching. Always watching.

Her son, vanishing into darkness.

The first night, she woke in a cold sweat, gasping for air with his name on her lips. Alvar had unsheathed his sword and was halfway across the room, Ornak appearing at the door, axe in hand, less than a heartbeat later, before Arian had waved them off. Then the Phoenix woman had put her arms around Renila and hugged her close through the storm of her weeping. And every night since, when Renila woke screaming, that warm hand found her in the darkness and held tight until the fear had passed, and sleep claimed her once more.

When morning came, Renila was starving. She'd always had a tendency to eat when she was upset or stressed, but this new voracious appetite had taken even her by surprise. When she'd mentioned it, Arian had only laughed and pointed to how much she and Ornak ate.

'Magic is energy,' she said. 'We have to fuel it somehow.'

Despite that, there seemed to be little risk of anyone going hungry. Ornak was not just a skilled hunter, able to produce fresh meat practically on demand, but an excellent cook, creating hearty and delicious meals from seemingly poor fare.

But Renila was growing impatient, and Alvar's memories churned in her mind. Her confusion mingled with frustration until her emotions were near boiling point. Her companions all seemed to sense it, but it was Ornak who took matters into his own hands – extending one of Arian's twin swords, hilt first.

'Time you learned how to use this.'

Alvar glanced up. 'She knows how to use it.'

'She *knew* how to use it,' corrected Arian.

Alvar glared, opening his mouth to offer a curt response. But Renila barely noticed, too busy eyeing the offered hilt with trepidation. Ornak watched her, ignoring the other two bickering, his head cocked to the side as he considered her. She almost flinched from that keen gaze. From the understanding that dawned there. Nodding to himself, he flipped the blade in his hand and buried the point in the soft earth, crouching down so he could look her in the eye.

'You're afraid you might hurt me,' he said. 'You can feel it now – that power pounding through your veins. It scares you. You don't know how to control it and that terrifies you. But your fear is the only thing stopping you. That power is as much a part of you as your hands or your feet. Accept it. Embrace it. Wield it. When you understand it, you control it, and it will never control you again.'

'What if I can't?'

'You can,' he promised. Then he stood and offered his hand instead. Renila looked up at him, vaguely aware that Alvar and Arian were watching the exchange, yet not really caring for their opinions. He had spoken with such unflinching belief, such quiet certainty, that her breath caught in her throat. Not words to soothe a damaged ego, to strengthen fragile confidence. Just the simple truth, as he saw it.

An image flickered through her mind.

An autumn afternoon – the training ring in Gaelan's keep bathed in golden light. Farran's steady, reassuring voice drifting across the courtyard, punctuated by the sound of wood striking wood. Erion grinning as he blocked an overhand blow, his eyes bright and cheeks flushed. Pride and happiness shining on Farran's face when he praised the boy for his rapid improvements.

The image faded. Ornak watched, a glimmer of understanding gleaming in his smiling eyes. His fingers fluttered in challenge, taunting her. Daring her.

She placed her hand in his. Allowed him to pull her to her feet. Returned his feral grin with a shy smile of her own. Took the offered sword.

'Show me.'

Ornak, it transpired, was a surprisingly adept teacher. He was patient, but firm. Tolerant, but unyielding. Arian's assessment seemed accurate – his instructions were punctuated with a broad range of colourful curses, and he had no manners to speak of. But Renila could tell his brusque demeanour concealed a kind heart. Not that the knowledge made his lessons any less painful. He pushed her hard, and she invariably limped away from their bouts.

Alvar tried to intervene all of once, before Ornak sent him packing, complaining the Immortal Prince unsettled his student. Renila had argued in Alvar's defence, though secretly she'd been quite relieved to lose the debate. Ornak, it would appear, was also perceptive. He was quick to play the fool, content to let people see him as a gruff, ignorant mercenary. But as her lessons progressed, Renila realised there was far more to the rough-spoken Dragon than he let on. She couldn't help but think how much Erion would have liked him – and how much he would have enjoyed watching her suffer through Ornak's sessions.

'You're getting better,' Ornak noted on the third day of their lessons, parrying.

She twisted away, but he caught her sword with his own and wrenched it from her grip. She could almost hear Erion laughing at her. With a sigh, she trudged across the muddy clearing to pick it up. Ornak got there first and grinned at her. Renila scowled. 'Clearly.'

'When I taught Arian how to use this thing, it took her a month just to figure out how to hold it properly,' he said. He threw a mischievous wink towards the Phoenix woman watching from a nearby rock.

Arian snorted, shaking her head in disgust. 'It was three weeks.'

'Pedant,' he chuckled. Then he held out the sword to Renila, his bright gaze serious for once. 'The point is – your body remembers what your mind has forgotten. The instincts are all there – how you hold the sword, how you stand, how you move – but you're overthinking it. Just relax. Trust yourself.'

She took the sword once more. 'How long did it take you to learn to fight like this?'

'I never stop learning,' he admitted, lunging for her. 'Every battle is a classroom. Every wound a lesson.'

She dodged, ducking under his arm and striking towards his exposed back. 'Except the fatal ones.'

'True for me – not so much for you.' He chuckled, twisting to block her.

She hissed in frustration, dancing back out of reach. 'How long until you learned enough to stay alive?'

'My father gave me my first sword when I was five years old,' he said, giving ground as she rushed him. He was bigger, true, but not as fast or nimble. 'Killed my first Darkling at fifteen. You do the maths.'

A hopeful smile rose to her lips when he struggled to parry. 'That's a long time.'

'That was a hundred years ago,' he countered, shoving her back and kicking her into the dirt. In her head, she could see Erion sighing in frustration at her mistake. Ornak waved a finger in her face. 'We went over this yesterday. You can't match me in brute strength. So?'

She picked herself up, gasping, 'So avoid putting myself in a situation where you can overpower me. I know. But I haven't had a hundred years to learn this stuff.'

'Yes, you have,' said a quiet voice from the cabin door. She glanced round to see Alvar leaning against the doorframe, his arms folded over his chest. 'You spent thirty years at the Academy, training under the supervision of the best tutors the Immortal Empire had to offer. Then you spent the next seventy years training with me.'

'Practice in a sparring ring doesn't prepare you for a battle,' Ornak argued.

Alvar's gaze didn't shift from Renila's face. 'I know. But I thought having the skill to knock my arse in the dirt would at least give her a fighting chance.'

'You think highly of yourself, don't you, princeling?' said Ornak. There was no denying the challenge in his voice.

Those thunderstorm eyes flickered to the Dragon. 'I've survived more battles and bloodshed than you've drawn breaths, boy. I haven't faced my equal with a sword since the day I taught Sephiron how to hold one.'

'Probably not something you want to brag about too much.' The taunting grin on Ornak's face was diabolical.

Thunder rumbled ominously in the background.

'Here's a thought – why don't you just whip them out and measure?' Arian sighed, getting to her feet. Ornak winked at her, a hand reaching for his belt. She levelled a flat stare in his direction. 'As entertaining as that might be, I'm not sure you'd like the result.' He opened his mouth to argue, his face reddening at the smirk on Alvar's face, but she continued. 'Stop wasting time. We've been here a week already – we should have moved on days ago. I only agreed to stay longer so you could make sure she wouldn't be a liability, and she looks competent to me.'

Ornak shook his head. 'She's not ready.'

'She doesn't need to be able to storm Dar Kual single-handed, Ornak,' Arian snapped, throwing her hands in the air. 'Darklings won't dare follow us any further into the mountains, and she'll have the three of us to guard her anyway.'

The Dragon hissed in frustration. 'My people might not suffer a Darkling to live, but I don't need to remind you that Nightwalkers rule Ciaron now. All it takes is one of them to get a good look at any of us, and we'll be up to our eyeballs in shit. She needs to be able to handle herself, especially since you're too scared to use the Casting.'

'It would draw every Darkling and Shade for miles around right to us, and you know it.'

Renila interrupted before Ornak could respond. 'Casting?'

'Elvish magic,' Arian replied, not taking her eyes off Ornak. 'Powerful, but not without its limitations – especially given that I am only part Elf. Not to mention, its easily tracked.'

Renila looked to Alvar for explanation as their companions continued to squabble. He sighed and rolled his eyes. 'Elves can use their power to manipulate the world around them. Control over the elements, if you like.

But they cannot create something from nothing. That power is unique to Immortals.'

'And the Shade,' Arian interjected.

'Their power is destruction,' he corrected sharply. 'We Wield the might of the Aether itself.'

She snorted. 'Whatever you want to call it, it works the same way. You both Wield a force not of this world.'

'Stop changing the subject,' Ornak growled. 'You know I'm right. And you're going to have to use the Casting to hide us at some point.'

'Compromise,' Alvar intervened. 'We move on, avoiding the towns for now, and she practises whenever possible. And my presence should help to hide all but the strongest of Castings. Acceptable?'

The Phoenix and the Dragon looked mutinous, scowling at each other, but eventually, they nodded.

'Where are we going?' Renila asked, handing Arian her other sword back once they looked less inclined to kill each other. She felt like Erion stuck in the middle of an argument between Suriya and Lucan.

'The Immortal says your boy was taken by a Shade Prince,' Arian said. 'Get a good look at him?'

Renila looked to Alvar. Her memories from that night were a haze. All she could remember was her fear. And those pale eyes.

Alvar only nodded and described him – slight, dark red hair and magic like black fire.

'Kieyin,' Ornak grunted, exchanging a long look with Arian.

The Phoenix woman nodded. 'The Shade King's chosen successor – in the absence of either of his true heirs. A Prince of the Shade Court, and one of three generals commanding the Shade King's armies. I've never faced him myself, but I've heard the stories. You were lucky to have escaped with your lives.'

'Not all of us did,' Renila whispered.

Arian watched Alvar for a moment before speaking. 'Your Captain gave his life for you. Do not dishonour that sacrifice with guilt for surviving when he did not. He made his own choices. You should respect that.'

Renila bristled at her tone. But something in her chest eased – the words soothing the harsh, bitter edges of regret and self-loathing that had been shredding her from the inside out.

'If Kieyin was the one who took the boy, he'll have handed him over to the Shade King,' said Ornak, glancing at Arian again. 'Only one place the King keeps a prisoner that valuable.'

She nodded. 'Elucion.'

Renila could feel the fist of fear closing around her heart. 'What can we do?'

'Doesn't matter if it was a Prince or the King himself. The Shade took your son.' There was no light in Ornak's eyes as he met her gaze. 'I say we go take him back.'

She stared at them in stunned silence. It was exactly what she wanted. She just hadn't expected it to be so easy. She glanced at Alvar, expecting him to argue. And though there was reluctance in his storm-cloud eyes, his jaw was set with determination.

'I promised you I would do everything in my power to return your son to you, and I will hold to that promise. If I have to tear the world apart, one rock at a time until I find him, that's what I'll do.'

She shivered from the force of his voice, at the promise of violence it held. A storm was gathering, thunder roiling behind his eyes and lightning sparking over his skin. She glanced at Arian. Her glorious golden eyes were burning, the flames of her strength and determination given form, and Renila felt something spark deep within her in recognition. A sliver of fear coursed up her spine as she looked around her. Here were two with fire and thunderstorms in their veins – who could ever hope to hold them in check?

She knew the stories. Magic was dangerous, a power so enormous it corrupted and destroyed all it touched. But as she thought of Erion, of her beautiful boy trapped alone and afraid in the dark, she found she didn't care. Alvar said he would tear the world apart to find her son? She would burn it to the ground if it meant she could pull him from the ashes.

Ornak smiled, a broad and bloody grin. 'I know what that look means.'

'The Shade will tremble in fear before the end,' Alvar murmured in agreement.

There was something akin to regret in Arian's gaze as she studied Renila. But she nodded. 'And so begins the Rising.'

They were another two weeks in the mountains, crossing the spine of Ciaron ridge and skirting south through the western foothills. It was a hard journey, though made easier by Starfyre. He'd given his master a reproachful look when Alvar first suggested it but had now grudgingly assumed the role of packhorse. Erion would have loved the gleaming stallion. It was easy to picture – her son, assuming responsibility for the horse, brushing him down each night, feeding and watering him whenever they stopped. It was an image that brought a tear to her eye.

As promised, they avoided all signs of civilisation – a harder task than she had first assumed. Mortals dwelt in relative safety in the mountains, protected by the presence of the Dragons lording over them from their castles.

'There are nine clans,' Ornak explained as they walked, 'each represented by an elected Chieftain who represents their interests at the Council of Nine.'

Alvar interjected, 'It's the same way the Council governs what's left of the Immortal Empire. Imagination was never a strength for your people.'

'Yes, a race of people who can shape-shift by visualising the form they wish to take must really lack imagination,' Ornak snapped.

'How does it work?' asked Renila before Alvar could respond.

Ornak grinned at her, flexing his arms. His bronze tattoos glowed in the sunlight, growing brighter and brighter until they almost obscured his entire body. His form shimmered and shifted, Changing slowly in a way that almost looked to be a trick of the light. Then it was over and, where Ornak had been, now stood a great, reddish-brown bear. Then the bear shimmered and shifted to reveal Ornak once more. A gasp of wonder echoed in her mind – the sound she'd heard from Erion's lips when he'd learned he was to be Farran's squire. She pushed the thought from her head. It was too painful.

'It's called the Change. I picture the form I want to take, and magic does the rest,' Ornak panted, his cheeks flushed as if from exertion. 'It has to be accurate though – if my mental image is off, so is what I turn into.'

Renila reached for him as he swayed. 'Are you alright?'

'It's draining,' he explained, waving her away. 'Magic is energy – it's tiring to use, and everyone has a finite resource. I wasn't blessed with the same kind of well to draw upon that you and Arian have. I'm more powerful than a lot of Dragons, but using that power still takes it out of me.'

She took his hand in her own until he was breathing normally, ignoring the suspicious frown creasing Alvar's brow. 'Tell me more about them? Your people?'

'Not much to say about them,' he snorted. 'Mine is a bloodthirsty, warmongering people. Even before the Fall, Nightwalkers were not uncommon, and they wore their curse like a badge of honour. It's even worse now.'

Renila frowned. 'Nightwalkers?'

'Murderers,' Arian growled, unable to hide the disgust and hate in her voice. 'They were Graced once, but when they turned on their own kind, they were cursed to endless night – banished from the light that once brought them strength. They're killers, traitors to their blood. Before the Fall, they were killed on sight in Elucion.'

Ornak's eyes were sad, but he didn't disagree. 'Nightwalkers rule Ciaron now. But even before the Fall, many admired them. They thought the curse a reasonable price to pay for vengeance, money, power – whatever drives them to kill their own kind.'

'And is it?'

He looked at the ground, refusing to meet her gaze. 'As a boy, I used to think not. I thought I would die rather than never feel the sun on my skin. I was sure there was nothing that would ever move me to murder my own kin. But now ... now I'm not so sure.'

They kept moving. Never staying in one place for more than a day. They passed through the lands of three different clans, giving their seats a wide berth. Ornak's continuous stream of information was surprisingly soothing, though it clearly irritated Alvar. Arian just watched, not bothering to intervene. Sometimes, when Renila wasn't paying attention, it was almost as if Erion was walking at her side – the incessant chatter an aspect of his personality he'd reserved for his mother.

The seat of the Tu clan was furthest north, Ornak explained. Their castle – guarding the entrance to a vast network of caves that ran through the mountains – occupied the whole of the first great chamber, which the Dragons called the Maw.

'Religious nutters,' was all he'd offered to describe the Maw's occupants.

She never saw the seat of Bán – the next most northern clan. Ornak just pointed to the twin peaks high above, shrouded in mist.

'The Horns,' he'd told her, shouting over a howling wind that came roaring off the mountains. 'The castle sits in the valley between them, and they keep a constant guard on the towers atop the peaks themselves. I flew the gap once.' He shuddered. 'Don't know how anyone can live in a place like that.'

A hundred questions would have risen to Erion's lips at that. Renila could hear his voice, whispering them in the vaults of her mind. One or two she even asked aloud, just so she might have something to tell him if they were ever reunited.

'So you can take any form you wish? Even something that can fly?'

Ornak nodded. 'Tricky, though. You need to visualise the wings perfectly, or risk crashing mid-flight … if you can even take off at all.'

'What form did you take to fly the gap?'

He grinned. 'A dragon, of course.'

They were now deep within Sil territory, on the Western Wing. Their seat was a sprawling splendour that spilled out of a secluded corrie, with the castle itself nestled at the centre, the ridge of mountains known as the Spine just visible through the cloud beyond. A wall of glittering granite blocked the entrance, and guard towers lined the upper ridge. But the town that had grown up around the castle stretched far out over the hillside. In her head, Erion's eyes were wide with wonder.

'Sil has always been a wealthy clan,' Ornak said, 'and safest of all from Darkling raiders. But even they didn't escape the Fall unscathed. Kah Thoran's mate was the Sil Chieftain's youngest daughter. She was our High Priestess, the Jewel of Ciaron. The Darkling Queens sacked the Temple, slaughtering her and all her handmaidens. Her daughter saw the whole thing. Sil Voren hasn't seen his granddaughter since. He's a broken man now, but he has no fear of the Shade. Besides my father's lands, this is probably the safest place for you in all of Ciaron.'

Renila looked up at the bustling settlement with trepidation. 'Is that where we're going?'

Ornak and Arian exchanged a long look, while Alvar crossed his arms expectantly.

'Voren remains Chieftain in name only,' Arian began. 'He's only been allowed to live because his other daughter Vella is wed to the leader of the Nightwalkers.'

Ornak grunted in disgust. 'Vella hated her sister – she was always jealous of Adara's union with Thoran. We'll get no help from that spiteful bitch. And even if we can get through her to Voren, which is unlikely, he won't aid us without Dorrien here to twist his arm.'

'We need supplies, Ornak,' warned Arian. 'And information. If she's left word for us anywhere, it'll be here.'

He grunted again, this time in agreement. Then he frowned. 'She might have gone to the Tail.'

'She wouldn't ask that of you,' Arian breathed, laying a gentle hand on his arm. 'No, if we've any hope – it'll be here.'

Then she looked at Alvar, who only nodded, understanding the exchange. He closed his eyes, frowning in concentration as sweat beaded on his brow. Slowly, painfully slowly, tattoos bloomed. More purple than grey, they forked and streaked like bolts of lightning over his softly glowing skin. Power churned like a thunderstorm beneath, but as the magic abated, so too did that ethereal aura. Panting from the exertion, he opened his eyes. They were wholly black, iris and sclera swallowed by night.

'Not quite what I was going for,' he complained, glancing down at his tattoos.

Ornak snorted. 'It'll do. Silver wouldn't have worked anyway – they'd have known you weren't one of their own and asked questions. Let's just hope there's nobody here from Io.'

Arian was busy braiding her hair back from her face, having discarded her headscarf for the first time since they'd left the cabin. Then she frowned and looked down at her arm, where ruby-red tattoos now blazed their way over her golden skin. Her eyes swirled to black, like Alvar's and with a wave of her hand Ornak's too were changed.

Then she looked more closely at Renila. Renila felt her skin tingle as the magic brushed over her, her own power sparking as if in answer. But when she looked down, rather than red tattoos to match Arian's, her skin was covered in black marks, curling over her like flames. Arian winced and glanced at Ornak. He was frowning in confusion, recognition sparking in his emerald gaze.

'Seriously?' he snapped, rounding on her.

Arian bristled. 'Too many of us from one clan will draw attention. If you don't like it, do it yourself.'

Ornak seemed to scent the lie – Renila could – but he let the matter drop. Instead, he pulled a jet-black cloak from his pack and handed it to Renila, watching in silence as Arian sat her down and wrapped her claret locks in a headscarf. There was no mistaking the suspicion and hurt in his now-black gaze, but he said nothing. Whatever secret Arian and Alvar were hiding from him, he seemed to understand that he would be told only if and when it was necessary for him to know. Renila envied him his trust, and his patience. Erion's voice was a constant whisper in her mind now, crying out in pain and fear. Whenever she closed her eyes, she could see his tear-stained face, his hands reaching for her. There would not be much of her mind left if they did not find him soon.

While Arian finished fixing Renila's hair, Alvar busied himself packing some of their more ostentatious weapons away, hiding the jewelled hilts of Arian's twin blades and the ornate scabbard of his Immortal-wrought sword from view. Ornak, on the other hand, was strapping more weapons to his body.

'Bloodthirsty and warmongering,' he reminded her, when he caught her watching him. He hefted the great, two-handed axe higher, running an assessing eye over the edge. Then he handed her a simple, vicious-looking dagger nearly as long as her arm. 'Violence is the only language my people understand. Stay close, and do not hesitate to use this if you have to.'

The town was a bustling hive of activity, the cobbled streets thronging with people. Farmers hauling produce for market, merchants and artisans carting their wares, mercenaries keen to spend hard-won coin. The Night-walkers were easy to spot, their clothing similar to that which Arian had given them. Hooded and cloaked, scarves drawn up over their faces and even their hands covered. Hiding from the sunlight that would turn them to ash.

A group of them stood in the shadow of a building, hoods down. Most bore the silver marks of the local clan. But there were a few others – flashes of blue and red, purple and green, and even one man covered in twisting black marks like Renila's. Ornak had given him a wide berth, a restraining hand on Arian's wrist until he was out of sight.

He led the way through the winding streets. The crowd parted for him, giving way to either his bulk or the promise of violence associated with the arsenal of weapons he carried. Renila followed closely, one side shielded by the gleaming flanks of the great white stallion and the other guarded by the grim scowl on Alvar's handsome face. Arian was not far behind, slipping smoothly through invisible gaps in the crowd.

They passed through the main gates without incident – though the sweat beading Arian's brow suggested it was no accident that the guards had overlooked them. A relieved gasp escaped the Phoenix woman when the throng swallowed them once more, and Alvar had to catch her arm when she stumbled. She flashed him a grateful smile that made Renila see red. But then that flash of hot anger was gone, and she was left wondering if she was indeed losing her mind.

Before she could think too much on it, Ornak glanced over his shoulder and jerked his chin in silent command. Renila followed the gesture and looked around in wonder.

The marketplace could only be described as the beating heart of the town. A hundred stalls – at least – lined the square, with more arranged in neat rows up and down the centre. But it was the variety of what was on offer that took Renila's breath away.

Food. Grocers' tables laden with milk and eggs and cheese and fruit and vegetables. Butchers' counters piled with everything from huge raw haunches to delicate slices of cured meat. Bakers' stands bursting with freshly baked bread and cakes and tarts and pastries – the smell of it enough to make her mouth water. Much of it packaged to be taken home, but some cooked and hot and ready to be eaten right away. And drink. Wine and ale and whisky and mead, bottled or served that very moment, and all available for tasting before purchase.

Fashion. Dresses and shoes. Scarves and hats and gloves. Fabrics like Renila had never seen, bought by the yard or incorporated into a garment of the customer's design – ordered now and delivered within the week. Perfume and cosmetics. Ribbons and feathers and lace and more. Jewellery befitting a dragon's hoard.

More practical clothing. Armour and weapons. Paintings and tapestries. Pots and pans, glasses and plates, cutlery and other utensils. Even a man selling pups sired by his prize hunting dog.

It was almost too much to take in. She didn't know where to look – it was so overwhelming. Alvar seemed to sense her distress and took her hand in his.

Arian appeared at her other side, a long-suffering expression on her face. 'Market day. I might have known – I thought there were too many people here. It only happens once a month, but of course, it would be today.'

'Don't start your whinging,' muttered Ornak, joining them. 'It helps us, and you know it. Less chance of awkward questions, and a simple answer, just in case.' He glanced around, eyes bright and assessing. 'Right. You three head to the tavern over that way and wait for me there. Shouldn't be too long.'

Arian nodded in agreement, but the frown on her face said she wasn't happy about it. 'Be careful.'

He winked in answer and sauntered out into the marketplace. Arian just shook her head in annoyance and led the way to the tavern he'd pointed at. Taking out her frustration on the first person to cross her path, she haggled so viciously over the price of stabling the horse that the poor stableboy left in tears.

The tavern had an area of seating outside and, despite the cool bite of mountain air on the wind, Arian insisted on dining there. Sheltered beneath a colourful awning, they were able to remove their various coverings. Any complaint Renila had was soon forgotten when the serving girl produced three steaming bowls of stew and a plate of crusty white bread. As she and Alvar tore into their meals with gusto, Arian picked at her food – too busy watching Ornak from the corner of her eye.

Renila followed her gaze, contemplating the big Dragon as he drifted through the crowds, pausing occasionally to examine wares or simply pass the time of day with the merchant. He bought some things now and then, including a new knife he didn't need, but he seemed to be more interested in information than his purchases. He avoided any stalls run by Dragons – Nightwalker or otherwise.

'There's a price on his head,' Arian said when Renila asked about it. 'Mortals won't know who he is, but Dragons recognise their own. Even with the glamour.'

Renila eyed him across the square. 'Why?'

426

'Because he didn't die when he was supposed to.' There was a finality in her tone, and Renila knew not to push the matter further. They finished their meals in silence.

Across the square, a Dragon woman was watching Ornak with a coy smile – her bare arms banded in the silver tattoos that marked her as a local. Not a Nightwalker. The first Dragon they'd seen who wasn't, and he made a beeline straight for her. Her body arched towardss him provocatively, and the lazy grin splitting his face gave some indication as to the topic of conversation. Sure enough, coins changed hands, and she pulled him back into the shadows of a nearby alley. Renila flushed with embarrassment and looked away.

A face in the crowd made her pause.

A pale, serious face – soft with childhood, but likely to be handsome one day. Nothing notable about it now; nothing that would catch the eye. A face born to blend into the background. Except for those eyes. Brightest amber, glowing like hot coals in the sunshine. Her own eyes staring back at her, out of her son's face.

'Mother.'

Alvar nudged her with an elbow, jolting her back to reality. 'Are you alright?'

She shook herself, nodding. She tried to speak, tried to tell him what she'd seen, but the words stuck in her throat. It was madness. It wasn't possible. But her eyes kept drifting back to that same spot. Where she'd seen him.

Erion.

Ornak reappeared from the alley after about ten minutes, fastening his belt, a satisfied smile on his face. Arian only snorted and downed the last of her ale.

'Come on,' she said, standing. 'He's got what he needs. Time to go.'

Renila blinked in surprise and allowed Alvar to pull her to her feet. But as soon as he released her, her gaze was drawn right back to the crowd. Searching.

A glint of crimson as a red jewel caught in the light; burgundy hair gleaming in the sun. Long, delicate fingers closing around a slender wrist. The Shade Prince, dragging Erion behind him. She blinked. No – a father and son, fighting their way through the crowd.

Arian and Alvar were moving now, skirting round the edge of the square, working their way over to Ornak. Renila followed, hardly looking where she was going. A tinkle of laughter snagged her attention. A smiling face – that impish grin, a rare but cherished sight. *Erion.* She shook her head in confusion. No. Just a boy, smiling at the gift his mother had just bought him.

Ornak was close now, his brow creased with concern and eyes flashing at something behind them. He seemed to be trying to signal Arian, but she couldn't see him through the crowd. Renila was about to say something when a voice made her turn.

'Mother.'

She stilled, her gaze wide with wonder as she reached for her son. 'Erion. How?'

'There's no time to explain,' he said, taking her hand in his own. His face was pale, drawn with worry and fear. 'Quick, come with me. It's not safe for you here.'

Renila frowned, confused. Her mind was so sluggish. 'What are you talking about?'

'The people with Alvar,' he whispered, drawing her close. 'They work for the Shade King. They're here to kill you.'

She blinked, shaking her head. 'No, that can't be. They're my friends.'

'It's true. I saw them talking to him, just before I escaped. He sent them to hunt you down and kill you.' A small voice in the back of her mind whispered that none of this made any sense. That she was being tricked somehow. But it was silenced when she registered the fear in her son's eyes. Erion was dragging her backwards now, pulling her with him as he melted back into the throng. Still, something nagged at her senses.

'What about Alvar? We can't just leave him.'

'It doesn't matter. They'll kill you and take me back to the King. I can't go back there. Please, Mother, please don't make me go back.'

Any hesitation that remained was drowned out by the desperation in his voice. She had never heard her son sound so scared. It broke her heart, and in that moment, Erion vanished. Panic gripped her like a fist around her chest, squeezing all the air from her lungs. She darted forward, pushing and shoving as she searched for him, trying to scream his name but unable to summon the strength. Her legs trembled, almost too weak to hold her. Her vision blurred, like she was wading through fog. There was a hollow ringing in her ears – almost drowning out the familiar voice roaring her name over the din. People were screaming, the crowd recoiling from something behind her, pressing so tight around her she could hardly breathe.

Then Erion was there, his hand somehow finding her through the crush. His bright amber eyes flashed with fear and relief. Then they were running, fleeing with the churning crowd from some faceless menace bearing down on them. Erion's grip on her hand was unyielding, a lifeline to cling to in a roiling sea that threatened to drown her.

Out of the marketplace, sprinting down the winding streets, they allowed themselves to be swept along by the screaming throng. Then Erion swerved hard to the left, dragging her with him down a darkened alley. There were fewer people here, but in the narrow street it was still difficult to catch her breath.

He veered right, down another alley. Then another right. Then left. Left again. And again. Right. Darting through the maze of dark, narrow streets with unerring surety.

Then they were through the great gates, twisting and turning through the town until there was nothing but open hillside in front of them.

Gasping from exertion they paused, hidden in the shadows of an outlying house. She swayed, but Erion held her tight. Too tight.

'Are you alright?' he asked. She nodded and tried to pull away, unsure.

He smiled, but her stomach shifted at the sight. There was something dark and malicious in his face that had not been there before.

His eyes swirled and changed – palest blue, shining like moonstone. Familiar, yet not. Suddenly, she realised that she was looking up at him. Dark hair faded to silver-blonde. The scrawny arms holding her, the slim chest pressed against her, filled out. Became the body of a man, strong and lean and corded in powerful muscle. A strange, star-shaped mark bloomed on his brow. That boyish face grew thinner, more handsome. Breathtaking. So stunning that she could only stare. He smirked, running gentle fingers down her cheek in a tender caress. Some instinct screamed at her to fight back, but she couldn't move. Couldn't even stretch her fingers towards the knife Ornak had given her, sheathed at her hip.

Two figures stepped from the shadows beside them. Cloaked in darkest grey, their faces hidden beneath hoods, one of them led a stallion by the reins. A magnificent beast, his coat glistening like quicksilver.

'They're not far behind you,' one figure warned.

The man smiled. It was an evil, wicked thing. 'I'm sure you can remedy that. I'm paying you enough.'

'You didn't tell us *who* we were delaying,' the other objected. 'The price is double.'

'The price is what we agreed,' the man breathed, his voice soft and all the more dangerous for it. 'If you want to earn some extra pennies, you can always deliver their heads to Elucion. The reward the King has offered for just one of them would keep you both in wine and women for the rest of your lives.'

The two figures hesitated, glancing sidelong at each other. Black eyes flashed beneath those hoods. *Nightwalkers*. One jerked his chin at Renila, still motionless in the man's arms. 'What about her?'

'What about her?' the man snapped. 'She's for the Princess, and therefore, none of your business. Now get a move on. The Hal bastard is close and Zorana will have your hides if I fail.'

The Nightwalkers hesitated, but they nodded and handed the reins over. Then they vanished back into the shadows. The silver-haired man looked back down at Renila, fighting against him with all her might but still frozen where she stood.

'Sleep now, little dove,' he murmured. 'Save your energy for later. You'll need it.'

Then his mind was inside hers, seeping in through her defences like smoke and smothering all resistance. She had never felt so helpless – he was in control, able to move her body like a puppet master twitching the strings of a marionette. And then with a simple whispered word, he soothed her fears; altered her emotions from terror and dread to trust and contentment.

'*What are you doing to me?*' she heard herself ask, though she no longer understood why she objected to what he had done.

The man chuckled darkly. '*You are mine now, sweet Renila. Sleep.*'

Unable to fight him, she did as she was bid.

CHAPTER THIRTY-SIX

A lexan would never know for sure how he evaded the Dragons hunting him. The echoes of their roars and the howling of Théon's Casting followed him for miles as he careered over rock and moor, but even they fell silent.

Théon. Gods, please let her be alright. He didn't think he could bear it if she was hurt protecting him.

You broke your vow.

He shoved the thought from his mind. She'd ordered him to run. He'd done as he was told. But now what? There was nowhere to hide. No way off the island either. Not unless he called for help, and he was damned if he was going to be the one to bring the Shade King to these shores. *Fuck.* How had he forgotten the damn ring? Or underestimated the Princess? Her Dragon lover and his sister? He knew better than that. Had spent long enough studying them all. *Know your enemy.* A lesson learned on the streets of Illyol as a child. One that had kept him alive in the Shade Court since the Claiming.

He dropped to a crouch and considered his options. Magic writhed in his veins, rising in response to his frustration. His fear. That dark behemoth of power waking from almost a century of slumber. It was a sign of his distress that it had stirred at all. For her. His Queen. The mark on his palm burning. *Please, Gods, keep her safe.* He reined it back in, but it did not go quietly. Once roused, it begged to be loosed. Gods, he was tempted to destroy the Dragons who had threatened his Queen, to watch them burn in magic more like a Shade Wielding than an Elvish Casting.

He uncoiled a small, searching tendril of power, searching for anywhere that might offer some shelter from pursuit. Sighed with relief when he found what he wanted. Then frowned when he realised what he'd have to do to get to it.

The sea cave was one of the biggest he'd ever seen, but that wasn't what drew him to it. No. Of far more interest was the freshwater cave adjacent.

Carved out by the river rushing down off the moor, now dropping through rock in a thundering waterfall. So either he'd have to follow that route, or else pick his way down the cliffs and then swim through the connecting chamber. Neither of which was appealing in the cold dark of the night.

Both, however, were better than facing the Dragons.

What if she was hurt? Trapped? Dying?

He shoved the thoughts away and chose the cliffs. Slower, but safer. Especially when he needed to conserve every ounce of power in case the Dragons found him. He was no use to his Queen dead.

The cave entrance was at the end of a long, broad gorge – no doubt carved out by the sea and perhaps once part of the cave itself. And if he thought the opening was big, it was nothing compared to the vast chamber beyond. It was remarkable. Breathtaking. And useless as a hiding place.

He prowled inside on silent feet, overwhelmed by the roar of the waterfall thundering down into the pool below. He peered through the darkness, thanking the Gods for his Darkling-heightened senses as they picked out the shore tucked behind the waterfall. With a grimace, he dropped into the water, sucking in a sharp breath at its cold bite, and swam across.

His body was aching by the time he pulled himself out of the water. Whether from cold, exhaustion or just the stress of the last hour, he wasn't sure. Perhaps a combination of all three. Whatever the cause, a wave of fatigue swept over him as he crawled onto the shore. He barely had the strength to warm and dry his clothes before passing out face-first on the rocks.

He was woken by the sound of footsteps echoing in the sea cave, though how he heard them over the roar of the waterfall he didn't know. Survival instincts were strange like that. He rolled to his feet, hunkered down between some of the larger rocks and waited with bated breath.

A familiar figure appeared above the rock pool, silhouetted against the moonlight spilling into the cave beyond.

Théon.

Relief crashed through him, and even in the darkness, he could see it mirrored in her as she sensed his presence. He was in the water and swimming to her without a second thought, desperate to hold her.

A desperation she seemed to share as she threw her arms around his neck, clinging to him. She was shaking. From cold or fear or relief, he wasn't sure. Didn't care. All that mattered was she was in his arms. Where she belonged.

'You're alright,' he murmured into her hair. 'Gods, I was so worried.'

'I'm fine,' she promised.

'What happened? How did you get away?'

She laughed breathlessly against his throat. 'My Shade magic might be bound, but my strength isn't. I might not have the Wielding, but my Casting is powerful enough to handle two Dragons.'

431

'You killed them?'

A violent shudder wracked her slender frame. 'No. Gods, I was tempted. When I realised they would kill you no matter what I said, the rage … If the Shade hadn't been bound … But no. They're family. By blood and more.'

He nodded in understanding and held her a little tighter. 'How did you find me?'

'Tracked down my magic,' she said, tapping the ring on his finger. 'Surprisingly effective.'

Then, before he could say anything more, she kissed him. With such unbridled passion it made his head spin. Her lips were soft and warm but insistent, and he almost gasped out loud when her tongue stroked his lips. He grabbed her by the waist and pulled her hard against him, sweeping inside her mouth with his tongue. Smiled as she moaned, her hands in his hair, crushing his mouth against hers.

Conscious thought was beyond him at that point, and his hands moved of their own accord, tracing over her hips until he grasped her firm arse. She squealed with delight when he lifted her and wrapped her thighs around his waist. Pinned her against the rocks as he revelled in the heat of her body against his. Her hands moved from his hair to grip his massive shoulders for support. Something inside him longed to throw his head back and roar as she dug her nails into his back. Instead, he kissed along her jaw and down her throat, for once ignoring her blood singing to him from beneath her skin.

Then her hands dipped inside his shirt. He groaned, desperate to touch her skin as he tore her clothes from her body. She ripped his shirt in her rush to remove it, but he barely spared it a thought. He wanted to be inside her with an urgent need, the like of which he had never experienced. A thought struck him in the moment before their joining, and he paused.

'Are you sure?' he groaned against her mouth. She pulled away long enough to look him in the eye.

'Yes,' she breathed. 'I want you.'

'I don't think I can be gentle,' he warned, quivering with the effort of restraint. The look Théon gave him was almost his undoing. Her eyes glowed with that terrible, pulsing light, the Shade threatening to surface, as some of that darkness locked deep within her was unleashed.

'Likewise,' she growled, her voice husky with desire. 'I'll try not to break you.' She moved, and Alexan surrendered to his impulses. His eyes rolled back into his head as he roared with the sheer pleasure of her. He wasn't gentle, not by any means, but neither was she.

It was perhaps an hour before dawn. They lay tangled together on the shore of the rock pool. She was dozing in his arms. They hadn't slept much. He'd had her against the rocks, and then again in the pool, and then beneath the waterfall itself. He'd got on his knees and worshipped her like the Queen she was, and when he was done, she'd repaid the favour.

His breath hitched as he remembered the sensation of her mouth on him. Gods above, he thought, where had she learned that? He'd been far from gentle, but she'd matched him every step of the way. His back was still stinging from her nails raking him from shoulder to hip. And her wrists were circled with bruises from where he'd pinned her arms above her head while he'd ravished her.

In an effort to distract himself from thoughts of tomorrow, he stroked a hand along the smooth curve of her side, trailing up from her hip to her breast. She stirred beneath his fingers, stretching as he coaxed her out of sleep. He palmed her breast in his hand, and she gasped, arching into his touch. He grazed his thumb across that peaked point, causing her to moan.

'You'd better be prepared to finish what you've started,' she warned him, not even bothering to open her eyes.

'And if I'm not?' he taunted, pinching hard. She hissed, and her eyes flew open, dark with desire.

'I'll make sure you regret it,' she growled. He chuckled again, moving his hand to her other breast, toying with her. She watched his hand, eyes snagging on the mark on his palm.

'What is it?'

His hand stilled. 'A birthmark.'

'Looks more like a brand.' She took his hand in hers, drawing it closer so she might inspect it. 'Like a snake, devouring its own tail.'

He loosed a slow breath. That was exactly what it looked like.

'I don't know what it is,' he admitted. 'I've had it as long as I can remember.'

She smiled then and pressed her lips to it. 'It's part of you, and that is all I need to know.'

Then she pulled him close to her once more. He still couldn't be gentle with her – his desire was too strong, too fierce for that. She stirred something primal and instinctive inside him that wouldn't be tamed. But he worshipped her with his loving, let his body tell her what his words failed to say. He wasn't sure if she understood. Part of him thought she did. Wondered if she felt the same way. Prayed to the Gods she didn't. It was her only chance at freedom.

<hr/>

They dressed quickly, Théon repairing the worst of the damage they'd done to each other's clothes with a hurried Casting. They were both reluctant to leave, hesitant to venture out into the world where anyone might be waiting. But dawn was a pale threat on the horizon. The Dragons would resume their search at first light … if they had stopped it at all. Each moment they waited brought death one step closer.

'So what now?' he asked.

'I have no idea.' Her voice was heavy, though there was no regret in her eyes.

'They'll kill us if they find us.'

'I know.'

'Is there any other way off the islands?'

She shook her head. 'They'll be watching every port, if we even make it that far. There'll be scouts scouring every inch of coast and moor.'

'A glamour?'

'Too many eyes. They work on mortals well enough, but Unicorns see right through them.'

He looked at her in surprise. 'There are other Unicorns here?'

'A few,' she admitted with a grim smile. 'The Fall wasn't quite as thorough as legend would have you believe.'

She didn't know the half of it.

'So what are our options?' he asked, steering the conversation away. 'Lay low until they give up?'

'I can't see that happening. No, we need to get out of here. I'm just not sure how.'

He hesitated, reluctant to push her this soon. When what was between them was so new; so fragile. But he was running out of options. 'I have an idea. But you won't like it.'

He held out the amulet. Didn't need to tell her what it was, not when she'd worn one as a child. The King still kept it by his bed, much to Jenia's disgust. There was no need to explain. She understood. A drop of blood, a whisper of magic, and her father would have her off this island before she could blink. Kill their pursuers too, if she asked it of him. Break whatever spell bound her power. Set her free.

She was tempted, that much was obvious. Not surprising when she'd spent the last century being judged and persecuted for who and what she was. She had to realise they'd never trusted her. Not fully. Not with that power sleeping inside her. And now? They'd never trust her again. Not after what she'd done.

'I can't. It would just be exchanging one cage for another. I'd rather die than give myself to him.'

'Gods, what is it about the King's blood that makes his daughters so damned stubborn?' he hissed in frustration. Regretting his words the moment he said them. But the damage was done. Théon froze, glaring at him with lethal focus.

'What did you say?' she breathed.

He took a deep breath. There was no avoiding it now.

So he told her. Told her how he'd chanced upon her sister in the Ravenswood. How he'd fought and captured Keriath. Lost her to Drosta and his Hunt. And when he was done, she slapped him clean across the face. He recoiled from the force of it but didn't retaliate. Gods knew he'd deserved it. She turned away, her shoulders shaking. With anger or fear, he wasn't sure.

'Théon, I'm sorry,' he said. 'But it's not too late. We can free her. We can

434

free you both. The King can break whatever spell they've bound you with, and then we can save Keriath. We can all be free.'

Her shoulders stopped shaking, and she turned to face him. Something had changed in her eyes. If he hadn't known better, he'd have said it was her father staring through them – they were so cold and full of hate.

'I will raze the whole world to ash before I let Keriath suffer like I did,' she snarled. He stepped back when he saw her eyes glow with that terrifying light as the Shade fought for freedom. Tried to stay calm in the face of that raging power.

'And if you had a choice?' he asked. 'If you could trade your place for hers? Would you do it?'

'Did you not hear me?' she hissed in a voice that was death. 'Or did I not speak plainly enough for you? I will die a thousand deaths before I go back to him, and I will burn the world down before I see Keriath endure that fate. Understand this, *Darkling*, I will kill us both before I allow either of us to stand at his side. I'll kill you too, if I have to. By the Gods, you'd deserve it.'

'I'm sorry, Théon,' he whispered. 'But you knew why I was here the day we met. You know I didn't have a choice, not in any of it. I've done everything I can to fight the Claiming, to prepare you as best as I can. To give you the best chance at beating me. I swear it.'

'You think that's why I'm angry?' she snarled, her aura raging like wildfire. In her fury, she had loosed her hold upon her glamour, revealing herself in all her wild savagery. She was beautiful and strong and fierce, and in that moment, he realised he loved her. Diathor was nothing more than a distant memory. A ghost that haunted his waking dreams. But here was a living, breathing woman who he would follow to the ends of the world if it was his choice.

'Why then?' he asked.

The Shade was raging to get free, pulsing behind her eyes. 'Of course I knew why you were here!' she spat. 'I've known this moment was coming for years – since the day I learned that the name of my father's new general was the same as the Lord Protector who gave his life to save me. No one else bothered to remember your name, but I did and I knew. I knew that somehow you'd survived and you'd tried to avenge her. How else do you think you've survived this long, when all your predecessors have fallen to Resari's blade? I've been ready for you for years now and I should have killed you on sight. But you showed me kindness when I didn't deserve it, and I owed you the same chance. And when I let you see the monster underneath, and you didn't flinch … Do you know how long it's been since anyone looked at me and didn't just see the darkness sleeping within? You gave me hope, made me care for you, made me think there was a chance. And then you shattered it all!'

'Théon, I'm sorry—' His voice hitched, the self-loathing like a fist around his throat.

'Don't!' she screamed. 'You don't get to be sorry. You gave me hope. And then with your next breath told me you'd sent my sister to the Darkling

435

Queens, to face Gods only know what! You could have done or said anything to get me to return, but you hit me where you knew it would hurt hardest. Do you think I need the monster to free her? Do you think I need my father to fight my battles for me? I will tear Dar Kual down with my bare hands and drag Keriath from the rubble. And when I am done, I will hunt down the bastard that sired me, and I will kill him for everything he has done.'

'That's why he sent me!' Alexan bellowed, tears in his eyes. 'He sent me because he knew I alone could break you. He knew I could get under your skin like nobody else, because I am the only one left living who has seen you at your weakest. I helped lead you back to the light; he thought it was fitting for me to lead you back into the darkness.

'I never had a choice, Théon. It's all been him since the first moment I walked into that blasted city. Why do you think he made me this in the first place? He looked into my head, a hundred years ago, and saw what we meant to each other. He's spent the last century breaking me, turning me into the perfect weapon to break you. It's all he cares about – having you back at his side. He wants his children safe. Is that so wrong?'

'He's a demon bent on ruling the world!' she yelled. 'He killed my mother, slaughtered my people! He doesn't get to care about things like family!'

A high, girlish voice interrupted them – echoing through the chamber. 'Oh, but he does, little Théon,' it crooned. 'He cares about his family very much.' Alexan's shoulders slumped in defeat when he saw the glint of blood-red hair in the shadows beneath the cave entrance.

Jenia.

The Darkling's smile was diabolical as she stepped out of the shadows. A vicious growl ripped from Alexan's lips at the sight of her. At the knowledge that Kieyin had either betrayed him or that the King's patience had finally run out. Either way, he knew why she was here. The day he'd been made a Darkling, the King had given his first order – the same order he gave every Darkling. Obey Jenia's word as though it was his own. When she spoke to him, she spoke with the Shade King's voice. The voice of the Claiming. It was a voice he must obey.

He shifted from foot to foot, hoping to remind Théon that he was behind her – that he was still a threat. But his Queen's attention was focussed on Jenia, putting pieces of the puzzle together.

'I should have known you were behind this,' she murmured, her voice barely more than a deadly whisper. 'It has your sick, twisted mind written all over it.'

Jenia's answering grin sent shivers down his spine. 'Much as I would like to claim credit, I had nothing to do with any of this.'

'Kieyin then?' Théon breathed. 'This doesn't seem like my father's style.'

'If you're looking for the architect of your destruction, I suggest you

436

look behind you.' Jenia hummed, cocking her head to the side as she considered her prey.

Théon looked at him, that evergreen gaze wide with betrayal. 'You led her here?'

He shook his head, not taking his eyes off Jenia. 'Not me.'

'Oh, come now, don't be shy,' purred Jenia, tossing something in the dirt at their feet. 'The mortal I took this from described you perfectly. Said you'd traded it for services rendered?'

Alexan tensed as Théon stooped to pick it up, but he didn't need to look to know what it was. Diathor's necklace. The one he'd given to Mari and Ana in exchange for their help in ferrying the mortal refugees off the mainland. Théon was staring at him, betrayal now mingling with hurt.

'It's not what you think,' he murmured, low enough that only she could hear. 'Illyandi wanted to help the mortals at the camp. The necklace was payment to get them to the islands. She told me you knew.'

Théon's gaze hardened. 'And you believed her?'

'I had to give the mortals to my Hunt to play with,' Jenia was saying. 'They were not best pleased with you, Alexan. They wanted to come with me, to make you suffer for the pain you caused, but I wanted to savour this moment alone. I just hope two can keep them occupied until I return.'

'Your Hunt are slow, lazy and predictable, Jenia,' he retorted. 'I've been telling you that for years.'

'Did you fuck her like one of your Elucion whores?' Jenia crooned, her eyes flashing with delight. Darkling senses were sharp, and only one thing made scents mingle that closely. 'I hope not, for your sake – the King won't be happy if you treated his daughter like a common slut.'

'Fuck you,' Théon hissed.

'Mmm. Perhaps I'd enjoy that. You tell me – did he make you moan? Coax delicious noises from you? I've never bothered with him myself, but you might just have perked my interest.'

'My father rarely likes to share. I might even consider going back to him, if he'd let me be the one to inflict your punishment for being unfaithful.'

It was only because Alexan knew Jenia so well that he saw her blanch at the thought. She was baiting Théon. Jenia's heart, black and callous though it was, belonged to the King. She'd never looked twice at another man. Théon's father was a jealous bastard, though not half as jealous as his lover.

'We could stand here and trade insults all day,' Jenia replied, her voice deeper and heavy with ancient weariness, 'but it will still come down to the same thing, Théon. You have a choice. Come with me, return to your father. You can be with Alexan; we will rescue Keriath, and you can do whatever you like to the Darkling Queens.'

'Or?'

Jenia heaved a great sigh. 'Or die.'

'Death it is,' Théon said. 'But I will not go quietly.'

Jenia smirked. 'I wouldn't expect anything less. Alexan, kill her.'

The order tore through him like a knife, piercing flesh and bone to reach his heart. His body moved of its own accord, even as he roared in warning. But she was faster than either of them expected and blasted him back into the rocks with a Casting. Fought her way past Jenia and vanished.

Alexan followed, the King's orders ringing in his ears. *Kill her.* But how could he bring himself to do the deed? No. No matter what, he wouldn't do it. Even if it meant sacrificing his own life.

Dawn was near to breaking as he scrambled up the cliffs after Théon. He'd been fast enough to chase down Keriath. He was as fast as any of the Graced. Faster, thanks to the dark magic that had corrupted him into this monster. He just prayed she was faster.

He'd never seen himself as clearly as he did now. Théon's eyes, with all the pain and fury they held, had been the mirror he'd needed. He tried to tell himself that was why he pushed himself so hard to catch her. He was a monster that needed put down, and Théon was the only one who could do it. But it was a lie. Jenia's orders – the King's orders – were singing in his blood, driving him onward.

Kill her. Kill her. Kill her. The words were a drumbeat as frantic as his racing heart. He wouldn't do it, he told himself. He'd find a way. Give her every chance to kill him first. He could smell her passage up the cliffs. The fear. The fury. Lust and rage. All of it mingled with his scent. He couldn't believe they had lain tangled together beneath the waterfall only hours ago.

There was no time to dwell on it. He had to catch her. He could claim purer motivations all he liked, but whether it was to kill or be killed, he had to reach her before Jenia. If Jenia got there first … Théon's death would become the stuff of legend. A warning to all who would turn their back on Sephiron's heir. Gods only knew what they'd do to Illyandi and Silvermane, if they found them. To the other Graced sheltering here.

He hauled his body up over the cliff edge and picked out the dark figure sprinting across the moor. Back towards the beach. Towards the Dragons. Towards their camp in the dunes. Spotted that familiar head of pale blonde hair amongst them. Sensed the hastily erected wards surrounding them. He hissed through his teeth in frustration, launching himself after her. He was close enough to see the sheen of sweat on her arms, to taste the tang of fear.

'Théon!' he roared, hoping she would stop and praying she kept going. He saw her flinch, though she didn't check her stride. But it was all the opening he needed. He crashed into her, tackling her to the ground. They rolled over and over, tumbling over the rough ground. Her knee came up, catching him in the gut, but he didn't retaliate. When they came to a halt, he sprang back and placed himself between her and the pursuing Huntress.

'I'm sorry,' he choked. 'I can't fight it.'

Théon smiled grimly, nodding in understanding. 'It's just another training session,' she murmured, 'just you and me.'

438

He wasn't sure who she was trying to reassure, but he felt himself calm at the sound of her gentle voice. He struck first, aiming for her beautiful face. She grinned, ducking and spinning away. He struck again, this time aiming to take her legs from beneath her, but she leapt clear and gave him a hefty kick in the ribs for his effort. They traded blows back and forth, probing but far from tentative. She was not holding back. Thanks to their training, she was stronger and faster than she'd ever been, understanding how and where to strike and blocking his every move. They were too evenly matched. It left too much to chance.

'Cast,' he gasped.

'I don't want to kill you,' she pleaded.

'No choice,' he panted. 'Kill or be killed. Do it now.'

He sensed the moment she reached for her magic. Faced with certain death, the Claiming took over. His own Casting exploded out of him, a storm of wind and ice, too strong for even Théon to block. She was blasted backwards, her body flying in a silent arc before crashing to the ground with a sickening crunch. His stomach heaved at the power coursing through him, but the Claiming was in control, and it kept him focussed on his prey.

Then he heard a sound he never wanted to hear again. Illyandi was screaming. She'd broken past the old man and was racing towards her sister lying in a crumpled heap just outside the wards. Silvermane was roaring at her to come back, to stay out of harm's way, trying to push his way past Dorrien even as Faolin sprinted after his lover. But the Princess couldn't hear them. Her green-and-gold eyes were fixed on her sister, her power shaking the earth.

He wasn't sure if it was the sound of her own name, or just the pure terror in Illyandi's voice that roused Théon to consciousness. But she surged to her feet, looking between him and Illyandi. He saw the moment she made her decision, saw the certainty in her lovely face. He roared at her to stop, begged her not to do it. A small, bitter smile twisted her lips, but there was forgiveness in her eyes as she turned her back on him.

She threw her hands up, flooding the wards with her power.

Sealing Illyandi inside.

Safe from Jenia.

Safe from him.

She'd known what it would cost her. She'd left herself exposed and there was nothing he could do to stop it. He slammed into her, fingers closing around her throat as he choked the life from her. He wanted to make it quick, but Jenia was guiding his hands – making Théon suffer, making Illyandi suffer. The Princess was screaming, pounding her fists against the now-solid wards, fighting her Dragon lover while he struggled to pull her back. There were only a couple of feet separating them, but it might as well have been a thousand miles. Not even Illyandi's magic could break through the spell Théon had worked.

He could only watch, a prisoner in his own body, as the light faded from Théon's beautiful eyes. Illyandi was begging him to stop. The sound of his name on her lips would haunt him for the rest of his miserable life. But it was the pathetic gasp of Théon's dying breath that cut the deepest.

It was done. His Queen was dead. He staggered back from her corpse, staring in horror at hands that were now his to control. His strength failed him. He crashed to his knees and roared up at the dawn in agony. On the other side of the wards, Illyandi was sobbing. Faolin held her to his chest, his eyes wet with unshed tears. Face twisted with hate and bloodlust.

But it was not for him.

He sensed the moment Jenia appeared at his side. She looked down at Théon's body and sighed. 'What a waste,' she said. Her eyes flickered up to Illyandi and Faolin, trapped behind the wards. 'I suppose there's always the consolation prize. I think the Dragon's head would be the perfect finishing touch to decorate the throne room back in Elucion, don't you agree, Alexan?' He didn't respond. He couldn't tear his eyes away from Théon's body. Couldn't believe she was gone. 'The Princess,' Jenia continued, eyeing Illyandi with distaste, 'is a different matter. The Dragon girl too. He'd want them alive. They're good breeding stock, if a little frigid, and he's just lost one heir. They could give him another.'

He only vaguely noted the bitterness in Jenia's voice. It was common knowledge that she couldn't give their master an heir. Why else would he have sought Princess Diathor and Lady Kylar and fathered children on them? No, Jenia wouldn't tolerate another woman in his bed – no matter the justification. She'd kill Illyandi rather than risk being replaced.

Alexan didn't know where he found the strength, what power he summoned to act. Perhaps it was the sight of the proud, haughty Illyandi on her knees, the sound of her keening as she screamed for her sister. Perhaps it was the memory of watching Diathor die for no other crime than loving her own child. Perhaps it was knowing that Théon had given her life to protect the Princess, and that he would not allow such a sacrifice to be in vain. Maybe it was none of those things, maybe it was all of them. He didn't care.

He stood. His hand snaked out and gripped Jenia by the throat, squeezing tightly. Just as she'd made him do to Théon. She couldn't speak, couldn't catch her breath enough to summon any sound, but her commands pulsed down the bond. His legs buckled from the effort, but he held fast. He had no idea how – he'd never known anyone to fight the Claiming and win. All he knew was that Jenia had to be stopped.

His gaze fixed on Jenia, savouring the panic in her bloody eyes, but he felt the moment the change began. His blood was boiling in his veins, changing in response to some other magic awakening within him. Something more powerful was Claiming him.

Théon was dead. The binding spell was broken. The Shade was loose. Her blood was in his veins. Had been for weeks. Strengthening him. Claiming him. And now it was free. He couldn't see the change, but he felt it. Deep within his soul. He was hers now. Her Darkling. Claimed by her Shade blood, even in death.

Jenia seemed to realise he was beyond her control, and she scrabbled for the amulet around her throat. Too late, he realised what it was as her bloody palm closed around it. The air beside her split open, and through it walked a nightmare.

Pale eyes and dark red hair, glinting like fine wine ...

Alexan released an explosive breath when he realised it was not the King who had stepped through the rip in the world. The look Kieyin gave him was one of hurt and betrayal. And, if there was any mercy in the Wielding blast that sent Alexan flying, it was only that he didn't kill him. Kieyin's arms wrapped around Jenia and then they were gone.

Dawn had broken, bathing the glen in the pale light of the morning. The sky overhead was clear and the soft breeze that caressed his cheek still carried the edge of night, even as the warmth of the sun kissed his skin. It was a vision of the world at peace. And as he gazed out across the ocean, Alexan felt all that remained of his tired and weary soul shatter.

His breaths came in furious pants as he stared at the spot where his prey had vanished. Transference. A growl of frustration rumbled in his chest. His fight with Jenia was far from over. After all she'd done, he would not rest until he was smiling down on her corpse. But as the peace of the morning seeped into the cracks of his broken heart, his rage turned to sorrow, and tears streamed down his cheeks.

Illyandi gasped. His attention snapped around, just as something stirred in the grass nearby.

Théon.

He didn't have the strength to stand, so he crawled instead. His hand found her wrist, searching for a pulse. *There.* A beat against his fingers. Faint but defiant. At his touch, he heard her take a shuddering breath and sobbed with relief.

He dragged himself up to sitting, leaning over her, cupping her face in his hands and murmuring thanks to whatever Gods watched over her. But his thanks fell silent as her eyes opened. They were not evergreen cat eyes that stared up at him. They were the pale eyes of the Shade.

CHAPTER THIRTY-SEVEN

I n the weeks since Erion had stood in the Shade King's throne room, Kieyin had done as his sovereign had ordered. Erion had hardly been allowed to leave his sight. Even when Seren joined them, the Shade had maintained a watchful eye on him. There had been that one day when, without warning, Kieyin had flinched and staggered to his feet, ordering Seren to stand watch before vanishing. He'd returned less than an hour later, and since then, he had been distant ... almost sullen.

His mood was infectious. Erion could feel resentment boiling in his weary veins. Even though Kieyin had ordered a hot bath drawn for him, provided him with clean clothes and a delicious meal of fried fish and steamed vegetables. Even though he'd let him sleep in his massive bed. It changed nothing. He was still a prisoner. Just because they made him comfortable didn't excuse them for taking him from his mother.

The Shade seemed to sense his unease. In some effort to make it up to him, he had promised Erion a treat he swore the boy would enjoy. Which was how Erion ended up climbing the one-hundred-and-sixty-two stairs to what Kieyin called the eyrie. It was an enormous tower that rose out of the centre of the Shade King's palace, a spiral staircase ascending the middle of it. He was breathing hard by about halfway, and by the time he reached the top, he was gasping through a stitch in his side. Kieyin walked behind him, not commenting or judging whenever he had to stop to catch his breath. Exhaustion pulled at Erion again, and he cursed whatever illness sank its claws into him. Cursed himself for tiring so easily.

He would have been breathless regardless, once he realised what they'd climbed to see. The top of the tower was open – a five-sided floor covered by a matching roof supported on struts. But the sides were open to the vast expanse of air between them and the ground below. On each edge was a V-shaped protrusion, making the pentagonal floor more of a five-pointed star. And inlaid in each ledge was a nest. Four of them were empty. But in one ...

He wanted to say eagle, but that would not have done it justice. The bird was large enough to carry a man – possibly two or three – and far more spectacular than a simple eagle.

'Her name is Amara,' said Kieyin, his voice tender and full of love.

Erion couldn't look away. She was beautiful. Her sleek feathers were pure white and swept back and off her neck, framing her head like a crown. Her beak gleamed like polished gold in the pale dawn light, and every breathtaking inch of her radiated blistering heat. The air around her shimmered with it.

Seeing them, she rose and stretched her mighty wings – knocking Erion over with the blast of air that they swept up – and screeched in welcome. The Shade chuckled and helped Erion to his feet without taking his eyes off the bird, murmuring to her all the while. Then she turned a dark, baleful eye on Erion. Acting on instinct, he stilled and stared back, dipping his head in respect. Then, without warning, she returned the gesture.

A breath of relief slipped out, and he could have sworn Amara gave him a mischievous wink. He blinked and shook his head. That would be ridiculous. 'What ...?' He couldn't find the words.

'Amara is a firebird,' Kieyin answered. 'One of the last, in fact.' He looked as though he were about to say more when his attention was drawn to a dark speck on the horizon, approaching fast. Amara clicked her beak irritably and gave Kieyin a reproachful look. Chuckling, the Shade murmured an apology and laid a reassuring hand on her neck. 'Behave yourself,' he admonished.

Then the dark speck became another firebird that shot towards the eyrie at breakneck speed. Amara huffed and shoved her noble head under one mighty wing, pretending she was fast asleep.

And as the other firebird swooped in and landed on the opposite perch, Erion understood why. This one was even bigger than Amara, with feathers of pure black and a beak and talons the colour of wrought iron. And astride its neck was the Shade King.

He looked younger than he had in the throne room. Happier and more carefree. And there was warmth in his gaze as he dismounted and stroked his firebird's beak in thanks. He glanced at Amara and smirked, but there was tenderness there too, though he said nothing to the bird feigning sleep. Then his gaze fell on Kieyin and Erion, and any thoughts of kindness vanished.

'How is she?'

There was a muscle leaping in Kieyin's jaw. 'Alive. She's waiting for you in your chambers.'

The King nodded. 'Thank you. For saving her. I don't know what I would have done—'

He broke off, looking to the horizon while he took a deep, shuddering breath. Kieyin only shrugged, as if to say that there was no need for gratitude, before producing an envelope from inside his jacket. Erion doubted the King missed the broken seal – he could see it from across the eyrie – but the Shade didn't comment on it. His gaze remained impassive while he opened the letter and read it. But as his dreadful eyes scanned the page, his gaze grew darker, and his brows furrowed in anger. All around him, his power crackled and sparked like a blacksmith's forge, and when he was done, the letter turned to ash in his hand. His gaze went to Kieyin.

'You read it?' he asked. Kieyin snorted and didn't reply, but the look he offered the King said the question offended him. The King nodded and gestured for Kieyin *to accompany him. 'Jenia will have to wait. Bring the boy,' was all he said, and they followed him back down the stairs and through the palace.*

The room to which he led them was large, but far less grand than the throne room. In it was a table upon which was a map. Erion shuddered when he noted that the corners of the map were pinned with four wicked-looking daggers. Chairs were placed around the table, but the King ignored these, standing as he pored over the map. Kieyin stood across from him, but he motioned for Erion to take a seat. He did as he was bid, even if it terrified him to sit at this table. So close to the Shade King.

'We've got Zorana and the Queens to the north – possibly joining forces – and we're hemmed in by the sea to the south. And now Mazron has cut us off from Ciaron. The only way out is east, and that means straying close to Revalla,' the King mused out loud.

Erion was speaking before he even realised it. 'What's wrong with Revalla?' He regretted his outburst as the King frowned, but Kieyin spoke before the King could punish Erion.

'It's haunted. Anyone who ventures there never returns, at least, not in any useful state. Gibbering wrecks, their minds melted in their heads. Long dead they might be, but the ghosts of Revalla's fallen are still a force to be reckoned with.'

The King nodded in agreement, his lip curling in distaste as he looked back at the map. 'We don't have the numbers to take her back by force. Not if the Darkling Queens have sided with him.'

'I don't think the alliance is set in stone,' Kieyin argued. 'Zorana doesn't trust them that much. She can't have told Drosta who he was hunting. He would have never taken her to Dar Kual if he'd known.'

The King frowned, studying the map. 'Drosta?'

'The Darkling who handed her over to the Queens,' explained Kieyin. 'He's one of theirs, but my sources seem to think he's working for Zorana – at least to some extent. He was also the one escorting the shipment of slaves from Ciaron.'

The King nodded. 'If Mazron is in Dar Kual, Ciaron is open.'

'I doubt it will stay that way for long.'

'Perhaps,' the King mused, studying the map through narrowed eyes. As if examining the pieces of a puzzle – all he had to do was figure out how best to fit them together. Erion studied it too, trying to make sense of the puzzle. 'Send Corrigan. Tell him to bring the Ciaron Nightwalkers back into the fold. Whatever it takes.'

'Mazron will get wind of it, eventually.'

There was nothing but the promise of violence in the King's gaze. 'I know.'

'You want him distracted while I slip in and steal her right out from under his nose.'

A thin, vicious smile. 'That's one option.'

'You want me to kill him?' asked Kieyin.

'I'd rather you brought him back here in chains, so I might have that pleasure myself,' the King mused. 'But if the opportunity arises, I don't care how it happens. I just want him dead.'

'What about Zorana? Killing him will give her the cause she's been looking for.

That's why she went after Keriath. She's trying to unbalance you – and it looks like it's working.'

A warning growl ripped through the room, and Erion quailed beneath the force of such a temper. But the King only said, 'Watch it.'

Kieyin's hands slammed down on the table, scattering a nearby pile of paper.

'Answer the fucking question,' he snarled. 'I don't care what I promised Alexan – if you think I'm putting my life on the line for her without knowing that you've thought this through—'

The King leaned over. 'You'll do as I tell you or—'

'Or what?' Kieyin interrupted, standing nose to nose with his sovereign. 'Even if I can get through Mazron, she won't come quietly. You know damn well what she says about you.' The King flinched. Infinitesimally, but Erion caught it. Kieyin did too and seemed to take it as a signal to keep pushing. 'Théon made her choice. She knew she could have come home any time she wanted. She chose death instead.'

The Shade King stepped back and sat down in his throne-like chair, his shoulders slumped with weariness. 'Théon is the reason we're safe from Zorana,' he said in a hollow voice. 'She's not dead. I'd know if she was. I felt her hovering on the brink. But she never crossed over. I don't know how, but she survived. And with Alexan at her side ...'

'She'll try to retake Illyol,' Kieyin said.

The King nodded, looking once more to the map. 'She was never going to tolerate a Shade on her mother's throne. Alexan's presence will ensure her success.'

'I can't take him with me to Dar Kual,' Kieyin said, gesturing at Erion.

The King turned to consider Erion and smiled. It made his blood run cold. 'Leave the boy with me. Have the rooms next to mine made up for him. I want to keep him where I can see him.'

'Seren won't like it,' Kieyin warned.

'Seren doesn't have to like it,' the King snapped, without taking his eyes off Erion. Then he looked back to Kieyin and stood. 'Leave Théon to Alexan. She'll find her way home eventually. It's Keriath who needs you now. Go.' Kieyin nodded and stood. But as he turned to leave, the King placed a firm hand on his shoulder. 'She may not come quietly, but I would trust no one else to do what is necessary. I would prefer that you spare her but, if it comes to it, swear to me you will make it quick. She's suffered enough.'

Kieyin bowed his head. 'I swear it.'

Then he was gone, leaving Erion alone with the Shade King.

It was almost sunset by the time Suriya crawled from the bed, having slept the whole night and the whole day following. Given how awful she felt, it would take even longer to recover all the energy she had channelled into her brother. She padded through the suite, on bare feet and wearing Gaelan's oversized nightgown, in search of food. She rubbed her eyes and stifled a yawn with the back of her hand. Despite her exhaustion, sleep had not come easily in this strange place. Even when she had drifted off, she

445

had been plagued once more by strange dreams that left her with an unshakeable sense of dread in her stomach.

The murmur of voices echoing from the dining room only added to that sinking feeling. She did not want to talk to anyone. Least of all Gaelan.

Reality was worse. She entered the dining room to find Prince Andriel seated at the table. Gaelan sat across from him, dressed as she had been when Suriya had last seen her. Lucan sat in the middle, wolfing down an enormous steak with a healthy portion of roasted vegetables and thick gravy, oblivious to the awkwardness of the situation.

'Good evening,' the Darkstorm murmured with a wry smile. She glared at him, squaring her shoulders and crossing the room to take her seat across from Lucan. Without a word, she snatched the bread from her brother's side plate and slathered it in butter. Lucan mumbled an objection around a mouthful of potato, but she only offered him a vulgar gesture in response. She was too tired for this.

'There's plenty of food in the kitchen,' Gaelan murmured, frowning with mild disapproval. Suriya didn't even look at her. She was not in the mood for any nonsense. Alvar's father watched her with interest, and she ignored him as she tucked into Lucan's supper.

Eventually, the Immortal grew bored and turned his attention back to Gaelan, continuing the conversation that Suriya had interrupted. 'I argued the point as best I could. The Frostfang backed me, as did the Blackfire and the Mistfury. But the others are all in her pocket, and with you absent, I didn't have the numbers to force the issue.'

Gaelan made a noise of disgust.

'You should have done it anyway,' she retorted. 'That she was allowed to go free is evidence enough she can't be trusted.'

'I'm well aware,' the Darkstorm assured her. 'That's why I've taken steps to ensure she is watched constantly. You don't really think Brer came up with that idea by himself, do you?'

Gaelan pulled a face that was one part horror, two parts pity. 'Raiden's hammer, you're a hard bastard. The Rebellion ruined you, didn't it?' she murmured, shaking her head. The Darkstorm's answering glare was rebuke enough, and Gaelan let the matter drop. Suriya couldn't even summon the energy to follow what they were talking about, let alone care.

'Any sign of my wayward son and his Graced pet?' he asked. Suriya was looking in Gaelan's general direction when he spoke, otherwise she would have missed the anger and worry that flashed across the Brightstar's face. But it was gone in an instant, replaced by a mask of brutal indifference.

'Running for their lives from a Darkling Hunt last I saw,' she said. 'I'm sure they'll return.'

The Darkstorm nodded in understanding, his attention drifting back to Suriya as she finished her brother's food. She kept her eyes on her plate, but she could feel his dark gaze boring into her. He looked so very like Alvar, but he had none of his son's kindness. There was nothing but seething wrath and ancient power churning in those storm-grey eyes.

'A painting would last longer,' Suriya snapped, raising her head to meet his gaze with a blistering glare of her own. She was tired. Tired of these people, tired of this place, tired of his curiosity – of the tension it caused in her. She let all her rage and anguish shine through her golden eyes and felt the air around her heat in response to her temper flaring.

Prince Andriel gave a dark laugh and leaned back in his chair. 'I see Phoenix tempers have not improved much. Little wonder your people met such a comprehensive end.'

Suriya blinked. *What?*

'Leave her alone,' Gaelan hissed, before Suriya could respond. 'She doesn't understand what you're talking about, and regardless, it's out of line. For Gods' sake, she's just a child.'

'She doesn't know?'

'Neither of them do. I haven't had a chance to explain it yet.'

The Darkstorm's smile grew thin. 'Can they control their power?'

'To some extent.'

He shook his head in disgust. 'You're tempting Caellach, Gaelan. I cannot shield you from the repercussions if this doesn't work.'

'It'll be fine.' Suriya opened her mouth to demand an explanation, but Gaelan's voice whispered in her mind. *'Don't. He's trying to provoke you. Just stay quiet, and I'll explain once he's gone.'*

'Is it true what he said? Am I really a Phoenix?'

'I sent word to Layol when I heard you'd returned,' Andriel continued, cutting off Gaelan's response. But not before Suriya sensed the storm of emotions that rose in response to that name. Whoever Layol was, the Princess of Brightstar both loved and feared him. And judging by the smug smirk on Andriel's face, he knew it too. 'I suspect he's already on his way – no doubt he'll be desperate to see you after so long. He's missed you.'

Gaelan smiled, though it didn't quite reach her eyes. 'And I him. How is he?'

'Much the same. He still has his father's temper,' the Darkstorm noted dryly. 'He had an argument with Emalia, two, maybe three, years back – almost destroyed the throne room before we dragged him away.'

'What was it about?'

'What is it always about?'

Gaelan snorted. 'I assume neither she nor the Council have reconsidered their position then?'

'Of course not. Still, he'll never convince them by behaving like that. A shame he does not take after his mother more. She was always far better suited to politics.'

'I doubt you'll find many who would agree with you on that.'

Andriel chuckled and stood to leave. 'Perhaps. But they do not know you as I do. Now you should rest. All of you. Whether or not the Council votes in your favour, you're going to need it.'

447

It wasn't long after Andriel had taken his leave that Brer stormed into the room in a terrible rage. Gaelan hadn't seemed pleased by his intrusion and dragged him out of the dining room, leaving Suriya and her brother to finish their dinner. But the almighty row that followed had echoed through most of the city, so if privacy had been her motivation she'd failed spectacularly. It seemed to clear the air, however, and he'd even joined them for dessert afterward.

Suriya had been too exhausted to join in with the conversation, but he and Lucan had got along well. Brer had even offered to take him out sailing. She'd declined to join them. Aside from that muttered response, she'd sat in silence through the rest of the meal, unable to summon the strength to even listen, let alone speak.

'I think you should go back to bed,' Gaelan murmured, rousing Suriya's attention back to the room.

She glanced up to see Lucan and Brer watching her. 'I'm fine.'

'You're exhausted. You need to rest – you both do.'

'No. What we need is answers. What was Andriel talking about?'

Gaelan sighed and leaned back in her chair. 'You know the stories. There are four Graced bloodlines. Dragon, Unicorn, Elf and Phoenix. Each one gifted with a different magical power. Dragons have the Change, Unicorns have the Enchanting, Elves have the Casting and Phoenix … the Rising.'

'And what are we?'

'I'm not sure,' she admitted.

Brer snorted, tapping his brow with a meaningful glance at Lucan. 'Oh, come off it. Magic always leaves a mark.'

The look she gave him in response was glacial. 'Each bloodline shows itself differently. The star-mark on his brow would indicate that Lucan is at least part Unicorn.'

Suriya pushed her hair back, revealing her pointed ears. 'And these?'

'Elf,' Gaelan admitted. 'At least in part. The mark of a Phoenix is much harder to spot.'

Brer snorted in disagreement. 'The hair and the eyes are a dead giveaway.'

'Anyone can have red hair,' argued Gaelan, 'and Phoenix eyes are not only shades of brown.'

Brer shook his head. 'If you call those brown, you need your eyes checked.'

Gaelan just sighed and turned her back on him. 'Of all the Graced, the Phoenix possess the most power. It shows. If you know what you're looking for, there is always something that sets them apart. So while it was Elf-magic – the Casting, control over the elements – that allowed you to defeat the Darkling in the Ravenswood, there is far more to you than that.'

'The bloodlines aren't supposed to mix,' continued Brer. 'After the Rebellion, the Graced scattered to the four winds. They kept to themselves – it was against their highest laws to mingle blood with others. Magic is

448

dangerous, and too much can be fatal. Mortal blood was never meant to hold such power, and whenever the bloodlines crossed, the effects were disastrous. That's what makes you so special – and so dangerous. You appear to hail from different lines, but the same blood runs in both your veins. Phoenix? Unicorn? Elf? That much power ... It's dangerous, not to mention it attracts things like Darklings. They can sniff out magic like scavengers after carrion.'

Gaelan nodded. 'That's why I didn't tell you about what you are until now. I was trying to keep you safe from others, and yourselves.'

Suriya was silent as those words, and all their meaning sank in.

But Brer wasn't satisfied. 'But the Graced have been all but gone for over a century. How could they possibly hail from those bloodlines? And how have they survived this long? Even without using their powers, that much magic shouldn't be stable.'

'I don't know. As I said to Emalia, they were entrusted into my keeping by one no longer able to care for them, but it was not their parents. I was told nothing of their origins.'

Silence followed. It seemed to stretch on for eternity, but Suriya couldn't find the words to break it. Across from her, Lucan fidgeted with his napkin. His mind was closed to her, but she didn't need to be inside his head to know what he was thinking. He was torn. Their real parents might still be alive, but he'd given Gaelan his loyalty. To search for them might hurt her, and he wouldn't want that. So she kept her mouth shut. Sacrificed her own desires for his happiness.

Gaelan sighed and looked up. 'Go on now. Back to bed. Both of you. Andriel might not be the most pleasant man in the world, but he wasn't wrong. You need to rest. Gather your strength. Whether or not they agree to shelter you, you will have a long road ahead of you.'

It was two nights later that Suriya woke screaming from another nightmare. One in which Erion had dined with the Shade King and his Darkling lover. She wrapped herself in the velvet robe Gaelan had given her and padded through the suite to her brother's room. Moonstone eyes glowed in the darkness, watching her as she slipped through the door.

'They're getting worse,' she said without preamble.

He nodded. 'We have to tell her.'

'She already knows,' she replied, flopping down on the bed beside him.

'She might be able to help. Even if she can't make them stop, maybe she can help us understand. Fear and ignorance go hand in hand.'

Suriya snorted. 'Gods, I hope they send us away if being here means you're going to talk like them. You'll be lording your superior intellect over your poor, uneducated sister before winter sets in at this rate.'

He hit her in the face with his pillow. 'Don't be stupid. Everyone knows you're the smart one.'

'Don't call me stupid then,' she retorted, throwing it back at him. Then she stood. 'Come on then, let's get this over with.'

They found Gaelan by the fire in the sitting room, drinking wine with Anwyn and Endellion. The two Immortal visitors paused in their laughter at the sight of them, prompting Gaelan to turn around.

'What's wrong?' she asked.

Suriya couldn't bring herself to say the words – not with the other two pairs of keen, Immortal eyes watching her. She looked to Lucan, begging him to answer for her. He grimaced, nodded, and took a deep breath.

'I think we need your help,' he began, his voice soft and tentative. 'The first night after we left the castle … the nightmare Suriya had. They're still happening, and I think they're getting worse.'

Gaelan gestured for them to sit. 'It's not surprising after all you've been through.'

'They were happening before though,' he said, sitting on the low settee across from her and pulling Suriya down beside him. 'They'd been happening for months before the Darklings. Just flashes at first. Glimpses. Back then, they were blurry though, and now they're so vivid it's hard to tell the difference between what's real and what's not.'

Gaelan's brow creased further. 'You're having these nightmares too?'

Suriya exchanged a long glance with her brother, and he nodded. 'We both have them. Always the same, like we share the dream. Every detail is identical.'

Then Endellion leaned forward. 'And what do you see?'

Lucan hesitated, glancing at Gaelan. But she only inclined her head, as if to indicate it was their choice. Suriya sensed the moment that Lucan decided to trust them. It was almost as though the ground shifted beneath their feet, so significant was the leap of faith.

'Lots of things,' he admitted. 'I don't even remember most of them, and then there are things that I see that I want to forget, but I can't. A woman with a scarred face, being tortured by Darklings. Renila being hunted by Nightwalkers. Erion being questioned by the Shade King …' He broke off, unable to continue. Anwyn frowned, tearing her attention from the hound draped across her lap to look at Gaelan.

'Erion?' she murmured.

Gaelan took a deep breath. 'Renila's son. A Shade took him during the Darkling attack.'

'Renila's *son*?'

Gaelan nodded, her eyes on her wine glass. Anwyn sat back with a soft curse, eyes wide with surprise.

'You know Renila?' Suriya interrupted.

Anwyn nodded absently, studying Lucan. 'Can you see where they are?'

'They're just nightmares,' he insisted. 'Bad dreams, that's all.'

Suriya stayed silent. The look Anwyn gave them said she shared Suriya's doubts.

Sure enough. 'Dreams that you both share? Seems a little strange, even for twins.'

'They're entwined?' Endellion asked sharply, peering at them. Then she looked to Gaelan for confirmation.

The Brightstar grimaced. 'Yes. But that doesn't explain the dreams themselves.'

'If they're not nightmares, then what are they?' Suriya asked, finding her voice. She'd ask what Endellion meant later.

'It's rare, but not unheard of to see things beyond what the eye beholds,' Endellion mused, leaning back and sipping her wine. 'Visions of past, present and future are possible – at the height of our power, there were plenty of Immortal seers – but it requires great strength. Most of the Graced do not possess the magic required …' She trailed off, examining the twins. 'What bloodlines do they hail from?'

Gaelan shrugged. 'At least three of the four. There could be Dragon in there too, but I can't be sure – I never knew who the parents were.'

Endellion nodded. 'That gift was always strongest with your people. And with that much magic in their veins, it's not beyond the realm of possibility.'

'You said mixing bloodlines is dangerous,' Suriya interjected, turning to Gaelan. 'That too much magic could be fatal. How is it we've survived?'

'I don't know,' she admitted. 'There are some rare examples of other children of mixed lineage surviving. Kalielle Half-Elven. Kah Thoran and his sister, the Lady Kylar. Even the Elvish Princesses Vianka and Velor.'

Endellion frowned. 'They were all twins, weren't they?'

'Yes. But I never figured out if it was cause or effect. Did they survive because there were two of them to share the magic, or did that much magic create the second child?'

'What about Kah Resari?' Lucan asked. 'She was descended from all four bloodlines, wasn't she? How did she survive?'

Anwyn let out a bark of laughter. 'Gods only know. That one defied all logic.'

'You knew her.'

It wasn't a question, but Anwyn answered anyway.

'Aye. A ferocious warrior and a good friend. The Fall made her a monster.'

Suriya blinked. 'What are you talking about? What's the Fall?'

The three Immortal women looked at each other, ageless sorrow in their ancient eyes. It was Endellion who broke the long silence, her voice soft and weary. 'The Fall of the Graced. When the Shade King's forces swept across the world, slaughtering every Graced man, woman and child they could find. His Darkling lover, Jenia, sacked Revalla and drowned the Unicorns in their holy city. He corrupted the Elf-Queen's own guard, turned them against her. They tried to slit their Queen's throat while she slept. The Nightwalkers overran Ciaron, stabbed the Dragon High Chieftain in the back, and the Shade King himself descended on Elucion. Nobody knows how he conquered the Phoenix, but only one survived the slaughter. The world drowned in blood that day, and all for the sake of one girl. A child, destined to bring an end to Sephiron's line. Just a child …'

Endellion fell silent, her eyes smouldering with unbearable pain as she gazed into the glowing embers in the hearth. Beside her, Anwyn stared blankly ahead. Gaelan stood and walked to the window, looking up at the stars that scattered the night sky with longing and sorrow.

And there they remained until Suriya fell asleep on the settee and slipped into a dream of blood and war, of a girl-child facing down a host of Sephiron's heirs.

Exhausted after another restless night, Suriya slept late and missed breakfast. Gaelan had cooked her a delicious brunch of poached eggs and ham on freshly baked muffins with a rich, buttery sauce. Unsurprisingly, Lucan had smelled the food and demanded a portion of his own. The sun was shining, so they'd eaten together at the wrought iron table and chairs outside on the balcony, still dressed in their pyjamas with thick, fluffy robes to ward off the chill of the brisk autumn morning.

Gaelan had said very little, sipping absently at her cup of tea while she gazed out across the city to the sheltered lagoon beyond. The white marble buildings gleamed in the sunlight and, this high up, very little of the noise from the city below reached them. Instead, all they could hear was the gentle breeze as it caressed their cheeks and the soft rushing of the open ocean beyond. It was so peaceful.

But something had been preying on Suriya's mind. 'How do Anwyn and Endellion know Renila?' she asked. Gaelan blinked, shaken from her reverie. But as Suriya's question filtered through, anger and frustration flickered across her face.

'Renila used to live here,' she said, her voice cold. 'She was just a baby, brought to the city for protection before the Fall.'

'Renila's Graced then?' Suriya interrupted. Not that she was surprised. But she wanted to hear it, if only to confirm her suspicions.

Gaelan nodded. 'Like you – a Phoenix, but with Elf-magic amongst other gifts. Andriel wanted nothing to do with a Graced child, but Alvar agreed to harbour her. He knew he'd never get the Council to agree without his father's backing, so he went elsewhere. He and Brer came up with the plan to hide her in plain sight – Anwyn and Endellion were in on it. She was enrolled in the Academy as a member of Blackfire. She went in an infant and came out a woman. The rest, as they say, is history.' Her tone implied that was the end of it, but Suriya's curiosity was not sated.

'Why didn't you offer to help her?'

Gaelan's eyes flashed, as if she were wounded by the challenge in Suriya's voice, but then her gaze softened, and she bowed her head with regret. 'I wasn't there,' she admitted. 'Even if I had been, I'm not sure I would have helped. Alvar and I were separated, had been for centuries. Our marriage broke down long before Renila came into our lives. Strong marriages can survive many things, but never secrets and lies.'

'But you still love him, don't you?' Suriya heard herself asking.

452

Lucan kicked her under the chair and shook his head. Gaelan caught the exchange and smiled.

'It's alright,' she assured him. She looked at Suriya then, her head held high. 'Yes. I do. And I suspect you will understand what Anwyn and Endellion do not – that sometimes, when you love someone that fiercely, you will put their happiness before your own. Alvar was better off without me in his life, so I let him go.'

Suriya inclined her head. She understood exactly what Gaelan meant. What would she not give for her brother? She had already killed for him, and she knew in her heart that she would die for him just as quickly. She considered the Brightstar in a new light. Considered that perhaps Immortality was a burden rather than a gift. Perhaps Gaelan's heart had been broken and pieced back together so many times that it no longer functioned as it should. And perhaps, because of that, she alone saw the world around her as it was and had the strength to do what needed to be done. No matter the cost.

Gaelan shook herself, taking a deep breath and offering a smile of reassurance to them both. 'Now, about these dreams,' she said. 'If the Council sanctions your entrance to the Academy, the tutors there should be able to help. It's unlikely the dreams will ever stop entirely, but I suspect you will find them far less daunting when you control them and not the other way around. I will forewarn you though, Graced magic works differently to ours, and it may be harder than learning from your own kind.'

'From what you said last night, I didn't get the impression that was an option anyway,' Suriya noted around a mouthful of egg.

Across the table, Lucan gave her a reproachful look. 'And what about if we don't get accepted into the Academy?'

Gaelan grimaced. 'I'll teach you what I can. There are others out there who may be able to help but finding them will be a dangerous journey.'

'What did Endellion mean last night when she said we were entwined?' Suriya asked.

Gaelan winced. 'It's difficult to explain … Do you remember the old apple trees that came down in the storms last winter?'

'The two that were joined together?'

'Precisely. Two trees, seeded from the same fruit. They grew so close to each other that over time it became difficult to tell one from the other.'

Suriya stared at her, understanding dawning. But the words caught in her throat.

'Are you saying we are like the trees?' Lucan asked.

Gaelan nodded. 'It happens sometimes – most common in twins really. But it can happen any time the bond between two people is strong, where one of them has the same gifts as you, Lucan. It's likely you touched Suriya's mind when you were still in the womb, and that link has only become stronger with time. You've grown up like that. Now your minds are so tangled together that you're almost conjoined.'

'So, what?' Suriya snapped. She knew better than to ask how to fix it. It would break Lucan's heart to think she might want free of him. Regardless of what she wanted, he needed her.

Gaelan frowned. 'It's not the healthiest existence in the world.'

'Is it dangerous?'

'Not exactly. But you saw what happened with the trees. When one fell, it took the other with it.'

'So if I die, Lucan will too?'

'Yes.'

Lucan interjected, 'But Suriya is a Phoenix? Won't she come back to life?'

'Yes,' said Gaelan, her voice grave. 'But without you, she would have only half her mind. Believe me, I have seen what happens when entwining is not corrected. It is not a fate I would wish on either of you.'

So the Council's decision was not just tied to their safety, but their sanity too. Gods help them.

'I guess we'd best hope they find in our favour then,' said Lucan with a quick grin – no doubt having sensed her unease, if not the dark thought. Then he frowned. 'What is the Academy anyway?'

Gaelan pursed her lips. 'We are not born Immortal. We have magic from birth, yes, but our Immortality has to be passed from one to another. Legends says this was a design of the Gods to ensure our numbers did not grow to a point where we might overwhelm this world. So, in order for us to bless another with the magic to live forever, we must sacrifice our right to do so. Over the aeons there have been many who proved unworthy of that gift. It was decreed that every child who aspired to Immortality, would have to be tested to see if they were worthy of the power that might be bestowed upon them. Tyrants are only dangerous if they can't be killed.'

'And the Academy is the test?' asked Suriya.

'Sort of. Children are enrolled before they reach their first birthday—'

Suriya cut her off. 'That's barbaric!'

'It's a necessary sacrifice. Love can be dangerous, Suriya. A mother's love most of all. What mother wouldn't sacrifice everything for her child? But to give a child that power, with no knowledge of who they might grow to be? I've seen the consequences. Trust me, that law is in place for a reason.'

'So, what – they just keep children from their parents until they're old enough to be made Immortal?'

Gaelan grimaced. 'It's a little more complicated than that—'

'For how long? How old are they when you decide?'

'Most Aspirants graduate in their third decade.'

Suriya blinked. 'Thirty years? You keep children from their families for thirty years?'

'Yes,' she snarled, 'because the alternative is another Sephiron.'

Silence.

'So, if the Council agrees, we have to stay there until we're thirty?' Lucan asked.

'Maybe longer. Some Aspirants can take fifty years to graduate. Many never make it.'

'And what happens if we don't?'

Gaelan ran a delicate finger around the rim of her teacup. 'If Emalia has her way, you cannot remain in this city. But you will have likely learned enough by then that you will be able to fend for yourselves beyond its walls. As you've heard many times since we arrived here, you are both extremely powerful. Once your magic has matured, and with the right training, Darklings will cease to be as much of a threat.'

'But all of that hinges on the Council agreeing to take us? Otherwise, we're back out in the cold?' Suriya snapped. 'Gods, your people are cruel.'

Gaelan snorted and lifted her cup to her lips. 'You'll hear no arguments here.'

The rest of the day passed in a haze. Brer appeared at lunchtime, agreeing to watch them while Gaelan ran some errands. She'd returned an hour later laden with new purchases, all of which she had handed to Suriya and Lucan. Mostly their gifts consisted of new clothes and shoes to replace what they'd lost. But there was also an exquisitely wrought sword belt for Lucan. And much to her surprise, a sheath for Suriya's dagger that could be strapped to her thigh and hidden beneath her dress.

Endellion visited around mid-afternoon. She had no update, save that the Council deliberations were ongoing. The Skyrider and the Wavebreaker appeared to be doing everything in their power to disrupt matters.

Anwyn too dropped in, with her massive dogs in tow, to check on them. It was only then that Suriya got the sense something was amiss. The dogs seemed agitated. Unsettled. She waited until Anwyn was gone before raising it with Gaelan.

'It's nothing,' was the curt reply.

But when all three joined them for dinner, Suriya's suspicions were confirmed. Brer's smile was just a little too broad, his laughter just a little too loud. Endellion chattered away like a caged songbird, while Anwyn swore so much she was practically using curses as punctuation. Gaelan, meanwhile, was subdued. Quiet and withdrawn, even. Lucan seemed to notice it too.

'Is everything alright?' he asked.

Gaelan glanced up from her plate. 'Of course. Why wouldn't it be?'

'You just seem a bit … out of sorts.'

Brer snorted into his wine glass but, at a warning glance from Anwyn, held his tongue.

'I'm fine, Lucan. Just distracted.'

Someone knocked on the front door.

The four Immortals stilled, three sets of eyes swivelling to Gaelan. One of the hounds at Anwyn's feet growled in warning, all three of them looking towards the main entrance.

The door swung open, and a man strode in without invitation.

He was tall – broad-shouldered and imposing – with dark hair and dark eyes. His head was shaved at the sides, ebony tattoos swirling over the bare skin and disappearing down under his shirt. There was something menacing about him that made Suriya's skin crawl. At the head of the table, Gaelan tensed but didn't turn around. The man didn't seem to care.

'Hello, Mother,' he said, his deep voice rumbling through the suddenly too-small chamber. 'Andriel said you were back.'

Gaelan looked round, body trembling with reluctance. 'Andriel likes to cause trouble.'

'I hear you had a run-in with some Darklings, and a Shade, no less,' the man said. 'How did that go?'

'I'm still here, aren't I?'

The man grinned. It was a terrifying thing. 'Well, if Sephiron himself couldn't bring you down, I doubt a few Darklings would have posed much of a threat. Even a Shade Prince is no problem for the mighty Gaelan Brightstar.' His dark gaze flickered over the table. Lingered on Suriya and Lucan. 'Still collecting strays then?'

'Suriya, Lucan,' she said, ignoring the jibe, 'allow me to introduce Layol. My son.'

The silence was deafening.

Her son?

Lucan could only stare in horror. It wasn't possible. She'd never said anything. Never even hinted at it.

He dared a sideways glance to Suriya frozen beside him. Her face matched the maelstrom of emotions rolling off her. Anger. Hurt. Betrayal. Fear.

The lazy grin spreading across Layol's face said he felt it too. So did the predatory glint in those dark, dark eyes. Lucan fought back the urge to place himself between his sister and this stranger. She wouldn't thank him for it. Instead, he took her hand in his beneath the table and squeezed tight.

'I'm here,' he whispered.

She seemed to settle, her rage hardening to armour as she stared Layol down. His taunting grin shifted to a smirk of admiration, and his dark gaze flickered to Gaelan – to his mother.

'I was graced with an audience with the Swansinger upon my arrival,' he announced, with the air of someone commenting on the weather.

'And the city is still standing? Your temper must be improving,' Endellion muttered.

Layol ignored her. 'She told me about your petition, your heartfelt plea to have two Graced fledglings enrolled at the Academy. Said you'd got on your knees and begged for them.'

'Watch it,' Anwyn growled.

Still, he ignored them, his attention on Gaelan now. 'She also told me that the Council was yet to reach a decision on the matter. Explained how the votes were split. Mistfury, Blackfire, Darkstorm and Frostfang for. Wavebreaker, Skyrider, Dovethorn and Ironclaw against. Swansinger and Shadowfox abstaining. Whitehart undecided.'

'Get to the point,' sighed Endellion.

Layol's smirk grew smug. 'I convinced her to reconsider her position.'

'You did what?' Brer snarled. 'How?'

That dark gaze flickered to him, glinting with spite. 'Turns out my tongue is more persuasive than yours, Shadowfox. She's agreed to vote in favour of the brats. I imagine your father will follow suit – anything to keep his precious heir happy, am I right?'

Brer's expression turned sour, but he didn't dispute it.

'If that's true then, even if Whitehart votes against, we'll still have the numbers to win the vote,' breathed Endellion, looking at Anwyn for confirmation. The Mistfury just nodded.

'What do you get out of this?' Anwyn asked, scowling in suspicion.

Layol spread his hands. 'Nothing. I only did what any dutiful son would do when he heard his mother was in need.'

'I'm grateful,' Gaelan murmured, though she sounded anything but.

Layol smiled and bowed his head. Then those dark eyes turned back to the twins, and there was nothing but bitterness and resentment in that gaze. 'Well, Suriya and Lucan *Brightstar*, it would appear you are to be enrolled in the Academy. Congratulations, and welcome to Khaladron.'

The distance from the abandoned croft nestled high up in the Nighthills, to the northern edge of the Ciaron mountains, was not insignificant. Travel by daylight was hard, forced back into her human form as she was. But night was worse. Her enemies were more active while the sun slept. All too often her choice was between a long detour to avoid their scouts or pausing to indulge her bloodlust. Both had resulted in equally lengthy delays.

So by the time she staggered into the cabin in the mountains, she was almost too exhausted to notice the lingering scent of strangers.

Almost. But not quite.

One smelled of smoke and ash. Eerily familiar and yet ... not.

The other ... thunder, lightning and the rising wind. She frowned. This one she had definitely smelled before, though when and where she could not remember.

Two more familiar scents mingled with those of the strangers.

Arian.

Ornak.

Checking beneath a loose floorboard, she found the hidden note. The scrawled handwriting more familiar to her than her own name. Coded, so that only she could read it, but she burned it anyway. Always better to destroy evidence of their presence. She was moving before the ash had begun to settle, ignoring the twinges of protest from her tired body.

So, they had found something in the Ravenswood after all. She had planned to infiltrate Dar Kual by herself, but perhaps ...

She staggered as that presence on the other end of the thread tugged hard on their bond.

'What is it? What's wrong?' she gasped, trying to catch her breath as his fear almost severed the connection.

Then his voice rang clear as a bell in her mind. 'Resari. I need you. Taelyr has betrayed us.'

CHAPTER THIRTY-EIGHT

Prince Mazron was not fool enough to leave her unsupervised again, even though she did not have the strength to escape and knew that it was hopeless to so much as try. Instead, he acquired four of the Queens' guards and Enchanted them to ensure their loyalty. They were standing outside the door now – the door which the Prince had locked and barred when he left.

Keriath's only company was the shy and somewhat skittish Darkling girl the Queens had sent. The Shade had taken one look at her, noted her short stature and scrawny, under-fed limbs, and he'd not even bothered with the Enchanting. Keriath didn't blame him. The girl was standing in front of her now, her red eyes wide.

'Will you not eat something, my lady?' she asked. Keriath followed her gaze to the table that the Shade had ordered the servants to set before his departure. A feast, compared to what she'd eaten since her capture. There was bread and cold cuts of meat, cheeses and fruits. There was even a knife for cutting her food.

That was enough to at least get her moving. She wandered over, legs shaking from the effort. The knife wasn't as sharp as her dagger, but it would do. She picked it up and tested the edge. She hesitated, looking around and trying to fathom the Shade's game. A single thought helped her decide. Food would give her strength. She fell on the meal, attacking it with all the grace of a ravenous wolf.

'You'll make yourself sick, my lady,' the Darkling girl admonished. Keriath scowled but took smaller pieces of bread, leaving the richer foods until later. She chewed them thoroughly before swallowing. It would not help strengthen her if she could not keep it down.

The Darkling was staring at her.

'What?' she snapped around a mouthful of food.

The girl said nothing, just stared at her with sad eyes while she ate.

When she was finished, the girl gestured to the bedroom. 'The Prince had a bath drawn for you, my lady, and clean clothes sent up.'

Keriath nodded and rose. Knife still in hand, she followed the girl through to the bathroom. The Darkling noted the knife but said nothing. Whether out of fear or a lack of it, Keriath couldn't tell. She wasn't sure it even mattered.

The clothes she discarded were little more than tattered rags, and the Darkling girl threw them on the fire without hesitation. Despite her weak appearance, her hands were surprisingly firm and gentle when she helped Keriath into the bath. A contented groan escaped Keriath's lips as she lowered herself into the steaming tub. It was heaven. The water was so hot that it almost burned, but the pain was nothing compared to all she had endured. Her tired body sighed as the water eased her aching muscles and lifted the dirt from her skin.

When she eyed the cloth with trepidation, the girl came closer. 'Would you like some help, my lady?'

'I'm nobody's lady,' Keriath whispered.

The Darkling girl smiled and picked up the cloth and the soap beneath it. 'That's not what I was told.' She pushed Keriath's hair to the side and began washing her back.

'And what were you told?' said Keriath, closing her eyes, revelling in that tender touch. 'That I am a Princess, daughter of the Shade King?' The girl was quiet as she moved to Keriath's arm. Then her other arm. Her legs. Her feet. Washed her hair.

'That you were the Lady of Revalla.'

Keriath stilled, eyeing the girl. 'There is no Lady of Revalla. My brother is unmarried and lord of a ruined city and a people who are dead and gone besides,' she said. It was painful to speak about her brother.

'I heard that Lord Taelyr gave up his right to that title when he betrayed you to the Princess Zorana. That some believe Lady Kylar's firstborn should have had it from the start. That your sister is the rightful Queen of Illyol, and together, you could rule half the world.'

She peered up at the servant girl through narrowed eyes, wondering where she had heard such things. Not in the bowels of Dar Kual. But as she looked a little closer, Keriath noticed something rather interesting.

The girl was wearing a glamour. A strong one at that. An ordinary Darkling would never have spotted it. Even a Shade might miss it if they didn't look close enough. But Keriath was looking very closely, and there was nothing ordinary about the power in her veins.

Unicorns had always been the first to spot glamours, though there were limits to their power. It was impossible to see through them, unless the magic was weak, but there was always a sense of *wrongness* – an instinct that said something was off. Glamours worked on the senses, and where most only had five to call upon, Unicorns had a sixth. And while the former five senses may be fooled, rare was the magic that could trick the mind itself.

This one was near perfect, but there was one flaw. She appeared weak –

shy and timid, with a small, scrawny body that looked like it might snap in the breeze. The tremble of her voice, even her smell – her fear was all too obvious in the air. All of Keriath's senses dismissed this girl, refused to see her as a threat. Except one.

Because her mind was calm. Cool and collected. It radiated a confidence that no Darkling servant should have. Not one who appeared so pathetic and skittish. Not when Keriath's presence made even the Queens nervous. It was a normal reaction for any creature faced with its natural predator, even when that predator was bound and broken. But despite that, despite the words she spoke and how she spoke them, despite all that her body language suggested – this girl had no fear of Keriath.

Keriath leaned back so the girl could rinse her hair once more. She didn't bother trying to peer into the girl's mind. If she was strong enough to conjure magic like that, or important enough that someone else would do it for her, her mind would be well guarded. So instead, she stayed silent while the Darkling helped her from the tub and wrapped her in a fluffy robe.

The girl led her back through to the sitting room and sat her in a comfy armchair by the fireplace where the heat from the flames would dry her. Then the girl stood behind her and began teasing a comb through the tangled mess of Keriath's hair.

'What do you know of my sister?' Keriath asked. 'What have you heard about Théon of Illyol?'

The girl smiled softly, pausing at a stubborn snarl. 'Many things. That she lives. That not even the Shade King's lover nor his favoured generals could defeat her. That she knows of your plight, that she is coming for you as soon as she is able. That she fears she will be too late, that she knows all too well the darkness that lingers in your heart. That she would kill you both, rather than see either of you resigned to this fate.'

Keriath nodded in thanks, not caring where the girl had heard such things. She sat in silence, allowing the warmth of the flames to wash over her, drifting in the peace and contentment of being cared for after so much suffering. When the girl was done, she led Keriath to the dressing room and held up the dress the Shade had laid out for her.

It was beautiful. Simple but elegant. A Unicorn design, made from translucent crimson silk and gathered at the waist and neck with a rope of golden thread. She took it from the girl, studying it with a frown. The colour was that of freshly spilled blood, and the rope all too reminiscent of a noose about her throat.

It slipped over her head, and the sensuous feel of the silk skimming over her skin made her stomach heave in revulsion. She ran her hands over her wasted curves, her lip curling in disgust at what she found. It was revealing enough that most would consider it scandalous, yet somehow, it hid the damage that the Queens' treatment had wrought on her once striking figure. It was a whore's dress, and part of Keriath rebelled against it. But she knew if she refused, she would only suffer more.

So she held her tongue and allowed the girl to lead her to the vanity table. She sat while the Darkling ran a brush through Keriath's now-dry hair, twisting it up and pinning it in place with a comb set with fat, gleaming pearls. Then she began on Keriath's face: rouge for her dry, cracked lips and hollow cheeks, and kohl to line her too-wide eyes.

Keriath watched the girl's hands in the mirror, not daring to even glance at her own reflection. But she could not avoid it forever. And when she brought herself to look, what she saw almost broke her.

The scars that Dell and Pria had carved into her flesh were awful. Far worse than the savage marks that marred her right side, because these were deliberate. They had been designed to maim, to disfigure and diminish her unnatural beauty. And beneath them, her skin was pale and drawn. All the softness was long gone from her face. Starvation and exhaustion had hollowed out her cheeks, her jaw, her eyes; even her brow and temples were sunken. A skull covered in tired and worn skin.

Her violet eyes were dull, all the magic and power faded from view. Lined with kohl, they regained some of their sparkle, but it was a farce. A mockery of what she had once been. Her hair was clean now, at least, but the strands that had been left loose to frame her face hung limp. Long gone were her lustrous raven locks, so glossy and full of life. The Darkling girl had done her best with what was left, but there was no way to disguise the horror of what Keriath had become. And yet, she was still beautiful enough to stop a man in his tracks. The curse of her kind.

'What does he want with me?' asked Keriath.

The girl winced. 'I think you know the answer to that.'

'What does he gain from that?' Keriath muttered, more to herself than anything else. 'Besides a pretty face to warm his bed.'

'He's not here to make you his whore,' said the girl, unable to meet her eyes.

'So you think he's here to collect me for the King?'

'No,' she replied. 'If he was here to take you to the King, you'd be in his hands already. The Prince has claimed you for himself, but it's a tremendous risk for him. He'd only do something like this if the reward was high enough. You're beautiful, my lady, but just having his way with you isn't enough. Mazron seeks a bigger prize.'

'What then?'

'Power. Enough to take control of the King's armies.'

'A Shade like him doesn't have that kind of power.'

'No. But a Shade like you might.'

'I'm not a Shade,' Keriath snapped. But then realisation hit her. 'But his child would be … and my child would have my power. He wants to use me to breed his heir.'

The girl nodded. 'The Prince will want to keep you away from the King until he can get you with child, until you can give birth.'

Keriath shuddered. A child with her bloodlines, bound to one as dark as Prince Mazron, that couldn't be beaten. The Shade would win. It wasn't as if she could even fight him. The mountain was still suppressing her power. Even with her power, she was no match. She rarely touched that magic, and he would not hesitate to utilise his full strength. He wasn't like her, hadn't been taught to use his power responsibly, had no sense of right and wrong. He would force her if he had to.

'What can I do?' whispered Keriath. The girl took her hands in her own, squeezing tight as she stared up into Keriath's face.

'Just hold on,' she breathed. 'Hold on just a little longer. I swear this will all be over soon.'

Keriath stilled, frowning as she asked, 'Who are you? What do you want from me?' The girl smiled and stepped closer, cradling Keriath's face in her hands.

'My name is Seren,' she whispered, 'and I am here to help you, Keriath.'

Keriath's mind was racing. Seren. The Shade King's Blade. His personal assassin. His spymaster. Little wonder she knew so much. It also explained the glamour ... not to mention the shields around her mind. But why was she here? To kill her? To claim her?

The sound of voices in the hallway outside interrupted her thoughts. Seren's eyes flickered over her shoulder to the door. 'Mazron's meeting with the Queens has finished. He's on his way now,' she muttered.

'He'll kill you when he finds out,' warned Keriath.

The Shade King's Blade smirked, her glamour slipping. 'He won't find out. Not until it's too late.'

'He will see this entire conversation in my mind!'

The glamour slipped a little further as the girl – no, the woman – winked at her. 'No,' she breathed, 'he won't.' Then she stepped back as a key turned in the lock and the Prince stormed into the room.

'Leave us,' he ordered, without even looking at Seren. With a low bow, she scurried towards the door, pausing only to let the Shade past. The Prince's gaze drifted over her, dismissing her as unimportant, his attention fixed on Keriath.

Seren hovered on the threshold, glancing back one last time – and let the glamour slip, revealing the woman beneath. She was tall and lean and devastatingly beautiful. Her hair was pure white, though her face was young and unlined. But she was ancient. There was always a weariness to those who had lived too long, and Keriath could see that weariness in her eyes. Eyes that were almost Darkling red, but not quite. As if some Shade had tried to claim her and found her too powerful to subdue. And little wonder, when the power that thrummed in her veins could be seen dancing beneath her skin. She offered Keriath a reassuring nod and slipped from the room.

Leaving Keriath alone with the Shade. He smiled. A slow, dangerous smile that made her heart race. Her legs were still weak, but she forced herself to cross the room and sit in a chair by the fire. The knife was still in her hand – Seren had not bothered to take it from her. She tucked it close to her leg, ready.

The Shade poured two goblets of wine and offered her one. 'Keriath,' he said, his voice a silky purr that sent shivers down her spine. She said nothing, blinking stupidly at him as she took it. Once upon a time it would have embarrassed her to be Enchanted so easily. But to feel shame would have required her to feel anything resembling pride, and the Queens had taken that from her. 'I trust you ate well?' She nodded. His grin broadened as he took in her appearance. 'And I see you enjoyed your bath?' She nodded again. And then she felt it. The gentle touch of the Enchanting, his mind caressing her thoughts and emotions.

A small smirk playing on his lips. Keriath forced herself not to look at or think about his lips. But the Shade had not yet left her mind, and he had other ideas. Her heart fluttered at the thoughts he inflicted on her. Thoughts of how his lips would feel on different parts of her body, thoughts of how his body would taste against her lips ...

Fury surged. She closed her eyes and took a deep breath.

'Get. Out,' she ground out from between clenched teeth.

'Your wish is my command, my lady,' he sneered, but he did retreat. She could still feel him inside her head, watching, but no longer Enchanting. Keriath looked at her goblet to avoid his gaze.

'Did the King send you to fetch me?' she asked.

Prince Mazron chuckled. 'You mean your father?'

Keriath glanced up. He was studying her, his gaze like that of a curious child.

'He's not my father.'

His eyes lit up as he read her thoughts. 'Interesting. You truly believe that,' he drawled, 'but your words are little more than a reflex.'

'He is *not* my father,' she repeated, firmly this time.

The Prince laughed at that.

'You're a fiery one, I'll give you that. Even after all this time with the delightful Queens,' he said with a feral grin. 'I just hope they haven't taken too much of your fight out of you. I prefer a challenge.'

Keriath glared at him. 'Sorry to disappoint you.'

'A pity. I expected better from you.' He sighed, his grin fading.

'Take it up with the Queens,' she retorted before looking away. But he was in her head. Saw her thoughts before she could act.

'Drop the knife, Keriath,' he ordered. She had barely moved, only gripping the handle tighter and readying herself to lunge. But at his instruction, she froze in place – her hand opening, allowing the knife to clatter to the floor. Prince Mazron's face broke into a broad, evil grin. 'That's more like it!' he laughed. But as he studied her thoughts, he sobered. 'But still a disappointing effort. The Queens were clearly unaware of your importance to have damaged you so much. I will speak with them about this later. Once I have you away from this place, that is. I can't risk them deciding to tell your father what I'm up to.'

'He's not my father,' she snarled. 'Now get to the point. What do you want from me?'

'Wouldn't that be telling?' he breathed. Then he cocked his head to the side, considering. 'You're hiding something.'

Keriath stilled. 'What do you mean?'

'Who was the servant girl?' he asked, searching through the parts of her mind he could reach. But as he neared the information he sought, a shield slammed down, blocking his advance. It mirrored her defences perfectly, hummed with her very essence. But it was not a shield of Keriath's making. Someone else was protecting her – hiding all trace of Seren from Mazron's sight.

The Shade growled in frustration, and a dark coil of power cracked against the shield. Keriath flinched from the blow, but the shield held firm. He struck again and again until it crumpled beneath the blow, revealing memories beneath. But the agony that should have followed never came, and that protecting presence slipped a little further inside her mind.

'Neres,' she heard herself say, and though it was her lips that moved, it was not her voice that spoke. 'Her name was Neres.'

The Shade scowled. 'You discussed my plans with her.'

It wasn't a question. He could see the evidence in her head. But the memory that he found was not the real one. The stranger in her mind had tricked him, baited and hooked him with a lie.

What do you think he wants with me?' asked Keriath.

The girl smiled. 'He wants to make you his Queen. You will give him heirs and stand by his side as he conquers this world for his own. Together, you will rule us all.'

'I will never join with him.'

Her smile faded. 'Then he will take you by force and get you with child. For his heir, birthed from your power, that child would be unstoppable.'

Prince Mazron snarled and pried further, searching for proof that they had plotted against him. Keriath screamed as he scoured her mind, the violation far worse than anything the Queens had ever done. As he rifled through her memories, she relived all the horrors she had fought to forget. The first time she'd felt the cold grip of the ruan – a sensation she now hardly noticed. The dread and fear as she approached the city, knowing she couldn't break free. The endless torture, the brutal floggings, the terrifying drugs, the agony of the Queen's blood … She relived it all, while the Shade watched with a smile. It went on and on, for there was nothing for him to find.

But he had to be sure. So he went back further, until she was nothing more than a frightened girl lying in the streets of Revalla, watching Jenia butcher her mother. Then further back still. A child curled on the forest floor, begging for mercy as Darklings burned her alive. She screamed in terror, collapsing to the floor, her body spasming and convulsing in agony at the memory.

'Stop!' she begged, her hands clawing at her scalp, as if she could reach into her head and tear the memories free. He did no such thing, delving deeper and deeper, right to her very core. His presence loomed in her mind, dark and menacing as he surveyed his prize. A tremor of wicked laughter echoed through her, sending her heart and soul trembling at the horrors it promised.

And it was there – right down at the centre of all Keriath was – that the other presence took over. Engulfed her whole. Hid her from Mazron's gaze. Shielded her from the lash of power he unleashed upon her. Mimicked her pain so perfectly he didn't notice the difference. Watched as her doom crept ever closer.

'Seren?' whispered Keriath.

A flicker of warmth and compassion washed over her as if in answer. Then, turning her attention back on Mazron, a growl of defiance ripped from Seren-as-Keriath. Power surged from Keriath's core. Not her own, but a perfect echo. An imitation so flawless that she almost believed it. But as she looked on, it changed. Warped and corrupted with the taint of Shade magic. Not truly tarnished – just made to seem like it. Then, as the glamour slipped down over her eyes, she saw Mazron's face contort with shock, and knew that her gaze of glittering amethyst had been replaced by one of pale fire.

Baring Keriath's teeth, Seren roared and lashed out. Mazron recoiled from the blow, flinching back as he raised his defences. Talons of Keriath-tinged magic gouged deep furrows in the wall surrounding his mind, and she scented his fear in the air. Seren pressed her advantage, striking again and again, unleashing a barrage of power against his defences. Not all she had – not even close, Keriath realised, judging by the strength enveloping her – but just enough to break through.

Keriath could feel how the temptation to shatter him threatened to overwhelm Seren. But with inhuman restraint, she leashed that urge. She could not kill him. *Not yet.* But Keriath could not have defeated him alone, and he could never suspect who had aided her. Better to make him believe she'd embraced her Shade lineage rather than submit.

Seren struck hard and fast, sending a wave of power rushing through the tattered remnants of his shields. Magic flickered into life, coating Keriath's clenched hand like a glove of amethyst flame, compensating for the lack of strength in her arm as Seren brought her fist down on his face. The power hit true, and when he crashed to the floor, he remained there. Motionless.

Keriath was panting. From exertion or fear, she didn't know. Her body shook and swayed as she looked down at the destruction Seren had wrought. The strange Darkling woman withdrew from Keriath's mind, and the sudden absence of that steady warmth sapped the strength from her legs. Keriath sank to her knees, trembling with raw terror. Seren's presence lingered, pulsing with power. Keriath took a ragged breath, tried and failed to swallow her fear. She'd never sensed anything like it in all her life.

'What are you?'

The presence pulsed once more, gently this time. 'A friend. Stay where you are, Keriath. Help is coming.'

Then she was gone, and Keriath was alone once more.

Keriath didn't know how long she stayed on the floor, quivering from exhaustion and dread. Mazron was unconscious, but alive. He would wake soon, and bereft of Seren's aid, she would suffer. Panic clawed at her throat, squeezing her chest tight in its icy grip. Sent her heart racing so fast she feared it might stop.

Then a strange warmth kissed her skin, drawing her attention. Soothing her fears. Blinking, she looked around.

The first light of dawn was streaming through the window. Keriath gasped at the sight – it was the first time she had seen daylight since she'd entered this accursed place. It burned her eyes, but she found she didn't care. The pain was nothing compared to what she'd endured of late.

Shielding her eyes with her hand, she drank it in. Sunlight. She had thought she would never feel it again. And yet here she was, absorbing its light and strengthening herself as if nothing had ever happened. A cool, easterly breeze swirled into the room, bringing with it the smell of the ocean. If she closed her eyes, she might almost believe she was home.

But it was a fantasy. The half-light of the dawn could not undo the months of damage and neglect. Not even the noonday sun would give her strength to fight the darkness of the mountain. Its hold was absolute, and without her powers there was no hope.

She opened her eyes and looked out across the Barren Lands. The dawn light softened the world around it, bathing it in an ethereal glow that seemed to touch her soul. And as she watched the beginning of a new day, certainty and determination settled within her.

All that made her who she was had been taken from her. She was a shell, holding nothing more than a shadow of what she had once been. She was just existing, clinging to life because she didn't know how to die. It was little wonder – fighting for survival was all she'd ever known. She didn't know how to stop.

But she had to. She knew what Mazron was after. Knew there was nothing she could do to prevent him. All Seren offered was a temporary reprieve. Mazron would wake soon enough. Even if she escaped before that happened, he would come for her. No matter where she hid, he would find her and use her, and the darkness she birthed would engulf the world. There would be no stopping it. The time for fighting was over.

Théon would understand. Théon was the only one who understood her burden. Resari would ask her to be brave. Her mother would ask her to be strong. Arian would ask that she had hope. Not one of them would ever stop fighting for survival. Not like Théon.

Keriath smiled as she considered her sister. Dawn had always been Théon's favourite time of day. After the Fall, she'd always risen with the sun. Always found some place to watch the coming of the new day. It had driven Silvermane to distraction, trying to keep his charge safe. If Keriath closed her eyes, she could see her. Standing tall, her face lit with anticipation while she waited for the sun to crest the horizon. They looked alike in many ways, though Keriath always denied it. They had the same dark hair, the same full mouth, often quirked into a sardonic smirk, the same intense eyes – though Théon's were green and Keriath's amethyst. In short, they looked like their father. But if either of them had ever admitted that, perhaps they would look even more alike, for the pale light of the Shade would be on them.

Théon had already known that horror. Keriath remembered the day her mother told her the truth about Théon's parentage. The day she'd explained why she was so different. Dark where Diathor and Illyandi were fair, wild where they were gentle, willing to kill where they were not. And she learned the truth about why Théon had done all those horrible things – that she was touched by darkness. None but Keriath knew it, but Théon had decided long ago that should the darkness ever rise again, she would end herself before allowing it to take root. She didn't ever want to go back to being one of his pawns. She would not let him use her to hurt the people she loved. No. If the Shade King came for Théon, she would go willingly into death's embrace rather than stand by his side.

They had always understood each other in a way that nobody else ever could. They shared the same burden, the same curse.

Keriath took a deep breath and stood.

She had nothing left. If she was honest, she knew she was already dead. Mazron would get her with child, and it would suck the life from her. And whether she willed it or not, its first breath would be her last.

She turned away from the dawn, squared her shoulders and walked over to the dining table. To the knife. She had to be quick – Mazron might wake any moment. There would not be another chance. She closed the distance, eyeing the blade in terror while she fought the rising panic in her heart.

Arian's song rose once more to her lips, barely more than a dying whisper as she picked up the knife. Murmured a prayer for her mother, her brother, and turned back to face the rising dawn.

She closed her eyes and savoured its warmth on her face as she pressed the tip of the knife against her breast. Her fingers trembled about the hilt, but she took comfort in her memories of all those she loved, all those she would die to save. She took a deep, shuddering breath and readied herself to meet oblivion. Steeling herself to drive the blade home—

But her hand did not move.

She tried again. Pressed harder. Still the knife did not move. She heaved against it, frantic for the end. Then she finally realised – Seren's presence had faded, but had never truly left. She was still there, in her head, holding her fast. Keriath strained against her, but she was far too powerful. Even at Keriath's strongest, she would have had no hope against that might.

'Please,' she begged.

Seren held firm. *'You only have one life, Keriath. Do not be so quick to throw it away. Not when salvation is so close at hand.'*

Then she heard it. The thunder of mighty wings, the rustle of feathers and footsteps on the flagstone floor, and a great gust of wind blew in through the open window. Warm fingers wrapped around her wrists, and the pressure on her mind relaxed.

'Now, now,' a male voice chided. 'There's no need for that, Princess.'

She opened her eyes.

And met the eerie, pale gaze of the handsome Shade holding her. He was staring at her with an intensity that burned, a gentle smile touching his lips. His burgundy hair glowed in the dawn light, and a blood-red gem glittered in his pointed ear, its twin hanging from a fine gold chain about his neck. He winked. She tried to flinch back, but his grip on her wrists was too strong. Then something moved over his shoulder, drawing her gaze to the gleaming, white firebird hovering beyond the window.

She heard the door open and then close behind her, the Shade's eye flickering up to the intruder, but Keriath did not dare turn around. Not until she heard Seren's firm voice behind her. The glamour was gone, the white-haired woman there for all to see. Her expression was grim as she ran an assessing eye over Keriath, wincing at the betrayal she saw there. Then she turned her attention back to the Shade. 'We have to go,' she insisted. 'Now.'

CHAPTER THIRTY-NINE

'*Wake up.*' The voice was sharp inside her head. Her eyes snapped open at his command, her mind jerking out of whatever haze he had dragged her into. It was enough to make her head spin. The silver-haired man was crouched in front of her, his head cocked to the side while he watched her. Rage, inexplicable but unrelenting, rose in her chest at the sight of him. But then her gaze met his and her anger ebbed.

He was breathtaking. His clothes were elegant and refined, though his shirt collar lay open, revealing graceful tattoos swirling over his chest. His silver-blonde hair, which looked almost white against his sun-kissed skin, fell across his forehead and into his eyes ... eyes like Renila had never seen before. They were pale, pearlescent blue and mesmerising. He was tall and broad-shouldered and moved with a confidence that unnerved Renila. He was stunning. The most beautiful man she had ever seen, except perhaps Alvar. But where Alvar – subconsciously or otherwise, she wasn't sure – hid his good looks behind a scowl and bad posture, this man did nothing to curtail the impact of his loveliness. He was devastating. Even weakened as she was, she couldn't stop thinking about how his hands had felt around her earlier.

He grinned and winked. 'That's better,' he crooned, satisfied that she was subdued. He stood. 'Your mind was well defended. It's taken me weeks to work my way into that pretty little head of yours. Who taught you to shield it so well?'

'Alvar,' she said. She blinked. She hadn't meant to say that. Didn't want to tell this man anything. She wouldn't. She refused.

The man laughed again and blew her a mocking kiss. 'Oh, little dove,' he assured her. 'You'll tell me everything. I don't even need you to say it out loud. I can see it all in your head. But where would the fun be in that?'

'We don't have time for you to play, Taelyr,' a crisp voice said from over his shoulder. The man turned to look at whoever had spoken. Seizing the opportunity of his distraction, Renila wrested some control to follow his gaze and look around. His quiet voice in her mind murmured that she could take nothing he was not willing to give, but she savoured the triumph. It was dark – long past sunset, but not yet midnight if she had to guess. They were in a clearing, deep in the woods. A campfire burned in the centre. More figures hovered around it, half shrouded in shadows as they hid from the oncoming dawn beneath the shade of the trees. A woman had spoken, her bare arms twined with azure tattoos. A Dragon. Her heart soared. But as the stranger stepped into the light, Renila realised her mistake. The woman's eyes were red. A Darkling. They flickered to Renila, and she thought she read pity in them.

'Jealous, lamb?' Taelyr breathed. The Darkling woman flinched and froze where she stood. 'If you're not, I can make you. Would you like that? Would you like your Hunt to see you beg? To see you get on your knees in front of me? To watch you crawl into my bed?' The Darkling was silent, but even Renila could see the rapid rise and fall of her chest betraying her fear. 'Well?' Taelyr roared. 'Answer me?'

She bowed her head, as though he had released her from his control. 'No, my lord,' she gasped. 'I only meant that my scouts report her companions are not far behind, and we don't have the numbers to match them.' Taelyr grunted in understanding and turned back to his prize.

'I guess we had better get this over with then. I had hoped the Night-walkers might have kept them occupied at least a little longer. Still, I guess I got what I came for,' he sighed, crouching down in front of Renila. He gripped her face between his hands and gazed into her eyes. 'Tell me, dove, who is this Alvar?'

'Prince Alvar Darkstorm,' she answered.

Taelyr grinned, sensing her evasion. 'An Immortal?' he chuckled. There was a collective intake of breath from the Darkling Hunt, and they inched closer in curiosity. 'Interesting. So you came from their city?'

'No.' He waited for her to elaborate, but she resisted. Pain erupted in her skull, and she screamed out in agony. Then it was gone, and Taelyr smiled patiently. 'I lived in the Lady Gaelan's castle – in the Ravenswood, on the edge of the Nighthills.'

'Alone?'

She ground her teeth as he dug deeper. 'No,' she hissed, fighting him with all she had. 'Lots of people lived there.'

'Including the Lady Gaelan's children, who look suspiciously familiar,' Taelyr noted with a frown, sifting through her memories, 'and your son.' He grinned at that. A cold, vicious thing. 'A mother's love is always so easy to exploit. You might as well have invited me into your mind the moment you thought you saw him. Who is his father?'

'I don't know,' she gasped. The admission hurt her more than she cared to admit. He laughed at her pain but read the truth in her mind.

'Oh, poor dove – you have no memories of your life before his birth? How interesting,' he mused. He delved deeper. 'A Darkling Hunt found you, flushed you out. How did you escape?'

Her memories engulfed her, a raging inferno fuelled by righteous fury.

471

Renila felt the heat building in her chest as she thrashed against his hold. 'Magic,' she spat. He flinched back, releasing her, as though her skin had burned him. He looked down at his hands in surprise – his palms were blistered where he'd touched her. She could see the fury sparking behind his exquisite face, as though he longed to punish her for the power she could not control. Then it was gone, smoothed away behind his polished exterior like creases out of a bed sheet.

'Now that is interesting. Not a dove, but a Phoenix. And blessed with the Casting power of the Elves,' he breathed. 'Few of those around now, are there?' The Darklings stirred, edging closer as they hummed in anticipation of the power in her veins.

Then Renila noticed a noise coming from the shadows: a rippling growl that had started low but was building to a terrifying snarl that tore through the quiet of the forest. Renila had never heard anything like it. All eyes turned to the source of the sound as a huge, hulking form stepped into the light.

It was a bear. Red-brown, with glowing eyes and long, knife-like teeth, gleaming like daggers in the firelight. It was enormous. Taller than a man at the shoulder, at least twice that standing on its hind legs. And laden with so much heavy muscle she had no doubt that a blow from one of those massive paws would mean instant death. Its entire attention was focussed on Taelyr. His eyes widened in recognition, and he whispered a curse under his breath.

Behind them, the campfire flared as a slight figure appeared at the bear's side. Her golden eyes burned with hatred, the blistering glare she pinned Taelyr with promising nothing but a violent death. Twin swords gleamed in her hands, wreathed in flame like her tawny skin, and her hair crackled and sparked around her, surrounding her face in a fiery halo.

Thunder cracked overhead and lightning split the sky as Starfyre stepped from the shadows to flank the bear, Alvar's storm-grey gaze murderous as he drew that beautiful blade. His power churned like a tempest beneath his skin, and his voice was the howl of the wind in the night.

'Release her now, and I will let you live.'

On the other side of the great bear, Arian hissed in disagreement. 'Speak for yourself. I spared your life once, Taelyr, and I've regretted that decision every moment since. Let her go, and I promise I'll at least make it quick.'

Taelyr snarled, dragging Renila upright and pulling her against him as he pressed his dagger to her throat. Alvar and Arian stilled, their expressions fixed in identical masks of fury and hate. The bear roared and took a lurching step forward, but when Taelyr hissed in warning and pushed the blade harder against her neck, it hesitated. She felt the sting as it broke the skin and saw the Darklings' eyes glow when they scented blood. The bear froze, the growl of fury that ripped out of its mighty chest as terrifying as the power raging around Arian and Alvar.

'I'll kill her,' Taelyr warned. 'Don't think I won't.' The bear huffed, a strangely human sounding noise that could almost be mistaken for a laugh. Because Renila was a Phoenix. Not even death itself could hold her.

Beside the bear, Arian chuckled too, though there was no humour to it. 'Go on then. She'll walk it off.'

Taelyr tensed. Renila could feel his heart thundering in his chest against her back, but his voice was steady – as was the hand he raised, displaying the ring on his finger.

'You should have walked away while you had the chance, songbird,' he breathed, the endearment filled with contempt. 'Know that you brought this on yourself.'

The jewel in the centre of the ring began to glow, sending a shiver down Renila's spine at the quiet rush of magic brushing so close. But it was not magic like her own. There was something about it ... something dark, tainted. Familiar. She shuddered, shying away from it.

As if in answer, the earth shuddered around them, and from the darkness a figure stepped.

She was lovely, for a nightmare. A golden-haired beauty, crowned and elegant. Graceful as she appeared, almost drawn from thin air. Clothed in an exquisite gown of green and gold brocade. Jewels glittering at her fingers, wrists, throat, hanging from tapered ears. Pale green light flickering in her hands. Pale eyes.

Renila's gaze met Alvar's across the clearing, and she forced herself to swallow the whimper of fear threatening to break from her lips. She would not let them break her. Thunder rumbled as he struggled to contain his temper, the winds rising as his fury raged on.

'Oh, come now,' the Shade woman admonished. 'Don't do anything rash. I would hate to have to hurt such a pretty face.'

Arian bared her teeth in silent challenge. 'Zorana. I should have known you were the one holding his leash. He always was a choosy bastard. Who else would he deign to whore himself for but a Shade Princess?'

'Arian,' the Shade purred, 'Taelyr has told me so much about you – his beloved songbird. It's a pleasure to meet you in person. My brother will be delighted. He's been so looking forward to getting to know you.'

The Phoenix spat at her feet.

Zorana flushed, a glimmer of haughty rage flashing in those pale eyes. 'Charming.'

'I warned you,' Taelyr murmured. Then he laughed, a sound that made Renila's stomach heave. 'At least Mazron can have some fun breaking her.'

The Princess smirked as she stepped closer, running a possessive hand down Renila's cheek. Renila forced herself not to flinch from that touch, but she could not keep the fear from her eyes when the Princess said, 'And now we even have a spare.'

The roar of thunder warring in the sky above was deafening. Lightning sparked and danced over Alvar's body, the winds howling through the forest.

'Touch her again, Shade,' he growled, 'and not even your power will be strong enough to shield you.'

Zorana laughed, her hand closing on Renila's wrist. 'I can be gone from this place before you can even draw breath – and you will never see her again. Or you can come quietly, and I promise that none of you will be harmed.'

'Your word is worthless,' Arian snapped. Beside her, the bear growled in agreement.

The Shade's pale eyes flickered to it. 'Rumour has it the bastard son of the Hal Chieftain is rather handsome. Why don't you stop hiding behind the fur and fangs and come out to play like a big boy?'

The bear shimmered and shifted, leaving Ornak standing in its place. He was panting, a rumbling growl building in his chest, but his hands were steady as he drew his axe from across his back. There was nothing but lethal calm in those bronze eyes as he stared the Shade Princess down and spoke with succinct brutality.

'Fuck. You.'

His oath was punctuated with a mighty roar followed by the great boom of beating wings, and all eyes snapped skyward. A cold shadow rippled overhead as a monstrous form glided over the treetops, blotting out the light of the stars and moon high above.

Ornak laughed, his eyes bright with the promise of violence, and he began backing up, dragging Arian with him. A feral grin twisted her lips as recognition danced in her golden gaze. Alvar too was smirking as he scanned the skies for that dreadful beast.

'You are *so* fucked now,' Ornak taunted. And with that he charged, bringing his axe down on the nearest Darkling. Arian followed, her blades flashing in the firelight, and Darklings died screaming wherever she went. Lightning streaked from Alvar's upraised palm towards Zorana and Taelyr – striking the ground between them with lethal precision. They were blasted back, Renila's wrist ripped from Zorana's grasp as the Shade Princess tumbled away. Taelyr's hold on her loosened, the dagger knocked from his grip, and Renila slammed her elbow back. He doubled over, winded, and she struggled free. Across the clearing, Zorana was screaming for him to grab her – the command drowned in the din of clashing weapons and magic. Snarling, he staggered to his feet.

Then he was in Renila's head, wielding her body like a puppet. Magic she didn't know she had flared at her fingertips – flames of brightest amber streaking towards Arian and Ornak. Arian blocked with a flash of crimson fire, but Ornak roared as the blaze slammed into him. The smell of burning flesh filled the air. Arian was screaming for him, battling her way through the Darklings as she tried to reach him. He was still alive, face down on the ground and struggling to rise. His side was a mess where the magic – her magic, Renila realised with horror – had struck him. Blistered. Charred. Smoking.

A voice she had never heard before, yet somehow recognised, echoed in her head. *'Shield.'*

Taelyr heard it, Casting a barrier of amber flames around them with Renila's power. Across the clearing, a dome of matching ruby fire flickered

474

to life over Arian and Ornak, while lightning sparked around Alvar. Then another roar shook the ground beneath their feet, and the air rippled as that beast dived from the sky, black flames spewing from its massive maw. The Darklings didn't even scream before they died. Only Zorana remained standing, her shield of pale green light flickering but holding against the onslaught.

Just as fast as it had started, it was over. Zorana stood in the centre of the smoking clearing, anger spitting from those pale eyes while she took in the carnage. Alvar lunged for Renila, but Taelyr forced her out of reach – used her magic to hold the Immortal off long enough for her to return to him. He was panting from the effort. But there was nothing weak about his grip when he pulled her back against his chest, this time holding her in place with her own amber flames. But before he could reach Zorana, a wall of black flame blazed into life between them.

Wings boomed again, that monstrous shadow engulfing the clearing. A gust of cold air whipped around them, and the earth trembled as the demon landed.

A dragon.

Black as night, monstrous in size. Ferocious-yellow eyes glowed through the shadows, teeth gleaming in the dark as a vicious growl ripped out of it. A blast of heat washed over them, and flames curled and smoked from between snarling jaws. Huge claws – hooked and as long as Renila's arm – gouged the earth. The rustle of leathery wings opening and closing hissed through the clearing, scales rasping as it shifted where it stood.

Those great eyes were fixed on Taelyr, another snarl of hatred rippling from between bared teeth. But a groan of pain had its massive head swinging away, looking to where Arian was helping Ornak to his feet – his wounded side healed, but brutally scarred.

Pale green light flashed towards them as Zorana struck. Renila tried to scream out in warning, but there was no need. One of those mighty wings flared out, and the Shade's killing blow slammed into a wall of leathery hide. The dragon did not so much as flinch. In fact, an eerily human laugh echoed from its mouth as it turned those baleful eyes on the Shade Princess.

Zorana held her ground, no hint of fear on her haughty face. 'Show yourself.'

The dragon considered her for a moment, and Renila thought for a moment that it had every intention of killing the Shade. But instead, it closed its wings in tight to its body and … Changed.

It was slow. Sluggish, almost. The dragon disappearing as the magic surrounding it grew, the silhouette blurring and shifting. Then light receded, and instead of a dragon, Renila found herself staring at a woman.

She was crouched low, panting from the effort of the Change, her face obscured by a peaked hood pulled down over her eyes. The rest of her face was hidden behind a scarf that covered her nose and mouth. In fact, Renila could hardly see anything of the stranger; she was dressed head-to-toe in black leather.

Taking a deep breath, the woman stood, her long, black coat swirling at her knees, gloved hands brushing the myriad weapons about her hips. Her sturdy boots reached her mid-thigh, and Renila saw more weapons strapped to her legs. There was a sword across her back, along with a bow and quiver full of arrows.

Something in Renila's chest tightened, as if in recognition. It was like the sensation of eerie familiarity she'd felt when she'd first laid eyes on Alvar, and yet this pull was so much stronger. She felt, more than saw, the stranger's eyes fix on her and shivered under the force of that predatory gaze.

Raising a hand to her face, the woman lowered her scarf. Revealed flame-like tattoos of pitch-black swirling over her jaw and down her neck, and lips twisting in an arrogant smirk. Then her other hand swept up to remove her hood.

Renila had to force herself not to scream.

Nightwalker. The woman was a Nightwalker. Her bronze skin was drab and muted, as if she had not seen the sun in a hundred years. Her eyes were black as the night she was cursed to. Her hair too was jet-black, bound in braids back from her face and cascading over her shoulders in a mass of wild ebony waves. Those fiery tattoos curled up over her forehead and cheekbones. And even her fingers, it transpired, as she tugged her gloves off with her teeth. Renila could not shake the peculiar sensation that she'd seen those marks before. A sensation that became a certainty when her gaze snagged on the Nightwalker's left hand. On the familiar ring there, the jewel held between two outstretched wings. Erion's ring. The one she'd given him the day he was born. But instead of a red gem, it was set with a shard of glittering obsidian. As though the curse had not only tainted her body, but all she touched.

At Renila's back, Taelyr trembled with fear.

Renila didn't blame him. That dreadful gaze was fixed on him, cold and hungry.

'Resari,' he breathed, his voice shaking.

Beside them, Zorana flinched. 'It can't be. You're dead.'

The Nightwalker smirked, black eyes flickering to the Shade Princess. 'Only on the inside.'

'The King told us you died – killed by your own people during the Fall.'

An evil grin split that otherwise beautiful face. 'He lied.'

'Why?'

The woman didn't answer. Her attention flickered back to Taelyr, staring him down. Renila could hear his heart thundering in his chest at her back, feel his panicked breath on the back of her neck. Another mind scraped over hers, vast and throbbing with power, like talons raking the mental barriers Taelyr had erected around them both. He shuddered from that touch.

476

'Because cursed to endless night, she's not a threat to him,' he gasped. 'But she is to you.'

Resari – Gods, was she really the legendary Kah Resari – chuckled. It was a dark, chilling sound. She glanced at Ornak, her eyes hardening at the sight of his scarred side before turning back to Taelyr. 'You should have run while you still had the chance, cousin. I might have spared you, for your mother's sake if nothing else. But you've dishonoured her memory. And now … now there is a debt to be paid, and it will be paid in blood.'

'But are you willing to pay the cost?' Taelyr breathed, tightening those amber flames around Renila's throat until she screamed from the pain.

'There is no price too high,' Resari breathed, taking a step forward, 'no cost too steep … nothing I will not give.'

She took another step forward, Arian and Ornak following to her right. Alvar's gaze met Renila's, and he smiled sadly, even as he moved to flank Resari on her other side. Arian's golden eyes caught hers, her lips moving in silent apology.

'Forgive me,' she mouthed.

Renila trembled in Taelyr's arms, suddenly afraid – certain that death now stalked towards her. That terrible presence brushed against her mind once more, whispering to her.

'It's alright to be scared. Bravery is not the absence of fear but looking it in the eye and refusing to let it control you. Time to be brave, Renila.'

Renila blinked in surprise, wresting control back long enough to ask, *'How do I know you?'*

'You tell me.'

Then Resari struck. Taelyr was ripped from Renila's mind by talons of pure night, even as blackfire and lightning twisted together, streaking towards Zorana. The Shade Princess whirled, vanishing into the air, and the combined might of Resari and Alvar slammed into the ground. Ruby flames caught Renila square in the chest, blasting her and Taelyr backwards. Then Zorana was above them, reaching for them. Renila thrashed, struggling to her feet as she tried to avoid the hand that would steal her away from this place. Taelyr's hand closed around her throat, only for him to be slammed back by another wave of black flame. His fingers caught her necklace, the fine chain snapping as he was thrown back. Zorana dissipated again, only to appear at his side a heartbeat later, her teeth bared in a furious snarl.

'So be it,' she hissed. Pale green light streaked towards them, slamming into barriers of black and red flames. But one bolt found its mark, and the Shade Princess smirked in triumph before melting into the darkness once more, taking Taelyr with her.

Darkness was closing in. Her legs gave way, knees barking in pain as she crashed to the ground and collapsed face-first into the dirt. She was vaguely aware of Alvar screaming her name, but he sounded so far away.

Her chest hurt. Not from the crimson flames – those had been little more than a sharp slap compared to this fresh agony. No, this wound was tainted. The touch of Shade magic, twisted and corrupt, burned far worse than the fire that had sprung from Arian's upraised palm.

Warm, steady hands found her – turning her over, jolting her back to waking for the briefest of moments. Then she was slipping away. Voices echoed above her, filled with despair and regret, but she could not make out the words. She was so cold. So tired. Oblivion beckoned – soothing, peaceful. She wanted to drift away into that quiet embrace.

That other mind caressed her own, gentle now as it soothed away the worst of her pain.

'She's at peace,' it said out loud. Darkness had its claws in her now, dragging her down into the abyss. The voice spoke again, the words echoing down as she drifted away. 'Burn the body. Let her rise out of ashes.'

And then Renila was gone, welcomed at last into the arms of her death.

EPILOGUE

The Shade King couldn't sleep. Moonlight streamed through the open window and a cool breeze stirred the heavy curtains. He lay stretched out in his bed, the silken sheets tangled about his waist while he scowled up at the canopy above him. One hand was behind his head, the other tracing pensive patterns on smooth skin. Jenia twitched beneath his fingertips, mumbling sleepy objections into the pillows. He glanced down, smirking. She was a sight to behold. Naked and draped over both him and his bed, a possessive hand splayed across his chest.

Even after all this time, she still made his heart stop. Petite and fine-boned, with blood-red hair and eyes to match. When he had first set eyes on her, they had been burnished copper with a core of gold – though those were nothing more than a distant memory. But it was not Jenia's beauty that he had fallen in love with all those years ago. It was her fire. A tempestuous inferno, churning and seething in her black heart … It was hypnotic watching the power warring beneath her skin. Power that simmered even as she slept, sated for now.

He sighed and extricated himself from her sprawling limbs. Her nails dug deep as he prised her hand away, leaving angry red furrows to match his crimson dragon-marks. His Queen in all but name. So greedy. So territorial. Even lost in her dreams she clung so tight. And for once, he was inclined to accommodate her. Her battle with Alexan had been brief but ferocious. Her throat was still tender where the Darkling's hand had almost crushed the life from her. The King repressed a shudder. The thought of losing her … It would be the end of him.

A flurry of night-kissed wind fluttered through the room, and his dark thoughts were chased from his mind as he watched Jenia's skin pucker from the cold. He eyed the coverlet they had thrown on the floor, along with the shredded remains of their clothes, but decided against it. The need to warm his lover was likely the only thing that would entice him back to

479

bed. Leaving her to her dreams, he lifted his robe from the hook on the wall and padded from the room on silent feet.

The bedroom gave way to a large and airy sitting room. Their personal dining room lay beyond it, with Jenia's dressing room to one side (not that she ever used it) and his study to the other. It was towards the latter he strolled, tying the robe about his waist. He paused by the sideboard, pouring himself a healthy measure of amber liquid from the crystal decanter. Anything to quieten the roaring in his mind. He ignored the mirror over the mantle, the reflection it held. Ignored the tall, broad-shouldered and imposing figure with dark hair and peculiar, pale eyes. Eyes that still unnerved him.

Taking a long draught, he gazed out the window, looking beyond the city below – across the sea, to the mainland beyond. Towards the power he could feel shaking the earth with every step. Power like he had not sensed since the Fall. Not since he'd ensured the only power that would ever threaten him had been broken and buried; ruined beyond all hope of rising. It had pained him to do it. The cost so steep it still haunted him to this day. The price paid in blood to ensure his own survival. Sometimes he wondered if it had been worth it.

Still. What was done was done. There was nothing he could do to change it. Which made this new power all the more unsettling. It could not be *her*. He'd made sure there was no coming back – had seen the evidence of her curse with his own eyes, had felt no whisper of her power since that day.

Although there had been that one night, a little over twelve years ago now. He frowned. The boy had said he was about twelve. Perhaps ... He shook his head. No, he'd studied the boy since his arrival. He was powerful, yes, enormously so. Almost bursting at the seams with untapped potential. Something was repressing it – some magic, no doubt designed to keep it contained, but which instead was killing him. That would need dealt with. Sooner rather than later too. But the boy was not the source of the power that kept him awake at night.

With a heavy sigh, the King slumped down into the chair behind his desk. Papers littered the work surface, one particular letter – the source of his irritation – pinned into the wood by the tip of an obsidian-hilted dagger. He scowled, repressing the snarl that rose to his lips as he wrenched the blade free. The message itself he burned with a wave of his hand. He didn't need it. They were not words he would forget in a hurry.

Forcing his anger down, he turned his gaze to the map on the wall, running a frustrated hand through his hair. It would take Théon time to clear Illyol, and the Darkling Queens were still an issue. And even without Mazron's influence, Ciaron was still a problem. Nightwalkers were easily bought. But even cursed, Dragons were fickle and proud – never a good combination. Any way he looked at it, the problem remained the same. He was boxed in. And his list of allies was dwindling. Losing Alexan had been a disappointment, but it was failing, yet again, to retrieve Théon that had hit hardest.

If he was honest with himself, he didn't know what else he'd expected of his daughter. She was too much like him – too stubborn, too proud. And if even half of what he had heard about Keriath was true, she was just as bad. He'd heard the rumours of a third child, another raven-haired daughter. He knew it wasn't true, much to his disappointment. So much bloodshed could have been avoided if she had been his – though she was too powerful to ever bring to heel.

Not that he'd say any of that to Jenia. The rumours grated on her. He knew what it would do to her if he ever admitted he wished them to be true. She had a hard enough time swallowing what he'd done to produce Théon and Keriath.

When he'd finally moved against the Graced, he'd offered her Kylar's life as a peace offering. The memory of what she'd done that night still haunted him. What she'd tried to do to Keriath. She'd never felt that way about Théon. She hadn't been welcoming, not by any stretch, but she tolerated Théon's presence in their lives.

The irony was not lost on him that she had found it in her heart to forgive him for raping Diathor. Something that still caused him to wake in a cold sweat a hundred years later. But she could not tolerate the fact that Kylar had come willingly to his bed. She was contrary like that.

But he'd needed heirs. And she could not give them to him.

Pursing his lips, he pushed those fears from his mind and reached out a tendril of power, tapping on the mental shields of the presence lingering in the hall outside. Corrigan answered the summons, slipping inside on silent feet and closing the door behind him.

'Sire,' he said, bowing.

The King did not take his eyes off the map. 'Any word from Kieyin?'

'Seren was successful in infiltrating the keep,' the Nightwalker reported, his voice as flat and unfeeling as ever, 'but last we heard, her search for the Princess was ongoing. Kieyin was to hold back and stay out of sight until she gave the signal.'

'And Alexan?'

'Back within the safety of the wards and beyond our reach for now.' Irritation flickered over his otherwise impassive face – as much emotion as he'd ever show. The King repressed a smile. His generals' hatred of each other was legendary, and a hundred years enduring each other's company had only made it worse.

'Do we know what happened?'

Corrigan's dead gaze sparked with annoyance. 'It appears he and the Princess had become lovers.'

The King tore his gaze from the map to glare at the Nightwalker. 'What?'

'The Steward didn't tell you?'

He glanced towards the bedroom. 'She's been a little preoccupied.'

'I see,' Corrigan said, a slow flush creeping over his cheeks. 'Her report stated that she found them together in a cave on the coast of Stormkeep. It was quite clear what had transpired between them. She ordered Alexan to kill the Princess, but after the deed was done, he turned on her.'

The King stilled, his voice nothing more than a deadly whisper. 'He was feeding from her.'

'Probably,' Corrigan admitted, crossing his arms over his chest. 'If Your Majesty remembers, I did suggest that perhaps Alexan might not have been the best choice to send after the Princess.'

'He was the only choice.'

Corrigan placed his hands on the desk and leaned forward. 'I fear that was short-sighted, sire. The Court chafes against your rule more and more every day. You barely won the last challenge; you are still weak from the battle. Not that you dare let even so much as a hint of it show. Now, with Alexan gone, Prince Kieyin and I are the only thing standing between you and utter ruin.'

'Don't push your luck,' the King hissed, magic flaring with his temper, with the fear lurking beneath it. 'I wear the crown, Corrigan. I give the orders. You follow them. Question me again, and I'll have your head mounted on a spike before you can blink.'

Corrigan held his ground. 'Ah, there he is, the dread Shade King. Power incarnate. All should bow before him in fear. Except we both know it's a lie.'

The King checked himself, freezing even as his blood pounded through his veins. 'Do we indeed?'

'I have served you faithfully for a hundred years, sire,' Corrigan breathed. 'Do you think me so ignorant that I would not see the heart of you in all that time? And yet I am still here. Still serving. As I swore I would be – until my dying breath. But I cannot protect you if I am kept in the dark.'

A vicious snarl ripped out of the King, but he looked away. Picking up the obsidian-hilted dagger, he was silent for a long time as he considered. Eventually, he nodded. 'Very well. You wish to know the truth? He did not kill Théon. Whatever spell was containing her power, it is now broken. The Shade is free. Just as I planned.'

The concession was difficult to swallow, but he could not afford to lose the Nightwalker. Shoving his frustration down, he looked back to the map, ignoring the sharp breath of relief that escaped Corrigan, and threw the dagger. End over end it spun, before impaling itself tip-first in the map – into the heart of the Ravenswood.

'What about the Ravenswood? Did you find out anything more about that?' he asked.

'Initial reports suggest you were right – it was the Rookery,' said Corrigan, straightening. 'It's sustained serious damage, but it is mostly still standing. The magic is strong.'

The King grunted. 'It would be. My father's power ran deep.' He paused. A possibility occurring to him. 'What about the Phoenix girl? Any sign of her?'

'Not since Arian helped destroy what was left of the Hunt Kieyin took.

There has been some movement out on Ciaron's Western Wing – likely just the Hal bastard causing trouble again, but I have sent a Hunt to investigate.'

The King made a sound of distaste. He would have to deal with the Dragon at some point. Arian too. She was one who had slipped through his fingers a few too many times for comfort. A shame that they had been unable to capture the other Phoenix woman. He could count on one hand the number who had survived the slaughter in Elucion. There was little doubt this stranger was linked to the new power rising. Then his attention turned to the final piece. 'What about the boy?'

'What about him?' Corrigan asked, feigning disinterest. It was an irritating habit he had – developed to get information from others in the Court, and now so ingrained, he did it without thinking.

The King rolled his eyes and let it slide. There was little to be gained from pushing him. 'I'm not sure what to make of him,' the King admitted. 'He's powerful, that much is obvious – though that containment spell will need to be broken if he's to survive. A sharp mind too. If a little timid.'

'I thought he was surprisingly brave,' countered Corrigan in a rare – and unexpected – display of perceptiveness. 'I doubt you would find many children that age who could meet either my eyes or yours and flinch as little as he has.'

Shrugging to concede the point, the King continued. 'I want to know where he came from. How he got into that room. There's something ... familiar about him. About his power. I don't like it.' He trailed off, lost in thought while he considered the puzzle the boy presented. 'I'll keep him here for now. See if I can break the spell, if I can get anything else out of him.'

'Seren isn't happy,' Corrigan began.

But the King cut him off. 'I don't care. If it becomes problematic having him here, I will send him to her, but for now, I want to see what I can find out for myself. Who knows? Maybe we can even persuade him to ally himself with us.'

Yet another lost child for Jenia to raise as her own. Just as she'd raised Kieyin – the closest thing he'd ever had to a son. His adopted heir, for now. Unless either Keriath or Théon were returned to him. He prayed it was soon. Otherwise, it would all crumble ...

He heaved a sigh and looked back at his general. 'Gather the Court. All of them. If Mazron and Zorana don't answer the summons, declare them traitors and sentence them to death. It's time we dealt with this uprising. And get word to Kieyin – tell him, if he's successful, take her to Ashmark. It won't be safe for him to bring her here with the Court gathered. If not, I need him back here as soon as possible.'

'And Alexan, sire?'

The King pursed his lips. 'Let him be. He will find his way home. The manner of his return will decide his fate.'

Corrigan inclined his head in acknowledgement, a muscle leaping in his jaw the only sign of his displeasure, and turned without a word. Then he

483

was gone, closing the door quietly behind him, and the King was alone once more with his thoughts. He took another sip of whisky, savouring the burning sensation as it slipped down his throat. The roaring had quietened to a purr for now, but his mind was never truly silent. Not since that day he had read those fateful words *Sephiron's heirs will rise … an ember may yet raze all to ash … only with faith can the Raven's line be cleansed … any price is worth paying to end Sephiron's line …*

His thoughts were cut off by a ripple of power that shook the very foundations of the earth. He lurched to his feet, gasping for air, the crystal tumbler smashing to the floor as it slipped from his grasp. That thrum of magic like a fist around his heart.

'Reith?' Jenia's voice echoed through their chambers, her voice heavy with worry. Then she was at his side. A wicked-looking dagger in hand – he wished she would stop sleeping with that thing under her pillow – and bloody eyes flashing as she searched for the threat.

'I'm alright,' he gasped, waving her away.

Jenia gave him a look that said she was unconvinced, but she lowered the dagger. 'What is it?'

He ignored her, collecting the various papers he'd knocked from his desk and clearing away the shards of shattered glass with a gentle sweep of magic. Jenia's expression was inscrutable, but there was a tension in the set of her shoulders that told him just how agitated his lover was. Finally, he met those red eyes.

'A Rising.' She flinched. Infinitesimally, but there was no hiding the naked fear in her bloody gaze. 'A powerful one.'

'Resari?'

He shook his head. 'She hasn't been able to summon that kind of power since the Fall. It's something else. Something new.'

'The boy's mother?'

'Possibly.' He didn't want to talk about it. Fear had frozen the blood in his veins. This was a power to rival his own. If it was fully fledged, it would be nigh on impossible to stop.

Jenia seemed to sense his unease, placing her dagger on the desk behind him as she pressed her body against his and kissed him. Filled him full of her fire. And when fear had loosened its hold on his heart, she pulled back and whispered against his lips, 'Reith, come back to bed.'

ACKNOWLEDGMENTS

I learned a long time ago that success is seldom single-handed. One does not get far in the sporting arena without recognising the invaluable contribution of others to the achievement of our goals, and though this work feels more my own than any medal I've ever won, I am under no illusion as to how many people have got me to this point.

Though it may seem strange, it's actually the people who helped me win medals rather than write manuscripts that I would like to thank first. To all those I worked with throughout my years as an athlete, who helped shape me into the person I am today. To Kris, Simon and Paul who did their best to keep me sane and taught me so much about myself – knowledge that I have used not just to make me a better writer, but hopefully a better person too. To Alison and Maggie, whose expert care and instruction continues to help me to this day – particularly after hours at the writing desk. And most of all to Colin, for everything.

Transition from athlete to author was never going to be straightforward, and the continued support of everyone at **sport**scotland, Team Scotland and my colleagues at STS means the world to me – the support of those athletes now under my care most of all. And to all those teammates – particularly Áedán, Fiona, Dave, Sheree and Sian – whose ongoing love and encouragement over the years has been a source of great comfort during some of the more difficult days.

But all the love and support in the world was never going to take my first draft and turn it into a publishable work, so to my editor, Sam Boyce, and proofreader, Kat Harvey, for that I say: thank you. Thank you for your patience and guidance while I navigate this new chapter in my life. Most of all, thank you for helping me make this story the best it can be.

Thank you to everyone who has bought, read and supported this book. I had two dreams growing up. Go to the Olympics. Become an author. Thank you to everyone who has helped me achieve those dreams.

Most of all, thank you to my friends and family, without whom I would be nothing. To Naomi, Petra, Snježana, Chelsea and Keri-anne – the best friends a girl could wish for (and a particularly huge thank you to Petra for helping with the production of the map). To my family – Caroline & Phil, Tommy & Mary, John & Frances. Grandma. Mum. Dad. Seonaid. There aren't really the words to express the kind of gratitude I hold in my heart for all of you.

And lastly. Andrew... and Brego. I love you. And thank you. For everything.

ABOUT THE AUTHOR

Jen McIntosh is a two-time Olympian and Team Scotland's most decorated female athlete. A lover of books and all things magical, she took to writing as an escape from the pressures of competing in one of the Olympics' more obscure and controversial sports – target shooting. Following her retirement from international competition in 2018, she escaped to the Scottish Highlands where she lives with her husband and their hyperactive spaniel.

To learn more about Jen and follow her journey from Olympian to author, check out her blog at:

<u>www.jen-mcintosh.com</u>

 facebook.com/jenmcintosh.oly
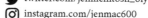 twitter.com/jenmcintosh_oly
instagram.com/jenmac600